Working systematically and with practised ease, they loaded their own animals with the loot and secured it with ropes in the manner of those long used to the exercise. Then they remounted, turned their steeds in the direction from which they had come, and headed back into the night. Within the hour they had merged once more with the mountains. Save for the rising wails of the wind and the restless moans of animals, all was again silent.

Quietly, cautiously, the men crept out of their hiding places. Beating their chests and foreheads with the palms of their hands, they surveyed their vandalised goods and the decapitated body of their companion and mentally calculated their losses. Thanking Allah that at least their own lives had been spared, they philosophically set about salvaging whatever was left of their cargo. It was not the first time they had been plundered on the Silk Road, nor would it be the last; with the mercy of the Prophet they would continue to survive. After they had re-packed their remaining goods and the animals had again been loaded, they finally directed their attention to their slain fellow traveller.

It was almost first light. The body still lay where it had fallen, the flesh stiff, the blood cold and congealed. As they gathered around the headless corpse they avoided each others' eyes, ashamed now in the brutal light of day of their willingness to betray their dead companion. Whatever quarrel the Hunza raiders might have had with Rasool Ahmed—for they had asked for him by name—they themselves had none. As far as they were concerned the man was courteous, reticent and had made neither complaint nor demand. Anxious to be on their way again, they set about digging a grave, reciting abridged prayers and hurriedly performing such rituals as were decreed for a decent burial.

The meagre ceremony over, they paused to confabulate. It would be compassionate, they decided—less for the benefit of the departed soul than for their own bruised collective conscience—to seek out the unfortunate Rasool Ahmed's family and to deliver to them his remaining possessions. However, never having set eyes on the man before Shahidullah and knowing nothing about him save his name, they had no information about his kinsmen. He could have come from anywhere.

In their final act of reparation, they searched the dead man's remaining belongings. Among the items of wearing apparel, toiletries and a book or two, they could find no personal information. Even the man's saddlebag produced little save old invoices, inventories and a few loose papers. The papers, they saw, were not in the Arabic script but in the Roman, probably English, a language with which they were only vaguely conversant.

Assuming that Rasool Ahmed was an educated man of high status with firanghi business contacts in India, they were again nervous. What if they were accused of stealing his property and of complicity in his murder? Rather than risk interrogation by the knife-tongued, hot-headed English Commissioner in Leh, they decided it would be safer to surrender the dead man's possessions to a known person of trust, the mullah at the Leh madrassa, for instance, who had some knowledge of English. Being a man of God, he would know not only what to do with Rasool Ahmed's effects but how to do it discreetly.

Although the effects were few and of little material value, there were among them two items that puzzled and disturbed the merchants greatly: a Buddhist prayer-wheel and a Hindu rosary of the traditional dried *rudraksha* berries. Refusing to touch either and even more alarmed, they wondered: What possible use could a devout Mohammeddan trader have had for these sacrilegious implements of the Hindu infidel?

The confusion of the merchants was understandable. They were not to know that Rasool Ahmed was neither a trader nor a Mohammeddan nor, indeed, a Hindu. So thorough was his knowledge of the language and manners of the region, so skilled his disguise, that not one of his fellow travellers suspected that he was, in fact, an Englishman. His true name was Jeremy Butterfield, although he was also known by others.

CHAPTER

Delhi
February 1890

Something was amiss, Emma saw, as soon as she turned the corner into Civil Lines.

Even though it was well past ten, reluctant remnants of winter mist still feathered the trees and the morning air was yet to lose its cutting edge. At the main gates of Khyber Kothi a hive of servants buzzed in aggressive debate, a most unusual occurrence in a residential enclave as fiercely possessive of its hush-toned privacy as Civil Lines. It being easy enough to procure neighbourhood news discreetly from friends without resorting to vulgar gossip, communal curiosity in servants was discouraged—except, of course, by the incorrigibly nosey Bankshall sisters, not averse to using whatever conduit offered the least resistance.

Riding past the animated group, Emma nudged Anarkali into a trot and turned into the driveway. Halfway down, adjacent to the rose garden, the sweeper and the gardener argued hotly, brandishing their straw brooms like weapons of war. Under the leafless gulmohar the gardener's youngest wife was locked in verbal battle with her sworn enemy, the bearer's eldest daughter, and in the portico Saadat Ali, the baburchi, sat slumped on the steps with a palm clamped to his head.

Emma surveyed the various vignettes in dismay. The last thing she had either the energy or the inclination for now was tedious domestic arbitration that would eat away hours of her working day. She had already had one unsavoury experience this morning; she could certainly do without another. It was as she was about to accost Saadat Ali and demand explanations that she noticed the constables. They stood concealed partially by the dreadfully overgrown bougainvillaea—which was why she had missed seeing them in the first place—and her irritation turned into alarm. Mama . . . ?

Dismounting hurriedly, she handed Anarkali's reins to Mundu, the sweeper's lad, and ran into the downstairs parlour converted temporarily into a bedroom. Her mother sat in her usual chair by the window sipping her cup of mid-morning milk. By the bed Mahima, the old ayah, stood patting the quilt and fluffing out the pillows. Undernourished and on the point of expiry, the usual apology for a fire flickered in the grate. The familiar signs of domestic normalcy brought a rush of relief; but then before she could speak, her mother did, and Emma saw that her relief was premature.

"Where have you been, dear?" Margaret Wyncliffe asked in a faint, quivering voice. "It's way past your usual time and I was worried stiff!"

Hurrying to her mother's side, Emma laid a reassuring hand on her shoulder. "I'm sorry, darling, but I was held up on my way back near Qudsia Gardens by a most unholy . . ." She cut short the remembrance and dismissed it. "Anyway, what's happened? What are these police constables doing outside? Have the servants had another set-to—or has Bernice Bankshall finally made good her threat to strangle our rooster because it woke her up at dawn once more?"

"No, no, nothing like that," Margaret Wyncliffe gasped, obviously about to have another of her dreadful turns. "It's . . . it's . . ."

"There, there, take your time, darling," Emma comforted, with a quick signal to the ayah as she stroked the heaving back to ease the breathing. "Whatever it is, it can wait."

As soon as her mother had gulped down the pills and the water the ayah presented, Emma walked to the fireplace and jabbed the dying embers with the poker. If the sturdy stone walls were ideal insulation in the searing heat of summer, in winter they turned Khyber Kothi into an igloo. The cost of fuel being what it was, the modest little fires they made do with were scarcely enough in a room of high ceilings, tall windows, threadbare curtains and a cold marble floor inadequately covered with rugs. Crisscrossing the few remaining logs over the wavering flames, she reached for the bellows.

Margaret Wyncliffe finally found her voice. "Someone broke into the house last night!"

Emma frowned. "Again?"

"Apparently. They came in the same way as before, through the drawing-room window overlooking the verandah. It was the sweeper who discovered the damage when he arrived this morning. You had already left so he woke up David."

"Well, that settles it," Emma said, more annoyed than alarmed. "I suppose we'll just have to install grilles on the downstairs windows whatever the cost. Was anything taken?"

"I don't know, dear, you'll have to see for yourself. David refused to let me look, although he did lodge a complaint at the police chowki and Ben Carter was kind enough to send an Inspector Stowe to interrogate the servants, which is why they are in such a frightful state. He is in the drawing-room with David, waiting to talk to you."

Emma sighed. The man would probably be here for hours and she did so want to get her papers done in case Dr. Anderson relented and sent for her. Giving a final stab to the fire, she asked for the remaining logs to be fetched from the stables, walked to her mother and draped a second shawl about her shoulders.

"Whatever you do you must *not* catch another cold or Dr. Ogbourne will be very cross. Don't worry, I'll take care of Mr. Stowe."

Mrs. Wyncliffe laid her head back and closed her eyes. "I'm glad you're home, dear. No one quite knew what to do while you were away and I could feel the palpitations coming on."

Personal feuds forgotten, outside the drawing-room at the furthest end of the back verandah the servants stood in a huddle exchanging apprehensive whispers. Inside the study, David was engrossed in brisk conversation with a solidly built, pink-faced young man in white police ducks. Pausing to speak a few words of reassurance to the servants, Emma stepped into the room.

"Ah, Miss Wyncliffe, we were waiting for you to return," the Inspector said as soon as David had made the introductions. "Perhaps you will be able to tell us now if anything is missing."

"Sorry not to have been more helpful," David apologised, "but I have no idea where anything is. My sister is more familiar with household stuff than I am."

Emma stared despondently at the shattered window; it would cost a packet to repair! Her eyes swept over the rest of the room. Apart from a few scattered cushions across the rug, shards of a china wall plate on the floor and an overturned glass paraffin lamp, nothing much appeared to have been disturbed. Her gaze swivelled towards the mantelpiece and her heart skipped a beat. She looked at her brother, but he evaded her eyes.

"I'm afraid I will have to leave you now, Inspector," David said quickly. "I have an appointment at the Red Fort barracks at eleven and I simply dare not keep my commanding officer waiting." He tossed a glance at his sister. "I'll see you at dinner, Em . . ."

Before she could make a response he had left the room.

Poking around in the debris on the floor, the Inspector turned to Emma and asked again if she noticed anything missing.

"The Dresden shepherdess." Emma indicated a side table. "She stood right there, between the paraffin lamp and the crystal ashtray, and I don't see her now."

"Just that one item?"

"Well, at first glance, anyway. I'll have a more thorough look later when I have the time." Walking over to a small rolltop writing desk, she ripped some sheets off the blotter and pressed them down on the table surface to soak up the spreading paraffin.

Inspector Stowe pointed to the mantelpiece. "Your bearer mentioned that a silver clock usually stands there in between the two vases."

"Yes, it does, but I sent it to the clockmaker yesterday to be oiled and cleaned."

"I see. So, nothing was stolen except this china figurine?"

"It would appear not." Emma smiled. "It was not a particularly attractive piece, Inspector. I doubt if anyone will miss it. I certainly won't."

An earnest young man with butter-coloured hair and large, serious eyes, he made no response as he set about perambulating the room. Peering under this and that and making jottings in his notebook, he threw Emma a sidelong glance. Having recently been transferred to Delhi, Howard Stowe had not yet had occasion to meet Emma Wyncliffe, although, of course, he knew her by reputation—who in Delhi did not? According to his sister, Grace, who made it her business to know everything about everyone, Emma Wyncliffe was a brazen "progressive" with a tongue like a wasp sting and a disposition to match. It was hardly surprising, Grace considered, that Emma Wyncliffe was still a spinster and destined to remain so. After all, Grace wondered, which man in his right senses would want to marry a woman with so few social graces and risk being stung to death in the bargain?

Howard Stowe cleared his throat. "Do you think they might have laid their hands on something not immediately visible, Miss Wyncliffe? Jewellery? A concealed cash box, perhaps?"

"We possess nothing of any great value, Mr. Stowe," Emma replied with a trace of impatience as she supervised the disposal of the remains of the wall plate. Struck by a sudden thought, she hurried into the adjoining room through a connecting door to return a moment later, her relief evident. "My father's American typewriting machine is still safe in the study, thank goodness. It would have certainly been a calamity if they had walked away with *that*."

"I understand from your brother that you had another burglary not so long ago?"

"Hardly a burglary, Inspector, since nothing was stolen."

"That is immaterial, Miss Wyncliffe. The point is—not to have iron grilles on ground-floor windows in Civil Lines these days is an open invitation to trouble."

"Whether they entered from here or elsewhere," Emma said wearily, wondering if he had any idea how much iron grilles cost, even second-hand ones, "there's little worth stealing anywhere in the house."

"What seems of no great value to a European, Miss Wyncliffe," he insisted in mild reproof, "could mean a month's subsistence to a poor native—a crystal ashtray, a pair of English scissors, that magnifying glass on the desk, indeed, even an unattractive china figurine—everyday articles that we take for granted. Sold for an anna or two in the thieves' market, any of these could fetch the price of several square meals."

"Well, I daresay you are right," Emma conceded reluctantly, hoping that he would leave soon, "but since only that wretched shepherdess was taken, a wall plate and window pane smashed, no great harm was done—as you can see for yourself."

Howard Stowe nodded absently and stroked his chin. An extraordinary report had arrived at the police station just as he was about to set out. If Emma Wyncliffe was, indeed, the woman involved in the incident near Qudsia Gardens earlier this morning—as he was beginning to suspect—then there was certainly something to be said for his sister's assessment.

"Your brother's room adjoins the study," he remarked merely to gain time, "yet Mr. Wyncliffe—or rather, Lieutenant Wyncliffe—maintains that he heard nothing, not even the sound of shattering glass."

"David is the English counterpart of Kumbhkuran," Emma informed him drily. "He once slept through an earthquake in Quetta."

"Er, Coomb . . . who?" The Inspector looked blank.

"A Hindu god notorious for the soundness of his sleep."

"Oh." He coughed politely. "Yes, well, to return to the matter in hand . . . your servants are all trustworthy, are they?"

"We don't have many servants, Mr. Stowe," Emma reacted sharply to the inference, "but those we do have are entirely trustworthy—if occasionally hot-headed with each other. Most of them have been with us since my father built this house and we've never missed anything." She added severely, "You can see for yourself how agitated they are even to be suspected."

Letting that pass, the Inspector walked over to the communicating door, pushed it open and peered within.

"That was my father's study," Emma said. "It's still in rather a mess,

I'm afraid. Since my father's"—she tried to say the word but could not—"over the past months I have been trying to put his books and papers in some sort of order." She smiled sadly. "However renowned he might have been for his work, my father was not the most organised man in the world."

"Few scholars are," Stowe said, closing the door and abandoning what he could see was a painful subject. "I understand from the servants that you dismissed your Gujar chowkidar last month?"

"I did not dismiss Barak! He wished to return to his village across the Jamuna, where his wife is very sick and will rejoin duty when she is better. I see no reason to malign him merely because he happens to be a Gujar."

"No, of course not," Stowe answered quickly, "but Gujars do have a bad reputation in Civil Lines, Miss Wyncliffe, as you must know. In any case I would strongly advise that you hire a substitute watchman while this fellow is on leave."

"We are perfectly secure with the staff we have, Mr. Stowe. I really don't see the need for panic. Since only a silly little china ornament was stolen, can we not simply forget the whole tiresome business?"

Howard Stowe could not have disagreed more but realised the futility of further argument. Tucking his notebook and pencil back into his breast pocket, he prepared to leave. "You may have been fortunate this time, Miss Wyncliffe, but I would advise strongly against taking future risks. If you subsequently find that something else *is* missing after all, I trust that you will contact me at the chowki. Please remember that I am always at your service."

"Yes, of course I will. And thank you."

She extended a firm hand. Howard Stowe shook it, picked up his solar topee and tucked his baton under an arm. He paused an instant in the doorway—should he question her about the Qudsia Gardens incident? he debated silently. But then, seeing how anxious she was to be rid of him, he found his courage lacking.

Yes, he had to admit, Emma Wyncliffe was certainly intimidating. At the same time he could not help a sneaking admiration for her. She was by no means a beauty—quite plain, in fact, almost dowdy in that limp beige shantung and the schoolmarmish topknot—but there was something about her that was undeniably compelling. She was intelligent, forthright and self-possessed. Faced with a burglary, every other young lady of his acquaintance (including his sister) would have either fainted on the spot or retired to her room to have hysterics. Emma Wyncliffe, on the other hand, showed not the slightest inclination to faint and there were certainly no symptoms of impending hysteria.

Noticing the look of diffidence on the Inspector's face, Emma was suddenly ashamed of her ungraciousness. After all, it wasn't the poor man's fault that he was here; he had come only to perform a duty—and she hadn't even offered him a cup of tea!

"Thank you for your concern, Mr. Stowe," she said with a sudden, spontaneous smile. "It was most kind of Mr. Carter to take personal interest in such a trivial matter considering his other pressing duties. My mother is not very well or she would have certainly thanked you in person."

The smile she bestowed on him was not only unexpected; it was unexpectedly radiant. In fact, it seemed to transform her personality altogether. Emanating from deep within her large, blue-green eyes, it dissolved the severity of her expression to soften her face quite considerably. Taken by surprise, Howard Stowe blushed. "Er . . . do have those grilles installed as soon as possible, Miss Wyncliffe," he said hurriedly. "In the interim I will instruct my constables to keep a special eye on your house after dark."

"Thank you. My mother will be relieved to hear that. Like most invalids, she tends to be unnecessarily nervous."

In the front portico where his escort waited, a constable crouched down beside the Inspector's horse to fashion a cat's-cradle with his fingers for a mounting block. For a split second Howard Stowe again pondered, then, encouraged by the lingering brilliance of her smile, he took the plunge.

"By the way, Miss Wyncliffe, you will be pleased to know that we are looking into that unfortunate incident near Qudsia Gardens this morning. In fact, some arrests are being contemplated. I would advise you for your own safety not to venture near the village for a few days. The men are still in a pretty belligerent mood."

Emma blinked. "How on earth did you know that it was I who was involved in the incident?"

"I did not know until I came here this morning. I do now. No other Englishwoman would have dared—or, for that matter, cared. Good day, Miss Wyncliffe."

Smiling faintly, Emma hurried back into the house. As soon as she re-entered the drawing-room, however, her smile faded. Walking up to the mantelpiece, she ran her fingers lovingly across the space occupied until yesterday by her father's cherished silver clock. She felt a rush of anger.

If David had been up to his old tricks again, she knew she would not find it quite so easy to forgive him this time.

*arrie Purcell held up a white muslin shirt and examined it with a critical eye. "Two buttons missing and a seam undone, otherwise perfect for summer. I should think some poor old man at our soup kitchen will be delighted to have it—unless you want to give this too to the cook?"

"What is Saadat Ali down for so far?" Margaret Wyncliffe asked.

"Two pairs of pyjamas, the checked shirt that was one of Graham's favourites and a pair of slippers. Whereas"—she consulted her notes—"poor old Majid only has that rather bedraggled coat and one pair of pyjamas."

"Well, we can let Majid have the checked shirt and half the number of lungis. He's got twice as many children as Saadat Ali and is consequently twice as poor. We can keep the remaining lungis for Barak when he returns."

"Right. One checked shirt and four lungis for Majid and the other four for the watchman." Folding the shirt and placing it in a half-full box, Mrs. Purcell picked up a pencil and made another entry in her book. "That's the lot where the *coolies* are concerned—except for the bow-ties, socks, hankies and cravats, all of which David will surely want. Now, while we're about it, let us also dispense with the *woollies* before the moths do."

Reclining under a light coverlet on the chaise-longue in the sun-dappled verandah, Mrs. Wyncliffe attempted a wan smile at her friend's little jest. The task in which her dear Carrie helped with such diligence was one that should have been done with months ago, but neither she nor Emma had had the stomach for it.

Helped by the ayah, Carrie dragged another trunk into position. "Now, let us see what we have in here."

As they went through the woollies she kept up a lighthearted patter, pausing every now and then to consult her best friend and her notebook. Finally she held up a deep maroon cardigan, the last of the woollen garments in the trunk. "It's *far* too good to give away—wouldn't David like to have it since it matches well with his new jacket?"

"We'll have to ask Emma about that," Mrs. Wyncliffe said. "She knitted the cardigan for Graham for his last expedition and you know how possessive she is about her father's things."

"Well, let's put it aside for the moment. Emma can go through the list whenever she can spare the time."

"Spare the time?" Margaret Wyncliffe gave a sad little laugh. "With the additional expense of the grilles and the broken window—to say nothing of the leaking roof—the poor girl will have even less time to spare than she does now."

Making another note, Mrs. Purcell nodded absently.

The day was drawing to an early winter close and with lengthening shadows on the back lawn the light was beginning to fade. Majid, the bearer, shuffled onto the verandah bearing a tea tray, placed it on a low table and set about lighting the sconces. Raising her bulk off the stool with an effort, Carrie Purcell stood up and stretched her creaking limbs. She was a large woman with an eternally cheerful disposition, a no-nonsense manner and an excess of avoirdupois that kept her in a state of permanent hostility with her weighing scales.

"Where *is* Emma?" she asked, surveying the plate of crumpets and well-filled butter-dish with hearty approval. "At the College?"

"No, at the Sackvilles'."

"On a Monday? Surely her day with the Sackville boy is Thursday?"

"It is, but Alexander starts his clerkship in Tom Tiverton's bank shortly and his Urdu is still not up to the mark. They've asked Emma to give him conversational practice twice a week until he achieves reasonable fluency. She should be back soon." Struggling up into a sitting position, Mrs. Wyncliffe lifted the teapot.

Carrie Purcell eyed the crumpets thoughtfully. Considering how uncooperative her scales had been lately, should she dare? No, she decided, she definitely should not, but by Jove she would! Quickly, before the exquisite anticipation of sin could vanish, she helped herself to a crumpet, buttered it lavishly, and bit deep into its heart. Heaven!

"Emma does take the sweeper's lad with her, doesn't she?"

"For whatever *that* is worth." Margaret Wyncliffe handed her a cup and took one herself. "Winter days are so short and she has such distances to traverse, I insist that she hires a tikka gharry back from the Nawab's house. She carries her father's Colt in her purse, of course, although, thank God, she has never had cause to use it yet."

"Oh, believe me, she will if she has to, considering Graham's tutelage in those rough-and-tumble camps of his. I *do* wish you would stop worrying about her, Margaret!"

Mrs. Wyncliffe closed her tired, worn-out eyes. Stop worrying? Good heavens, how could she . . . how could any mother with a headstrong spinster daughter on her hands?

"What is all this about Papa's camps?" Emma asked, catching the remark as she stepped onto the verandah. Pulling up a cane stool, she sat down, her freshly scrubbed face more honey-brown than ever and her hair brushed back and up in the usual topknot.

Her mother's face brightened. "Carrie was just reminding me of the liberties your father allowed you in his camps. How you endured all that uncivilised living I still cannot understand."

"I endured it very well, thank you," Emma retorted. "It was David who could not, spoiled rotten as he was by your pampering."

"I never pampered him more than I did you, never!"

Emma smiled. "Of course you did, Mama. You still do." Bending over, she lovingly fingered one of the woollens ranged on the sheet. "I'm glad this is behind us now. We've been putting it off for weeks and Papa did so hate procrastination." She gave a small shiver. "Why is Jenny not with you today?"

"Because Jenny is where she always is these days," Carrie Purcell crimped her lips, "with the most important man in her life."

"John Bryson?"

"Oh no, her tailor. They're locked in another battle, this time over the mess she says he's made of the gold *tarkashi* embroidery on the bodice of her wedding dress. Apparently, he's also stitched the wrong sequins on the gown she plans to wear to Georgina Price's supper, to say nothing of one frill too many—or is it too few?—on her going-away blouse. I don't know who's right and who's wrong and, frankly, I'm past caring. All I know is that by the time Jenny's trousseau is done, one of us will be in the asylum, in all probability me—or poor Archie who's footing her unbelievable bills. I hope you are coming with us to the Prices, Emma dear?"

Emma shook her head. "I have a tuition on Saturday evening. Besides," she made a face, "considering what happened at her last dinner party, I doubt if Mrs. Price would welcome me."

"Oh, fiddlesticks! Georgina can hardly remember what happened at breakfast, let alone at a party two months ago. And you were right, of course," a chuckle rumbled in her cavernous throat, "why don't we try to learn the language of the land? I agreed with everything you said to that insufferable female."

"Well, a great many people didn't," Mrs. Wyncliffe said crossly, "and the poor woman—what was her name, Duckworth?—was most offended. Georgina was very put out, she told me so."

"Well, what about my poor Em? Why should she have taken what the silly old bat said without retaliation?"

"It doesn't matter one way or the other," Emma intervened quickly, "since I've decided not to go anyway."

"Of *course* you must go!" her mother insisted. "Alec has already been round twice to ask if he may escort you. Can't you take the Granger lad on Tuesday?"

"I've only just started at the Grangers', Mama," Emma protested, tucking a strand of hair behind her ear, "and I've already had disapproving looks for being late the other morning." Then, seeing that her mother was spoiling for another of their frequent arguments, she heaved a sigh and surrendered. "Oh, all right. If it pleases you, I will go. I'll hate it, of course, but I shall try to tolerate the evening—and Alec Waterford—somehow."

"It may not be as intolerable as you think," Mrs. Purcell said. "Georgina says Geoffrey Charlton will be there."

"Geoffrey Charlton?" Interest sparked in Emma's eyes. "I didn't know the Prices were acquainted with him?"

"Reggie is. Apparently they met in London at the Geographic Society. Considering the stampede to lionise Mr. Charlton, I should imagine even a casual brush translates into usable social currency. Jenny says John is escorting you both to his lantern slide lecture at the Town Hall this weekend?"

"Yes." Emma drained her cup. "Anyway, I'd better get back to work if I want to have that study in reasonably good order by the end of the week." She jumped up and with a cheerful wave vanished through the doorway.

Margaret Wyncliffe's sallow cheeks quivered as she pressed a handkerchief to her forehead and opened her mouth.

"Don't start your usual nonsense again, Margaret dear," Carrie Purcell warned pre-empting the remark, "or I promise I shall be very, very angry."

"It's *not* nonsense!" Mrs. Wyncliffe sniffled tearfully into her hanky. "If I were well enough, would Emma need to lower herself with these humiliating tuitions? And would my darling David have to leave home?"

"Emma is only doing what any sensible, practical girl would. By feeling sorry for her—and yourself—you simply humiliate her more. As for David, a posting away from home will do your darling son a world of good. He's very lucky—far more than he deserves, I might say—to have secured a commission through Colonel Adams's good offices."

"Oh, I know, I only meant . . ."

"I know what you meant, dear, and I'm all for occasional self-pity, but let's not overdose ourselves, shall we?" Carrie reached out and gave her friend's hand a sympathetic squeeze. "At least you're not faced with eviction like the poor Handleys, entirely at the mercy of that pernicious bania landlord of theirs. At least you *do* have a roof over your head—leaky but nevertheless your own."

Mrs. Wyncliffe blinked and dabbed her eyes. "You're right, Carrie, dear, you always are. I shouldn't really be whining and wailing but sometimes I do feel so . . . *frustrated,* especially for Emma. She, poor dear, never complains, never, either by word or deed." She stopped and blew noisily into the hanky. "Anyway, talking about leaky roofs, we will simply have to have ours re-tarred before David is posted away. Emma will not have the time to manage on her own and I certainly am no help."

"Any decisions yet?"

"On the posting? No. David has his own ideas about what he wants. I only hope they don't send him too far from Delhi."

"Army discipline will be good for him, Margaret. It will keep him out of mischief and he does need to toughen up. I told you what Colonel

Adams said to Archie the other night at the Club, didn't I? Your David is very clever with languages and easily outclimbs everyone else at their mountaineering camps."

"He gets that from his father, of course. Graham was as nimble as a mountain goat and he spoke dialects like a native."

Noticing a renewed tremble in her friend's lips, Carrie Purcell decided it was time to change the subject. "Tell me, my dear, who did Ben Carter send this morning from the chowki? Not that silly little man with pigeon toes and chronic garrulitis, I hope?"

"No, someone called Stowe who has just been posted to Delhi."

"Howard Stowe?" Mrs. Purcell's eyes gleamed. "Hmmm. *Very* eligible, you know."

"Oh?"

"Twenty-seven and a competition-wallah. Winchester and Oxford, both with flying colours. Comes from Warwickshire, Indian Civil Service family. Did a stint in Simla last year at Viceregal Lodge with Lord Lansdowne's entourage, Eunice Bankshall was saying. Quite the rage with the lassies during the Season, his sister Grace tells Jenny. Bit dull and an occasional stuffed shirt, I think, but then nobody's perfect. Considering the quality of merchandise in the marriage market here, who can afford to be picky?"

"Surely Jenny was never interested in Howard Stowe, was she?"

"As it happens, no." Carrie Purcell whisked up a pair of long johns and held them aloft. "He came to mind because of Emma."

"Emma?" Mrs. Wyncliffe sat up quickly. "I didn't know Emma had even met him before this morning!"

"Well, she hadn't, at least not that I know of. I merely mention him as a possibility."

"Oh, a possibility." Margaret Wyncliffe sank back again into the pillow. "Knowing Emma, I've long stopped counting *possibilities*."

"My dear Margaret," Carrie frowned at the note of disapproval, "your daughter is better educated than most, with a good brain between her ears which, what is more, she knows how to use. There can't be many young girls—if, indeed, any—who read, write and speak two languages with such facility." Helping herself to another crumpet, she added a rather daring pat of butter.

"Education and intelligence are all very well, Carrie," Mrs. Wyncliffe replied with sudden animation, "but they don't help girls find husbands! If it's not money or political influence, it's looks and a certain . . . well, feminine manner that count. As it is, all the nice young men are starting to look elsewhere."

"What you should be worrying about is whether Emma will ever find a man interesting enough for her. I should imagine she'd be bored to distraction with someone merely nice."

"Well, what's wrong with Alec Waterford?"

"Nothing—if you're willing to put up with a son-in-law as dull as last week's leftovers who still dangles by the apron strings of an insufferable mother. *I* simply can't imagine your Emma and Daphne Waterford co-habiting under the same roof—any more than I can Emma as a curate's wife. But then, as Jane Granger was saying the other day, compared with Calcutta, the male crop Delhi reaps is decidedly bleak and," she stabbed the air with a finger, "that goes even for my Jenny's John Bryson. Mind you, I love John like a son and I would rather die than have Jenny know what I think—but he does tend to be so terribly . . . what is the word I want? . . . passive. Yes, that's it, passive. No spirit at all."

"Spirit is all very well, Carrie," Mrs. Wyncliffe said despondently, "but that's hardly what men look for these days. Quite the contrary. And then people do talk, you know . . ."

Despite her staunch sense of loyalty to her goddaughter, that was something not even Carrie Purcell could deny. People did talk about Emma Wyncliffe, and that too not kindly. Maintaining a discreet silence, she consoled herself with a final crumpet, vaguely surprised at how little remained of the butter.

*T*he Daryaganj man refuses to come down even a pice," Emma told her mother that evening as they waited to start dinner. "Prices of building materials being what they are, he says roof repairs for less barely make up his costs."

"And the Sudder Bazaar man Norah Tiverton recommended?"

"Considering the construction boom, Mama, it will be six of one and half a dozen of the other. Everyone seems to be building annexes in the Chandni Chowk area. Anyway, David said he'd have a word with the Sudder Bazaar man on his way back from the barracks."

The wall clock chimed once and Margaret Wyncliffe looked up. "David didn't say he would be late this evening, did he? He's usually back by seven."

"It's only half past, Mama. He may have been detained by Colonel Adams or decided to stay back at the barracks with his friends. He's twenty-three, you know—old enough to lead his own life."

"Oh, I know, I know—it's just that I can't help wondering if he's . . . well, you know where."

"Of course he isn't! He gave his word, remember?" Nagged by the thought of the missing silver clock, Emma spoke sharply, but more to convince herself than her mother.

As it happened, it was not until an hour and a half later that David strode noisily into the dining room just as his mother and sister were about to sit down to a belated meal.

"Couldn't wait for the prodigal to return to tuck into the fatted calf, eh?" he remarked sternly. "Well, just for that I have a good mind to forfeit these humble offerings." He waved two elegantly wrapped packets in the air, then whisked them behind his back.

"I'm sorry, dear, but it *is* after nine, you know," his mother pointed out, despite her relief.

"Ah, eaten away by remorse, are you?"

"What we are eaten away by is hunger," Emma informed him acidly. "Humble offerings notwithstanding, the Bible says nothing about prodigals not being punctual."

"Alas, true, too true." He broke into a grin. "Being of an uncommonly forgiving nature, I therefore overlook the discourtesy provided it is not repeated." Bringing both hands forward with a flourish, he placed a parcel before each of them and sat down with his arms crossed. He was in marvellously high spirits.

"My goodness." Mrs. Wyncliffe looked very pleased indeed. "How nice to be given presents outside Christmas and birthdays! Is today a special occasion?"

"I suppose you could call it that." He paused, enjoying the suspense as he helped himself to the mutton stew Majid offered. "After all," he added airily, "a first posting *does* call for some sort of celebration, wouldn't you say?"

"You've received your orders!" Emma exclaimed.

"Indeed."

"Where to?"

"Leh."

"Oh David, that's exactly what you wanted!"

"You can be sure it is! I am to report to Maurice Crankshaw, British Joint Commissioner." He sat back and beamed. "What do you think of that?"

"Leh? That's in *China,* isn't it?"

"Only in Chinese maps." David laughed. "Oh Mama, when will you come to terms with geography? No, it's in Ladakh, not China. Anyway, I am to be a courier and an interpreter and I am to have—wait for this— half a bungalow and half a bearer all to myself." Vastly chuffed, he laughed again. "The other halves are for the office."

"On a first posting?" Emma inquired. "Isn't that unusual?"

"No more unusual than the talents of your brother."

"Or, indeed, his modesty!"

"But it's still so . . . so *far* from Delhi!" Mrs. Wyncliffe wailed. "When will we ever see you again?"

"Come, come, Mama, no tears. You promised, remember?" He jumped out of his chair to give her a reassuring hug. "If all goes well, we can be together in Leh next summer—now, isn't that something to look forward to?"

"When do you leave?" Emma asked.

"I have a few weeks of instruction in Dehra Doon at the Survey of India. After that, hopefully, they'll give me a week or two off before I leave for Leh." He glanced at the gifts. "Well, aren't you going to open them to see what the generous prodigal brings?"

Brushing aside her tears and trying hard to smile, his mother unwrapped her packet and her hand flew to her throat. In an elegant leather box lined with purple velvet reposed a pair of silver-backed hairbrushes with matching mirror and comb. "Oh my goodness, they're . . . they're lovely! They must have cost an absolute fortune!"

"They did," he agreed, "but a fortune well spent."

Emma examined her own gift in silence: a scarlet Chinese silk kimono with brilliantly coloured motifs embroidered all along the hem and down the front. Biting back her astonishment—and alarm—she took care not to let her smile slip. "It's very pretty, David. Thank you. As it happens, I do need another kimono. The one I have is falling to pieces."

Glowing with pride, Mrs. Wyncliffe examined her gift from all angles, then set the box aside. "While I think of it, dear, did you remember to talk to the Sudder Bazaar man about the repairs?"

"Blast! I knew there was something I should have done and didn't. Tomorrow, 'pon my word of honour." Giving himself a second helping of the stew, he doused it liberally with hot lemon pickle.

"We can't put the repairs off much longer," Mrs. Wyncliffe said.

"Nor the grillework," Emma added.

"The roof simply must be resurfaced before we have another downpour," Mrs. Wyncliffe said. "The last one all but ruined the piano and the carpets. It should have been re-tarred much earlier, but your father never seemed to have either the spare time or the spare money. Perhaps we should sell the piano? It's hardly of any use now anyway."

"Oh no, we *can't*, Mama!" Emma protested. "Papa bought that piano out of his very first salary from the Archaeological Survey."

"Well, then, have you thought about the Nawab's offer?"

"Yes." Emma paused, then said, "I've decided to turn it down. Once the book is compiled, I intend to submit it to the Royal Geographic Society."

"My dear, are you sure that is the right decision?"

"Yes, Mama. I know that the Nawab means well, but I doubt if the cognoscenti of the Delhi Literary Society would have the slightest interest in Buddhist esoterica from Himalayan monasteries."

"But dear, the Society does enjoy very high repute among intellectuals," her mother persisted, "and the Nawab himself is considered quite a scholar."

"Whatever meagre notes Dr. Bingham brought back are still in a mess. Even if worthy of being included in a compilation, they will first have to be edited."

"Has Theo Anderson agreed to help you?"

"No. He was very upset about what happened to Papa, of course, but he's off to Tibet again and frightfully busy. He said he simply did not have time for extra work."

"Perhaps just as well." Taking note of his sister's disappointment, David joined the conversation. "Anderson is an old fuddy-duddy and notoriously absent-minded. Once he's off, those notes would probably sit on his shelves for months collecting dust."

"True, but without professional guidance I'll never be able to compile Papa's papers into a book up to the standard of the RGS."

"In that case, dear," Margaret Wyncliffe interposed, "would it not be better . . . ?"

"No!" Emma cut her off and laid down her spoon. "Papa's work cannot be assessed in terms of money, Mama. He put his life into it, took terrible risks for it, *died* for it. . . ." She broke off and cleared her throat. "I refuse to let everything Papa achieved be sacrificed for financial expediency."

"Well, I agree with Em," David said, mopping up the last of his stew with a hunk of bread. "The RGS funded Papa's expeditions, gave him their gold medal for his discoveries in the Tian Shan. As such, they do have prior right to the manuscript. Em knows how Papa's mind worked, Mama, and the book is her project. She should be allowed to tackle it the way she wants."

With a resigned nod, Margaret Wyncliffe deferred to her children. "In that case, we will just have to sell the Georgian tea service to pay for the roof and the grilles."

"Nobody will have to sell anything!" David sat back and tucked his thumbs into the armholes of his waistcoat. "It just so happens I already have funds for the repairs."

There was a moment of surprised silence. "No more loans, David dear," his mother warned. "It's difficult enough to clear what we already owe."

"I haven't taken another loan, Mama. In fact, I've already repaid what we borrowed."

Mrs. Wyncliffe stared. "Where is all this money coming from, dear?" she asked nervously.

"Bit of a windfall, really." He dabbed his mouth with a napkin and pushed away his plate. "We arranged a lottery down at the barracks to mark the end of training and the start of postings. As luck would have it, I drew the winning ticket."

"Oh." His mother's face cleared. "In *that* case I suppose it's all right. I must say, it couldn't have come at a better time, could it, Emma? It is such a relief to have those wretched moneylenders off our backs!"

Emma remained silent.

Dinner over, David opened the atlas and pointed out Leh to his mother. "Not much of a town, just a village at the base of the hill, but the air is pure and the summers are as cool as in Simla. Old Cranks is a bit of a curmudgeon, Nigel Worth says, quite a slave driver, in fact, but he's a very good political officer and speaks the lingos fluently. Having served a couple of years in Leh, Nigel should know."

"But are you confident you'll be able to translate as well as they expect you to, dear?" his mother asked anxiously.

"Of course I am! Do you think Adams would have given me the posting, or Old Cranks would have accepted me, if they'd had any doubts? Border problems being what they are, they do need men they can trust." He stretched his legs and yawned, his arms held high above his head. "Later, if my stars continue to shine, I might even be permitted to take the two-year course in Dehra Doon to train as a cartographer."

Devastated by the prospect of his imminent departure, Mrs. Wyncliffe did not notice her daughter's silence. If David did, he took good care not to remark on it. Emma knew that she would not be able to talk to her brother privately, as she must, until their mother had retired. Forbidden by Dr. Ogbourne to climb stairs until her heart had mended, their mother was housed for the time being in the downstairs parlour, with David installed in the adjoining small spare room.

It was only after her mother was comfortably settled in bed with all the necessary medicines ingested and the mosquito-net securely tucked under the mattress, that Emma could make her way to her brother's room. She found him sprawled on the bed, book in hand, gazing blankly at the ceiling. He started as she entered.

"Em? I thought you'd gone to sleep."

"I'm glad *you* haven't," she replied. "I want to talk to you."

He groaned. "Again?"

"Yes, again." She positioned herself on the edge of the bed and took the book away from him. "*You* staged that absurd burglary last night, didn't you?"

"I?" He struggled up on an elbow. "No, I certainly did *not!*"

"And you took Papa's clock off the mantelpiece," she went on angrily. "You know that it's sterling silver and would fetch a pretty penny once the Archaeological Survey citation is removed. It's just as well I concocted that tale about the Dresden shepherdess the ayah broke last month, otherwise the Inspector would have been here all morning. How *could* you, David?"

"You think I took that clock?"

"Yes. You're in trouble again, aren't you?"

"I didn't and I'm not!"

"Well, I wish I could believe you, but I don't." She stared hard into his defiant face. "Where were you last night?"

"Here. Asleep."

"No, you were not. You didn't get back until past two. I know because I heard your horse stumble just past the front steps."

"That's not true . . ." he began, then stopped. "All right, so I did come home late. So what?"

"So where were you—and don't say it's none of my business because it is! If not from the sale of that clock where did you acquire all this sudden largesse? It wasn't from a winning lottery ticket, was it?"

"What difference does it make so long as I have the money—and I bloody well do! I didn't need to pinch that clock." He flung himself off the bed, dug into the top drawer of the table, withdrew from it a cloth pouch and strewed its contents on the bed. "See?"

Emma scanned the display of currency, and her brother's flushed face, with dismay. David lied so often she was never sure when he spoke the truth.

"You went to Urdu Bazaar," she said flatly.

He did not deny it. "Yes, and as you can see, it was damn well worth it." Sitting down next to her, he ran his fingers through the scattered coins, delighting in the sounds and feel of the metal, his pale, thin face alive with triumph. "My luck has finally turned, Em," he said dreamily, "finally!"

"Because you had one win against a hundred losses?"

"Oh come, come, Em, don't be such a wet blanket. It was just a casual flutter to celebrate a posting after my own heart."

"How many times have you been to Urdu Bazaar since you promised Mama you wouldn't?"

"Oh, for goodness' sake, Em," he snapped without answering her question, "it was just a spur-of-the-moment visit, so don't go making a mountain out of a molehill. What was the harm anyway so long as I won?"

"The harm? *You* should know the answer to that better than I, David. Besides, a promise is a promise. Mama would be heartbroken if she heard you had been gambling again."

The familiar pout returned to his mouth. "I told you I'd pay you back for the ring," he muttered sullenly. "Once the repairs are taken care of . . ."

"I don't want to be paid back, you know that, but neither do I have any more rings to sell. With Mama's medical bills pending . . ."

"Dammit, Em," he cut her off with an oath, "can't you understand that even in the army there is such a thing as keeping up with the crowd? That if chaps treat me, they expect to be treated in return? That I too have social obligations? I can't just accept hospitality without ever returning it, can I?" He clenched his fists. "My God, how I hate never having enough money! You don't know what it's like to count every penny, to buy the cheapest cheroots and pretend the man made a mistake, to manipulate it so that you're out of the room when a collection is made . . ." Trembling, he turned away.

Emma's anger melted. Once again she filled with a familiar ache. "You're wrong, David," she said tiredly. "I *do* know what it's like, but running after easy money is not the answer."

"Then what is?" he tossed back bitterly. "Tutoring cossetted brats? Teaching fat, rich Indians English and fat, rich Europeans Urdu? Is that a solution? And is that how *you* want to spend the rest of your life?"

Emma's face fell, suddenly dispirited. "No, David. Since you ask, no, that is not the way I want to spend the rest of my life. That, however, is the way circumstances force me to spend it at the moment. Until we can somehow improve those circumstances, until Mama is back on her feet, until your position in your regiment is secure . . ." She gave a shrug and left it at that. "Anyway, the fact is that at the moment neither of us can afford financial irresponsibility."

"Look at this house, Em, just look at it!" He waved his arms about, not listening. "It's too big to live in and too damn expensive to maintain. If, as rumoured, a house-tax is introduced, we're done for. Why then don't we sell the blasted property? Why do we continue to pour money down a drain we know to be endless?"

"We can't sell Khyber Kothi," she said. "Mama would never agree to live anywhere else. I'm not sure that I would. Papa built this house when they married. This is where their happiest memories—*our* happiest memories—are. It would be heartbreaking to have to move." Going up to him, she put an arm around his shoulders. "I know how you feel, my dear, believe me, I do. Don't you think there are times when I too feel frustrated?

If only you knew how much *I* hate this . . . this pointless, joyless, hand-to-mouth existence. But what are our options? At the moment, none. We simply have to try to rise above our feelings and make the best of what there is."

"As easy as that, eh?" he asked sarcastically.

"No, it isn't easy, but it has to be done." Gently she stroked his hair, sensing his yearnings, his deprivations, his raring hopes and ambitions and bitterness. "Now that you're posted, your allowances and salary will increase."

"Ha! Ever heard of a second lieutenant becoming a millionaire on his allowances and salary?"

"You don't have to be a millionaire to . . ."

"No more pious lectures, please!" He shook off her arm. "I'm sick and tired of hearing how little filthy lucre matters, how unimportant money is in the grand scheme of things." He flung himself on his bed and trickled the coins lovingly through his fingers. "Let's take one day at a time, Em. And today, let's just be grateful that I *have* been able to raise the money for the repairs. How, when and from where are immaterial." He attempted a smile and thrust out his hand. "And now, if you don't mind, I'd like to have my book back."

Silently, Emma studied her brother's thin, discontented face, the sullen droop of his mouth as it struggled to lift in a smile and the shining, unconcealed wildness in his eyes. He was only a year younger than she, filled with an abundant, nervous energy that showed in the constant restlessness of his hands. She loved him dearly, of course, as she knew he did her, and had always protected him fiercely. At the same time she recognised that in spite of his strapping, well-muscled body, David was weak of will, easily influenced by glib patter and still too immature to be able to assess and evaluate on his own.

"Do you swear that you did not take that clock, David?" she asked quietly.

"Of course I swear!" He sat up and, perhaps in relief that the argument was over, finally smiled. "Let's be happy in our good fortune, Em, however brief. Let's not think of anything beyond that. Agreed?"

Forcing herself not to say more, she sighed and handed him back his book. She still did not believe him but she did not tell him that. "Agreed, but *please* keep away from the gaming-house, David!"

He did not reply as he evaded her eyes and a certain look flashed across his face. Emma knew that look, she had seen it many times before, but she also knew from experience that the more she said, the less likely he was to listen.

"The trouble with you, Em," he said, reaching out to give her ear a playful tweak as good humour was restored, "is that you take your pleasures too heavily."

"And you too lightly!"

"Perhaps." He laughed. "Anyway, who else have you been fighting today—apart from your angelic little brother, eh?"

"Who said I had been fighting?"

"Mundu. Apparently, you had angry words this morning near Qudsia Gardens and one of the men was a firanghi. Anyone I know?"

"I hope not. Anyway, it wasn't a fight, just a silly argument over something inconsequential."

"But nonetheless you read the fellow his fortune!"

"Had he merited more of my time I might have, but he didn't."

He grinned, leapt off the bed, gave her a gentle pat on the rump and pushed her through the door. Emma smiled. For all his weaknesses there was something very lovable about David. Devastated as she was by the loss of that treasured family clock, once again she decided to give him the benefit of the doubt. The familiar disquiet, however, persisted.

*T*he incident to which David referred was unsavoury and had left an ugly taste in Emma's mouth. Preoccupied with other matters, however, she had had little time to dwell upon it; now, with the day's work done, her brother's reminder returned the scene to her mind in all its sordid detail.

On her way back from her tuition that morning she had been thinking about Nawab Murtaza Khan. Much against the wishes of his conservative family, the Nawab had decided that his only daughter must have some education. Hard-pressed for time and reluctant to fit in an extra assignment so far from Civil Lines, Emma had eventually succumbed to his persuasions. Much to the Nawab's delight, the child responded remarkably well to her coaching.

A typical example of Delhi's fast-eroding Muslim aristocracy, like many others the Nawab had fallen on hard times after the disbandment of the Moghul court. Despite his reduced circumstances, however, he continued to pursue his varied literary interests with great dedication. Refined and well educated, he was a founding member of the prestigious Delhi Literary Society, an acknowledged authority on the Koran and an Urdu poet of some celebrity.

Aware of the family's modest means and appreciative of the strong stand Murtaza Khan had taken regarding his daughter's education, Emma had asked for a modest fee for her services. Being a man of fierce pride, he now sought to make recompense by offering to purchase and publish her father's papers under the aegis of the Literary Society. Emma was genuinely touched by the offer; but knowing that to raise the money he would have to sell yet another family heirloom, she had decided not to accept it. The problem was, how to decline without injuring the Nawab's all too fragile pride?

As she rode through Qudsia Gardens that morning cogitating over various possible solutions, she suddenly became aware of a commotion on the river bank ahead. Spurring her horse in the direction of the clamour, she arrived presently on the outskirts of a village—to find herself confronted by a most horrific sight.

At the head of a procession of about fifty villagers were two men beating enormous drums. The centrepiece of the parade was a donkey on which sat a young woman clad in rags that barely covered her nakedness. Her long hair was spread across her breasts and her face was blackened with charcoal powder; pale streaks on her cheeks marked the passage of her silent tears and in the biting cold of the winter morning she shivered convulsively. Alongside the donkey walked a man holding a stick with which he rained lashes on the woman's bare back. From the expressions and gestures of the men, it was evident that they not only endorsed but, indeed, encouraged the proceedings.

Without a second thought Emma dismounted, purse in hand, and pushed her way through the crowd to position herself directly in the path of the procession. Startled, the men came to an untidy halt. Removing her own shawl, she draped it about the shoulders of the woman, then turned to the chief perpetrator. Without raising her voice or displaying her anger, she commanded him to stop beating the defenceless woman. Confused by the unwarranted intrusion, that too by a white mem who spoke fluent Urdu, the man gaped for an instant, then started to bristle.

"This is not a matter that concerns you, memsahib," he said huffily. "Considering her crime, she warrants no sympathy."

"Whatever her crime," Emma insisted, still without anger, "to parade her in this barbaric fashion brings shame not only to her but to your entire community."

Seeing that if he backed down before this interfering woman he would lose face in his community, the man placed his hands on his hips and assumed a posture of defiance. "How she is to be punished is *our* business, memsahib, not that of an outsider!"

Emma's own temper stirred. "Do you consider that the ends of justice are better served when you punish one crime by perpetrating another?"

"This woman is my wife. I have a right to punish her as I wish so long as the panchayat approves!"

Amidst some incoherent mumbles, one or two voices rang out in instant agreement. Frightened and uncomprehending, her arms crossed tightly over the shawl that covered her naked breasts, the woman continued to stare in silence.

"If she is your wife," Emma pointed out, taking a step forward, "all the more reason for you to defend her honour and dignity. Lay down that stick and let her go."

"For what she has done she must be punished," the man snapped. "It may not be your way, memsahib, but it is ours." There were louder cries of support this time. Reassured, the man triumphantly urged the donkey forward and again raised his stick. Before he could bring it down, however, Emma had opened her purse, extracted her Colt and aimed it at him.

"If you touch her again, I promise I will shoot."

The man's eyes dilated and his supporters hastily stepped back. Was this firanghi woman mad? someone whispered. Naturally, someone else whispered back, were they not all?

"Since I am mad," Emma said, picking up the exchange and raising the barrel so that it was aimed at the centre of the man's forehead, "I advise you not to put me to the test—or you will have at least one man less in your community."

The man's arm dropped and the stick fell to the ground. Throwing her a venomous look and cursing under his breath, he retreated. Turning her attention to the silent victim, Emma nodded, and the woman sprang back to life. Gathering the shawl close about her, she slipped off the donkey, darted off into the trees and vanished from sight.

No one made a move to follow her.

Emma replaced the Colt in her purse. "I am aware that you fear the police and that you have good reason to, for they are not always fair with you. However, if you repeat this savage act I will report you to Carter sahib personally and ensure that you have even better reason to fear them than you do now."

She started to walk away and, silently, the crowd parted to clear a path for her. In a nearby thicket, quaking with fright, Mundu stood clutching Anarkali's reins to his chest. As Emma turned to mount her mare, she stopped. Concealed partially by a tree trunk with the reins of his own horse held lightly in one hand was a firanghi. He wore a riding-habit, high black boots and a navy blue silk cravat adorned with paisleys. His head was uncovered. As Emma paused uncertainly, he started to clap.

"Who are you?" she asked, taken aback.

"As of now, an admirer." Pulling himself up to his full height, he gave a courtly bow. "It is not every day that one comes across so impressive a performance, a display of such commendable courage. Those men could have attacked you."

"An admirer from a safe distance, I see!" Emma scoffed, gathering from his speech that he was English. "If you were so concerned for my safety, why did you not step forward and intervene?"

"Considering the adequacy of your own formidable resources, I saw no need to. I doubt if I could have done a better job myself. Besides," he tilted his head and smiled, "it is possible that the woman deserved what she was getting."

"You *approve* of what those men were doing?" Emma asked, outraged.

"Well, if she has been unfaithful to her husband—which I think is the case—then certainly."

"You do not consider corporal punishment abhorrent, especially when perpetrated on a woman with no means of defence?"

"Not if it proves to be an effective deterrent. I doubt if she will dare to stray again." The appraising smile lingered on his lips but made no effort to reach his eyes.

Emma surveyed him with distaste. "Since you speak with such authority," she said, "is one to presume that your extraordinary conclusions derive from personal experience?"

She had the satisfaction of seeing him flush. "I note that your reputation does not belie you, Miss Wyncliffe. You do have a decidedly wicked tongue."

Emma frowned, again taken by surprise. "How do you know my name?"

"How?" He laughed. "If it is supposed to be a secret then it is not a particularly well-kept one. You are, believe me, a lady of quite remarkable renown."

She gave him a cold look. "Well, I do not know who you are, nor have any particular wish to, but I do feel obliged to say that I find your attitudes quite repellent."

Without waiting for his response she climbed into the saddle and galloped away, followed on foot at breakneck speed by a highly relieved Mundu. What an insufferable man, she thought, as she headed back towards Civil Lines. Who on earth was he, anyway?

She was soon to find out.

CHAPTER

2

ot many outside Indian government circles are familiar with the name of Hunza. Those who might be are not inclined to pay it much heed. A minuscule apology for a kingdom, Hunza perches atop a cliff at the end of a topographical cul-de-sac. Tucked away among the protective lower folds of the western Himalayas, it is as unknown to the outside world as it is unknowing of it.

Bounded on the north by the Roof of the World, on the east by the Karakoram ranges, and in the west by the mountains of the Hindu Kush, Hunza is divided from its sister kingdom of Nagar by the six hundred foot–wide Hunza river that thunders down between formidably high cliffs. The surrounding terrain—skeletons of dead glaciers and gigantic moraines—appears untouched by the living world. Towering in the distance above is the giant peak of Rakaposhi, known locally as *Dumani,* Mother of Mist, 25,550 feet of perpendicular rock entombed eternally in shimmering snow. Frequent avalanches cascade down the mountainside, crash into the gorge and produce deafening echoes. A single precarious swing bridge of rope intertwined with birch twigs high over the gorge is the sole means of entry into Hunza.

Unable to discover a name in existence for the region, some years ago a German anthropologist named it Dardistan. The Dards who inhabit this vast, unexplored territory claim direct descendance from Alexander the Great. Judging from their physiognomy—fair hair, light eyes, and pale skins as translucent as alabaster—their resemblance to their European cousins is certainly striking. Despite the ancestral connection, however, the Dards despise the white infidel and have little cause to trust him. Hunza and Nagar pay token allegiance to the Maharaja of Kashmir and to the Emperor of China, although with characteristic arrogance they snap their fingers at both.

Like the rest of the Dards, the Hunzakut—as the people of Hunza are called—are obsessively independent, as inhospitable and hostile as the glacial world in which they live. Those few outsiders who have managed to survive a visit have not been in a hurry to return. As nimble as deer, as surefooted as rock lizards, and as instinctive as mountain spirits, the Hunzakut are superb mountaineers. With only marginal cultivable land, the population of about ten thousand subsists mainly on fresh and dried fruit, especially apricots, and on local wines derived from them. Untouched by the trappings of alleged civilisation, the Hunzakut are among the healthiest, hardiest and longest-lived people in the world.

They are also among the most bloodthirsty.

The favoured occupation of the Hunzakut is plunder, their targets the rich caravans that traverse the Silk Road routes between Leh, Yarkand and Kashgar. Indeed, if the name of Hunza is known at all beyond its frontiers, it is as a synonym for brigandry, slaughter and the slave trade.

Understandably, therefore, it was on precisely these less palatable aspects of the Hunzakut character that the thoughts of Colonel Mikhail Borokov of the Russian Imperial Army dwelt as he sat one cold winter mid-morning facing Safdar Ali Khan, the Mir of Hunza.

The long, drawn-out ceremonial meal had finally concluded. As guest of honour, it had been Colonel Borokov's privilege to be served the head of the suckling yak that had formed the main ingredient of the stew cooked in apricot kernel oil. Neither he nor his guard of ten Cossacks had tasted such tender meat since they had left Tashkent weeks ago, and they had eaten extremely well—rather less well, however, of the extraordinary dessert: grated glacier ice sweetened with fruit juices.

The Mir expressed himself honoured by the justice his guest had done to his humble offerings. Borokov accepted the compliment with a wan smile. The large room in which they sat atop the Mir's stone fort balanced on the edge of a cliff was icy, the oily expressions of friendship not to be trusted, and he was undeniably ill at ease. However, to display diffidence now at this vital juncture in their negotiations was unthinkable. As Alexei Smirnoff had instructed, the best way to deal with this barbaric dictator would be to appear fearless and give him no quarter.

In any case, Borokov was tiring of the fulsome conviviality. They had spent two hideously cold days searching for ibex in the frozen ravines; another day had passed in inspection of the irrigation system which was the lifeblood of the people. Skilfully planned, the canals had been excavated a thousand years ago by hand with tools made from ibex horn, and Borokov's admiration had been genuine. One of the water channels ran along the top of a wall forty feet high, others across sheer rock or through long tunnels painstakingly bored. The headwaters were about half a mile up the ravine on the edge of which Hunza rested, below the massive glacier that fed the system through twelve months of the year.

Borokov hated mountains. He hated the thin, frozen air, the terrifying heights and the glassy, slippery tracks. He and his Cossacks had been expertly escorted by Safdar Ali's men through a fairly low pass that was still negotiable, but now if they dawdled and the pass became snowbound, he would have to remain in this frightful place until at least May—and if the cold didn't kill him, then the boredom surely would. With the midday meal over, as soon as the mountainous pile of dried fruit arrived with carafes of local mulberry wine, he made another determined bid to settle down to business.

"Being aware of Your Highness's extreme perceptiveness," he said resolutely before the Mir could broach some other trifling matter, "I am curious to learn the impression Your Highness formed of Colonel Algernon Durand."

The unlettered savage had no right to the exalted form of address but Borokov knew that it would please him, as would the flattery. From the pyramid of fruit and nuts he carefully selected an apple and took a bite. It was as sweet as nectar.

"The Englishman from Gilgit?" Safdar Ali's expression clouded as he bit fiercely into something fat and purple like a prune. The pulp from the fruit splashed onto his scanty, pointed beard and then onto his lap. He did not bother to wipe it. "The man is a fool," he said with open contempt, "and an arrogant one at that."

"And the terms he offered, Your Highness found them generous?"

"The terms?" An expression of cunning flashed across the Mir's face. For a moment he played with the turquoise and coral clasp of the belt that held his heavy Chinese silk dress about his waist, then shrugged. "Certainly. I have no cause for complaint."

Of course he lied through his teeth! According to Borokov's informant, the Mir had flown into an insane rage with Durand, threatened to cut off his head and return it to the Indian government on a plate. "In that case"— Borokov smiled—"Your Highness will have even less to complain of after hearing the terms that I have been authorised to offer by my government in St. Petersburg. As I had mentioned to Your Highness's emissary in Tashkent . . ."

"What you mentioned to my emissary is unacceptable!" Safdar Ali snapped. He had no idea where St. Petersburg was, nor did he care. Having been assured by his advisers that like Peking, Kabul and Calcutta it was no larger than his own kingdom, he saw no reason to show this man any more latitude than he had the Englishman. "If your raja wants our co-operation, then he must be prepared to make adequate recompense." He brought his sword down sharply on the table and sent the fruit skittering.

Borokov did not react to the show of temper. He was already aware of the size of the carrot the Angliski had dangled: twenty-five thousand rupees annually contingent on several conditions.

"May I ask how much Your Highness might consider adequate?"

The Mir looked him straight in the eye. "The English have offered thirty thousand."

"We would be willing to match that," Borokov intoned smoothly.

Safdar Ali thrust out his lower lip in a pout. "If I accept your offer, then the Englishman will retract his."

"I was about to add that *should* our conditions be met, my raja might see his way to making a higher offer."

"Well, before I can give you an answer, naturally I will have to hear your conditions and consult my Wazir."

Standing deferentially behind his master's chair, the old prime minister nodded.

"Naturally." Borokov rose and strolled across to the edge of the open platform outside the room on the top level of the fort. In the light of early afternoon the frozen vistas of the valley, the village below and the towering grandeur of Rakaposhi beyond were magnificent, but he was unimpressed. In fact, he shuddered. "We would also be willing to grant a subsidy to your son."

Borokov knew that the English had refused this particular demand of his and that Safdar Ali was peeved about it.

"Well, how much?" the Mir asked baldly.

Borokov walked back and sat on the edge of his seat as an indication of his urgency. "Considering that the prince is only four years old, my superiors consider five thousand rupees annually to be a reasonable amount."

He was again irritated by the need to converse through two interpreters. The Mir spoke only Burishaski, the Hunza dialect, and not a word of Russian, Turki, Persian or Hindustani. The German anthropologist might have considered Burishaski "the cradle of human thought as expressed in language," but to Borokov it sounded like guttural gibberish. The Mir, however, did understand Pushtu, the language of the Pathans. His interpreter, a Pathan, translated the Burishaski into Pushtu, which was then further translated into Russian by one of the Cossacks who had lived among Pathans long enough to be passably familiar with their language. It was a slow, cumbersome process and the Mir's span of concentration was deplorably brief.

Borokov waved an arm at the display of lavish offerings he had brought. "Apart from the subsidies there will be many more gifts, Your Highness. My raja can be extremely generous."

With the tip of his sword the Mir picked up a heavy sable coat, swung it around in the air and draped it across his knees. He skimmed a palm across the silky soft fur. There was no doubt that compared to the offensively cheap baubles the Englishman had brought—which the Mir had tossed out of the room in a rage—the Russian's gifts held greater promise for the future.

"Whatever else the Englishman offered," Borokov continued, "I doubt if it included what we are prepared to give."

"Guns on wheels?" the Mir asked.

"Yes, those can be arranged. Also," Borokov hesitated, as if reluctant to say what he was about to, "modern magazine rifles of small calibre and the smokeless powder we have recently developed. At present Your Highness's troops have nothing but matchlocks, breechloaders and jezails."

Safdar Ali concealed his elation behind a frown. "The other man who came from your raja . . ."

"Captain Grombetchevsky?"

"Yes. He made no mention of all this."

"With the arrival of Durand in Gilgit, circumstances have changed. Your Highness needs to be forearmed against attack."

"Bah! Durand has no army with which to attack."

"On the contrary, with the creation of the Imperial Service Corps he now has all the Kashmiri troops in Dardistan under his command."

Safdar Ali assumed an expression of solemnity. "We are a peace-loving people." He sighed sadly. "We abhor violence. Why should we wish to fight the British who come to us in friendship?"

Borokov regarded the pale, delicate face before him and tried to reconcile it with the man's reputation as a vicious cutthroat. No more than twenty-two, fair-complexioned enough to pass for European, Safdar Ali had an effeminate face, slitted Mongolian eyes and light brown hair and beard. Patricide and fratricide being among the devout traditions of Hunza, three years earlier he had honoured them by murdering his father, Ghazan Khan; strangling and dismembering two of his brothers; and tossing a third off a cliff to grab the throne for himself. Borokov let the blatancy pass.

"Gilgit is only fifty-two miles from Hunza, Your Highness," he pointed out instead.

"But two hundred and twenty miles from Srinagar!"

"As head of the recently revived Gilgit Agency, Durand already builds roads for his troops and his supplies and extends the telegraph from Srinagar with the added funds sanctioned. Your Highness is far too erudite not to recognise the motives behind these sudden developments on the doorstep of Hunza."

"Pshaw!" His host waved the observation away with a rude gesture. "The British will not get past Nagar."

"The British will swallow Nagar and not even belch."

"Are you suggesting that as fighters we cannot match the British?" Safdar Ali asked more in astonishment than indignation.

"On the contrary, I know that you can—but only if you give your troops modern weapons."

"The British will use that as an excuse to attack us!"

"The British will attack anyway. They will not need an excuse."

Borokov refrained from reminding the Mir that his father had suffered no qualms when asking the Chinese for arms to fight the British. In exchange he had permitted them to claim Hunza as part of their Celestial Empire, which the Chinese still did. It was only because the guns had got inextricably stuck in the Himalayan snows that a confrontation with Britain had been averted.

"We have signed a treaty with Durand," Safdar Ali said.

"The treaty is not worth its paper since neither Durand nor Your Highness has the slightest intention of honouring it." Borokov's patience was again wearing thin, but he knew that if he were fool enough to lose his temper he might also lose his head. "The British do not trust you," he said, adding quickly, "any more than Your Highness trusts the British. Last August, Durand threatened to withhold your subsidy until his compatriot, Lieutenant Francis Younghusband, was granted safe passage through Hunza on his return from the Pamirs."

Safdar Ali flushed. "How do you know all this?"

The Russian leaned forward, ignoring the question. "I also tell you, Your Highness, that Durand came not to befriend Hunza but to reconnoitre, to learn the terrain, to assess where roads could be made, bridges strengthened, positions effectively defended in the gorge, and to gauge the vulnerability of your forts. Did he make notes during his visit?"

Safdar Ali remained silent.

Borokov laughed. "Colonel Durand is headstrong, ambitious and dying for a scrap. He also happens to be the brother of the Foreign Secretary in the Indian government—a dangerous combination."

Safdar Ali's mouth turned down further. "I do not wish to take the offensive."

"But you do need to defend yourselves—and the British *will* attack Hunza. They will trap you in your forts and overrun your country. They will forcibly convert you to Christianity, defile your traditions, confiscate your lands, rob you of your independence and your dignity and treat you with contempt, as they do the Indians. In time, the name of Hunza will vanish from the maps and your ancient kingdom will simply cease to exist. Once they are here, like locusts they will devour everything. As they have India they will strip Dardistan clean."

Had he gone too far? Borokov cast a surreptitious glance at the Hunza guards ranged at the far end of the platform out of hearing, their breech-loaders (all looted from caravans) at the ready, but the sight of his own well-armed Cossacks ranged alongside reassured him. However unpredictable his moods, Safdar Ali would not, he hoped, be fool enough to provoke an "incident." And despite his childish posturings, the man did desperately want those guns.

"If there is anything that gives the British sleepless nights," Borokov continued softly, "it is the nightmare of a Russian invasion. They will not rest until they have secured all the passes in their frontiers. . . ."

"These are not their frontiers!" The Mir struck his fist against his palm. "These are our frontiers, our mountains, *our* passes!"

"Unless adequately defended they will soon be theirs. As for that subsidy Durand promised, you will not receive it until your people stop raiding the caravans. Is that not the main condition Durand imposed?"

"If we do not raid, how do we survive?" the Mir asked petulantly, confirming both the charge and the contention. "Neither the English nor you have a right to deprive us of our livelihood!"

"My raja has no wish to interfere in your internal affairs."

"Oh?" Safdar Ali was briefly amused. "Then what exactly does your raja wish in exchange for all this bounty—apart from my help in keeping the English away from our passes?"

"The weapons will need to be brought through a pass that is both safe and secret."

"The Shimsul is safe."

"But no longer secret. Younghusband has recently negotiated it."

"There are other passes. . . ."

"All of which will be soon known to Younghusband and his masters. When he visited you recently, he came with instructions to explore *all* means of entry into Hunza from the north. Apart from the Shimsul he has successfully explored others, even the Mustagh. The Hindu Kush passes are lower than those of the Karakoram and easier to traverse. Indeed, some are open the year round; to cross others one need not even dismount and can be in the Kashmir valley in a few days to water the horses in the Wular lake."

"And you think that is all we have?" the Mir offered slyly. "There is not a Hunzakut alive who does not know every Himalayan valley, every trough, every precipice and ledge and crevasse, who cannot negotiate the mountains with his eyes shut."

"The British learn fast."

"Not so fast! They cannot defend those passes without our help either."

"Not at the moment, perhaps, but the weapons cannot arrive in Hunza until late summer. In the meantime the British will not remain idle." Borokov's tone hardened. "It is mandatory, as much in your interest as in ours, that a safe route unknown to the British be made available for the guns on wheels."

"You will have no need for passes. We will take delivery at our fort at Shimsul. Transporting them here will be our concern."

Borokov's eyes narrowed. "That will not be acceptable to my raja," he said shortly. "The delivery to Hunza will be made by us through a clandestine pass. Or not at all."

There was a thick, pregnant silence during which neither man spoke. Safdar Ali peered into the distance and caressed his beard.

"You already have such a pass in mind, Colonel Borokov?"

The icy winds that whipped across the platform were excruciatingly cold against Borokov's skin. Even so, he felt his neck prickle with sweat. This then was the crux of their negotiations, the reason why he had waited so long for this encounter, travelled so far and so hard in this diabolical land.

"Yes, we do have such a pass in mind." In the sudden silence came the boom of another avalanche as it crashed down thousands of feet into the gorge. Borokov waited for the echoes to die down, then took a deep breath. "It is the Yasmina."

"Ah!"

The Mir expressed no other reaction, but as Borokov spoke the name the air around them turned even more arctic. Looking startled, the old Wazir slowly sank down on a stool. The interpreters stopped shuffling their feet and stole uneasy glances at each other. Borokov kept his bland gaze fixed to the middle distance, his breath trapped in his throat. The Wazir opened his mouth but the Mir silenced him with a gesture.

"How is it, Colonel Borokov," Safdar Ali asked with a mocking smile, "that of all the great white men of knowledge in your country, not one has yet discovered the Yasmina? That this one little pass has actually escaped your untiring surveillance?"

"Your Highness knows full well why the Yasmina has not been discovered." Borokov kept his face impassive. "Indeed, why it might never be discovered. The secret of its location is known only to your people. To sustain the secrecy every Dard has been nurtured for generations on stories of malicious, vengeful spirits said to haunt the Yasmina. Across the length and breadth of the Himalayas one is constantly assailed with legends of ogres and fairies and evil demons and mysterious abductions, of people who have vanished from the Yasmina never to be seen again."

"You believe these legends to be untrue?"

"What I believe is of no consequence. It is what your people believe that matters. Even if its location were known, there is not a single porter or guide or pack animal in Dardistan that can be hired for the Yasmina. Not even Younghusband has been able to find it—and the British have searched for it for years. There are many rumours, but since they conflict with each other it is impossible to sift truth from conjecture." He took a handful of pine nuts and tossed them into his mouth, marvelling at the richness of their taste. "Durand too sought the Yasmina, did he not?"

Lifting a walnut from a large basket of the most exotic dried fruit Borokov had seen outside Afghanistan, Safdar Ali pressed it hard between his palms and, with astonishing ease, cracked it open. He did not rise to the bait and the question went unanswered.

"You want to use the Yasmina to pour troops into my country?"

"Only if the British do, and only to assist in your defences."

"How then are your people different from the British?"

"Come to Tashkent and see for yourself," Borokov urged. "We Russians treat our allies with respect. We make no effort to change their ways into ours. With our modern methods of irrigation we merely teach them to produce bigger, better crops, to green barren lands, to eat well and to live more fully. There is no starvation in our empire as there is in India. Wherever there is Russian presence in Central Asia there is prosperity. My emperor's emissary in Tashkent, the Governor-General, His Excellency Baron Boris von Adelssohn, would be honoured by a visit from a Mir of Hunza to see for himself what Russia has achieved in Asia."

Unimpressed, Safdar Ali pincered the Russian with a haughty stare. "Kings like myself have no need to travel outside our kingdoms," he said, tossing aside the sable coat as he rose. "Anyway, I am tired of all this talk. We will resume the discussion later."

Borokov cursed inwardly, but having no option he too rose. In silent frustration he followed his whimsical host through the trap-door in the floor down the thick log of wood that functioned as a stairway. As they reached the chamber below, Safdar Ali halted.

"The Yasmina Pass is our sacred legacy from our forefathers, Colonel Borokov," he said. "It belongs to us and only to us. It is our secret and will remain so." He walked another few steps towards a second trap-door leading further down and again stopped. "At least, until after we have received the guns."

Borokov felt a surge of exhilaration. Safdar Ali would continue to use delaying tactics, hedge and evade and make further demands, prolong the cat-and-mouse game with tiresome tantrums. Then just before they reached breaking point he would agree to everything.

No, the negotiations for the Yasmina were by no means over.

*I*t was Saturday morning.

In her room Emma prepared to leave for St. Stephen's College, where she had an appointment with the librarian. The morning sky, dazzlingly blue and typical of a North Indian winter, held promise of a perfect day. As she dressed, Emma hummed to herself and considered what lay ahead with pleasurable anticipation. Following her visit to the College she was to accompany Jenny Purcell, her closest friend, on one of the would-be bride's interminable shopping expeditions. At four in the afternoon, after luncheon at the Purcell home, John Bryson, Jenny's fiancé, would come to fetch them to the Town Hall for Geoffrey Charlton's talk about his journey across Central Asia on the recently completed Transcaspian Railway. The ancient civilisations of Central Asia were a subject close to Emma's heart; she had been looking forward to the lantern slide lecture for days.

As she was about to put her papers in her portmanteau, she heard the rumble of carriage wheels on the drive. Assuming that her tikka gharry had arrived, she looked out of her window to see that the carriage in the driveway was not a tikka but an unfamiliar and quite smart brougham with matching greys. Her mother had not mentioned that she expected callers this morning, and in any case it was time for the daily mid-morning nap Dr. Ogbourne had stipulated. Intending to summon Majid and instruct him accordingly, Emma opened her door to be confronted with the bearer holding an envelope. It was, she saw with some surprise, addressed to her. Wonderingly, she slit it open and from within extracted an elegantly printed ivory visiting card, accompanied by a brief note:

Mr. Damien Granville begs to be permitted to call upon Miss Emma Wyncliffe, the most admirable memsahib in all of Delhi.

The name of the sender was repeated on the card, together with an address, Shahi Baug, Nicholson Road, Delhi.

Emma was not familiar with the name, but some curious instinct told her that this was the same impossible man with whom she had crossed swords some days earlier near Qudsia Gardens. She marvelled anew at his audacity; obviously, he was blessed with even less sensitivity than he had displayed on that unmemorable occasion. Tearing the note and the card into small pieces, she replaced the fragments in the envelope and handed it to Majid to return to the waiting messenger as a fitting response to the impertinence.

Unable to conceive of any situation in which she would wish to see Damien Granville again, she dismissed him from her mind.

*D*elhi's Town Hall, seat of the local government, was a colonial edifice typical of Victorian architecture. Set in the heart of the city, the gargantuan structure contained offices of the Municipality, the Chamber of Commerce, the Delhi Literary Society, a museum, a library, and a European Club. It stood within Queen's Gardens—colloquially known as Company Baug—at the eastern end of Chandni Chowk, nub of the commercial district close to the East India Railway station, and was the venue of many formal gatherings.

Geoffrey Charlton's lecture, organised by the Delhi Literary Society, was a popular draw and the hall was filled to capacity. Having arrived early, John Bryson had managed to secure for them seats in the third row from the front, with a good view of the dais, where a large black apparatus had been placed on a table. The Rudge magic lantern—John explained—was the most modern of its kind and was being seen for the first time in Delhi. Suspended on the wall behind was a large canvas on which images from the glass slides were to be projected.

First to take his seat on the dais was Delhi's Lieutenant-Governor, a portly man with beady little eyes, known for the great reverence in which he held the sound of his own voice. He was followed by the Commissioner, other government officials and leading lights of the Society, including Nawab Murtaza Khan. Finally, and somewhat modestly, came Geoffrey Charlton.

"My goodness, he's dreadfully young, isn't he?" Jenny's gasp was embarrassingly loud. "I thought he'd be an old fuddy-duddy like the others John drags me to listen to."

"He's thirty-four," Emma answered, pointedly lowering her own voice to a whisper.

"Oh? How do you know?"

"The *Sentinel* carried a biographical note on him when they ran his articles about the trip."

"What does he write about?"

"Mostly Central Asian affairs."

"Is he based in London?"

"I would imagine so."

"Married?"

"How on earth should I know?"

"You certainly seem interested enough to have found out."

"Geoffrey Charlton is a widely read journalist," Emma said severely. "You would be interested in him too if you didn't keep your head buried in those dreadful romance magazines you buy by the shovel load."

"Oh, I also have it buried in the hatched, matched and despatched every morning," Jenny retorted cheerfully. "Anyway, who cares about silly old Central Asia?"

"Well, then, why bother to come at all?"

"Because everyone else has and I'd rather be bored than left out." She cast an admiring glance at the dais where Charlton was arranging his equipment. "He's *not* married, you know," she declared firmly.

"You can tell just by looking at him?"

"Just by *sniffing,* my dear. Don't forget whose daughter I am—Mama can tell a bachelor at a hundred paces with her eyes closed."

"Well, even if he is unmarried," John said, "*you* certainly won't be for long, so save your soulful looks for someone able to reciprocate better."

"Spoil sport!" Jenny gave his hand a fond squeeze and with a smile of perfect contentment settled back to listen.

Expectedly, the Lieutenant-Governor's "few words" stretched to fifteen minutes and the audience clapped vociferously out of sheer relief when he finished. Sensing the mood in the hall, however, the remaining speakers kept their speeches brief. Finally, to the accompaniment of prolonged applause, Geoffrey Charlton rose to take his position by the table.

"Whatever its political implications, or the motives behind its construction," he began, "the Transcaspian Railway is an engineering achievement of remarkable ingenuity, foresight and determination, and only the most churlish amongst us would deny Russia her moment of glory. By establishing an effective means of communication across a region as vast, mysterious and unexplored as lies between the Caucasian and the Himalayan mountain ranges, she has earned the admiration, gratitude and, no doubt, envy of the world.

"Plans for the railway were first evolved in 1873 by Monsieur Ferdinand de Lesseps of Suez Canal fame, who envisaged a line from Calais to Calcutta. Considered over-ambitious, the plan was abandoned, as were several others. Eleven years ago General Annenkoff, then Comptroller of the Transport Department of the Russian Army, was invited by the Commander-in-Chief to take charge of the construction of the Transcaspian, for this is essentially a military railway. Annenkoff completed the project in record time, and on 27, May 1888 the inaugural train carrying a contingent of Russian soldiers steamed into Samarkand, its present terminus, opening a revolutionary new chapter in long-range land transportation.

"Now, as printed in the Russian Bradshaw, there is a daily service from the Caspian to Samarkand. An uninterrupted journey takes seventy-two hours over nine hundred miles with sixty-one halts. A second-class one-way ticket costs thirty-eight roubles—three pounds and sixteen shillings—which works out to about a penny a mile." He smiled. "A very worthwhile bargain, I assure you."

The audience agreed heartily.

Charlton continued, "Many will be relieved to hear that I do not intend to linger over dreary statistics and technical data. About those I would be happy to answer questions later. What I intend now is to allow my slides to speak for themselves and to invite you to join me on the actual journey. As you will see, the photographs present astonishing and unexpected aspects of a region so far believed to be bare, with not much to offer a tourist. I consider myself privileged to have had the opportunity to verify just how inaccurate these preconceptions are.

"Central Asia is the meeting point of four great religions—Buddhism, Islam, Christianity and Zoroastrianism—and a multi-cultural delight rich in history and archaeology. Its oases are marvellously fertile, its soil a treasure house of minerals and the varied ethnicity of its people of great historical significance. Indeed, there is so much here to captivate and inform that one hardly knows where to begin."

The wall lamps dimmed; a strong beam of electric light from within the apparatus was switched on and the projector came alive. As Charlton inserted the first slide in the machine, a magically enlarged street scene in St. Petersburg, capital city of the Tsars, appeared on the screen with perfect clarity.

"Once all requisite permissions have been secured in St. Petersburg," Charlton resumed, "to all intents and purposes the starting point of the Transcaspian Railway is Baku, on the western shore of the Caspian. From here a boat takes one to Uzun Ada, which is the first halt in the Central Asian region."

As one mesmerising slide followed another, the audience plunged deeper into the mystique of lands strange and sprawling and breathtakingly exotic. Spellbound, they were whisked across lofty mountains, legendary rivers, sinister deserts, verdant valleys, lush oasis towns and a hundred other aspects of the burgeoning Russian Empire. It was an ever-changing kaleidoscope of alien communities, of ancient cities half buried in the sands, of walled capitals with noble squares, ornamented minarets, mud palaces, blue-domed mosques and mausoleums, and bewildering bazaars selling everything from pigeons to porcelain. With a minimum of rhetoric, Charlton brought within touching distance many forgotten civilisations, arcane cultures and nomadic lifestyles of Central Asia. It was an entrancing itinerary of places most knew merely as names in a newspaper or a history book: Askabad, Kandahar, the oasis town of Merv, the Ferghana valley—cradle of the Moghuls and their heavenly horses—Bokhara and Samarkand, the twin cities of Tamerlane, and Tashkent, once the capital of Alexander the Third and now the centre of Russian military might in Asia.

As a travel guide Charlton was compelling, his attention to minutiae both academic and anecdotal. The knowledge he had acquired was prodigious, his delivery confident and yet modest. As did everyone else, Emma listened and watched with unmoving attention, marvelling at Charlton's prodigious memory, which allowed him to speak at such length with only occasional glances at his notes. Nobody, not even Jenny with marginal interest in the subject, noticed that more than an hour and a half had elapsed by the time the lamps were again brightened and Charlton declared the floor open for questions.

Immediately, a dozen hands flew up. A wizened little man with ginger hair whom Emma knew to be an engineer with the railways asked the first question. "Since there is no coal in the region, what fuel do the Russians use to run their locomotives?"

"They use *astaki* from the oil fields of Baku," Charlton replied. "The residue of petroleum after distillation is said to be six times as economical a fuel as coal. Since the Russians are sufficiently blessed with it, they now plan to illuminate the entire town of Bokhara with petroleum."

In response to other questions the audience learned that each piece of timber, iron and steel used for construction had been transported from the forests and workshops of Russia; that the labour force had consisted of twenty thousand men; and that the total cost of the project was approximately five thousand pounds sterling per mile for the tracks and another half million for sidings, stations and ancillary structures.

A Parsee gentleman who owned a prosperous wine shop in Chandni Chowk stood up to inquire what effect the Russian railway might have on British exports to the region.

"A very profound effect," Charlton replied. "Russia now has a monopoly of imports into Central Asian markets. Until very recently, goods manufactured in Manchester and Birmingham were plentiful in Bokhara's twenty bazaars. Now, few English wares are to be seen and shops are flooded with Russian manufactures. Fifteen years ago, there was only one Russian merchant in Bokhara; today, the town has branches of the Imperial Russian Bank, the Central Asian Commercial Company, the Russian Transport Society and private Russian enterprises thrive. In 1888," he ruffled his papers and pulled out a sheet, "Russian trade with the khanate of Bokhara alone was worth a grand total of about a million and a half pounds sterling."

"And the reasons for this dismal state of affairs from the Indo-British point of view?" The shopkeeper posed a second question.

"Several. Cargo from Europe and India is caravan-borne. There are delays due to bad weather, accidents and prohibitive duties to be considered. Russian goods on the other hand now travel swiftly and safely on the Transcaspian and are exempt from levies. In her search for new outlets, Russia cuts into traditional British markets as far afield as Afghanistan, Baluchistan, Persia and, indeed, our own border towns, where smuggling is rampant. Add to that the systematic, well-planned caravan raids by Hunza bandits, encouraged tacitly by the Russians, and the picture turns even grimmer."

Having scant interest in politics and commerce, Emma waited impatiently for a return to history. What she wanted to hear about were the ancient cities of Merv, the human hecatombs of Genghis Khan, and Huang Tsang, the seventh-century Chinese Buddhist monk who journeyed hundreds of miles on his own through the region. At one point she swallowed her shyness and almost put up her hand to ask a question, but then a determined brigadier with a martial moustache and a monocle leapt up and it was too late.

"Do you consider, sir, that a Russian military invasion of India is feasible?"

It was, Emma knew, the most hotly debated question of the day and an expectant murmur rippled across the room. She sat back again, heaved a sigh and resigned herself to listen.

"Russia has dreamed of invading India for over a century, ever since the reign of their empress Catherine," Charlton said. "The fact that none of her plans materialised is due more to Russian contingencies—and our own good fortune—than to British counter-tactics." He paused to allow his criticism of the government to be absorbed. "Now, with the successful commissioning of the railway, the prospect of an invasion assumes greater urgency. Fifty years ago, Russia's frontier was a thousand miles from Kabul. Today, with the conquest of Kokand, Samarkand, Bokhara and Khiva, it lies only three hundred miles away from Peshawar. With Russia now extending the railway to Tashkent, who can tell where the frontier will be fifty years from now?"

"What might be an accurate assessment of Russian military forces in Asia?" the brigadier asked.

Charlton scratched his chin. "Well, the Russians are reluctant to reveal exact figures, naturally, but as far as I could gather they number about forty-five thousand."

"As against our own seventy thousand British soldiers and double that number of Indian sepoys, sah!" a major in uniform pointed out with righteous pride.

"True, but let us not be dazzled by numbers," Charlton warned. "Rightly or wrongly, since the Mutiny native sepoys are not permitted to bear modern arms and this embargo seriously depletes our firepower. All Russian troops, on the other hand, are equipped with modern weapons, and, I might add, live extremely well, indeed, far better than do our own."

"How so?" the major demanded.

"Well, each Russian barrack, for instance, has its own dining room in which the food served is plentiful and of good quality. If armies march on their stomach, then none more so than the Russian. Horse-drawn field kitchens equipped to cook for two hundred at a time travel with the army and provide ready meals at all times of the day or night. Compared with our own average soldier, therefore, the Russian is not only better equipped but healthier, sturdier, more capable of enduring long marches in sub-zero Himalayan temperatures and more content with his lot."

"Why could we not also introduce the same sensible system in our own military forces?" the major persisted.

Charlton smiled. "Of course we could—if in its great wisdom Whitehall did not consider otherwise. I duly made the suggestion on my return to London, but the War Office threw up its hands. Sixty pounds per field kitchen? They were horrified at what they considered wanton expense!" He spread his hands and smiled wryly. "Nothing better exemplifies the shortsightedness of our penny-wise, pound-foolish military policy in India."

He paused for a sip of water, then continued. "The truth is, ladies and gentlemen, that Russian presence in Central Asia is almost entirely military. Although friendly and hospitable, Russian officers were perfectly frank about their impatience to expand southwards across the Himalayas. Already Russia strengthens and flexes her muscles, today she claims this, tomorrow she usurps that—and so it will go on. The richest target for her in Asia is India. With the Transcaspian Railway virtually at our doorstep, what better conditions could exist for an invasion?"

"But surely our intelligence agents are alert enough to detect clandestine incursions and encroachments in the Himalayas?" a sprightly little man asked from the rear.

"Undoubtedly, and I am glad of the opportunity to say a few words about our Military Intelligence Department, Political Department and the Survey of India, whose agents—British as well as Indian—gather information at such peril to themselves. Incredibly courageous, constantly under threat from assassins and brutal climatic extremes, they explore and chart and relay back vital news from Central Asia. Some never return, others suffer imprisonment and savage torture to limp back to a premature death, irreparably damaged in mind and body. Indeed, you would be appalled to learn at what human cost intelligence is sought, collected and sustained in the Himalayas and beyond."

"Hear, hear, sah!" someone shouted and the audience took up the cry with vigorous applause.

"However, even these valiant efforts," Charlton resumed when the clapping had subsided, "are not enough. It remains the duty of each one of us to remain individually vigilant. Russia plants agents in India to spread disaffection and misinformation, to perpetuate the myth that Britain rules India through tyranny. These agents work secretly, labour hard to manufacture mischievous rumour, to exploit human greed, to gull the uninformed and to seek covert means of entry into India."

"The rumours that you have been reporting recently in the *Sentinel,* concerning this murder in the . . ."

"Ah, thereby hangs a tale, sir!" Charlton quickly raised a hand to halt the question from the gentleman in the rear. "A tale I would rather not discuss at the moment. When the rumours are substantiated and the facts confirmed—as they will be—everything will be exposed in print down to the last detail. On that you have my word."

One or two more attempted to raise the same question, but Charlton refused to relent. The remaining questions were concerned mostly with the railway and the logistics involved in running it. Finally he glanced at his pocket-watch and started to shuffle his papers.

"The note on which I would like to end," he said, "is, inevitably, the threat of Russian aggression to our Empire. Like all of you here and many others, I find myself gravely concerned about our government's policy of 'masterly inactivity.' Russia creeps forward inch by inch, claiming and attacking and annexing with impunity. We watch, turn away our faces and mumble diplomatic inanities. I believe sincerely, indeed passionately, that unless we take action now, unless we abandon our attitude of apologia, unless we stop pretending to be blind, deaf and mute in the face of this very real threat, the British Empire in Asia may well be rubble by the end of the century."

His voice faded away and the audience rose to its collective feet in a rousing ovation. If Charlton had ended on the dramatic note for effect, he had certainly achieved it. A few in the audience made for the exits to avoid getting caught in bottlenecks, but a veritable sea of admirers surged towards the dais to deluge the speaker with a hundred further questions. As they threaded their own path through the crowd towards the main doors, Jenny gave Emma a sharp nudge in the ribs with her elbow.

"So, now are you persuaded to join us at the Prices' burra khana next Saturday?" she whispered with a sly grin.

Emma shrugged. "Perhaps. We shall see."

Jenny laughed, knowing that with Geoffrey Charlton as the bait, wild horses would not keep Emma away from the evening.

Colonel Mikhail Borokov was bored, so bored in fact that he doubted if he could survive another day in Hunza. A further week had passed since their discussion and Safdar Ali still showed no inclination to return to the all-important negotiations for the Yasmina. Each time Borokov made an effort to reopen the topic, the Mir postponed the discussion until after "the entertainment."

The previous morning Borokov had arrived at the fort early from his encampment, determined to continue the dialogue. The Mir, however, with other tiresome diversions in mind had insisted on explaining to him every detail of the cannon that had greeted his arrival in Hunza with a thirty-one-gun salute. Since the only man in Hunza who could be trusted and knew how to fire it was the prime minister, it was he who had performed the honours. The massive weapon had been cast by an ironsmith from Wakhan and all available household utensils had been melted down to supply the metal for it. The ironsmith had done an admirable job, everyone agreed, but to prevent him from repeating the feat for the benefit of Hunza's enemies, he had subsequently been beheaded.

In between compilation of a report for Alexei Smirnoff, cautious sorties along the fearsome glaciers, and keeping an anxious watch on the leaden skies for worsening weather, Borokov worried vaguely about the mysterious "entertainment" upon which the Mir appeared to place such importance. Winter ice prevented tedious chukkers of polo, the national sport of Dardistan, and there was precious little else in Hunza that could be called amusing.

Finally the great day arrived.

The entertainment was to take place in the flagstoned courtyard—covered in powdery snow and absolutely freezing. Crowds surged in a high state of excitement around two iron stakes grouted in the centre of the courtyard, between which was tied a figure with a gag stretched across his mouth. As Borokov took his seat beside the Mir, he guessed that the "entertainment" was a routine execution. Sparing only a passing thought for the unfortunate wretch who was to be deprived of his life, he heaved a sigh of relief.

The victim strapped to the posts was little more than a boy, for his face was still hairless. As the Mir approached, he thrashed his head about and screamed through the gag, obviously pleading for mercy. Safdar Ali did not even spare him a glance. Instead, with a hand he made some slight signal: the lone drummer sounded a vigorous roll the echo of which rumbled into the gorge and sped away down the river. As the echoes died, the crowd started to chant in rhythm. It was a call for blood.

The Mir raised a forefinger. Someone from the crowd stepped forward and the chanting rose to a crescendo. Ripping off the gag, the man pressed the boy's head back against one of the stakes. At the same time he brought up his other hand, thrust it inside the shrieking mouth and wrenched out the tongue. The spongy flesh, spurting blood and still twitching like an amputated reptilian tail, flip-flopped on the ground almost at Borokov's feet. The screams turned into incoherent splutterings, the eyes closed and the body sagged as the boy lost consciousness.

A second man bearing an iron rod stepped forward, grabbed the boy's hair and thrust the rod through each of his closed eyes. Both men were obviously expert at their job for the entire exercise could not have taken more than five minutes. The lad's head lolled forward against the dripping red chest; his body, either dead or dying, slumped and he made no more sounds. The pool of viscous, sweet-smelling blood at his feet spread steadily outwards as his life's fluid drained. Triumphant cheers rent the sombre, steely skies and the entertainment was over.

Borokov felt sick. He had seen plenty of savagery in the khanates and, indeed, at home where the serfs were fair game, but now his stomach revolted. If there was a point to this barbaric execution—and he was sure there was—he had a horrible suspicion that it had to do with him.

Gulping down his nausea, he asked in a voice thick with bile, "Who is this boy, a trespasser?"

"No," the Mir replied. "He is one of us."

"Why has he been executed?"

"He has sinned against his kinsmen." Safdar Ali's face was as blank as the wall behind him. Not daring to voice a question, Borokov waited. From the folds of his voluminous gown the Mir produced a pair of binoculars and thrust it at him. "To acquire this cheap toy he betrayed a sacred trust. He revealed the Yasmina to an infidel and then absconded. The punishment, therefore, is no more than he deserves." He bunched his cheeks and spat hard on the ground.

Keeping his eyes fixed on the binoculars in his hand, Borokov remained silent. Safdar Ali pointed curtly to the fort and strode off towards it.

Borokov followed. It was only when they were once more seated in the room upstairs that the Mir chose to speak again. Apart from the interpreter—a new man, Borokov noticed—and his own Pushtu-speaking Cossack, there was no one else present.

"You will deliver the agreed subsidy before three months are over," the Mir ordered. "More than the guns on wheels we are particularly anxious to acquire the new magazine rifles and the smokeless powder that you mentioned."

Borokov's heart skipped a beat—the bait had been swallowed. "I apologise to Your Highness, but I fear that my government's offer will not go as far as the new rifles." He sounded genuinely regretful. "They have only recently been developed and the field trials are incomplete. Indeed, even the rearmament of our own infantry and cavalry is in abeyance."

"What we offer to your country in return is not worth a few rifles and some powder?" the Mir asked coldly.

"Undoubtedly it is, Your Highness, but it would be dishonest of me to make promises that my government will refuse to honour. They will not consider including those rifles in the consignments."

Safdar Ali's face darkened. "Then why were they mentioned?"

"I spoke out of turn, Your Highness," Borokov said, trying to look abashed. "Once again I beg forgiveness. Because they are of such high standard, the magazine rifles are expensive to manufacture and in extremely short supply."

Safdar Ali rose, stood with his feet apart and his hands on his hips. "If the rifles are not included, Colonel Borokov, there will be no bargain!"

"Let us at least discuss the matter, Your Highness," Borokov said hastily before the annoyance could explode into a murderous tantrum. "It is possible that a solution may emerge. . . ."

The Mir re-seated himself, one hand still on a hip dangerously close to the hilt of his sword. "Well?"

"First, a question." Borokov scrutinised his nails with concentration. "This infidel to whom the boy betrayed the secret of the Yasmina—who was he?"

"He was what you would call an Angliski."

"Was?"

"Like the boy, he is no longer of any consequence."

"Ah." Much relieved, Borokov settled back more comfortably. "If I am to try to persuade my government to include a few of the new rifles in the consignment, I would be reluctant to do so without some—" He broke off and pursed his mouth.

"Some what?"

"Some substantial proof of Your Highness's good intentions."

Safdar Ali slowly eased himself back in his seat. There was no change in his expression. Borokov hardly dared to breathe as, heart pumping ferociously, he waited for a response. Finally the Mir moved. He again fumbled within the folds of his silken dress and then jumped up so suddenly that the Russian was startled.

"Arrange for Colonel Borokov to be escorted back to his camp," the Mir barked to the interpreter. As he walked purposefully past Borokov, he paused, took hold of Borokov's hand, curled his own round it and held it for an instant.

"I will send an emissary to Tashkent shortly," he said. "In the meantime, you will start preparations for the delivery. If the weapons are according to the agreement and to our satisfaction, you will be escorted to the Yasmina and allowed to occupy it." He stepped onto the ladder in the trap-door leading to the floor below. "But if we are being deceived . . ." He did not need to complete the sentence; the savage contortion of his features said it all. "Our business is over, Colonel Borokov. I would be obliged if you would leave my country before sunrise tomorrow."

Borokov scrambled to his feet, cautious jubilation superseding even the nauseous memory of the execution. Seeing that he still held the binoculars in his left hand, he quickly handed them to the waiting interpreter. Frantic to be away, he ran down the succession of ladders holding his breath against the sickly sweet stench that still clung to the courtyard as he ran across it. It was only when he was halfway down the slope on the way to his encampment that he stopped, unclenched his right fist and examined what the Mir had placed within it. Something cool and smooth and metallic glittered in the centre of his open palm.

It was a nugget of gold.

Borokov started to tremble, so much so that he was forced to sit down by the wayside to resuscitate his limp knees. It took full five minutes for his senses to recover and only then did he allow free rein to his soaring spirits. Raising his face to the icy, insipid greyness, he expelled his choking tensions with a roar of a laugh. It reverberated through the ravines like a bolt of thunder.

The time he had spent in this miserable hellhole of a country had not been wasted, after all.

CHAPTER

As Emma walked into the parlour Mrs. Wyncliffe regarded her with surprise. "Very fetching, my dear," she murmured, hiding her surprise well. "I've always said aquamarine was your colour. It sets off your lovely hair and deepens the greeny-blue of your eyes."

"Well, it's been hanging in the almirah for so long," Emma said off-handedly, "I might as well put it to good use before it disintegrates."

"Very sensible, dear—no point in having pretty clothes if one doesn't wear them." Privately she wished Emma would let her hair hang loose—how she hated that topknot!—but knowing her daughter's intransigence, she held her tongue. She asked instead, "Am I mistaken—or did Carrie say something about this man Charlton being at the burra khana?"

"Yes, I believe he might."

"That would be nice, dear, since you found his talk so entertaining. You'll see Howard Stowe too, I'm sure." She added hastily, "He might have some news of those wretched intruders. Will David be coming home to change?"

"I don't know, but if he's not here by the time the Purcells and Mr. Waterford arrive, he can reach there on his own later."

Emma walked to the window thinking again of the many questions she intended to ask Geoffrey Charlton this evening. He would be the focus of the evening, of course; she would be lucky to have even a few moments of his time. All the same, his mere presence would be enough to help her endure the occasion with acceptable grace.

As it transpired, however, Geoffrey Charlton was not destined to be

Emma's saviour after all. They were informed on arrival by a distraught hostess that Charlton had sent his regrets at the eleventh hour and taken the evening train to Umballa on his way to Simla. Having lost so precious an opportunity to steal a social march over her peers, Georgina Price was devastated.

"Oh dear, Emma was so looking forward to making Mr. Charlton's acquaintance," Jenny remarked. Noting Emma's expression, she amended that quickly to, "We *both* were."

Concealing her disappointment under a bleak smile, Emma surveyed the other dinner guests without enthusiasm. The fact that the larger the crowd the less the need for small talk brought only marginal relief. With the soulful-eyed, heavy-breathing, tediously correct Alec Waterford hanging on to her for dear life, the hours between arrival and departure seemed interminable.

"Why is it that I can never find Reggie when I need him?" Georgina Price asked no one in particular as she flew past Emma. "I simply cannot remember if it's Rob Granger who breaks out in hives if he has fish or Nigel what's-his-name, and Reggie would kill me if either were to take ill."

Obviously, she didn't remember Emma's unfortunate earlier argument with Felicity Duckworth either, for as she passed she flashed a generous smile in Emma's direction. No such amnesia afflicted Mrs. Duckworth, judging by the succession of venomous looks she aimed in the same direction. Sighing to herself, Emma made a vow; however arduous the exercise, she would be pure sweetness and light this evening, with not a single sharp word to anyone.

Above the hum of conversation she heard someone call out her name. She turned to see a familiar figure with balding head, a vague smile and shambling gait wave from across the room. It was Clive Bingham, a geologist who had been with her father on his last tragic expedition. Having returned afflicted with severe frostbite, he had been hospitalised in Delhi for weeks and had left for England shortly after discharge. She noticed that he still walked with the help of a stick. Fond as she was of her father's old friend and colleague, the prospect of reviving a topic she still found painful dismayed Emma. However, seeing that escape was impossible, she assumed a brave smile and greeted him cordially.

"What a pleasant surprise, Dr. Bingham—I thought you were away in England."

He confirmed that he had been, having returned only last week, and mighty glad to be back. "Dreadful weather, freezing, in fact. Whether or not the sun sets on the Empire it certainly doesn't rise much in Britain, I can tell you." He laughed, then quickly sobered and lowered his voice. "I heard at the RGS in London that Graham's death had been confirmed and read the details, such as they were, in *The Times* obituary. I was inexpressibly saddened, inexpressibly. After all, one never does lose hope, does one?"

Mumbling something inaudible Emma quickly inquired after the frostbite, relieved to learn that his feet were almost as good as new. He in turn asked after her mother, declared himself delighted that her health improved, promised to call on her soon, then again turned sombre.

"They say it was some tribesmen who eventually found Graham?"

"Yes."

"They did not say precisely where."

"No."

He shuddered. "A ruthless, vicious region that, a veritable death trap. I tried my best to dissuade Graham from venturing onto the glacier with the blizzard pending, but he refused to listen. You know how stubborn he could be once his sights were set."

Having heard it all before, Emma maintained a stoic silence.

"He was determined to cross the old trade route, determined to find that monastery, certain that he could by-pass the storm." Steeped in his own distress, he did not notice hers. "Now when I look back, I wonder still if I should not have tried harder to stop him, if there were not other means by which I could have forced him to abandon, or at least defer, the search."

"You did everything that you could, Dr. Bingham," Emma said, suppressing her own emotions in a bid to soothe his. "No one else would have taken such terrible risks to mount as extensive and as thorough a search as you did. Often it is only hindsight that makes us consider the impossible as an overlooked probability."

"Still wise beyond your years, eh?" The sag of his jowls lifted and he smiled. Whisking two glasses of wine off a passing tray, he handed her one. "My dear, your father's pride in you was as justified as it was deserved. Theo Anderson tells me that you now plan to compile a book of Graham's papers?"

"Yes." She was relieved at the marginal change in topic. "Papa never seemed to have the time to publish all his papers—the Mongolia lectures delivered at the Asiatic Society in Calcutta, for instance. I thought it might be a good idea to compile a volume of unpublished and some published papers and submit it to the RGS for assessment."

"Well, I must say I do admire your initiative, my dear. Most young girls would baulk at such a daunting task."

"Far less daunting if Dr. Anderson would agree to guide me," she said wryly. "About to set off again for Tibet he is, understandably, extremely short of time. Without his help I'm not sure I would be up to the task at all."

"You do yourself an injustice, my dear. The considerable practical experience you gained with your father counts for a great deal, you know. After all, degrees and diplomas do not supplant what you possess in abundance, a true love of the subject, an instinctive understanding of the country's history and culture and an unusually methodical mind."

Emma coloured at the compliment. "Whatever modest knowledge I may have acquired, Dr. Bingham, is due more to Papa's encouragement and patience than to excessive virtue in myself."

"Oh, come, come!" He waggled a finger. "I remember that dig up north when you were what—nine, ten? You were already jabbering away in Urdu with the best of them and rattling off Sanskrit shlokas verbatim. I was most impressed."

She laughed. "I was only parroting what I'd heard my father recite—and, of course, showing off outrageously."

He stared into his empty glass and his eyes turned dreamy. "When we were at Cambridge, I remember how fired Graham and I were by Cunningham's Buddhist excavations at Sanchi. Young and foolhardy, we later shared impossible dreams and adventures on those digs mounted by the Archaeological Survey. At one lamasery in the Zanskar, I recall, the lamas had picked up European bits and pieces and placed them reverently on their altar—empty brandy bottles, East India Company coins, a silver cuff link. . . ." He broke off to chuckle briefly. "And then when we photographed the Ajanta cave frescoes for the Survey, I remember Graham saying to me . . ."

His reminiscences about the halcyon days seemed to Emma from another age, another planet, and the evocations brought a return of the sweet-sour aches. It was only much later that, catching sight of Jenny and John, she could excuse herself and flee from memories that still smarted. By the time she had negotiated the length of the room, however, the couple had vanished from sight and she was left scanning her only other option. A knot of frisky, fashionably dressed young girls chattered and giggled and exchanged flirtatious glances with a group of subalterns, and next to them sat a forlorn Alec Waterford, waiting patiently for her return to the fold. Sighing inwardly, Emma walked over to join them.

"Why, how charming you look this evening, Emma my dear." Prudence Sackville smiled. "I do like the cut of that dress and you carry the colour so well."

"Yes, doesn't she?" Stephanie Marsden agreed, leaning forward in a provocative bid to show her shapely bosom off to best advantage and surveying Emma from topknot to toe. Flaxen-haired, blue-eyed and dimpled,

Stephanie was the station beauty and a practised flirt well aware of her good looks. "On the other hand, after one has passed a certain age, perhaps grays and beiges befit one far better, would you not agree?"

True to her promise to herself, Emma ignored both Stephanie and the remark and sat down next to Prudence, a pleasant, unpretentious girl whom Emma liked and whose brother, Alexander, she tutored in Urdu. Once again hanging worshipfully onto every word that happened to drop from her lips, the ubiquitous Alec Waterford quickly positioned himself on her left.

In another corner assorted mothers and aunts discussed, as always, the inclemencies of the weather, aberrations of servants and insects, the recent visit of the Prince of Wales to whom a blessed few had been presented and the latest bulletins on the station's allegedly covert romances. Among them also sat Mrs. Waterford, highly disapproving of her besotted son's infatuation with Emma Wyncliffe, a girl she considered utterly unendowed with the virtues expected in the wife of a man of the cloth.

"*Fifty* rupees is what he charges us every month, my dear. The harassment, of course, comes free." Also as always, Peggy Handley held forth on their much hated landlord. "He knows he can get fifty-five, what with everyone wanting to move to Civil Lines. It's bad enough living next door to people from the railways and the mills, but mark my words," she warned darkly, "when those *nouveaux riches* natives move in one of these fine months, the cat will be among the pigeons, won't it?"

Everyone agreed that it would.

A somewhat awed group surrounded a Mrs. Belle Jethroe, leading light of Delhi's amateur stage in winter and, in the Season, of Simla's Gaiety Theatre. Because of her passion for tragic roles, behind her back she was known as "Mrs. Death Throes." Among her adoring entourage was the young army captain from Simla whose name, Emma had learned from their host, was Nigel Worth. With the annual governmental migration to Simla— and her own months of seasonal glory—round the corner, Mrs. Jethroe held forth in deep tones loyal to both contralto and bass but with commitment to neither, on the subject of Queen Elizabeth. Having been told recently that she bore a marked resemblance to the Virgin Queen, she had started to rehearse a play for the Simla stage—written by herself—which paid elaborate court to Elizabeth's amorous dalliances with Walter Raleigh, if rather less to history.

"It's exhausting, positively *exhausting,* to wring oneself dry of emotion night after night," she boomed as she struck a tragic pose against the mantelpiece. "But then what is one to do when one's public *demands* it?"

Listening with scant attention to the chatter of girls with whom she had so little in common, Emma looked around the room with some desperation. Jenny and John were deeply engrossed in conversation with a couple from Calcutta, where John was to be posted shortly. Under the verandah arch near the bar table some young officers from David's regiment stood drinking and laughing. Mrs. Purcell sat too close for comfort to Mrs. Waterford and Mrs. Duckworth, and the men were all outside on the lawn. There was still no sign of her brother. In the meantime, Alec's heavy breathing in her ear was beginning to unnerve her beyond tolerable limits, but fortunately divine intervention was at hand.

A Canadian missionary couple en route to Assam to establish a mission school endowed by the residents of Toronto arrived. Determined to divert at least some of the Canadian bounty into other pockets, the Reverend Desmond Smithers, Alec's superior, aimed several pointed glances in the direction of his lovelorn curate. When they could no longer be ignored, Alec assumed a martyred look and reluctantly went off in pursuit of the Canadians to attend to duties of a less lustful nature.

Heaving a sigh of relief, Emma started to circulate among the contingent of businessmen, bureaucrats and army personnel with many of whom she was already acquainted. Someone introduced her to a general on his way to Gilgit and then to the rather shy Captain Worth—miraculously prized apart from Mrs. Jethroe—who stood conversing with Howard Stowe. Following an exchange of courtesies, they resumed their discussion of common friends and events of mutual interest in Simla where Stowe had served on the Viceregal staff and Captain Worth was now posted.

"How is that old walrus, Hethrington?" Stowe asked with a laugh. Colonel Wilfred Hethrington, he explained to Emma, was Nigel Worth's commanding officer in Simla.

"Sniping away as usual," Worth replied cheerfully. "Still, heart of gold and all that rot."

Remembering that David had mentioned Captain Worth the other night, Emma said, "I'm sure you already know that my brother has just been posted to Leh where, I believe, you too were stationed until recently?"

"Yes, ma'am."

"Well, from your own experience would you say that Mr. Crankshaw deserves his reputation of a curmudgeon?"

Worth grinned, answered in the affirmative, went on to relate an amusing anecdote or two about the crusty Commissioner and they laughed. Then, perhaps to ensure that no other courtier took advantage of his absence to replace him in her affections, he excused himself and hurried back to Mrs. Jethroe.

"No arrests have been made," Howard Stowe informed Emma in a low voice as soon as they were on their own, "but stiff warnings have been issued to the men of the village. Any repetition of the incident will have them behind bars."

"Well, I am relieved to hear it," Emma said. "And the woman?"

"It seems that she has finally eloped with her paramour."

"Oh." She felt a small sense of disappointment. "Then she *was* unfaithful to her husband?"

"It would appear so. No news, however, about your burglars, I'm afraid. Once you have those grilles installed and the . . ."

"Talking shop again, Stowe?" A middle-aged man who obviously knew the Inspector well sauntered up and cut into the conversation. He was introduced to Emma as Charles Chigwell, an actuary, who had recently rented premises in Civil Lines. "Miss Wyncliffe, did you say? Ah yes, wasn't it your home that was broken into recently?"

In Delhi's limited European community, since even the tiniest scrap of information about one's own kind was shared as selflessly as carrion among carnivores, it was unlikely that this too should not be in the public domain. Emma nodded briefly.

"I suppose it's those blasted Gujars, as usual?" Ignoring her, Chigwell addressed his question to the policeman.

Stowe cast a nervous glance at Emma. "Well, one can't say . . ."

"Oh balderdash, of course one can! They're a notoriously bloodthirsty lot, those tribals, far more than the average native. They've been terrorising our neighborhood for years."

"Since they have been deprived of all their land," Emma pointed out pleasantly enough, "they merely try to earn a living. It's unfair to blame all crime in the Civil Lines on the Gujars."

"Unfair? They make it impossible for residents to hire any but a Gujar chowkidar and in *my* book that's pure and simple extortion."

"Well, they do have a legitimate grouse against us," Emma replied, still pleasant and patient. "All our houses were built on land that originally belonged to the Gujars for which they received minimal compensation. That includes the two hundred acres of Thomas Metcalfe's estate, still the most expensive English residence ever built in northern India."

"Good grief, Metcalfe died years ago, during the Mutiny!" Waving his brandy glass about, Chigwell glared. "Are you saying that you approve of the slaughter of the family merely because they lived on Gujar land?"

"No, of course not! But that was war and there was brutality on both sides. In any case, the Gujars paid heavily for it with the confiscation of their village. Now whatever little land remains to them has been acquired for the waterworks. The least we can do is to employ them as nightwatchmen. In my book that's not extortion, Mr. Chigwell, that's justice."

The actuary snorted. "I must say that for an Englishwoman you have an extraordinary perception of justice, Miss Wyncliffe. How on earth are we ever to remedy the ignorance of this country if we ourselves persist in remaining ignorant of the realities?"

"There are many kinds of ignorance, Mr. Chigwell," Emma heard herself snap, much to her surprise, "some easily remedied, others not. I find it amusing that people too ignorant to recognise even their own ignorance should launch crusades to remedy that of others." Spinning on a heel she walked away, leaving the man wordless, red-faced and spluttering.

By now several of the other guests, including some of the girls, had gathered around them to listen to the debate. As Emma walked away, nettled by all the male attention she seemed to be attracting, Charlotte Price was livid. "One must not be too hard on poor Emma, Mr. Chigwell," she said witheringly. "Being country-born, without the advantages of a civilised English education at home, she is to be pitied rather than pilloried for the extraordinary opinions she holds and inflicts on others."

Looking like a harassed sheepdog rounding up an errant flock, Mrs. Price swept up and down the garden frantically trying to get everyone inside and the dancing going. Grabbing the advantage provided by the confusion, Emma made good her escape towards the refreshments table in a far corner of the dining room. More angry with herself than with Charles Chigwell, she stood by the table glowering at a glass of green sherbet.

No, she decided, she had not conducted herself well. Having vowed not to argue, she had done precisely that. Greatly annoyed by her lack of restraint, she was about to lift a glass from the table when she suddenly found herself staring into the all too recognisable face of Damien Granville. Formally dressed, he was an elegant—if flamboyant—figure in scarlet evening jacket, ruffled silk shirt and a spectacular foulard. Taken quite by surprise, Emma stood rooted, her hand frozen in mid-air.

He bowed, handed her the glass, stood back smiling and crossed his arms.

"I see that I have surprised you, for which my apologies."

Emma was flustered but not enough to lose her wits entirely. "You . . . you flatter yourself if you believe that you have the capacity to surprise me." Then she asked rather foolishly, "What are you doing here?"

"Hoping to meet you again."

She glared at him, not believing a word of it. "Really!"

"Yes, really. Incidentally, I approve of the manner in which you demolished that pompous ass, Chigwell."

Once again in control, she returned his gaze evenly. "Your compliments are of little consequence, Mr. Granville. I am entirely unconcerned with your approval."

"But at least you do remember my name."

"Only because I have a good memory for the inconsequential."

His smile faded. "Why did you tear up my card?"

"Because I do not wish you to call on me."

"Why not?"

"I see no reason to cultivate an acquaintance I find distasteful."

He lifted an eyebrow. "Because I happen to endorse corporal punishment for unfaithful wives?"

"No, because I do not like you, Mr. Granville. Your opinions are of as little consequence to me as your approval. Since we are on the subject, Mr. Stowe informs me that the woman has eloped with her lover after all. So you see, corporal punishment is not as effective a deterrent for wayward wives as you seem to believe."

He shrugged. "One cannot win every bet, Miss Wyncliffe. Even the best of us have been known to make mistakes."

The best of us! She was amused by his conceit. "As you did in presuming that I would receive a call from you with delight?"

He raised his hands in surrender. "Well, since you obviously will not, I suppose I will have to wait until *you* call on *me*."

"*I* call on *you*?" The idea was so preposterous that Emma laughed. "I see that despite your less appreciable qualities, Mr. Granville, you do have a sense of humour."

"Also a sense of the inevitable, I assure you."

"Oh? And how am I to be persuaded to recognise this inevitability when it manifests itself?"

He regarded her curiously. "The human brain is a surprisingly versatile organ, Miss Granville. No doubt it will devise suitable means of persuasion."

"Well, in the unlikely event that I do call on you at all, Mr. Granville, it will be on the day the sun chooses to rise in the west."

She started to turn away, but just then their hostess came rushing up and took hold of Granville's arm.

"Oh, Mr. Granville," Georgina Price cooed, "I am delighted that you decided to join us after all—I had *quite* given up on you. Charlotte, my daugher, awaits you with all manner of questions about . . . Oh!" She broke off, suddenly aware of Emma's presence. "Oh, I do beg your pardon!" She looked from one to the other in confusion. "Am I interrupting a private conversation?"

"Not at all, Mrs. Price," Emma replied. "Mr. Granville and I have nothing more to say to one another."

"Have you two already met?" Mrs. Price's fan flapped faster and in direct proportion to her disapproval. "I had no idea."

"Oh, indeed we have," The enthusiastic response came from Granville. "You might even say that we are . . . old friends."

"Might we now!" Mrs. Price looked even more put out at the prospect of such unlikely competition for her daughter.

"No, we might not," Emma clarified immediately. "I barely know Mr. Granville." Nor, her tone implied, had she any wish to. Excusing herself, she moved away from them both.

Georgina Price's relief was all too obvious. "Well, then, as I was about to say," she gushed, "Charlotte has been *so* looking forward to meeting you, Mr. Granville—as, indeed, everyone has. Er, shall we?"

Jubilantly, she bore away her trophy to the corner where Charlotte awaited, signalling in transit to the hired quartet to strike up a waltz. If God had chosen not to give her Geoffrey Charlton, her manner proclaimed, He had made restitution by landing in her lap a prize of even greater potential.

Once again left on her own, Emma set out despondently in search of Alec Waterford. It seemed to her that wherever she went this evening she ended up ruffling feathers. The silly argument with Charles Chigwell had been bad enough, but how childishly she had reacted to Damien Granville. She had allowed him to upset her, allowed him to *see* that he had upset her, and that upset her even more. Determined not to court any more controversies, she meekly positioned herself again by Alec's side—much to his delight and his mother's annoyance—and prayed for dinner to be announced.

Regardless of Emma's disenchantment, there was little doubt that the Prices' unexpected guest was quite the man of the evening, Geoffrey Charlton's absence already a fading memory. Emma watched with silent disgust as, egged on by assertive mothers and aunts, the female component jockeyed and jostled for Granville's attention, fawning and flirting and fluttering lashes as they twirled about the dance floor in his arms. That he appeared to enjoy the attention did not surprise Emma in the least; from a man such as he she could hardly have expected otherwise.

"He's very attractive, isn't he?" Jenny whispered as she watched Emma watching him while pretending not to.

"Is he? I hadn't noticed."

"And that scar across his chin makes him positively mysterious."

"Really?"

"Well, he does have a sort of air about him, a sort of indefinable *je ne sais quoi,* wouldn't you say?"

"If by that you mean he's impertinent and presumptuous, I am entirely in agreement."

"I saw him talking to you near the refreshments table. What did he say?"

"Nothing worthy of repetition."

Jenny gave her a curious look. "You've met him before, haven't you?"

"No."

"I watched your face as you talked. You looked quite angry."

"Well, I wasn't," Emma said irritably. "Why on earth *should* I have been? I hardly know the man."

Just then, dinner was announced. Grateful for the timely interruption, Emma again searched the room for David but there was still no sign of him. Where on earth *was* he? She had a momentary pinprick of unease, but dismissing it she laced her arm through Jenny's, and with the loyal Alec and the Canadian couple close on her heels walked into the dining room.

Having helped herself to the somewhat flattened fish mousse, pallid chicken curry, glutinous rice and a spoonful of unidentifiable vegetables buried under a cheese sauce, Emma positioned herself close to an open window waiting for the others to join her. As she stood picking at her food, she listened with half an ear—and quite unintentionally—to a conversation taking place outside on the verandah.

". . . couldn't agree less, sir," someone was saying in response to an unheard remark. "With unemployment rampant and factories over-producing, Russia tramples all over Central Asia frantically seeking new markets."

"As does England in India," answered a confident voice Emma had no difficulty in identifying. "Conquest through commerce merely tries to legitimise colonisation through the back door."

There was an instant of hushed silence. "Are you suggesting, Granville, that we have no legitimate right to India?"

"As much as, or no more than, Russia has to Central Asia."

"Good God, you actually equate us with them?"

"Why not? We are both equally greedy. The only difference is that with our customary skill in the art of self-delusion we persuade ourselves that *our* lust for power enjoys divine sanction." An almost audible smile, a brusque "Excuse me," and then receding footsteps.

There followed a bristling silence and then a nasty laugh. "By Jove, he does have a bloody nerve—I'll say that for him!"

"Naturally. Why else would he elect to live in Kashmir under the patronage of that Rusky stooge of a maharaja? If he's grata here at all it's by the bare skin of his teeth."

"I say he deserves to have the hide whipped off his arse—and by Christ, I'd be happy to be the one to do it!"

"Well, what else can one expect considering his background, eh? Anyway, enough of Granville. I say"—the voice lowered itself to a conspiratorial but still audible whisper—"I suppose you've heard about poor Butterfield?"

"The Simla chap?"

"Yes. Old Jeremy."

"What about him?"

"Well, he bought it."

"Butterfield? *Bought* it?"

"Somewhere in the Karakorams, they say."

"Good grief! Why, I was splitting beers with him only last—when was it, April?—at the Gymkhana Club in Simla."

"Well, the bubble burst about a month ago, you know. It appears he was on his way back when they got him."

"Oh dear me, how frightful! So that's what Charlton is on about in the *Sentinel*, is it?"

"Undoubtedly. Still all very cloak-and-daggerish, you know, secret maps and suchlike. In Simla, naturally, it's the silence of the graveyard. Buttoned lips, 'no comments' all round, the usual." An anxious pause. "I say, old chap, don't breathe a word to anyone, will you? From what I heard said it's a hell of a prickly business with them that knows."

"Wouldn't dream of it. Not one for speaking out of turn, old boy, you know that. Where did *you* hear it?"

"Ah, ask me no questions and I'll tell ye no lies." A laugh. "They also say that . . ." Whisper, whisper.

Realising suddenly that she eavesdropped, and not particularly interested anyway, Emma quickly moved away from the window. She did not see Damien Granville again that evening. By the time they had finished dinner, he had left.

Sitting beside her in the carriage on the ride home, Alec said with uncharacteristic spirit, "I heard about your contretemps with Chigwell, Emma. Everyone did. Was it necessary to be quite so hard on the poor man?"

"No, it was not," Emma acknowledged mildly. "I simply lost my temper. I should not have."

"He had almost agreed to a donation for the repair of the front pews, you know, and the argument quite ruined his mood."

"Well, I'm sorry, truly I am." She changed the subject. "Tell me, did you have any luck with the Canadians?"

His face brightened. "They've asked us for luncheon tomorrow at the Mission House for further discussions. Reverend Smithers says it was a most fruitful evening, *most* fruitful."

Well, for the Church, perhaps; for her, it could not have been more of a disaster. The sole crumb of comfort Emma saw in it was that by accepting the invitation she had pleased her mother.

*I*t was a matter of relief to learn as soon as Emma returned home that David was safely back and asleep in his room. Tomorrow being Sunday, there would be time enough to find out why he had not put in an appearance at the burra khana. That, however, was easier said than done. Leaving the house early on Sunday, David did not return home for the next three days. According to their mother, he was staying at the barracks to complete his paperwork before he left for Doon. It was on the fourth night, as Emma was about to go up to her room, that her brother called softly from the foot of the stairs.

"Em? I say, come in here a moment. I want to talk to you."

"Is Mama all right?" she asked as a matter of habit.

"Yes, yes, Mama is all right, probably asleep by now. I . . . There's something I have to tell you."

Hearing the strangeness in his tone, her grip on the bannister tightened but she replied calmly enough, "I'll be with you in a minute, just as soon as I've taken a fresh mosquito-net out of the linen cupboard. Mine has so many holes last night I barely slept a wink for the bites."

Ten minutes later when she entered his room, David was sitting at his writing table with his back to the door. When he turned, she saw that he was holding a brandy glass and his face was haggard.

"What is the matter?" she asked, alarmed. "Are you ill?"

Going up to him, she put a hand on his forehead. He shook it off. "No, I'm not ill, but I wish I were dead." He buried his head in his arms, tipping over the brandy glass in the process.

Forcing herself to stay calm, she fetched a duster and took her time to mop up the spilt drink. She then sat down on the bed. "All right, tell me what this is all about."

"I've done something terrible, Em," he whispered.

"You've been to Urdu Bazaar again," she said tonelessly.

He made no verbal response but the slump of his shoulders was answer enough. Restraining both her anger and her disappointment, she waited for the usual excuses to follow.

The gaming-house in Urdu Bazaar near the Jama Masjid, the city's largest mosque, was a notorious den of cutthroat professional gamblers. There had been a time when, in the company of highly undesirable acquaintances, David was seen there often. The habit had started with innocuous flutters and a few lucky wins, but then, just before he received news of his commission, he had begun to incur heavy losses. After his last escapade, unknown to their mother, Emma had sold a much loved gold ring inherited from their grandmother in England in order to settle his debts. Repentant and ashamed at the ignominy of having his sister bail him out, he had promised never to gamble again. Obviously, the promise had not been kept. The "casual" visit of a few days ago had led to others. None of this Emma needed to be told; the guilt on his stricken face was testimony enough.

"Well, how much have you lost this time?" she asked sharply when no explanations appeared to be forthcoming.

"Everything," he mumbled. "Everything . . ."

"Everything? What on earth is everything?"

He told her and, for a moment, she stared in incomprehension. "Khyber Kothi?" she echoed. "What do you mean, you've lost Khyber Kothi?"

"Just that," he said dully. "Just that."

Her temper rose. "How many brandies have you had?"

"For God's sake, Emma, I'm not drunk, I know what I'm saying!"

"Then what is this, some sort of silly joke?"

"If only it were!" He drew a deep, ragged breath. "I ran out of money. All I had left to stake was Khyber Kothi, so I did. I lost the hand and the house." He laid his forehead down on the table and started to cry. For a moment there was no sound in the room save that of his dry, rasping sobs.

"Pull yourself together, for heaven's sake!" Still not able to absorb the extraordinary announcement, Emma drew up a chair and sat down beside him. "Now tell me everything that happened, right from the beginning."

"There's nothing to tell. I staked the house on a bet and lost, that's all."

"When, tonight?"

"No, two nights ago. I didn't have the courage to tell you—or to show my face at home."

"Were you drunk when you played?" she asked angrily.

"Yes. No . . . I don't know. I was . . . befuddled. I didn't seem to be aware of what I was doing." He choked again. "Oh God, I must have been mad. . . ."

"You haven't said anything to Mama, have you?"

"No, of course not." He lifted his head and wiped his eyes with the cuffs of his shirt. "How could I?"

For a while Emma sat in silence, outraged not so much by his absurd contention—which she did not take seriously—but by the fact that he had gone back on his word. However, to vent her temper on him in his present frame of mind, she knew, would be futile.

"Who were the men you played against?"

"Man. Singular. The devil himself, Em." He shivered in remembrance. "He didn't say much, but his eyes, Em, his eyes . . ."

"Don't make it worse by spouting fanciful rubbish!" Her hands itched to grab his shoulders and shake them hard. "One doesn't need to be a Lucifer to gull an unthinking fool!"

"Not this time, Em, not this time, I swear it." He stared up at her, still fearful. "I didn't want to play, Em, on my heart I didn't, but it was as if I had no will left of my own, as if I played mechanically. He made me obey him, Em, he *willed* me to play. I kept losing and he kept winning and still I could not stop—and then there was nothing left to stake except the house. . . . Oh God, oh God!" He convulsed again. "I don't deserve to live, Em. I wish I were dead!"

"Oh, do stop feeling sorry for yourself," she snapped, furious. "And don't credit a seasoned criminal with Satanic powers merely because he made an ass out of you."

"You can mock all you want, Em, but you don't know him. Nobody does. He's . . . he's a magician, a mesmerist. . . ."

"And does this magical mesmerist also have a name?"

"What does it matter?" He shook his head and moaned. "He doesn't live here, he's a stranger in Delhi. Granville."

"Granville?"

"Yes. Damien Granville."

Emma bit back her shock and stood up. "You played against Damien Granville?"

"Yes."

"You've played against him before?"

"Twice. I won both times."

"Those were the winnings you brought home the other night?"

"Yes." He buried his face in his palms. "Granville has every intention of making me honour the debt. He . . . he warned me when . . . when the wager was laid."

"And yet you played?"

"I tell you, Em, the man is the devil incarnate. He *urged* me to go on, he simply took control of my mind, my will, my senses. . . ."

"You played because you wanted to. He had nothing to do with your mind!" She started to pace. "This . . . this Granville—is he a habitual gambler?"

"I don't know, but he's been there every time that I have. The wager was laid before Highsmith, I can hardly deny it. And Highsmith employs men, terrible men, to make his collections. Besides, if it ever came out that I reneged on a bet, what would . . . ?"

Emma stopped listening. All this had happened before Granville accosted her at the party! She was appalled that even someone as silver-tongued as he could be capable of such duplicity.

Panic-stricken, David clutched at her arm. "My God, how am I ever going to tell Mama?"

"You won't need to." Emma's face set. "No one, not even a hardened professional gambler, could expect such a debt to be honoured." Honoured? She winced at the irony of the word. Convinced that in his naïveté, David had simply been made the butt of a particularly tasteless prank and too tired to think clearly at the moment, she made a move to leave.

David clung to her arm, refusing to let her go. "What are we going to do, Em?" he asked, again close to tears.

"Do?" She wrenched her arm free. "I don't know about you, but I'm going to bed. I suggest you do the same. We'll talk about it in the morning." As she went through the door a question occurred to her. "What did Damien Granville stake in this travesty of a game?"

"His estate in Kashmir."

"And if he had lost, do you seriously believe he would have kept *his* side of the bargain?"

"He would not have lost," David said bitterly. "Damien Granville loses only when he chooses to. The man is a born winner."

"Oh?" Emma's eyes narrowed. "Well, we will just have to see about that, won't we?"

That David had been to the gaming-house and got himself into trouble, Emma had no reason to disbelieve. The rest of his bizarre tale, however, reeked of improbability. Damien Granville might be a seasoned adventurer with little to commend him, but David certainly provided a willing target for even lesser villains. By pleading coercion, her gutless brother simply sought to place elsewhere a blame that sat squarely on his own shoulders. He was rash, unthinking and callow, an unformed youth out to prove himself through what he mistakenly believed to be masculine pursuits. Unfortunately, he was also a fool soon parted with his money—or in this case his house, which their father had lovingly transferred in his name when he turned twenty-one.

Recalling her conversation with Damien Granville at the burra khana, Emma marvelled anew at his audacity. Obviously well accustomed to using his shallow charm to advantage, he had been forward and entirely out of line. Despite that, however, she simply could not bring herself to believe that even a philanderer with an overdeveloped sense of pride and underdeveloped scruples would challenge an unthinking young man—yet to learn how to hold his liquor—with so frivolous a wager and expect it to be honoured. It was preposterous!

Furious as she was with David, she refused to take the matter seriously.

Despite her scepticism, however, that night Emma's sleep was far from peaceful. When she finally rose red-eyed and heavy-headed, it was with the reluctant realisation that perhaps it was unwise to take either David's sorry tale or Granville's intentions too lightly. The first step, therefore, was to reinforce her armoury.

"You want information about Damien Granville?" Jenny Purcell could not have been more astonished.

"Yes."

"You are interested in him?"

"I am not at all interested in Mr. Granville," Emma clarified. "Indeed, I have never been less interested in any man, I assure you. What I am interested in is information about him for reasons that are not half as salacious as you would like to believe."

"What reasons?"

"I'd rather not say yet. When it's all over, I'll tell you everything."

"When all *what* is over?"

"Whatever."

There were few secrets between their two families; the Purcells were already aware of David's earlier misadventures in Urdu Bazaar. Much as she loved Jenny, however, it was because of her congenital incapability to hold a secret that Emma hesitated to reveal everything yet. The reason for her early morning visit was that Jenny got on well with Grace Stowe, who possessed (and nobly shared with the community) a formidable repository of gossip about everyone in Delhi. It was this repository that she was anxious to tap. To ensure privacy she had insisted that they talk in the summerhouse at the back of the Purcells' garden.

Knowing that at the moment she would extract nothing further from her friend, Jenny sighed. "Well then, what exactly *do* you want to know about him?" she asked grumpily.

"Everything that you do. Apart from the fact that he lives in Kashmir, the man is a total stranger to me. What is his occupation?"

Jenny snorted. "With his money, he doesn't need one! Grace says he owns an estate outside Srinagar called Shalimar, after the gardens. If anything, I suppose one would call him a gentleman-farmer."

A euphemism for a hedonist! "Foreigners are not permitted to own land in Kashmir," Emma said. "How does he manage to have an estate in forbidden territory?"

"I have absolutely no idea, but manage it he does. Someone was saying last night that his father enjoyed the friendship and favour of the late maharaja. I presume royal patronage is extended also to the son."

Emma suddenly recalled the conversation she had unwittingly overheard at the burra khana. "Why is he non grata with the Indian government?"

"Because of his political opinions, Grace says. He has sympathies with the Russians and doesn't care who knows it."

"Is he not English?"

"Well, his father was, although his mother, they say, came from Europe. Austria, I think." Even though no one was listening, out of habit Jenny lowered her voice. "There was some sort of scandal about her, Grace says. Apparently, she ran away with another man but it was all hushed up." She stretched and yawned. "She's dead now so I don't suppose it matters any longer."

"Does he have other family?"

"You mean, is he married?" Jenny gave a knowing smirk. "No."

"What did his father do?" Emma ignored the smirk.

"He was an officer in the army, Grace says."

"In the Kashmir Army?"

"No, the Indian Army. Oh, for heaven's sake, Emma, who cares?" Jenny said crossly. "It's not important what his father did, is it, so long as he is still unmarried!"

"Who, the father? Yes, that I find perfectly believable."

Jenny dissolved in giggles. "The man himself, silly! His father died years ago."

"Well, I'm not surprised the son is still a bachelor," Emma said severely. "Which sane woman would want to cast her lot in with a conceited philanderer anyway?"

"Charlotte Price would. She's vowed to have him, you know."

"I said 'sane' woman. He lives alone then, does he?"

"That depends on what you mean by alone." Jenny's eyes twinkled. "Charlotte says her mother knows someone who confirms that he's *very* popular with a certain type of lady and is certainly never short of company."

"Oh, that I don't doubt, even though his morals—or lack of them— are hardly my concern. Why should they be, anyway? I hardly know the man."

"Uh-oh, do I sense that the lady doth protest too much?"

"No, you do not!" Emma said, exasperated. "Why must you make romantic capital out of everything? And just what is so special about this odious man that all of Delhi falls over itself to gain his attention?"

"Odium notwithstanding, he's young, he's rich and he's willing to be fallen over." She laughed. "Oh, come, come, Emma, you have to admit that the man is attractive, a good dancer and immaculately mannered. Charlotte Price, desperately smitten, thinks of him as a modern musketeer, quite the most dashing man she has ever met."

"Charlotte Price would find a scarecrow dashing so long as he wore trousers," Emma retorted. "To get back to the point—what is he doing in Delhi?"

"Who knows?" Jenny shrugged. "According to Grace's gardener, whose brother works at the Nicholson Road house he's rented, he has very strange visitors from very strange places and sends and receives a great many letters. Much of his time is spent closeted in the study with his private secretary."

"An Englishman?"

"No, someone called Suraj Singh."

"Does he intend to stay long in Delhi?"

Jenny struggled to contain another yawn. "Well, he seems pretty well settled for the moment. At least, that was the impression he conveyed that night according to Grace."

"How does he spend his evenings, does Grace know?"

"Not at burra khanas, I assure you. Mrs. Granger was saying that everyone has asked him to theirs but he avoids them like the pestilence. Why he accepted the Prices' invitation no one knows, not even Grace, and consequently Mrs. Granger's nose is most severely out of joint." Seeing the touch of colour her remark brought to Emma's cheeks, Jenny pounced. "You wouldn't know why he accepted the Prices' invitation, would you?"

"No, I would not!" Emma said warmly. "Why should I?"

"Well, you were the first person Granville talked to and he seemed to smile a good deal."

"I thought you said I looked angry!"

"*You* looked angry, *he* smiled a good deal."

Emma cut short the exchange with an impatient "*tch!* What else is rumoured about his pursuits?"

Jenny gave her a sidelong glance but got nothing further from Emma's expression. "Well, Grace's gardener's brother reports that he seems to prefer staying at home—except for visits to some gaming-house in Urdu Bazaar."

Emma's heart plummeted. "So then he *is* a gambler!"

"I presume so—why else would he go to a gaming-house?" Jenny was beginning to look irritated. "Don't you want to know anything really important—like how he got that wildly attractive scar on his chin?"

"No, but I can see that you are going to tell me anyway."

The animation returned to Jenny's face. "Well, everyone has a theory about that. Charlotte, with whom he danced thrice, believes he got it in a duel defending the honour of a lady love, while Prudence says it is most definitely the mark of a cuckolded husband's vengeance. Grace on the other hand, who always knows best, prefers a more heroic explanation. He was in a Himalayan war, she says, fighting Afghan tribesmen single-handed. So take your pick."

Emma had to laugh. "What did the Bankshalls have to say?"

"Oh, they disdained to offer any theory. Eunice swore she smelled native blood in him since no true Englishman would dare appear in public wearing scarlet velvet, let alone frilled collar, cuffs and an unbelievable foulard, and Bernice thought he was a dago from South America and so naturally a mountebank. Origin of scar notwithstanding, the consensus in the zenana is that Damien Granville is maddeningly attractive."

"And in the mardana?"

"Slightly less ecstatic," Jenny said sadly. "The consensus among the men, John says, is that Damien Granville is a bounder."

Emma could not have agreed more.

What made Simla—summer capital of the government of India—a most desirable home away from home for burra sahibs and memsahibs was its essential Englishness. Situated in the Himalayan foothills at an elevation of more than seven thousand feet, Simla boasted pine-scented air, cultured valleys, shaded glens and sylvan glades, all perfect antidotes to the dreadful lethargy induced by the intolerable heat and grime of the plains. Cool, therapeutic and marvellously reviving, its climate during the Season could not be faulted any more than could its English ambience.

In the north, it was overlooked by towering Himalayan peaks; to the south, wooded slopes rolled down foothills to merge with the flatlands of the Punjab. Thick forests of deodar, pine, oak and ilex were nesting grounds for flocks of chakore, and in the leas and meadows and along brooding precipices enormous banks of scarlet rhododendron ran wild. To those fortunate enough to be posted here during the Season, Simla was a Mount Olympus. Others, left to their prickly heat and perspiration down in the dustbowls, dismissed it as a bureaucratic monstrosity. A satirist had dubbed it the "Abode of Little Tin Gods," and those driven by envy agreed feelingly.

Whatever else the summer capital lacked, however, it certainly was not entertainment. Away from the searing winds and administrative drudgery of Calcutta, it offered unending prospects of fun. The Annandale Club grounds were an ideal venue for gymkhana racing, picnics, polo, croquet, charity bazaars, fairs, fiestas, and the civilised excitement of the Durand Football Tournament. Indoors, there was gaiety galore to be had at the galas, dances, dramas and fancy-dress balls, and interminable burra khanas presented cosy occasions for more private conviviality. Most enjoyable of all in a bureaucratic milieu beset by cliques and coteries, intrigues and innuendos and eternal requests for appointments by favour, was the rare promise of romance without commitment or castigation.

The heart of Simla palpitated most strongly on the Mall. Here fashionable commercial establishments afforded opportunities to see and be seen, admire and be admired, talk and be talked about and to arrange clandestine assignations through discreet eye contact. Located also on the crescent-shaped street were the town's prominent institutions—the Civil Secretariat, the Imperial Bank, the Military Office and army headquarters, the Roman Catholic Cathedral, clubs, libraries, hotels, restaurants and tea-rooms. At the end of the Mall was the new Viceregal Lodge, a six-storeyed, fortlike structure replete with towers and cupolas. Despite its baronial air—or perhaps because of it—its present incumbent, Lord Lansdowne, was said to be pleased to have at last a truly *English* residence rather than merely an Indian home.

It seemed an unceasing marvel that in this once primitive wilderness of slushy tracks and crude wooden cottages, such sophistication should have arrived in so short a time. Taken now entirely for granted were brass bands from London, salmon from Scotland, sardines from the Mediterranean, champagne and wines from French vineyards, tinned delicacies from Fortnum & Mason, patisserie and chocolates from Switzerland and the latest fashions offered by Savile Row and Parisian haute couture. Tidy little English homes with tidy little English gardens sported white picket gates bearing English names like "Dove Cote" and "Green Acres," "Dingley Dell" and "Briar Rose Cottage." Not the least of Simla's claims to celebrity was the fact that it was in these pristine environs that Lola Montez, one of the most notorious courtesans of the century, had first practised and honed her pubescent skills.

In between the frolic and frivolity there was also work to be done, of course, and if some government officers elected not to overburden themselves during the jolly Season, Colonel Wilfred Hethrington, Director of Military Intelligence, was certainly not one of them. Deeply conscious of his Department's pivotal role in the matter of gathering intelligence along the sensitive northern borders, Colonel Hethrington took his responsibilities extremely seriously. It was because of Simla's proximity to strategic Himalayan kingdoms that the Department was based here throughout the year, as were the headquarters of the Commander-in-Chief of the Indian Army under whose ultimate authority it functioned.

Having arrived early at his office on the Mall one particularly fine, pine-scented Monday morning at the inception of the Season, Colonel Hethrington sat thoughtfully surveying the assortment of objects laid out on his desk: sextant, compass, field glasses, a sealed cowrie shell, a collapsible walking staff and a slim thermometer case. The cleverly disguised tools of trade of intelligence agents had been packed in the false bottom of the large, woebegone wooden travelling chest that stood to one side of the desk and had been delivered to the Department not so long ago.

Retrieving a sheet of paper from his desk, the Colonel re-read it and banged hard on his bell. The door opened with an agonised creak and his personal chaprassi appeared bearing a tea tray.

"Sir?"

"Has Captain Worth sahib returned from Delhi?"

The liveried peon confirmed that he had.

"Ask him to come in, will you?"

The peon set the tray on the desk, dabbed with a white napkin a few drops spilt into the saucer, salaamed and withdrew.

Solid-chested, with thinning hair used with artistic imagination to reduce the blank spaces (his sole concession to vanity), Colonel Hethrington had the kind of face of which he secretly approved. It was unremarkable and forgettable, which in his line of work he considered to be an asset. Behind the unremarkable features, however, reposed a needle-sharp brain, energetic, meticulous, and indeed seldom in repose. As he sat sipping his tea and waiting impatiently for his confidential aide to arrive, he stared abstractedly through the bay window. Against a spectacular view a family of macaques fidgeted restlessly on the windowsill. He did not notice them.

Like many others, Colonel Hethrington considered the annual migration to Simla of the entire government a waste of time, energy and public money, a whimsicality initiated by a Viceroy who found Calcutta's summer heat intolerable. Well, who the devil didn't? For his part, what Hethrington found intolerable—unlike some of his colleagues—was the Season. He never ceased to be amazed at the transformations wrought in otherwise respectable, God-fearing men by mere geographical relocation. Whereas in Calcutta most minded their p's and q's pretty well, one whiff of Himalayan air seemed enough to send decorum flying out of the window. Those who had left wives and families behind were, naturally, the prime offenders. Cavorting with abandon and impunity with women they had never seen before the Season started—nor would again once it ended—they became total slaves to carnal desire. The women, if possible, were worse. To the hardy annual crop of widows, grass widows and spinsters, anyone white, willing and whiskered (bachelor, husband or widower) was fair game in the hunt for seasonal liaisons.

Thinking in general of the scandal-filled months ahead and in particular of the Viceroy's inaugural costume ball in his immediate future, Colonel Hethrington scowled into his cup. His wife, an otherwise blameless lady of prudence and piety, had set her heart on dressing up as Queen Elizabeth to his Walter Raleigh, and no amount of pleading could dissuade her from the fixation. His irritation mounting by the minute, he was about to give another punishing thump to his bell when the door opened with its customary squawk and Captain Nigel Worth appeared.

He saluted smartly. "Sir! I was just about to . . ."

"Where the devil were you?" Colonel Hethrington interrupted testily. "I've been waiting a good hour for you to put in an appearance."

It was a gross exaggeration, but Captain Worth knew better than to challenge it. "I was instructing Burra Babu on the *Kashmir Military Gazetteer,* sir. It needs to be brought up-to-date, which is why I felt I should . . . ah, sh-sh-should . . ." He broke off with a hiccup and quickly covered his mouth with a hand. "Beg pardon, sir, but we were rehearsing till all hours of the morning and I was unable to catch much sleep."

Efforts to explain away the yawn cut little ice with the Colonel. Obviously, that god-awful Jethroe woman had accompanied him back from Delhi and the damn fool had *again* been up all night—not rehearsing, either! On the impeccable authority of his wife, Colonel Hethrington had it that the Captain's hazel eyes were memorably soulful, his nose classically Roman, and the oceans of brown waves that caressed his head irresistible to female fingers. Unimpressed, the Colonel scanned the bleary eyes, reddened nose and undulating hair with chilly disapproval. It was a face he decided, not for the first time, most *ill* suited to Simla in the Season.

Hethrington bitterly regretted that it was not within his purview to sanitise the morals of his staff. Given a free hand, by Jove, he'd soon have the whole jing bang lot back on the straight and narrow. Unfortunately, he had had to fight tooth and nail to get Crankshaw to release Worth for Simla. It was just his luck that having finally found a first-class aide, he should turn out to be an amateur actor who couldn't keep his trousers buttoned. If Worth weren't such a past master at subterfuge with a mind as devious as a minotaur's maze, he would have kept him chained to his desk until the locusts swarmed back down the hills and the Season concluded.

"Sit down, sit down," The Colonel growled, sliding the tea tray with the message halfway across the desk.

"About the project, sir."

"Later, Captain, later." The Colonel dismissed the project with a wave. "As you can see, I have again been summoned by the QMG. He wants *another* discussion about Hyperion's ghastly murder."

Worth cast a wistful eye at the tea tray, but sensing his commanding officer's querulous mood did not dare reach for it. Instead, he picked up and read the message from the Quarter Master General, their direct superior. "I should imagine he would, sir. Some loose ends undoubtedly remain."

"A masterly understatement!" Hethrington rose, opened the travelling chest, returned to it the various objects displayed on his desk, replaced its false bottom, and sat down again. Picking up a sheet of paper, he tapped it with a forefinger. "I wish Hyperion could have sent a more comprehensive message with his box. We got everything from his Gurkha before he was packed off to Cawnpore, did we?"

"Yes, sir. Lal Bahadur's interrogation was very thorough. In any case, Hyperion would not have entrusted sensitive details, even in code, to the man, since he himself was on his way to deliver the papers in person."

The perfectly logical explanation did little to improve the Colonel's mood. "So in the meantime, what the hell am I expected to say to the QMG? That we know where Hyperion's papers are but Crankshaw let them slip through his fingers? How do you think *that* little gem would go down with H.E., the C-in-C and the Foreign Secretary, eh? To say nothing of blasted Whitehall!"

"In all fairness, sir, Mr. Crankshaw went to the caravanserai in Leh as soon as he received our telegraph. It's hardly his fault that by the time he persuaded the merchants to talk, it was already too late." Worth gave a polite little cough. "All said and done, sir, it could have been worse."

"Could it now?"

"Well, considering how frightened the Yarkandis were of being implicated, they needn't have troubled to turn in any of Hyperion's possessions. They could have buried the carpet bag with the body, or simply abandoned it in the Karakorams. We learned about the raid only because Mr. Crankshaw was quick off the mark."

"And fat lot of good that's done us so far!"

"Well, sir, had the mullah not been in such a tearing hurry to push off to Mecca, Mr. Crankshaw would have . . ."

"All right, all right, I know all that."

Draining his cup, Hethrington rose to his feet and started to pace. One of the macaques on the windowsill, obviously the pater familias, tapped on a glass pane. Deep in thought, Colonel Hethrington still did not hear him. Seeing his chance, Worth quickly poured himself a cup and took a reviving sip.

"Hyperion was by no means a careless man, sir."

"You think I need to be reminded of that? All the same, it was sheer bloody luck that the raiders were impatient enough to get to the loot to destroy only the papers they could see."

"They were also illiterate, sir," the Captain reminded him mildly, "and there is another possibility we may have to consider as a last resort."

"Well, what?"

"Knowing that he was being followed and that his life was in danger, Hyperion must have been under diabolical mental stress. In the final analysis, sir, even agents as sharp as Hyperion are human and capable of error."

Resuming his seat, the Colonel buried his chin in his chest. "True," he conceded sorrowfully, "even though that is the one possibility I find most difficult to accept." He sighed deeply. "He was a good man, Captain, one of the best. I can't tell you how grieved I am to lose him." He sucked in his cheeks and tapped the desk with a fingertip. "And now, to cap it all, we have Charlton to contend with."

"He merely reports rumours, sir."

"Only until he gets at the truth!" Hethrington was once again irritated by his assistant's habit of always looking on the bright side of everything. There was, after all, a time and a place for optimism. "Given the fact that the Yasmina *was* located and the papers *are* missing, Charlton's snide little darts land too close for comfort. He asked too many questions here, sniffed around a little too hard at the Club. I do wish you wouldn't take it quite so lightly." Restless again, he drummed the desk with his fingers. "And I warn you, if Charlton gets even a whiff of this hare-brained project you've bullied me into . . . what name did you give it?"

"Janus, sir. The Janus project."

"Yes, and I can see why!" Hethrington's smile was pure acid. "Well, if Charlton puts your bloody project on the front pages, you can count on transfers for both of us to the Meerut cantonment mess kitchens. I must have been temporarily insane to let you talk me into it."

"Well, sir, since nothing else has worked . . ."

"And you think this will? Hah!"

"If we fail, we will be in no worse a position than we are now."

"We damn well *will* if Charlton finds out!" Hethrington sat down heavily. "You think we might? Fail, I mean?"

"Hopefully not, sir, but . . ." Worth faltered.

"Exactly!" The Colonel pounced on the pause. "It's that damned 'but' that refuses to go away, isn't it?" He propped his chin up with his fingers and closed his eyes. "There's a stench about this that sticks in the craw, Captain. Too many variables. Besides, I don't trust your man. I didn't when I met him and I don't now. Anyway"—he pulled in a long-suffering breath—"I suppose I might as well hear what you've been up to so far."

Nodding occasionally, Hethrington listened with tightly pursed lips, then slumped back and relapsed into brooding silence. Wisely, the Captain allowed a moment or two to elapse before trying the delicate little cough he usually gave to regain the Colonel's attention.

"About our side of the bargain, sir."

"Oh yes, there's that, too." Hethrington's face turned even sourer. "The man has left for Kashgar, hasn't he?"

"Oh yes, sir, with the medical supplies Capricorn ordered. Mr. Crankshaw and I saw the caravan off from Leh before I went to Delhi. With luck, by now they should be across the Chinese border."

"Well, then?"

"I think we need to send some basic explanations to Capricorn."

"No." Hethrington shook his head. "Not yet. The less he knows, the fewer the risks. Herbal digestives, eh?" He gave a snort of disgust. "Capricorn really thinks this Indian voodoo stuff can counter the Russian consul's clout in Kashgar? Mark my words, Captain, Capricorn won't even get within farting distance of the Taotai!"

"Capricorn is very resourceful, sir."

"Well, I still think he's in for a wild goose chase, but I suppose it's too late to worry about that now."

"Yes, sir. Now we have no option but to wait and see."

Hethrington gave him a cold look. "If that was by way of reassurance, Captain, I'd rather you refrained from insulting my intelligence by stating the obvious."

He shot out of his seat and strode across the room to open the window outside which the macaques still patiently awaited their daily due. From a bunch of bananas in a bowl on a side table he plucked a few and tossed them out one by one. Leaping joyously from the sill, the monkeys ran off with shrill cries of excitement as they battled and jostled for the fruit. Hethrington stood for a while listening to the familiar sounds of morning—the drone of bees, the cawing of crows and whinnies of distant horses. Breathing in deeply, he let the cold gusts refresh his lungs, calm his mind and settle his nerves. A further thought occurred and he turned—to surprise his aide in the middle of a full-blown yawn.

Leaving the thought unspoken, he stalked back to his desk. "That will be all for now, Captain," he said frigidly, pleased to have a legitimate reason to vent his spleen. "Since I am obviously keeping you awake, I suggest you return to resume your nap over the *Kashmir Gazetteer*. In the meantime I would deem it a favour to myself, to the Department that pays your salary and to the Empire, if you could force yourself to get some sleep tonight."

Worth blushed furiously, leapt to his feet and hurried towards the door. As usual it squawked itself open as if in the final throes of death.

"Requisition some oil for that infernal racket, will you?"

"Yes, sir, I will see to it immediately."

"And Captain?"

"Sir?" He halted in mid-flight.

"What did you say was the name of this play you claim to have been rehearsing all night?"

"Er, *Elizabeth and Raleigh,* sir."

"That's what I thought." The Colonel smiled grimly. "As it happens, Mrs. Hethrington and I need Elizabeth and Raleigh costumes for His Excellency's fancy-dress bash on Saturday. Considering your clout with the leading lights at the Gaiety, I have no doubt you will know *exactly* how to procure them."

He watched with sadistic relish as his stricken aide turned tail and fled.

CHAPTER

4

The assorted titbits Jenny had provided were of marginal interest to Emma, but she had at least confirmed that part of David's story was true. Damien Granville was indeed a gambler and did frequent the gaming-house. Now it remained to verify the rest as best she could, however unsavoury the prospect.

When summoned by an awed factotum, Bert Highsmith, the Cockney owner of the gaming-house in Urdu Bazaar, was startled to see an Englishwoman, a lady to boot, in his less than modish office.

"Yuss?" Having been roused from his bed, Highsmith's manner was anything but cordial. "Wot can I do fer yuh, miss?"

Wasting no time on preliminaries, Emma gave him her name. "I have come about a game allegedly played here some days ago between Lieutenant Wyncliffe and a certain Mr. Granville."

"Well, wot of it?" he countered, not bothering to conceal a wide yawn that revealed tobacco brown teeth and a furry tongue. Then, as her name registered, he turned wary. *Oh Lawd,* he groaned silently, *a bleedin' rel'tive!* "You connected wiv the gent?"

"Yes. What was the game that was being played between them?"

"Pontoon."

"And were you present throughout the game?"

"Yuss, I always am for every gime that . . ." He stopped, his expression rife with suspicion. "Wot's all this abaht then, eh? Anything wrong with the gime?"

"That's what I've come to find out," Emma said. "*Was* there?"

His face darkened. "Are yer s'gestin' that . . . ?"

"All I want to ensure, Mr. Highsmith, is that the game between Lieutenant Wyncliffe and Mr. Granville was fair." She saw the absurdity of the question but nevertheless watched him closely.

If anything, he bristled. "*All* my gimes are fair, mike no mistike! Wyncliffe is an old customer, *'e'll* tell yer that."

"And Mr. Granville? Is he also an old customer?"

"No, worse luck." He shook his head ruefully. " 'E's a true gennelman, we don't get many of 'em in 'ere." Emma wondered grimly what David would have to say about that. " 'E's also shrewd, *very* shrewd. Senses 'ow the cards're goin' ter fall."

Emma leaned forward on his desk. "Can anyone else vouch that it was a fair game? Surely there must have been other witnesses?"

"No." His eyes were again cautious. " 'Igh-stike gimes are private like, see? The pliyers sit in an hinner room, not ahtside. They don' want strangers breathin' dahn their necks." His face darkened. "I dunno what yer lookin' fer, miss, but like I sed, if *hanyone* sez I run a dishonest house, then 'e's a bloody liar!"

"In that case, I reckon Mr. Ben Carter is," Emma said with blatant untruth, aware of Highsmith's dubious reputation. "Mr. Carter appears to hold a somewhat different opinion." A navvie from Liverpool who had jumped ship in Bombay years ago, Highsmith also organised *satta* gambling, dog and cockfights, pigeon races and kite-flying competitions, all at very favourable odds to himself. According to what Emma had heard, he was an out-and-out rogue and often in trouble with the law.

Hearing the police chief's name mentioned, Highsmith's colour deepened and again his manner changed. His astonished staff crowding the doorway, marvelling at the rare presence of an English lady on their premises, moved back a step.

"Wot 'appened wuss only the once," he muttered sullenly. "This gime I supervised pers'nally. Yuh ask Wyncliffe, ask Granville, ask *hany* of my staff." He waved grandly at his bedraggled employees.

Emma stared at him hard and his shifty eyes dropped. Whatever he concealed, how was she ever to find out? "How many days are given to losers to pay their debts?"

"Fifteen. That's fair, ain't it?"

"I have no idea. And is this period ever extended?"

"That's nuffin' to do with the management," he said with a lofty shrug. "That's fer the winner ter decide."

"Can debts be paid in instalments?"

"Sime difference," he shrugged again, his impatience showing. "Why don't yer ask Mr. Granville, eh?"

Unable to think of any more questions, Emma swallowed hard and asked the one she had been postponing. "What was staked in the game they played?"

So, he 'adn't told her—typical! "It's not the management's policy . . ." he started stiffly, then stopped, remembering this aggressive woman's association with the blasted police chief. "Their 'ouses," he said, glowering. "They stiked their bleedin' 'ouses, that's wot!"

"And you *allowed* such a monstrous bet to be placed on your premises?" she asked angrily. "You did nothing to discourage it?"

" 'Ow could I?" he whined. "I *tried* to stop 'em, so 'elp me Gawd. It was young Wyncliffe 'oo wuss too plastered ter lissen. 'E pliyed and 'e lost 'yer 'ouse. Khyber Pass or some such . . ."

Emma returned home despondent. The encounter with the seamy side of Delhi and the lowlife that inhabited it had left her shaken. Had the visit been worthwhile? She had no idea—any more than she had about what was to be done next.

At dinner that evening, a sorry affair, a gaunt-faced David sat submerged in silence, his gaze lowered, and toyed with his food. His eyes, sunken and dark-ringed, were haunted and the cutlery he held clattered against the china with the tremble of his fingers. Engrossed in relating Carrie Purcell's most recent battles with Jenny about the mounting bills for her trousseau, fortunately Margaret Wyncliffe did not notice.

"But what the devil am I to *do*, Em?" David cried when Emma cornered him in his room after the meal. "I've already had two messages from the manager of the gaming-house about the settlement—the second with all kinds of threats." So much for Highsmith's pious protestations about "the management." "Do you think I should go and see Granville? Perhaps if I explained . . ."

"No!" Emma silenced him angrily. "You've demeaned yourself enough—how dare you think of grovelling! Have you no self-respect left?" She did not tell him about her visit to Highsmith. He had already crumbled under his burden of guilt; however well deserved, further decimation would be cruel.

"Then what?" His relief at having been saved seeing Granville was pathetic. "I can't just sit here doing nothing!"

"You've done enough already," she said bitterly. "Just leave the rest to me. I'll think of something."

He turned away, crushed. "Yes, I know you will. You always do."

As it happened she already had, but it only served to sharpen her resentment against her brother. The following morning, however, an unexpected ray of sunshine brightened the gloom: a letter from Dr. Theodore Anderson asking her to see him at the College with her papers.

I suppose I will have to wait until you call on me. . . .

Gritting her teeth, that afternoon Emma sat down to compose a letter to Damien Granville. She kept the note brief, simply requesting an interview at his earliest convenience. Before her resolve could weaken, she addressed the envelope, summoned the gardener and despatched him to Nicholson Road to deliver it.

She still had no doubt that the unscrupulous Mr. Granville was playing some particularly devious game with her brother. Despite his alleged wealth, the man was obviously a chiseller, and like all chisellers he too would have his price. What she had to do was to find out what that price might be and pray that they would be in a position to pay it. Sweeping aside the sordid affair, she plunged into resolute activity.

The study was still not presentable and papers needed to be sorted and filed. Also, letters of sympathy that had arrived belatedly awaited replies on behalf of her mother. Seating herself at her father's typewriting machine, which she had taught herself to use with fair proficiency, Emma was soon engrossed in her labours. As she re-read the letters and the tributes from her father's colleagues in foreign universities, her memories started to unwind and she was engulfed by nostalgia.

Once again she was ten. Once again she was with her father in remote regions history acknowledged as the cradles of human civilisation. Cascading back came tastes, sights and sounds of the joyous summer holidays of childhood, the wonderful relief from orthodox routines, the easy camaraderie of the camps, the freedom to ramble, to explore, to observe, to question and to learn. She remembered noontime picnics amidst wild flowers and bedtime stories by campfires under open skies. On her tongue she again tasted the curious tea served in high lamaseries, sour and buttery and brewed with vegetables, and she recalled how refreshing she had found it.

Submerged in her evocations, she once again felt the impossible thrill of a rare find—a dusty shelf in a secret Himalayan monastery packed with ancient texts; a heap of rubble that had once been a living stupa; a dark wall alive with forgotten frescoes. She relived the breathless wonder of being able to touch artefacts that had existed three centuries before Christ, two centuries before the Roman invasion of Britain and seven hundred years before England had seen a single face that could be called English.

The fearlessness with which she swam and rode and fished and hunted delighted her father and sent her mother rushing for her salts. Aware that girls at school feared the sun because it browned their skin, she herself suffered no such apprehensions as her own complexion turned rich and honeyed and aglow with health. Romping across sprawling plains, scrambling up fearfully angled slopes and splashing about in legendary rivers where crocodiles watched from afar with lazy detachment, she thrived in the open.

If camp life was uncomfortable, Emma neither noticed nor minded, able to tolerate the lack of urban conveniences far better than her less robust brother. Fortunately for her, the family budget was limited and it was only David who could be sent to boarding school in England. Admitted into a Delhi convent, she rejoiced to be able to remain in India and spend time with a patient and instructive father. Indeed, it was during these years that he taught her to cherish the treasures of this maddeningly diverse land he had chosen as his own, and he who encouraged her to think of its complex heritage as also part of hers.

Alive with images and remembrances of days long gone, the hours flew by unnoticed. By the time the letters were written, the papers arranged and the study a shade tidier, Emma's heart was again heavy with grief. She desperately missed her father: she was still unable to accept that a man so vital, so essentially decent and with so much more to contribute to the treasuries of human knowledge, should have died alone in some unmarked land, on some unnamed day, friendless and separated from his family. It seemed to her a terrible irony that he should have met his death among the mountains that he loved, those very mountains that had given him the happiest days of his life.

So deep had Emma's thoughts recessed into the past that it was only as she started to light the paraffin lamp on her desk that she remembered the note she had sent to Damien Granville, a note to which he had not responded. The gardener, when summoned, reported that he had been asked to leave the letter with the watchman at the gate and told that "huzoor"—as the staff addressed their employer—would reply to it the following day.

No word came from Damien Granville the following day.

The delay, Emma saw, was intentional, the suspense sustained out of sheer perversity. Considering the circumstances, however, she also saw that all she could do was hold on to her patience and wait. Damien Granville's silence persisted over the next two days. Then, just as she was considering the humiliating need for a reminder, he broke his silence and a response arrived.

Mr. Damien Granville would be pleased to receive Miss Emma Wyncliffe at the above address at eleven A.M. on Thursday next.

The note was signed by one Suraj Singh, who, she had learned from Jenny, was Damien Granville's private secretary.

Well, that was that, the die was cast; there could be no going back now. Emma had never doubted, of course, that Granville would agree to see her—how could he not with such a perfect opportunity to gloat? Two days remained until Thursday. Refusing to brood, she concentrated her energies instead on preparations for the all-important interview with Dr. Anderson.

I heard about your frightful experience, my dear," Dr. Anderson said as soon as Emma entered his room at the College where he taught. "You lost nothing of value, I hope?"

He was referring, of course, to the burglary. "Fortunately not," Emma replied. "It was more of a nuisance than cause for serious worry."

"Well, I am relieved to hear it." Having got that out of the way, he waved her into a chair. "I had not considered, my dear, that I would have the time to give your project adequate attention. On reflection, however, I feel that I have been a trifle hasty. A project in memory of a dedicated scholar and a dear friend who did much to expand awareness of Buddhist culture, and died in the process, deserves to be encouraged. So, if you think that an hour or two a week of guidance might help, I would be pleased to supply it. Alas, with the expedition to consider, that is all that I can spare at the moment."

Emma accepted the offer with gratitude, adding that she hoped she would prove worthy of it and measure up to his expectations.

He gave her a piercing look. "Even as an editor, my dear, are you aware of the considerable complexities involved in the task you confront?"

"Only too aware," Emma admitted, "but those of Papa's papers that have been published are already well edited and need only footnotes to be brought up to date. It is the unpublished papers, of course, that will certainly need attention."

"Graham talked to me about his intentions before he left. I advised him to think very carefully before venturing onto the glacier, but he was obsessed with that monastery and nothing would distract him." He clucked and gave his head a sad shake. "To return to your book—I know that Graham was meticulous about recording details, but to be academically credible one will need to interpret them accurately. Even as an editor you risk controversy."

"So did others far more experienced and learned than I, Dr. Anderson. Alexander Cunningham's twenty-three volumes, for instance, have been widely criticised as amateurish—and he was director-general of the Archaeological Survey of India!"

Dr. Anderson nodded. "Yes, your point is well taken. On the other hand, even though you were close to your father and his work, to do justice to a publication such as you attempt, dear child, you have to be nothing less than totally confident. Are you?"

"I don't really know," Emma replied honestly. "Sometimes I fear that perhaps I have bitten off more than I will be able to chew. At the same time I feel that I must at least make the effort. Papa would have wanted me to."

She could hardly tell him without making a fool of herself that while working on his notes she felt close to her father, that she could hear his voice through his handwriting and that the exercise made it easier for her to come to terms with her bereavement.

"Without in any way claiming academic distinction," she said instead, "I feel I know the subject reasonably well. My abilities may be limited but neither my enthusiasm nor my sincerity is."

"Necessary and commendable, of course, but when dealing with esoteric, highly specialised subjects, they can be inadequate. At one time Buddhist history was unknown to the outside world. Today, interest in it is growing, especially in the West. Buddhist and Hindu practices and philosophies are being studied very seriously. Now intellectuals find inspiration in Asia. In his *Parsifal* libretto, for example, Wagner included an episode from the *Ramayana,* and the paintings of Odilon Redon and the literary works of Tolstoy show unmistakable . . ." He stopped, remembering that he was not in class delivering a lecture. "I'm afraid I digress—what were we talking about? Ah yes, your ability to compile this book."

"Or lack of it," Emma said wryly.

Dr. Anderson studied the anxious face before him and his tone softened. "You may consider my remarks harsh, my dear, but I merely point out that justice will be better served if you are able to view Graham's work with dispassion. Professionalism will have to be placed above sentiment."

"Given a chance, you will not find me lacking in professionalism," Emma assured him, "any more than in endeavour and the will to work hard. With the added benefit of your tutelage my efforts will not be entirely worthless."

"Splendid." He rubbed his hands together. "Well, before I can make evaluations, I need to examine what you have brought. Understandably, it is his last expedition that will be of greatest interest to the academic community."

"Well, Papa hardly had time for extensive exploration before the tragedy struck, but I have brought most of what Dr. Bingham carried back with him. The remaining notes I will bring when we meet next. When do you plan to leave for Tibet?"

The question did not please him. In fact, he frowned. "Our funds are still not adequate and our departure has had to be deferred—which is why I am able to find time for your project. If the money arrives soon and we set off before your project is complete, I will leave written guidelines on how to proceed."

It was as satisfactory an arrangement as circumstances permitted and Emma agreed to it eagerly.

"Now then, just as soon as I can find my spectacles . . ."

Noticing them on the chair on which he was about to sit, Emma rescued them in the nick of time. He smiled, patted his desk top, and she placed on it the neatly bound sheaf of papers, charts, maps and photographs on which she had worked so hard.

"Papa's handwriting being what it is . . . was, I have deciphered his more recent notes as best I could and printed them out on my typewriting machine."

Already engrossed, he nodded absently.

Delighted to have been accepted as a protégée, Emma felt a surge of confidence. An authority on ancient texts in Pali, Kharosthi and Aramaic, Theo Anderson was an expert on Central Asia and a respected Tibetologist. An early contender in the race to reach Lhasa and the Potala palace of the forbidden city, he had not yet succeeded in his quest. Nevertheless, he had surreptitiously traversed parts of western Tibet often and his knowledge of Buddhism as it had once flourished in Central Asia was extensive. As, indeed, appeared to be his patience.

Through the next hour, in painstaking detail, without irritation at her many questions, Dr. Anderson explained to Emma many of the finer points of her father's work. In the process he revived much in her memory, provided her with forgotten or fresh insights, and imparted advice on how best to coordinate and edit the scribbled notes to make them acceptable to a highly critical academic community. By the time her tutorial was over, her morale had received a much needed boost and she was hugely elated.

Later, after they had conversed about matters rather more mundane and sipped lemon tea prepared by Dr. Anderson's devoted Pathan khidmatgar, Ismail Khan, the professor leaned back and beamed.

"I have to confess, my dear, in my initial estimate of your capacities I was mistaken. I am impressed by your approach to your father's work. You appear to have a good grasp not only of the subject but also of the way in which Graham's mind worked. And in your own right, of course, you are intelligent, perceptive and unusually well informed for your age."

She was very pleased by his commendation.

"However," he held up a warning finger, "I request that you keep to yourself our little arrangement or I will be inundated with similar requests which I simply cannot accommodate." He got up from his chair. "I shall expect you at the same time tomorrow morning."

"Tomorrow?" Emma was flustered. "I'm dreadfully sorry, Dr. Anderson, but tomorrow morning I have . . . another appointment. Would you be able to see me on Friday, the day after?"

"Good grief—is tomorrow Thursday?" He was seized by alarm. "I had quite forgotten that in a weak moment—an extremely weak moment!—I had agreed to judge a flower show at the Town Hall on Thursday. That frightful Duckworth woman badgered me into it, refused to take no for an answer." He subjected a flower vase to a venomous glare. "So it will have to be Friday after all. In the meantime I suggest that you go through"— he waved his hands about vaguely, then stopped, having forgotten what he was about to say.

*H*olbrook Conolly liked Kashgar.

Situated strategically on the north-south, east-west axis of the Silk Road, Kashgar was the capital city of Chinese Turkestan now renamed Sinkiang, the new dominion. Enclosed on three sides by the Pamirs, the Tian Shan and Karakoram ranges, in the east it was fringed by the Taklamakan desert. Unlike Yarkand a hundred miles to the south, Kashgar was not a pretty town. The forty-foot-high city walls, the Taotai's palace and most of the squat dwelling houses were of mud, the roads were badly rutted and bar one or two monuments there was little of historical interest. Winters, brown and drab and ice-sheeted, were miserable, with not a blade of grass to be seen, and permanently leaden skies resounded with the mournful cries of pochard, mallard and grey geese as they fled to the warmer climes of India.

In spring and summer, however, the Central Asian capital of the Celestial Empire exploded with colour. The trees shimmered with new leaf; the willows and lucerne assumed myriad shades of green. Grape vines and fig trees buried underground for protection against frost were excavated and the markets overflowed with summer produce. There were twenty-six varieties of melon alone, some with a girth of as much as five feet.

For this and various other reasons, Kashgar suited Conolly well. Whereas in Yarkand polluted water tanks spread virulent diseases, here the water was potable, and despite the lack of hygiene in the crowded bazaars, Kashgarians were less afflicted with the goitre rampant elsewhere and therefore reasonably healthy. The comparative lack of serious sickness was for Conolly a great advantage, for although he ran a thriving, successful medical practice he was not a qualified physician.

Nevertheless, he suffered no qualms of conscience. His father had been a medical missionary in China and this had equipped him with both a knowledge of basic medicine and colloquial fluency in Mandarin. Three subsequent years in a London medical college had provided enough practical experience for the confident treatment of minor everyday ailments. In this sprawling, underinhabited region of wandering tribes, peripatetic traders and widespread illiteracy, no one bothered with academic qualifications anyway and Conolly's skills were widely in demand. More importantly, his bustling clinic constituted a perfect front for the discharge of duties of a more clandestine nature.

Apart from Conolly, there were only five resident Europeans in Kashgar: the Russian consul, Pyotr Shishkin; his wife; their two Imperial Service officers; and a Dutch consul who, for some curious reason, was also an amateur barber. There was no British consulate in Kashgar for the very good reason that the Taotai refused to permit one. Conolly himself was yet to be granted permanent residency status and was forced to travel in and out of town frequently, which, as it happened, suited his purposes well. Aided and abetted by the shining innocence of his cherubic face, his charming manner and his energetic youthfulness—for he was not yet thirty—Holbrook Conolly plied both his trades with commendable success.

The fact that people tended to drop their guard when talking to a doctor was, of course, an invaluable tool of his covert trade. As a political agent (code-named Capricorn), Conolly gleaned much useful information for his superiors in Simla through sagas of domestic woe, travellers' tales, commercial chit-chat and bazaar gossip. Through his competence at chess, he had even managed to gain tenuous entry into the Russian consulate as occasional doctor to Pyotr Shishkin. However, his energies at the present time were directed towards a different objective: to win the confidence of the Taotai, the Governor of the Chinese dominion.

In his distrust and loathing of white foreigners, until recently the Taotai had depended solely on indigenous medicine for his health problems. It was only last month that he had, suddenly and surprisingly, sent for Conolly for a first consultation. Now, much to Conolly's delight, he had been summoned again, this time with an invitation to dine at the palace—a most promising development in view of his latest instructions from Simla.

Hethrington's orders—received via a Baluchi trader from Leh together with medicines smuggled inside a pair of leather boots—baffled Conolly. No reasons had been given for the curious mission, although that was neither here nor there. As a foot soldier of the Department, it was not for him to question its whims, however rum. Tonight after dinner, therefore, he intended to have a quiet post-prandial tête-à-tête with the Taotai. Since his fluency in Mandarin eliminated the need for an interpreter, Conolly had every hope that their little chat would be in private.

As he threaded his way through the crowded bazaar on his way to the palace, Conolly exchanged frequent greetings and pleasantries with passers-by, for he was a popular and well-known figure. His thoughts, however, were focussed elsewhere—on the lavish feast that awaited him at the palace. According to Chin Wang, the Taotai's head cook (and a source of frequent information), the Governor had ordered a meal of thirty-seven courses to be served and the menu Chin Wang had related had Conolly extremely worried.

The unhappy fact was that the Chinese Governor suffered from chronic flatulence; the slightest hint of oil on the stomach lining had him teetering on the brink of disaster. Obliged to entertain frequently and eat rather better than advisable, at formal banquets he was often driven to excuse himself from table in order to perform certain unmentionable (and uncontrollable) bodily functions out of hearing. It was embarrassing. Worse, it was undignified. If the Celestial supremo's lack of gastric control were to become public it would not only undermine his authority but make him a laughing-stock, the butt of crude jokes in the marketplace. The very fact that he had finally been driven to send for a despised Anglo-Saxon round-eye (on condition of strict confidentiality, of course) was a measure of the stricken man's desperation.

The Taotai received Conolly cordially and with a smile, a good omen. Since Chinese custom decreed that wines be served at table between courses, they sat down to dine immediately after drinking cups of the mandatory green tea. Conolly noted with relief that the usual coterie of mandarins and officials was absent, perhaps in view of the delicate nature of the Taotai's ailment. In spite of the early spring, flurries of snow spilled in from under the door and the room was draughty and uncomfortably cold. However, a brazier had been lit under the large circular table and this kept the lower extremities from freezing.

The first course, a minute portion of sliced ox tongue and apricot jam, was superb, as was the thimbleful of steaming rice wine not unlike an English hot toddy. There followed a succession of dainty dishes in the manner of hors d'oeuvres, each tastier than the last. If the English were skilled in conversing interminably about the weather, the Chinese had refined the practice into an art. Over the stuffed quails' eggs, fried deerskin and Peking duck, they talked of the unseasonal snow and little else. The delectable shark's-fin soup, pig's trotters, lotus root and bamboo shoots in hot, piquant spices came and went. And still the Taotai did not excuse himself from table!

After the fourteenth course, Conolly's nerves started to ease; after the twenty-fifth—sea slugs and hot, doughy bread—he allowed himself a small, cautious smile. The acid test, however, was the thirty-second course, crackling of suckling pig deep-fried in sesame oil, according to Chin Wang. When the platter finally arrived dripping with grease, the Taotai helped himself to it liberally and demolished the lot without even a belch. Even ten minutes after his plate was wiped clean and the chopsticks set to one side, he displayed not the slightest sign of discomfort.

Holbrook Conolly was jubilant. Not by word, deed or expression, however, did he make the mistake of showing it. Smothering a strip of oily crackling with a last mouthful of clammy dough, he inquired in the most euphemistic terminology at his disposal if His Excellency's internally inclement weather showed signs of improvement.

The Taotai's expression remained inscrutable. "With the blessings of my ancestors, yes. The four winds appear to have receded."

Conolly chuckled to himself—ancestors my left eye, blessings of good old British charcoal tablets and Ayurvedic digestives more likely! Outwardly he kept his face blank; the matter he knew would not be discussed further. The conversation veered into other channels and his host's good humour persisted. Nevertheless, it was not until later as they sat smoking their aromatic opium pipes that Conolly considered it safe to abandon Chinese euphemism and revert to European bluntness.

"There is a small matter in which I am obliged to crave the assistance of the Celestial Empire, Excellency."

The Taotai's smile turned wary. "Yes?"

"It is a personal matter," Conolly said.

"Oh, a personal matter." The smile returned. "A matter of the heart perhaps?"

"Well—" Conolly coughed and assumed an air of embarrassment. "It *is* about a woman, Excellency. I need help to locate her."

"Locate her? Ah!" The Taotai chuckled knowingly. "Your concubine has run away with your neighbor. You wish me to catch them and have them beheaded?"

"Er, not exactly, Excellency."

"What then?"

"The woman I seek is being held in bondage, possibly in Sinkiang."

The Governor was annoyed. "There are no slaves in Sinkiang."

"Undeniably many thousands have been freed over the years," Conolly conceded soothingly, "but some still remain in domestic positions in the households of rich merchants."

"Are you aware of the size of Sinkiang?" the Taotai asked irritably.

"I am aware of it, Excellency."

"Who is this woman you wish to trace? Is she English? I was not aware that any of your people are being held in bondage."

"No, Excellency, she is not English. As a matter of fact, she is," he gulped, "Armenian."

"A Russian subject!"

"Only through conquest," Conolly pointed out quickly.

The Taotai's expression continued to chill. "Be that as it may, I recommend that you approach Mr. Shishkin. I have no desire to meddle with Russian subjects whether through conquest or not."

"I am reluctant to approach Mr. Shishkin, Excellency," Conolly said carefully, knowing how profoundly the Chinese hated and feared the Russian consul and his country. "I am of the opinion that, unlike Your Excellency, Mr. Shishkin is not a man of compassion. Besides, he dislikes the English as much as he does Excellency's Celestial people. If the woman *is* being held captive in Sinkiang, he will make political capital out of it to the detriment of your great Chinese nation."

It was an argument that appealed to the Taotai, as Conolly knew it would. Tapping the bowl of his pipe against the edge of the table, the Taotai smiled slyly through the haze of smoke. "Your opinion of the Russian consul is very erudite. Nevertheless, it astonishes me. I was under the impression that you are a friend of Mr. Shishkin, which is why you choose to dine with him once a month."

Conolly was unsurprised that his movements were monitored. "We share a common interest in chess, Excellency. Also I have had occasion to provide professional services to Mr. Shishkin."

The beady eyes gleamed. "For what ailment?"

"I regret that I cannot discuss Mr. Shishkin's illness, Excellency," Conolly said loftily, "any more than I would your own. To betray a patient's confidence is contrary to the spirit and letter of the Hippocratic Oath."

Never having heard of the Hippocratic Oath, the Taotai was nonetheless impressed. He eased back against his bolster. "This woman you seek— your interest in her is of a romantic nature?"

Conolly engineered a maidenly blush and dropped his gaze.

"Yes, yes!" The Taotai waggled a skittish finger. "Most definitely a matter of the heart." His smile dropped and once again he frowned. "I would not like to offend Mr. Shishkin. It would not be politically . . . judicious."

Had he not been a doctor privy to the intimacies of his bowels, Conolly knew that the Taotai would never have made such a damning admission. In view of the gross inadequacy of their defences and consequent vulnerability, the Chinese took good care never to cause the Russian consul the slightest offence. With their troops massed permanently in Ferghana just across the border, Tashkent loomed very large indeed on the Celestial horizon.

"There is no reason for Mr. Shishkin to learn of my request," Conolly said. "Indeed, I would beg Your Excellency to keep it as confidential as I would a, ah, medical consultation."

The point was not lost on the Taotai; his lips tightened. "Looking for a woman in Sinkiang is like searching for a tea leaf in the China Seas. You bring details of her?"

"A few, alas, not nearly enough, which is why I need assistance." Conolly extracted an envelope from his pocket and placed it on the low table between them. The Taotai ignored it.

"How do you know that she is not one of those already freed and returned to her homeland?"

"Inquiries have eliminated that prospect, Excellency. All indications so far are that she remains still in Central Asia."

"To make overt inquiries about a Russian subject possibly held in Sinkiang would be embarrassing for my government."

"Your Excellency has a most splendid network of *covert* informers renowned for their discretion."

"As has Mr. Shishkin," the Taotai reminded him sourly. "These medicines that you have prescribed for me . . ."

"Yes?" Conolly held his breath. It appeared to be an abrupt change of topic, but he knew that the question could not have been more pertinent. He waited.

The Taotai stared hard through the window. "You have a good stock of the black tablets and brown powder?"

"So far, yes."

"Enough to keep me supplied should the, er, winds rise again?"

"That would depend, Excellency."

"On what?"

"On how freely my medical supplies are allowed into Kashgar." Conolly looked him square in the eye. "Since British goods are unwelcome and preference is given to Russian manufactures, the import of medicines is erratic and I am asked to pay heavy duties."

"Only on those that are imported legally," the Taotai pointed out drily. "Those that are smuggled in by caravans do enter freely."

Conolly remained prudently silent.

The Governor's bulbous fingers drummed on his knee as he sucked at his pipe and mulled over the problem. "Very well, Dr. Conolly," he then said briskly. "I will do the necessary with regard to your medicines and give the matter of the woman some thought."

It was the closest, Conolly knew, that he would come to a commitment. "Thank you, Excellency. I am most grateful."

He rose to his feet, withdrew from his pocket a bottle and a packet of powders and placed them before the Governor. "As a mark of appreciation for a gracious hearing and a most enjoyable meal."

All said and done, Conolly reflected as he walked back home, it had been a successful evening. He wondered uneasily, as he often did, how much the Taotai knew of his true occupation. Certainly, there were moments this evening when he was worried by the Taotai's manner. The medicines sent by old Cranks from Leh provided some insurance for his immediate future, but from now on he would have to be careful, live only one day at a time. If the business of the woman could be successfully concluded and the providential winds disappeared permanently from the gubernatorial tum-tum, he would then consider asking the Taotai for a residential passport.

What the devil the Department could possibly want with an unknown female Armenian slave, however, was a question to which Conolly could not even begin to hazard an answer.

With its influx of merchants, traders and professional people from other provinces, Delhi was the seventh richest city in British India. Nowhere was this mercantile prosperity as evident as in Chandni Chowk—Silver Street—the main commercial thoroughfare. Localities on either side of the street boasted the highest land values in Delhi, the properties belonging to wealthy Hindus, Muslims and immigrant Marwari families from Rajputana. It was a long, wide avenue with a canal flowing down the middle and tall trees providing cool shade for passers-by. The smarter shops owned by Europeans and Parsees stocked imported luxury goods that were much in demand in the pursuit of urban sophistication.

Emma had passed through Chandni Chowk a thousand times and it never failed to thrill her, but today the elegant parades went by unnoticed. As she sat carefully back in her rented carriage, unseen and anonymous, she thought only of the coming encounter.

In acknowledgement of the fact that Damien Granville had a keen eye for the ladies, this morning she had taken considerable pains over her grooming. Hating the hypocrisy, she nevertheless accepted it as necessary under the circumstances; it would have been childish not to merely in order to express pique. With so few arrows in her quiver she could not afford to overlook anything that might work in her favour. However, when she scrutinized her image in the mirror before leaving the house, it seemed to her that despite her laborious efforts her physical shortcomings remained exactly as they were. Her face was too long, her mouth too wide, her forehead too high and her manner—she had been told often enough by her mother—too forthright for those used to feminine submissiveness. To add to all that she was too tall, with too little flesh on her bones to round the too many angles into the too few soft curves.

With a rare stab of envy Emma thought of Stephanie Marsden and her luminous beauty, her petite figure and china blue eyes, her seductive pout and the permanent look of helplessnesss she cultivated with such success. Her own unremarkable features, it seemed to Emma, looked plainer than ever this morning. Even her large blue-green eyes, her head of lustrous hair and her smile—her best assets, according to her mother (for whatever that was worth)—failed to inspire her. Besides, her simmering resentment was all too evident in her expression. Too sensible not to realise that anger at this juncture was self-defeating, she made a determined effort to put it behind her.

All the same she decided that, successful or not in her mission, she would return with her dignity intact. She would make compromises if necessary, but she would not grovel, nor prime Damien Granville's already inflated sense of self-worth.

Once again surprised by her daughter's uncharacteristic chic, Margaret Wyncliffe accepted without question her explanation of a visit to Mr. Lawrence, the family solicitor. Privately, however, she wondered if the well-cut turquoise shantung suit with lace cuffs and collar, the burnished chestnut hair, freshly turned curls and subtle use of cosmetics might not be in honour of—dared she hope?—a worthier, younger gentleman such as Howard Stowe?

The mansion Damien Granville had rented from an avaricious Begum was one that only the rich could afford, considering the exorbitant rent she charged. It was an ugly structure cluttered with a dozen styles ranging from Ionic to Moghul, but the gardens were well kept and the flowering trees that bordered the lawn were studded with pretty little spring buds. As the carriage came to a halt in the portico, Emma took a moment to fend off the sudden assault of butterflies in her stomach, but by the time she alighted she showed no sign of nervousness. Waiting to receive her on the front steps was a man dressed in starched white drill and scarlet turban.

"Suraj Singh at Miss Wyncliffe's service." He introduced himself with a crisp bow and a military click of the heels. "I am Mr. Granville's private secretary. Huzoor regrets that he is presently occupied with an urgent matter that has just been brought to his attention. He presents his apologies and begs the honourable memsahib to await him in his private apartment.

He will not be delayed more than a few moments." With a very elaborate flourish he again bowed and indicated that she should accompany him.

Obviously aware of Emma's fluency in the language, he had spoken in Urdu. He appeared to be of middle age, sturdy and spry. His temples were flecked with grey, as were his trim beard and moustache, and he had the martial bearing of a Rajput warrior. His manner was extremely courteous without being obsequious.

"Please wait for me in the driveway," she instructed her coachman, adding pointedly, "I do not expect to stay long." Then she turned and followed Suraj Singh into the house. He walked, she noticed, with a slight limp.

The interior of the mansion was as bizarre as the facade, with a surfeit of bric-à-brac, Italian statuary in impossible postures and gloomy, undistinguished oil paintings. It was a dark, brooding house, hardly a place to inspire confidence in one already ill at ease. The first-floor chamber into which she was eventually ushered was more pleasing. Furnished like an English office, it was airy and its bay window overlooked the river. Behind the outsized mahogany desk the walls were thick with bookcases.

"Perhaps the honoured memsahib would care for some tea?" Suraj Singh asked.

"Thank you, no." Emma seated herself in the chair he indicated and started to remove her dainty lace gloves.

Repeating the flowery apologies for his employer's absence, he added, "Should the honoured memsahib change her mind about refreshments she has only to command. The khidmatgar awaits her pleasure." He bowed, excused himself and left as the khidmatgar materialised to take up position outside the door.

Rather relieved to have a moment to herself, Emma looked around, then rose and walked over to a wall mirror to ensure that her coiffure was still tidy. Through the window she gazed down upon the pleasing prospect of the river which lapped at the walls of the compound. Just beneath the window a group of fishermen sat repairing their fishing-nets. In the distance were the hazy outlines of the Red Fort, stronghold of successive Moghul emperors.

Mentally, Emma reviewed the proposition she intended to place before Damien Granville—should all else fail. She still could not believe that anyone could take such a scandalous wager seriously, but then this was a strange man of extraordinary perceptions; there was no knowing how he would choose to react. The ormolu clock on the wall chimed the half-hour; she had been waiting thirty minutes and there was still no sign of her host— if that was indeed the apt word. The discourtesy was, of course, deliberate.

However, if it was Granville's intention to abrase her into losing her equanimity, she was determined not to give him the satisfaction.

The encounter, she saw, promised to be even more difficult than she had imagined.

The door opened abruptly. "Forgive me for having kept you waiting, Miss Wyncliffe." The deep voice preceded Granville into the room. He walked with long strides towards the window, took her hand and bowed over it at just the right angle. The touch of his hand made her shiver; he noticed it at once. A faint smile came and went with the arch of an eyebrow. "Yes, it is rather chilly this morning, isn't it? Perhaps a warming cup of coffee might help."

Emma did not return the smile as she quickly—not too quickly!—withdrew her hand from his. "No, thank you. I am warm enough and perfectly comfortable."

"Some Turkish coffee, Maqsood." Discounting her refusal, he ordered it anyway. "We must not allow our very special guest to catch cold, must we? And, of course, some baklava. I am ashamed to confess, Miss Wyncliffe, that I have an appallingly pampered sweet tooth. I hope that you will not inflict on me the punishment of having to indulge it alone."

Resisting the charm with ease, Emma ignored the remark. "I was beginning to believe that you had forgotten about the appointment," she said. "As arranged, I arrived on the stroke of eleven."

"So I was told. Well, I have already apologised, but if it pleases you I will happily do so again."

She was saved the need to reply by the entry of a second attendant bearing a tall silver hookah. He waited and looked uncertainly at his master. "Would you permit me to smoke while we have our little chat?" Granville asked.

Little chat! The attempt to reduce her visit to the level of a casual call was another insult. "You are free to do as you wish in your own home, Mr. Granville," she answered distantly.

"Thank you. Not many English women tolerate this contraption but then you, I know, are of quite a different breed, Miss Wyncliffe." He laughed and waved her into a particular chair. "I think you would be better seated facing the window. The rest of the chairs, like the house, are uncomfortable and in atrociously bad taste."

Emma did as advised and Granville settled himself opposite in a leather armchair. Sensing that his eyes were on her and missed little about her appearance, she kept her own resolutely on the servant as he set about arranging the hookah. Granville sucked at the mouthpiece gently and the water-bowl gurgled into life. Her father had sometimes indulged in a hookah smoke while sitting and chatting with the workers during digs, and the evocative aroma of tobacco wafting across the room suffused her with nostalgia.

"No, I had not forgotten about the appointment," Granville said in response to her question. He added softly, "It would, indeed, be difficult to forget a day when the sun has risen in the west."

Well, there it was! She had expected the taunt, of course—how could he have resisted making it? She did not give him the pleasure of a reaction. "I would not have dreamed of seeking you out, Mr. Granville," she said calmly, "were it not for certain unfortunate circumstances."

"Oh? And what might these be, may I ask?"

"You are as aware of them as I am, therefore let us not waste time in unnecessary word games. I have come about Khyber Kothi, our property. I understand from my brother that you claim to have won it from him in some sort of card game?"

"That is not entirely correct, Miss Wyncliffe," he said and Emma's heart leapt. "I do not claim to have won it, I *have* won it."

"You intend to take the wager seriously?"

He looked surprised. "How else are wagers to be taken if not seriously?"

"You mean to recover these alleged winnings even though this particular wager was frivolous and utterly unethical?"

"Winnings are meant to be recovered, Miss Wyncliffe. And all wagers are frivolous and unethical when they are lost—as every loser will tell you."

She regarded him with acute dislike. "The wager was made by an immature, irresponsible youth in a state of inebriation."

"So, presumably, were those on the previous evenings when the same immature, irresponsible youth claimed his winnings with considerable despatch." He paused to give his full attention to the adjustment of his hookah mouthpiece. "Your brother's alleged lack of maturity has not prevented him from visiting the gaming-house with devotional regularity, I believe. As to his proclivity for alcohol, Miss Wyncliffe, that is your problem, not mine."

With great effort she held on to her temper. "You *forced* him to drink!"

"Hardly! I have no apparatus with which to pour liquor down the throat of a grown man. Your brother drank willingly, Miss Wyncliffe, indeed, too willingly."

"I know that David is impulsive and rash," she conceded, "and I am not condoning his foolish behavior, I cannot. But you exploited his weaknesses, incited him to play, tempted him to place increasingly wild bets."

"Is that what he told you?" His smile was contemptuous. "Mature or otherwise, your brother is over the age of twenty-one. In the eyes of the law, at least, he is responsible for his actions and liable for their consequences. As for forcing his hand . . . come, come, Miss Wyncliffe. Not even a doting sister, certainly not one as intelligent as you, could possibly take that seriously."

Emma flushed but withheld the retort that sat on the tip of her tongue. "The stakes with which you played were extortionist. No one could possibly accept such a game as fair."

"It was a perfectly fair game, Miss Wyncliffe," Granville said with a first touch of sharpness. "The man you saw the other morning, Highsmith, has already testified to that. He will also testify that I warned your brother repeatedly before the wager was laid that should the cards fall in my favour I had every intention of claiming his house."

"Had they not done so, would *you* have surrendered your property without protest?"

"Certainly!" His lips thinned. "There is a universal axiom that gamblers are expected to follow, Miss Wyncliffe—if you don't have the stomach to lose, don't play."

There was no rejoinder to that—or, indeed, to any of Granville's arguments. She had made her allegations only to test the waters, to see if any trace of humanity lay hidden behind the hardened exterior. It didn't. The khidmatgar returned bearing a silver salver with two tiny porcelain cups of Turkish coffee and a plate of baklava wedges. He laid the tray on a table beside Emma's chair and withdrew. Damien Granville rose and offered her the baklava. She shook her head. He then picked up a cup and offered her that, and this Emma accepted. He helped himself to two wedges of the sweet, took the other cup of coffee and again arranged himself comfortably in the armchair.

"Drink it while it's hot. Cold, it never tastes quite the same."

Emma started to sip. The coffee was superb, sweet and bitter at the same time, and its strong flavours loosened her constricted throat. She sipped in silence until the brew was reduced to its thick sediment, then returned the eggshell-thin cup to the tray. Since it had given her time to recapitulate the offer she had come to make, the interlude had been welcome.

"If you are under the impression," she said, now brisk and businesslike, "that I have come to make excuses for my brother and cast ourselves on your charity, I must inform you that you are mistaken."

"Oh? Well, then, why exactly have you come?"

"I have come to make you an alternative offer."

The eyebrows shot upwards. "You intrigue me more and more, Miss Wyncliffe. I can hardly wait to hear it."

Emma ignored the sarcasm. "Since I have no doubt it is the considerable sum of money involved in the wager that is of interest to you, I suggest that you appoint a surveyor to assess the value of our property. Whatever its worth, we will undertake to pay the amount within a period of one year from now."

"And from where, may I ask, will you get this money?"

"I don't consider that to be any concern of yours, Mr. Granville. I assure you that we do have resources to clear the debt."

"What if Khyber Kothi is assessed at more than these alleged resources?"

"We will make good the difference somehow. Again, the means need not concern you."

He sat back and flicked a spot of ash off his jacket. "Your scheme would be perfect, Miss Wyncliffe, were it not for one flaw."

Her pulses quickened. "Flaws can be rectified by mutual consent."

"The flaw is that it is unacceptable to me."

Under the folds of her skirt she clenched her fists. "Why?"

"I am not convinced that such a tenuous arrangement guarantees payment of my dues. Besides, what I want is the house."

"But you do not live in Delhi!" she cried. "I hear that you already have a home in Kashmir and that you find this town distasteful. Surely it is the money that matters to you most?"

"You conclude wrongly, Miss Wyncliffe. However unpleasant I may find Delhi, I do require a residence of my own here. I dislike living in rented premises. Indeed, your house could not have become available at a more convenient time."

Nothing so far had shocked her quite as much as what he had just said. "You intend to *live* in our house?"

"That is the general idea," he confirmed equably. "Given a healthy infusion of funds, Khyber Kothi is potentially a most desirable residence with the right social address. I like the fact that it is private, stands in its own grounds and is well endowed with fine old peepul and ashoka trees. All said and done, it should satisfy my requirements admirably."

"Khyber Kothi is our home, our *only* home!"

"I take it that your brother was aware of that before he placed the bet?"

"My mother is confined to the house with a heart ailment and the trauma of having to leave would kill her," Emma burst out, despising herself for the note of entreaty that she heard in her voice. "Surely there is room for some compromise?"

"I am distressed to learn of your situation," he said, giving scant indication of it, "and I am embarrassed that it should fall on me to deprive you of the roof above your head, but," his own tone hardened, "the blame for your homelessness must belong not to me but to your brother. Indeed, it is he who should be here this morning instead of you, Miss Wyncliffe. I find sympathy difficult for someone willing to hide behind the skirts of a sister."

"David has no idea that I am here, I . . . I came of my own accord. I had hoped to strike a mutually beneficial bargain, but I see that I have been guilty of a serious miscalculation." Swallowing her despair, Emma gathered up her gloves, her poche and the remains of her self-respect and rose to her feet. "There appears to be little point in continuing this discussion."

"Well tried anyway, Miss Wyncliffe. Your spirit is certainly to be saluted. Indeed, you may yet engineer the salvation of the English memsahib in India."

She was enraged by his patronising manner. "I doubt if you would do likewise for the English sahib, Mr. Granville," she snapped. "You played a dishonest game and nothing will convince me that it was otherwise. However mindless, self-centred and irresponsible my brother might be, you, sir, are a cheat, a liar and a parasite scavenging on decent society."

To her horror, pinpricks behind her eyelids heralded the arrival of tears. Resisting with supreme effort the urge to either shed them or flee, she turned slowly and walked unhurriedly to the door. With one hand on the door knob she forced herself to halt. "You will *not* succeed in driving us out of our home, Mr. Granville," she flung back. "To thwart your nefarious scheme, I promise I will fight you with every last breath in my body!"

She was about to slam the door behind her when he spoke.

"Wait." The single syllable was said softly but it emerged as a command. Without meaning to, Emma stopped. Granville rose out of his armchair, walked to the door and pulled it open. "Please come in and sit down."

"Why? You have made your intentions eminently clear—what else remains to be said?"

"Something does."

Her heart lurched with painful hope as she took a few tentative steps back into the room—he was about to accept her offer after all!

"Please sit down."

"I can hear just as well standing up."

"As you please." He closed the door behind her, then turned and strolled back to his desk, sat down and faced her across the length of the room. "I too have an offer to make."

The spark of hope flared but she concealed it well.

"There is one condition under which I might be willing to cancel your brother's debt."

Her heart stopped. "Yes?"

"As you are evidently aware," he said, his eyes never leaving her face, "I live in Kashmir. I do not know if you are at all acquainted with the Vale, but it is wild and beautiful, endowed by nature as no other place on earth. I live surrounded by everything that a man could possibly want—material security, a fertile estate, a home arranged and furnished to my own taste with every creature comfort I require. I live as I please. I call no man master." His dark eyes were alive with pride. "There is, however, one vital component that my life still lacks." He hesitated a minim. "A woman."

The words took an instant to register. Emma stiffened, her cheeks flooded with colour to match the crimson of the curtains and her gaze buried itself in the floor. Continuing to observe her intently from behind his desk, he allowed her a few moments of silence. Her sense of shock finally receded; she thrust her trembling hands beneath her poche.

"If I understand your drift correctly, Mr. Granville," she said in a voice acceptably steady, "I find it unworthy of comment. Indeed, I find both you and your proposition contemptible."

"Oh? Just what do you think my proposition is?"

"That in exchange for the cancellation of my brother's debt I should agree to become your mistress," she said, bluntly refusing the refuge of euphemism.

"My dear Miss Wyncliffe!" He threw up his hands in mock horror, a model of outraged innocence. "You astonish me more and more. I find it difficult to believe that a pure, untouched English rose like you could even be aware of such dreadful creatures as mistresses." He laughed and crossed the length of the room to where she stood, his thumbs tucked in the arm-holes of his waistcoat. He halted so close to her that whiffs of his tobacco-tinged breath fanned her face.

"No, Miss Wyncliffe," he said, "mistresses I have galore. I doubt if I could accommodate more without inviting serious damage to my health. You will therefore be relieved to know that I do not want you for a mistress." His manner was casual but his eyes held a curious, piercing intensity. "I want you for a wife."

For an eternity, it seemed, the words remained suspended between them. The silence expanded and then thickened, punctuated only by the *tick-tock* of the clock. Emma stared at him wide-eyed and incredulous, unaware in her astonishment that she had folded back into a chair.

"So, Miss Wyncliffe," he murmured. "It appears that I do have the capacity to surprise you, after all."

Rendered speechless, she continued to stare. This unprincipled philanderer, this seasoned, dissolute gambler, proposed marriage to her?

She started to laugh, and unable to stop, continued to do so. As her peals reverberated through the room, Damien Granville stiffened and his face, dark and unamused, flooded with rich colour. He walked over to where she sat in helpless hilarity, and before she could even begin to guess his intention, his hand had lashed out in a resounding slap. The laughter died deep inside her throat and she gasped. Her own hand flew up to her cheek; it felt numb. For a moment they stared wordlessly at each other, he in rasping fury, she in cold, creeping fear.

"You laughed in my face once before, Miss Emma Wyncliffe," he said, again lethally calm. "Well, you will not do so again. Please remember that in future."

She stumbled to her feet, and without looking at him fled towards the door. He made no move to stop her. As she wrenched it open, she turned and gave him one last poisonous look. "On the contrary, Mr. Granville, I will remember nothing of you in future! I despise you. Indeed, I am astounded at your inability to see just how much."

She slammed the door behind her and swept out into the corridor past the waiting khidmatgar, down the marble staircase and into the front hallway. She did not look back. Walking up to her carriage waiting in the portico, she stepped inside and ordered it home.

CHAPTER

5

he manoeuvres of the Jutogh Mountain Battery and a company of the Wiltshire Regiment were well into their second hour. The seven-pounder screw guns on mules, the ammunition carriages and the soldiers had passed the saluting point where the Viceroy, the Commander-in-Chief, the Quarter Master General, the Commandant of the Simla Volunteer Corps, the Lieutenant-Governor of the Punjab, members of Council, assorted secretaries, high government functionaries and their guests were seated. Opposite them was Jakko hill, with its small Hanuman temple and bands of resident monkeys. As the assembled guns fired busily (and noisily) at screens arranged on the hillside, there was shrill protest from the simian community.

Glancing once again at his watch, Colonel Hethrington thought of his overladen desk and cursed quietly. There were despatches to be read, circulated and returned, responses to be considered, composed and despatched, and telegraphs wired to London, Leh, Srinagar and, no doubt, Timbuctoo. Out here in the open the sun was unendurably warm, the umbrellas lamentably inadequate and the infernal racket an aggravation to the headache he had acquired last night smothered in his Walter Raleigh suit.

Where the blazes was that jackass Worth? He had given instructions that he was to be summoned on some pretext or other no later than eleven a.m. It was now almost noon and there was no sign of the man. He was on the point of standing up to scour the multitudes when, like a genii emerging from a magic lamp, his aide materialised soundlessly by his side.

"Sorry to be late, sir, but I was decoding a cipher just received from Mr. Crankshaw which I think you should see at once."

The cipher, Colonel Hethrington discovered half an hour later in his office, was by no means a pretext but genuine and also alarming. Geoffrey Charlton, Crankshaw informed them, had arrived in Leh and intended to proceed to Yarkand.

Hethrington closed his eyes and pressed his eyelids down with his fingertips. "Damn!"

"We could stop him from going further, sir."

"And be pilloried for obstructing a free press in its duty to the populace? Don't be daft, lad, that would only confirm that we *do* have something to hide."

"Well, then, we could at least delay him."

"Or try to! Yes, I suppose that's the best we can, under the circumstances. Draft a cipher for Crankshaw, will you? Any word from Capricorn yet?"

"No, sir, but we should have news soon."

Hethrington cursed some more. "And in the meantime what do we do, eh? Confess everything to the C-in-C and QMG and get ourselves cashiered?"

"Perhaps not to the C-in-C, sir," the Captain said thoughtfully, "but to the QMG, yes. Sir John seldom questions your decisions in matters of Intelligence. Once he is informed of the project and approves it, we would be adequately protected against potential censure should anything go wrong."

"Really! And what if he doesn't bloody well approve it?"

"With Charlton already on the prowl?" The Captain smiled. "He would have no choice, sir."

The Colonel tented his fingers and half closed his eyes. "Enlighten the QMG but keep the C-in-C in the dark, eh?"

"We have no other option, sir. The C-in-C would abort the project and order forcible confiscation of the papers—with inevitable and highly embarrassing fanfare."

"And if the QMG orders likewise?"

"Sir John has never let the Department down when it came to the crunch, sir, and if this isn't a crunch I don't know what is."

Still not convinced, Hethrington stroked his chin. "Withholding information from a superior officer is a misdemeanour, Captain."

"Not by a Department where secrecy is the norm, sir. Besides, the misdemeanour has already been committed. The QMG should have been informed *before* the project was initiated."

Hethrington relapsed into meditative silence.

It was well known that the Commander-in-Chief of the Indian Army, General Sir Marmuduke Jerrold, was an aggressive, unabashed hawk who lived by the book. The QMG, on the other hand, Major-General Sir John Covendale, had an instinct for Intelligence and all it entailed and had been known on occasion to show a surprising flair for the unconventional. So far, the project remained between the two of them and Maurice Crankshaw; but if the QMG were to be put in the picture, it would certainly help save hides later if things did get out of hand. Yes, Hethrington decided, the Captain's suggestion made good sense.

"Anyway," shaking the matter out of his mind for the moment, he turned to his despatch box, "on now to other business."

"The Hunza affair?"

"Yes, Captain, for our sins, the Hunza affair." He struggled briefly with the lock of the red despatch box, then gave up. "Imagine how much easier our lives would be if our frontiers were as well secured as our infernal despatch boxes!"

Worth leapt up to do the needful, unlocked the box and then resumed his seat, pencil in hand.

"Needless to say, everyone from here to Whitehall and back is in a flat spin about Borokov's little jaunt."

"True to form, sir."

"Quite." The Colonel rummaged through the papers and extracted a thin folder stamped "Secret & Confidential." "The QMG wants to review every scrap we have on the visit and there's precious little. The first thing he will want to know is—why the hell didn't we hear of it earlier? The Russian was there when?"

"Mid-January, sir. Safdar Ali's emissaries escorted him through the Boroghil, which was still open. According to our informant in the Baron's outer office, the emissaries had been camping in Tashkent for weeks."

"Francis Younghusband was in Hunza when, November?"

"Yes, sir, three months after Colonel Durand."

"Communications—or lack of them—being what they are, delays are to be expected, but surely not over so many weeks, Captain?"

"You may recall, sir, that the message was carried from Hunza to Srinagar by a Balti porter employed on the new mule road. Landslides made the going even slower, although our Resident in Srinagar wired us as soon as he had the message in hand. Knowing how unreliable most of these ad hoc couriers are, I'd say we were lucky to have received it at all."

"Borokov is the second Russian in Hunza during the past eighteen months—and Grombetchevsky still wafts about the Raksam valley, I believe. That aside, three other parties—Russian, French and English—have been seen recently in the Pamirs. How the devil do we explain that to Whitehall?"

"Well, sir, Grombetchevsky hated Hunza and refused to return, which presumably accounts for Borokov's trip. The other Russian party was more of a scientific expedition assigned to chart the Sino-Tibetan frontier. The Frenchman was a carpet-maker under contract to the Kashmir government and the two Englishmen merely did sport chasing the ovis poli sheep."

"And Borokov, what does he chase?" Colonel Hethrington asked cuttingly. "Kashmiri papier-mâché finger-bowls?"

Captain Worth sighed. "We know what he chases, sir, but surely there is no immediate cause for alarm."

"You and I may believe that, Captain, but I wouldn't recommend suggesting it to Colonel Durand—or to those pin-striped paper-pushers in Whitehall who smell Tsarist bogeymen in every crack and crevice of the Himalayas. Of course, the fact that the Pamirs become more like Paddington Station every year doesn't exactly help. Who is this Borokov, anyway?"

"A career officer in the Russian Imperial Guards, sir."

"Background?"

The Captain opened his folder. "According to our military attaché in St. Petersburg, he is about fifty and was born in Kharkov to poor parents who died early. He was shunted from one foster home to another till he attracted the attention of General Nicholai Smirnoff."

"Alexei Smirnoff's father?"

"Yes, sir. Smirnoff senior was then Minister of War. He arranged a place for Borokov at Moscow University, from where he took a degree in engineering. Smirnoff senior's wife hailed from Kharkov and had a distant family connection with Borokov's mother."

"Mmm, very fancy. Anyway, go on."

"After he was commissioned, also with Nicholai Smirnoff's influence, Borokov was sent to Central Asia with the rank of Captain as part of the Khiva campaign. For a while he was posted at Petro-Alexandrovsk outside Khiva with the Russian garrison. Later, he was in charge of the double-storeyed residential train for officers while the railway was being constructed. After a spell at the oil installation in Baku, he was recalled to St. Petersburg by the Foreign Ministry. Currently he is ranked a Colonel and heads the general staff of the Baron in Tashkent. His visit to Hunza is rumoured to have been instigated by General Alexei Smirnoff, Military Controller of the Emperor's Household. Smirnoff and Borokov are said to be privately and politically close."

"No wonder Borokov had the authority to dangle all these carrots before the Mir! He's not been known to have visited these parts before, has he?"

"No, sir. According to our military attaché, he is fairly new to the Intelligence game. He is, naturally, influenced to a great extent by Alexei Smirnoff who, as we know, has been itching to grab a piece of the Himalayas. It was Smirnoff, if you recall, sir, who created the diplomatic incident with Afghanistan on the Murghab when he was posted in Tashkent as a junior officer."

Hethrington eased himself slowly back in his chair, his brows knitted. "Not a happy situation, Captain. If Smirnoff does replace the Baron as Governor-General, we can certainly expect some pyrotechnics in the Pamirs."

"So our embassy in St. Petersburg warns, sir."

"It's the lack of telegraphic communication that compounds the problem, of course. Once Durand has his mule roads and his telegraph lines going, I daresay the situation will change. For one, he will certainly not waste a moment in marching his troops into Hunza."

"He will have to find a reason to do so, sir."

"Reason?" Colonel Hethrington gave a nasty laugh. "Since when does political insanity need a reason, eh? In any case that rascal Safdar Ali will give him one soon enough and Durand knows it."

"Younghusband considers that the Hunza gorge is impassable."

"Neither impassable nor impossible, laddie! Half the staff at the Gilgit Agency belongs to Algy Durand's old-boy network. They all speak the same language, subscribe to the same tub-thumping views. When the time comes, he will insist on more officers, more Gurkhas, more mountain batteries, even a Gatling gun—and he'll get them, too. It certainly hasn't done his career any harm to have a brother for a Foreign Secretary." He gave a snort. "Anyway, what else do we have on Borokov's meeting with Safdar Ali?"

"Very little else, sir. Our man on the spot received information secondhand through one of his cousins who is a bodyguard of the Mir. Unfortunately, the men were positioned out of earshot and the interpreter was a Pathan with limited knowledge of Burishaski. Our man was forced into considerable guesswork and, consequently, so are we. Their final encounter after the execution was secret, with a new interpreter in attendance."

"Secret, my foot! Safdar Ali asked for the moon and the Russian promised it, what else? They could conceivably transport heavy weapons on that railway without our knowledge, but they still have to lug them through a high pass they fondly hope will be the Yasmina. In any case, Calcutta would consider such a delivery an act of war and certainly Durand would refuse to wait a moment longer. Borokov—and Smirnoff—must be aware of this."

"That execution, sir," Worth mused, "jolly rum show, what?"

"That's all it was, son, a show, arranged as much for Russia's benefit as ours. Borokov is now in St. Petersburg, is he?"

"Yes, sir."

"Well, then, for both our sakes, Captain," Hethrington said softly, "I hope he stays there a good long time."

He leapt out of his seat to measure the length of the room in quick, even paces, restless fingers plucking at each other behind his back. Thick veils of Simla mist had descended with customary suddenness to obliterate the world and the blank opacity outside seemed to Hethrington depressingly symbolic.

"The Hunzakut believe that the Yasmina is a gift from the spirits of the mountains," he said. "Its secret, they say, is known to them and them alone, never to be revealed to an outsider. In local legend the pass is always referred to as female, a *purdahnasheen,* who must never reveal her face to a stranger. Apparently, a Sufi mystic predicted years ago that when the Yasmina becomes known to the world, the Hunza nation will cease to exist. It's all twaddle, of course, but that's what they believe."

He tapped on the window pane. Immediately a little head with large anxious eyes appeared. He fumbled in the fruit bowl and tossed out a fig.

"They'll push us to the brink, no doubt, but in the end Safdar Ali will not get a single weapon from the Russians, not one, any more than the Russians will get the Yasmina." He shook his head, raised a hand to dismiss his assistant, then stopped with an afterthought. "By the way, Captain—"

"Sir?" Worth halted on his way to the door.

"Those costumes filled the bill admirably. Mrs. Hethrington was very pleased when Lady Lansdowne commended her on her choice. I felt a right twit in mine, of course, but no one seemed particularly bothered about that except me. Anyway, thanks." He smiled affably. "Our compliments and gratitude to the owner of the costumes. It was most kind of the lady to have loaned them. Arrange for a tasteful bouquet to be delivered from Mrs. Hethrington and myself, will you? And let me know the damages."

"Yes, sir." Captain Worth's good-looking face remained carefully expressionless. "I will see to it at once."

Behind him, as smooth as skates on ice, the door closed without a murmur.

By the time Emma arrived back home, the numbness had passed. All that remained was profound outrage. Crushing her handkerchief to her cheek, she ran up to her room to examine her face in the mirror. The livid imprint of Granville's fingers was still discernible. She stared at it weak with anger, weak with a crippling sense of defilement. Damien Granville had dared to strike her!

Throwing herself down on her bed, she burst into tears.

To her good fortune, her mother had guests for luncheon and they had already eaten. David, of course, was away at the barracks. When Mahima knocked at her door with a belated tiffin, Emma used the excuse of a headache and declined to eat. For the moment even the fate of Khyber Kothi seemed secondary to the monstrous humiliation to which she had been subjected. Oh, that she could somehow undo the inglorious morning! But, of course, she could not—any more than David could his unforgivable act.

Unable to show her face while the telltale marks persisted, Emma hid behind her headache all evening, secure in the knowledge that her mother could not venture up the stairs. Lying on her back staring up at the ceiling, she whiled away the angry hours in trying to devise means of vengeance, but could think of none. Driven by bravado, she had promised to fight back with every last breath in her body. What hollow words, what an absurdly inadequate weapon—and how hard he must be laughing!

Marriage to Damien Granville? She would see him in Hell first!

Concerned about Emma's absence and disappointed at missing their evening game of backgammon to which she was addicted, Mrs. Wyncliffe sent up a bowl of lentil soup and two hot chappatis. Not wishing to provoke further inquiries, Emma forced down the frugal supper on her verandah, shadowed by its darkness.

"Is my brother home yet?" she asked Mahima as the ayah turned down her bed and arranged the mosquito-curtain around it.

When told that he would not be in for dinner, she was not alarmed. Considering Highsmith's ominous warnings, the last place David was likely to be seen was the vicinity of Urdu Bazaar.

Filled with unholy spectres, her sleep that night was haunted by bizarre, incomprehensible and unwarranted images of Damien Granville. Sometime past midnight she awakened with a start; a horse neighed below her window, David's gelding. For the first time that she could remember, she dreaded, truly dreaded, seeing her brother. Having so confidently taken upon herself the burden of a solution, what was she to say to him now?

To her great relief, David did not seek her out.

With morning, however, came a return of reason and a fresh surge of courage. The bright cornflower blue sky looked cheerful and the air resounded with birdsong. Sights and sounds of the March morning, so incompatible with defeat, pushed aside the dejection and forced Emma to regroup her resources. She had, she now saw, allowed her sense of personal outrage to run away with her reason. The truth was that she had overestimated her capabilities—and underestimated Damien Granville. Vicarious dreams of retribution, however satisfying, resolved nothing; the problem remained exactly where it was. What she had to do now was to set aside her damaged pride, review the situation pragmatically and put it in rational perspective. That decided, she set about investigating the one option left to her that still gave hope of success.

"The Kutub Minar land?" James Lawrence echoed Emma's question with surprise when she went to see him on her way back from the Nawab's house. "You are seeking to sell the plot?"

"Yes. As you know, since you arranged the purchase, Papa bought it many years ago purely as an investment. Having lain vacant all these years, I believe that it has appreciated considerably in value."

"Yes, in essence that is correct. Have you talked to Margaret about this?"

"Well, no. As you know, we try to save Mama as much financial worry as possible. The fact is that we need the money."

The solicitor gave her a searching look. "Are you having any fresh problems that I should know of, Emma?"

"No, just the old one," she replied quickly. "As I've mentioned to you on occasion, the house is too large and cumbersome for our needs. Maintenance costs rise every year and repairs are becoming impossible to manage."

"Yes, that I can appreciate. Do you have any particular objective in mind?"

"Well, David and I have been thinking that, if we could sell this plot at a good price, we could purchase a smaller house in which to live."

"But, my dear, why not simply sell Khyber Kothi?"

"Oh, Mama would never agree to that, Mr. Lawrence," Emma answered easily. "You know how sentimental she is about her home. I suppose we all are. What we were considering was to rent it."

"You have a prospective tenant in mind?"

She disliked lying to the grizzled old solicitor, loyal friend and confidant that he had always been, but at this juncture she could hardly afford the luxury of a conscience. Besides, the ploy might work—if Granville could, somehow, be persuaded to declare himself a tenant, at least for public benefit. It was, at best, a tenuous device, but it was the only one she had. Taking a deep breath, she answered him with confidence.

"Yes."

"I see." Lawrence took off his pince-nez, polished them, then replaced them on his nose. "Well, it is certainly a sensible, practical plan, my dear, but"—he looked uncomfortable—"I regret that it is not feasible."

"Why ever not?"

"Because, my dear, that plot has already been sold."

"Sold?" Emma was stunned. "When? By whom?"

"Early last year, by your father. He feared that the Geographic Society grant would not cover all the costs of this last expedition. He hoped that the sale would subsidise the expenses. I could not persuade him to request more funds. You know what a proud man he was."

"But none of us knew anything about it."

"You find that surprising?" James Lawrence smiled. "You know very well that when it came to mounting an expedition, Graham forgot everything else. And it was hardly ethical for me to take it upon myself to reveal a client's transactions."

Emma stared at him in dismay. She had counted heavily on the availability of that plot. Indeed, the bargain she had tried to strike with Granville was solely with the Kutub Minar land in mind. Supposing her offer had been accepted? Immeasurably dejected, she slumped back in her chair.

The solicitor opened a drawer and extracted from it an envelope. "My dear child, if it's only a matter of repairs . . ."

Emma quickly shook her head. "By waiving your dues and giving us free advice, you already do enough for us, Mr. Lawrence. Your kind offer is greatly appreciated, but as it happens, David has made provision for the repairs. I simply had the idea that, with David posted away and a wealthy tenant in view, I could persuade Mama to live in more practical premises." She got up to go. "The move will have to be made some day but the matter is hardly one of urgency."

She walked out of the solicitor's office sick with disappointment.

*T*he following afternoon, when Emma returned from a tuition, the bearer presented her with an envelope addressed to her mother. The memsahib had been having her morning massage when the note arrived, he said, and he had forgotten to give it to her later.

Immediately recognising the ivory envelope, Emma took it up to her room and opened it with unsteady fingers. He was, Damien Granville wrote, an admirer of Dr. Graham Wyncliffe and his work. Having learned only recently of his tragic death, he begged for permission to call upon Mrs. Wyncliffe to present his condolences.

Something cold touched Emma's heart; for the first time she felt the stirrings of panic. The intention behind the hypocrisy was only too obvious. Shaken by the callous lengths to which he was prepared to go in pursuit of his ill-gotten dues, she quickly composed a reply on her mother's behalf and used the excuse of ill health to defer the proposed visit.

Through sheer chance, disaster had been averted on this occasion. What about the next?

Time was running out; Highsmith's deadline had already come and gone. It seemed hardly worthwhile to chase the remaining slender options; none had the remotest chance of success. Even if she could secure another loan to rent a smaller property—how on earth were they ever to repay it? And how long would it be before rumours from the gaming-house started to circulate around town and were conveyed to their mother?

With no immediate way out of the morass, Emma saw that their mother had to be prepared for the truth.

"If we were to move out of Khyber Kothi and rent smaller premises," she asked Dr. Ogbourne as he was on his way out after his evening visit, "what would be Mama's reaction?"

"Move out?" He looked puzzled. "Why?"

"Well, we are no longer in a position to maintain a house as large as this. Finances simply will not permit it."

"Margaret mentioned nothing to me about moving out," the doctor said, somewhat peeved. "In fact, she tells me you are about to have the roof re-surfaced and re-tarred."

"Those are just patchwork repairs." Unable to meet it, Emma avoided his direct gaze. "There are plenty more that await attention. Also, with David now posted away, we have no use for all this space. Mama must be persuaded to move to more affordable premises."

He was not at all pleased. "Well, I must say, this is a fine time to pull rabbits out of a hat, my girl! Your mother's heart mends well, indeed, far better than I had anticipated. A move would not only be physically demanding but emotionally distressing. Surely the matter can be postponed for a month or two?"

"I was thinking that perhaps she might not react quite so adversely if *you* could be the one to recommend the move to her."

Dr. Ogbourne was very cross indeed. "I am in the business of trying to save patients, not bump them off! I will do no such thing. And if you want your mother to recover, which I take for granted to be the case, I strongly advise that you do not, either."

Refusing to discuss the matter further, he left in a huff.

There were no more options left. For the first time in her life, Emma felt truly at the end of both her wits and her resources, and her resentment against her brother soared. The burden this time was too heavy to be borne alone; besides, she now saw no reason why it should be. David *had* to be told the truth, made to accept his share of the responsibility.

Once again, however, that was easier said than done. These days they were hardly ever at home at the same time. When they were, he avoided her by skulking behind locked doors or gave her the benefit of his company only in the presence of their mother. Finally, even Mrs. Wyncliffe noticed the odd behaviour of her cherished son.

"What on earth is wrong with the boy?" she asked anxiously. "I've never known him to be so . . . so withdrawn. Do you think something has gone wrong with his posting orders?"

"His orders are perfectly secure, Mama," Emma replied. "He frets because he leaves home—you can hardly expect him not to."

Entirely trusting of her children and easily satisfied, Margaret Wyncliffe asked no more questions—at least for the moment.

*T*hat night, as usual, David returned home late and went directly to his room. Having waited up, Emma hurried down to the verandah, relieved to find his door unlocked. She found him sitting in the near dark by the table, his back to the door. Before him was a saucepan of water in which he was dousing swabs of cotton wool to carry to his face. To one side was an open bottle of dark-coloured liquid and she got a strong whiff of tincture of iodine.

He started as she entered. "You could at least knock," he muttered sullenly.

"What are you doing?" she asked, walking up to the table.

"Cleaning my face."

It was such an odd answer that she frowned and turned up the lamp on the table. Above his right eyebrow, she saw, was an ugly bruise. It was discoloured, still raw and had obviously been bleeding. Taking hold of his chin, she forced him to face her.

"Where did you get that?"

"I had a fall."

"No, you did not—you were in a fight!"

He shrugged. "If you must know, I was attacked on the way home. Highsmith's thugs got to me in a gully behind the Fort."

"Did you lodge a complaint at the chowki?" she asked, unthinking in her alarm.

"And have it all over town that I can't pay my debts? No, I did not lodge a complaint at the chowki. They've given me until Saturday to clear the debt. Granville will not wait any longer. The next time, they promised, it would be worse." He dabbed the bruise, winced, and asked with over-done offhandedness, "Have you had any luck anywhere?"

She shook her head, all at once swamped by hopelessness. "Why don't we just tell Granville to go to hell?" she asked fiercely. "What can he do, take us to court? Have us forcibly evicted and publicly declare himself a villain?"

David laughed. "Don't be silly, Em. All he has to do is to see Colonel Adams. I will be cashiered, of course. We both know what that would do to Mama."

Emma sat down heavily on the bed and stared at her brother. There was a strangeness in the way he spoke, without emotion, without inflection, as if he were drained of energy.

"Well, what do you suggest then?" she asked, wanting to shake him out of his apathy and force him into action. "Just sit here and wait for that to happen?"

"There's nothing we can do. It's all over, Em. My career in the army is finished, *I'm* finished."

He was prepared to simply lie down and die?

"Well, if you are, then it is no more than you deserve!" The pent-up frustration of days exploded as she exercised on him her own sense of defeat. "If Mama's well-being were not at stake, I'd let it happen. To face disciplinary charges would at least force you to grow up, to be a man instead of a snivelling pup waiting to have his nose wiped by others!"

She had never before spoken to him quite so harshly, but his face showed no change of expression as he silently continued what he was doing. His lack of response fuelled her temper further.

"Why should I always be the one to scrounge around for solutions?" she raged. "It's *you* who should be foraging for answers instead of crawling about the house with your tail between your legs like a damp cat. Doesn't it bother you that one of these days you might end up with Mama's death on your hands?"

She spun on a heel, went out of the room and slammed the door behind her. He did not look up as she left.

Upstairs in her room, Emma flung herself on her bed and wallowed in rare self-pity. She spewed hatred on her uncaring brother, on Damien Granville and even, in a flash of supreme irrationality, on her ailing mother on whose account they were having to bear this intolerable cross. But later, when her tears were spent, her energy squandered and the storm had blown itself out, the person Emma hated most was herself.

However responsible David was for their situation, family difficulties had to be shared and overcome jointly. That had been her father's most abiding principle, indeed, the very foundation of family life as he saw it. "Why should I always be the one to do favours for him?" she had demanded once when a childish disagreement with her brother had been, in her opinion, inequitably resolved. "Because some day his son might do the same for your son," her father had replied, "and so level the scales of justice."

It was a lesson she should not have forgotten.

She had wounded David further and achieved nothing—what had she said that he did not feel already? His crime was unforgivable, but as always his resources were inadequate. That was the way it had always been, that was the way it was now.

The bedside clock showed three A.M. The house was dark and still. In the dense silence of the night, Emma's ears picked up a sound that came from the back of the house. With the recent break-in still fresh in her mind, she lit a lantern, slipped on her kimono and hurried downstairs. David's light was burning but the room was empty. Uneasily, she turned her attention to the garden. It was deserted. At the far end of the back garden a sliver of light showed under the stablehouse door. *Another* intruder?

Extinguishing her lantern, she took her courage in both hands and tiptoed across the grass. While Barak was on leave it was the duty of the gardener's lad to lock the stables at night, but the doors were open, she noticed with alarm. Holding her breath, she applied minimal pressure to one of the door panels. It moved back soundlessly; with a gasp of relief she recognised the figure inside as that of her brother.

"It's only me . . ." she said quickly as he whirled round. "I heard a sound in the garden so I came down to investigate."

He was standing near the decrepit hulk of a carriage that had once been a prized possession but was now too expensive to maintain. The two horses tethered in the stalls shuffled restlessly and as she walked over to soothe them she did not look at him.

"I'm . . . sorry for all the terrible things I said, David. You must know that I didn't mean them. My only excuse is that, like you, I'm tired and depressed and in my dejection I lost control of my tongue. I'm sorry, desperately sorry."

"They're true, nevertheless," he replied tonelessly. "I'm not a man, Em. I deserve your contempt."

"Don't!" She was again close to tears. "Don't make me feel worse than I do already."

"Ever since Papa's death, it is your wide shoulders that have borne the burden of a provider. It is you who have always been the sensible one, morally strong and emotionally impregnable. I remain the encumbrance I always have been." He whipped round in a brief burst of animation. "Don't dismiss that as an exercise in self-pity, Em. It isn't."

"I love you very dearly, David," she said miserably. "You must know that—just as you must know how unfettered my temper can be." Walking to where he stood, she reached out to take him in her arms. "Forgive me, darling. Of *course* we're in this together, and of *course* you're not an . . ." She stopped. As he resisted her arm, something he appeared to have been holding clattered to the floor. She half-bent to retrieve it but before she could do so he did, and then whisked it out of sight.

"Go back to sleep, Em. I just want to be left alone."

"Not until you show me what you're hiding!" He still resisted, so she grabbed his forearm hard and wrenched it forward, forcing him to release what he held. It again dropped to the ground and she saw that it was his service revolver. Just for an instant she failed to react, then she went rigid.

He bent down, picked up the weapon and with an elaborate flourish laid it back on the table next to a long brush and a cloth duster. "I was cleaning it."

"At this time of the night? Here?"

"I couldn't sleep and it needed cleaning. This seemed as good a time as any to do it. Why the fuss?"

"If you were just cleaning it, then why did you hide it from me?"

"Because I knew exactly how you would react—exactly as you have reacted!" He took the revolver, picked up the long brush, thrust it down the barrel and resumed his labours.

She stared at him stupidly. "Is that . . . all you were doing? Cleaning it?"

"Yes. Oh, don't worry"—he gave a humourless laugh—"I wasn't about to shoot myself, although if I did, that certainly would be a solution, wouldn't it? No David, no debt. No ruined lives. As simple as that."

Trying to recover her wits, she struggled for normalcy and sank down on one of the shafts of the old carriage. "And that would make everything all right? Reverse that alleged ruin of our lives?"

"Well, it would be a damn sight easier than to watch you run around trying to scrounge money to pay off my debts." He raised the barrel and peered down it with one eye closed.

Despite the lightness of his tone, Emma was cold with horror. "And what about Mama and me?" she cried. "Have you spared a thought for what that would do to us?"

"Oh, you will survive, Em—and Mama will know everything soon enough anyway. Neither you nor I can do anything more to protect her. As you so rightly pointed out, I already have her death on my hands."

Overwhelmed with pity, with remorse, with love and devastating fear, she wanted to shelter him within her arms and stroke away the deadness from the dear, despairing face she loved so much; but she could not move. "How can you think of punishing us with such undeserved cruelty?" she asked, trying not to give in to panic. "I won't let you!"

He laid down the revolver and turned to face her. "If I really wanted to shoot myself, Emma," he said quietly, "you would not be able to stop me. You might tonight and tomorrow night and the night after—but there would be too many nights to keep vigil. There would be one when you looked the other way."

"You would think nothing of taking a coward's way out?"

"Well, that's what I am, Em, a coward." His mouth twisted in a travesty of a smile. "I'm not a fighter like you. I don't have the strength. I never have, I never will."

Numbly she stared at the revolver, marvelling at how brightly it gleamed. Suddenly she saw that if in a moment of insanity he did kill himself, her life too would be over. In his defeated eyes she saw her father's, and somewhere in the depths of his despair she heard a whisper of her father's voice. She got up, took hold of her brother's hand and interlaced her fingers with his.

"It doesn't matter if you don't have the strength," she breathed, "I have enough for both."

*E*ven though it is believed that those who proclaim their intention to commit suicide seldom do, overnight Emma's priorities changed. Consumed by David's tottering mental balance, she ceased to think rationally. Much in the manner of a drowning man shown a straw, she no longer cared who offered it.

She had to see Damien Granville again.

Before she could set the seal of doom on her self-respect and write to him to request a second interview, however, once again he took her by surprise. The following morning he suddenly materialised out of thin air, or so it seemed to her, in a narrow lane in the heart of the native area as she walked towards Company Baug where Mundu awaited with a tikka gharry.

"Since there appears to be little likelihood of your paying me a second visit," Granville said as he dismounted his chestnut Arab, "I was hoping I could intercept you on your way home."

Emma halted, covered in confusion. "How . . . how did you know that I would be coming this way?"

"I know the homes you frequent. I followed you from the Grangers' knowing that you have no fear of Delhi's back lanes."

He had been following her—why? She was seized with apprehension.

"I wanted to apologise for having struck you," he said in direct answer to her unspoken question. "It was an unpardonable act. I am deeply ashamed. Can you possibly bring yourself to forgive me?"

If he had surprised her before, now he truly astounded her. So unexpected was the apology—and, indeed, his sudden presence—that she could think of no appropriate response to make.

"I also wanted to assure you that I had nothing to do with the attack on your brother," he said, grave and unsmiling. "That was entirely Highsmith's doing and he has been suitably reprimanded. Now, do I merit a pardon?"

Emma searched his face for signs of mockery; there were none. Unaware in her confusion that she did so, she nodded and lowered her eyes. With her thoughts tumbling over each other in a bid for coherence, she resumed her walk.

"Miss Wyncliffe, please wait."

"You have made your apologies and they have been accepted," she called over her shoulder without reducing her pace. "As far as I am concerned, the matter ends there."

"But not as far as I am concerned! That morning I made you a certain proposal. You have yet to give me your answer."

She again came to an abrupt halt. "It appears to me, Mr. Granville," she said, colouring, "that a public street is an extraordinary place for this equally extraordinary conversation."

He shrugged away her observation. "This is essentially an Indian locality. Europeans are not only reluctant to venture here but also embarrassed in case they should be seen. As for the Indian residents, I doubt if they give a damn about our matrimonial plans."

"We have *no . . .*"

"Why don't we sit and make ourselves comfortable?" he interrupted smoothly before she could complete the indignant protest. "Then we can proceed with our discussion in a relatively civil manner."

Taking her elbow, he guided her towards a small paved courtyard enclosed between two houses where a bench had been grouted into the flagstones. It was quiet and secluded—probably because it was private property—but he was unconcerned that they trespassed. The humility subsumed in the apology had vanished; in his audaciousness he had reverted to type. Sorely tempted to give him short shrift, she realised it would be foolish to spurn an encounter she was about to solicit anyway. Relieved that the humiliation of a second letter, at least, had been averted, she seated herself on the bench without softening her expression. He positioned himself on a low wall and looked at her expectantly.

"Now, what was it that you were about to say?"

"I was about to express my astonishment that you should consider a further response necessary, Mr. Granville," she said, wishing that her voice would stop shaking. "I had thought I had already made my feelings abundantly clear."

"That you despise me?" He swept it aside as a trifle. "You don't really expect me to take that seriously, do you?"

"Why not? It was meant seriously enough."

"It is still not an answer. What I need is a plain yes or no. All things considered, I hardly expect it to be the latter."

She was nettled by his conceit, but sheer self-interest forced her to keep her tongue reined. "Tell me, Mr. Granville," she asked, "why *do* you want to marry me?"

"Dear me, what a strange question." He was amused. "Because you are an adorable creature, Emma Wyncliffe, why else?"

"No, I am not an adorable creature," Emma retorted. "At least credit me with enough intelligence to recognise that. You could have your pick of simpering dollies who are adorable creatures, who wait with bated breath to be invited to grace your hearth and home. Why, of all women, should you want me for a wife?"

He regarded her curiously. "You value yourself so little that you can ask such a question?"

"It is because I value you so little that I wonder!"

"Well, then, would you believe me if I said that I was passionately in love with you?"

"No, I would not! I know that you are not—any more than I am with you."

"You consider love a necessary ingredient in every recipe for marriage? Happy enough alliances are forged every day without emotional excesses."

Having already heard some of his bizarre opinions, his cynicism did not shock her. "It does not trouble you to consider as wife a woman who does not even *like* you?"

"I do not seek to win a popularity contest, Miss Wyncliffe. Emotions are neither white nor black, and love and hate are meaningless extremes that have little to do with reality."

"You find it meaningless that a man and woman should have some affection for each other before they commit themselves to a lifetime together?"

He dismissed that with a shrug. "Love grows with age."

"You mean, like gout?" She almost laughed but did not dare.

He looked irritated. "Why such an animated debate? As you yourself pointed out, there are plenty of women in Delhi who would be delighted to accept my proposal."

"Well, then, why not choose one of them and put the poor creature out of her misery?"

He gave her a long, hard stare. "You really cannot understand why I find you the most appealing?"

Embarrassed by the stare, she shook her head and looked away.

He continued to observe her closely for a moment, then suddenly arrived at a decision. "All right then, I suppose I will have to spell it out." He sprang to his feet and started to stroll with long, impatient strides. "I am thirty-two years old. One might say that I am at the prime of my life. Unfortunately, I am also the last surviving male in my family. If I were to die now, my lineage would be extinguished, my property in Kashmir would revert to the state and eventually fall into alien hands. The prospect is unacceptable to me. It is therefore necessary for me to have a son."

"You want to marry me only for that?" She could hardly believe her ears. "Giving birth is hardly a specialised skill, Mr. Granville, any reasonably healthy young woman could provide you with an heir without the slightest difficulty."

"No, not only for that." He clarified further. "You see, Miss Wyncliffe, I am a dedicated believer in inherited virtues, and you possess many that I would like to see in my son. You are intelligent, you have spirit, you pursue your principles with determination and you appreciate the value of learning. You are also fearless, uncaring of narrow social prejudices and you do not cower in the face of ignorant public opinion."

He stood still with his hands clasped behind his back and his eyes glued to the flagstones beneath his polished boots.

"I want my son to love this land as I do—as you do. I want him to grow up proud of his inheritance, part of the people around him. I want him to speak their tongue, enjoy their food, understand their customs and accept their traditions, to treat them as equals with respect, not as inferior beings with contempt. I want him to be humble enough to remember that here it is *he* who is the transgresser, not they." There was a strange tremble in his voice. "Above all, Miss Wyncliffe, I want my son to honour Kashmir as did his father and grandfather, and be grateful for the manner in which it illuminated their lives."

He looked up and there was a shine in his eyes. "Shalimar is my home, my sanctuary. It is paradise on earth, but it takes blood, sweat and tears to keep it so. Most memsahibs look upon having to dress themselves as penal servitude. You, on the other hand, having been forced by circumstances to do so, know what it means to work hard. Indeed, all said and done, I can think of no more fitting wife for myself, mistress for Shalimar and mother for my son than you, Emma Wyncliffe." In a lightning swing of mood he abandoned the solemnity and once again turned flippant. "And in the final analysis, you might as well know, you are the only woman I have ever met who does not entirely bore me to tears."

It was an extraordinary confession, startling and unexpected. In her surprise Emma had listened to it in stunned silence. Now, with an effort, she shook herself out of her trance.

"Thank you for that 'not entirely,'" she said shakily. "I suppose I should be flattered by these extravagant commendations, but I am not sure that I am. You view marriage as a genetic experiment to breed a champion son as one would a thoroughbred horse or dog. I do not. To me, such an alliance would be a travesty."

"A highly profitable travesty, nonetheless."

"Its only virtue, perhaps."

"Well, then, thank you for that 'perhaps'! So, when may I expect your answer?"

"You do not consider that you have already received it?"

"I have yet to hear a plain yes or no, Miss Wyncliffe."

Dazed, Emma ran the back of her hand across her eyes. "I . . . I need time to consider."

"When?"

"In a month. Two, maybe . . ."

"Three days, Miss Wyncliffe."

"Three days?" She was aghast. "Three days are simply not enough!"

"They will have to be because three days are all you will get. I wait to hear from you on Friday," he looked at his pocket-watch, "by noon. Good day."

He turned and left.

hat was she to say to David?

He had not spoken to her since last night. When she ventured into his room later that day, she found him preparing his traps for Dehra Doon. Still gaunt and knotted with tension, he barely glanced at her as she entered. Having no idea how to phrase what she needed to tell him, she watched for a moment in silence, then seated herself at the foot of his bed.

"I went to see Damien Granville this morning," she said in a slight variation of the truth.

The hands packing the case faltered but he offered no comment.

"He received me . . . well."

He went on with his packing.

"He heard me out with considerable patience, David. Indeed, I had not expected him to be so understanding." Once started, the fabrications flowed. They were, at best, flimsy. Had David not been so profoundly out of kilter, he would have certainly questioned them, but lost in his own turbulences he did not. Beneath the feigned indifference, however, his eyes were watchful. "There is a chance that we can come to a mutually accept-able settlement."

"Why should he compromise?"

"Because I have offered him a good bargain—the Kutub Minar plot instead of Khyber Kothi. The idea seems to appeal to him. He said he would consider it seriously. He will inform me of his decision by Friday."

"I won't be here. I leave first thing in the morning."

"I will write to you as soon as I hear from Mr. Granville." She laid a hand on his arm. "In the meantime, *promise* me you won't do anything . . . foolish, David."

He remained briefly silent, then gave a curt nod.

Early next morning he left for the Fort en route to Dehra Doon. Two days later, just before noon, Emma sent Damien Granville a one-line letter to inform him that she accepted his proposal.

CHAPTER

Damien Granville lost little time in responding to
Emma's message. The following day Suraj Singh arrived with a letter for
Mrs. Wyncliffe and presented it with due ceremony.

Margaret Wyncliffe had, of course, heard about the mysterious stranger
from Kashmir who had rented the Begum's mansion on the Jamuna. Indeed, Carrie Purcell was a veritable walking encyclopaedia of rumour and
conjecture and Jane Tiverton—who had three young daughters to en-
dower—had spoken of little else at luncheon the other day.

"Do you know why Mr. Granville should wish to see me?" Mrs. Wyncliffe asked Emma, fluttering with nervous excitement.

"No."

"Perhaps he was acquainted with your father and simply wishes to
express his condolences?"

"Perhaps."

Her mother cast an anxious glance at her taciturn daughter. "You will
be home in the afternoon when he calls, won't you, dear?"

"Yes."

That settled, her mind went to other matters. "Do you think we should
ask Saadat Ali to make some jam tartlets for tea, dear?"

"If you wish."

"And perhaps a dozen vegetable samosas? Your father was very partial
to them, remember? Tuna-paste sandwiches too, I think, which Saadat Ali
does quite well. Ask the gardener to pluck one or two bunches of lettuce,
will you, dear? The crop this winter is wonderfully crisp." She reflected a

moment. "Carrie says he lives in Kashmir, where they eat very spicy food. Do you think we should substitute potato and onion bhajias for the sandwiches?"

"I'll order both, if you like," Emma said, "although I hear Mr. Granville professes contempt for social niceties. He'll probably be in and out like a dose of salts."

But, as it happened, Emma was wrong.

Damien Granville arrived at the stroke of four, not informally on horseback as she had expected but in the splendid brougham with matching greys and a liveried coachman she had seen once previously. He was dressed very correctly in a navy blue woollen suit, white silk shirt and cravat, and his unruly dark hair, brushed back down to the nape, was immaculate. Black boots in quite the latest style shone like mirrors and sported brilliantly polished brass buckles. As always, his head was held arrogantly high when he alighted from his carriage, but his manner was perfectly charming. Standing by in freshly laundered uniforms resurrected from various storeroom trunks, the Khyber Kothi staff was both impressive and impressed. Not since the passing away of the burra sahib had a man of such sartorial elegance been seen on the premises.

Stone-faced, Emma received Damien Granville in the porch. He paused to survey her carefully from head to toe, his expression solemn. Seeing no reason to waste time and energy on her toilet now that the bargain was sealed, she had deliberately—and much to her mother's horror—worn her oldest, most faded, least attractive dress of printed mull. Their gazes met and held an instant, his quietly triumphant, hers defiant and challenging. He bowed, reached for her hand and retained it lightly in his, a performance, no doubt, for the benefit of the avid audience. In an instant reflex Emma shivered, then closed her eyes to hide the inadvertent response that lurked behind the fragile facade.

I will have to spend the rest of my life with this arrogant man—dear God, how will I bear it?

"I would not have believed," he said with a suave smile, "that we would meet again so soon and in such auspicious circumstances."

"Would you not have?" She pulled her hand out of his. "You may have blackmailed me into accepting your proposal, Mr. Granville, but make no mistake, not even blackmail can force me to like you!"

Without giving him a chance to retaliate, she spun on her heel to stride on ahead towards the drawing-room where her mother waited. Judging by the buoyancy of the footsteps that followed, he appeared undaunted by the frosty reception.

What subsequently transpired between Damien Granville and her mother Emma did not know, nor tried to. Having performed the mandatory introductions, she excused herself while the conversation still hovered on polite exchanges about the weather. It was, of course, a temporary respite; half an hour later Mahima's knock on her door announced that the moment of reckoning had arrived. Reconstituting her features into the semblance of a smile for the benefit of her mother, Emma grudgingly made her way down the stairs.

Damien stood by the open window gazing out into the overgrown garden. On the sofa, her face flushed and her fingers knotted into a tight ball, sat Margaret Wyncliffe. The remains of the lavish tea gave ample proof of how wrong Emma's assumptions had been. Considering the detritus on the table, Damien Granville's appetite had extended well beyond a cup of tea and a token morsel or two. As Emma entered he turned and, arms crossed, leaned back casually against the window-ledge. She did not look in his direction.

Mrs. Wyncliffe beckoned her daughter to sit beside her on the couch. "I . . . I hardly know what to s-say, dear," she gulped, unaware that her wide-eyed disbelief was anything but complimentary to her daughter. "Indeed, I am almost speechless. Mr. Granville has asked for my permission to . . . to make you his wife!"

Emma broadened her smile and hoped that it would be accepted as one of joy. Keeping her eyes riveted to her demurely folded hands, she merely nodded. The figure filling the window might not have been there at all.

"And . . . what do *you* have to say about it?" Mrs. Wyncliffe asked, continuing to look bewildered. "Are you inclined to view Mr. Granville's proposal favourably?"

"Yes." The smile adhered to her lips with the same tenacity as her gaze did to her lap. The minimal hesitation went unnoticed.

Margaret Wyncliffe patted her moist brow with a handkerchief. "But, my dear, I was not aware that you were even . . . acquainted with Mr. Granville."

Raising her eyes, Emma stared straight ahead, wondering in a flash of irrelevance how long it would take her mother to notice the absence of the clock from the mantelpiece. "I . . . we . . ." Refusing to be dislodged, the words stuck in her throat.

"We happened to meet once by, ah, accident and then again at the Prices' dinner party," Damien stepped in smoothly. "Our encounters have been brief but quite enough to confirm a true meeting of minds—would you not agree, Emma dear?"

In an agony of embarrassment at the charade with which they were deluding her poor trusting mother, Emma prayed that the rush of colour to her cheeks might be blamed on maidenly modesty. She again nodded.

"Well, since you seem to have already arrived at a mutual understanding," Mrs. Wyncliffe said faintly, "I . . . I suppose you do have my permission." Struggling to resist one of her terrible turns, she revived herself with deep lungfuls of air and fanned herself vigorously. "I assume . . . at least I hope, that my daughter is better informed than I am, Mr. Granville, but whatever little I know about you is only from hearsay."

He came immediately to position himself in the chair opposite. "What would you like me to tell you about myself, Mrs. Wyncliffe?" He gave no indication of impatience. "Naturally, there are questions you need to ask and naturally I am only too happy to provide the answers."

Emma rose to her feet and whisked the empty teapot off the table. "I'll ask Saadat Ali to brew a fresh pot," she muttered. "This one is stone-cold." Before her mother could protest, she had again made good her escape.

Outside on the back verandah she leaned weakly against the wall. There was a dreamlike unreality about the afternoon and she almost convinced herself that she was asleep, that soon she would awaken and everything would be as before. Trying to ride the storm within her own head, she listened despondently to the gales of merriment blowing out from the room. Her mother had not laughed as heartily since her father died; welcome though the sound was, the source of the hilarity was not. That Damien Granville should want to capitalise fully on his facile charm she could understand, but that her mother should respond with such excessive enthusiasm was to her the ultimate betrayal.

"Emma, dear?"

Thrusting the teapot she still held into the hands of the waiting bearer, she returned to the drawing-room. Margaret Wyncliffe no longer looked bewildered. On the contrary, she looked animated and perfectly at ease with her guest. Wide smiles wreathed her thin, pale face and her eyes shone with a rarely seen sparkle.

"Well, dear, we've had our little tête-à-tête," she announced happily, "and I must say, I am impressed, most impressed. Perhaps now you would like to take Mr. Granville into your . . . ?"

"Please do call me Damien," he suggested silkily.

"Yes, of course . . . er, Damien, into your rose garden, dear?" Turning to him, she added, "The rose garden is Emma's special preserve. It's very pretty and also very, well, private."

"It's just a nondescript little patch," Emma said ungraciously, annoyed by the bald device, "but if you feel you absolutely must, you are welcome to examine it."

"Nothing would give me greater pleasure," Damien exclaimed as he sprang to his feet, "although I cannot imagine that anything to which you apply your mind, my dear, could possibly be nondescript." Ignoring her glare, he bent over Mrs. Wyncliffe's hand and skimmed his lips over it. "We will meet again, of course, perhaps tomorrow, if that is convenient? Once again, thank you for a most enjoyable tea, and above all, for your gracious permission to make your daughter my wife. I am honoured."

Having had time to recover from the shock of her daughter's extraordinary windfall and quite bowled over by the charm being dispensed in such lavish proportions, Mrs. Wyncliffe simpered. Who would believe that this most eligible, most-sought-after young man blessed with such good looks and so much fortune was soon to be the husband of her homely daughter? Why, Emma would be the envy of every young girl in Delhi and she of every scheming mother; she could hardly wait to communicate the news to Carrie, to the insufferably smug Betty Marsden, indeed, to the entire station!

In the privacy of the rose bower heavy with the perfumes of spring, Emma surveyed Damien with ill-concealed contempt. "You didn't waste much time in exacting your dues, did you?"

"I never do," he replied. "I saw no reason to wait."

"So, having won your pound of flesh, you intend to lay claim to it immediately."

"Well, perhaps not quite immediately. I would hate to outrage your gardeners."

"There is no need to be coarse," Emma countered frigidly. "Your stock with me is low enough as it is."

He laughed and without warning reached out to stroke her cheek. "Can you not let bygones be bygones, Emma, and truly forgive me for this?"

She recoiled at his touch. "Don't be a hypocrite—you have already made your views on corporal punishment for women abundantly clear." She changed the subject. "Well, I have fulfilled *my* side of the bargain. What about yours?"

He dug his hand into his pocket, withdrew an envelope and handed it to her. Within were David's IOUs, and an affidavit to the effect that all debts owing to Mr. Damien Granville of Shahi Baug, Nicholson Road, Delhi, by Lieutenant David Wyncliffe of Khyber Kothi, Civil Lines, Delhi, hereby stood cancelled. A note from the gaming-house owner, Bert Highsmith, confirmed the same.

"Satisfied?"

"Satisfaction has very little to do with it, Mr. Granville, but yes, the bargain appears to be legally sound." She added bitterly, "I see that ours is to be a unique marriage, forged not in heaven but in a gambling den!"

"Well, better a known devil than an unknown angel," he offered cheerfully. "What does it matter anyway so long as two kindred souls are united in blessed matrimony?"

"We are not kindred souls," Emma said crossly, knowing that he mocked. "And if there is an example of matrimony more unblessed than this, I have yet to hear of it."

"Had the circumstances been different, would you have agreed to marry me at all?"

She disdained an answer.

"I believe it is the custom to give one's intended bride a ring." Before she could react, he had taken her left hand and slipped a ring onto the third finger. Emma stared at it an instant, taken aback. It was a platinum circlet set with a line of small sparkling diamonds on either side of a gem the size of a pea. It was impossibly expensive and, of course, quite beautiful. The thought of an engagement ring had never even occurred to her and she hated the sight of it on her finger.

"To prove your proprietorship?" she asked, as she wrenched her hand free.

"And my honourable intentions."

"A marriage contracted at gunpoint can hardly be called honourable, Mr. Granville!" Removing the ring off her finger, she slipped it carelessly into a pocket of her dress.

Refusing to take offence, he tilted his head to one side. "Tell me, Emma, if only to satisfy academic curiosity—is the prospect of marriage to me as abhorrent as you so stridently proclaim?"

"No, but if I were to reveal the full extent of my abhorrence, my mother would forbid the farce and we would be homeless."

She had longed to wound him and this time she succeeded. Warm colour flushed his cheeks in a first show of anger. "Oh, the farce will be a marriage all right," he snapped. "Let me assure you that I meant what I said. I have *every* intention of exercising my conjugal rights as your lawfully wedded husband."

"The prospect of taking a woman by force, even a wife, does not diminish you as a man in your own eyes?" she cried, filled with despair.

"I have never taken any woman by force, nor will I you."

The iron restraints sustained with such difficulty over the past few hours crumbled; for a moment she thought she would faint. As she swayed his hand reached out instinctively, but she steadied herself and leapt back like a startled rabbit. Even so, his face was suddenly very close; he held her gaze with such persistence that she could not look away. Helplessly she watched as his lips hovered above hers, then settled lightly and his arm encircled her waist. For an instant, just an instant, she stood absolutely still. Then in a lightning recovery she flung out her hands and pushed him away. He released her immediately and with such suddenness that she stumbled back against the trunk of an acacia tree.

"How dare you!" she gasped, rubbing her mouth with the back of her hand. "Oh, how *dare* you!"

He stood with an elbow on the wooden fence enjoying her outrage. "I dare because whether or not you choose to wear it, you have accepted my ring—not to mention your brother's IOUs."

"Under duress, Mr. Granville," she whispered, tight with tears, "only under duress!"

"Well, then, would you grant me a further concession under this same duress?" She stared at him in alarmed silence. "Could you possibly force yourself to call me Damien?"

She did not smile.

For a long moment he stood in silent study of her profile. When he did speak again, it was softly, "You are a girl of rare spirit, Emma, but you are still a girl. I shall enjoy making a woman out of you."

*I*t did not surprise Margaret Wyncliffe in the least that her daughter should have chosen the wildly attractive Damien Granville for a husband. Why he should have chosen *her,* however, did—although she would rather cut off her tongue than say it. Nevertheless she soon talked herself out of her misgivings. The human heart, she reminded herself, had an intelligence of its own even though its divine logic was not available to all. Who was she to question the hidden designs of the Lord?

In spite of her anxiety to deliver the news to the world at once from her rooftop, Margaret Wyncliffe reined her excitement and decided that at least some social proprieties needed to be observed. On Damien's second visit the following day, therefore, she decreed that formal notice of the betrothal should be published the very next day in the *Mofussilite*. Subsequently the couple should be seen together at church and at burra khanas (suitably chaperoned, of course) to establish the bona fides of the engagement. When asked for an opinion, Emma merely shrugged; one act more or less in the pantomime made little difference to her either way.

Impatient to return to the Vale—as the Kashmir valley was sometimes called—now that spring was on the doorstep and the high passes would soon be clear, Damien reluctantly agreed. He insisted, however, that the wedding should take place soon, be on a modest scale with the guest list restricted to family and close friends. This Emma endorsed heartily. Given free rein, her mother would want the world and its brother to celebrate the unexpected end of her daughter's spinsterhood—but where was the money for such self-indulgence?

"Would you consider next Saturday week a convenient day for the wedding, Mrs. Wyncliffe?" Damien asked.

"Oh dear me no!" Mrs. Wyncliffe was horrified. "That gives us no time at all for preparation!"

"What is there to prepare?" he asked irritably.

"Why, a thousand matters, Damien dear. A coat of whitewash for the house, a *shamiana* for the garden in case it rains, suitable caterers for the reception, invitation cards—and even a pared-down guest list will need some thought, after all." She cast a beseeching glance at her daughter but received no support from that quarter. "And what about a trousseau? Surely, Emma must be given time to prepare at least that?"

"Well, can't she find something suitable to wear from her—what do you women call it?—hope chest?" He was uninterested in the purely feminine problem.

Mrs. Wyncliffe fell silent. She could hardly disclose that due to Emma's refusal to have one there was no hope chest, and resigned to her daughter's spinsterhood she herself had long ceased to insist on one. She stole another glance at Emma's ungiving face as if to say, "Oh, men!" but could not catch her eye.

The announcement duly appeared in the *Mofussilite* the next morning. Considering the limited time at her disposal, Margaret Wyncliffe leapt into immediate action, determined to make the most of her moments of glory in the eyes of Delhi's colonial society.

As for Delhi's colonial society, it was frankly electrified. Ruining digestive processes at many a breakfast table the bare announcement sent every mother of a marriageable daughter reaching for her salts and every marriageable daughter for her handkerchief.

"It's not fair," sobbed a devastated Charlotte Price. "Damien Granville danced with me three times and with Emma not at all! Oh, how could he deceive me so cruelly?"

"There is more to this than meets the eye," her mother hissed, livid at the blatant abuse of her hospitality. "She went after him with a grappling iron, that's what. How else could a man like Damien Granville even *conceive* of settling for a woman as plain and perverse as Emma Wyncliffe? Why, it's . . . it's . . ." Words failed her, at least for the moment.

"I sensed it that evening, I swear I did," wailed her inconsolable daughter. "I could tell by the way she looked at the poor helpless lamb that he was headed for the trap. And everyone *knows* she has no portion save that hideous Georgian tea service Grace says they pawn every month to pay the grocer."

"Maybe he likes her," her husband suggested mildly when he could get a word in. "Emma may not be the world's greatest beauty, but however unbridled she's certainly a brainy filly."

"You mean a dark horse!" his wife snapped, throwing him a murderous look as Charlotte burst into renewed tears. "Well, I for one am not going to *rest* until I get to the bottom of this plot, so help me God."

With minor variations much the same scene was repeated in several other households.

Arriving at Khyber Kothi immediately after breakfast, Mrs. Purcell smothered Emma with kisses. A tight-lipped Jenny pecked her coldly on the cheek.

"I told you so, Margaret, didn't I?" Carrie Purcell bubbled, genuinely thrilled. "All that worry for nothing! I guessed right away that something was afoot at that burra khana. Why anyone could see that they had eyes only for each other." Lowering her voice, she winked, "And such an attractive brute, too!"

Emma smiled and remained modestly silent.

She had not looked forward to the Purcells' visit. It was one matter to beguile her mother with well-rehearsed responses but quite another to placate an intimate friend.

"My, my!" Jenny confronted her with blazing eyes the instant they were on their own. "So, the much maligned Mr. Granville is not *quite* so odious, after all. I had no idea you were capable of such lightning changes of mind—or such barefaced duplicity!"

Emma gave her a hug. "It all happened so suddenly, Jenny dear, that my head spins. I said I would tell you everything when . . ."

"But you didn't!" Jenny's eyes brimmed. "I was reduced to reading it in the newspaper like everyone else. Tell me, how do you contemplate marrying a man you profess to hate so soundly?"

"I was wrong about Damien," Emma said. "When I came to know him better, I discovered that he was really quite . . . appealing."

"Oh? And this unsuspected appeal of his true self was revealed to you within a fortnight?" Jenny hooted. "Don't lie to me, Emma, and don't you dare claim you are madly in love with him because I know you are anything *but*."

"No, I am not in love with him at all, madly or otherwise." Emma heaved a convincing sigh. "Well, if you insist, I suppose I have no option but to confess the truth."

Jenny's shrewd eyes gleamed. "Yes?"

"The truth is that Damien Granville is well educated, personable and rich. In marriage market terms I suppose one would call him a 'catch.' When he expressed interest in me at the burra khana, I made a pretence of anger but I am ashamed to admit that I was, well, flattered—and too embarrassed to say so."

"Ah."

"In fact, there is a question I have been waiting to ask you, Jenny dear, a question I could never dream of asking anyone else."

Injury forgotten, Jenny eagerly leaned closer. "Yes?"

"Would you consider me dreadfully mercenary if I confessed that I accepted Damien because of his money?"

"No, not at all." The answer came with expected promptness. "There's nothing wrong in marrying for financial betterment."

"Oh I'm *so* glad you think so! I can't tell you how hard I've been battling my conscience over that."

"To tell you the truth, Em," Jenny said wistfully, "if my John had happened to be better heeled, I would have loved him all the more without the slightest twinge of conscience."

They looked at each other and smiled happily.

*I*t was to be an extraordinary courtship—if, indeed, it could be called that.

Still winded by the swiftness with which everything had happened and still somewhat puzzled by her daughter's silent compliance in all matters, it eventually occurred to Margaret Wyncliffe that perhaps all was not as well as she had blithely assumed. There were occasions when she sensed strange undercurrents beneath the smiles and she was concerned.

"Are you *quite* sure, dear, that this is what you want?" she asked Emma anxiously.

"Quite sure." If Emma was irked by her mother's unqualified acceptance of Damien so far, she was equally annoyed by her belated doubts. "Why—do you not consider him a worthy candidate for a son-in-law?"

"Most certainly I do. But you seem so . . . so unusually submissive, so strangely withdrawn, that it troubles me. Besides, I am quite baffled by the hurry with which you appear to have arrived at such a vital decision. It's so unlike you, dear."

"Since I agree with most of Damien's views, I feel there is no need to keep repeating my approval. As for the hurry—to marry at leisure doesn't always prevent one from repenting in haste, Mama."

"But . . . could you both not wait until you are at least better acquainted? If there is any reservation I have about your decision, Emma dear, it is this."

"Would you rather I waited until he proposed to someone else?"

"Dear me no, of course not!" Shocked at the very idea, Mrs. Wyncliffe hastily revised her stance. "On second thoughts, dear, perhaps an early wedding is a more sensible decision. After all, one can't put anything past Betty and Georgina, can one?"

She did not raise the topic again.

Reluctant to commit more lies to paper, Emma did not write to David as she had promised to do. He arrived home at the end of the week and cornered her almost at once in the rose garden. However well her sly devices had worked with Jenny, Emma knew she would have to do better with her brother.

"Mama tells me you are going to marry Damien Granville?" He demanded, aghast.

"Yes."

"*Why,* in heaven's name?"

"Why?" She did not look up from the bush she sat pruning. "My word, what an extraordinary question!"

"And just how extraordinary is the answer?"

"I am going to marry Damien because I want to, why else?"

"Good grief, you hardly know each other."

"He still wants to marry me."

"What on earth for?"

"You'll have to ask him that—but thank you anyway for the vote of confidence in your sister's eligibility," she remarked drily. "If you must know, we plan to marry because we find that we do have . . . feelings for each other."

"Feelings? What feelings?"

"Respect, admiration and, I suppose, a certain mutual attraction. Damien's proposal was as much a shock to me as it is to you, David." Well, that much at least was true. "My instant reaction was to refuse it, and I did. But then, there were other considerations that outweighed my reluctance. Believe it or not, there can be reasons to marry other than instant passion."

Taking hold of her shoulders, he forced her to her feet. "Do these 'other considerations' have anything to do with my gambling debts?"

"No, of course not."

"I may be an occasional fool, Emma, but I'm not entirely without brains. Tell me truthfully what transpired between you when you met him about the debt."

"I've already told you what transpired—I offered him the Kutub Minar plot and he agreed to consider it."

"When did he ask you to marry him, at that meeting?"

"No, he proposed later."

"Proposed marriage—or the cancellation of the debt? Or did they come together?"

"The debt has nothing to do with my decision. If you must know, Damien never intended to collect it anyway. He merely wanted to teach you a lesson."

"Uh-oh! Is *that* what he told you?"

Silently she handed him the envelope kept in her pocket in readiness for his return. He flicked through the papers rapidly as if ashamed of the sight, then thrust them in his own pocket.

"Now do you believe me?" she asked.

He ruffled his hair with a hand. "I know you've never lied to me, Em, but frankly I don't know what to believe."

"Well, believe me when I say that I consider his intentions to be honourable, David."

"Damien Granville has the reputation of a debauch, an out-and-out cad, Em. How can you even think of him as honourable?"

She cleaned her secateurs and replaced them in the pocket of her gardening-apron. "Well, as it happens, there is another reason why I agreed to marry him."

He paled further. "What reason?"

She walked to the stone bench, sat down and patted the space beside her. He joined her grudgingly.

"Do you remember a question you asked me that night when you showed me the money you had won?" He obviously didn't. "You asked me if this was the way I wanted to spend the rest of my life."

"And?" He frowned, still not remembering.

"I said no, this was not the way I wanted to spend the rest of my life. At the time it was not a considered answer, but since then I have thought a great deal about your question. The truth is, David, that in my own way I too am frustrated. I'm merely more accomplished than you at concealing it." She turned so that she faced him. "I am twenty-four years old. I'm not like Stephanie or Jenny or any of the other girls who have had men hot on their heels since they were fifteen. Being neither the most eligible nor the best endowed spinster in town, I am unlikely to drive men to put pistols to their heads if denied my favours. So far, I've had one proposal of marriage, from Alec Waterford, who for some wondrous reason appears to find me irresistible." Listening intently, David did not share in her smile. "Before I met Damien, I was resigned to the prospect that I would never marry. Rather than enter into matrimony for the sake of convenience, I had convinced myself that I would be content to remain a spinster. But now." She looked away. "Now I wonder."

Trying hard to comprehend, he merely stared.

"You see, David," she said gently, "I too am tired. I'm tired of having to scrape the bottom of empty barrels, tired of trying to eke out a paltry existence that has neither meaning nor dignity, tired of not having a future. Like you, I too feel that life is passing me by, that I am stagnating. I see myself doomed to a solitary old age living one lonely day at a time, and suddenly, David, the prospect of my unlived life fills me with dread. . . ." She was surprised at what emerged from her mouth, even more surprised at the sting of tears behind her eyes.

"To put it bluntly, David," she concluded thickly, "I accepted Damien's proposal because it is the best offer I'm ever likely to have and I simply cannot afford to spurn it." Blinking hard, she sat back and stared blindly over his shoulder. "There! Now that I've bared my soul to you— do you still believe that I'm lying?"

He had never before heard her speak with such openness about her intimate thoughts, certainly never with such feeling, and he was shocked. She had revealed to him an aspect of herself he had never suspected. To him, Emma was self-sufficient, indomitably independent and entirely invulnerable; he had never considered that she could be otherwise. Naive and untutored in the minds and motives of women, for a moment he was at a total loss.

"Do you swear, Em," he finally whispered, "that what you have told me is the truth?"

"Yes."

"You swear that your acceptance of Damien's proposal has nothing to do with my gambling debt?"

"Yes, I swear it."

He nodded and walked away.

Trembling, Emma sank back on the bench. She was shaken by what she had said, shaken by the effortless fluency with which the words had flowed off her tongue. It was as if they had sat poised in her mouth for days waiting to explain thoughts she was not even aware existed.

Could it be that the alibis concocted merely for her brother's benefit were true?

No, that was preposterous. Her pride refused to let her even consider that.

Two days before the wedding, Emma's panic revived. "Tell me truly, Damien," she asked, worn out by yet another trivial argument, "why in heaven's name do you want to marry me?"

"I have already told you."

"You know nothing about me!"

"I know enough to ensure a worthy son."

"Through snippets of gossip picked up here and there? You consider these sufficient to convince you that we are destined for each other?"

"Well, except for the fact that we disagree on appropriate punishment for wandering wives, I'd say we were remarkably well matched."

"If I could profess to know even half that about you," she said, "I might agree that we were adequately matched—or, more likely, confirm that we are not. I still think that your genetic theories are absurd."

"They work pretty well for horses. I see no reason why they shouldn't for us."

"But I know *nothing* about your family, your habits, what you do, what you read, your taste in food!"

"Had you been interested to, you would have asked."

Emma flushed. It was true; if she knew little about the man who was to be her husband and his family it was because sheer intransigence refused to let her ask questions, and on his own he volunteered little.

"Well, it doesn't matter. I'll find out soon enough, I suppose."

"As I have already explained to your mother," he said, without reacting to her bad temper, "my parents are dead. I live well and comfortably, and so will you. My occupation is my estate, which also you will get to know in time. My reading tastes are catholic, as my library at Shalimar will tell you. I enjoy everything that finds its way into print. As for what I eat, well, everything, really"—he thought a moment, then amended that—"except aubergines. I cannot abide aubergines, never have. My favourite dish is gushtav, traditional Kashmiri meatballs, the best in the world. Anything else?"

"No, of course not," she said crossly. "That remarkably explicit autobiography says everything any woman could possibly want to know about a future husband."

He flung up his hands. "Doesn't it seem extraordinary to you that a man and a woman about to enter into the most intimate relationship possible between them should find it impossible to conduct a civil conversation even about a safely neutral topic?"

"I can think of no topic neutral enough to induce civility."

"Tell me about your father."

"My father?" She was taken aback.

"Well, I know how deeply attached you were to him."

He had never before shown the slightest interest in her father—except in that presumptuous letter she had intercepted. She was incensed that he should pretend to do so now and reduce the hurtful subject to an expedient conversational gambit.

"What is there to say? He lived, he worked, he died."

"I see. An even more remarkably explicit biography about a future wife's father."

Again they were teetering on the brink of an argument. With no stomach for more, she diverted the subject. "Whether or not you approve," she announced, "I intend to resume work on my father's papers as soon as we reach Kashmir. I also intend to make certain that I have the time to do so."

"By all means—so long as your intellectual endeavours remain secondary to your essential duties."

"What essential duties?"

"To cater to the needs of your hearth, home and husband."

She flounced out of the rose garden back into the house.

*D*etermined not to be denied her moment of triumph despite the shortness of time, Margaret Wyncliffe made certain that the roof of the house was tarred, the outside walls of the bungalow given a quick coat of whitewash and the front gates repaired. Going through some of the bills with Emma on the eve of the wedding, she suddenly asked after the silver clock.

"I've packed that to take with me to Srinagar," Emma said. "That is, if you have no objections."

"No, of course not, dear," her mother hastened to assure her. "We'll just have to sell the Georgian tea service instead to pay for whatever we can't purchase on credit."

"Yes, I suppose we will," Emma agreed glumly.

The wedding morning in early April, a Saturday, dawned fine and clear, bathing the city in pale gold sunshine. The lingering freshness of winter in the air was heavy with seasonal scents of new leaves and spring blossoms. At Khyber Kothi, frenetic activity had started at dawn with a steady procession of tradesmen bearing the thousand and one items on Margaret Wyncliffe's sheaf of lists. With a chorus of voices demanding, debating and denouncing all at once the din was ear-piercing. As always in India during even the simplest of operations, confusion reigned supreme.

Imperiously enthroned on a high-backed chair in the crowded compound with her faithful lieutenant Carrie Purcell by her side, Mrs. Wyncliffe directed operations with the purposefulness of a general marching troops into battle. Gone were the turns and twinges, the sallow cheeks, the perennial pains and palpitations. Surprisingly energetic, her voice rang out as strong as a bull frog.

Well, something good has come of all this, after all, Emma thought, watching from her balcony with a curious sense of detachment.

Dragged early from his bed, David received his orders for the day with a series of yawns. Since their conversation in the rose garden, he had avoided speaking to Emma except when necessary. He also avoided Damien, Emma noted, as persistently as Damien did him. Neither ever mentioned the other to her.

Today she was to be married, Emma marvelled, wondering what normal brides felt on their wedding day. Nervousness? Heartbreak at leaving the nest? A rapturous urge to sing and dance and float on air? Looking within herself in an effort to identify her own feelings, she was unable to sift her mélange of emotions into individual recognisability.

The private wedding ceremony, conducted by the Reverend Desmond Smithers assisted by a woebegone but manfully stoic Alec Waterford, took place in the drawing-room at Khyber Kothi, attended by a few close to the family. From the bridegroom's side there was only Suraj Singh, Damien's private secretary, whose selection as best man had sent shudders of horror through the community.

"A damn disgrace, sah, an outrage!" Despite not being on the guest list, Charles Chigwell delivered the consensus at the Officers' Mess. "You give them an inch and they take a flaming mile. Next they'll be asking for membership of our clubs, what?"

Damien dismissed Margaret Wyncliffe's cautious protest with impatience. "Suraj Singh is not only an employee, he is also a friend, and twice the man any of your strutting sahibs profess to be. I don't give a damn what anyone thinks."

The bride was given away by her brother.

The reception, somewhat less austere than the wedding ceremony but still modest, was held on the back lawn—hastily mowed, trimmed and swept—and David had managed to arrange his regimental band at generously reduced rates.

Enduring with grace the enforced gaiety and fulsome good wishes, and with forbearance the murderous looks, whispered barbs and expressions of incredulity, Emma clung tenaciously to both her smile and her poise. If anyone noticed her stiff lips, blank eyes and waxen pallor as she danced the first waltz in the arms of her dashing groom, they put it all down to understandable grief at the parting with her mother and, of course, prenuptial night nerves. Everyone agreed, some grudgingly, that if Emma Wyncliffe did not make a ravishing bride, certainly the dignity and decorum with which she conducted herself could not be faulted.

What flowed more freely and furiously than the limited liquor was the gossip, the bridal jewellery exciting far more comment than the bride. It was very striking and very expensive, a wedding gift from the doting groom—as Margaret Wyncliffe lost no time in informing all who cared to listen.

"What a waste!" Charlotte Price briefly set aside heartbreak to hiss in a vicious undertone. "One might as well load diamonds onto a Rajputana camel."

"And isn't that gown the limit?" Stephanie Marsden asked. "I believe they picked it up cheap from a lace-maker near the Jama Masjid. Typical!"

"Well, they probably couldn't afford the genuine stuff from Brussels anyway—not that she would be able to tell the difference."

Everyone looked to Grace Stowe for her contribution. "I've heard it said," Grace said, sounding very mysterious indeed, "that in Srinagar there is a certain lady who—" she paused, leaving unspoken nuances to convey potential delights.

The excited little group closed in around the station's high priestess of gossip. "Oh, *do* tell—lady who what?"

"—shall remain nameless for the moment, who—" Grace's voice relapsed into a whisper for the benefit of a privileged few.

"We must not lend our ears to mischievous hearsay," Alec Waterford remarked, sad and saintly in his acceptance of defeat. "Let he who is without fault cast the . . ."

"Shut up, dear," his mother ordered. "If you had any sense, which you haven't, you would be lighting candles for a thanksgiving instead of a wake."

Long before the guests departed, the newly-weds did so amidst a shower of rice, confetti and good wishes dispensed by Jenny and other loyal friends. Margaret Wyncliffe wept inconsolably.

"What will I do without both my children?" she sobbed.

"You will do very well indeed, thank you," Carrie Purcell snapped, putting an end to the mourning.

The night was cool but still and airless. In the coach, the bridal couple sat side by side and unspeaking. The relief both felt was one of the few feelings they shared as they gazed out of opposite windows.

Damien slipped his finger inside his collar and loosened it. "Thank God that's over and done with," he muttered. "It would have been less of a nightmare simply to have eloped."

"If you had, you would have had to elope alone," Emma replied.

He grunted. "That Price woman was very rude, do you know why?"

"Probably because she had rather hoped you would marry her daughter," Emma informed him, her tone suggesting that she wished he had.

"Which one, the girl with the protruding teeth?"

"No, the girl with the large nose. The mother of the girl with the protruding teeth simply cut you dead. You see? You leave Delhi littered with the broken hearts of many adorable creatures."

"Adorable and with pleasant dispositions."

"Well, you wouldn't want a son with an outsized nose or buck teeth, would you?" Emma asked nastily.

"No, but it seems I will have to settle for one with a foul temper instead."

Emma tossed her head and looked away. Not another word was exchanged between them for the rest of the journey to Shahi Baug.

At the Nicholson Road mansion, a freshly prepared suite of rooms adjoining that of huzoor awaited the bride. Emma's personal staff, she discovered, was to consist of a buxom elderly woman called Sharifa, with apple cheeks and a forthright manner, and a very young girl with shy eyes who was presented to her as Sharifa's niece, Rehmat. Both had been summoned from Srinagar to supplement the entirely male staff of the mansion. Emma would have preferred to have Mahima with her for at least a few days, but knowing that her mother's need was greater than hers, she did not suggest it.

Weak with nervous exhaustion, she sank into the brocaded upholstery of a sofa in her sitting room. The suite, consisting of a bedroom, a sitting room and the usual offices, was appointed with the oppressive lavishness displayed in the rest of the house. Damien strode across the room to throw open the windows, then waved away the contingent of waiting attendants.

"I hope the accommodation is to your satisfaction?" he asked, as he opened cupboards and drawers and inspected fittings.

"Perfectly." She answered mechanically, without interest, wanting only to be left alone—if now such a luxury was to be had at all.

"This is a temporary arrangement, as you know. We will be leaving for Kashmir within the fortnight. You will, I hope, find Shalimar more to your taste."

"A fortnight?" She sat up with a jolt. "I thought we were to be here at least a month. I . . . I haven't had enough time with my mother or with David, who leaves shortly for Leh. And I am to be matron of honour at Jenny's wedding next month—how can I possibly let her down at this eleventh hour?"

"I regret that you will have to. Later, perhaps, after you have settled down well, you can entertain your family and friends in Kashmir. I would be happy to make the arrangements."

"And, what about the arrangements I have to make for my mother?" Emma demanded, close to tears.

"Arrangements for your mother are already in hand. You have no need for concern."

"In whose hand?"

"Well, your mother's, for one."

Her mother had made arrangements without consulting her? Emma flooded with resentment, but fatigued, she lacked the energy even for revolt. Having removed his jacket, rolled the sleeves of his white-ruffled shirt up to his elbows and undone the buttons down its front, Damien had made himself comfortable on the sofa with his legs stretched across a stool in front of the fireplace. If he noticed her wretched state, he did not remark upon it.

"Come and sit by me." He indicated the space beside him. It was a command but his tone was not imperative.

With her throat dry and her heart thudding, Emma moved closer to where he reclined, but deliberately chose the chair opposite. He watched her silently, taking in the slender figure outlined by the silk and lace dress and the deep neckline that accentuated the rise and fall of her bosom. Quickly, she drew her scarf closer around her shoulders. He leaned forward and gently covered the fist clenched in her lap.

"Why are you nervous of me? I am not known to bite—unless invited to."

She stiffened and pulled at her hand but he would not release it. "I am not at all nervous of you! I am merely . . . indifferent."

"Are you, now? I've been accused of many crimes but never of inducing *indifference*!"

"Well, there is no accounting for female perversity. It is a curse of our sex. Besides, you did say I was unlike other women you had met, didn't you?"

Annoyed, he released her hands and stood up. "There is a messenger who has just arrived with news I have been awaiting. I may be late in coming up." Her heart leapt with pathetic relief; even an hour of blessed solitude would be a merciful reprieve. "But come up I will," he added. "Make no mistake about that."

She turned away, trying to devise a suitable barb with which to pierce his conceit, but could not find the words. By the time she had found them, he was no longer in the room.

Disconsolate, she summoned Sharifa and set about unpacking. The woman and her niece turned down bedclothes on the enormous fourposter, removed empty boxes and arranged her toilet articles in the bathroom. On top of her clothes in the trunk her mother had packed a bridal nightgown and matching peignoir, frothy, diaphanous clouds of apricot pink ordered from the most expensive lace-maker in Delhi, who for double wages had stitched them in record time. Had they not been for so distasteful an occasion Emma would have considered them ravishing, but now she shuddered.

"Begum sahiba cold?" Sharifa inquired.

Begum sahiba? Is that what she was to be called? Emma shook her head and smiled wanly. "No. Somebody just walked over my grave."

"Please?"

Realising that the woman's English was limited, Emma changed to Urdu. "I am not cold, thank you, just tired. I shall not require either of you tonight. You may leave. Goodnight."

Sharifa's eyes shone with surprise and approval. "Begum sahiba speaks the language of our country well," she said with new respect. "In Kashmir, very few people speak English."

"What do they speak then, Kashur and Dogri?"

"Yes, begum sahiba."

"Are they difficult to learn?"

"Not for one as clever as begum sahiba. She could learn in no time at all." She salaamed, grasped Rehmat's hand and withdrew.

Emma unpinned her hair, luxuriating in the feel of it on her shoulders. With a groan of relief she kicked off her shoes, stepped out of the uncomfortably heavy formal gown and removed her jewellery, vowing never to wear it again. With no more than a cursory glance at the ornaments, she repacked them in the velvet-lined box and pushed it down to the bottom of her trunk. If Damien considered diamonds and rubies adequate compensation for a marriage by blackmail, then he knew her even less well than she had suspected.

Today was the culmination of one nightmare, but it also marked the start of another. The band she wore on the third finger of her left hand reminded her that she was now the wife of a stranger. Her vows bound her to him till the end of her days, gave him legal sanction to do with her as he pleased. Forcing herself not to cry, she repaired to the bathroom to bathe, using the blissfully cool water to wash away the tiredness. Scrubbing herself dry, she returned to the bedroom and dismally slipped into the beautiful apricot nightgown. It did little, she noted, to improve either her spirit or her appearance. As she stood before the mirror taking careful inventory of herself, she decided that she had never looked worse.

The tensions of the past weeks were all too evident in her face and in the weary stoop of her shoulders. Underneath the golden tan, her skin looked lifeless and blotchy and her lustreless eyes were circled with coffee-coloured rings. Her body, naturally tall and slender, seemed thinner, more angular. By honing selective thought into a skill necessary for sheer survival during these past weeks, she had deliberately refused to dwell upon the prospect of intimacy subsumed in a marriage. But now with the hour of reckoning almost upon her, she could evade it no longer.

A bride on her wedding night—or a lamb to the slaughter?

That Damien had no love for her, she had always known. Yet, much to Emma's secret distress, of late she had begun to find his lack of feeling hurtful. The more she steeled herself, the more disturbed she was by his proximity, reacting to his touch with a response she considered shameful. Even fleeting contact—a brush of the shoulder, a feel of his hand, an arm about her waist when they danced—provoked sensations she had never before experienced, sensations she was unable to understand, unwilling to accept and loath to encourage. Once when he had no more than cupped her elbow as she alighted from the carriage, she had shuddered so violently that he had noticed it.

"Why do you recoil at my touch?" he had asked, misunderstanding her reaction. "Is your dislike of me so totally uncontrollable?"

"Yes," she had retorted to cover her embarrassment, "but time, no doubt, will give me the means to conceal it."

He had gone red and she had felt a small rush of triumph at having dented the outsized pride of a man who had thought nothing of exploiting her desperations. Determined to keep her secret responses to herself, she had continued to counter his flippancy with indulgence and match his indifference with her own.

As she must tonight!

For a long while Emma sat by the open window brushing her hair with absent strokes and battling private furies. From the courtyard came sounds of singing and drums and tinkling bells as the staff celebrated the end of their huzoor's bachelordom. She listened with half an ear, waiting with ever-growing apprehension for the return of her husband. *Husband!* How strange that word sounded, how frightening! Would she ever get used to saying it?

Trying to calm her rampaging nerves, Emma suddenly noticed a glass-fronted cabinet that displayed several decanters. Sniffing each in turn, she took a tentative sip from one; it tasted strong and dry, a Bordeaux wine such as was served at some of the burra khanas. She poured herself a glassful and started to sip. As the warm, nutty flavour percolated downwards, her limbs started to loosen and her panic receded to acceptable levels. By the time Damien came up at half past two in the morning, justice had been done to more than half the carafe.

She heard the door of the adjoining apartment open. Standing by the window, watching the watery reflection of a solitary light in the river, Emma held her breath. Soft footfalls paused by her door—and passed on. Her trapped breath erupted in a fervent prayer. *O God, let it be that he has changed his mind!*

But Damien had not changed his mind. A few minutes later came the *click* of a latch being lifted. The connecting door between their suites opened and Damien walked in. Without giving her time to react, he moved towards her, coming to a halt so close that she felt his breath on her face. Smelling the telltale whiffs of wine in hers, he laughed.

"You *are* nervous of me!"

There was triumph in his voice as his lips brushed swiftly across her brow. Startled, she tried to step back, but one of his arms was circled about her waist. The other rose lazily to stroke her neck with feathery fingertips. Clenching her teeth to hold back the cry that rose in her throat, she closed her eyes and blotted out his face. His lips slid downwards to the hollow of her neck; his fingers, splayed against her back, seemed to draw her closer without the slightest use of pressure.

She tried to step back but the fender obstructed her escape. In revived panic she struggled for release, but he only laughed softly against her skin. Knowing that it was futile to try to match his superior strength, Emma willed her body into unfeeling stone and wiped her face clean of expression. He covered it with languid kisses, lingering at the corners of her mouth, on her determinedly closed eyelids, along the outer edges of her earlobes.

He lowered his hands and withdrew. "Women who resist are even more desirable," he said. "Did you know that?"

"Desirable?" She managed a laugh of sorts. "Of course, that is all that is important to you since you do not recognise the need for love!"

"I have never met a woman capable of your brand of love. Mine, I have had in plenty."

"You mean your brand of lust!"

"If you wish. It doesn't matter what you call it. What matters is that it pleases. It engages the senses without disturbing the heart."

"And that is all that you want of marriage?" she asked. "To engage the senses without disturbing the heart?"

"Well, since you profess to despise me, you should be grateful for that."

Dismayed at how much his remark had wounded her, she walked away. "You may have acquired my body with your reprehensible bargain, Damien, and much as I might want to I see that I will not be permitted to deny you that. *More* than that, however, you will never own. That much I promise."

He covered the distance between them with rapid strides and his hand tightened around her wrist. "But I will never let you forget that I do own your body, that much *I* promise!"

She snatched her wrist out of his grip. "An act of rape given the sanction of the law!"

"Rape?" He shook his head. "As I told you, I have never yet taken a woman against her wish, nor will I you."

Before she could prepare herself, she was again in his arms. This time his mouth on hers was minimally more demanding, his tongue tip slightly more inquisitive. Emma shuddered but did not withdraw. Stiff and unresponsive, she suffered his lips to nibble at will as they explored the hollows behind her ears, the denseness of her hair, the bony ridges of her shoulder blades. The explorations were gentle, not at all what she had anticipated; the assault, persistent and subtly persuasive, was not on her body but on her senses. Taken by surprise, she was even more alarmed.

Gradually, almost imperceptibly, urged by forces unseen yet frighteningly tangible, an echo of a sensation stirred somewhere in the soles of her feet. Sinuously, it crept up her limbs, threading its way through her veins, threatening every remote niche of her body. Within her began a tumult, a civil war, as she battled to hold on to herself. She might as well have conserved her energy, for it was like trying to halt a hurricane with a hand. Gradually her control ebbed. Helpless against the tightening knots of pleasure, she started to dissolve. The muscles forced into tautness went limp, the breath forcibly fashioned into even cadences, broke loose. For a moment more she struggled but then, all at once, it was over. Like a bud tricked by a wicked summer sun, her mouth opened under his and the battle was as good as lost.

His arms tightened. Rejecting her weight, her knees wavered and she stood crushed against his heartbeat. Transfixed by a force beyond her capacity to resist, she could not move nor, amazingly, did she appear to want to. Together with her conscious mind her strength eroded and, all too fast, the last of her willpower. Even as some distant command sounded in her brain forbidding them to do so, her arms lifted and wound themselves about his neck.

Gently, without releasing her mouth, he worked her nightgown off her body. In a swirl of apricot mist it floated to the floor to settle about her feet. His hand touched her breast and produced a cloudburst of feeling, a feeling so acute, so agonising, that without knowing it she whimpered. As easily as if she were a leaf, he lifted her and laid her on the bed. His face, a blur of heat and breath and glowing eyes, loomed above her in the half-dark. She made a last-ditch bid for salvation.

"Damien, no, please wait, for pity's sake, *wait.* . . ."

"Why?"

"I can't . . ."

"You can, you will. I will make you. Trust me."

"Not yet, not *yet!*"

The remainder of the protest died unheard. Large brown hands, rough and incredibly tender, roamed across the lines and planes of her body, leaving a trail of wondrous disaster. A strange mix of inner sound rose and fell in her throat, cries of surprise, gasps of pain, incredulous rapture releasing prodigious, primaeval energy. Her own caressing hands turned more daring, more demanding, her responses increasingly urgent. Wanting him never to stop she willed him on, stunned at the speed with which she learned to savour that which she had never tasted. She was being ravished, and one infinitesimal part of her was aghast that she should enjoy it so. She heard herself cry out in anguish, no longer owner of her mind, much less of her body. Without conscious effort she matched his kisses and caresses, shocked by her wantonness but unable and unwilling to contain it.

Guided expertly through the byways of unknown heavens, she floated up slopes, skimmed unassailable peaks, stroked the skies and pierced diaphanous clouds, soaring, ever soaring. Then when she felt she could bear the torment not an instant longer came the impossibly exquisite pain of release, and her body turned lifeless. Warm and languid and resting in peace, she slipped into the dreamscapes of the valley of a little death. There was no more time and no more reality, only sensation. Eventually she slept. When she wakened again, her head was on his shoulder and invisible fingertips trailed through the abundance of her hair.

She raised her head and, disoriented, stared into the unknown face next to hers. The movement produced a sharp pain and she winced. Turning on his side, he cradled her in his arms, kissed her on the lips one last time and laid her back on her pillow. She gazed up at him through the vapours of sleep, frowning at the unfamiliar contours.

"Damien?"

"Hush. Go to sleep."

Without knowing it she smiled and then slept again, deeply and dreamlessly. When she awakened, she knew not how much later, he was no longer beside her. She was alone in the dark.

Without resources to think, for a while she lay still, dazed by the mass of exposed nerve ends in her body. Then she crept out of bed and stumbled into the bathroom. Despite the sharp, raw edges of the night, she bathed with cold, cleansing water, enjoying its feel, luxuriating in the miracle of revival.

For a long time she remained seated by the window, staring unseeingly into the night. If she had any awareness at all of reality it was that from now on nothing for her would ever again be the same.

CHAPTER

7

ilfred Hethrington had not looked forward to the meeting called by General Sir Marmaduke Jerrold, Commander-in-Chief of the Indian Army, to whom the Department was ultimately accountable. Because of the sensitive nature of the agenda they had been ordered to convene in the C-in-C's private study at Snowdon, his official Simla residence, rather than at the office.

"However hard you may try, Colonel," Sir Marmaduke began brusquely, tapping the folder in which reposed Hethrington's report, "the stink produced by this particular kettle of fish can no longer be sweetened by perfumed prose—at least not to *my* satisfaction. Whitehall thirsts for blood and by God, I'll be damned if I let them have mine!"

Smarting under the spate of incendiary questions in the British press, sharp exchanges with the Foreign Secretary, outraged inquiries from London and a rap on the knuckles from the Viceroy, the Commander-in-Chief was far from done.

"Considering the motive for Hyperion's murder," he continued, "the uproar can hardly be dismissed as unjustified. Have you read what is being suggested in the press about the loss of those papers?"

It was a rhetorical question. The preposterous insinuations had the Russians conniving with Safdar Ali to murder Hyperion, and the Yasmina papers variously in Afghanistan, China, Germany and Turkey. Most absurd of all, it was hinted that Hyperion himself had secretly sold the papers to Russia.

"Only by the less responsible rabble-rousers with an even less responsible readership, sir," Hethrington replied mildly. "I do not consider that the imaginative conjectures need to be dignified by an official response."

"As it happens, Colonel, I agree with you—although I wouldn't go so far as to call Geoffrey Charlton an irresponsible rabble-rouser. Are you aware of how many people subscribe to these 'imaginative conjectures'? Half of Whitehall and Simla, and one can scarcely blame them." Eyelids half lowered over smouldering eyes, he leaned forward. "Tell me, Colonel, while we are on the subject, how *did* Charlton come to learn so much, considering how jealously you guard your Department's little secrets?"

Colonel Hethrington coloured at the sarcasm. Catching a warning glance from the Quarter Master General, however, he resisted the temptation of a rejoinder.

"As everyone else does, sir. Walls in Simla have ears, eyes and tongues and Charlton has the memory of an elephant and the nose of a bloodhound. All he needed was to scout around, buy a few doubles at the Club, pick up a two here and there to make twenty-two and publish inspired guesswork as fact."

"Well, can you blame him in view of your own tight-lipped official statements? Besides, the questions he raises are perfectly justified. For instance, knowing that the region is crawling with Safdar Ali's thugs, how *did* Hyperion . . . ?" He stopped. "I know how cagey you are about the identities of your agents, Colonel, but since the unfortunate man is dead, I think we can dispense with the code. How the devil *did* Butterfield turn so damn careless?"

Hethrington bristled, but quietly. "In all fairness, sir, Jeremy Butterfield was a meticulous officer. If he . . ."

"Ah, so it was meticulousness that made him carry secret papers in a carpet bag as casually as he would his underwear, eh?"

Hethrington fell silent. He had had previous occasion to differ with Sir Marmaduke across the conference table, but considering the thin ice on which the Department presently skated it would be self-defeating to provoke another confrontation. Seated by the window next to the C-in-C's military secretary, Captain Worth's head remained safely buried in his notebook.

Reprieve came with the arrival of Sir Marmaduke's personal chaprassi bearing a tray of coffee, biscuits and a box of thumb-tacks. Before the military secretary could make a move, Nigel Worth had leapt up, appropriated the tacks and set about securing a loose corner of the large wall map behind the desk. Working as slowly as he dared, he gave his C.O. time to devise appropriate responses.

While Hethrington pondered, his eyes flicked morosely over the belligerently masculine room with its scuffed leather chairs, unadorned carpets, Ordnance Survey wall maps, abundant trophies of war and military memorabilia. His gaze settled on a familiar face in a proudly framed photograph, that of a previous Quarter Master General and founder of the Intelligence Department, Major-General Sir Charles MacGregor, under whom also he had served. The reminder brought him little pleasure.

While still in office Sir Charles had written a report, *The Defence of India,* in which he had said: "I solemnly assert my belief that there can never be a real settlement of the Russo-Indian question till Russia is driven out of the Caucasus and Turkestan." Having expressed the inflammatory opinion while still in uniform, Sir Charles had compounded the indiscretion by leaking the document to the press.

The report had created a furore both in Westminster and in St. Petersburg. An incensed William Gladstone had taken it as a direct criticism of his Liberal policies and copies of the book had been withdrawn, but not before a few had found their way into Russian hands, necessitating the humiliation of a diplomatic apology. Severely reprimanded, Sir Charles had been allowed to save face by serving out his full term as QMG but had subsequently been relegated to a minor post that had ensured the end of his career.

Even though a junior on Sir Charles's staff, Hethrington had come in for an ill-deserved rebuke and the memory still smarted. Charles Mac-Gregor was now dead but there were many in high office in India and Britain who heartily endorsed his virulent mistrust of Russia. Among them was General Sir Marmaduke Jerrold, the present Commander-in-Chief.

A big-boned, solidly built man, with an aggressive military brain beneath a fine head of hair that showed not a strand of grey, Sir Marmaduke boasted a medal-encrusted chest, a fiery temper and a thin, determined mouth that housed a lacerating and energetic tongue. As a dedicated Russophobe, he often made it abundantly plain that if it was war England wanted, nothing would delight him better than to give her one.

No, Hethrington had not looked forward to this meeting.

"As I have already mentioned in my report, sir," he resumed when Nigel Worth had re-seated himself and the coffee cups and biscuits were in place before them, "for obvious reasons Butterfield's final message to us sent with his Gurkha, even though in code, was brief and worded with extreme caution. He suspected that what had been discovered was the Yasmina, but without proof we cannot be certain." Resisting the urge to clench his hands, he merely clasped them. "I have to repeat, sir, that Butterfield was a responsible agent. Whatever decisions he took were for a carefully evaluated purpose."

The Commander-in-Chief's stony face showed no signs of relenting. "I have no need to remind you, Colonel, of my own horror at what happened.

Certainly, I would never question Butterfield's loyalty to Queen and country. However"—the stare above the rim of the half-moon glasses hardened—"in view of proliferating rumour and innuendo, old questions need to be revived and resolved, as much in the interest of the army's credibility as in deference to the British taxpayer."

Pushing back his chair, he rose to his feet and strode up to the wall map. "Butterfield's brief was to investigate the feasibility of establishing a supply depot in *this* region," he stabbed the map with a forefinger.

"Yes, sir. The Survey plans to explore the Hispar/Biafo glaciers later this year. At thirty-six miles, they comprise the longest sub-polar glacial system in the world and an accessible supply depot at Ashkole was considered essential. Because of its proximity to the Hunza gorge, it has always been assumed that it is somewhere in this region that the Yasmina is located."

"If Butterfield suspected that what he had stumbled across *was* the Yasmina, why did he not head straight back to Simla or Doon or even Leh—why the detour north-east to Shahidullah?"

"Well, sir, as we have already surmised, Butterfield changed both direction and identity because he feared he might be followed. He backtracked to Shahidullah to join a caravan in the belief that with it he would be safer." They had been over this before, of course, and Hethrington held on to the tail of his patience with effort. "That he miscalculated we know only through hindsight."

"In situations as mercurial as this, Colonel, no allegedly responsible agent can afford the luxury of a miscalculation! The questions Charlton asks are uncomfortably pertinent and the general sense of alarm in Whitehall most certainly justified."

"The fact that Charlton—and Whitehall—have reacted with such extravagance," Hethrington replied with a first sign of sharpness, "is only to be expected, sir. It is simply a symptom of the irrational delusions that appear to have become a national affliction."

"Irrational delusions, eh?" Sir Marmaduke returned to his chair, eased his enviably trim frame back into it and latched his ice blue, limpetlike gaze onto Hethrington's face. "You consider that to be concerned about defence against a highly possible Russian invasion through a pass unknown to us is a symptom of an irrational delusion, Colonel?"

"With due respect, sir, I consider that *whatever* concerns we have should be within sight of the existing realities." Evading the QMG's worried glare, Hethrington continued to sip unhurriedly at his coffee. "So far, we have no reason to panic, no evidence to prove that what Butterfield found *was* the Yasmina, and certainly none to indicate that his maps are in Russian hands or, indeed, likely to be so in the immediate future."

"You offer these consolations, Colonel, without even knowing what is contained in those papers that have, apparently, evaporated into thin air?"

Hethrington shifted a little uneasily in his seat. "What we have been forced to presume, sir, is that the papers were . . ."

"With the predators in London about to chew off my tail, Colonel," Sir Marmaduke snapped without letting him finish, "presumptions no longer suffice. Whitehall doesn't give a tinker's cuss about presumptions or about where the papers were, only about where they *are!*"

It was at this volatile juncture, quite unexpectedly, that Sir John decided to enter the fray.

"Jeremy Butterfield's papers are where the Colonel's report says they are, sir," he said with astonishing firmness, "scattered to the four winds in the gorges of the Karakorams."

So far, the Quarter Master General had remained a passive listener, contributing only with nods and monosyllabic mumbles, allowing his Director of Intelligence to bear the brunt of the inquisition. The decisive rescue mission took Hethrington by surprise.

Sir Marmaduke transferred the rapier gaze to the QMG's face. "Well, are we quite convinced, John, that *all* of Butterfield's papers were destroyed in that raid?"

Eyes fixed unblinkingly at the charming views of Swiss chalets and deodar groves outside the French doors, Hethrington waited with held breath for the response.

"We have no reason to believe otherwise, sir," the QMG said smoothly, and Hethrington exhaled again.

"Crankshaw's sketchy inventory of whatever else Butterfield carried—is that the only one compiled?"

"Yes, sir." Sir John's face remained impassive. "As mentioned in the report, fearing implication in the murder, the merchants simply bundled all of Butterfield's belongings in the carpet bag and dumped them at the madrassa in Leh. By the time Crankshaw reached the mosque, the mullah had given the bag and its contents away in charity and left for Mecca. Crankshaw finally persuaded the merchants to help him compile the inventory from memory."

Sir Marmaduke frowned, obviously unconvinced, but before he could voice any more questions, Sir John snapped his folder shut.

"I have to say, sir, that I fully endorse Colonel Hethrington's assessments in the matter. There is no way that we can know what terrible compulsions Jeremy Butterfield suffered just before his death, but to doubt his decisions now would be to perpetrate an injustice to a man of proven competence who can no longer defend those decisions."

Effectively silenced, at least for the moment, the C-in-C eased himself back in his chair and relapsed into thought.

Hethrington was jubilant. When informed of the Janus project, Sir John had declared himself appalled and had refused to give it his approval. Indeed, until a few moments ago Hethrington had not had the remotest idea how much Sir John would elect to conceal—or reveal—at the meeting. The fluency with which the half-truths tripped off the QMG's tongue left him speechless. And, of course, vastly relieved.

"Very well then," Sir Marmaduke said grudgingly, in a tone noticeably less abrasive, "let us move on to the other matter." He raised a finger and Colonel Hartley hurried up to place before him a flimsy sheet of paper. "This telegram from Whitehall about the Borokov business—how do you suggest we respond to it?"

With a rustle of paper, they turned to their own copies of the telegram. Knowing that the C-in-C would have his own preconceptions in the matter, neither Sir John nor Colonel Hethrington risked a suggestion.

"Do we have an acceptable explanation for the fact that shortly after Butterfield's papers vanish, this fellow Borokov turns up in St. Petersburg and the Russian press falls over itself to predict an invasion through the Yasmina?"

Having done his bit for the Department, the QMG left Hethrington to field that one.

"The British press enjoys no monopoly on rumours, sir," Hethrington was pleased to point out. "Russian papers have often been known to go one better. Both their principal dailies, *Novoe Vremya* and the *Morning Post,* for instance, recently reported that Her Majesty is addicted to the bottle and retires each night in a state of intoxication—and Russians believe it. As they believe that Britain's press is controlled by the government, which is why English newspapers in Russia are caviared so ruthlessly. Lord Castlewood is the only . . ."

"Are *what* so ruthlessly?"

"Er, caviared, sir. Departmental colloquialism for censored."

"Oh."

"Lord Castlewood is the only Englishman in Russia to receive his newspapers in one piece. Even though naturally concerned about Borokov's visit, his lordship is aware of no Russian activity to support rumours of an impending invasion."

A moderate, a self-confessed Russophile and enormously popular at the Russian court, Britain's ambassador in Petersburg was a man with whose every opinion Sir Marmaduke disagreed vehemently. "What sort of activity does his lordship expect—an announcement in the St. Petersburg Court Circular?" He gave a bark of a laugh. No one dared to echo it. "All these

Rusky contingents that are suddenly sprouting all over the Himalayas like bloody mushrooms—how would his lordship account for them, I wonder?"

"The spurt in Himalayan exploration is due partly to widely published reports of the extraordinary exploits of Younghusband, Ney and other British mountaineers, sir. Besides," Hethrington cleared his throat, "Himalayan ranges are still open territory, sir. We are hardly in a position to dictate who should or should not explore them."

"Not yet, Colonel, not yet," Sir Marmaduke said complacently. "Nevertheless, the fact that these Russians roam the Pamirs as if it were their own back garden and Safdar Ali sends regular emissaries to Tashkent, is . . ." He broke off as his military secretary approached. "Yes, Colonel, what is it?"

Colonel Hartley bent down and murmured something in his ear. The C-in-C glanced at the clock and replaced the flimsy in the folder.

"I have to leave for Peshawar in an hour for this meeting about our defence schemes. We will have to defer further discussion on the Borokov matter until my return. However, let me warn you, gentlemen, that I have every intention of resuming the debate. The loss of the papers, the situation that has developed in St. Petersburg consequent to Borokov's visit, the fact that Alexei Smirnoff is being tipped off as the next Governor-General in Central Asia—all warrant serious attention. I am not in a position to issue reassurances to the Viceroy and the Foreign Secretary unless I myself am convinced that there has been no breach of security. I need hardly add that I am *not*. Good day, gentlemen."

They rose, shut their folders, saluted and stepped out onto the Mall into the late spring sunshine.

As always during the Season, the Mall was crowded with noonday shoppers and strollers. Briskly, the trio walked back to their own office, past the government secretariat and Christ's Church, said to have five of the finest stained-glass windows in the country. Despite Simla's ambience as a holiday resort, not for a moment could it be forgotten that here among the sylvan glades beat the heart of an empire. Weaving in and out of summer hats, frilly parasols, leashed dogs and mountainous shopping bags, liveried peons scurried along carrying locked red despatch boxes within which reposed the destiny of a nation. Of the three hundred and fifty million people belonging to that nation, however, there were few signs. Indian civilians were discouraged from strolling on the Mall alongside their white masters and certainly never in traditional dress.

"Well, Wilfred, one more nail in the coffin, eh?"

Sir John's acerbic comment came as soon as they were seated in the privacy of his personal office.

"Your timely support was greatly appreciated, sir," Hethrington murmured.

"Especially since you hadn't the foggiest that it was coming, what?"

Hethrington blushed.

"Well, we've already been over that enough," the QMG said, "and I don't want to waste time in recrimination, except to remind you that I still consider your project outrageous. You had no business to initiate it without my prior sanction."

"If I had asked, sir, would you have sanctioned it?"

"No. I have no great desire to commit professional suicide." The QMG regarded him coldly. "It is one thing to withhold information temporarily from a superior officer in the interests of what one considers—rightly or wrongly—a greater and justifiable cause, Wilfred. We've all done that in our time. But to lie to the Commander-in-Chief of the Indian Army, to actually *lie* . . ." Words failed him.

"We both know, sir, that to tell Sir Marmaduke the truth is to abandon all hope of recovering the papers with even a modicum of discretion," Hethrington said bluntly. "Are we in a position to risk losing them altogether?"

"No. In any case we're too far in now to back out." Sir John pressed his fingertips deep into his temples and closed his eyes in a moment of silent thought. A deceptively small, wiry, mild-mannered man, with square hands and pale eyes, Sir John had proved his mettle in the Second Afghan War and was perceived by many as a possible Commander-in-Chief after Sir Marmaduke's retirement.

"There are three reasons, Wilfred, why I eventually decided to approve your scandalous scheme," he finally said. "First, having known and respected the man, I cannot bring myself to doubt Jeremy Butterfield's claim. What was found *was* the Yasmina, I am convinced of it. Had it not been, he would not have been killed; it's as simple as that. However, until those papers are in our hands we must, absolutely must, persist with our denials.

"Secondly, I have always delegated considerable independent authority to you because I do have faith in your judgement. And for my sins," he added drily, "quite awesome regard for the skill with which Captain Worth spins his little webs of intrigue."

Standing stiffly with his back to the wall as if awaiting a firing squad, Worth's shoulders relaxed in acknowledgement of what he chose to take as a compliment.

"And thirdly," Sir John sat back and sighed, "I happen to believe that empires are neither made nor maintained merely by following regulations." In his pale blue eyes there was the whisper of a twinkle. "I believe that in a curious occupation such as ours with no manuals to refer to in a crisis, imagination and innovation are of the essence. As a dash of chillies does to common fare, a touch of unorthodoxy adds zest to an agent's life, puts shine in the dreary business of gathering intelligence. The risks involved in your cheeky little caper may give me peptic ulcers but at the same time I see that it might, just might, succeed."

Hethrington looked very pleased indeed and Nigel Worth beamed.

"On the other hand," the twinkle vanished, "it might not, and I don't need to remind you again of the consequences. I take it Crankshaw has been adequately briefed?"

"Yes, sir," the Colonel said.

"Well, what does he think?"

"He has expressed some reservations, sir."

"Ho, ho, I bet he has!" Sir John chuckled, but only briefly. "We must be very careful, Wilfred. If this project springs a leak, the Department sinks—as do all who sail in her. Apart from the sheer ignominy, our budget will be slashed and it's spread thinly enough as it is."

"We will not sink, sir," Hethrington maintained stoutly. "We will sail back into port with all hands safe on board."

Having spoken impulsively with far more conviction than he felt, Hethrington returned to his office vaguely discomfitted. In the eventuality of failure, quite apart from the blow to the Department, he had few illusions about his personal fate.

All at once the army mess in Meerut's dusty cantonment loomed very large indeed. He tried not to think of it.

*T*he noon sun rode high in the heavens and the room was flooded with glare. Emma winced, pulled the coverlet over her head and lay back with her eyes closed. Her gently aching body felt unfamiliar, as if no longer hers; her limbs were heavy with drowse, suffused with a pervasive languor that was strange but not entirely displeasing. For a while she remained thus, dispossessed and disembodied, savouring the liquid sweet-sour aches, hovering on the rim of wakefulness, somnolent within a hazy dream. She could not remember where she was.

Then recollection came flooding back and she jolted awake, her memory tingling fresh and her mind whipped into alertness. She remembered everything, most vividly her own participation in the night's adventure, and in the relentless light of day she felt denuded. Damien had taken her knowing that she had no love for him. He had used his practised hands on her like an expert musician manipulating an inanimate instrument—and how willing she had been to be manipulated! Stricken and ashamed, she mourned the fickleness of the flesh, mortified by the ease with which it had surrendered to its baser instincts. At the same time she marvelled that an act of such coarseness, such gross unsubtlety with so little to commend it, should have the power to produce such a dazzling array of sensations. It was a stunning discovery of the arcane, unimaginable dimensions of the human body, *her* body. Oh, that she should know her mind so well and her flesh so little!

The fierce inner conflict left her drained and she slept again, or merely dozed. When she reopened her eyes, the tempest had passed. All that remained was a dull discomfort, aching testimony of the fact that, as promised, the girl had indeed been transformed into a woman. And if Damien had enjoyed the metamorphosis, so, for her sins, had she.

Dragging herself off the bed, she surveyed with distaste the apricot nightdress lying in a heap on the floor. Tossing it into the laundry bag in the bathroom, she splashed her heavy-lidded eyes with cold water and rinsed out the sour taste from her mouth. She bathed again with lashings of cool, purifying water and scented sandalwood soap, trying to wash away the feel of his hands on her body. She dabbed herself dry, combed out the knots from her wet hair and slipped into a cool, printed linen dress. Smoothing out the dishevelled sheets on the bed, she composed her features into a mask of dignity and rang for Sharifa.

Of Damien there was neither sign nor sound, for which she was grateful. How, she wondered in hot-cheeked embarrassment, could she ever look him again in the face?

A soft knock on the door heralded the arrival of the maid and her niece. They entered with heads lowered, the fingertips of a cupped hand touching their foreheads in the traditional salaam, then stood awaiting further orders.

"I would like some tea, please, Sharifa," Emma said, pretending to be engrossed in the arrangement of the pleats of her dress.

Sharifa bowed. "I will fetch it immediately. Rehmat will remain here to see to begum sahiba's requirements. Some breakfast also?"

"Just tea will do nicely, thank you," Emma said. "I am not very hungry." Aware of the women's searching looks and knowing smiles, she did not raise her eyes.

However, when Sharifa returned a while later bearing a tray of food, she was surprised to find that she was ravenous. While the women set about tidying the room, she gulped down the pale tea perfumed with mint leaves, then ate of the fruit, nuts, toast, scrambled eggs and preserves with relish.

"Perhaps begum sahiba would prefer to rest today?" Sharifa asked as she cleared away the remains of the meal. "She must be tired."

"I am not at all tired," Emma said with more sharpness than the remark warranted. "Indeed, quite the contrary."

For a moment she debated if she should ask where Damien was so that she could be prepared for his return, but then decided against it. Wherever he might be she had no desire to see him and an inquiry would unnecessarily fetch him up. Feeling lost and vaguely forlorn, she did not quite know what to do now. She longed to return to Khyber Kothi to be with her mother for a while, but she dared not; if Damien came up and found her absent he would be annoyed, and she simply did not have the stamina for another argument. As it happened she need not have worried.

"Important messages have come from the valley," Sharifa informed her, "and today huzoor is very preoccupied."

Emma was relieved to hear it. "Will he come up for luncheon?"

"I cannot say but I will ask siccaterry sahib to . . ."

"It doesn't matter," Emma said quickly. "It was an idle inquiry."

She spent whatever remained of the morning on the balcony, contemplating the pleasing vistas on the Jamuna. A group of dhobis squatted on the river steps thrashing the daylights out of a pile of clothes against large, smooth stones, then rinsing them out in the water. A pot-bellied boat lumbered past, its deck crowded with passengers bound for the opposite bank, and a lone fisherman sat with his rod in the water, singing. While observing the changing vista, Emma chatted casually with the woman who cleaned and dusted and brought efficient order to the room, pleasing her by asking questions about her home and family. Sharifa answered eagerly, informing her that she had come to Shalimar as a very young bride of one of the cooks and had been there ever since. Her husband was no longer alive; Rehmat was her sister's child and her son, Hakumat, was huzoor's personal khidmatgar in Srinagar.

"They played together as boys," she added proudly.

"You were in employment when the late begum sahiba was alive?"

"No. The late begum sahiba had already left by then."

"Left?" Surely she meant died? "Left for where?"

"Well . . ." The maid cast an uncertain glance at the door. "Begum sahiba must ask huzoor about his late mother."

Emma remembered that Jenny had said something about a scandal. She waited, hoping the maid would continue, but no further information appeared to be forthcoming. Kashmir, Emma knew, was a state of turbulence and mystery that very few Europeans had visited until fairly recently. The scene of many battles, the state had a bloody past left behind by a succession of despotic rulers. Impersonal history, however, was a matter of public record; what Emma suddenly found herself wondering about was the personal history of the family whose name she now bore, a family of strangers about whom she knew nothing.

Damien did not come up for luncheon. According to Sharifa, he had left the house and would not return until evening. A merciful release! From the bookcase in her sitting room Emma selected a translation of *Rajtarangini,* a definitive history of the valley by the twelfth-century sage Kalhana. Lingering over a late luncheon of boiled rice, mutton curry, yoghurt and fresh spring vegetables, she read while she ate and absorbed the account with deep interest.

After luncheon, marginally more at peace with herself, she stretched out on her bed so as to read in greater comfort. Before she had completed even a page, however, the book slipped from her hands and she was fast asleep.

*T*he confident knock on the door Emma had been dreading all day came as she enjoyed a cup of afternoon tea following her long, restful siesta. The door opened. Looking hot, bothered and dusty, Damien stepped into the room. Her cup halfway between the table and her lips, Emma's hand stilled even as her stomach lurched.

He flung himself on the sofa. Pulling a handkerchief out of his pocket, he wiped his forehead. "It's devilish hot out there. Absurdly so for April."

She made no response, continuing to sip her tea while keeping her eyes fixed on her book. Sensing from the warmth in her cheeks that she was blushing, she lowered her head over the pages. If Damien noticed her discomfiture or, indeed, had any recollection of the night before, he gave little indication of it. Sprawled in his favourite position, he stared blankly into the lifeless grate. In fact he appeared troubled, so deeply engrossed in his own thoughts that he was hardly aware of her presence.

Should she ask him about the message from Srinagar, or wait until he introduced the topic? While she was still debating the question a knock heralded the arrival of the khidmatgar she had seen on her first visit to the mansion, bearing a tray of fresh tea. Without hesitation, he placed it on the table before Emma. Now that huzoor had acquired a wife, the gesture appeared to suggest, it was only proper that she should have the honour to pour. Emma waited a moment; still lost in his solitary meditations, Damien gave no sign of having noticed the refreshments.

"Would you like some tea?" she asked.

He nodded without looking at her. She poured out a cup, then again paused uncertainly. Did he take milk? Sugar? Or did he prefer his tea with a sliver of lemon? Never having bothered to notice, she couldn't quite decide which.

"No milk. Just a twist of lemon. Half a spoon of sugar."

Emma bit her lip; obviously, he had been observing her. Cup in hand she rose, went to where he sat and placed it before him. She made to return to her seat but he stopped her with a gesture.

"Why do you always sit so far away from me?"

"I . . . have my book on the table," she mumbled, unable to look him directly in the face.

"Damn your book! You will have plenty of time without me to read as much as you like."

Her heart leapt. "Oh?"

It was unlikely that he would not notice the spark of hope in her eyes although he did not remark on it. "I have to leave tonight," he said shortly, stirring his tea. "Something urgent has come up."

He did not explain further and she did not ask. "And . . . I am to stay on in Delhi?"

"Much as it pains me to ruin your tender hopes, no. You will leave for the Vale, as planned, after a fortnight. Suraj Singh will remain behind to escort you and to make all the arrangements."

The spark of hope died. Emma averted her face so that he could not see the despair in it. "A fortnight is not enough, Damien! With David due to leave tomorrow, I have to stay back to see my mother well settled."

"I have already told you that arrangements are being made for your mother's future."

"What arrangements?"

"You can ask your mother about them when you see her. She is, I might point out, neither a child nor an imbecile. I therefore suggest that you stop treating her like one. Whatever decisions have been made are hers as, no doubt, she will tell you herself."

Two weeks—that was all that was left to her of the easy familiarity of her beloved Delhi!

"The prospect of being without me doesn't fill you with delight?" he asked.

The mockery brought back all the resentment of the morning. The flashes of tenderness, the velvet-soft caresses, the murmured endearments, all had been given to many before her. If his lovemaking had meant little to her apart from base sensation, then to him it had meant even less.

"Oh, it does," she retorted. "It is only because the prospect is so brief that I am disappointed."

"Really!" His eyes gleamed. "In that case, the performance you put on last night was merely a tribute to your histrionic abilities, was it?"

Knowing that he would not rest until he had made the taunt, she was prepared for it. "Another tribute," she amended, not dropping her eyes. "You've already had enough proof of my skill as an actress. Why, all of Delhi believes that I am madly in love with you!"

"And . . . aren't you?"

She laughed. "If you believe that, Damien, it is only because conceit provides you with such convenient blinkers."

"Even after last night?"

She shrugged. "Last night was of as little consequence to me as it was to you. It merely engaged the senses without disturbing the heart—*exactly* according to your recipe for a satisfactory marriage."

This time the dart went home. His bronzed complexion deepened, turning the scar on his chin livid, but hoist with his own petard he could think of nothing to say. Visibly fighting anger, he walked over to where she sat, placed a finger under her chin and roughly jerked it up.

"One day," he breathed, "it will disturb your heart as nothing ever has, Emma. I wager my life on that."

"Don't." She neither moved her head nor looked away. "Despite your skill as a gambler you will lose both, your wager as well as your life."

He released her chin, grasped her forearms and pulled her to her feet. His hard, angry mouth was on hers before she could turn away. She closed her eyes, refusing to weaken. The hands that cupped her face were not gentle and his lips were punitive. She clenched her fists, her nails sharp against the softness of her palms, but she gave him the pleasure of neither response nor reaction.

"You perform well," he said. "It will be good to have you with me at Shalimar. I can hardly wait for a repeat performance."

"Really? And how will you fill the intolerably lonely hours until then— with willing substitutes?"

"Would that trouble you?"

"Not in the least. Indeed, I would rejoice that it is not only I who must put up with your tedious demands."

Before he could retaliate, a knock sounded on the door. He made no move to release her.

"There is someone at the door." She struggled to free herself.

"Whoever it is can wait."

"Let me *go*, Damien!"

"Why?" His hold tightened. "Are you ashamed of being seen in the arms of your husband?"

"Yes . . . no . . . oh, do leave go of me!" With a burst of strength she broke away and stepped back, panting.

He laughed but did not reach for her again. Instead, his voice rang out with a command and Suraj Singh entered. "We need to hurry, huzoor," he said with a bow in Emma's direction. "The train departs in less than an hour."

"Then why the devil didn't you tell me earlier?" Damien grumbled, quite unreasonably, it appeared to Emma. Suraj Singh, however, gave no sign of having taken offence. "Has everything been loaded?"

"Yes, huzoor."

"Good. I shall be downstairs in a moment." He turned to Emma. As Suraj Singh withdrew, his entire appearance changed. The look of only a few moments ago vanished; his eyes were again clouded and his expression distant. "Suraj Singh will arrange for the packing of whatever effects you wish to take with you."

"There is no need for . . ."

"There is need! The journey is long and improperly packed boxes are easily damaged. My men have special steel-lined trunks that will protect your belongings well. Besides, you will want to spend time with your mother and brother, not waste it in drudgery that can safely be left to others."

Surprised by the thoughtfulness, she accepted the good sense of that with a nod. Secretly, however, her mind raced to devise ploys to delay her departure from Delhi.

"Don't bother to concoct alibis to postpone your journey," Damien said quickly, picking the thought right out of her mind. "You will leave exactly as planned, a fortnight from today."

Without another word, not even a gesture of farewell, he turned and walked out of the room.

*D*eliverance!

After the terrible trauma of the past weeks, once again Emma was in charge of her destiny. In spite of the brevity of the respite, she revelled in her sense of liberation.

As soon as Damien left she sent a note to her mother, then sat down to a substantial supper. Retiring early, she resumed her reading of the *Rajtarangini,* her buoyant spirits keeping her up well past midnight. Having the spacious bed all to herself she slept extraordinarily well, awakening many hours later to the sound of curtains being drawn and the cheerful rattle of teacups on her bedside table. She sat up and yawned, revived herself with a sip of the fragrant brew and set about planning her first day of freedom.

"Was my . . . was huzoor in time for the train last night?"

"Yes, begum sahiba," Sharifa replied, "but only barely. The train was already moving when they arrived at the railway station."

"Then how did they manage to catch it?"

"Huzoor asked the guard to stop the train."

"And he did?"

"Oh yes." Sharifa looked surprised. "Nobody would ever think to dis-obey our huzoor."

Well, nobody except his wife!

It was another unblemished morning, sunny but not yet unbearably so, and humming with sounds from the river. Emma was to spend the day at Khyber Kothi, where Jenny would join them for luncheon. Following a leisurely bath, she slipped into a plain skirt and muslin blouse and asked for breakfast to be served on the balcony. As she sat down to eat, she noticed a green paper packet tied with gold thread lying half concealed by the serviette.

"It was left by huzoor," Sharifa said, "to be delivered to begum sahiba this morning."

Wonderingly, Emma undid the parcel. Inside, within a wrapping of red tissue paper reposed layers of an embroidered fabric that was quite the softest she had ever touched. The shawl, for that was what it turned out to be, was creamy white and beautifully embroidered. So fine were the stitches that at first glance it gave the impression of an elaborately woven tapestry or a painting executed by some divine brush. Emma had seen many Kashmiri shawls in Delhi but never one quite as exquisite.

"It is a *shatoosh* shawl," Sharifa explained, well satisfied with the re-action, "woven from the under-fleece of the *chiru,* an antelope found in Tibet."

Silently, Emma skimmed her palms across the rippling folds, too taken aback to speak.

"In Kashmir we call it a ring shawl, I will show begum sahiba why." Gathering one of the narrower ends of the shawl in pleats, Sharifa slipped a ring off her finger and threaded the pleats through it with the greatest of ease. She added proudly, "This was woven by our own weavers on the estate."

"There are weavers at Shalimar?"

"Oh yes. The weavers' village on the estate was started by burra hu-zoor. In those days he and Qadir Mian used to gather the pashmina and *shatoosh* wool themselves from the mountains."

"Who is Qadir Mian?"

"Huzoor's chief weaver, an Afghan. He was brought to Kashmir from Peshawar as a young man and trained by burra huzoor. It is he who wove and signed this. See?" She turned a corner of the shawl to reveal a silken signature. "Shawls that carry Qadir Mian's name fetch very high prices."

Embroidered all over, the shawl was reversible, with not a knot to be seen on either side. Standing before her mirror, Emma draped it about her shoulders, revelling in the feel of it against her neck, a feel as soft and warm as a kitten. She had never possessed an article of clothing quite so splendid, quite so regal.

If only it had not come from Damien!

The return to Khyber Kothi was for Emma joyful and at the same time depressing. Everything looked the same, yet nothing was, nor ever would be again. She arrived to find Suraj Singh already on the premises with the packers awaiting her instructions and soon saw that the very quantum of effects to be transported confirmed the good sense of Damien's suggestion.

It was just before Jenny arrived for luncheon that Margaret Wyncliffe made her extraordinary announcement.

"Sell Khyber Kothi?" Emma was astounded. "When did you come to that decision, Mama?"

"Well, I haven't exactly come to a decision, dear," Mrs. Wyncliffe said. "I . . . I wouldn't, not without first talking to you, but I have been thinking about it a great deal lately." She looked around her sadly. "I do love this house and everything in it, but one can't live in the past forever. There comes a time when one must rearrange one's priorities and move on—that is, if neither you nor David objects."

"The house might be in David's name," Emma said, still quite shocked, "but Papa built it for you. Of course we don't object."

Mrs. Wyncliffe looked relieved. "What both of you have been saying for so long is perfectly true—the house *is* too large for us, certainly for me on my own. I shall rattle around in it like a stone in a tin can and I shall hate it. Besides," her voice trembled, "now you both have your own lives to lead, and I feel the time has come when I must start to lead mine. Having been a burden long enough, I must let go. And so must both of you."

"But if you sell the house, where will you live?" Emma asked.

"Didn't I tell you? But of course I didn't. Where has been the time with so much happening? Anyway, with Jenny's suite soon to fall vacant in the Purcell bungalow, Carrie has suggested that for the time being I move in with them."

"And later?"

"Well, dear, you know that summerhouse the Purcells have in their garden? Carrie suggests that with the money I get from the sale, I enlarge it into a cottage and build quarters for the servants at the back. Once the cottage is ready, I can purchase the plot from them and be independent. The little nest egg left over from the sale of Khyber Kothi will help clear the debts from the wedding and be quite sufficient for my living expenses." She threw Emma an anxious glance. "Well, what do you think, dear? Does it not resolve everything?"

It certainly appeared to. "You thought all this out on your own?" Emma asked slowly.

"Oh, dear me, no." She looked flustered. "As a matter of fact, it was Damien who suggested it."

"Damien?"

"Yes." She reached out and squeezed Emma's hand as if in apology. "Well, he does seem to have such very practical ideas, dear, and you seemed so preoccupied I didn't want to trouble you. Dr. Ogbourne agrees that a smaller house without stairs to climb would be medically advisable, easier to manage and, of course, cheaper to run. With Archie and Carrie, bless them, right next door, Barak back and dear old Mahima and the other servants to look after me, I will be perfectly secure."

"And the sale? How will you manage that on your own?"

"James Lawrence will take care of the legalities."

"Before that, Mama, we do have to find a buyer!"

Margaret Wyncliffe dropped her eyes. "We don't have to worry about that, my dear. You see . . . Damien has offered to buy Khyber Kothi—if you and David agree, naturally. Wouldn't you say that that is enormously generous of him?"

For a wordless moment Emma stared and then started to laugh. Having started, she found that she simply could not stop. Unaware of the irony of the situation, Mrs. Wyncliffe looked on in puzzlement as she waited for the hilarity to cease.

"Damien made me promise not to tell you until later," she said. "He said he wanted it to come as a surprise."

"Oh, that it has," Emma assured her, wiping her eyes. "That it certainly has!"

Luncheon over, Emma broke the news of her departure to Jenny.

"A fortnight?" Jenny looked devastated. "You will not be here for my wedding!"

"I'm afraid not. You see, dear, my life is no longer in my hands. Indeed, nothing seems to be any more. Now I am expected to do only as I am directed." She tried not to sound bitter but did not quite succeed.

"Uh-oh!" Forgetting her own enormous disappointment, Jenny peered into Emma's face. "Do I detect a note of disenchantment in the new bride?"

"No, of course not." Emma was quick to smile. "I merely meant that it feels odd to have to fashion my life according to someone else's wishes. I suppose I'll learn soon enough, you will too, never fear. Anyway, Damien has asked me to invite John and you to be our guests at Shalimar whenever you have the time and the inclination. Do come, Jenny," she pleaded, squeezing her hand, "it would mean so much to me—to us—if you would."

Despite the brave facade, all at once it was intolerable not to have Jenny near to exchange confidences, to giggle over silly things, to reach out to each other for consolation. Once they went their separate ways they would be divided by a subcontinent, denied a share in each other's day-to-day lives. Then, seeing that she had alarmed her friend unnecessarily Emma laughed, quickly made a jest and lightened the moment.

It was almost time for David to leave for the station on the first leg of his long journey to Leh. He had not been round to see Emma at the Nicholson Road house nor, she knew, would he. Despite the fact that he was still avoiding her, as soon as Jenny left, Emma cornered him in his room one last time.

"Do you know the plans Mama has made about the house?" she asked.

"She mentioned them, yes." Engrossed in last-minute chores, he spoke offhandedly.

"I wish she had talked them over with me," Emma said, realising that he must also know about Damien's participation.

"Why? It's a perfectly good arrangement and it suits everybody, especially Mama."

His tone and his expression were closed. No, he had not forgiven Damien yet.

"You don't like Damien much, do you?" she asked impulsively.

"No. But for your sake I suppose I shall have to learn to."

"Damien may have many faults," she said, surprising herself, "but he can also be very . . . considerate."

"Considerate?" He lifted an eyebrow, smiled and walked away.

They were both, Emma knew, responsible for the schism between them. Whatever he held against Damien, he had not forgotten the terrible words she had spoken that night in the stables. Despite her own simmering resentment against her brother, she was profoundly hurt by his coldness, for beneath the ill feeling their love for each other was unquestionable and deep.

At the moment of parting at the Delhi railway station, David could no longer sustain his pretence of indifference. He put his arms about her and hugged her, unable to withhold either his emotions or his tears.

"Be happy, my dearest sister," he said thickly. "Promise me you will take good care of yourself."

"I will, darling, I will," Emma whispered back returning the hug. "God keep you safe in Ladakh. *Write.*"

He hesitated an instant. "Be careful of him, Emma," he blurted out. "Damien is a dangerous man."

Her eyes widened. "Dangerous?"

"He is not what he seems."

She forced a light smile. "Well, come to think of it, darling, which one of us is? Damien too must have his little secrets like everyone else."

"You don't *understand*," he said fiercely, "they say that he . . ." The railway guard's shrill whistle cut off the rest.

"They say what, David?"

Mouthing something which she could not hear, he leapt onto the carriage steps and disappeared within. Emma stood and watched the tail end of the train vanish through a film of black smoke and tears. When would she see her brother again?

In the overwhelming sorrow of parting, his remarks about Damien she pushed to the back of her mind to be considered later.

So! You finally remember the commitment you made with such sincerity and enthusiasm, eh?" The tone was curt, the manner glacial. Dr. Theodore Anderson was extremely angry.

Deserving as she was of the reprimand, what could Emma possibly say in her defence? She had not been to see Dr. Anderson since that initial occasion when she had mouthed such heartfelt assurances. Indeed, she had entirely forgotten the subsequent appointment made for Friday. When she finally had remembered it and sent him a note of abject apology, he had not bothered to respond. To compound it all, in her distraught frame of mind she had forgotten even to send him an invitation to the wedding. Living as he did in an academic ivory tower, she hoped that he had not heard of it, but he had.

"It's always the same with you women," he raged. "Marriage, marriage, marriage at all costs—that's all you want out of life. And that is *precisely* why I draw the line at taking women students. No sense of responsibility, no academic integrity, no . . ."

After he had expended his wrath with considerable eloquence, he paused to take a breath and await her explanations, such as they were. Meekly, Emma embarked on a doctored account of the events of the past four weeks—was it only a month since she was last in this room? It felt like a lifetime! As she spoke she squirmed, deeply ashamed of the excuses she manufactured for the benefit of her kindly mentor.

"I have no words with which to beg your forgiveness, Dr. Anderson," she concluded humbly. "All I can say in my defence is that when I approached you for help, I had no idea that unforeseen circumstances would arise to make a mockery of my intentions."

Having listened to her in frosty silence, he grunted, partially mollified. "So, you are abandoning Delhi to live up north, eh?"

"Yes. My . . . husband has preceded me." She made a valiant attempt to sound joyously bridal. "I am to follow on Saturday."

"You say he lives in Kashmir?"

"Yes."

"Well, then, I presume this marks the end of your noble endeavours on behalf of your father, eh?"

"Not at all, Dr. Anderson," she assured him. "Even without your valuable help I have every intention of continuing what I have started. I hope that greater effort will compensate, at least in part, for what I have lost in enlightened guidance."

"Hmph." He sat for a moment in frowning thought. "In that case, perhaps we could move the papers back and forth through reliable dak runners?"

"In spite of your plans for Tibet?"

"Since the funds expected have not arrived, the expedition has been postponed indefinitely."

His tone was clipped. She realised that his anger this morning was not directed entirely at her. Knowing how galling must be his disappointment, she appreciated his situation. She murmured her sympathy but saw that the offer of postal guidance, however generous, was hopelessly impractical. "I have to confess, Dr. Anderson, that I do not place much faith in dak runners. The best I can suggest under the circumstances is that I take advantage of your kindness the next time I am in Delhi."

The next time. When? In another life . . . ?

"As you wish." He shrugged, having already lost interest. Rising to his feet, he went to his filing cabinet and from it withdrew the sheaf of folders she had left with him. "I have made some notes in the margins and suggested further reading, but as I pointed out earlier, only unpublished papers of fresh explorations would be of interest to academe. And now, if you will excuse me. . . ."

He escorted her to the door, muttering vague good wishes for her future happiness.

As soon as he had seen Emma off the premises, Dr. Anderson returned to his desk and sat down, his mouth set and his brow furrowed in thought.

For a while he remained thus, unmoving and unseeing, deep in meditation. Presently he got up, summoned the stalwart Pathan sitting outside on a stool and closed the door behind them.

"An urgent message needs to be away this evening, Ismail."

"Very good, sahib."

"You will take the usual route and deliver it to the usual contact."

"Understood, sahib."

"And Ismail?"

"Sahib?"

"See that I am not disturbed for an hour or so, will you?"

"Very good, sahib."

As Ismail left, the professor bolted the door behind him and re-seated himself at his desk. For a moment or two he stared at the virgin sheet in front of him, then picked up his pen and thrust it into the inkwell. He started to write:

"My dear Colonel Borokov . . ."

CHAPTER

8

*T*he two weeks passed even before Emma knew they were gone. Deeply despondent, she completed domestic arrangements for her mother's move, packed her own personal possessions and bid farewell to old friends. Then, it seemed to her, before she could turn round and regain her breath she was standing once again on the platform at Delhi's railway station where she had said good-bye to David a fortnight ago. Surrounded by mountainous baggage, a large entourage and moist-eyed family and friends, she felt as if her heart would break.

"For goodness' sake, Em," Jenny hid her own heartbreak behind a damp smile, "you're going to the most beautiful valley in the world to live in luxury with the most deliciously exciting man in the world—not to be guillotined!"

"I don't know when we will see each other again," Emma said, holding back her tears with difficulty. "Kashmir is at the other end of the earth, in quite another space and time."

"Oh, fiddlesticks—why, there isn't a girl in Delhi who isn't eating her heart out with envy! Charlotte Price, I'll have you know, says since she can't have Damien Granville she will renounce the world and enter a nunnery. Now doesn't that warm the cockles and make you feel better?"

It did not, but Emma raised a bleak smile.

The parting with her mother was particularly agonising. That her health was now vastly improved and dear, devoted Carrie Purcell promised to care for her well were matters of relief, but there was still a searing finality to the separation. Emma clung to her tight and tried not to cry.

"Write to me soon, darling. Let me know everything about your move, every *single* thing. Don't overstrain yourself, don't try to do too much, don't . . ." She broke down and they sobbed quietly into each other's shoulders.

The whistle blew and the station master waved his green flag. Lurching and hissing and belching coal dust, the train started to move. As the carriage filled with acrid smoke, Emma clapped one hand to her mouth and nose and waved through a window with the other. The figures on the platform receded, diminished into specks of greyness and then dissolved into nothing.

Another chapter of her life closed forever!

Behind her lay Delhi, her loved ones and a cherished past; ahead loomed an emotional wilderness. Kashmir, as alien as a moonscape, was where she would spend the rest of her life in bondage to a man she neither knew nor liked nor understood.

All at once she was very frightened.

*H*is Excellency Baron Boris von Adelssohn, Governor-General of Russia's Central Asian empire, was an extremely worried man. An enthusiastic amateur zoologist with a great love of fauna, he took immense pride in his private zoological garden in Tashkent. This morning when he had gone to the aviary to supervise the first feed, he had found one of his cherished golden orioles looking poorly, with a droop in its wings and a dull film over its usually bright little eyes. Knowing the delicate disposition of these beautiful, fragile creatures, the Baron was deeply concerned. The army veterinarian, for whom he had sent immediately, had diagnosed a stomach infection but had been unable to prescribe a remedy.

Therefore, when informed that two men of doubtful origin had been caught without papers in Russian territory, the Baron was understandably irate.

"Ask Colonel Borokov to deal with the matter," he ordered from behind the wire mesh. "Can't you see that I'm busy?"

"Colonel Borokov has not yet returned from St. Petersburg, Excellency," his aide-de-camp reminded him.

"Well, what about Captain Vassily or the ten thousand others? Is there not one officer in station able to deal with the triviality?"

"The men insist on a personal audience, Excellency, because of the animal."

"Animal?" The Baron's ears pricked up. "What animal?"

"I cannot say, Excellency. I have not seen one like it before."

"Well, what does it look like, man? Is it a fox?" He had been promised a pair of silver foxes and delivery was imminent.

"No, sir. I have seen foxes in Russia. This one looks like a goat, a large goat. If Excellency commands, I could ask . . ."

"Never mind, never mind, I'll ask them myself. Fetch them to the front verandah, will you?"

A few moments later, enthroned in the usual high seat in which he received the hordes of petitioners that were part of the daily cross he bore, the Baron surveyed the pair of culprits with distaste. They were shabbily clothed, ill-kempt, generally unprepossessing and stank all the way up to the ceiling. Had he received them indoors, the stench would have taken days to clear, and with their farewell ball round the corner his Olga would have had a fit.

"They were caught loitering in the officers' residential locality without papers, Excellency," the captain of the Cossacks said. "When questioned, they . . ."

"What language do they speak?" the Baron interrupted impatiently.

"Turki, Excellency."

The Baron surveyed the two men sternly. "What are you doing on Russian soil without proper authorisation?" The older of the two made a response in the peculiar Turki spoken by many in Asia that bore not the slightest resemblance to Turkish. "What did he say?"

One of the Cossacks stepped forward. "He says they meant no harm," he translated. "They came to deliver a gift to Your Excellency but got lost on the way."

A likely story! The Baron subjected their baggy trousers, loose shirts and badly stained quilted overcoats tied with string to another stern inspection. In the manner of all Muslims, they wore embroidered skullcaps around which were wound turbans with the customary forty folds that might have once been white. Their high boots were covered in dried mud and their faces, half obscured by straggling beards, had probably not been washed in days. There was no sign of any animal.

"If I find that you come from that fat old Chinksky in Kashgar to spy on us, I will have you beheaded immediately!"

"We are not spies," the older man pleaded. "Knowing Your Excellency's great love of animals, we come only to deliver one such as Your Excellency has not seen before."

"Well, where is it?"

The captain of the guards signed to a Cossack and the man stepped off the verandah. He returned a moment later leading the creature by a rope. About three feet high, with a greyish pelt, it was a young male with a pair of horns which when fully matured would be triple-twisted. The animal appeared to be quite tame, for it promptly set about grazing on the stubbles of grass bordering the verandah unworried by the presence of a gardener who worked close by.

A Kashmiri markhor!

The Baron struggled to contain his elation. Being a favourite target of hunters in the Himalayas, the Kashmiri markhor was a sadly depleted species. Indeed, he had given up all hope of securing one before he left Tashkent. "Where did you find this animal?"

"In the Kaj Nag, Excellency. He was abandoned by his mother while still a suckling. We have cared for him ever since."

Since the markhor was known to rut in December and kid in June, this specimen could not have been more than ten months old. The Baron rose, walked up to it and tentatively stroked its ears. The markhor tossed its head but did not shy away.

The Baron was entranced. "Well, how much?" he asked, taking care not to reveal his exhilaration.

"We do not want money," the younger man replied.

"What then?"

"A favour."

"Oh, a favour." The Baron's mouth drooped. He knew all about favours, of course. A job for my brother, a plot for my father, a license to trade for my friend. A passport. "No, no favours," he said firmly. "Absolutely out of the question."

"If you will hear us out, Excellency," the man persisted, "the favour is a simple one."

"All favours are simple to begin with, but they have a nasty habit of turning into headaches later." He battled within himself a moment, then sighed. "All right, what kind of favour, man? Be quick. I can't stand about all day with a sick oriole on my hands."

The man looked at the waiting Cossacks. "What we have to say is confidential, for Your Excellency's ears only."

The Baron was about to erupt again at this further insolence when the markhor lifted its snout and with every sign of trust and affection nuzzled the back of his hand. Shooing his Cossacks away out of earshot, he again sat down. "Now, you scumbags, any sign of trickery and I'll . . ."

"We plan no trickery, Excellency. As your guards have already ascertained, we are both unarmed."

"Where do you come from anyway?"

"We are Dards, Excellency. My uncle belongs to a village in Chitral. I myself live in Wakhan."

"Well?"

The younger man spoke in rough Russian. "We request Your Excellency's help to locate a missing person."

"A missing person? Who?"

"A slave, Excellency."

"There are no more slaves in Russian Turkestan."

"I use the term loosely, Excellency. She could be simply a domestic servant in the employ of . . ."

"She?" The Baron was even less pleased. "A woman!"

"Yes, Excellency. She is Armenian and originally from Khiva. Her trail from St. Petersburg leads back to Tashkent."

The Baron scanned them with renewed astonishment. "You have travelled to St. Petersburg in search of this woman?"

"Not us, Excellency, but others, good friends, who are the ones anxious to locate her. They have been given to understand that she is presently employed in the household of a Russian Army officer."

Naturally, the Baron did not believe a word of the farrago. Indeed, he was beginning to find something altogether fishy about the visitation. Obviously criminals, the fellows had learned of his love for animals and used the markhor merely to gain an audience. The woman they sought could be an accomplice, possibly a traitor, a thief, a murderess or, indeed, all four, and he certainly had no wish to be involved in anything unsavoury. His five-year tenure was almost over and blissful retirement awaited, as did the Moscow house, the dacha on the Black Sea, his grandchildren and long, uninterrupted hours with his menagerie. With so few weeks left in office, he would be a fool to jeopardise retirement perquisites through hasty miscalculation.

"Quite apart from the fact that I do not trust you," he said sharply, wrenching his eyes away from the markhor, "I am not prepared to waste government funds on a highly suspect wild goose chase. Therefore, you may remove your animal and leave." He rose to go inside. "If you are not off Russian soil within forty-eight hours I will have you arrested."

"A moment, Excellency!" The younger man held up a hand. About to summon his guards, the Baron paused. "We are in a position to offer compensation that would make the trouble worthwhile."

Digging inside his voluminous coat, the man extracted a sheet of paper from one of a dozen pockets and handed it to the Baron. Holding it gingerly by a corner, the Baron read the Cyrillic characters at a glance. Oh dear, dear, not *again*!

"Is this a jest?" he asked irritably, crumbling the paper and tossing it over his shoulder.

"No, Excellency, it is not a jest."

"Do you know how often each year I am offered maps of the Yasmina Pass and by how many?"

"By crooks and charlatans, Excellency. The maps we have in our possession are genuine."

"Really! And how, may I ask, were these genuine maps denied to the rest of humanity acquired?"

"By accident, Excellency," the younger man replied. "An English agent was killed on the Silk Road some months ago by Hunza raiders. I was a camel groom with the caravan and the maps happened to be in his possession."

"And now they are in yours? How?"

"I stole them, Excellency."

The Baron had heard of the raid and the murder of the Angliski from Borokov, of course, but how the devil was he to be sure that these men spoke the truth? Stroking his chin, he stole a covetous glance at the markhor. It still grazed happily. Realising that the matter appeared to be more complex than he had imagined, he was uncertain what do so next.

"Er, you bring the maps with you?"

"No, Excellency. They will be presented for inspection only at the time of the exchange, after the woman has been found."

"Well, why is this woman so important as to merit such a transaction?" he asked in gathering perplexity.

"She is not important at all, Excellency, except to our friends."

That the two men were scoundrels the Baron did not doubt. At the same time there was something about them that disturbed him. Silently cursing Colonel Borokov for being away, he finally decided that although he did not believe them, neither did he understand the situation. If this was a trick he could see no motive behind it, and if it was not a trick, what then? Knowing Borokov's obsession with the Yasmina and his closeness to Alexei Smirnoff, he decided to play it safe. When Borokov returned he could tackle the business as he thought fit.

"You have details about this woman?"

"Yes, Excellency." The man again burrowed inside his filthy coat, withdrew a second paper and handed it to the Baron.

As he read what was written and noted the diagram on the paper, the Baron's brow creased. He perused both at great length and then scratched an ear. Could it be? No, surely not!

Trying not to show his confusion, he said casually, "Well, I will have to make inquiries. It will take time. In the interim both of you will remain in Tashkent until my chief-of-staff returns from St. Petersburg to conduct a proper interrogation. The markhor I will take charge of personally."

Once again the younger man stopped him as he was about to summon his guards. "Regretfully, Your Excellency, we cannot stay. We will return later for the interrogation."

The Baron positively bristled. "What do you take me for, a fool?" he demanded angrily. "Of course you will stay!"

"Should the woman be found, Excellency, we will have to return to claim her anyway. If we are detained now and the eggs are laid and hatched in our absence, the fledglings will either be abstracted or be old enough to fly away."

"What fledgings?"

"In the nest of a golden eagle. While reconnoitring in the late autumn we . . ."

"A golden eagle nest?" The Governor-General half rose out of his chair. "Where in heaven's name did you find a golden eagle nest?"

"In Hazara, Excellency, on the forests along the precipices. Had the matter of the woman not been so important to our friends, we would have remained in Hazara to keep watch over the nest. The mission to secure the fledglings has been given to us by an English general sahib in Rawalpindi who, like your honourable self, is a collector of animals. We are poor men, Excellency. If imprisoned now, we stand to lose not only the fledglings but also the very handsome reward promised."

A golden eaglet! The Baron could hardly breathe for excitement. In that moment he couldn't have cared less about the general in Rawalpindi or Mikhail Borokov or, indeed, the blasted Yasmina. The *Aguila chrysaetus* was the rarest of rare winged creatures to be seen in the Himalayan ranges. Many had searched for years without even a sighting, let alone locating a nest. To be able to rear a golden eagle in his own private aviary—why, he would be the envy of every ornithologist in Russia! But then how to handle a situation of such extreme delicacy?

It was, in fact, the older man from Chitral who handled it. "A suggestion, Excellency."

"Yes?"

"It does not take *two* men to guard a nest. If my nephew might be allowed to proceed to Hazara to resume his watch, I will remain behind as hostage to ensure his return with the fledgling. That will also give Your Excellency time for inquiries about the woman."

The Baron pondered. It seemed a perfectly reasonable solution, one that satisfied both sides, and what the man said was true—to claim the woman they would have to be in Tashkent anyway. The dubious credentials of the men ceased to bother him.

"How long will it take you to return?" he asked the nephew.

"I will be back before Your Excellency departs Turkestan."

The Baron gave a nod. "All right. But the first sign of mischief and I will have your uncle strung up and flogged to death."

"We are not mischief-makers, Excellency," they protested in unison. "We are poor men, we can hardly . . ."

"All right, all right, let us get *on* with it!" Button eyes gleaming, he leaned forward hardly able to contain himself. Even the Kashmiri markhor paled somewhat in importance. "Now, about these fledglings . . ."

The Kazakh gardener still sat quietly weeding the verge. As the men discussed details of the arrangement, quite unnoticed he continued to listen with the closest of attention.

*T*he long train journey to Amritsar, where the railway line terminated, was hot, dusty and uncomfortable. The square wooden bogies shook and rattled, their balance precarious at the high speed of twenty miles an hour. Sharifa and Rehmat attended to Emma in her first-class compartment, which Suraj Singh had thoughtfully provisioned with milk and soda water bottles, bread, butter, tins of beans, tuna and ham, a basket of fruit and reading material. Travelling in an adjoining bogey Suraj Singh remained the epitome of concern, arriving at every stop to inquire after their well-being.

Having traversed it before with her father, Emma was not unfamiliar with the Punjab, the land of five rivers. The stretch between Delhi and Amritsar was dull, flat country with not much of interest to offer. Even though a tub of ice had been placed in the compartment for relief from the persistent heat, by the time the train staggered into Amritsar station the next day, Emma felt soiled, drained of energy and her head ached. There still remained the long journey ahead across the arid plains before they arrived at the Pir Panjal range for the arduous climb up to the pass. A day's rest at Amritsar could not have been more welcome with its promise of those most basic of creature comforts, a cool bath, a hot meal and a bed that did not threaten every bone in the body.

Installed in the dak bungalow and with little to do through the day, Emma divided her time between necessary ablutions and recovering lost sleep. In the evening after the dust had settled and the air was comparatively fresh, Suraj Singh arranged a carriage ride through the city and a visit to the Golden Temple, the domed shrine held most sacred by the Sikhs.

Early the next morning even before the sun rose, the commotion in the compound indicated that the pack beasts and teams of coolies that were to constitute their caravan had arrived. Up with the lark and much refreshed, Emma eyed without enthusiasm the litter Suraj Singh had ordered for her.

"I would prefer to ride," she declared, having no intention of being carried on men's shoulders like a sack of coals.

"Huzoor will not approve," Suraj Singh warned nervously.

"Huzoor will not know," Emma reminded him, determined to have her own way for as long as she could.

"Begum sahiba will not be able to tolerate the heat . . ."

"If everyone else does so can I."

". . . and the dust will be insufferable."

"It already is, a little more makes no difference."

Suraj Singh sighed. "Well, if begum sahiba insists . . ."

"Begum sahiba does indeed!"

"In that case," he surrendered with infinite courtesy, "I will make the necessary arrangements."

In Moghul times the Vale of Kashmir was much favoured as a summer resort by the emperors who made incredible journeys across these very routes accompanied by thousands of animals and attendants. Remembering her father's habit of travelling light with a handful of porters and only essential baggage, Emma was amazed at the assortment of conveyances that comprised their own caravan: horses, camels, two elephants, Punjabi mules, porters and coolies. In addition there were grooms for the animals, goats to provide fresh milk and meat en route, baburchis to cook, khidmatgars to serve, armed guards in case of attack by dacoits and, of course, assorted camp followers.

The mount Suraj Singh selected for her was a blue roan mare with an equable temperament. Never having felt secure riding side-saddle, Emma chose to sit astride, like the men, wearing divided skirts designed for the purpose. Galloping up to join her, Suraj Singh offered her a solar topee.

"It may not look elegant," he said apologetically, "but it will help to keep the head cool."

She was touched by his concern but declined the offer. "I am used to the sun far more than to topees, but thank you anyway."

"Begum sahiba is very . . . adventurous," he commented sadly.

Reading "stubborn" for "adventurous," Emma laughed. "Well, my mother would certainly agree with you there, Suraj Singh, perhaps with a greater degree of disapproval."

For a while they followed the bed of a minor river with not a hill in sight across the dustbowl that was the Punjab plain. To compensate for the heat, however, a pleasant spring breeze blew across the corrugated landscape and the journey was not intolerable. Cantering up and down frequently, Suraj Singh kept a stern, tireless eye on his flock, barking instructions and issuing sharp reprimands if any lagged behind.

They stopped at noon for luncheon and a much needed siesta, then set off once more towards their distant destination, the Himalayan foothills soon to be outlined against the shifting skies. The heat and dust of the dry plains, the meandering streams and coarse scrubland across which they passed were for Emma achingly evocative, and she rode along at a comfortable pace lost in her own thoughts. Before she knew it, the sun had slipped behind the distant hills and Suraj Singh had called a halt for the night in one of the many caravanserais that dotted the route. Built by the Moghuls for the convenience of travellers, each caravanserai had a quadrangle, stables and suites of living rooms, although now most were in shocking states of disrepair wrought by heavy rains and floods.

For the retinue and pack beasts a camp was pitched outside on the river bank. Before long a kettle bubbled on the paraffin stove, a goat was milked and a welcome cup of tea arrived to whisk away the tiredness. The meal of vegetables, rice and lentils eaten against the clatter of kitchen utensils and the general bustle of camp life were comfortingly familiar and Emma felt completely at ease. Later, as she sat on a boulder by the edge of the rivulet idly watching the shifting patterns of the water, she was joined by Suraj Singh.

"Is there anything else begum sahiba might require tonight?"

"Thank you, no."

She smiled, motioned for him to sit and he positioned himself gingerly on a nearby stone. "I understand begum sahiba has travelled this way before?"

"Yes, twice. The first time was many years ago when my father explored the site of the ancient Buddhist university of Taxila. He took me up to Koh Murree, I remember, to see the high mountains. Before then I had never seen snow." She sipped at her tea, its flavour strongly reminiscent of all the others she had tasted from a common camp kettle.

"Begum sahiba did not miss the city?"

"Sometimes, but on the whole it was wonderfully tranquil to rise and rest with the sun, to sleep in the open under the stars and to learn the joys of solitude."

Suraj Singh nodded. "Huzoor too prefers the solitude of the mountains to the humdrum existence of the city."

Well, that at least was something they had in common.

She did not add that it was also in Koh Murree that she had first heard of Kashmir from her father and learned of the unique ring of lofty peaks that surrounded the valley. Suddenly, regardless of her fears and the circumstances, the prospect of penetrating beyond that childhood glimpse into the guarded Vale was exciting. Indeed, for the first time since her father had died, she again felt the thrill of an explorer on the threshold of the unknown.

She asked for a second cup of the refreshing brew and took another sip. The taste of crushed cardamom made her mouth tingle. "You, of course, must know this territory extremely well, Suraj Singh."

"Indeed, begum sahiba."

"And my . . . husband?"

"Huzoor also. He was born in Kashmir, as begum sahiba already knows, and travelled often to India. This area is as much home to him as it is to me."

Emma had not known but she did not say so. A thought occurred; in the half dark she covertly studied Suraj Singh's face.

About fifty-five, strong-muscled and intelligent, with deep, watchful eyes, he had a sun-hardened, well-weathered skin that spoke of a life spent in the open. Unvaryingly formal in her presence, this evening he seemed less so. With David's parting words now again in the forefront of her mind, it was too good an opportunity not to exploit.

"You have been in the Granville family's employ many years, Suraj Singh, have you not?"

"Yes, begum sahiba."

"Since the time my husband's father was alive?"

"No, begum sahiba. I joined after Major Granville passed away."

"My husband's mother died earlier, did she not?"

"Yes, begum sahiba." Was there a slight shift in his posture or was it her imagination? "She died before I came to Shalimar."

"Now, let me see"—brow creased, she appeared to search her memory—"when my husband was . . . ?"

Her pause was long and the intonation that of a question. "Huzoor had just turned twelve," Suraj Singh supplied willingly. "He was sent away to school in England the same year."

Damien went to school in England? That too she had not known. "Did he never consider a career in the army, like his father?"

"Huzoor is not enamoured of the Indian Army," he replied. "In any case, his obligations to Shalimar have always been his first consideration."

"Major Granville was posted in . . . Rawalpindi, I believe?"

"No, begum sahiba, Peshawar. He was with a Gurkha regiment."

"Yes, of course. And that was where he met the late Mrs. Granville, where they eventually married." He nodded and, as if in affirmation of what she already knew, she did too. "Major Granville retired rather young from the army to settle in Kashmir when he did, did he not?"

"Burra huzoor took early retirement."

Noting the slight hesitation, she risked a shot in the dark. "Because of . . . that business?"

"Unfortunately, yes."

She sensed an undertone of unease. The "unfortunately" was a clue, but since he presumed that she knew the reason, she could hardly pursue it.

"It was all rather unpleasant, my husband said. But perhaps in the long run," another daring little nudge, "it was worth it."

"Oh yes. His Highness approved wholeheartedly of his scheme and I am told burra huzoor never regretted his resignation. To his good fortune, the weavers' village took fast and firm root in the valley. Since then it has done much to encourage the weaving industry. The long-term success of the project, he felt, had more than compensated for the loss of an army career."

So that was how Major Granville managed to have his Shalimar! It was not difficult to read between the lines. "Since foreigners are not allowed to own land in Kashmir, the maharaja's concession of such a large estate to an Englishman could not have been viewed very favourably in the valley."

"It was not, I believe. Voices were raised, indeed, still are. But in those days the political climate in Kashmir was very different to what it is today. The British were not so firmly entrenched and Maharaja Ranbir Singh exercised enough power to be able to sanction the scheme. As long as the property is used to provide employment to skilled artisans and to increase the prosperity and prestige of Kashmir, the family will continue to enjoy the status of *mulkis,* state citizens."

"And if not?"

"If they bring Kashmir into disrepute or happen to die without leaving an heir, perish the thought," he gave a small, delicate cough, "then the estate will revert to the state."

"And has it?" Emma asked with a heightening of colour and glad of the dark. "Increased the prestige of Kashmir, I mean?"

"Undoubtedly. The weaving project still produces very fine quality shawls and there is no dearth of discerning buyers. However, nothing can truly compensate for what was subsequently lost."

Subsequently lost? Suraj Singh's expression was unsuspecting; certainly he appeared not to question her right to further information. Even so, she did not dare ask for an explanation, at least not yet, and took refuge in a nod and inaudible murmurings.

"Huzoor has never recovered from the shock, as begum sahiba must already know."

Shock of his mother's death? Of that mysterious scandal?

"My husband was saying," she ventured, "that it was his great love for his estate and his work that helped his father to carry on after ... it happened."

"Very possibly."

"Were they happy in their marriage?" she asked boldly.

Another hesitation, a perceptible stiffening. "I am not in a position to say. I have always assumed so."

So, they were *not* happy!

"I'm sure the late Mrs. Granville must have found much to interest her in the valley," Emma murmured as she foraged for other questions. "Certainly the mountains must have reminded her of her own country and its beautiful Austrian Alps."

"I ... I ... beg your pardon?" He seemed startled. It was the wrong remark to have made! "Perhaps it would be more appropriate for huzoor to acquaint begum sahiba with the rest."

Thrown off balance by his reaction to her innocuous comment, Emma started to improvise reparation but then stopped. The damage was done, and in any case it was too late; Suraj Singh was already on his feet and his expression had closed. Assuming a light smile, she looked around her, remarked on the serenity of the night and asked when they might expect to reach the foothills. Visibly relieved, he informed her that the Pir Panjal range was still some days' travel away and asked, hopefully, if the begum sahiba were tired of riding and might consider making use of the palanquin that followed.

Amused by his persistence, she thanked him but declined. "Not being entirely unused to long hours in the saddle, Suraj Singh, I assure you I do not tire easily."

He pulled in a long breath. "If I may be permitted to say so, begum sahiba is a very courageous lady and huzoor a very fortunate husband."

Quickly he slipped away.

*F*ollowing the defeat of the Sikhs by the East India Company's forces at the Battle of Sobraon in 1846, Lord Hardinge, the Governor-General, recommended that the wings of the Sikhs be clipped for the future security of the British. The best means of achieving this, it was decided, was to deprive them of Kashmir.

Consequently, Kulu, Mandi, Nurpur and Kangra were amputated and retained by the East India Company. The Kashmir valley, Ladakh and Baltistan were sold off to their loyal Dogra ally, Maharaja Gulab Singh of

Jammu, for seven and a half million rupees as a reward for his support during the conquest of the Punjab. Under the Treaty of Amritsar, Gulab Singh became the first Dogra maharaja of Kashmir, ruler of two and a half million subjects across eighty-five thousand square miles of some of the most coveted and spectacular country in the world.

What concerned the British far more than scenic beauty, however, was the strategic importance of Kashmir as a frontier state. In their determination to secure the northern boundaries, and using the threat of a Russian invasion across the Himalayas as an excuse, they appointed a Political Officer in Srinagar in 1870. It was only a matter of time before their grip tightened. In 1887, the Political Officer was replaced by a full-fledged Resident armed with enough powers to overrule the maharaja and fully and firmly exercise Calcutta's will.

As they arrived at the summit of the Pir Panjal Pass and she had her first look at the country below, however, none of this political history was of the slightest interest to Emma.

If the approach to the pass with its deep oak woods, scarlet rhododendron and yellow campanulatum was picturesque enough, the view from the hospice fairly took her breath away. There was light snowfall in the pass; the air was crackling fresh and gusting winds lifted little flurries of snow high into the skies. Emma untied her woollen scarf from her head, removed her leather gloves and let the snowflakes play in her hair. Picking up a fistful of snow, she held it between her bare palms until her flesh turned numb, marvelling at the panorama unfolding before them.

"No valley the length and breadth of Kashmir with an unbroken ring of high mountains exists anywhere else in the world." Suraj Singh said. "Looking at it today it is difficult to imagine the valley as a lake, as it was thousands of years ago."

> *Enclosed on all sides like a precious jewel*
> *Learning, lofty houses, saffron, icy water and grapes*
> *Things that even in heaven are difficult to find . . .*

Emma's quotation of the lines by a sixth-century poet invoked Suraj Singh's immediate approval. "Begum sahiba has studied Kashmir well. It is unusual to find such scholarship in a European lady. No wonder begum sahiba has earned the admiration of huzoor."

Had she? she wondered.

On the descent the vast grassy carpet was woven in a thousand shades of green, lavender and gold; the vibrancy of the flora was amazing. Threading their way through sprawling meadows, shadowed glades and emerald forests were streams fluffy with foam, their banks ablaze with honeysuckle, jasmine, azalea, clematis and wild roses. Fruit trees were heavy with blossom—apple, pear, peach, apricot, cherry and mulberry. Waving fields of paddy, saffron crocus and wild flowers covered the slopes, making them seem enamelled. And on all sides, reaching high into the intense blue of the sky above this unique valley of eternal spring, were the snowy peaks of the Himalayas. It was like a shop-window so laden with splendid wares that one did not know where to look first, and the sight brought tears to Emma's eyes.

She had always suspected that the descriptions she had read of the Vale of Kashmir were imaginative excesses. She saw now that they were not so. If anything, the reality exceeded her expectations. It seemed to her incredible that here ordinary people could lead ordinary lives as humdrum as in a less endowed world. So much beauty concentrated in one blessed valley—why, it seemed quite unfair to the rest of the world.

"Begum sahiba is impressed?"

Emma nodded, unable to tell Suraj Singh that perhaps for once in her life begum sahiba was speechless.

As they ate their last outdoor meal of the journey beside a brook in a meadow covered in wild violets and narcissi, Suraj Singh pointed out peaks considered sacred by the Hindus: Harmukh to the east and Mahadeo to the south. To the east and north rose the ranges beyond which lay Zanskar, Ladakh and the giant Karakorams.

"Many of these peaks have never been scaled," he said.

"Nor, perhaps, should be," Emma declared. "It seems unthinkable that human footprints should defile virgin slopes many believe to be the abode of the gods."

It was as they were almost upon the town of Srinagar and could catch glimpses of Dal Lake upon which it stood that Emma felt a return of the earlier nervousness.

"How far are we now from Shalimar?" she asked.

"About fifteen miles, begum sahiba. It is situated to the west of Srinagar on the road to Baramulla."

"The estate must be a matter of great pride to my husband."

He considered a moment. "To huzoor, Shalimar is more than a matter of pride," he said quietly. "Shalimar is his life."

She was surprised to see that his usually impassive eyes were suddenly very troubled.

*I*t was dusk by the time they arrived at the outskirts of Srinagar. Situated at an elevation of just over five thousand feet above sea level, the ancient city was founded by the Buddhist emperor Ashoka in the third century before Christ. Calling a halt in a large meadow, Suraj Singh started to reorganise the caravan. Sharifa, her niece, one khidmatgar and he himself were to remain with Emma for the night and escort her to Shalimar the following morning. The rest were to continue to the estate with the baggage.

"My husband has a house in Srinagar?" Emma was pleased at the prospect of an overnight stay in the town.

"Not a house, begum sahiba, a houseboat. It is called *Nishat* and it is moored on the Dal."

She was even more pleased. The floating homes on the lakes of Kashmir, said to have been first suggested by the Moghul emperor Akbar, were known to be picturesque and comfortable.

Once in the town they dismounted and walked, for the streets were narrow and crowded. There was brisk selling in the stalls that lined the cobbled lanes. Local people in skullcaps, turbans and flowing robes stared unabashedly, still not used to the sight of white-faced women in their streets. Not minding the stares in the least, Emma stared right back and equally hard.

"What do they carry inside their *phirrens*?" She pointed to the curiously bulging stomachs beneath the long garments. *"Kangris?"*

"Yes, begum sahiba."

The bulge did look comical, but Emma had read that few Kashmiris would dream of abandoning the little earthenware pots of glowing coals fitted into wicker baskets that they wore suspended from their waists in order to stay warm.

"What do they use for fuel?"

"Huk, begum sahiba—charcoal made from driftwood and dried chinar leaves. Both burn long and provide good heat."

"Is it not dangerous to keep the stoves under one's clothes?"

"Well, accidents do happen," Sharifa admitted cheerfully, "but every Kashmiri child learns early to be careful."

The air had freshened. Emma pulled her thick fleece-lined jacket closer around her as from a rough timber jetty they stepped onto a wooden stairway leading up to the *Nishat.* The waters of the lake were thick with lotus leaves and alive with the reflected lights of the town. Faint streaks of colour still touched the western horizon and the snowy caps of the mountains were pink, like luminisent cones.

Identified by a neat sign on the prow, the *Nishat* sat high on the water. It was flat-roofed and a composite establishment of several boats tied together. In the master boat was a sizeable sitting room, two bedroom suites, a dining room and a covered deck aft and fore. The kitchens, storehouses and servants' quarters were on the auxiliary boats attached alongside. Comfortable furniture, deep pile Ispahan carpets, drapes, walls adorned with paintings and bookcases, and every possible domestic convenience gave the rooms a feel of home.

"Does my husband stay here often?" Emma inquired.

"Whenever he passes through Srinagar," Suraj Singh replied. "Huzoor has many business interests in town."

Her travelling bags had been arranged neatly in the dressing-room that adjoined the master bedroom, obviously the suite that Damien used during his visits. Unlike the furnishings in the Delhi house, here the materials were light, flowery chintzes and the carved furniture was of honey-coloured walnut wood. The fourposter that dominated the room had a fringed canopy and the vases were filled with spring blossoms. On a desk stood a pipe-rack, as well stocked as the bookcase. Some of Damien's clothes hung in the large almirah and a pair of fleece-lined slippers peeped out from under the bed. The room had a pervasive scent of tobacco such as she had noticed in the Delhi mansion.

It felt strange to be among Damien's personal belongings, for in the Delhi house they had not shared a bedroom. Also, mundane mementos of Damien's powerful personality brought home the fact that what had been a leisurely interlude of personal independence was soon to end. Tomorrow she would be at Shalimar, once more at the beck and call of a stranger, once more expected to don the mantle of a dutiful, subservient wife. On the one hand, the prospect was touched with a strange sort of hesitant expectancy; on the other, she dreaded the inevitable tensions, the constant friction and the debilitating arguments. The inescapable intimacy of the nights! She would be forever on her guard, forever suppressing rebellion. It was a depressing thought, but then she remembered that tomorrow, at least, was still hers and the depression lifted.

After a warm bath and a satisfying meal of freshly baked Indian bread, spiced lamb chops and fruit, Emma climbed up to the terrace roof of the houseboat to sit in the open and watch the stars mirrored in the waters, to inhale the cool, moist fragrances of spring and to imbibe the feel of a new culture in a new environment. However, no sooner had she settled in her chair than her eyelids drooped. Trying to stay awake and not succeeding, she eventually gave up the struggle and returned to the bedroom. It was the first time in days that she was to enjoy the feel of a truly comfortable bed; she was asleep almost as soon as her head touched her pillow.

She awoke early to the glorious light of morning. Through the bedroom window the lake shimmered like cloth-of-gold. Large pink and white lotus blossoms bobbed up and down on the ripples and an astonishing variety of vessels navigated the waters. Several other houseboats, some unoccupied, were moored along the banks being prepared for the annual influx of tourists. Revived and full of energy, Emma greeted the day with enthusiasm.

"Since I would like to see something of the town," she said after breakfast, "I suggest that the journey to Shalimar be postponed by a day."

Suraj Singh showed immediate alarm, as she knew he would. "Huzoor has ordered that . . ."

"Huzoor will understand my keenness to explore Srinagar," she insisted. "One day here or there will make little difference."

Having already learned that argument with the intractable begum sahiba was a wasted exercise, he capitulated with his usual grace and offered resignedly to order a palanquin.

"I will walk," Emma declared firmly. "It would be foolish not to use one's legs in a town so specifically designed for them." Without giving him a chance to protest, she ran down the stairs and onto the shore.

In the narrow, meandering lanes, a jumble of wooden houses lined the cramped, cobbled byways. They had peaked roofs, latticed windows with intricate shutters and gave the town a look of quaintness. At one time, Emma had discovered, there were as many as seven hundred Moghul gardens in Kashmir. The most famous of these, the Shalimar Baug after which the estate was named, was located on the rim of the Dal, as were several others. With so little time at her disposal, the most Emma could hope for on this initial visit was a whirlwind tour of just one garden.

"It would be disrespectful not to give the gardens the attention they deserve, begum sahiba," Suraj Singh protested when she expressed her intention. "There is much to be admired in each."

"I can always return for a second visit later, Suraj Singh. Surely we can spare an hour or two for the Shalimar Baug today?"

"Not if some of the shops are also to be explored, for they are in quite another direction. I understand begum sahiba wishes to purchase a gift for huzoor?"

Since it was the first Emma had heard of it, she wondered just how Suraj Singh had come to "understand" that. However, placed in an awkward position, she had no choice but to concur. "Very well," she sighed, not wishing to appear churlish. "I suppose we shall have to keep the Shalimar for another occasion."

Mention of a gift for Damien suddenly brought to mind the exquisite shawl he had left for her in Delhi. It had not occurred to her to reciprocate, but now that she had no choice in the matter, she decided to make the gesture with good grace.

The small, dark shops of the bazaar were again crowded with shoppers. In pursuit of the gift he had obviously decided that Emma should buy, Suraj Singh guided her to an emporium where, he maintained, only goods of the highest quality were to be found. They entered a house through a low doorway, crossed a courtyard and climbed a stone staircase into a bright, airy room filled with colorful handicrafts. There were shawls, carpets, papier-mâché artefacts, walnut-wood carvings, silver trinkets and cupboards full of coats, jackets, *phirrens* and bolts of shimmering silk in every conceivable shade.

The owner of the emporium, a squat, balding Kashmiri with a handlebar moustache and small, podgy hands, was, she was informed, chief art adviser to the maharaja. All smiles and sweeping bows and flowery words of welcome, he received them effusively. His name, he informed Emma, was Jabbar Ali. His family had come from Bokhara many decades earlier to settle in the valley. His emporium, he added grandly, like those of Pestonjee and Abdoos, was an establishment renowned across the length and breadth of Hindustan, the property of himself and his brother Hyder Ali, who was away at present. All that explained, he settled down to business.

"A gift for huzoor?" Jabbar Ali was rapturous. "As it happens, I have *just* what the begum sahiba seeks."

Since Emma had not the vaguest idea what it was she sought, she waited with some amusement to see what the wily Kashmiri would produce. He disappeared into an inner room and appeared almost immediately with a large leather box. Before displaying his wares, however, he arranged his important customer comfortably on a thick floor mattress lined with bolsters and ordered a samovar of *qahwa,* traditional Kashmiri tea served steaming hot and heavily laced with spices. Then he opened the box and from within extracted an armful of embroidered woollen jackets. They were sleeveless, high-collared, with two pockets on either side. The wool was as smooth as cream and the silken embroidery, deft and delicate, was expertly executed. On the inside, the jackets were lined with silk which gave them a most superior finish.

"Is this pashmina wool?" asked Emma, fingering the fabric.

"But of course!" Jabbar Ali was shocked that she could have thought otherwise. "I would not dare offer anything but the very best for a gentleman of huzoor's discernment."

The jackets were admittedly beautiful, but Emma had absolutely no inkling of Damien's likes and dislikes in the matter of colours and designs. She looked uncertainly at Suraj Singh and held up two of the most striking examples for his inspection.

"The pale blue with the saffron and white embroidery," Suraj Singh declared promptly. "As begum sahiba must have noticed, huzoor dislikes the colour beige. He maintains that beige is for beige people." He allowed himself the rare luxury of a smile. "Huzoor is extremely partial to these jackets. Unfortunately, he very recently destroyed the only one he possessed by putting in its pocket a pipe that was not fully extinguished. He was very upset at the loss."

The matter settled nicely and quickly, Emma was much relieved. She might have been manoeuvred into buying the gift, but now that the deed was done she was well pleased with her purchase. While the jacket was being parcelled, they sipped tea and Jabbar Ali made impassioned efforts to tempt her with other offerings, from daggers to dressing-table sets. Knowing the ways of shopkeepers only too well, she fielded his persuasions with a question.

"Oh yes, begum sahiba," he said proud to be asked, "The chinar leaf and the paisley have always been motifs greatly favoured by our weavers. Also the *jigha,* of course, the almond-shaped ornament with an aigrette of feathers first worn by the Moghul emperor Babar in his turban. One of the weavers imitated the design in a royal scarf and it was so well liked that the emperor ordered the design to be copied all over Hindustan and Persia."

Flattered by Emma's genuine interest, he went on to inform her that the art of weaving in Kashmir went back four thousand years, had been put to many uses, and that Maharaja Ranjit Singh's royal tents, for instance, were made from *kani* and *jam-e-war* shawls.

"Indeed, our Kashmiri shawls have also been high fashion in Europe since Napoleon bought many for his empress Josephine on a state visit to Egypt."

The transaction—and the mandatory social chit-chat without which no sale in India was considered complete—having finally concluded, they rose to leave.

"On behalf of myself and my absent brother, Hyder Ali," Jabbar Ali said, his voice hushed with reverence, "I offer humble felicitations to begum sahiba and huzoor on the joyous occasion of their nuptials. *Mahshallah!* It is truly a match made by the angels of heaven."

Or more likely, Emma thought with grim amusement as she stepped out into the sunshine, *by the devils of the other place!*

CHAPTER

9

$\mathcal{S}$halimar!

The wrought-iron gates, tall and painted black, stood between two tidy lodges festooned with creepers and tumbling white blossoms. Well oiled, they swung open to receive the cavalcade and the liveried watchmen manning them offered salaams. Emma peered through the curtain of her palanquin but was unable to discern much from her cloistered seat. On this occasion, much to Suraj Singh's relief, the use of the hated contraption was not rejected. Whatever her private feelings about Damien, Emma conceded readily that it would be unseemly for his bride to arrive astride a horse. Whether or not huzoor approved, certainly the conservative staff would not, and she had no desire to add to her troubles by starting a new life on the wrong foot.

From what little she could see through the swaying chink, the winding drive was lined with chinars bordering an impossibly green parkland. Tall flowers, large and fluffy as feather-dusters, waved from well-ordered beds. Packed in tight profusion, nascent pink and lemon and ivory white spring blossoms almost suffocated budding branches. Against a chorus of birdsong, deer grazed, plump brown squirrels scampered up and down contorted tree-trunks and an army of gardeners paused in their labours to stare with unashamed curiosity. Of the house itself, Emma could see nothing.

The palanquin finally came to rest. Relieved to be done with her cramped quarters, Emma tied a scarf about her head and stepped out into a pillared portico. A flight of stone steps leading up to a pair of stained-glass doors was lined with men, women and children standing three-deep in hushed silence with their eyes lowered. As she started up the steps, they bent in well-orchestrated unison.

"Who are all these people?" Emma asked Sharifa nervously, responding to the greeting with a nod, a smile and folded hands.

"Huzoor's staff and their families who live and work on the estate. They come to present their respects to huzoor's wife."

But of huzoor himself, Emma noticed, there was neither sight nor sound.

In her privileged position of personal maid to the lady of the house, Sharifa issued imperious orders and everyone scurried about fulfilling them. While the luggage was being unloaded, Suraj Singh ushered Emma through the entrance to the accompaniment of a hum of comments, the gist of some she caught.

"She has a brown skin," a woman whispered in Urdu.

"If she were not so tall," came the response, "she could almost be one of us."

"Well, perhaps she is not a firanghini after all," remarked a third. "She certainly is not as pretty as the others."

The others! Emma bit on a lip, lowered her own head and quickly passed into the house. High-ceilinged and well proportioned, the entrance hall had polished parquet flooring partially covered by geometrically patterned Bokhara carpets. She had a tumbling impression of radiating corridors, great banks of flowers in gleaming bronze vases, tapestries and paintings against pale walls, delicately carved furniture in rich maroons and light walnut, and splashes of buttery spring sunshine. In the tranquil coolness even as a first impression she discerned good taste, elegance and understated wealth. On the carpeted wooden staircase burnished copper vessels held sprays of ferns like dancers in a choreographed ballet; framed photographs dotted the walls. On the landing of the first floor, a pot-bellied porcelain mandarin smiled slyly from a low table as if privy to salacious secrets.

Emma's own apartment across the landing appeared to run at least half the length of the floor. The sitting room, rectangular, breezy and southeast facing, was awash with sunshine. In contrast to the overwhelming opulence of Delhi's rented premises, here there was a sense of discretion, a serene moderation that was restful to the eye. The furnishings were of subdued designs and in pastel shades; antiques in ivory, porcelain and bronze arranged with economy and discrimination compounded the flavour of well-bred refinement. Even the flames in the open fireplace burned with lack of excess. The air was faintly scented. Indications here were of a lived-in home—a home, she recalled with sinking heart, of which she was now the mistress. A large bedroom, a dressing-room and a bath with excellent modern fittings, adjoined the informal sitting room. A glass door led onto an open balcony.

Beyond the bedchamber was a smaller room full of brilliant light, and it brought Emma to an astonished standstill.

"Huzoor ordered a study for begum sahiba," Suraj Singh explained. "If anything has been inadvertently overlooked I am instructed to rectify the omission."

Emma stood in the doorway and stared. A desk. Two glass-fronted cupboards. A revolving bookcase, wall shelves, pictures, a swivel chair, deep pile carpet, velvet curtains, more space than she had ever imagined or, indeed, ever had at her disposal—everything, in fact, that she had ever hoped for in a workplace.

She was overwhelmed.

All in all, it was a beautiful apartment. What brought it truly to life, however, was the vista through the large-paned windows that ran the length of the suite. The verdant slopes outside spilled down into a valley clothed in a patchwork of fields. At the far end, a huddle of slate roofs peeked from behind bottle green trees and tall, cascading rhododendrons. There was living colour everywhere; shades of yellow and pink and cinnamon melted into each other like patterned dyes in a giant mantle. A riot of wild flowers floored one side of the valley in the dip of which gleamed the waters of a lime green stream. And beyond in the far, far distance, majestic and blinding white against a sky of sapphire, towered the guardians of Kashmir, the Himalayas, abode of snow.

And this was what she would awaken to each morning!

The sound of a cough returned Emma to reality. Sensing her unspoken inquiry, Suraj Singh shuffled his feet and dropped his eyes. "I learn from the staff that huzoor is away."

She had half guessed that already, but the confirmation brought a sharp pinprick of something. Relief? Disappointment?

She scanned Suraj Singh's highly embarrassed face. "You did not know that when we arrived he would still be away?"

"I had hoped that he would have returned by now."

"Returned from where?"

"From Leh. Huzoor has gone to receive an urgently awaited consignment of wool."

"He went directly from Delhi?"

"Yes." He handed her an envelope. "This letter arrived from Leh with a courier. Perhaps it contains some further explanations." The soul of discretion, as always, he left her to her letter and positioned himself outside the door.

The envelope was addressed to her not by name but as "Begum Sahiba." The note inside contained just a few sentences:

I am unavoidably delayed by a matter of business and will return as soon as I can. Suraj Singh knows that he must treat your every wish as a command. The staff is entirely at your disposal. Please do with them exactly as you please. I apologise for my absence.

The letter was signed with the initials "D. G." There were no other explanations. The involuntary disappointment disappeared, superseded by relief. A few more days of blessed independence!

"So much for huzoor's orders to hurry back," she remarked tartly as Suraj Singh returned. "We could well have stayed on in Srinagar and visited the gardens."

"Huzoor's orders to me in Delhi were quite clear," he maintained doggedly. "They could not be disobeyed." *Huzoor's orders*—it was a phrase she was beginning to dislike heartily. "Begum sahiba approves of the accommodation?"

Seeing his anxiety to please, Emma bit back a retort and smiled. "How can I not? I have seldom seen a suite with as many delightful aspects, much less lived in one."

He walked to a connecting door at the far end of her sitting room and flung it open. "Huzoor's apartment adjoins. Naturally, begum sahiba is free to make such use of it as she wishes."

Emma nodded but made no move to enter. The tensions of her arrival having dissipated, suddenly she was overcome with fatigue. Assessing that the constantly attentive Suraj Singh with a thousand duties done and a thousand still awaiting must also be tired, she dismissed him as well as the maidservants. Closing the door behind them, she sank into a settee and laid her head back.

For a while she simply sat and savoured her surroundings, inhaling deeply of the scented air, basking in the touch of sunshine on her cheeks, revelling in the views. Then, kicking off her sandals, she wandered about the room to luxuriate in the deep, warm softness underfoot, the smoothness of the furnishings, the crisp crackle of taffeta as she swung the curtains back and forth. Enjoying the rare gift of unlimited space, she revelled in the sight of the drawers and shelves in the dressing-room almirahs, and marvelled again at the mountains, reaching out in her mind for a touch of snow on her fingers. Finally, unable to repress her curiosity, she opened the connecting door and went into Damien's apartment.

In size and shape it was a mirror image of her own, but very much a male preserve. The parlour was furnished with tan leather armchairs, sober furnishings in unadorned earth colours and well-filled bookcases. Without being austere it had a look of formality, of function rather than cosmetic appeal. Whiffs of a now familiar tobacco and a silver hookah by the fireplace accentuated the masculine flavour. Even though Damien was away, a low fire burned in the grate, perhaps as a contingency for an unexpected return.

The rooms contained many of Damien's belongings Emma remembered from the Delhi house. From a hook behind the bathroom door was suspended his silken robe; by the side of the washbasin rested a Meerschaum pipe, half-filled and forgotten. A pocket-watch, no doubt wound daily by Hakumat despite his master's absence, lay ticking on the dresser. In a double-fronted, mirrored mahogany almirah with carved panels, among several others hung the dove grey suit he had worn for the wedding.

A small room, Damien's study, led off the bedchamber and corresponded to her own; the door was not locked. What caught her eye immediately and held it was a grouping of family photographs in papier-mâché frames on a shelf behind the desk. A well-built gentleman in army uniform wearing a jaunty hat stood stiffly at attention against a tent surrounded by forest. Edward Granville? He was a handsome man, with stern, piercing eyes, but his features bore little resemblance to those of his son. The other two photographs were of Damien with his father, one on shikar holding the rifle responsible for the mound of partridges at their feet, and the other in blazer, trousers and tie against a brooding Gothic structure—his school in England? There was a third figure in the picture, a boy of about Damien's age also in school uniform. Emma stared for a while at the youthful image of her husband. The gawky, angular schoolboy with the rigid neck, melancholy eyes and hesitant half smile seemed so different from the self-assured man she knew that she could barely reconcile the two images. There were no photographs of the late Mrs. Granville.

On a sloping draughtsman's table were boxes of calligraphy pens and an array of artists' tools. Shelves held books on wool weaving and shawls, local flora, fauna and history. A large, tissue-paper-leaved album enclosed intricate hand-painted diagrams and designs. Correspondence was stored in alphabetically marked pigeon holes and several fat folders were stacked on various other shelves.

Standing amidst personal souvenirs of a man she still viewed as an enigma, Emma suddenly felt out of place, a trespasser in forbidden territory. Quickly she left the room and the apartment to return to her own. At a loss over what to do next, she wandered into her own study. Perching on a corner of the desk for a while, Emma stared out at the distant mountains. Reflected vermilion light washed over them as the sun, done for the day, slid into the snowy troughs behind and an indigo blue night descended upon the ranges.

The gathering dark accelerated a sense of rare self-pity. However welcome she chose to consider the solitude, Damien's absence was humiliating. That he should not be here to welcome her to her new home was an act of indefensible insensitivity. Brought up in modest circumstances where lack of money was an everyday fact of life, she was awed and intimidated by this affluent, elegant mansion she was now expected to run. She knew nothing of the routine of the household, nothing about its inmates. What exactly were to be her duties in an establishment already well ordered and competently serviced? How was she expected to behave, and who was to tell her what caused offence and what did not? If nothing else, Damien's presence would have helped her to tide over the inevitable awkwardness of the early days.

Had none of this occurred to him when he took off from Delhi without so much as a look over his shoulder?

Feeling desperately alone, indeed abandoned, Emma's eyes thickened with tears. She ran a forefinger around the clean, straight lines of the desk as if to gain reassurance, and impatiently blinked away the tears. Closing her eyes, she forced in them a vision of herself hard at work at her new desk. However beloved and well used, the study in Khyber Kothi she had inherited from her father had been inadequate, eternally short of storage space and working surfaces. Here, there would be no such constraints.

In her imagination, behind closed lids, she arranged the study to her satisfaction. She littered the desk with her father's papers; a pile of reference books she placed to her right next to his folio of maps and charts and diagrams; behind them she made space for her favourite family photograph. Her father's treasured collection of Buddhist relics collected from far-flung, little-known lamaseries—images and icons, birchbark scrolls, tankhas, oil lamps, instruments of worship and ritual—she neatly labelled and indexed and arranged in the glass-fronted cupboards along the far wall. The slim drawers of the tallboy proved perfect for his collection of photographs and sketches. His books, catalogued and marked, fitted nicely into the many shelves available in the bookcases. The small table in the far corner she placed next to her desk and on it positioned her cherished typewriting machine.

The vivid exercise in fantasy proved to be salutary; it brought a touch of reality to the moment, a renewed focus to her mind. Surrounded once again by what was comfortably familiar, she rectified her tilting balances and regained her sense of purpose. Jumping off the desk, she shook off her despondency and tugged at the bell-rope beside the desk. As Sharifa appeared, she asked for a pot of lemon tea, hot water for a much needed bath, a light supper of vegetable broth, toast and fruit, and ordered the sconces and paraffin lamps to be lit.

Tomorrow she would start to reorganise her life and rearrange her perspectives. And tonight, she promised herself, she would neither think nor dream of Damien.

*N*or did she.

Rested, refreshed and full of bounce, she awoke, quite literally, with the birds. A perky blue and yellow pair fluttered against the window, making shrill noises which Emma interpreted as a demand for breakfast. The distant mountains were awash with dawn orange. A first ray of sun touched a peak and set it ablaze, and in a matchlight effect the entire range burst into flame. Springing out of bed, she threw open the window, tossed a handful of biscuits up into the dew-fresh air and laughed at the shrill scrambles below.

She bathed, breakfasted on surprisingly English fare of porridge, eggs and fresh cottage cheese from the dairy, and started to unpack her trunks. While she stacked books and papers on the desk and shelves, Sharifa sorted out the mountain of soiled clothes accumulated during the journey and despatched them to the dhobi house with her son, Hakumat. He was, Emma observed, a well-behaved young man with agile fingers, a quiet intelligence, abundant energy and an eagerness to please. Having brought some semblance of order to the apartment, Emma sent for Suraj Singh and pronounced herself ready to receive the staff that waited to be presented.

Apart from those who worked within the house, there were a host of others employed on the estate: Brentford Lincoln, the Eurasian estate manager, and his staff; agricultural workers and gardeners; dairymen; compounders from the dispensary; servants with multiple functions and many with wives or husbands and families. The weavers in the village on the edge of the estate were a separate community and would be visited later. Emma asked questions, ventured comments and tried to play the châtelaine with grace. Privately, however, she was dismayed; how on earth could she ever get to know each one individually as she would be expected to?

And so many to serve just one man! The involuntary thought touched her heart with unexpected sadness.

Her first essential duty concluded, it was time, Suraj Singh said, for a conducted tour of the house. Not quite as large as she had earlier envisaged, the house was symmetrically built, its two wings divided by a wood-panelled formal salon on the first floor and a corresponding dining room below. Both wings contained a succession of long corridors and high-ceilinged rooms. The north wing was kept locked. At the back, some distance from the house, were the servants' quarters and compound, the dairy, kitchens, store and dhobi houses. The granaries, stables, carriage house and other outhouses were to the west between the orchards and the main building. The master kitchen and pantry on the ground floor showed commendable signs of spit and polish under the supervision of the senior cook, a Kashmiri Brahmin, and the larders were filled with large, clean vats stocked with rice, wheat, lentils and a variety of cereals that showed no signs of weavils. The estate offices, Suraj Singh informed her, were some distance away from the house and screened from view by a grove of plane trees.

On closer examination, Emma realised, the house revealed an aspect not included in her hazy impressions of the day before. What she had interpreted as pleasant tranquillity then was in fact something quite different, a feel of apathy, indeed, a sense of decay. Well appointed and meticulously maintained, the rooms were nevertheless cold, impersonally arranged shop-windows assembled for the benefit of passers-by, waiting rooms in which no one waited. The salons and reception rooms rang hollow, like vast shells resounding with echoes of forgotten, long-vanished seas. The pall of melancholy lay everywhere, as inescapable as the all-pervasive scent of pine. Motes of dust dancing and diving in the thrusting swathes of sunlight appeared to be the only movement in a still world bereft of life.

At the same time there was in the rooms an odd, almost eerie, sense of expectancy. The grand Steinway in the music room, long out of tune, pleaded mutely to be played. Untouched in years, the racks of stiffly erect billiard-cues and shrouded table seemed poised and ready for the game to begin. On the polished mahogany dining table for twenty-four, unlaid in decades, the candles appealed for just a touch of a match to spring to life, as did the chandeliers, and a mere chord or two, it appeared, was all that was required for heels to start tapping on the dance floor and the ball to begin.

Once again Emma had an involuntary vision of a man sitting and eating alone in his apartment surrounded by flurries of servants and layers of unbroken silences, and once again something unexpected tugged at her heart.

The tour concluded in the basement, cleverly built into a rockface, that served as a wine cellar and did duty as a natural icebox for storage of the estate's perishable produce. As they eventually re-emerged on the ground floor, Emma turned to proceed to the left and found herself confronted by a padlocked grille.

"The apartments along this corridor were occupied by burra huzoor and his wife," Suraj Singh explained in answer to her query. "Unfortunately, the parquet is riddled with woodworm, which has rendered it unsafe. Huzoor ordered the corridor to be locked after a servant boy fell through the floor and broke his leg. One of these days, no doubt, huzoor will find time to consider repairs."

The locked section of the house, Emma calculated, lay directly beneath their own apartments on the first floor.

"Did you say that my husband is in Leh awaiting a consignment of wool?"

"Yes, begum sahiba."

"The pashmina for the weaving comes from Leh?"

"Well, it comes from the mountains. Huzoor usually receives it personally to ensure that it is of the requisite quality."

She was about to remark on her brother's posting in Leh, but recalling the hostility between Damien and David, she left the thought unsaid. "I believe there was a time when the only way to secure this wool was to gather it from the plateaux of Tibet?"

"Yes, begum sahiba, but now it is simpler to hire tribesmen to do the job since they know the mountains well."

"The goats are sheared in the wild?"

"Mountain goats do not need to be sheared. In winter, they grow extra layers of down on their underbellies. When the weather turns warm, they shed the extra layers by rubbing themselves against rocks and thorny bushes. It is this discarded fleece that the tribesmen gather and deliver in Leh."

"Surely local goats also produce under-fleece?"

"Yes, but of an inferior quality. Burra huzoor tried to breed mountain goats here, but because of the lack of extreme cold the animals had no need to grow extra coats and the experiment failed. What was comparatively successful was a project to cross-breed wild goats with our own. The fleece they produce is nothing as fine as pashmina or *shatoosh,* but then there is also a demand for medium-quality shawls that are relatively inexpensive."

"Well, I am most intrigued by the processes that produce these exquisite garments. When do we go to the weavers' village?"

"This afternoon after luncheon, if begum sahiba wishes."

They had been walking down yet another long corridor, having traversed several of similar length, and Emma remarked on the fact.

"All told there is a half mile of corridors on the three floors of the house," Suraj Singh informed her.

"Good heavens! You have actually measured them?"

"Yes, begum sahiba."

"With a tape measure?"

"No, begum sahiba. With my paces."

Puzzled, she was about to ask another question, but she saw that he was uncomfortable with the subject, perhaps because of his limp. "How very ingenious," she murmured and left it at that.

Following a cursory luncheon, Emma changed into her riding-habit in preparation for their visit to the weavers' village. It was a demure habit meant for riding side-saddle; recognising that to undermine Damien's dignity on the estate would be to undermine her own, she again compromised willingly. In deference to local custom, once more she covered her head with a scarf.

They were about halfway to the stable house when Hakumat came hurrying after them to announce the arrival of a visitor.

"A visitor?" With some surprise Emma examined the card the bearer presented. "Who is Mrs. Chloe Hathaway?"

"Mrs. Hathaway is a widowed lady resident in Srinagar," Suraj Singh said. "Mr. Hathaway was revenue commissioner at the time of his death three years ago and a friend of huzoor."

"Well, since she has taken the trouble to come all this way, I suppose I had better receive her. Tell me, Suraj Singh, is it customary in the valley to call without prior intimation?"

"No, begum sahiba, it is not customary." Suraj Singh looked most put out. "But then Mrs. Hathaway is a lady not particularly concerned with what is customary."

"Oh?" Emma's eyes twinkled. "In that case I absolutely must meet the poor old dear! Apart from being my very first visitor, a woman unconcerned with custom is someone after my very own heart."

A few moments later—after a swift change back into a dress and sandals—as Emma stepped into the formal reception room, she halted in surprise. For some reason she had presumed Mrs. Hathaway to be a lady of advanced years; she saw now that she could not have been more wrong. The person confronting her was not only young but striking—as far removed from a "poor old dear" as anyone could possibly be. The tall, lissome figure was well contoured, the coiffure chic and the smartly cut blue linen suit with its trimmings of Brussels lace very modish indeed. Curved in a smile of great charm, the luminous pink lips were full and the pencilled eyebrows quite expertly trimmed into perfect arcs. Indeed, Mrs. Hathaway's grooming was impeccable enough not to be faulted even in the fashionable salons of London and Paris. For an instant Emma remained transfixed; then, hastily recovering her composure as well as her manners, she smiled, extended a hand and stepped forward.

"Mrs. Hathaway? I am Emma Wyn . . . er . . . Granville." She coloured faintly at the slip. "How very kind of you to call. I am delighted to make your acquaintance."

Chloe Hathaway enclosed the proffered hand between cool palms and subjected her to a deep and long look. Finally, she relaxed her scrutiny and widened her smile. "Thank you. I believe Damien is away again?" Unsurprisingly, her voice was as carefully modulated as her appearance.

"Yes, but I expect him to return any day now," Emma replied, without abandoning her own smile.

"Well, I have to say that the man is really quite impossible!" Mrs. Hathaway lowered herself gracefully into a wing chair and let her lace shawl slip off her shoulders. "He promised to come and see me when he returned from Delhi but then went off again without a peep. I shall have words to say to him when I see him, I promise. So must you, my dear," she advised sternly. "Not even Damien should be forgiven for abandoning his bride to the tender mercies of an empty house."

"Hardly empty, Mrs. Hathaway," Emma pointed out with a half laugh to cover her embarrassment. "I should imagine there are at least one third as many people at Shalimar as in Srinagar. As it happens, Damien went to Leh on urgent business directly from Delhi without returning home." Even as she said it she wondered why on earth she should bother with excuses for one who so little deserved them.

"Oh, phooey—Damien's business is always urgent." Chloe Hathaway dismissed the alibi airily. "If I were you, my dear, I wouldn't believe every excuse the man offers—take it from me, he has an entire treasury of them, some quite rare gems of ingenuity. Anyway," she flashed even, well-graded teeth, "I am pleased to have met you at last, Mrs. Granville. After having heard so much about you, I have to confess my curiosity was quite feverish—which accounts for my barging in rudely without notice."

"Heard about me? From whom, may I ask?"

Chloe Hathaway's tuneful laugh, like very tiny bells, was as alluring as everything else about her. "Ah! That would be telling . . . but we do have common friends in Delhi." She hesitated a minim, then relented. "As a matter of fact the Prices, Reggie and Georgina, among others. I believe you do know them?"

Emma nodded, well able to imagine the accounts Mrs. Hathaway had received of her from them! She turned to search for the bell-rope, but watching discreetly from somewhere, Hakumat materialised in the doorway unsummoned. Not knowing precisely what to order, Emma simply asked for tea and refreshments. She experienced a moment of uncertainty wondering what the cooks would produce without specific instructions, but then decided to leave the tea to fate and returned her attention to her visitor.

"And what are your early impressions of Kashmir?" Mrs. Hathaway was asking. "Are you already in love with it as everyone else appears to be—or do you find yourself missing the social whirligig of Delhi?"

"Since I arrived only yesterday, it would be rather presumptuous of me to express a categorical opinion," Emma replied, "but I can see how easy it would be to surrender one's heart to Kashmir. As for the social whirligig of Delhi, as you call it, no, I don't miss any of it and doubt very much if I will."

"And the estate? What do you think of Damien's Shalimar?"

"That, too, I have not yet had time to explore. In fact, I was about to be escorted around just as you were announced."

Chloe Hathaway took the remark in her stride by ignoring it. "Well, it's a place *I've* always adored," she declared. "Such order, such privacy, such heavenly solitude—so removed from the filth and clamour of Srinagar."

"You know Shalimar well?" Emma asked, trying to size up her vivacious visitor without appearing to do so. At close quarters she was older than she had initially seemed. A network of small lines appeared at the corner of her eyes each time she smiled. If not entirely successful, the effort to conceal them with cosmetics was certainly very skilful.

"Oh yes." Mrs. Hathaway's eyes rounded in surprise at the question. "Almost every inch of it, I should say. This was one of Claude's most favourite places, you know."

Assuming that Claude was her late and perhaps not greatly lamented husband, Emma murmured something by way of sympathy, then asked, "You yourself have elected to stay on in Srinagar because the country pleases you?"

"Well, places are really people, aren't they? Much as I love Delhi and Calcutta and Simla, after Claude passed away I simply couldn't bring myself to abandon a place where I have so many caring friends."

"No, I'm sure you could not," Emma agreed, wondering not too kindly if Damien might also be included in the list. "My husband often says that he would find it impossible to live anywhere else."

"Well, Damien is, of course, besotted with his Shalimar—and one can hardly blame him, can one, dear?"

As Mrs. Hathaway's eyes turned towards the doorway, so did Emma's, to see a tall figure being ushered in by Suraj Singh. "May I present a dear friend, Mrs. Granville?" Chloe Hathaway asked, obviously having expected the new arrival. "I wasn't at all sure if he would agree to come in, which is why I didn't mention him earlier. We happened to be returning from Baramulla and it was my idea to stop and present my salaams. Too shy to intrude, he insisted on cooling his heels outside, but I'm pleased that he changed his mind. Perhaps you are already acquainted with Geoffrey's reputation?"

Geoffrey Charlton!

"Oh, indeed." Taken quite by surprise, Emma was flustered. "I'm really very . . . pleased to be meeting Mr. Charlton at last."

"At last?" He clasped her hand and waited for amplification.

"Well, I've read your articles in the *Sentinel,* of course," Emma said breathlessly, trying hard not to sound juvenile. "Your most recent series on Central Asia was admirably informative. And, of course, I immensely enjoyed your lantern slide lecture in Delhi."

He smiled that shy, boyish smile she remembered so well. "Thank you for your commendations, Mrs. Granville. I'm not sure I merit such extravagant praise, but being deplorably human I cannot deny that I am pleased to receive it." The smile turned faintly anxious. "I hope you do not consider my unannounced arrival a rude intrusion, Mrs. Granville? If so, I do beg your forgiveness."

"Indeed, I do not!" Emma exclaimed. "I am delighted Mrs. Hathaway persuaded you to accompany her, Mr. Charlton. Perhaps now I will have a chance to ask all the questions I wanted to in Delhi and was denied the opportunity of doing so."

"Oh, Geoffrey would be only too happy to answer them, I promise," Mrs. Hathaway remarked with a touch of coyness. "Indeed, he's been dying to make your acquaintance, haven't you, darling?" Without waiting for his response, she again turned to Emma. "My dear, I warn you, Geoffrey is known to charm the female of the species with laughable ease. The only ones disinclined to laugh, of course, are the men. They find the charm definitely unamusing."

Geoffrey Charlton had been dying to meet her? Immensely flattered, Emma blushed. She could think of not a thing to say.

"As always, Chloe exaggerates." Taking the banter in his stride, Charlton stepped into the gap without embarrassment. It was obvious that they knew each other extremely well. "Nevertheless, I must plead guilty to the charge. Having once had the honour of meeting Dr. Wyncliffe in the Zanskar valley I have indeed looked forward to making your acquaintance, Mrs. Granville. Like everyone else, I was shocked to learn of his untimely death."

They talked for a moment or two about her father, then in the interests of social correctness Emma asked, "Are you also acquainted with my husband, Mr. Charlton?"

"Well, we have met, of course. It is impossible to be in the valley and not be acquainted with Damien Granville." He left it at that. "You mentioned that you were at the lantern slide lecture and had questions to ask?"

"Oh, hundreds!" Emma laughed, hardly able to believe that she was finally facing the great man in her own home. "I couldn't bring myself to voice any at the Town Hall and after the lecture you were inundated with admirers. And then, of course, you were unable to attend Mrs. Price's burra khana the following week."

"Ah yes, unfortunately I had to leave that very day for Simla. Anyway," he sat back, "now that we have finally met, I place myself entirely at your disposal."

"Dear me!" Mrs. Hathaway replaced a wisp of hair that had dared to stray. "You're not going to talk shop again, Geoffrey dear, are you? I warn you, Mrs. Granville, once Geoffrey boards that Russian train of his, wild horses can't drag him off until every stop is explored, every heap of rubble probed and every last political nuance dissected."

Emma couldn't imagine a more enthralling prospect but refrained from saying so.

"What I've been longing to hear from you, my dear," Mrs. Hathaway continued resolutely, "is the latest *gup-shup* from Delhi. Now tell me—is it true that young Charlotte is sweet on a certain Captain O'Reilly from the Royal Irish who has the most dazzling red hair and is absolutely on the brink of popping the question?"

"I'm afraid I don't really know," Emma confessed. "I am not acquainted with Captain O'Reilly and there was no news of an engagement at the time that I left Delhi."

She had a sudden and quite mischievous urge to add that what Charlotte was absolutely on the brink of was taking holy orders because she had missed netting Damien. However, once again she restrained herself. Undaunted, Chloe Hathaway fired another cannonade of questions about common acquaintances. Woefully ill equipped to provide answers, Emma nevertheless battled valiantly to conjure up little titbits to satisfy her visitor's curiosity.

The door opened and Hakumat entered at the vanguard of several bearers wheeling trolleys of refreshments, bringing to a halt Mrs. Hathaway's eager demands for gossip. As far as the food and its service were concerned, Emma saw that she need not have worried; both were eminently satisfactory. Busying herself with the teapot, she signalled Hakumat to pass around the miraculously produced cake, sandwiches and cheeseballs, and before Mrs. Hathaway could resume the conversation quickly turned to Geoffrey Charlton.

"I appreciate that you needed to condense a great deal in order to remain within the time allocated for the lecture, but I was disappointed that you mentioned so little about the ancient civilisations of Central Asia."

"The omission was deliberate," Charlton replied. "I felt that the audience expected to hear about living, topical matters rather than about the dead bones of history."

"My father often wondered if the Russian government would permit a British team to excavate the three ancient cities of Merv, for instance. I know he would have dearly loved to."

"Well, I doubt it. Russia guards her annexed territories very jealously and Britons, more than others, are naturally suspect. Besides, since the Russian authorities have little interest in conservation, most of the monuments are in a sorry state. The crops are plentiful and there is economic prosperity in the region, but gone, alas, is the splendour of ancient palaces and gardens that have bedazzled travellers for half a millennium."

"Oh dear, how very distressing. Tell me, Mr. Charlton—are you here on some special assignment from your newspaper?"

"Well"—he scratched an ear—"I suppose you could say that."

Emma smiled. "I have heard that journalists dislike revealing details of their work so I will refrain from impolite questions, but I assume that the assignment is to do with Kashmir and that you intend to stay for a while?"

"Oh yes. Quite a while."

She could not have been more pleased and said so. "You have, of course, been to Srinagar before and know it well?"

"Reasonably so. I was here last autumn on my way to Gilgit to meet Algernon Durand. As you must have heard, the defunct Agency has finally been revived."

She had not heard, but then not knowing who Algernon Durand might be or what purpose the Gilgit Agency served, she merely nodded.

"With good reason," Charlton said. "Russian influence in the north grows at an alarming rate. Certainly Durand is most uneasy about infiltrations from across the Pamirs." He sipped at his tea and frowned. "As he is about the misleading information being spread by Russian sympathisers in India."

"Really?" Emma recalled that he had touched upon the subject during his lecture. Not particularly interested then, she tried to appear so now.

He inched forward in his seat. "The problem is, of course, the vulnerability of Kashmir. Were it not that . . ."

"Don't encourage him, Mrs. Granville," Chloe Hathaway interrupted with a gesture of mock horror, "or we'll be here until Christmas! Geoffrey sees Russian agents behind every chinar in the valley."

Quite good-naturedly, Charlton shared in the laugh. "I'm afraid Mrs. Hathaway is right. I do sometimes tend to get carried away."

"Well, so do a great many others, it would appear," Emma commented in swift support. "Certainly in Delhi the men talk of nothing but politics."

"Or business, both equally tiresome! Anyway," Mrs. Hathaway

focussed her attention again on Emma as she nibbled on a slice of plum cake, "did you have occasion to see something of Srinagar on your way up to Shalimar?"

Realising that a more serious conversation with Geoffrey Charlton would have to be kept for another time, Emma sighed inwardly and abandoned the effort. "Not very much, I regret, but I do hope to make a more satisfactory visit later with Damien. Apart from its visual quaintness, Srinagar does offer much by way of history."

"Well, I suppose it does," Mrs. Hathaway crinkled her nose and Emma noticed how perfectly shaped it was, "even though the dirt and lack of hygiene are appalling. The people never wash, you know. And I must say I do find their features rather . . . coarse."

"Coarse? On the contrary, even during our brief stay in town yesterday many of the Kashmiris we saw were extremely handsome."

"Some, perhaps," Chloe Hathaway conceded, "particularly those with pale skins, fair hair, and traces of European blood." She leaned forward, speared a cheeseball and carried it to her plate. "Nazneen, for instance, who only has to change her mode of dress to pass for a European."

Obviously not interested in their conversation, Charlton excused himself and sauntered away to investigate the wall hangings.

"Who is Nazneen?" Emma asked.

Chloe toyed idly with a morsel on her plate. "Oh, Nazneen is a . . . a common friend of ours, mine and Damien's." Leaving reams unsaid, she gave her entire attention to the cheeseball.

"In that case I look forward to meeting her," Emma said steadily, "as I do all my husband's friends in the valley."

They went on to more small talk and Emma tried hard to make her responses sound enthusiastic. Behind her fixed smile, however, she could not help wondering—how well *did* Chloe Hathaway know Damien? She would have been a fool not to see (as she was meant to) that they were better than casually acquainted.

Strolling around the room, Charlton looked greatly impressed as he inspected the tapestries, the Kasan wall hangings, the fine French furniture, the tasteful collection of clocks and Chinese porcelain, gilt mirrors and Belgian glass. Kneeling on the floor, he fingered the scattered carpets to calculate the number of knots per square inch, and then studied each of the photographs in filigreed silver frames arranged on the side tables. Finally, he stood a while in mute thought examining a large portrait of Edward Granville before returning to resume his earlier position.

"I hope you will forgive my unseemly curiosity, Mrs. Granville," he said, seating himself opposite Emma, "but I have heard so much about your husband's estate that I feel I must pay due attention to everything I see."

"Please do feel free to indulge your curiosity, Mr. Charlton," Emma assured him, relieved by his return. "Had my husband been here I'm sure he would have appreciated your interest."

"That portrait of Edward Granville is certainly very skilfully executed," Charlton said. "A similar-sized painting, I note from the faint outline on the wall, has been removed. Was it, by any chance, that of the late Mrs. Granville?"

"Yes, I believe so. A corner of the painting was damaged by damp and it has been sent to Lahore for restoration." Emma repeated the explanations she had received from Suraj Singh when she had remarked on the telltale patch that morning.

"Well, I must say it appears to have been gone a very long time," Mrs. Hathaway murmured as she exchanged a quick look with Charlton.

Intercepting the look, Emma reddened but made no further comment. However well acquainted Mrs. Hathaway might be with Damien and his background, she had no intention of discussing the Granvilles with her or, for that matter, with Geoffrey Charlton.

Mrs. Hathaway smiled, dropped the subject, and the conversation again turned unremarkable. Finally, after a few more moments of casual talk, she rose to leave.

"Come on, Geoffrey dear," she commanded, dusting the front of her dress and patting down her perfectly turned hair, "we really must be away before we outstay our welcome—and before it gets too dark for Mrs. Granville to resume her tour of the estate which, I believe, we interrupted."

"The interruption could not have been more pleasurable, I assure you," Emma offered politely. "The tour was of no great consequence, it can wait till tomorrow." She turned to Charlton and smiled. "Determined as I am to have answers to my questions, Mr. Charlton, you will not be permitted to escape quite so easily the next time we meet."

"I would consider it a privilege and a pleasure." He bowed and his smile was most winning. "But I must warn you, Mrs. Granville, that when talking of Central Asia there is little I enjoy better than the sound of my own voice."

"I take note of the warning, Mr. Charlton," Emma returned gaily, "and remain unalarmed, knowing that in me you will find a most attentive and patient listener."

"Well, should you consider that I can be of any other service, a note sent to the dak bungalow in Srinagar will reach me."

"Thank you." For some reason she was relieved that he was not staying as a guest of Chloe Hathaway. "I shall remember that."

"I wonder if Damien will take you to call on Walter and Adela Stewart when he returns," Chloe Hathaway mused as Emma escorted them to the front of the house where their horses and attendants awaited. "Walter is the Resident here, you know. Quite lively and a very good dancer. Adela tends to be a bit of a bore, poor darling, although she does try, I'll give her that." Since no response was called for to the instant demolition of the hapless Adela Stewart, Emma made none. "Unfortunately, Damien and Walter don't see eye-to-eye on everything, which is why I wonder. Anyway, you must both dine with me one evening soon. Damien is convinced that my cook makes the best gushtav in Kashmir. It's his favourite dish, you know."

In the privacy of her apartment a few moments later, Emma settled down to ponder the visit. On the whole, she decided, she had conducted herself well. She had not reacted to Mrs. Hathaway's subtle little digs and attempts to stir mischief, indeed, had fielded them with fair dignity. How disappointed the clever lady would be if she only knew with what disinterest she viewed Damien's liaisons, past, present and future! Chloe Hathaway herself, quite obviously, was one such liaison, and this Nazneen equally obviously another. How could she not have guessed when Mrs. Hathaway went to such lengths to deliver precisely that information?

Amused by her visitor's wasted efforts, Emma was far more exercised over the fact that she had not been able to talk to Geoffrey Charlton and that her visit to the weavers' village now had to be deferred to tomorrow.

*T*he sun was starting to set. In her apartment the beautiful Venetian glass lamps were being lit, the fire stoked and fed with pine-cones and the windows shut. Opening the glass door into the small balcony off her bedroom, Emma stood for a while gazing into the darkening distances, lost in private thought. Her father had believed that the Himalayas had the extraordinary power to expand human consciousness, to help put oneself into proper perspective. Watching the faraway peaks now, she saw what he had meant.

She returned to sit by the fire, and while waiting for her bath water to arrive, began a conversation with Rehmat. The child, she had noticed, was shy and unduly timid.

"Have you ever been to school, Rehmat?" The girl blushed, lowered her eyes and shook her head. "Do you know how to read and write?" Again the girl made a gesture of denial. "Would you like to learn?"

Raising her head, the girl gave her a nervous look, then nodded. "If Abba permits it," she whispered.

"Why should your father not permit it?"

"I am not a boy. Everyone will laugh."

"He will permit it if you were to learn from me."

The child's eyes lit up. "Begum sahiba would teach me?"

"Why not?" Emma stood up. "Now, if you will help me to look, I'm sure we can find a copybook and some pencils in the study and start right away."

By the time the writing materials were found and *aleph,* the first letter of the Urdu alphabet, written out, the child had lost her shyness and was chattering away nineteen to the dozen. Her parents lived in Srinagar, she informed Emma, and her father owned a tailoring shop in the bazaar. She had five brothers but no sisters; she had been brought to Shalimar three months ago by her Sharifa khala—her mother's sister—in order to serve huzoor's begum sahiba and be trained as a lady's maid.

"Where is your house in Srinagar?"

"Not far from Naseem Baug."

"Naseem Baug?" Emma frowned, trying to recollect her brief glimpses of Srinagar. "Now where might these gardens be?"

"On the same lake as the Shalimar Baug. Our house is halfway down a lane just opposite the new masjid with the green glass windows." In an effort to make Emma understand better, she added, "Our lane is next to the one in which Nazneen Bibi has her *kotha.*"

Kotha? Emma was startled; Nazneen was a dancing girl with an establishment in the bazaar? The remark revealed not only the woman's profession but also that her association with Damien was well known to the staff.

Unnerved by the innocently delivered information, Emma took a moment to recover. She wondered, how *did* wives react to news of their husbands' past (and no doubt continuing) peccadilloes? Normal wives, she knew, were expected to swoon, rail and rant, go off their food and ultimately die of a broken heart. Searching within herself for these accepted signs of normalcy, she could find none. She felt no immediate compulsion to swoon, nor to shout and scream, and nothing indicated that either her appetite or her heart was on the verge of collapse. Pleased that she could accept Damien's waywardness with such admirable maturity and lack of emotion, she resolutely returned her attention to Rehmat's initial lesson. By the time Sharifa ushered up the water-carriers with hot water for her bath, she had cast both Chloe Hathaway and Nazneen out of her thoughts and focussed them elsewhere.

That night after she had bathed, eaten and dismissed the servants, Emma again ventured into Damien's apartment, this time in search of a particular book, Godfrey Thomas Vigne's *Travels in Kashmir, Ladakh, Iskardu, Etc.* After browsing a while, she was about to replace some books on the shelf when she accidentally dislodged a slim volume and it fell to the floor. As she picked it up to return it to its place, she noticed that it was in an alien script with a handwritten inscription on the flyleaf in the same script. Russian? Having no idea that Damien knew Russian, she was vaguely surprised, but then she wondered why she should be; she knew so little about him anyway.

Shrugging off the matter and still wide awake, she strolled into her study, sank into her comfortable swivel chair and started to read. Even though Vigne's book was fascinating, she felt oddly restless, out of sorts and unable to concentrate. Had she been accustomed to self-deception, Emma would have fabricated any number of excuses to account for her malaise. Being essentially honest with herself, she did not.

The truth was, she was mortified to have to concede, even privately, that she was not able to dismiss Chloe Hathaway quite as blithely as she would have wanted to. Her inner vision, in fact, was alive with images of the merry widow and her knowing smiles, and her ears still rang with the many pointed innuendos she had delivered. Lurking also in the shadows of her mind was the anonymous face of this woman called Nazneen. All at once furious—as much with Damien as with herself for her reaction—Emma flared up in rebellion. How dare he lay her open to such humiliation at the hands of his mistress, how *dare* he!

Re-seating herself at her desk, she pulled out the virgin pad of very stylish letterheaded notepaper she had found earlier in a drawer and started to write a letter. It was to Geoffrey Charlton. Hoping maliciously that Damien would be back in time to savour the occasion, she told Charlton again how delighted she had been to meet him, how much she would like to see him again, and asked boldly—would he be free to have tea with her—at Shalimar the following Wednesday?

CHAPTER

10

*J*f Wilfred Hethrington had looked forward to the C-in-C's earlier meeting with something less than joy, its continuation did even less to improve either his temper or his ability to control it. A timely affliction would have helped, but as luck would have it, he had never felt or looked better.

Ensconced once again in Sir Marmaduke's study at Snowdon, they received a summary of various defence plans discussed at the Peshawar meeting in the event of a Russian invasion. Having met Francis Young-husband and received a first-hand account of his successful explorations of several new Himalayan passes—including the treacherous Mustagh—Sir Marmaduke appeared to be in a comparatively benign mood this morning. No one, however, made the mistake of taking its continuance for granted.

"To return to what we were about to discuss on the last occasion—Whitehall's request for our assessment of the situation building up in Hunza." The half-moons of the C-in-C's glasses caught the light and glinted as he scanned the cipher in his hand. "When I say 'request,' I use polite terminology which, as you may have noted, the India Office does not. Neither, I might add, did the Foreign Secretary when I dined with him in Peshawar. As the Americans would put it, gentlemen, the time for pussy-footing is over. Sir Mortimer wants a comprehensive, accurate and author-itative response drafted to London. Before we commit anything to paper, however, the situation needs to be reviewed from all angles." He replaced the flimsy and sat back. "Now, about this fellow Borokov—I want to know what the devil he has been up to in St. Petersburg." Once again the stiletto gaze was aimed at Hethrington.

Hethrington riffled through his folder. "According to the military attaché at our embassy, sir, Colonel Borokov has been visiting various military establishments in the company of General Smirnoff. One such visit was to the training camp at Krasnoe Selo outside the capital to watch secret trials of the new rifles and smokeless powder."

"The issue has already commenced, I believe. When is it expected to be completed?"

"By their own estimates, sir, not for another five years. Present Russian production is unable to match the demands of the army. At least, that is what our military attaché surmises."

"Can we believe then that they are re-equipping their infantry and cavalry merely for the fun of it, Colonel?"

"Every army re-equips its troops as a matter of course as and when better weapons are developed, sir," Hethrington pointed out. "Twenty years ago we ourselves replaced the Snider rifle with the Martini-Henry, which we now abandon for the Lee-Metford."

"Well, I wish I could be as easily satisfied as you, Colonel. Anyway, we will return to that in a moment. What else?"

"Two of the visits Smirnoff and Borokov made," Hethrington continued, "were to an ordnance depot near Moscow."

"The devil they were!"

"From information gleaned at the Yacht Club—of which Borokov and our attaché are both members—Smirnoff and Borokov have also been seen together at the baccarat tables and at private dinner parties among Smirnoff's elite inner circle."

"I see. So they're still good chums, what?" Sir Marmaduke propped his elbows on the desk and cradled his chin. "I think that confirms that the purpose and timing of Borokov's visit *are* significant—he was summoned by Smirnoff to select arms for Hunza."

"That certainly appears to be the impression the Russians wish to convey, sir."

"Is that all it appears to you to be, Colonel, an impression?"

"So far, sir. The possibility of the Russians actually being able to deliver weapons to Hunza is remote. If by some miracle they do succeed, the consignment is unlikely to include the new rifles, which are in short supply. Safdar Ali's men still use matchlocks, breechloaders, jezails and home-made ammunition. He would be happy to get just about anything that fires, and like ours, Russian ordnance depots are packed high with obsolete weaponry. It is possible, sir, that this is what Smirnoff has been investigating"—

Hethrington coughed politely—"naturally, to the accompaniment of orchestrated fanfare meant to be heard in London."

The C-in-C stared at a beautifully carved wooden cigar box on the desk. "You are aware, I presume, that Smirnoff's appointment as Governor-General in Tashkent has been confirmed in the Russian Court Circular?"

Of course he was bloody well aware! Hethrington remained silent.

Flicking open the box, Sir Marmaduke considered the cheroots ranged inside but then changed his mind and snapped it shut again. "The reputation of Central Asia as a favourite hunting ground of headstrong Russian officers is well known, Colonel. Smirnoff's earlier antics there prove that he is ambitious, aggressive and reckless. Coupled with the fact that Butterfield's papers are still not accounted for—at least not to my satisfaction—the matter of *any* delivery to Hunza assumes serious dimensions. I wouldn't advise minimising those alleged orchestrations, Colonel."

Sir John opened his mouth, thought better of it, nodded in Colonel Hethrington's direction and returned the ball to his court. Reluctantly, Hethrington retrieved it.

"The Russians derive considerable pleasure from rattling their sabres in order to watch our excessive reactions, sir," Hethrington said, struggling to balance honesty with tact. "The cordite and fixed-cartridge incidents are both cases in point. I suggest that this time we deny the Russians that pleasure."

"Ah yes." The C-in-C gave an affable nod. "We return to the irrational delusions, do we?" Reaching for the cheroot after all, he took one and nudged the box in Sir John's direction. "You consider that what our governments here and in Whitehall react excessively to is mere sabre-rattling?"

Declining the offer of a cheroot, Hethrington evaded the question. "I do not doubt the possibility of a shipment of arms being despatched to Hunza, sir, only the probability of its ever arriving. Safdar Ali's father had made a similar request to the Chinese—who claim Hunza as theirs anyway—in order to keep us out. Two Chinese cannons, duly despatched, got stuck in the snows of the Hindu Kush and in all probability are still there."

"That was years ago, dammit! Today, the railway network makes it easier and faster for Russia to expand her sphere of influence and the political equations in Asia are radically changed, Colonel."

"But not the weather and topography, sir. The Himalayas still remain a natural, impenetrable barrier that forms a more effective defence system than any we could hope to construct."

"Not quite so effective if they gain access to the Yasmina!" Pulling hard at his cheroot, the C-in-C balanced it on the rim of the ashtray, then rose and turned to the map on his wall. "Younghusband confirms that the

Hindu Kush passes, along here, are absurdly easy to negotiate. Light artillery has been taken successfully through the Boroghil into Chitral and through the Darkot into Yasin. We have a road straight into Gilgit, Chilas and down the Indus. For the Russians to bring a column down from Kokand to Wakhan, here, would entail less than fifty miles of road—a damn sight quicker than for us to send a column up from the Punjab to Yasin or Hunza."

"In case of the eventuality of an invasion, sir," Sir John hastily intervened, nervous of what Hethrington's bluntness might drive him to say next, "surely we would have enough advance information to prepare a better counter-offensive?"

"Not if they used routes that are unfamiliar to us." The C-in-C stabbed several points on the map. "Don't forget there are passes here no more than a day's ride from Gilgit and there are others that can be used throughout the year."

"None that could secretly support a sizeable army and heavy artillery, sir, a fact confirmed by General Lockhart and Ney Elias. Of the forty or so passes Elias explored, he reported that one or two in the Hindu Kush could conceivably accommodate a small contingent between July and December, but to cross Badakhshan, the Russians would have to win over the Amir, which seems vastly improbable. In the final analysis, therefore, the only two passes capable of accommodating a sizeable army remain the Khyber and the Bolan. Neither can be used without Afghanistan's cooperation."

"Should the Russians invade, John," Sir Marmaduke said, "they would not be foolish enough to concentrate all their strength in one pass. As General MacGregor pointed out in his book, they would start with minor, multi-pronged incursions by small combat groups—as I would were I on the other side—which is why the Yasmina is vital. A pass close to Hunza and unknown to us gives them the advantage of surprise."

"Nevertheless, sir, the prospect of a Russian assault through any combination of Himalayan passes is"—Sir John hunted for a word that would give the least offence—"dubious at best. But," he quickly added, "I express that as a purely personal opinion."

"A half-baked one, John! We have only seventy thousand British troops in India. Double that many sepoys are forbidden modern weapons, which renders them more or less useless. In a country of a hundred and eighty million, we have an average of one armed man to fifteen hundred civilians and our communication and supply lines to the north are impossibly long. The Russians have forty-five thousand troops in Central Asia to control a mere two and a half million. Not only are their men superior in mountain training, but geographical considerations, the Transcaspian Railway and the political realities of Central Asia all work in their favour."

Sir John scratched his chin. "True, sir, but these factors would count only in the event of a full-scale war, which . . ."

"I am not stupid enough to believe, John," the C-in-C cut in irritably, "that Russia envisages conquest. What she has dreamed of for more than a century is invasion. Planned forays—a jab here, a thrust there, a feint in between merely to embarrass us. You must see that even a minor incursion into the Hunza gorge would be an insufferable slap in the face to which we would be forced to give a fitting response." His eyes gleamed at the prospect.

"Russia's posturings could be a smokescreen, sir, to . . ."

"Keep us busy in Calcutta rather than Constantinople? No, John." Sir Marmaduke shook his head decisively. "I have never subscribed to the theory that all Russia wants is to rule the Bosphorus. Borokov's flirtation with Hunza has a serious purpose behind it, as has Alexei Smirnoff's appointment to Tashkent. Frankly, I would prefer to err on the side of safety rather than smugness. I do *not*," he thumped the desk hard and an onyx inkwell jumped, but fortunately did not spill over, "want us to be caught with our trousers down as we have been in the past."

"No, sir." The QMG retreated. "Of course not."

"To return to Smirnoff, it is mandatory that we know every damn thing the fellow does from the moment he arrives in Turkestan. Is that clearly understood?"

"Yes, sir."

"Who do we have there at the moment?"

"Colonel?" The QMG returned the floor to Hethrington.

"Since Tashkent is almost entirely a military station and always on the alert, it is risky to plant one of our pundits there on a permanent basis. Therefore we are forced to rely on ad hoc information from an Uzbek clerk in one of the Baron's less important departments and on bazaar gossip carried back by travellers."

"The Uzbek, is he the same contact established by our military attaché in St. Petersburg when he was invited to Tashkent?"

"Yes, sir. Since the man has some English, the Russians used him as an interpreter during the visit."

"Has he proved to be reliable?"

"Fairly so, sir. It was he who alerted us to the fact that Safdar Ali's emissaries had arrived to meet the Baron—which flagged off Borokov's visit to Hunza."

"Well, I want Smirnoff and Borokov watched. Anything out of the ordinary, however trivial, must be reported at once."

"The Uzbek has been instructed accordingly, sir."

"What about their new road from Osh?"

"Its progress is being monitored by one of our men, sir, a new recruit but on good terms with the local people. Any unexpected military activity will be brought to his notice."

Aware of the secrecy the Department maintained with regard to its operatives, and often irritated by it, Sir Marmaduke scowled but did not probe further. "When was it that Safdar Ali's emissary arrived in Tashkent—before Durand's visit to Hunza or after?"

"Shortly after, sir." On comparatively surer ground, Hethrington spoke with confidence, even a touch of malice. His distrust of Colonel Durand's methods at the Gilgit Agency was no secret in official circles. "Safdar Ali was piqued by both Durand's superciliousness and his point-blank accusation of duplicity."

"Oh?" Sir Marmaduke's eyebrows shot up. "You don't find it intolerable that the damned fellow has the gall to footle around with Russia?"

"The damned fellow also footles around with us, sir," Hethrington pointed out pleasantly. "Had Durand been less arrogant and more accommodating we might have cut more ice with the Mir. With due respect, sir, duplicity is often the only resource left to small kingdoms trapped between hostile giants."

The observation did not go down well and the steely glint in the General's eyes said so. "Then what do you suggest we do, Colonel—pamper the scallawag while he flirts with the enemy? Sit back and turn a blind eye to a Russian delivery of arms?"

Noticing that the QMG had again shifted uneasily in his chair, Hethrington swallowed his rejoinder. "No, sir, but as long as it *is* only a flirtation . . ." He shrugged and let his mumble trail away.

The C-in-C's eyes narrowed. "You might be interested to know, Colonel, that despite your own optimism, at the defence meeting there was universal consternation at the recent succession of events—events that many considered sufficient even for mobilisation." He held up a hand and picked off his fingers. "Butterfield's murder, the mysterious loss of his papers, Borokov's impertinent visit to Hunza, his closeness to Smirnoff and the summons to St. Petersburg, Smirnoff's unsavoury reputation and his imminent arrival in Tashkent, issue of the new rifles and smokeless powder." He threw up his hands. "What more would it take to shake us out of our complacency, goddammit—a broadside on Simla?"

George Aberigh-Mackay, as incisive a satirist as Rudyard Kipling, had dubbed an erstwhile Commander-in-Chief "the revolver of the Government of India." The description fitted the present incumbent equally well. Even though Hethrington felt the heat rise to his face, he accepted the tirade in silence. To argue further, he knew, would be to ensure a transfer.

Breathing hard to contain his rising temper, Sir Marmaduke snatched a second cheroot from the box, lit it and puffed vigorously. "Now, to return to the Butterfield matter . . ."

The QMG did not bat an eyelash, but Hethrington had the presence of mind to drop his pencil on the carpet, bend down and take his time fumbling around for it.

"I know that your Department professes reservations about Butterfield's claim, John, but tell me—do you personally believe that what he found *was* the Yasmina?"

Sir John fingered an ear and assumed an air of deep reflection. "It could have been, of course; we certainly can't dismiss the claim entirely. On the other hand, neither can we confirm it."

"You mean because the details are lost to the four winds in the Karakoram?"

The question was laden with sarcasm, but to his credit Sir John did not flinch. "Yes, sir. Regardless of what Butterfield might have thought he had found, personally I am confident that the loss of the papers constitutes no immediate danger to our security."

"I would have slept better without that 'immediate,' John," the Commander-in-Chief returned with a narrow look. "Is that assurance strong enough to be conveyed to Whitehall?"

"No, sir. I consider that it would be unwise to commit ourselves to more than an enlightened opinion of the probabilities provided by our own instincts within the boundaries of the information available. Aware, in any case, that we are hardly in a position to provide guarantees, all Whitehall asks for are assessments."

The bureaucratic gift of verbal excess without content produced a smile within Hethrington. He did not let it surface.

Clearly sceptical, Sir Marmaduke nevertheless gave a grudging nod. "All right. Go ahead and draft a cipher for the approval of H. E. and the Foreign Secretary, would you please, John? And make sure that I get it by this afternoon."

"Yes, sir."

"It might be a good idea to re-emphasise your doubts, John, if only to protect our own damn arses. Insist that they be circulated to the press to squash whatever other imaginative rumours might be rolling off the print mills. For the rest we will just have to wait and watch once Smirnoff arrives. Well, anything else?"

It appeared not. There was a rush of sound of throats being cleared, folders snapped shut and chair legs scraped back. Hethrington heaved a sigh of relief. It was only a brief reprieve, of course, but at least it was a reprieve. With luck, it might even allow time for the project to come to fruition.

If at all!

*T*he stables were well stocked and the mount Suraj Singh selected for Emma the following morning was a light brown mare that was even-tempered and obeyed instructions well.

"Unlike her neighbour, I see," Emma remarked, eyeing a splendid and spirited midnight in an adjoining stall, tossing his mane about and snorting angrily.

"Oh, that is Toofan, huzoor's favourite horse. He certainly does not obey instructions well—except from huzoor." Recognising his name, the midnight flared his nostrils, scraped the floor with a hoof and glared at them both. Suraj Singh laughed. "Now you see why he is named Toofan. His temper is as fierce as a storm but so is his stamina, which makes him ideal for hard riding. At home huzoor uses Sikandar, an Arab with less energy but better manners."

They started off at a slow trot and from a distance Emma observed the clean, square lines of the main house. The outside walls were painted sun-shine yellow with the shuttered windows picked out in green, the colour of sage. The overall effect was most attractive. To her many questions about the estate, Suraj Singh provided ready answers. Familiar with every last detail, there was no doubt that he took great pride in the property.

"Do you yourself belong to an agricultural family, Suraj Singh?" she asked.

"No, begum sahiba. My father was a soldier."

"From Rajputana?"

"No, begum sahiba. We come from Jammu."

"Oh? You are a Dogra then, are you?"

"Yes, begum sahiba."

Respecting his aversion to personal questions, she did not ask if his limp was the consequence of a war wound. Instead, she let drop casually that she had invited Geoffrey Charlton to tea the following week. It was unlikely that Suraj Singh had not already been informed of the despatch of the letter to Srinagar early that morning, but he made no immediate comment. In the brief incline of his head, however, Emma sensed disapproval.

"Mrs. Hathaway is also expected?" he asked.

"No." Did she imagine a flicker of relief in his eyes? Without having to, she explained further. "Mr. Charlton is a correspondent of considerable repute and an expert on Central Asia. I would like to learn more about his experiences in the region. Mr. Charlton mentioned that he is acquainted with my husband."

"They have met, yes." He hesitated. "Without intending any impertinence, begum sahiba, I feel obliged to point out that huzoor is not . . . well disposed towards the gentleman."

Which, of course, instantly made the prospect of entertaining Charlton even more desirable. "And Mrs. Hathaway?" she asked in all innocence, enjoying his discomfiture. "Is huzoor also not well disposed towards the lady?"

"I cannot say," Suraj Singh replied with distant formality. "I am not privy to huzoor's opinion about all his acquaintances."

So Chloe Hathaway was just an acquaintance, was she? Emma was amused by his loyal choice of terminology.

"Would begum sahiba wish me to arrange for tea in the withdrawing-room, as usual?"

"No, I think the orchard outside the summerhouse might be rather more pleasant. It would be a pity to miss the sunset on the western mountains."

It was a considered decision. If Damien returned by next week—which she hoped he would if only to be irked by Charlton's presence—it wouldn't matter where they had tea. But if he didn't, it certainly would. Geoffrey Charlton was young, personable and a bachelor, and attitudes here were conservative. To entertain a male visitor in the open in full view of the staff was less likely to cause a sensation.

They travelled through a field of delicately tinted purple saffron, a monopoly of Kashmir from ancient times. Used in worship by the Greeks and Romans, saffron yielded a perfume which, legend had it, the Greeks sprinkled in their public places and the Romans in the streets each time the emperor entered the city. In India, the aromatic spice was used mainly as a culinary garnish to add colour and bouquet to traditional dishes. Among the trees Emma could identify willows, chinar, poplar, cypress and cedar, but many others were unfamiliar. If the proliferation of blossom was to be believed, the orchards promised a veritable explosion of fruit this summer. In the Vale, she had learned, the seasons changed at every thousand feet of elevation. One could have snow, spring blossoms and summer fruit all at the same time, depending upon the altitude.

The huddle of cottages in the weavers' village had traditional roofs of slate, wooden shingles and thatched reeds from the lake. In a brick-laid yard, weavers sat under apple and apricot trees plying looms back and forth as if in rhythm with an invisible metronome. A group of women squatted around a mountain of white fleece, separating the kemp into two piles. Others sat cross-legged at spinning wheels drawing fine threads out of fleece, doubling and twisting strands as they spun. Behind the village ran a narrow stream, its grassy banks streaked with coral from the willow roots. The surrounding fields were alight with bronze rice blooms that shone like polished metal, and a family of ducks waddled past on their way back from the stream, their orange beaks clacking like castinets. To one side among tall grasses was penned a large contingent of goats.

As Emma approached, the weavers rose, stood with heads bowed in greeting and then waited to be presented. Hidden eyes peeped curiously through the slatted chiks in the doorways and a host of children, awestruck and tongue-tied, giggled. First to be introduced was Qadir Mian, the ageing Afghan weaver Sharifa had mentioned with such pride in Delhi.

Speaking in Urdu, Emma complimented him on the beautiful *shatoosh* shawl he had woven and which huzoor had given her as a gift. He received the compliment with an offhand inclination of the head, but she could see that he was pleased. "Do carry on with your work," she said. "I do not wish to disturb your labours."

They resumed their seats, three men at a loom, and the staccato rhythm continued. The superior pure white fleece, she learned, was reserved for the warp threads in the finest quality of shawls; the inferior grey was dyed and used for the weft. As they wove, they wet the threads continuously with thin rice paste to prevent them from fraying. The pattern master, *talim guru,* had written his instructions in explicit detail in the traditional "shawl alphabet." The colours expert—*tarah guru*—recited them aloud, calling out the colours and number of warp threads under which the bobbins of weft were to pass. The instructions were placed in stands before the weavers much in the manner of music sheets on a piano.

Once the shawl was ready, Emma was told, it was washed in the river, then stamped on with bare feet and finally slapped hard against a stone slab to remove the rice starch from the thread. The process was repeated several times before the shawl was set out to dry in the shade. When Emma expressed astonishment at such brutal treatment of so fine a garment, Qadir Mian chuckled.

"It is this final stage that gives the Kashmiri shawl its inimitable soft-ness, begum sahiba. There is magic in our rivers, a magic not found in waters anywhere else in the world."

"How long does it take to complete one shawl?"

"Anything up to a year and a half."

Sadly but inevitably, years of such arduous and precise labour left the eyesight impaired and some of the older weavers wore glasses. Qadir Mian's, Emma observed, were especially thick.

"It is because of Qadir Mian's genius," Suraj Singh said, "that the annual gifts for the English Queen are prepared at Shalimar." Noticing Emma's incomprehension, he raised an eyebrow. "Huzoor has not mentioned these to begum sahiba?"

If only he knew how much his huzoor had *not* mentioned to begum sahiba! Emma shook her head.

"Under the Amritsar treaty the maharaja agreed to make a symbolic annual gift to the Queen of a horse, twelve shawl goats—six male and six female—and three pairs of cashmere shawls. When our project started to do well, the maharaja requested late huzoor to undertake the preparation of these gifts at Shalimar. The shawls are woven here and the horses are bred and reared at huzoor's stables in Gulmarg."

"The goats survive the sea journey all the way to England?"

"Alas, no. So many perished that finally the Queen herself suggested the practice be abandoned on humanitarian grounds. The gifts now consist of ten pounds of natural pashmina, four pounds each of packed black, grey and white wool, and one pound each of the three best qualities of yarn. Those, together with one horse and three square shawls, are now accepted as adequate proof of Kashmir's loyalty to the crown—such as it is."

Knowing how strongly the Kashmiris resented the British presence in their state, Emma was not surprised by the cynicism. "How many professional weavers are there in the valley?"

"Twenty years ago there were forty thousand, but only four thousand survived the famine of thirteen years ago, which is why master weavers like Qadir Mian are difficult to find. Altogether two hundred thousand people are said to have died that year."

They talked of the terrible disaster for a while, then Emma asked, "Since shawls are impractical to wear over bustles which are currently much in vogue in Europe, has the demand for shawls not decreased over recent years?"

"Unfortunately, yes. Today the average weaver in Kashmir earns no more than one and a quarter annas per day, works in appalling conditions and dies young of malnutrition. But," he shrugged, "fashions are fickle. They come and go with the seasons. For finely woven shawls with beautiful designs such as these, huzoor believes, there will always be a demand from those of discrimination."

"Wool weaving seems so far removed from the pursuits one would expect a military man to follow," Emma said. "How did Major Granville develop such an abiding interest in it?"

"Late huzoor's mother was French and one of her brothers owned shawl-weaving factories in France. When he went to Paris for one of the

Great Exhibitions, he took his young nephew with him. It was then that burra huzoor first developed a passion for fine weaves."

"And my husband continues the tradition with the same passion?"

"Begum sahiba can judge for herself." He indicated one of the looms. "The pattern they weave was devised by huzoor. He is an excellent artist."

"After his father?"

"No. Late huzoor had a keen eye for design and texture but he was not an artist."

"After his mother, then?"

"Yes, begum sahiba."

"Was she a trained painter?"

"No, begum sahiba, but they say she had an inborn flair for art."

Before Emma could voice any more questions, Qadir Mian approached to ask if she would care to watch the dyeing process, and once again she was forced to relinquish the subject of the late Mrs. Granville.

All in all, it proved to be a most informative morning. The estate, Emma learned, was almost self-sufficient in its requirements of food and it contained an astonishing variety of activity. Mulberry trees bred silkworms for Kashmiri silks; a three-acre plot was devoted to the cultivation of plants used for medicinal purposes by the estate dispensary. There were fish in the streams, a thriving dairy, a grinding mill, a walnut forest with three varieties of nut, several orchards and a cannery for excess fruit.

"Who looks after all this apart from my husband and yourself?" Emma asked, marvelling at such disparate industry.

"Lincoln, whom you have already met, the estate manager. The estate itself is run on somewhat unorthodox lines. Everyone who works here has some share in the profits and so has an incentive to work hard and stay honest."

Riding through waist-high fields of wheat and rice and skirting neatly tended kitchen gardens, they returned to the house by a different route in time for luncheon. In the flourishing vineyards, great clusters of grapes hung in red and white profusion. Encouraged by the Kashmir government, Suraj Singh said, huzoor had planted hops and now planned to experiment with winemaking.

"Grapes today are not as plentiful as in the time of the Moghuls when eight seers could be bought for one-fortieth of a rupee. Later, Maharaja Ranbir Singh imported vines from Bordeaux and a distillation plant was set up at Gupkar. The experiment continues but has not been a success as the plants are prone to Phylloxera."

"And the vines here at Shalimar?"

"These were imported from America. They are believed to be sturdier, less susceptible to disease."

"Is there a demand for wines in Kashmir?" Emma asked.

"Only in Srinagar. There is a demand in India, of course, but the cost of transportation and customs duty at the frontier makes the trade unprofitable."

"Well, then, why has my husband embarked at all on a project that has little hope of commercial success?"

Suraj Singh sighed. "For precisely that reason, begum sahiba. Huzoor is as unable to refuse a challenge as to accept the prospect of failure."

*F*or heaven's sake, man," Sir John said in mild irritation as they sat down to draft the telegram, "is it necessary to rub him up the wrong way at every meeting? It wouldn't hurt to be diplomatic once in a while. The cordite and fixed-cartridge matters, for instance, it was particularly tactless to bring those up."

"I consider it as dishonest to voice an insincere opinion, sir, as not to voice an honest one," Hethrington replied.

"Oh tosh!" Sir John laughed good-humouredly. "Not with a little practice, you wouldn't. In all fairness, Wilfred, what Sir Marmaduke said was not unreasonable. The combination of events *is* worrying and precautions *do* need to be taken."

"To endorse a foreign policy fashioned by rumour is, in my opinion, wrong, and to jump each time the Russians blow the whistle is humiliating. In any case, I certainly don't express views not held and voiced by a million moderates in Britain."

"Moderates! Voices in the wilderness, Wilfred—and we both know what Sir Marmaduke thinks of them!"

"There must be some sane politicians who . . ."

"Politicians and sanity?" Sir John chuckled. "Dream away, Wilfred, dream away—I can tell you there's not a chance in hell of finding such an animal. In any case, policies and politics are way off our preserve—and well you know it."

He returned to his draft and Hethrington sank into silence.

The readiness of the government to believe the worst of Russia on the strength of random tittle-tattle never ceased to amaze him. Half information, misleading information, outright untruth, all were grist for the gossip mills. For example, a mere whisper that Russia had stolen a sample of British cordite produced mayhem in Whitehall. Subsequently, a German scientist working for the French War Office on France's smokeless powder—melinite—exposed the British powder as chemically useless and the usual red faces resulted.

The "fixed"-cartridge affair was even more embarrassing. Asked to confirm the rumour that Russia had introduced "fixed" cartridges in their artillery, the British military attaché in St. Petersburg replied in the affirmative. The usual panic followed—until the attaché confessed that he had boobed. Not being an artillery man, he had presumed that "fixed" cartridges were those of which the patterns and shells were "fixed" for each type of gun. In point of fact, cartridges were said to be "fixed" when the shell was fused with the casing to make one unit to ensure more rapid firepower. Needless to say, they had not been introduced in the Russian artillery and the last smirk was again had by St. Petersburg.

Sir John laid down his pen and sat back. "All right, Wilfred, let me ask you this—are you, in all honesty, truly as unworried about Smirnoff's arrival as you appear to be?"

"No sir. I am, in fact, extremely worried. I know that something is brewing in Tashkent and that after he arrives it will brew harder, but conjecture clouds the issue, not clarifies it. We have to be alert, granted, but not hysterical and hawkish. Have you taken note of Lord Castlewood's long cipher?"

"I have, but Sir Marmaduke dismisses it. He believes that when the issue of the new rifle is completed, Russia will go to war, possibly with England and most probably in India. Russian firebrands in Central Asia *are* stoking trouble in their hunt for medals, Wilfred."

"Do you consider Colonel Durand any less of a firebrand, sir, any less greedy for medals?" The QMG shrugged but remained silent. "I don't deny that Smirnoff comes to make trouble, but whatever the trouble it will be without the Tsar's blessings."

"Well, all right, even if we accept that he's acting against orders, isn't it curious how St. Petersburg has reacted to disobedience in the past? For his skirmish with the Afghans on the Murghab, for instance—an act of rampant irresponsibility—Alexei Smirnoff was actually promoted!"

"Well, his father was Minister of War at the time."

"And you consider Smirnoff minor any less influential in his own right as Military Controller of the emperor's household?"

Hethrington shook his head. "In Russia, there is only one centre of power, sir, Alexander the Third, with very little delegation of authority. Even the expense vouchers of a military attaché have to be approved and initialled personally by the Tsar. Officially, the Russian Army in Central Asia has strict orders not to set foot in any disputed territory."

"What about unofficially?"

"Unofficially, if a Russian officer oversteps his bounds, it is an act of individual indiscipline, not a prelude to war, which is the only point I make.

Stray acts of belligerence are no more part of official Russian foreign policy than Sir Charles's *Defence of India* is part of ours.''

Sir John threw up his hands. "It doesn't matter what you and I think, Wilfred," he said wearily. "Algy Durand, the C-in-C, the Foreign Secretary and Whitehall think otherwise, and that, my friend, is what counts. Let me also remind you, Wilfred, that the Intelligence Department is new, still to earn its laurels, still on approval, so to speak. Our budget is a thorn in many a side and I am sure I have no need to . . ."

"Sorry to interrupt, sir"—having knocked briefly, Captain Worth entered flourishing a paper—"but this just arrived from Leh."

The QMG and Hethrington looked up simultaneously. "What does it say?" they asked in joint alarm.

"Mr. Crankshaw informs us that having returned from Yarkand, Geoffrey Charlton has now arrived in Srinagar."

There was a moment of hushed silence, then Sir John put a hand to his forehead. "Well, I would say that completes a perfect day. Wouldn't you agree, Wilfred?"

Hethrington did not even have the heart to nod.

*T*alking about Merv," Geoffrey Charlton said, "I think you would be disenchanted with it as it is today."

"Really?" Emma leaned forward to listen better. "And its three old cities? Surely something still remains of their successive civilisations?"

"Only the ruins ten miles from the new township, which stretch all the way to the horizon. Indeed, there is scarcely a square foot where one does not stumble across some half-buried, forgotten relic." Hakumat approached and Charlton paused to accept a plate of freshly sliced peaches and cream. "During the construction of the railway the town did enjoy some importance, but now most of the traders have left. The new town is a huddle of huts, a straggly stream, a few unremarkable wooden houses and a garden or two."

"What about Koushid Khan Kala's magnificent mud fortress?"

"The railway now runs through it after it leaves Merv. Other old structures house Russian Army offices, the residence of the provincial governor, small military garrisons and perhaps a nondescript garden or church."

"And the ancient cities attributed to Alexander, Zoroaster and the Macedonians?"

"All crumbled into dust, I regret to say."

"What a pathetic end to a traveller's delight!" Emma exclaimed sadly.

"Tell me, Mr. Charlton, why do local people not protest about the wanton neglect of their monuments and their historical heroes?"

Charlton smiled. "I see, Mrs. Granville, that you are a romantic."

"Why? Surely everyone with regard for history laments such ruination? Don't you, Mr. Charlton?"

Charlton shrugged. "It is a matter of allocating one's priorities. Being a journalist, I am essentially a realist. What concerns me more than the unchangeable past is the rapidly changing present—and how successfully Russia moulds it into a profitable future for herself."

"You call this destruction a matter of success?"

"Destruction?" He laughed. "On the contrary, Mrs. Granville. The oases today are more productive than ever before, which is why local people don't think to protest." He pushed aside his cup and dabbed the corners of his mouth with a napkin. "Modern legends recognise only one hero, General Konstantin Kaufmann, the first Russian Governor-General. Tamerlane and Alexander might ring a bell here and there, but no one really has time for antiquity. However unscrupulous and acquisitory, Mrs. Granville, unfortunately the Russians are also good colonisers." He rose, stretched himself and gazed appreciatively at the distant ranges dazzled by the sun.

"You mean as opposed to the British?"

"As opposed to any other colonisers. For instance, long before Merv was annexed, St. Petersburg sent down teams to rejuvenate the oasis. The region is naturally rich; sixty million new trees planted made it even richer. Neglected waterways were revived, irrigation projects initiated and the Sultan Bend dam on the Murghab repaired. In the past five years cotton production in Ferghana has increased twenty-five-fold and exports thrive. Turkoman carpets, for example, sell in Europe for as much as thirty thousand pounds." He turned and gave her a look of amusement. "So you see, Mrs. Granville, today a refreshed and revived Merv flourishes. If trade expands and people prosper—why should anyone bother about the dead past with such profit to be had in the living present?"

Emma was disappointed by the cynicism; it seemed somehow incongruous. "You consider that material prosperity justifies the neglect of antiquity?"

"I do not justify it, Mrs. Granville, I merely present to you the realities as they exist today. Russians are not interested in preserving history, only in making it. Such excavations as have been attempted are halfhearted and ham-fisted."

"But then why do they not permit outsiders to excavate? Many would jump at the opportunity."

"Merv's annual trade is estimated at five million roubles, Mrs. Granville, and all of it goes into the private purse of the Tsar. The Russians will not permit any activity that might wean the attention of the people away from their daily labours."

"But surely that is exploitation?"

"The people do not think so. They know that it is because Merv makes the Tsar richer that its economic development—and theirs—is assured."

Emma frowned, confused by the logic. "Am I to understand then that you *approve* of Russian colonisation?"

"On the contrary. Because Russian Transcaspia thrives, it starts to appeal also to many natives of British India, especially in the border states." His gaze wandered off in pursuit of a giant yellow and purple butterfly that fluttered past the table in search of a landing site. "Dazzled by the superficial quality of life in the Russian Empire, the Indians forget that man does not live by bread alone, that the one who puts food on his table eventually owns his soul."

"Is not the same true of all colonisers?" Emma asked. "One way or another, they all play Mephistopheles!"

"But the Russians, you see, play it better. For instance . . ." He broke off sharply and frowned. "How on *earth* did we manage to arrive at this interminable debate from the old cities of Merv?"

Emma laughed. "I was beginning to wonder about that myself."

He was instantly contrite. "If it was my doing, I do apologise. It would be unforgivable to waste a perfect afternoon and an idyllic environment in insoluble political debate. Now," he sat down again, all attention, "what was it that you asked me earlier about Bokhara?"

Since neither politics nor Russian colonisation methods interested her in the least, Emma was relieved. The erstwhile khanate of Bokhara built largely by Indian engineers derived its name from the Sanskrit *vihara,* a college of wise men. She had merely asked if evidence remained today of this wisdom. Pleased to have the conversation move into more agreeable, less controversial channels, she repeated her question.

It was indeed a perfect afternoon, cool and balmy, filled with the humming of bees, the gushing breath of spring breezes and the thick, sweet perfume of ripening fruit. As arranged, Charlton had arrived punctually at three, hatless and dressed informally, genuinely delighted to have been invited. Thoughtfully, he had come armed with several books on Central Asia which he felt would be of interest to her. The tea table, covered with starched white damask and laid with fine bone china, a silver tea service and delicate lace doilies edged with glass beads to keep the insects away from the food, had been supervised by Hakumat and Sharifa. Before they sat down to tea, at Charlton's request Emma had guided him on a tour of the estate. His enthusiasm for everything was almost schoolboyish; he was all praise for Damien. Following at a discreet distance, Suraj Singh was at his inscrutable best.

Politics forgotten, they talked now of Bokhara and Samarkand, the magical river Oxus born in the glaciers of the Pamirs, and of many other exotic places. Even though his knowledge was vast, Charlton's manner remained as modest as at Delhi's Town Hall. Listening to his painstaking answers to her abundant questions, Emma again marvelled at his articulacy and his memory for detail. He spoke in measured cadences, rarely searched for words and his voice never rose above polite levels. In the course of the conversation Emma also learned something about Charlton. He had, she gathered, been brought up in a Yorkshire mining town and had won a scholarship to grammar school and then to Manchester University.

Strolling up to a peach tree, he turned and looked at her in inquiry. Emma smiled and nodded. Jumping up, he plucked a high peach and bit into its sweetness. Having demolished it, he took aim and tossed its stone deep into the undergrowth. As he glanced at his soiled hands, Hakumat leapt forward with a jug of water, a soap dish and a fresh napkin.

"When the Moghul emperor Akbar was asked on his death bed what he desired as a last wish"—Charlton sighed—"he said, 'Only Kashmir.' "

"By that I presume that life in the valley is also to your own taste?" Emma asked.

"Yes. I like it in the valley." He washed his hands and wiped them dry carefully, finger by finger. "It is a convenient base for Central Asia. Here, in the perfumed quiet, one can write without interference and Walter Stewart, the Resident, is kind enough to allow me access to his telegraph to despatch my reports to London." Raising his face to the mountains, he breathed in deeply.

Emma smiled at his lack of artifice and his ingenuous enjoyment of everything around him. Yes, she decided, there was something truly charming and unspoilt about the man, perhaps because of his modest beginnings. She signalled Hakumat for a fresh pot of tea.

"As I mentioned the last time," Charlton said, "I had the privilege of meeting your father once. I was greatly impressed by him, both as a man and as a scholar. I would have liked to know him better. At the time he was searching for ancient monasteries along the old trade routes followed by Buddhist pilgrims."

"Yes." Emma heaved a small sigh. "The monasteries buried inside the mountains along the Silk Road were a lifelong obsession with Papa. He had discovered one in the Tian Shan, what the Chinese call the Heavenly Mountains, and in the Magar caves he later found the oldest and most extensive collection of Buddhist murals and scriptures anywhere in the world. He loved the alpine meadows of the Tian Shan," she added wistfully. "He said it was impossible to take a step without crushing some of the pansies that grew in such wild profusion and every conceivable colour."

They talked for a while of Graham Wyncliffe's life, of his passion for secret cachets of ancient wisdom, and then, to her surprise, Emma found herself talking also of his death. Considering how hurtful she still found the memory, it astonished her that she should revive it with an acquaintance, someone she barely knew. But there was something about Geoffrey Charlton that was comforting and immensely sympathetic. Not only was he easy to talk to, but as a good journalist he had a habit of listening with flattering attention.

"Papa was fiercely jealous of his privacy and often wandered off on his own," she said. "His team respected his need for solitude. Sometimes he stayed away from his base camp for days and they never worried. This time, sadly, he failed to return. It seems so intolerably cruel," she added, trying to keep the pain out of her voice, "that we should be denied even the small comfort of laying flowers on his grave—if, indeed, there is a recognisable grave."

Her eyes were bright but there were no tears, for the unburdening was cathartic; as she talked, she felt solaced. She was so tired of letting it fester within and in any case it was all common knowledge now. She laid her head against the back of her chair and stared up at the russet sky.

"We had lived in hope for so long, praying for a miracle, but it was not to be. We learned much later that Papa's body had been discovered by mountain tribesmen who also found it in their hearts to bury it, although we have no idea where."

Taking note of the distress she could no longer hide, Charlton got up to wander around the orchard to allow her a few moments on her own. When he returned to resume his chair, he did not revive the topic. He asked instead, "Mr. Granville is in Leh, I hear?"

Emma wrenched her thoughts away from the past. "Yes, but due to return soon."

"Your husband is an extremely clever man, Mrs. Granville."

Was that said as a compliment? She was not sure.

"I am told he knows the name of almost every plant, animal and bird in Kashmir and every track into the mountains. Of course, he is also fluent in several languages."

"Well, he was brought up in Kashmir. His Urdu is as perfect as his Kashur and Dogri." She almost added, "so I'm told," but didn't.

"As, of course, is his Russian."

She happened to be bending down to retrieve a fallen napkin, which saved her the need for an immediate response. Her startled thoughts flew back to the Russian book she had seen in Damien's library, but an instant later when she raised her face it gave no hint of surprise.

"Of course." She smiled. "That too."

"As it happens, it was at the Yacht Club in St. Petersburg that I first met your husband, Mrs. Granville." He gently lifted a tiny ladybird off his knee onto the back of his hand.

"Oh? Well, he was probably on one of his business trips. Kashmir shawls, I believe, are prized even in Russia."

"Yes, probably."

Not quite understanding the drift, Emma said nothing more. For a while Charlton sat engrossed in the progress of the ladybird as it crawled slowly up his coat sleeve, then he lowered his head and blew it away softly. Dusk was falling. Withdrawing his watch from his waistcoat pocket, Charlton suddenly voiced an exclamation and leapt to his feet.

"Good heavens! I had no idea it was so late. I hope I have not overstayed my welcome?"

Emma assured him that he had not. Indeed, privately she was disappointed that he did not stay a while longer. She had enjoyed the afternoon immensely and the hours had flown by unnoticed. Even though this was only the second time they had met, she felt completely comfortable in Charlton's company. He was extremely well read, and when one got used to it, even his cynicism was curiously engaging. She was relieved that during the course of the afternoon no mention had been made of Chloe Hathaway.

Damien had not returned after all. Still violently unforgiving, Emma decided that the exercise of entertaining Charlton at Shalimar would have to be repeated.

Becoming aware that Charlton's gaze was fixed on her face, she coloured. "I am so pleased that you took the trouble to come all this way just to satisfy my curiosity, Mr. Charlton. I hope I did not bore you too much with my endless questions?"

"On the contrary, Mrs. Granville, as I have already confessed, one of my greatest pleasures is to pontificate before a rapt audience—and as rapt audiences go, you are not to be faulted."

Emma smiled; the self-deprecation was characteristic and rather appealing. "You must dine with us one evening when my husband returns," she suggested boldly.

He made no response, but his eyes, suddenly serious and troubled, continued to study her face. "I would be privileged, Mrs. Granville," he said all at once, "if you would grant me a very special request."

"Heavens, how solemn you look, Mr. Charlton!" She laughed. "Considering how long I have waited to meet and talk to you, I would be happy to grant almost any request you care to make."

"In that case I request that you consider me your friend." He remained unsmiling. "Some day soon you may need one."

CHAPTER

11

Colonel Mikhail Borokov strolled down the wide, graceful avenue in Tashkent known as Romanov Street. The avenue was lined with quadruple rows of geometrically spaced acacia, poplar and willow, a fact he noted with pride, for he approved of geometry.

By and large he also approved of martial law and the sense of discipline that it brought to Tashkent, capital of Russia's Asian Empire and nucleus of Central Asian trade. There was no doubt that military rule had effectively modernised the "city of stone" and brought to it a taste of European living. As widespread as Paris, but with one tenth its population (less than one hundredth if one discounted the hundred thousand indigents), Tashkent was now a capital city almost as much to be envied as Calcutta, centre of Britain's empire in Asia.

As he walked past the parade ground and barracks, an orderly formation of soldiers saluted and Borokov tipped his cap with a finger and sighed. The honest truth was that despite its regimented discipline and his endorsement of it, privately Mikhail Borokov found Tashkent joyless. The military club and its incessant balls and buffets were dreary, the officers who frequented them even more so. The twenty thousand men stationed here he dismissed with contempt as intellectually retarded and unworthy of fraternisation, as he did the indigents of every breed, colour and origin imaginable. What Tashkent sorely lacked, much to his regret, was a class of educated, prosperous and refined natives such as was found in the cities of Britain's Indian Empire. Ironically enough the city's shortcomings, he saw, were a consequence of precisely those aspects of urban society that martial law had destroyed—individual vitality, intellectual friction and social sophistication, aspects that gave such a heady flavour to European cities like St. Petersburg.

Secretly, Mikhail Borokov longed for a return to St. Petersburg. He missed the gaiety and glitter, the soirées and suppers and the exclusive Yacht Club, where among the polished Russian elite one met genuine elegance and style. He also missed, he could not deny, the privileged luncheons at the imperial palaces arranged now and then by Alexei Smirnoff. Whatever his own personal opinion of Alexei, there was no gainsaying that the man was a true aristocrat. Born to riches, he had the social confidence that went with privilege, and this Borokov envied immensely.

Regardless of his longings, however, he also knew only too well that the life for which he yearned would have to wait. He had unfinished business in Central Asia, a plan to implement, a mission to complete. He heaved another silent sigh, cast aside his visions of St. Petersburg and again consulted his pocket-watch.

Still early for his appointment with the Baron, he strolled into a small roadside park, one of many such in Tashkent, and sat down on a bench. A bumbling old fart who couldn't see beyond his ovis poli, the Baron was nonetheless a stickler for punctuality who disapproved as much of latecomers as of those who arrived early. Borokov was grateful, of course, that Ivana never allowed him to miss an appointment, but sometimes her efficiency irritated him. Instead of sitting and twiddling his thumbs here in a park, he could have been spending a profitable half hour in his office completing his St. Petersburg report.

Abstractedly watching the antics of a young boy at play with his dog, he thought of his secret confabulations with Alexei Smirnoff. Alexei had considered it dangerous to try to procure even a few of the new magazine rifles without official sanction, and how Safdar Ali was to be persuaded to accept obsolete guns, Borokov failed to see. Another problem, of course, would be the timing. Safdar Ali would not lead them to the Yasmina before the guns were reassembled and tested; they on their part would refuse to complete the assembly without prior access to the Yasmina. And what if the bastard killed them off as soon as they had occupied the pass? Borokov relieved his frustrations with a silent oath; until Smirnoff arrived, everything was up in the air! He had no idea whether it would eventually land neatly at his feet or explode above his head. Trying to shake off his apprehensions, he leapt up, glanced once again at his watch and continued morosely towards his destination.

The so-called palace of the Governor-General of Russian Turkestan was, in point of fact, not much of anything but an eyesore, partly relieved in its ugliness by the splendid gardens at the rear. Spread around an artificially created stream and waterfall with mountains of flowering shrubs, the acres of lovingly nurtured greenery were indeed a sight to behold. To one side of the enclosures housing the Baron's menagerie was a bear pit. Because the bears had taken to eating the gardeners and had been destroyed, they had recently been replaced by a pair of less hostile silver foxes.

Since it was in these gardens that the Baron spent many hours of his day, it was here that he received Colonel Borokov.

"On time, I see." The Baron nodded with approval. Extricating himself from crowding canines of every shape, size, breed and colour imaginable, he shifted the falcon perched on his gloved right hand to the left. "I like a man who respects time, Colonel. There is still an hour left to the next feed, but be a good fellow and try not to dawdle."

Losing interest in his visitor, he transferred his attention to a cage of rare partridges from the Chimgan hills, leaving Borokov to glare into the face of an unblinking Oxus pheasant. The Baron was a short, fat man, with a monocle, pendulous jowls, and a drooping mouth with rather the look of one of his despondent spaniels, even more so now that he was in mourning for his beloved golden oriole. He finally noticed Borokov again.

"Well, man, speak up, speak up—what brings you here?"

"You asked me to report to you, sir, as soon as I returned from St. Petersburg."

"Oh yes, that. Well, how did everything go?"

"As well as could be expected, Excellency." There was no point in recounting details about his discussions with Alexei; the old fool would not remember more than one word out of ten. "The weapons have been selected, listed and are now in the process of being dismantled."

"Weapons?"

Borokov sighed. "For Hunza, sir."

"Ah!" The Baron held up a forefinger as proof of comprehension. "Of course. But why dismantled?"

"We would not be able to transport them across the mountains without provoking a strong reaction from the Angliskis, sir. Once dismantled, the component parts will be easier to disguise."

"I see. But not these new rifles, I trust?"

"No, sir. General Smirnoff is doubtful if they will be sanctioned."

"I should think not! So, when do the deliveries start?"

"Later this summer, sir, by which time, unfortunately, Your Excellency would have already left Tashkent."

The Baron's frown vanished; he smiled happily. "Pity," he murmured in an effort to look regretful. "Pity. I would have liked to see our commitment concluded before I left. What did you say the man's name was?"

"Safdar Ali, sir." Borokov tried to shake off a huge male canine of indeterminate breed that humped his right leg in the belief that it was a willing female.

"Isn't he also expecting some money from us?"

"Yes, sir. St. Petersburg will send that only after the bargain is completed."

"Bargain?" The Baron looked blank, then grimaced and hastily returned the falcon to its perch. Kneeling down, he vigorously rubbed his glove against the grass to rid it of the reminder of the bird's visit. "Er, refresh my memory, will you?"

"In return for the weaponry and subsidy, sir, we have demanded access to the Yasmina Pass."

The Yasmina!

The Baron gave a start. "Oh yes, I remember now." His eyes flew to the enclosure where the Kashmiri markhor grazed. He noted again with pride that the horns would indeed be triple-twisted. As full memory returned, his mouth drooped. He was certain that the wretched Dard would arrive shortly with the golden eagle fledglings, but the other man appeared to have vanished in the bowels of Tashkent. However, he was not truly worried. One of them would have to return because of that woman, wouldn't he?

He reinforced himself with a breath. "There has been a rather, ah, *curious* development while you were away, Borokov," he began nervously. "Therefore, let us retire to the smoking-room where we can talk freely."

Borokov followed him out of the garden and in passing landed a hefty kick on the amorous dog's rump, which effectively settled its ardour. It yelped and slunk away in the opposite direction. The rest of the brigade, yapping and nipping and snapping joyously at his heels, trailed them all the way into the house.

The Baron's inner sanctum was a cosy private chamber which not even his wife entered without his permission. Its wood panelling and coffered cornices had been painted by local Sart artists, its divans upholstered in red velvet specially woven in Bokhara. The sanctum led off the Baron's main reception room where enormous oil portraits of the late Tsar and Tsarina and the present royal couple decorated the wall above a dais. Even though it was a warm, temperate evening, a fire had been lit in the grate. The dogs raced towards it, fell in an untidy heap on the hearth and jockeyed noisily for favoured positions.

"Curious development, sir?" It was only after they were seated before their glasses of slivovitz and bowls of roasted almonds, and the dogs silenced, that Borokov could ask his question.

"Yes, very."

"Curious to our advantage, sir?"

"Curious because I do not know. Nor am I certain how you will choose to regard the matter." Increasingly uneasy, the Baron fidgeted with an unlit cigar. "I have had a visitation from two men claiming to be Dards. They made a most astounding proposition."

Borokov's heart sank—what unholy mess had the idiot gone and landed them in now? It was uncomfortably warm in the room. He rose, threw the window wide open, marginally loosened the neckband of his uniform and returned to his seat prepared for the worst.

Outside the open window directly beneath its protruding ledge, the Kazakh gardener crouched in the grass pruning rose bushes. Borokov did not see him.

The Baron crinkled his eyes and stared hard into the fire. "Tell me, Borokov, if someone were to offer you a young markhor buck, golden eagle fledglings and . . . and God's gift on a platter, what would be your instant reaction?"

"I would be instantly suspicious, sir."

"Quite." The Baron nodded unhappily, struck a match and lit the tip of his cigar. "And if that someone were to offer you all these in exchange for something that *he* wanted—then what would be your reaction?"

With no idea what the man was babbling on about, Borokov was exasperated. "Well, I suppose I would conclude that whatever it was that *he* wanted was of considerable value to him, what else?"

"Precisely!" The Baron looked relieved. "That precisely is my interpretation, although I'm damned if I can understand any of it."

"Perhaps I could be of some assistance, sir?" Borokov offered, trying hard not to clench his teeth. "They say two heads are always better than one."

"Well, I certainly hope so, Borokov, I certainly hope so." He puffed even more vigorously. "I have been offered detailed, authenticated maps of the Yasmina Pass."

Borokov felt his tensions loosen. "I see. This new animal in the garden—these men brought it, did they?"

The Baron flushed. "A Kashmiri markhor, Borokov, with triple twists in his . . ."

"And, incidentally, also offered maps of the Yasmina?"

"Well, not quite like that."

"How much money did they demand in exchange?"

"They didn't want money, they asked for a . . ."

"They said they were Dards?" Borokov cut in impatiently.

"Yes, but under all that hair and grime all these people look the same to me. One of the men—the nephew I think—said he came from Chitral."

"How did they happen to acquire these alleged maps?"

"They said they stole them."

"From where?"

"The nephew claims to have been a camel groom with the caravan in which that Angliski traveled, the one who was killed—what was his name?"

"Butterfield?"

"Yes, that's the one."

Borokov sat up slowly. "He mentioned Butterfield by name?"

"Yes . . . no. I can't remember, but he said he stole the papers from his bag during the raid."

Borokov frowned. He himself had heard of the Angliski's murder from an occasional informant, a horse-dealer, who had heard of it at the caravanserai in Leh. Now, of course, it was all over the English and Russian papers, despite Simla's frantic efforts to keep the lid on the affair. About the contention of the Dards he was frankly sceptical, but he was also puzzled.

"I wonder," he mused, "if there is a connection?"

"Connection, what connection? Stop mumbling, man!"

About to explain, Borokov stopped. It would be a waste of breath to explain details of what he had accidentally stumbled across in Hunza. He asked instead, "You let the men go?"

"Only one of them. To guard the nest and then abstract the eagle fledglings when the eggs hatched. And to fetch the maps, of course. The other man is still in Tashkent."

"Where?"

The Baron waved a vague hand. "Somewhere. What does it matter as long as he is within our jurisdiction?"

"You did not have him taken into custody?" Borokov was amazed at the sheer stupidity of the man.

"There was no need to. I told you they wanted something in return, didn't I?"

"Whatever they wanted, they will not show their faces again," Borokov said disgustedly, "with or without the fledglings and the maps."

"They will *have* to if they want her."

"Her? Who?"

The Baron coughed at some length, then rose and stoked the fire. He did not look at Borokov. "It appears that they came to locate a woman believed to be working somewhere in our territory. When the woman is delivered to them, they will give me the golden eagle babies and the maps." He resumed his seat and lifted a small, fluffy white Pomeranian onto his lap.

"Who *is* this woman they want in return for all this bounty?" Borokov asked, bewildered. "And how is she to be located?"

"I have already located her."

"Where?"

Engrossed in examining the Pomeranian's paws the Baron jerked off a tick, tossed it into the fire with a grimace of distaste, and replaced the dog on the hearth. "Here, in Tashkent. They left behind this information about her." He extended a piece of paper.

Borokov made no move to take it. "Well, what am I expected to do about it, Excellency?" he asked, extremely irate. "I already have my plate full with other responsibilities."

The Baron refolded the paper and placed it carefully on the table. "I think you should take a look at this, Colonel. They said that she is Armenian and might be wearing a pendant such as is drawn on this piece of paper. You see, Colonel," he stared hard at Borokov, "I am convinced that the woman they seek is Ivana Ivanova."

Outside the window the Kazakh gardener picked up his implements and departed as silently as he had arrived.

*E*mma had been on her own at Shalimar more than eight weeks before Damien returned.

Since their marriage, she calculated, they had spent less than forty-eight hours together. If their courtship had been a succession of hollow words, false smiles and meaningless charades, the marriage was certainly an appropriate corollary. She was aware that there were whispers at Shalimar about Damien's absence; much as they rankled, she had no means to counter them, for his virtual abandonment of her was proof enough of his unconcern. Why then, she wondered again and again, had he bothered to marry her at all?

Far more disturbing than Damien's absence, however, was the fact that it was beginning to stir unwanted emotions in her. She had deluded herself into believing that her present freedom to do as she pleased was a blessing; now, after weeks on her own at the core of a large, unfamiliar household in an alien country, she could no longer sustain the lie. The truth was that however much she fought the feeling, she found Damien's callousness deeply hurtful.

To add to her sense of insecurity, Charlton's visit had left her vaguely disturbed. He was undoubtedly an entertaining raconteur, invigorating company and a sympathetic listener; even after so brief an acquaintanceship, between them there already appeared to be an empathy. Nevertheless, she was mortified by his curious request as they parted. Was it so obvious even to an acquaintance that she was lonely and desperately in need of a friend?

Regardless of her misgivings, Emma filled her days with self-devised activity. Indulging her natural curiosity, she set about familiarising herself with the estate. Forever questioning and peeking and probing, she explored every corner, spent long hours in the office with Lincoln, the estate manager, visited the homes and families of the workers in an effort to absorb as fully as she could the flavour of this wild, beautiful place to which perverse fate had brought her.

She watched the paddy being threshed to provide fine rice for the fastidious tables of India and Afghanistan; fresh saffron was being planted and would be harvested in October when the stigma turned scarlet. She helped to sort out, weigh and list excess fruit for canning and learned about indigenous accounting methods. Much to Qadir Mian's amusement, she insisted on practical instruction in how to shear and card the wool of the long-haired mountain goats before it was transformed into yarn.

There was to be a wedding soon on the estate. Intrigued by the customs and rituals of a Kashmiri Brahmin ceremony of which she knew little, she made notes in her diary for future reference. To be able to communicate more easily, she recruited a shy, scholarly *munshi* from the estate office to instruct her in Kashur, the unique dialect of the valley derived from Sanskrit and influenced by many other languages during the centuries of its existence.

When the weather proved inclement, she studied Dr. Anderson's annotations and worked on her book. Delighting in the luxury of space the study offered, she labelled, catalogued and exhibited to her heart's content. Her father's Buddhist artefacts were already proudly on display in the glassed-in cabinets, his library neatly arranged in the bookshelves and his fine Tibetan silk tankhas hung on the cream walls. To fill the solitary hours of evening, she ordered Kashmiri dishes and accustomed herself to new tastes, scoured Damien's library for reading material and embarked on a serious study of Kashmir in an effort to convert a necessity into a virtue and benefit from it. At night before going to bed, she wrote long, ecstatic letters to her mother, the Purcells, Jenny and John and David, extolling the virtues of her new home and husband, fabricating plausible details such as they would want to hear.

Still fascinated by their expertise, however, it was at the weavers' village that she spent most of the hours of her day whenever it was fine.

"You ask questions like *she* used to," Qadir Mian said one morning over a tangy cup of *qahwa*. The old man had started to address her with an informality that was, Emma saw, an indication of his increasing acceptance of her daily presence.

"Who?" She paused in her perusal of a folder of designs.

"The late begum sahiba." He took a pinch of snuff, inserted it into one nostril and sneezed with great satisfaction. "She too wanted to know everything, see everything. At least in the early years."

"Not in the later years?"

He shook his grizzled head. "In the later years she was beset with many sorrows. She too was a fine lady and as you can see"—he pointed to the book in her lap—"a gifted artist."

"These patterns were created by her?"

"These and many others. Her designs were like butterfly wings, light and delicate and filled with colour, just like those of our chota huzoor. You see, she understood the mysteries of the Kashmiri pine, the patterns of which are sung like fine poetry. Later, she painted to soothe her grief, sometimes for many hours every day, with her head bent low over her table and tears pouring down her cheeks."

"What was the cause of her grief?"

Lost in his own thoughts, the old man did not hear her question. "Often she sent for me in her room as she sat painting by the window and talked to me of her own country, her own people, telling me tales about her home, her childhood."

"She spoke your language well?"

"No, not well, but the language of grief is universal."

Emma repeated her earlier question.

"The cause of her grief? That too was universal. She was a stranger in Kashmir, she longed to return to her own kind."

"Were you here when she went away?"

"Oh yes." He replied willingly, accepting her right to ask him whatever she pleased.

"And chota huzoor and his father?"

He sucked in a breath, making his jowls quiver. "Had they been here that night they would not have permitted it, but they were in Bombay for the *numaish* and returned only after she was long gone." Emma presumed he was referring to one of the frequent trade exhibitions held in Indian cities. "Two of our craftsmen demonstrated the weaving of a *tilikar* in Bombay, a shawl of small, square woven patterns like this. They were much praised."

Emma admired the shawl he held up. It was truly exquisite, but her mind was elsewhere. "She left alone?"

"Alone? Oh no. She left with the man who came to fetch her."

"Who was he, a firanghi?"

He nodded.

"Was he young?"

"Who can tell with firanghis? Only Zaiboon saw him and she was already half blind."

"The late begum sahiba's maid?"

"Yes. She became dear to Allah five years ago." He nodded and peered as he searched his clouded memory. "It was a cold night. We were all in our warm beds, even the chowkidars. Heavy rains had produced fearful landslides and floods in the middle of the apple harvest. I remember this well because some of our sheep broke loose during the storm and we had to wade through slush *this* high"—he circled his knee with a hand—"to find them."

"Does anyone know where she went?"

He looked up into the blue of the sky and spread his palms. "Where her kismet took her, poor lady. Now she is dead and will never return." Even behind his thick pebble glasses, she could see that his eyes were moist. "I shall never forget that night. It took burra huzoor's life and changed all of ours forever. As for our chota huzoor"—he shook his head—"he was only a boy then, too young to understand, too old to cry. Burra huzoor sent him away to *bilait* soon after. We managed as best we could, but it was not the same, it was never again the same. There was a time when shawls were valued like jewels. Not any more, not any more."

He lovingly stroked his *tilikar* shawl, and losing the thread of the conversation bemoaned the lack of the rare wool—"soft gold," the Tibetans called it—from the goats of Ush Tarfan.

It was futile, Emma saw, to question him further.

With her curiosity about Damien's dead mother again raring, a bold plan stirred in her mind. Suraj Singh would not approve, of course, but so long as she chose her timing with care, Suraj Singh need not know at all.

*I*t was a pleasant night, clear and tranquil, and the whispering air was as warm as a sheath. Galleons of clouds sailed across nocturnal oceans and clusters of stars, not yet diminished by the melon moon entangled in a chinar, sprinkled enough light for Emma to pick out a path across the gardens. Except for the cries of night creatures and distant echoes of music and chanting, the silence was untrammelled.

Tonight was the night of the wedding. The staff, in particular Suraj Singh, were occupied with the festivities. As chatelaine and principal guest, Emma had offered her good wishes to the families, blessed the couple, and, as advised by Suraj Singh, made her presentation of twenty-one silver rupees, embroidered *phirrens* and *poots,* a silk turban, a pair of gold bangles and trays of sweets. Once the marriage had been consecrated with the seven perambulations round the fire and token sweets eaten, she had excused herself to allow the more informal festivities to commence.

It was now well past eleven. Without fear of discovery, Emma marched out of her apartment armed with a low-burning lantern, a box of matches and a screwdriver. Sharifa and Rehmat, who slept in an anteroom at the end of the corridor, were at the wedding and not likely to return for hours. Suraj Singh lived in an independent cottage on the estate; with Damien away, unless summoned he would not visit the house after dark. The staircase and cavernous entrance hall were hushed, devoid of human presence. With their attention focussed on the celebrations, and sated with food and drink, the chowkidars were unlikely to notice her little expedition. Through a side door in the downstairs scullery, she slipped out into the garden.

Breaking into the ground-floor apartment proved easier than Emma had anticipated. On an earlier exploration she had observed a pair of locked doors at the back of the house, each leading into one of the apartments. With the screwdriver she carried in her pocket, she now tackled the hasp on one of the doors. It was old and rusted and the screws came away with minimal resistance. She gave the door a gentle nudge; it swung inwards with no more than a modest creak of disuse. She slipped inside, closed the door behind her and raised the flame in her lantern. As she had calculated, the room was a bathroom, congruent with Damien's on the first floor, and the layout of the apartment was easy to guess. Without wasting time in the derelict bathroom, she slipped off her shoes and stepped through the adjoining dressing-room into what had once been Edward Granville's private parlour.

She raised her lantern and looked around, noticing with relief—and some surprise—that the paraffin lamps on the tables were well filled with fuel. She pulled the heavy curtains across the windows, struck a match and held it to a well-trimmed wick; it burned cleanly and brightly. She sniffed the air; it smelled fresh, as if the rooms had recently been aired. Recalling Suraj Singh's words of warnings, she proceeded cautiously, testing the parquet flooring with tentative steps. No protesting creaks came from beneath the carpets; the floor appeared to be in perfect condition.

Why then had Suraj Singh lied to her?

Emma surveyed her surroundings with interest. The furniture in the apartment was unremarkable, almost Spartan, making few concessions to elegance. There were no dust sheets anywhere nor, indeed, dust, and in the deadly hush somewhere in the entrails of the apartment sounded the heartbeat of a well-wound clock. Far from being damaged and dangerous, as Suraj Singh had implied, Edward Granville's apartment appeared to be not only in good condition but also in frequent use.

The most attractive piece of furniture among the nondescript rest was a desk. Rectangular, of gleaming mahogany with a beautiful grain, it had columns of drawers on either side that supported the top. As she placed the lamp on the mirrored surface, the well-polished brass handles twinkled. The columns of drawers, she saw, were protected with locked, vertical hinged flaps running down their outer edges. The locks that hung on the latches felt oily to the touch, with no indication of rust. For what purpose was this desk used, she wondered, and why a locked desk in a locked, allegedly unusable apartment with abundantly secure storage upstairs and in the estate office? Lowering herself into the swivel chair in front of the desk, Emma eyed the locks thoughtfully.

Should she . . . ?

Her motive in breaking into the apartment was innocuous and, in her opinion, justifiable—to learn more about the Granvilles. The desk might conceivably contain books, paintings, photograph albums and other relics that would reveal at least some of the background of the mysterious family into which she had married. If, indeed, there were any secrets to be had, well then, as Damien's wife surely she had a right to share in them?

Abandoning her scruples, she reached for her screwdriver.

Before she could take it to the latch, however, her ears picked up a sound. She froze into immobility and listened. Yes, there it was again, a single creak, then a succession of identifiable noises: a key grating in a lock, a chain being released, grilled iron doors being swung open and clanging against walls, heavy, booted footsteps. Someone had entered the corridor that led to the apartments, someone making no effort to conceal his presence.

Damien!

Biting back a gasp, Emma blew out the lamp, whisked it off the desk, picked up her lantern and ran into the bathroom. The lamp would be missed, of course, but rather that than the telltale smell of the burning wick and the feel of the hot chimney. Behind her, softly, she closed the bathroom door and leaned weakly against it to retrieve her vanished breath. She heard the door to the apartment open and heavy boots traverse the floorboards until the footfall was deadened by the carpet; then silence. The steps had sounded uneven. Emma realized that her unsuspecting companion in the apartment was not her husband but Suraj Singh, unfortunately not quite as engrossed in wedding festivities as she had assumed.

She waited, expecting him to burst into the bathroom any minute and find her crouching in a corner—the ultimate humiliation! How would she explain her surreptitious entry? But the minutes passed and nothing happened. Had Suraj Singh left? Opening the bathroom door a hairline chink—praying that it would not creak—she peered into the gloom. In the far distance she discerned the glimmer of a light and concluded that he was still there.

Less nervous now and once again consumed by curiosity, Emma opened the door wide enough to slip through. Inching across the dressing-room to avoid unseen objects, she crept to the doorway that led into the sitting room and peered round the curtain.

His back to her, Suraj Singh stood bent over the desk examining some papers in the light of the lamp positioned at his elbow. With one of the hinged flaps unlocked and the bottom drawer pulled open, he seemed deeply immersed in whatever he was doing. The absence of the lamp, she assumed, had not been noticed.

One of her bangles hit the wall with a faint tinkle and she held her breath, but he did not turn. Why should he? Not expecting a visitor, it would not occur to him that he was being watched. By his gestures and the easy confidence with which he removed and replaced papers, Emma saw that he was familiar with the desk and its contents. He sat down and started to write, the scratchy noises from his pen bearing testimony to the speed with which it raced across the sheet. A few moments later he extracted an envelope from the drawer, inserted the letter within, addressed it, then sealed it with a stick of red wax melted over the lamp.

That Suraj Singh enjoyed the confidence and respect of Damien Emma already knew, but that he should be privy to the hidden pockets of Damien's life suddenly seemed insupportable, and she filled with resentment. How ironical that she, Damien's wife, should have to enter the apartment in stealth whereas he, an employee, had free run of it!

His task concluded, Suraj Singh straightened, slipped the envelope into a pocket, shut the drawer and locked the hinged flaps. His keys, Emma noticed with disappointment, were fitted onto a large ring attached by a chain to a buttonhole of his jacket. He picked up the small lantern he had brought with him, blew out the lamp, went out of the door and closed it behind him. As he did so, he hummed; whatever it was that he had been doing, he was obviously well satisfied with it.

Riven as she was by curiosity and longing to investigate the adjoining suite as well, Emma saw that it would be risky to resume her explorations. If Suraj Singh were to return and find her in either apartment, she would be in a pretty pickle. Swallowing her disappointment, she decided that her voyage of discovery would have to be kept for another, more opportune occasion. She waited fifteen more minutes to ensure that Suraj Singh had left the apartment, then returned the way she had entered, through the bathroom. She replaced the screws on the hasp of the door, slipped back into the scullery and ran back upstairs. The festivities were still on and Sharifa and Rehmat had not returned.

Her absence had passed unnoticed.

*T*he following morning, to her great joy, Emma received two letters. It was her first packet of post since she had arrived and all else was forgotten. One letter was from her mother; the other, from her brother, had come from Leh.

David's pique obviously persisted, for his letter was stiff and formal and gave only basic news of his new life. His bungalow was adequate, his Ladakhi bearer a thief and Maurice Crankshaw a demanding officer. There was a great deal of paperwork to be done, but not much by way of other activity. The monastery on the hill was an interesting retreat with a good library of old texts and the summery weather was holding. He had been on a recce, had established good contacts during his travels and was now about to leave on a first real assignment (he did not say where). He hoped she was well and that Kashmir was to her liking.

He did not ask after Damien.

Her mother's long letter, on the other hand, was filled with news and warmth. She had moved in with Carrie and Archie and was most comfortable. Jenny's wedding in St. James was appropriately solemn, the reception a splendid bash and the dancing had gone on till well past breakfast. The Purcells, especially Jenny, had missed her dreadfully. Georgina had hinted at Charlotte's imminent engagement without revealing the identity of the suitor (in case he backed out at the last minute), but everyone knew it was that young O'Reilly boy who had courted the Drabble girl before she ran away with what's-his-name from Karachi. No more was being said about Charlotte's renunciation of the world. Everyone assumed that her plan to give herself to God had been indefinitely postponed.

Rumour had it that Stephanie Marsden was finally about to put young Alexander Sackville out of his misery (although she'd said that before and it had always come to naught). The Lieutenant-Governor had attended the wedding (Jenny's, that is) and asked after her (Emma). Alec Waterford had gone one over the eight and keeled over the drinks table, spraying red sorbet all over poor Carrie's new dress. Daphne had had hysterics but not before delivering a mouthful. There had been tight lips all round, the tightest those of Reverend Smithers in spite of the Canadian donation. The newly-weds had left for a honeymoon in Agra (where John had a sister), from where they would proceed directly to Calcutta.

Dear Clive Bingham was off on another expedition but poor Theo Anderson still awaited funds for his, and the Handleys had finally been evicted. They had found temporary refuge with the Bankshalls but were having to pay even for *matches,* which everyone thought scandalous. It looked like Howard Stowe would finally settle for Prudence. She, her mother, missed both of her children desperately—when would they ever meet again?

Starved of news, Emma avidly devoured the morsels of gossip. The spidery handwriting, the familiar turns of phrase and the abundant expression of affection brought on waves of homesickness. Overcome, she started to cry. Later, when Sharifa came in to light the lamps, Emma stopped her, knowing that her eyes were red and puffy. Even though the cry had made her feel better, swamped by memories of home, she continued to sit in the dark with her eyes closed.

When she opened them, it was to see Damien framed in the doorway.

Not having known that he was expected this evening, and with the glimmer of light in the corridor behind him, it took Emma a moment to recognise the apparition. When she did, her heart missed a beat. Hastily, she composed herself and brushed a hand across her eyes. How long had he been standing there?

He walked up to her and peered into her face. "Why are you sitting in the dark?"

"No . . . no special reason." She trembled with the effort to sound normal. "I was watching the sunset and must have dozed off."

He peered closer. "Have you been crying?"

"Of course not!" She managed a smile, then ran into the bedroom to wash her face and grab a few moments to recollect her wits. On her return she tugged at the bell-rope for Hakumat, ordered the lamps to be lit and a tray of refreshments to be brought up.

"Or would you rather I ordered dinner?" she asked. "You must be hungry."

Sitting with his arms crossed behind his head and his eyes closed, he shook his head. "Not yet. For the moment some tea and a bath will do."

She fell silent, fumbling frantically for topics of conversation. "Your trip—was it successful?"

"Yes." Sprawled across the couch with his legs extended, he looked weary. There was a dark stubble across his cheeks. His shirt was patchy with sweat and his boots covered with mud. Behind him, Hakumat moved quietly about the room lighting and re-positioning the lamps.

"Did you get the wool?"

"Wool?"

"The wool you went to receive in Leh?"

"Oh that. Yes. Yes, I did." He used the tip of one boot to push off the other. It fell to the floor with a thud. "The fellows bringing the consignment arrived late. Apparently they were caught in a landslide and barely escaped with their lives."

She hesitated. "Did you see . . . David?"

"No." His eyes were again closed, his fingers laced behind his head.

"And Mr. Crankshaw?"

"Who?"

"His superior officer in Leh."

"No." He made a face. "I've never met the man—and have no desire to. You know what I think of these British agents."

"I would have liked to know how David was faring in his work. He says so little in his letter."

Damien made no response. Still flustered by his sudden presence, she rose, signalled Hakumat to remove the discarded boots and turned up the lamps; the room flooded with light. Damien watched in silence as she placed a fresh log on the dying flames in the fireplace. He spoke again only when she was seated.

"Your own journey, was it comfortable? I take it Suraj Singh saw to all your needs as instructed?" He patted the seat beside him.

"Oh yes, thank you, on both accounts. Suraj Singh could not have been more attentive." She pretended not to notice the mute summons and remained where she was.

"Well, what do you think of Kashmir?" He waved a hand at the window. "Does it not please you, this place where the heavens are said to meet the earth?"

"It does, but I see that you have answered your own questions."

He leaned forward to stare intently into her face.

"And the house? The staff, your apartment, especially the study? Are they all to your satisfaction?"

She was disarmed by his steady gaze, but maintained her poise.

"How could they not be? Your Shalimar has every comfort one could possibly ask for, and your staff are most admirably diligent."

They spoke cordially enough but like two acquaintances exchanging small talk. To the many questions that followed she gave careful, precise answers, realising with wry amusement that this was the first conversation they had ever had that could be called even remotely civilised. Because of its very banality the exchange sounded strange, making her even more stilted. If he did notice her cultivated responses, however, he did not comment upon them.

"I'm sorry that I could not be here when you arrived."

Emma had not expected the apology; she received it without reaction. "It didn't matter. Your staff took good care of me."

"You mean, you did not miss me at all?"

"Not at all," she assured him, matching his light tone. "I am accustomed to making do with my own company and the process of getting used to your Shalimar left little time to brood."

He raised an eyebrow. "*My* Shalimar, *my* staff?"

She coloured. "An unthinking choice of pronoun. Unused as I am to such affluence, it will take me time to adjust to it."

Before she could anticipate the move, he had leaned forward and taken her hand in his. "Whatever is here is also yours," he said matter-of-factly, indeed, with a trace of annoyance. "I would like you to be happy at Shalimar."

"Really? Is that why you awaited my arrival with the intolerable impatience you promised in Delhi?"

"My absence was not of my making." He released her hand. "It could not be helped and I have already apologised. This is a new place for you, Emma, it is natural that initially you should feel unsettled. You will grow into it soon enough. This is, after all, your home."

"Oh? Well, in that case, you must ask your mistresses not to make it a habit to call on me without being invited."

As it slipped out, Emma almost bit off her tongue. She certainly had had no conscious intention of lowering herself by bringing *that* up. However, once said, it could not be retracted; she assumed an attitude of defiance.

"You mean Chloe? Yes, I heard that she had called with Charlton in tow." He made not even the pretence of a denial. If anything, he sounded amused. "You must not let Chloe upset you. She's really quite harmless—and she does have her occasional uses."

"About as harmless as a banded krait," Emma snapped. "As to her 'uses'—as you so tactfully put it—yes, I'm sure we *all* have our uses, she perhaps more than others."

"You equate yourself with Chloe Hathaway? You are a wife, not a mistress."

"So, you admit that she is your mistress!"

"Yes—except for the tense. Chloe *was* my mistress at one time. The relationship was of no great consequence."

"You mean," Emma said nastily, "she satisfied the senses without disturbing the heart?"

He was irked by the reminder. "Since you ask, yes, but I have not seen her since I left for Delhi." He suddenly flung up his hands. "Would you rather I lied to you, Emma? You know that I have not been a saint—which unencumbered man is? Surely you are old enough to know that there are certain physical . . . appetites that demand to be satisfied? That men need to expend some energies in order to preserve others?"

He was patronising her again!

The tea arrived with a plate of freshly fried samosas. Obviously, the cook was better prepared for the master's return than she was, Emma thought sourly as she served the samosas, handed him the plate and started to pour the tea.

"And would you as a husband," she asked when Hakumat had left the room, "accept that same explanation from your wife about the needs of the female body?"

He bit into a samosa with relish. "To satisfy those, a wife is expected to go to her husband."

"And what if she preferred to satisfy them elsewhere?" she demanded, as incensed by his masculine conceit as by his earlier admission.

He finished the rest of the samosa, replaced his plate and, smiling faintly, reached for the pipe tucked in his belt. "With whom, for instance?"

"With"—in rising anger she said the first name that came to mind— "Geoffrey Charlton?"

For a split second his hand remained where it was, in mid-air, then he returned his attention to his pipe. It was only after he had filled the bowl with tobacco, picked up a burning branch from the fire and lit it to his satisfaction, that he spoke again.

"If she claimed that, the husband would hope that she was lying."

Emma's eyes glittered. "And if she were not?"

"Well, then, I suppose like any other self-respecting cuckold, the poor man would have to do something dreadfully tiresome—take a horse-whip to the man."

"Even though it takes two to make a cuckold?" she asked maliciously, enraged that he should not take her seriously.

He leaned back to study her face. "If the wife we speak of is you, Emma, then I suggest that you refrain from this particular game. At least until you learn how to play it." In no way perturbed, he laid his head back and continued to suck pleasurably at his pipe. "Apart from the fact that you already know my views on wayward wives and how to deal with them, unworldly women like you are liable to make fools of themselves."

She longed to wipe the complacency off his mouth, to wound him, so that he would take her seriously. "And what about worldly women like Nazneen?"

An instant or two passed before he replied, "Who told you about Nazneen?"

Again, no word of refutation, not a whisper of an excuse!

"As among thieves," she said scathingly, "there appears to be little honour among mistresses, too. Mrs. Hathaway was kind enough to enlighten me also about Nazneen—indeed, it seemed to be the chief purpose of her visit." She stood up abruptly and made to leave the room. "I will ask Hakumat to bring up some hot water for your bath and order dinner in an hour."

Regardless of tiredness, Damien was disinclined to retire meekly. He uncoiled himself, laid his pipe on the mantelpiece and leapt out of his seat, all so swiftly that she had no time to react. Before she knew it, he had barred her way and cupped her face between his hands.

"I have already told you that I have had many mistresses," he said softly. "Why should this upset you so much now?"

"Your appetite for mistresses is of no concern to me." Taking care not to move, she met his gaze coldly. "You are welcome to as many as your health and time will accommodate—so long as they don't defile *my* door-step. Kindly note the amended pronoun. You see? I do learn fast."

"Ah, but it is of concern to you!" The amused eyes told her that he still made sport. "It couldn't be, could it, that the uncaring, self-sufficient Emma Wyncliffe is actually *jealous*?"

She laughed. "No, Damien, it could not! If it appears so it is only because, as usual, your conceit blocks out the reality."

"Does it, by God!" Gripping her waist with both his palms, he bent down and kissed her hard on the mouth. Unmoving, she stiffened inwardly but registered no noticeable response. He did not repeat the performance. Instead he stepped back, propped an elbow on the mantelpiece, and grinned. "I see that my absence has given you time to hone your histrionic abilities even further!"

"Or, more likely, you are not quite as irresistible as you would like to believe!"

"Well, we will have to see about that tonight, won't we?" He reached for the bell-rope and Hakumat appeared. "Tell Lincoln to be ready with the files about the revenue dispute. I will be down shortly. And get the *bhisti* to bring up my bath water, very hot and plenty of it." He turned to Emma. "Don't wait dinner for me. Hakumat will fetch me something in the office." He disappeared through the communicating door into his own apartment.

Emma sank into the chair and stared blankly into the fire. She had let the conversation run out of control and she was very cross with herself. She wished she could have behaved with less spite and more dignity— certainly, she had not intended to fling accusations about the moment he returned home. At the same time she had meant what she had said—she was not prepared to tolerate his partners in profligacy (past or present) in her home and be reduced to a laughing-stock!

With no appetite left for dinner, she dismissed Sharifa, extinguished the lamps, quenched the fire and firmly locked both doors into her apartment.

She washed, changed and lay down in bed, shivering against the cold touch of the sheets. There was no point in courting sleep; she knew that it would not come.

It was as the chimes of midnight resounded through the dark silences that Emma finally heard the tentative turn of a door knob. Gritting her teeth, she lay still in bed with the quilt pulled up to her chin. The knob turned once more, then fell silent. She listened for a moment hardly daring to breathe, but the sound was not repeated. Her taut muscles slackened; with a sob of relief she slid under the bedclothes.

Her relief was short-lived. Barely a minute later came the crack of a gunshot and amidst a shower of splinters the communicating door flew open to a resounding kick. Throttling a cry, Emma leapt out of bed intending to flee into the study. Before she was even halfway there, Damien strode into the room and barred her path, the revolver still smoking in his hand. The acrid smell filled her nostrils and she started to cough.

He stood by the bed, legs apart, hands on hips, and waited for her paroxysm to subside. When it did, she groped for the bed, sank back into it and pulled the quilt up to her neck. Even without being able to see his expression in the half dark, she could tell that he was furious.

"Don't ever, ever again," he said, his voice all the more menacing for its quietness, "lock your door on me."

Badly frightened, but trying not to show it, she buried her face in the quilt. "Leave me alone, Damien, oh leave me *alone*! Can you not see that I do not want you near me?"

He thrust the revolver back under his belt roughly. "If you still choose to believe that I took you against your will, Emma, you are welcome to your self-deceptions. But remember"—he walked back towards the connecting door—"I will not come to you again until you ask me to."

"I will never ask you, *never*!"

He turned and in the shadows the whites of his eyes glistened. "You may be a woman, Emma, but by *Christ* you have a long way to go before becoming a wife!"

"Why should I bother when you have willing substitutes like Nazneen to satisfy what you call your physical appetites?"

"A woman of discernment knows when to show spirit and when to be tender. That is certainly something Nazneen could teach you well."

"Then go to your Nazneen, go to this . . . this paragon of perfection," she cried, "and leave me to my own inadequate devices!"

"Yes, perhaps I will."

Spinning on a heel, he walked back into his room.

She heard the next morning that he had risen early and left for Gulmarg.

CHAPTER

12

his, then, Emma saw bitterly, was to be the pattern of her marriage: an errant husband, an empty house and ugly scenes whenever they were together. It appeared that their lives were destined to run on parallel lines ordained never to meet. Regardless of gossip, Damien would continue to come and go as he pleased, continue to lead an independent existence as he always had. And what sublime joy it would bring his assorted women to learn that Damien and his wife did not care to share a bed!

Much as she regretted having provoked the demeaning scene, Emma vowed again that she simply would not condone his debauchery. Nor ask him to return to her bed!

Waiting in the paddock to commence their daily round of the estate the following morning, Suraj Singh wore his usual ungiving expression. How, she wondered uneasily, had Damien explained away the shot in the night and the shattered door? An unthinking accident? Ignorance that the revolver was loaded? A lost key?

In his hands, Emma suddenly noticed, Suraj Singh held the reins of an unfamiliar horse, a chestnut mare with light beige mane, socks and tail and moist, soulful eyes. Her leather saddle was hand-tooled and quite magnificent.

"Huzoor feels that begum sahiba will require a mount of her own on the estate," he said. "The mare has been reared from very fine stock and brought from Gulmarg to fulfil that requirement."

Emma was taken entirely by surprise.

"Since she is well disciplined but also has a mind of her own, huzoor believes that she will suit begum sahiba well." He made the comment without smiling. "Huzoor has named her Zooni, after Kashmir's most famous poetess, who lived in Gulmarg."

The unexpected (and quite generous) gift brought back the discomfitting memory of another, the *shatoosh* shawl. Emma remembered that she had not thanked Damien for the shawl, nor, indeed, had she given him the jacket she had bought in Srinagar. As she stroked the mare's forehead and marvelled at its softness, she felt a pinprick of guilt.

"How far is Gulmarg from here?"

"About twenty miles."

"My husband returns soon?"

"That is difficult to say. The cottage needs repairs, as also the outer walls. Much work needs to be done before . . ." He stopped.

"Before?"

"Before the rains. I myself leave for Gulmarg in the morning."

It was not what he had been about to say and Emma sighed to herself; another innocuous remark and another nerve touched?

"This cottage, is it as comfortable as the house here?"

"Oh yes, as comfortable but smaller. It is constructed of wood and has fewer rooms. Huzoor enjoys the privacy it allows on his occasional sojourns."

Sojourns with Chloe? Nazneen? The flicker of guilt died without trace and the taste in Emma's mouth soured.

As it happened, all night long the seed of an idea had lain gestating in her wide-awake brain. It was a daring idea, so daring as to be all but unthinkable. Nurtured now by resurgent anger, the seed suddenly took root and flowered.

"I read somewhere," she said, "that the very first coach in Kashmir was brought up by Henry Lawrence many years ago?"

"Yes, begum sahiba," Suraj Singh affirmed, "but since there were no roads in Kashmir at the time, it was kept as a showpiece in Srinagar. Nevertheless, it created such a sensation that our own burra huzoor was inspired to import one from Lahore."

"Oh yes, I saw a carriage in the barn at the back. The component parts were brought up and assembled on the estate, were they?"

"Yes. As begum sahiba must have noticed, it is very small."

"Safe enough to be used as a conveyance?"

"Well, only on the new road between Baramulla and Srinagar. It is a mere track, but it can take wheels. As a matter of fact, huzoor has used the carriage once or twice to go to Srinagar."

"How far is Srinagar from here?"

"About ten miles from the turning at Narabal."

Emma remarked that it sounded like a most uncomfortable journey. Suraj Singh agreed that it was indeed, and there the matter ended.

A woman of discernment knows when to show spirit and when to be tender. That is certainly something Nazneen could teach you well.

The taunt, not one Emma was prepared to forget, still stung badly, but to the wounded anger of last night, curiosity had been added. Who *was* this Nazneen? What was it that made Damien admire her enough to flaunt her in the face of his wife? Despite her burning resentment, Emma was consumed by a perverse desire to know more about this alleged paragon.

The next morning she rose at dawn. After having ensured that Suraj Singh had indeed departed for Gulmarg, she informed Sharifa of her intention to drive to Srinagar in the carriage to explore the Shalimar Baug. Sharifa was in turn surprised, alarmed and delighted. The surprise and alarm, however, dispelled with the assurance that huzoor had given his consent to the journey.

"Since Hakumat is in Gulmarg with huzoor, we will get two of the other fellows to escort us on horseback," she suggested enthusiastically. "Huzoor would be annoyed if we went unescorted."

It was, Emma agreed, an excellent idea. "We will take Rehmat with us. While I explore the gardens, both of you can visit your family. Later, I could meet your brother-in-law and persuade him to permit the child to be coached by me."

All of which Sharifa accepted most willingly.

"Just one thing more while I remember," Emma added as an afterthought. "When we return, my almirah will need to be sprayed with disinfectant. Last night I noticed a cockroach in one of the lingerie drawers and I am very concerned."

"A cockroach!" Sharifa was horrified. "*Toba, toba!* Where did the little devil come from? Huzoor is most particular about cockroaches and mice, *most* particular. I don't think I could bear to wait a moment longer to clean that almirah, begum sahiba. There can be no question of my going to Srinagar, no question at all! Why not just take Rehmat? The girl is good company and will entertain you well."

And that, of course, settled that problem nicely.

As she prepared herself for the trip, Emma wondered—not without a certain dark humour—what might be considered appropriate wear for a visit to one's husband's mistress. Formal, informal? Flamboyant or sedate? Eventually she chose a rather modish dress of chartreuse velvetine with a saucy little hat to match. She teased and brushed her hair until it positively twinkled, arranged it with unaccustomed care and treated her face to a patina of cosmetics. When she was ready, she stared mutinously at the mirror and took careful inventory. The darkened sockets had lightened and filled out, as had her cheeks. Her skin, once more honeyed, glowed from the many hours spent in the sun, and the sharp, bony angles of her body had softened; the collarbones no longer stuck out like ridges. Consciously or unconsciously, she had started to hold her head confidently erect and there was a sparkle in her eyes she could have sworn had not been there before.

All in all, the image that stared back at her was reassuring. Whatever virtues the matchless Nazneen might possess, she would not emerge too poor a second. Even though the prospect of coming face-to-face with yet another of Damien's mistresses was highly unpalatable, knowing herself, she saw that she would not rest until stubborn curiosity had been satisfied.

Small but snug and in mint condition, the coach was as sprightly as the pony that pulled it—which was more than could be said of the liveried coachman. Inexperienced and nervous at suddenly being called to active duty, he started off precariously and almost landed them in the ditch. Emma would have far preferred to hold the reins herself or, even better, ride on horseback, but such forwardness would appall the staff and she had no wish to stretch her luck further. Following one or two more near mishaps, however, the coachman rallied and they proceeded at a reasonable trot without undue risk to life and limb. The two chowkidars rode on ahead to reconnoitre for hidden dangers. Frankly petrified, Rehmat clung to Emma's hand, chanting prayers. A minefield of ruts, ridges and potholes, the track had them bouncing along rather more than necessary, but the early summer morning was cool, the panorama magnificent and eventually even Rehmat's nerves adjusted to the unfamiliar experience.

Just before noon, they reached the outskirts of Srinagar and alighted in a field on the southern rim of the Dal lake. One of the chowkidars was despatched to hire a shikara to ferry them to Naseem Baug near which Rehmat lived. Emma herself would have preferred to walk round the lake, but time was short and she had to get the encounter over and done with before her courage failed. To the other chowkidar she handed a swatch of material to match with a yard of silk from the shop of the Ali brothers in town. Giving them both money for food, she instructed the coachman to water the horse and wait by the carriage for their return.

"This is where I live," Rehmat exclaimed, hugely excited as they disembarked from the shikara near Naseem Baug. "There, down that lane just around the next corner."

"Good." Emma pressed a coin into the child's hand. "I will wait for you near the entrance of Shalimar Baug at two o'clock. Don't be late. We must be back home before dark."

As Rehmat ran off with the other chowkidar dutifully in tow, Emma waited a few moments. When they were no longer in sight, she slipped over her head the burqua she had brought with her, walked onto the road and then down the lane, at the end of which she could see the minaret of a mosque. All around, crowds jostled, but engrossed in their own business no one gave her a second glance. She stopped by a small silver shop to confirm her directions. Taking her to be a customer, the shopkeeper put on his most persuasive smile and began to unlock his wares. When he heard her question, however, his smile vanished.

"Nazneen Sultana's house?" he asked curtly as he replaced his trays of silver jewellery. "Next to the mosque, the one with the green shutters." Turning his back on her, he retreated, grumbling.

The double-storeyed house adjoining the mosque was tall, narrow, and painted cream. Without allowing herself time to think, Emma pushed open its green door and entered a brick-lined courtyard. Her heart thumped hard as she marvelled anew at the insanity that had brought her here. Supposing the woman was rude and offensive? Supposing she refused to see her at all? An elderly woman, fat and half asleep, rose from where she sat cleaning a tray of rice.

"Yes?"

Emma removed her burqua and introduced herself. "I have come to see Begum Nazneen Sultana."

The woman's flaccid, betel-stained mouth slackened further as she conducted a surprised appraisal of the visitor. Then she turned wordlessly, waddled up a narrow stone staircase and beckoned Emma to follow. From behind green-painted chiks hidden eyes watched and Emma's nervousness returned: what would Damien have to say if he ever found out about her inexplicable mission?

Through an archway curtained with strings of coloured glass beads they passed into a salon furnished with an ornate Persian carpet, thick mattresses draped in red velvet embroidered with gold thread, and plump bolsters. In a corner stood a selection of traditional musical instruments and a basket of brass ankle-bells.

A courtesan's tools of trade.

A second, similarly curtained doorway led into an inner chamber and Emma's steps faltered. What was she to say to the woman; how was she to explain an incomprehensible urge she could barely understand herself? Had the old crone not been so close behind, she would have turned and fled. And then it was too late.

"Please do come in, Mrs. Granville. I am Nazneen Sultana."

The glinting, tinkling screen parted and a woman stood in the doorway. Emma found herself ushered into a smaller, more intimate chamber furnished in the Western style with chairs, tables, a sofa and a low divan before which the woman positioned herself. She was dressed in the traditional

Kashmiri *phirren* and baggy trousers. A veil of flimsy rose-coloured gauze was draped over her head. She was of medium height, slight and small-boned; even her minimal movements were performed with a grace that confirmed her profession, as did her slow, supple salaam.

"Please do be seated, Mrs. Granville. I am honoured that you should choose to call on one as unworthy as myself." She kept her kohl-lined eyes lowered. "Had I received advance intimation, I would have prepared myself better to entertain you according to your status." She looked at the old woman and with a touch of imperiousness ordered a samovar and plates of sweets.

She had spoken in English to Emma in tones that were pleasant and cultivated. There was no trace of mockery in her manner, only an undertone of deference which emphasised the untenability of Emma's own situation. Trying to arrive at the modalities of a conversation with one's husband's mistress, Emma was momentarily rendered speechless. The woman—girl!—who sat facing her was astonishingly young, perhaps younger than herself. She had deep grey eyes and thick, henna-tinted brown hair woven into a plait that reached down to her knees. Her skin, pale and pink, had the smooth gloss of blossoming youth, like a ripe apple, and the full lips were shaded coral. She was unmistakably Eurasian and, not surprisingly, quite beautiful. Even in the presence of a visitor so unexpected and perhaps intimidating, she showed no signs of discomfiture. Indeed, she appeared supremely composed, far more so than Emma herself.

She raised her eyes and lightened the heavy silence with a smile. "I have heard a great deal about you, Mrs. Granville, but I had not thought that we would ever meet."

Emma found a voice. "A great deal about me from whom?"

"Why, from huzoor."

She said it without self-consciousness, as if it were the most natural thing in the world for them to talk of the man they shared. In fact, it was Emma who blushed. Thrown even more off balance, she was annoyed that she should feel large and gauche and devoid of the grace this wraith of a girl radiated with such ease.

"How does my country appeal to you?" Formal and yet at ease, the girl asked the inevitable question. "Not many Europeans have been to Kashmir, but those who have are enchanted."

Emma eased the constriction in her throat with a swallow. "Justifiably so. Your valley is, indeed, quite uniquely blessed."

"And Shalimar? Is that not an equally unique world in itself?"

Emma chilled. "You have been to Shalimar?"

"Oh no. It would not be proper for huzoor to take me to his home. That is the preserve of his wife." She said it simply, without artifice or rancour. "Huzoor has talked of it so often that I have learned to visualise it well."

Despite her overt discomfiture and rather more covert resentment, Emma felt her curiosity revive. It seemed to her incredible that in spite of her profession there should be about this girl an air of such unassumed *innocence*. No doubt a facade, another useful tool of trade!

The old woman came in again bearing a samovar and refreshments. Carefully, as if performing a ritual, Nazneen poured the *qahwa* into dainty little copper cups, then rose to offer a plate of sweets to Emma. Declining the sweets with a shake of her head, Emma accepted the tea and sipped if only to lubricate a gravelled throat. It slid down warming her from within, providing marginal confidence.

"In what way may I be of service, Mrs. Granville?" The question came as soon as the old crone had left the room.

Service? The presumptuousness subsumed in the word brought a fresh surge of colour to Emma's face. What possible service did she expect of this girl? All at once she saw even more clearly the absurdity of her situation; without even knowing why she was here, she had merely made a fool of herself. Replacing the cup on the table, she stumbled to her feet.

"I should not have come," she said, horribly embarrassed. "Indeed, I am as much at a loss to explain my presence as about what to say. You will have to forgive me for having intruded upon your privacy."

Before she could flee, however, Nazneen Sultana too had risen. "Huzoor said that you are an uncommonly courageous lady. He was right. To make this visit could not have been easy."

"Neither easy nor wise," Emma murmured, as perplexed about how to conclude the abortive encounter as she had been to initiate it.

Not permitting the silence to expand, Nazneen stepped into it deftly. "You and I both are part of a curious situation, Mrs. Granville," she said, making a tacit gesture for Emma to re-seat herself. "It is one that English women, even those born and brought up here, find difficult to comprehend. Or accept." She spread her henna-patterned palms and smiled, "In the East we are taught that there are many compartments to a man's life, each separate, each with its own function. I see that you are embarrassed to have come. Please do not be. You have questions that you need answered, questions that you have a right to have answered. Please ask me whatever you wish. I will not take offence."

Questions? Oh yes, she had questions—but how in heaven's name could she demean herself even further by asking them? At the same time, too confused to realise that she did so, Emma retraced her steps and resumed her seat.

"My husband visited you last night?" Emma saw the absurdity of her question instantly—how could he have when at midnight he was at Shalimar and by morning had left for Gulmarg?

Nazneen, however, accepted the inquiry quite naturally. "Huzoor has not been to see me since he left for Delhi. That essentially is what you came hoping to hear, Mrs. Granville, is it not?"

"No. I was . . . curious about you, that is all."

"Huzoor spoke to you of me?"

"Hardly! I learned about you from . . . someone else."

"Ah!" She did not elucidate, but in the solitary syllable lay a wealth of understanding.

"How long have you known my husband?" Emma asked, emboldened.

"Two years. I was brought to huzoor's notice by his good friend, Hyder Ali Mian, who was acquainted with my mother."

Damien had been visiting this girl for two years! The revelation brought an involuntary ache to Emma's heart.

"For women like me, Mrs. Granville, this is the only profession available." She was referring, of course, to her mixed parentage. "I was born of an English father and a Kashmiri mother. They were not married. My father was an officer in the army on leave from Umballa, my mother an untutored Kashmiri girl who worked as a washerwoman in the dak bungalow. She was very young and very simple." Absently, she turned a gold ring back and forth on her finger. "A child born out of wedlock between two cultures is without a future in India. For girls, it is worse. They have no choice but to . . ." She broke off with a slight heightening of colour, a fine trace of anger. "Make no mistake, Mrs. Granville—I offer no excuses, ask for no sympathy. Ours is an honest profession. There is no shame in giving pleasure to someone, even if it is for a price."

Alarmed in case she provoked intimacies she had no wish to hear, Emma raised a hand, but the woman gave an impatient shake of her head.

"You have a *right* to know. You are his wife." She paused to refill their cups, then leaned back against the bolster and laced her long, well-shaped fingers in her lap. "I have been luckier in my life than most, Mrs. Granville. I have had the good fortune to enjoy the attentions of only one man, and he has been kind."

Kind?

Catching Emma's fleeting reaction, Nazneen smiled. "Your husband is a man of obdurate opinions and violent extremes, Mrs. Granville. His shell is hard, for it covers many wounds, but within he is soft, like molasses, and often as sweet. Since he does not reveal himself easily, to disagree with him one must first agree."

"He appears to have revealed himself easily enough to you," Emma remarked with involuntary sharpness.

"For that there is a reason." Nazneen's gaze again dropped to bury itself in the intricacies of the carpet. "You see, Mrs. Granville, men who come to us do not consider us individuals of any great account. Consequently, with us they tend to drop their guard." A first flash of bitterness came and quickly went. "They reveal themselves without knowing, often without caring, and we are taught early how to accept and respect confidences." The lowered gaze rose to meet Emma's. "In the past two years I have seen many aspects of your husband, Mrs. Granville, aspects that perhaps even his wife has yet to see."

It was said with complete ingenuousness, but even so Emma felt a shock of betrayal. Apart from his body, Damien had allowed this girl to share his private thoughts, his hidden emotions. She was overcome with fierce feeling, a feeling so alien to her nature that she failed to recognise it as jealousy. Watching her intently, Nazneen took silent note of the reddening cheeks, the angry flash of eyes and perhaps even the underlying pain.

"In our profession, Mrs. Granville," she said gently, "it is considered foolish to transgress beyond certain prescribed limits. Huzoor accepted me for what I am. He made no demands beyond those that my position allowed me to fulfill, and I neither expected nor asked for anything in excess of my due."

Trying to comprehend that, Emma frowned. "You considered such a relationship satisfactory?"

"Relationship?" Nazneen was puzzled by the word. "Relationships are possible only between equals, Mrs. Granville. Huzoor is my mentor, my benefactor, and perhaps also a well-wisher, but it would be highly improper for me to think of myself as his—or, indeed, your—equal. If he has regarded me in any manner beyond what is prescribed, it is not due to his lack of rectitude but because of my own good fortune."

As an exercise in candour, it was admirable. In some subtle way, Emma saw, she was being reassured—and at the same time being taught to identify *her* place in Damien's life. In this bizarre, mannered game she had set out to play, it was obvious that there were indeed rules and she was yet to learn them. The realisation that Nazneen had sensed the motive behind her visit where she herself had failed to, was humbling, and Emma felt further reduced in her own estimation.

"In a few days I leave for Lahore to join my mother and sister," Nazneen said. Another reassurance. "I will continue to dance in the hope that by the grace of Allah, someday, I will find another mentor who will be kind to me and my family." The girl's pewter grey eyes were proud and somewhere in them was a trace of amusement touched faintly with scorn. "I have given huzoor pleasure, as was my duty, but on his heart you will not find a single mark left by me. You may return in peace, Mrs.

Granville. I have no place in your husband's life. He will not come to me again."

What was there left to say? The girl had answered everything, asked and unasked. Only one clarification remained to be made.

"You say my husband spoke to you about me?"

"Yes."

"When?"

"Before he left for Delhi." Smilingly, Nazneen uncoiled her legs and stood up. "I pray that Allah will bless your union, Mrs. Granville," she said. "I pray that you will give huzoor many sons."

Emma walked back down the stone staircase in a daze. Damien had spoken to Nazneen about her *before* he left for Delhi? How extraordinary—before he went to Delhi they had never set eyes on each other!

*A*s soon as he was ushered into the Governor's presence, Conolly saw that all was not well. In fact, the Taotai was in a rage.

However, as Chinese etiquette demanded, regardless of circumstances, they first drank tea and conversed only about the weather. Conolly disliked green tea. To him, it tasted like flavourless hot water, but trying hard to appear unperturbed, he kept his forefinger on the lid of the cup and sipped through the chink with every sign of enjoyment. They were on their own, but, somewhat pointedly, outside the door two of the Taotai's most trusted courtiers stood in watchful attendance.

Finally the tea ritual came to an end. "I have learned something that has disturbed me greatly, Dr. Conolly," the Taotai said.

It was an ominous start. Ignoring the missed beat of his heart, Conolly clung to his smile and waited.

"As you are aware, Dr. Conolly," the Governor continued, "the English are most keen to establish a consulate in Kashgar."

Of course he was aware! "Are they?" He looked politely surprised. "Well, that would be rather jolly."

"No, it would *not* be rather jolly, Dr. Conolly! I do not want foreigners, particularly *English* foreigners, in my territory. The Anglo-Saxon has a talent for even greater mischief than the Slav."

Conolly assumed the sins of his race in meek silence.

"Four years ago," the Governor went on, "when Mr. Andrew Dalgleish was here and before he was so unfortunately murdered in the Karakorams, the Indian government sent a delegation to Kashgar. We did not consider permitting Mr. Dalgleish to stay because we had already learned not to trust your people. Now another request has been received for the entry of

Mr. George MacCartney of your Political Department, and Captain Francis Younghusband. No doubt you are aware of the request."

Conolly was again about to profess ignorance but thought better of it. "A consul would help mutual trade, Excellency," he made bold to suggest, taking care not to sound too enthusiastic, "and benefit both our great nations."

The Taotai raised a pencil-thin eyebrow. "As the East India Company has benefitted Hindustan, Dr. Conolly?"

"Ha, ha!" With no intention of jeopardising his future post with a political debate, Conolly laughed good-naturedly and raised a finger. He did not overdo the amusement. "You certainly have a point there, Excellency. But then, as Excellency knows, I have no interest in politics. I find it tedious in the extreme."

"Do you really, Dr. Conolly?" The Taotai did not share in the amusement. "Do me the honour of not lying to me or underestimating my intelligence. I know that you are an English agent sent by your government to spy on us." Conolly opened his mouth to protest but then quickly shut it. "I have summoned you today to tell you that permission for Mr. MacCartney and Captain Younghusband to enter Kashgar will not be granted." He paused to examine his fingertips and Conolly's breath caught. "Unless certain conditions are fulfilled."

The held breath trickled back slowly. "Conditions, Excellency?"

The Taotai rose with an effort, pulled himself up to his full height and towered over his seated visitor. "First, I want to know more about this Armenian woman that everyone seeks."

Everyone? Conolly's stomach gave a sickening lurch. "Er, wh-who else, Excellency?"

"Even though that is not your concern, Dr. Conolly, I will provide an answer purely as a favour. A request identical to yours has been received by the Russian Governor-General in Tashkent."

Conolly was aghast. "From . . . whom?"

"I was hoping," the Taotai said drily, "that you could tell me that." Rendered speechless, Conolly remained silent. "Well, Dr. Conolly? Who exactly is this woman?"

"She is just an . . . an unimportant slave, Excellency," Conolly said faintly, groping for explanations, "one of the, er, thousands still held in bondage in Sinkiang."

"Pshaw, lies, all lies!" The contention was dismissed with an angry gesture. "Anyway, I have not summoned you here to waste time in dignifying vile rumours, Dr. Conolly, but to find out more about this mysterious woman."

"Apart from the details I have already provided," Conolly protested, heaping every imprecation he could devise on the head of Colonel Heth-rington, "I know nothing, Excellency. To tell you the truth, I made the request on behalf of . . . a good friend."

The Taotai lowered his lids and reduced his eyes to slits. "You made the request on behalf of your superiors in Simla," he hissed.

"I have no superiors in Simla."

"I want . . . no, demand, to know who she is!"

Conolly almost laughed. If only the Taotai knew what *he* would give to know precisely that!

"Don't push me too far, Dr. Conolly," the Taotai thundered, "or the consequences for you will not be pleasant."

"I cannot betray a personal . . ."

"Why should your government press for the release of 'just an unim-portant slave,' eh?"

"I have no connection with the . . ."

"Enough!"

Expecting the Taotai to fly into an almighty rage, Conolly almost pan-icked when, to his surprise, the Celestial manner suddenly changed. Re-seating himself, the Taotai laced his squat, stubby fingers across his ample stomach and shrugged.

"Well, have it your own way, Dr. Conolly. Both you and I will have the answer to that question shortly. You see, I have already located the woman."

Conolly gasped. "Blimey! *Where?*"

"That information will remain in abeyance for the moment."

Conolly spread his hands in genuine helplessness. "I . . . I cannot reveal more, Excellency, because I do not know more." Well, that at least was true. "I merely perform a service for a friend."

"Indeed!" Pointedly, the Taotai averted his face and immersed himself in haughty inspection of the opposite wall.

"In all fairness, Excellency," Conolly pleaded, "surely I have a right to know at least who has asked for this woman in Tashkent so that I can pass the information on to my, ah, friend?"

After a brief inner struggle, the Taotai relented. "The request was made through two Dards, no doubt hired mercenaries, who offered the Russian buffoon vital information in exchange."

"What vital information?"

"Authentic maps of the Yasmina Pass."

Conolly sank back into his chair. Dards, hired mercenaries, the Yas-mina? Ye gods, what was all this about, anyway? He was both flabbergasted and furious at his lack of information. As a political officer, however, he had been taught never to be surprised into showing surprise. He hid his bewilderment under a grim smile.

"Through unimpeachable secret sources," the Taotai informed him, "I have come to learn that the English have successfully located this pass."

Conolly almost laughed. Unimpeachable secret sources, his arse—the rumours had been all over the English papers for weeks. Nevertheless, he remained suitably grave. "Have they, by George!"

"Your show of innocence does you credit, Dr. Conolly." The Taotai smiled sadly. "However, now I suggest that you stop pretending. Your Military Intelligence people in Simla may be past masters at intrigue, but a nation that gave the world chess and gunpowder should not be dismissed as stupid. Therefore, Dr. Conolly," he gave a tight, triumphant little smirk, "if you wish to take charge of this woman, you will have to secure from the government with which you say you have no connection the authority you presently claim not to have."

"Take charge of her in exchange for what?" Conolly asked unhappily, already knowing the answer.

"Maps of the Yasmina Pass. I expect them to be delivered as soon as possible to a constituted representative of the Celestial government, namely, myself. The woman will be handed over to you only after the delivery has been made and we have had time to verify that the maps are genuine."

Conolly mopped his brow. "I wish I could be of assistance, Excellency," he persisted stonily, "but I cannot deliver what I have no means of acquiring."

"I will give you the means. You will send a message to your people from Shahidullah—from where you usually send messages to Mr. Crankshaw in Leh—to apprise them of the situation. If within eight weeks you have not received those maps you say you know nothing about, you will be executed." A sinister pause. "As will this woman your government seeks. If you choose to abscond, she will be executed anyway."

Despite the frightening ultimatum, Conolly felt a quiver of excitement—was the woman already in Chinese custody?

"I have been very tolerant with you, Dr. Conolly," the Taotai concluded, "mainly because of your medical skills. You have performed well in the service of my people, but now my tolerance is at an end." He leaned forward, beady little eyes again narrowed into glittering crescent moons. "You will also inform this government with which you have no connection about my decision not to allow Mr. MacCartney and Captain Younghusband to set foot in Kashgar until such time as those maps are in my hands."

Conolly thought fast. Excuses and alibis, he knew, were now futile. The cat was out of the bag and his days in Kashgar were numbered. "I will see what I can do, Excellency," he said, all at once brisk and businesslike, "but I can make no promises. As it happens, I too need some answers."

"Well?"

"The Russians want a secret pass through which to pour troops into Kashmir, the British want it in order to stop them. The Celestial Empire, however, has no territorial ambitions beyond the Himalayas. Why the interest in the Yasmina?"

"The Celestial Empire already extends beyond the Himalayas," the Governor amended coldly. "If Hunza is ours, so also is the Yasmina. We ask for nothing that we do not already own legally."

Conolly risked a small smile. The pompous explanation was not, of course, the true reason.

The undemarcated fifty-mile gap between Sinkiang and Afghanistan was the meeting point of three empires and a potential flashpoint. South of the Himalayas lurked the despised British; in the west permanently massed Russian armies breathed down Celestial necks; and ever present in Kashgar, reducing Chinese nerves to shreds, was the much feared Pyotr Shishkin. What better means to balance the power scales (and clip Shishkin's overgrown wings) than access to the Yasmina?

Conolly kept his thought to himself. "The two ounces of gold dust from Hunza is only a token, Excellency," he pointed out instead, "exactly the same that it pays to Kashmir."

The Taotai surveyed him with distaste. "For a man who finds politics tedious, Dr. Conolly, you appear to be remarkably well informed. Anyway," he made to rise, "unless my demands are met as stipulated, after two months you may consider both your stay and your life at an end. You can now leave."

He got up and left the room.

Walking back through the bazaar, Conolly could not deny that he was alarmed. He was being used as a pawn by Simla in some sinister plot of which he had no knowledge. He knew nothing about this Armenian female, nothing about the blasted Yasmina or the Dards. Even if he had the faintest notion where the maps were—which he hadn't—he had absolutely no means to secure them. In the English newspapers he occasionally received through caravans, he had read about poor old Jeremy Butterfield and the lost papers, of course, but about what had happened since he was entirely in the dark.

While Conolly wended his way home and reflected glumly on his precarious situation, at the palace the Taotai issued secret instructions to his two most trusted courtiers.

"There is a woman in Tashkent who is to be brought to Kashgar as soon as possible. The means used to abduct her are immaterial. She may be drugged but she is not to be harmed. Her name is Ivana Ivanova and she will be found at the house of a certain Colonel Mikhail Borokov, where she is employed as a housekeeper."

"It is as good as done, Excellency."

"Is Padshah Khan still here?"

"Yes, Excellency. He awaits permission to rejoin his post in the Baron's gardens before he is missed."

The Taotai nodded. "Tell him to return immediately to Tashkent and prepare for the coming mission. See that his reward is more generous than usual, will you? This time he has earned it."

There was no sign of Rehmat or the chowkidar at the entrance to the Shalimar gardens and Emma was relieved. She needed to be alone; she needed time to think, to regain her equilibrium. Slipping into the gardens, she set off on a brusque, solitary walk.

She was stunned by the revelation that Damien had known of her long before they had met. Under the impression that their initial encounter near Qudsia Gardens was by accident, she was now inclined to believe that it was not, that perhaps Damien had manipulated it solely to cultivate her acquaintance. She had always been sceptical about the reasons he had enumerated for wanting to marry her. Could it be, she now considered, quite dazzled by the thought, that she *had* valued herself too little? That Damien had pursued her with such tenacity because he truly found her appealing?

Unimaginable as the prospect seemed, it was at the same time immensely flattering. A quiver of something pleasurable touched her heart; hugging herself, she shivered.

For other reasons too, Emma conceded, the encounter with Nazneen had been extraordinarily revealing. Having convinced herself that her brazen mission was provoked only by defiant curiosity, she was amazed that Nazneen should have abstracted her true motive with such ease—to seek reassurance. She had been determined to dislike her as much as she did Chloe Hathaway. It surprised Emma now to find that she did not, that the encounter had left her not only reassured but also with a most unexpected feeling of humility.

One way or another, Damien had been right; she *had* learned a great deal from Nazneen.

"Mrs. Granville? I say, Mrs. Granville!"

Emma turned to see Geoffrey Charlton striding up behind her.

"Why, what a pleasant surprise, Mr. Charlton," she called back gaily. "As it happens I have been thinking about you."

"Oh? And to what do I owe such an undeserved honour?" He fell into step alongside.

"Well, I have been thinking about our conversation of the other day and wondering when we might have occasion to resume it."

"Any time you wish. I am always at your service." He looked around. "Surely you are not in Srinagar on your own?"

"No, on the contrary I am extremely well escorted. I came to . . . to make some purchases and, of course, to see these gardens. The little girl and one of the chowkidars who have accompanied me should be here presently."

"I am relieved to hear it. In spite of the comforting fact that there is almost no crime in Kashmir and the police enjoy generous sinecures, it is not a good idea for a lady to wander about unaccompanied. Would you have any objections if I did escort duty until your attendants arrive?"

"No, of course not. Indeed, I am pleased to have congenial company with whom to share these remarkable delights."

"My pleasure, entirely."

With tacit consent they started to stroll side-by-side surrounded by a proliferation of scenic beauty. The seventeenth-century gardens were designed by the Moghul emperor Jehangir. Landscaped with symmetrical precision, the terraces cut deep into the mountain slopes. Artificial channels were edged with chinars and studded with fountains. Each marble terrace was joined to the next by steps, pillared porticos and miniature waterfalls. Two tiny islets connected by a bridge terminated the view downhill. Beyond lay the placid jade green Dal into which the streams flowed.

"The Moghuls practised formal landscaping and horticulture as an art form unique in India," Charlton remarked, and for a while they spoke of this and other royal gardens in the state, said to be as many as seven hundred.

"I have read two translations of the word *Shalimar*," Emma said, "each different to the other. One maintains that *Shalimar* means a hall of love, the other that the word is a combination of *shala,* 'mountain,' and *mar,* 'beautiful.' Which in your opinion is the more apt, Mr. Charlton?"

"Does meaning matter so long as it is beautiful?"

"No, perhaps not." She conceded the point with a smile, then halted abruptly in her steps. "You made a strange remark the other day as we parted, Mr. Charlton. May I ask what you meant by it?"

"About your imminent need for a friend?" He made no pretence of forgetfulness. "I'm afraid I spoke purely out of impulse and also out of turn. I should not have." Somewhat embarrassed, he walked on.

"But the fact that you did make the observation," Emma insisted, "surely entitles me to an explanation?"

He slowed his pace. "I meant nothing very significant, Mrs. Granville, only that since you are a stranger in the valley, you might welcome the friendship of a like-minded soul. As any friend might, I offered my services should the need for them arise."

Emma subjected him to a look of some severity. "If you do want us to be friends, Mr. Charlton, you must refrain from devaluing my perceptions. The other day you seemed to imply that the need *would* arise, and that too soon."

A little boy accompanied by his parents ran between them and earned a sound box on his ear from his father. Waiting for the child's howls of outrage to subside, Charlton relapsed into thought.

"Yes," he finally admitted, although with reluctance, when the family had passed, "perhaps some explanation is due to you for my impertinence."

"Well, then, why do we not sit down and make ourselves comfortable while you make it?" Spying a bench not far from where they stood, she promptly occupied it, giving him no chance to refuse.

With a slight inclination of his head, he smiled and surrendered. "As you wish, Mrs. Granville." He seated himself carefully at the far end of the bench. "I regret, however, that I cannot make an explanation without committing a further impertinence. Do I have your permission to ask an extremely delicate question?"

Emma nodded.

"How well did you know your husband before you married him?"

"Well enough to have married him, Mr. Charlton!"

If she made light of the interrogation, Charlton chose to remain solemn. "And how conversant are you with the history of the Granville family?"

"Well, I do know that Damien's parents met and married in Peshawar where Major Granville was posted at the time, and that he resigned shortly thereafter to settle in Kashmir."

"Do you know why Edward Granville resigned?"

She hesitated. "Because life in the army seemed less attractive than the life that beckoned in the Vale?"

"Edward Granville resigned because he was asked to."

"Oh."

"You did not know that?"

"No." She added quickly, "But only because the subject has never really come up. I did hear, however, that there was some sort of . . . scandal in the family."

"Yes, I suppose you could say that."

He proceeded unwillingly, Emma saw. Part of her urged to let matters rest, but now well aroused, her curiosity refused to permit it. "Whatever happened happened many years ago, Mr. Charlton. I would not like you to feel that you are betraying anyone's trust, because you are not. I could have as easily found out from Damien had I thought to inquire."

"I still consider that it is not my place to reveal details, Mrs. Granville," he said uncomfortably. "Family matters should be discussed within the privacy of the family. I suggest you leave it to your husband to enlighten you when he returns from Gulmarg."

How did he know that Damien was in Gulmarg? she wondered in vague surprise.

Aloud, she asked not without a trace of wistfulness, "If the scandal involved another man, Mr. Charlton, surely lovers and mistresses are de rigueur even today?"

"The scandal was of a different nature, Mrs. Granville."

"Well, then, something equally salacious, perhaps? Gossip, after all, comes in many shades and colours."

"No, it was not gossip." He halted and stared hard at the ground. "Even though it embarrasses me to be the one to tell you, Mrs. Granville, on second thoughts perhaps in your own interests you are entitled to know more. I must insist, however, that you forgive me for revealing what is not my business."

In her own interests?

"Your late mother-in-law, Countess Greta von Fritz," he began, "arrived in India when she was only nineteen. She was, it was alleged, an Austrian aristocrat from Vienna, very wealthy and widowed at a tragically young age. She was also very beautiful."

"It was *alleged*?"

"Yes." He evaded her eyes. "In actual fact, Greta von Fritz was Russian. Her real name was Natasha Vanonkova."

Somehow, Emma concealed her surprise. No wonder Suraj Singh had almost thrown a fit when she had mentioned the Austrian Alps! "So the scandal was simply the fact that she was Russian?"

"Well . . ."

Emma laughed. "Mr. Charlton, as you know better than anyone, all Russians are automatically suspect in India. I can hardly believe that the late Mrs. Granville too didn't come in for her fair share of suspicion."

"Her case was not quite as simple as that," he said. "You see, Mrs. Granville, thirty years back, Natasha Vanonkova came to India illegally as a member of the Russian Intelligence Service. She was brought here by a certain Igor Petrovsky, an officer in the Kiev Dragoons posing as an Austrian nobleman and her uncle. They entered India from Bombay with forged papers, travelled up the Jhelum and established themselves in Peshawar where there was, still is, quite considerable Indian Army presence."

He spoke in a monotone and continued with the same flatness. "While

Petrovsky secretly reconnoitred mountain routes, allegedly studying local flora, Natasha Vanonkova befriended army officers to extract information about British troop movements along the vulnerable north-western borders with Afghanistan. She was young, attractive, vivacious, and a gifted pianist and artist. She could produce a lifelike sketch of any face in a matter of minutes. This not only provided amusement at parties but also subsequently helped St. Petersburg to identify top-ranking Indian Army personnel."

Charlton paused to throw her an oblique glance. She did not return it.

"Using these many talents," he went on, "Greta von Fritz soon established herself as a popular addition to the social circuit in Peshawar with an entrée into most military homes. Money for her affluent lifestyle was no problem; it came from Russian government funds. One of the British officers who happened to befriend Greta von Fritz was Major Edward Granville. As his bad luck would have it, he fell hopelessly in love with her."

He stopped, allowed a group of chattering women to pass, and then carried on.

"Eventually, rumours started to circulate about the mysterious Austrian countess. Despite being warned by his commanding officer, Edward Granville refused to believe them. When the whispers became ubiquitous and the situation difficult for young Greta, Granville asked her to marry him. Nothing could actually be proved against her and the army brass had no desire to provoke a public scandal. Granville was quietly asked to resign his commission, leave Peshawar and take up residence outside British India. After a hasty marriage, the couple left for Amritsar en route to Kashmir where, because of his long-standing interest in weaving, Granville enjoyed the patronage of the ruler. Relieved to have avoided a sticky situation, the army swept the matter under the rug and left it there. Natasha Granville was given permission by the maharaja to stay and the Granvilles settled in Kashmir. Petrovsky vanished without trace from Peshawar. It was assumed that he had made his way back to Russia through Afghanistan."

A blue-breasted kingfisher swooped into the grass not far from where they sat, then shot off into the sky with a shrill cry. Following its path until it disappeared into the clouds, Emma concealed her shock with considerable effort. Only her hands clasped in her lap tightened against each other. She realised now why Charlton had been reluctant to speak. She had forced him into an awkward position—but to apologise would be to place herself in one.

"I cannot tell you how deeply sorry I am that it should have fallen upon me to tell you this, Mrs. Granville," he said gently.

Putting a brave face on her own embarrassment, Emma smiled. "Well, I should imagine it's all water under the bridge now, Mr. Charlton," she returned lightly. "However, I must say I do feel sorry for poor Natasha. Goodness knows under what terrible pressures she did what she felt compelled to."

Torn between wanting to know everything and guilt at an indiscretion that smacked of disloyalty to Damien, Emma struggled in silence. She need not have bothered; sensing her discomfort, Charlton himself resolved her dilemma.

"I suggest that you appeal to your husband for the rest, Mrs. Granville. I have exceeded my limits enough for one day, for which I beg forgiveness. Thank you for giving me the benefit of your company. If I am not mistaken, I see that your escorts have just entered the main gate to the gardens. My offer of friendship, incidentally, still stands. Good day, Mrs. Granville."

Not waiting for her to respond, he hurried away.

On the path behind her in the distance Rehmat, the chowkidar, and an elderly bearded man—presumably the child's father—were walking toward where she sat.

Natasha Vanonkova.

Emma rolled the name around her tongue. Despite her immediate reaction to what had been revealed, her sense of shock was starting to soften and she was moved. There were poignant undertones to the tale, hints of a profound family tragedy, and she was even more intrigued. Considering the impossible tensions between them, however, her pride refused to let her consider the prospect of questioning Damien.

Whatever else there was to know she would have to search for on her own.

*E*mma's second nocturnal journey to the apartments below presented no problems. Suraj Singh was safely away and Sharifa and Rehmat snored on happily. Screwdriver, matches and lantern in hand, that night she again made her way to the back of the house.

She did not doubt that Charlton had spoken the truth. He had no reason to lie, after all, and hushed-up scandals were not difficult to confirm if one knew the right people. With no interest in political intrigue and the covert games governments played, Emma restored her own perspectives with remarkable ease. In the playground of politics, today's allies were tomorrow's enemies and one man's traitor was another's hero. The fact that Damien's mother had spied for her country was to her immaterial.

What troubled Emma far more than what Geoffrey Charlton had said was what he had left unsaid. The decades'-old scandal was dead and forgotten, as were its protagonists; yet in some curious, unstated way, Charlton had implied that the events of the past were still linked to the present.

Through Damien?

The hasp on the second back door was as easy to remove as had been the first and Emma entered Natasha Granville's bathroom without trouble. There was mildew on the tiles and a strong smell of must, but the brass taps were elegantly fashioned, the towels hanging on the brass rails faded but exquisitely embroidered, and the decor distinctly feminine. Eager to explore the rest, however, Emma hurried through the adjoining dressing-room into the parlour.

The inadequate flickers of illumination from her lantern did little to lighten the unrelieved darkness. In the parlour, a facsimile of hers, she drew aside a curtain from the window. A cloud of dust attacked her nostrils and almost blinded her. She coughed, covered her face with the edge of her gown and opened a shutter. The slatted moonlight that fell across the floor was enough for a cursory survey. There were lamps on the tables but all bone-dry, their clogged wicks brittle to the touch. She raised the flame of her lantern and, like a flat picture given a third dimension, the room assumed discernible perspective.

Regardless of the dust covers over the crowded furniture, the difference between this and Edward Granville's sitting room next door was striking. Indeed, Emma's first startled impression was of an Aladdin's cave appointed with cloying lavishness. Heavy gilt clocks stood beside onyx and marble figurines, their ticking hearts long stilled; jewelled snuff boxes tarnished by years of neglect squatted among Chinese jade dragons and burial urns and a range of exquisite glassware. Under a dust sheet the brocade upholstery on a beautifully carved loveseat was tarnished, but the heart-shaped satin cushions were still glossy with the conserved brilliance of a bygone age.

Tightly drawn across all the windows, the floor-length curtains were fashioned with fringed pelmets and tasselled rope. Well protected from the devastations of sunlight, beneath the layers of dust every bird and flower on the richly patterned silk carpet was alive with colour. Two glass chandeliers, coated with grime, swung from the wooden beams overhead, and on the walls, patterned with lilies-of-the-valley, there were faded water-colours of ice-white lakes and skeletal trees denuded by an arctic winter. A gilt triptych of a Russian Madonna and Child peered bleakly through its murky laminations. Above the desk, a calendar with Russian lettering gave information no one had needed for twenty years.

Here too the parquet flooring beneath the carpets was perfect; there were no intimations of decay.

In gathering confidence Emma moved towards the draughtsman's board on the desk, to which was pinned an unfinished design of stylised pines and entwined leaves. The paper had turned yellow, its unsecured edges curled upwards. A portfolio propped against a wall contained more designs neatly stacked between tissue paper that crackled with age. A calligrapher's pen, its nib encrusted with ink, still reposed in the groove of a palette next to coloured pencils and other tools. Behind the desk, almost concealed by a curtain, were the outlines of a large gilt picture frame. . . .

She moved into the bedroom. A lacy peignoir and negligée were folded into a satin case on an embroidered quilt; a pair of fleece-lined bedroom slippers adorned with red rosettes were half hidden under the fourposter; an open book lay face-down on the brass-cornered commode by the bed. Emma rubbed a finger across the stained cover and saw that the title was in Russian. Bunches of spring flowers, withered and shrivelled, were massed in vases. On a table, lovingly wrapped in a dusty length of purple silk, was a balalaika, its broken strings twisted and curled in a confusion of tendrils.

Returning to the dressing-room, Emma slid back one of the cupboard panels. Amid clouds of clinging must were suspended dozens of dresses, sequinned evening gowns, smart jackets and skirts, embroidered and printed day dresses, all encased in protective sheaths of muslin. On the shelves there were shoes stretched across iron trees, handbags, satin pouches, an incredible variety of hats. A scarf carelessly discarded lay on the floor next to a hastily removed pair of leather gloves cuffed with lace.

Out of a corner, Emma's eye caught a sudden movement. A ghostly vision formed before her and her hand flew to her throat in cold fear. But then, almost immediately, she saw that what moved was her own clouded reflection in the triple mirrors of the dressing-table, and her breath revived.

Cosmetics, toilet articles and perfume sprays were ranged before the mirrors next to silver-backed hairbrushes and combs on embroidered lace doilies. She picked up a comb; strands of pale hair were entangled in its teeth, reminders perhaps of the very last occasion that it had been used. Incredibly enough, a mist of perfume still hung in the air, faint but evocative, like a stubborn spirit that refused to go away. She tugged at the glass knob of a drawer; it slid open to reveal purple velvet–lined compartments meant for jewellery, all empty.

Emma quickly pushed the drawer shut and ran back into the parlour, trembling.

Natasha Granville had lived in beauty surrounded by elegance. Neither the dust of ages nor the mustiness could obscure her essential good taste, her passion for beautiful things, her love of life. But cossetted and loved and cocooned in luxury, she had not found happiness. There was sadness everywhere—a deep, lingering melancholy that not even two decades could erase.

Inevitably, Emma's eyes swivelled towards the half-concealed picture frame behind the curtain. As she pulled it out from its hiding place and turned it around, Natasha Granville's face sprang to life before her. The portrait, in oils, was a pair to that of Edward Granville in the withdrawing-room.

Suraj Singh had lied to her about that too!

For a long while Emma sat staring at the face, mesmerised by its loveliness. Pale, flaxen hair in fashionable kiss curls across a clear, smooth forehead; crescent lips touched with a smile; high cheekbones and deep, laughing Slav eyes sparkling in a celebration of a time when there had been joy. Around a long, alabaster neck in the dip of a tantalising neckline she wore a strand of pearls and a filigreed pendant. Held in tapering, bejewelled fingers was a painted Japanese fan with an orange base and tassel. Contemptuous of death, she looked alive and invincible, a woman destined for immortality. Emma was surprised at how much Damien had taken after his mother. His colouring was his father's, but the fineness of his features came from his mother.

Who had removed the picture from its assigned place in the withdrawing-room upstairs, Damien or his father? An act of rage or of grief?

Natasha Granville had fled in a hurry, her apartment left exactly as it was on that night. In one way it was like a ritual burial chamber with only the coffin missing. In another, curiously enough, each priceless piece she had collected had a quicksilver presence of its own, a presence as palpable as that of the unfortunate woman herself. The very atmosphere held a sort of hopeless expectancy, as if awaiting an erstwhile occupant destined never to return.

Emma again felt the onset of dread and her skin erupted in a rash of goose-pimples. To stop her fantasies she gave her head a hard shake, threw back her shoulders and took a deep breath. She returned to the desk and pulled open a drawer. It was filled with letters written in Russian. Official or private? She had no way of telling. Disappointed, Emma shut the drawer and tried another. Here she was luckier: a few scattered untidy packets were loosely tied with ribbons. She undid one. It contained lined sheets scribbled over in Russian letters and a childish scrawl. Damien's? Unable to read it, she replaced the papers with a cluck of frustration.

There is new leaf on the chinar...

She suddenly came across a sheet that started abruptly in English. Her eyes flew to the date: 4 May, 1870. Was it a letter? An essay?

There is new leaf on the chinar. The snows swell the streams and the toads croak. There will be rain tomorrow. The spring breezes rise with the cherry blossom but I do not like them. The touch of the wind is sharp and it stings. Sasha barks all night. When the owls hoot I am frightened and I lie awake to listen. I think I hear her voice on the stairs. Is it coming up? No, it is only a bird call or a trick of the night. She will not see the new leaves and the cherry blossom, nor be here when I return. Good! [The last word underlined thrice] *The eyes that hold evil do not deserve to perceive beauty. Neither do they . . .*

The jottings ended as suddenly as they had begun and were unsigned. There were no letters in English, but an old school notebook was filled with other disjointed notations in a strange mélange of English and Russian. She picked out a sentence:

What is the colour of water, the taste of fire, the feel of the wind in the hand? No one knows but she [underlined twice] *, for now she has gone where all is revealed and nothing is secret.*

Sensing rather than comprehending, Emma read a few more, knowing that she trespassed over a private wasteland of torment. On another page:

Today the first yellow rose bloomed on the bush she had planted. I crushed its fangs and tore it out by its roots. I burned it behind the stables and stamped its ashes into the earth. I hate it, it repulses me.

Strangely enough, this reference Emma understood. Ancient Egyptians considered the yellow rose a symbol of perfidy, of betrayal. In her mind's ear she heard the echoes of loneliness, the outpourings of grief and bewilderment and rage and, inevitably, hate. Ramblings from many years ago, unaccountably preserved, souvenirs of pain from the soft underbelly of a deserted child.

Too young to understand, too old to cry . . .

Emma tried to imagine that night twenty years ago when a knock on the door had brought the child's world to an end. He had returned to a home hollowed of its essence, left only with material mementoes of a bereavement too gross to absorb. What were the reasons for the abandonment? Were they ever explained, understood? Could they ever be . . . ?

The vision brought a burning to Emma's eyes. She felt resentment against the woman who had laid to waste two lives and a home. Then, realising the unfairness of so peremptory a judgement, she cleared her own mind of anger. How could she, all these years later, assess the desperations of Damien's mother? How could anyone? That Damien should blame his mother for her betrayal was understandable—how could it be otherwise when he was only twelve and still innocent of the ways of the world?

In the adjoining apartment a clock struck twice and Emma started. With her concentration elsewhere she had not heard it strike before. It was late and her eyelids smarted with sleep. She yawned, replaced everything in its original position and looked around in case she had left telltale signs of her visit. Satisfied that she had not, she returned the way she had entered. By the time she had replaced the screws of the latch on the outside door, it was almost half past two.

If there were other insights into Damien's childhood to be found, Emma sensed that they would not be in his mother's apartment. Bitter about her desertion, he had obviously not stepped foot in it for years, not since having written and secreted his initial cries of pain in her desk. Now wildly curious about the unfolding family saga and even more compelled to resume her search before either Suraj Singh or Damien returned, Emma determined to do so the following night.

But that, as it happened, was not to be. The next morning when she awoke and stepped into her parlour, she was confronted with the sight of a pair of black leather, mud-encrusted high boots standing on the hearth awaiting Hakumat's attention.

Sometime during the night Damien had returned.

CHAPTER

13

"Slept well?"

Fresh from a bath, Damien stood in her parlour vigorously towelling his hair. As Emma came to an abrupt halt in the doorway, he peered at her through the folds; briefly wordless, she nodded.

"Well, you don't look as if you have. What have you been doing—fighting the demons of hell single-handed in your slumbers?"

Having neither washed nor combed her hair, she retreated hurriedly to gather her wits. When she returned a few moments later scrubbed, brushed, clad in a lemon quilted dressing-gown and reasonably composed, he was reclining in his favourite chair by the hearth going through a pile of letters. Still damp, his dark hair stood up in spikes and his towel was slung about his shoulders.

"What time did you return from Gulmarg?" she asked, positioning herself opposite him nervously, hoping—God forbid!—that it was not during her nocturnal explorations.

"Early, just after three," Damien replied, and she loosened.

On the one hand (remembering the circumstances of his stormy departure), she was wary of his sudden return; on the other, with her covert discoveries still fresh in her mind, the wariness was not unmixed with hesitant pleasure.

He tossed an envelope in her direction. "Letter for you. If it's from your mother, I hope she is well and not too worried about her daughter whisked away into the wilderness by a big bad wolf."

The uncharacteristic humour was as surprising as his return. She had not ever seen him so lighthearted.

"Thank you." Intending to read it later, she set the letter aside. It was, she saw, not from her mother but from Jenny.

It was still very early, not long after dawn. Breakfast, evidently already ordered, was served by Hakumat. It seemed to Emma strange to be sharing, for the first time, an ordinary, everyday meal. The sudden plunge into domesticity was unfamiliar and brought a touch of awkwardness; grateful that the demands of housewifery provided a momentary diversion, she busied herself with her immediate duties.

"Well, aren't you going to read it?" Looking up from his letter, Damien glanced at the envelope at her elbow.

"I thought I would keep it for after breakfast," Emma said.

"You have the patience to wait that long to know what your mother has to say?" With obvious relish he heaped his plate with devilled kidneys, wild mushrooms, scrambled eggs, and started to eat.

Emma stole an uncertain look at the letter. "Well, actually, I don't," she admitted with a smile and picked up the envelope.

Jenny's letter contained more details of the wedding, more news about mutual friends and more titillating fragments of Delhi's gossip. Written in her characteristic style, it brought a smile to Emma's lips and once or twice she giggled. Halfway through the letter, she paused to lift her cup and saw Damien watching her.

"It's from Jenny—Jenny Purcell," she explained quickly. "Perhaps you remember her?"

"Yes. I remember her."

"They must be well settled in Calcutta by now. John Bryson, her husband, has a new job with the sales department of a Scottish jute company. Jenny writes very amusing letters."

"Evidently, since they bring a smile to your face." He added, "I only meant that since you smile so seldom, spontaneous amusement makes a refreshing change. I don't like to see you going around like a dying swan."

"Oh?" His lightheartedness was infectious; she decided to match it. "I thought you were going to say, like an angry goose. Temper is what you usually accuse me of."

"Well, that too." He laughed and combed his damp hair back with his fingers.

If he had never seen her laugh with genuine amusement, Emma could return the compliment with equal truth. This morning he appeared to be in very high spirits indeed. Pretending to be immersed in her letter, she made a covert study of his face as he munched on a piece of toast and read his own correspondence. Despite the cheerfulness, deep creases scored his forehead; there were dark smudges of exhaustion beneath his eyes and faint ruts at the corners of his mouth. Travel weariness? Worry? She had not taken note of the signs before.

The childish scrawl, the pain-filled words and aching inadequacies of expression all came leaping back into focus and Emma's heart twisted with sudden—what? compassion? Compassion! It was the last emotion she would have expected Damien Granville to invoke in her, or anyone else, and Emma was surprised at herself.

Mercifully, it appeared that the ugly scene of the other night was to be consigned to oblivion. He neither made mention of it, direct or oblique, nor seemed inclined to. Relieved, Emma finished reading her letter and helped herself to a substantial bowl of broken wheat porridge, tangerine honey and goat milk. Damien had ordered huge clusters of grapes from the vineyard; they were tart and sweet at the same time and, she agreed in answer to his query, perfectly delicious. Indeed, his manner was so cordial this morning that Emma wondered, rather unkindly, if there might be a motive behind it, even though she could think of none.

"I have to leave for Srinagar in a short while to see Jabbar Ali about a shipment of shawls for Lahore," he said as they finished breakfast. "Would you care to accompany me?"

Her heart skipped a beat—was he aware that she had made a journey on her own yesterday? Probably not, at least not yet. "I would like to very much indeed," she said. "Thank you."

"We can stay the night on the houseboat and return tomorrow, if the idea meets with your approval."

She assured him that it did.

Mention of Jabbar Ali brought to mind the matter of the jacket. She fetched it from her bedroom and offered it to him with sudden shyness. "I . . . I bought this when we passed through Srinagar on the way here. I hope it fits well and that it is to your taste."

"For me?" He could not have been more astonished. "Good heavens, it must be years since anyone bought me a present!" Quickly he undid the parcel, whisked out the jacket, then held it up and examined it from all angles.

"*Just* what I need!" His pleasure was so excessive that recalling the offhandedness with which the purchase had been made, Emma felt small. "I've been meaning to get one of these but never seemed to have got down to it. How ever did you guess that I needed a new jacket?"

"Well, Suraj Singh mentioned that you had burned a hole in the pocket of the one you already have."

Slipping it on at once, he declared it a perfect fit, then patted down the pockets and flicked a bit of fluff off the lapel. "I can see that there are advantages in having acquired a wife after all—if only to dispense with the dreadful business of shopping."

"I have not had the opportunity to thank you for the *shatoosh*," she said, determined to be done with that too, "and also the chestnut mare. I . . . you must not feel that I expect to be spoiled with expensive presents." In her embarrassment she knew that she sounded stiff and ungracious.

"You know what they say about gift horses," he replied, as awkward to receive gratitude as she was to express it. "Besides, you will need one of your own on the estate."

"Only on the estate?" She grabbed the tangential shift of topic. "Nowhere else?"

"Well, only if you are escorted. In Kashmir a woman gallivanting about on her own is looked upon with disfavour."

"I thought you did not care about anyone's favour."

"I don't, but neither do I wish to hurt anyone's sensibilities. We are strangers in Kashmir; we must do as they do, we must respect *kashmiryat*— do you know what that means?"

"The essence of being Kashmiri?"

"That and more. It subsumes all the intangible nuances of their codes of thought and behaviour. In any case, where is it that you wish to go on your own?"

"Nowhere. It's just that I'm not used to crowding attendants."

"There will be no crowds. If that is what you wish, your single escort will be ordered to maintain a discreet distance." Slitting open another letter, he glanced through it, then started to make notes in the margins. The subject, she saw, was closed.

To disagree with him, one must first agree . . .

She made no further protests.

Unwilling to be consigned to the tender mercies of the coachman, Damien took charge of the reins himself as they commenced their journey to Srinagar. Emma sat up front next to him and Sharifa was installed in the back with the luggage. Hakumat, the coachman and two other attendants followed on horseback trailing Toofan, Damien's stormy stallion.

"Why do you need Toofan in Srinagar?" she asked. "You can hardly ride him in those narrow lanes without endangering people."

"I may have to go to Gupkar, to the winery. Toofan will get me there and back faster than any of the other horses."

Suraj Singh, she presumed, was still up in Gulmarg. She did not ask after him.

Damien drove with care and his skill at manipulating the carriage over the rutted track was a relief. It was not yet eight. In the delicate mist that veiled the countryside, the valleys looked opalescent. The almond gardens, still in blossom, showed light pink for the sweet almonds and dark pink for the bitter. It was a very pretty display. Yesterday, preoccupied with her impending mission, Emma had noticed little of the journey. Today, surprisingly at ease, she took care to miss nothing.

With the passage of the day, Damien explained, the countenance of the hills would change dramatically. The distant ravines, patched with indigo, would lighten into pale blues and greens and lavender. Later, when the shadows slid down the slopes, they would transform into ochre and bright yellows.

"Did you know that Kashmir is said to have connections with three prophets?" he asked.

"Three? Two, as far as I recall," Emma replied. "The mosque at Hazratbal houses what is believed to be a hair of the Prophet Mohammed, and legend has it that Christ once came to the valley. Who is the third prophet?"

"Moses." He was pleased at her astonishment. "Thirty miles from here is a place called Bandipur, once known as Beth-Poer. Many Jews believe that Moses died here. A grave in the jungle marked by a black rock, still looked after by an old man of the faith, is said to be his final resting place. I will take you there one day." He looked around with obvious complacence. "The problem with living in Kashmir is that it ruins you for every other place on earth—it certainly has me!"

She had heard him say that before, of course, but only now was she beginning to appreciate the sentiment.

"I am told that the Gulmarg valley is particularly enchanting at this time of the year," she said, "with its huge varieties of plants and fine views of Nanga Parbat and Harmukh. Would it be possible to go up there too someday?"

"Yes. When the repairs have been completed." He reined sharply and pulled up on a verge.

"Why do we stop?" For no reason she was alarmed. Was it something she had said?

"Don't you want any refreshment?" he asked.

"Refreshment?" Emma looked around. "Where?"

He waved a hand at the orchard spilling down the hill by the side of the track, its trees laden with spring fruit. "Here."

"Whose property is it?"

"It doesn't matter. In Kashmir one is permitted to eat in any orchard provided one doesn't abuse the privilege. Come."

They nibbled with relish on fat, beaded mulberries, plums, cherries and sweet strawberries from an over-endowed bed, larger than any Emma had seen. On the pomegranate trees the fruit was still green and would not ripen until late summer. Emma listened to Damien's enthusiastic explanations about everything, as astonished by the extent of his knowledge as by his ebullience. There was much about him that puzzled her. Sometimes she despaired of ever knowing him fully, surprised now that she should want to. Most surprising, however, was that his bruised childhood should have touched her own heart with such pain. Should she ask him about his mother? At one point she almost did, but then bit back the question. The understanding between them was still nascent, far too fragile to be disturbed by clumsy probings.

They alighted in the same field on the outskirts of Srinagar where she had stopped the day before and walked to the lake where a shikara awaited.

"Hakumat and Sharifa will escort you to the *Nishat*," Damien said. "Apart from Jabbar, I have to see one or two others. I will have to leave you to your own devices until dinner."

Who were the "one or two others"? Forcing away the swift, piercing stab of jealousy, she climbed meekly into the shikara.

On the open deck of the *Nishat*, the staff and the inevitable samovar of *qahwa* awaited. There were fragrant bunches of flowers everywhere. The curtains and bed linen were freshly starched and pressed and the dining table had been laid for two. Around them the lake shimmered, white and sapphire blue from the cloud-dusted noon sky it mirrored. Feeling marvellously content, Emma returned to the deck to observe the panorama better and Hakumat sprang to attention with a cup of very welcome tea.

There was brisk daytime activity on the lake. Boats of many kinds plied the placid surface, some swiftly, others taking their ease with unhurried grace. Still others at anchor bobbed up and down with the waves as did beds of lotus and water-lilies and swards of duckweed. Fruit and vegetable sellers in shikaras hawked their wares from houseboat to houseboat, their decks loaded with fresh seasonal produce.

The Dal was dotted with islands spiked with hefty chinars, firs and pines. Some were flat and covered with melon and cucumber, others still awaited planting. These, Emma knew, were the "floating fields" of Kashmir, formed by densely packed water-plants and reeds. On one such island stood the maharaja's pigeon-house, the *kotar khana,* where thousands of birds came to roost. A shy little boy, no more than ten, slid his shikara alongside the *Nishat*. Staring up at Emma from beneath impossibly long black lashes, he smiled and she smiled back. Encouraged, he stood up and held out a pink lotus bud. She leaned over the rail and took it. He gave a cheeky laugh and without waiting for payment paddled away, thrilled at his daring.

Along the broad promenade to the north were the banks, the post office, European shops and establishments. The tall, narrow wooden houses had their first storeys built above the level of the water as a precaution against annual floods precipitated by melting summer snows. The windows of the houses were latticed, the shingled roofs covered with grass and thriving flower beds. Dominating the horizon were two isolated hills, one crowned by the state prison and the fortress of Hari Parbat, and the other by an ancient temple known as Takht-e-Suleiman, the Throne of Solomon. On the lake bank opposite the *Nishat* a row of other flat-roofed houseboats awaited the influx of summer tourists.

Enjoying the different vignettes and her own musings, Emma reclined on the chaise-longue in a pleasant state of drowse, eating freshly roasted water-chestnuts, too replete to contemplate luncheon. As the afternoon waned, an idea occurred to her. Summoning Hakumat, she asked him to inform the cook that she wished to help him prepare an evening meal of traditional Kashmiri fare.

Very pleased with her brainwave, she went inside to change into a housegown in readiness for her kitchen chores. In the master dressing-room she saw that her box had been placed alongside Damien's and she went still. They were to share the bedroom . . . ?

Not having foreseen this entirely unexpected aspect of the trip, Emma went slightly cold. All at once she was overwhelmed by a wild tangle of emotions: dismay, apprehension, anticipation?

She could not tell one from the other.

*I*vana Ivanova?

The more Mikhail Borokov thought about the extraordinary business, the more bewildered he became, and over these past days he had thought of little else. As he sat abstractedly sipping his vodka on the verandah of his modest residence late in the evening and eating the triangles of toast, Beluga caviar and chopped eggs that Ivana prepared so well, he again hunted for answers. And again they eluded him.

Someone wanted Ivana in exchange for maps of the Yasmina? He simply could not believe it!

During his two years in Tashkent, they had been approached many times by men who claimed to have discovered the Yasmina. Not one of the claims had been substantiated. Initially he had conducted the interrogations himself, but then, disgusted with the lies, evasions and outrageous bids for money, he had passed the duty on to Captain Vassily, his deputy. The claims made by the two Dards, however, he had been unable to dismiss.

As also the matter of Ivana.

The Baron was familiar with her sad history, of course, and details about her left behind by the Dards could not be discounted as circumstantial, nor the diagram of the pendant and the Armenian connection waved away as coincidences. Had that prime imbecile not sent one of the rascals back and set the other loose with such dispatch, the truth could have been thrashed out of them in no time at all. Borokov found it laughable that anyone could even consider poor Ivana worthy of such an extraordinary bargain.

But obviously someone did. *Why?*

"Am I to remove the tray, Colonel sir, or should I leave it be?"

Borokov started. He had not heard her come into the room, but then he never did. She had the habit of walking on cat feet, as if equipped with special pads under her soles. At one time, when she was still a child, her soundless comings and goings had made him nervous and he had insisted that she wear heeled boots around the house. However, over the years he had come to appreciate her cat feet as highly as he had her other virtues— respect for his privacy, an unspoken understanding of his needs, admirable domestic competence and, most blessed of all, discretion.

Servants of other officers he knew lied, stole, cheated on groceries, chattered endlessly and broadcast their employers' private affairs around the neighbourhood. He had no such complaints about Ivana. She spoke only when necessary and then too sparingly. Indeed, in all the fifteen years that she had been with him, he could not remember having had other than a trivial domestic conversation with her. Nonetheless, her instincts about him were uncanny; he needed only to think of a requirement and it was fulfilled. Let alone his money, he had learned to trust her with his life. Indeed, if there was anything that truly shocked Mikhail Borokov about this preposterous business, it was that anyone could have ever thought of Ivana as a slave.

For a while he wondered whether to question her about the strange offer, but then decided against it. He was certain that she had no knowledge of it and he did not wish to alarm her unnecessarily.

Now clad in her usual faded grey baboushka, Ivana set about emptying the ashtray, plumping up the cushions and brushing the crumbs off the table. Borokov observed her closely, as if seeing her for the first time. To him, women simply did not exist as individuals; save as occasional interludes, they had no place in his well-planned, carefully calculated life. If he thought of them at all, it was collectively, as a nameless, faceless breed tolerated now and then to perform duties essential for the upkeep of his health.

Therefore in all these years it had never occurred to him that Ivana Ivanova might have a gender, perhaps because she possessed none of the cunning, coquetry and avarice he associated with the sex. To him, she was merely a pair of dextrous hands and sturdy feet fashioned for his comfort, a domestic convenience like the flat iron or the thermantidote or the kitchen stove. He did not remember ever noticing her face. Had he been asked to describe her features with his eyes shut, he would have been hard put to do so.

When he had chanced upon her in Khiva sixteen years ago, she was no more than four or five, one of thousands of orhpaned children in slavery, and he had inherited her by default. She had simply appeared one morning with the housekeeping couple he employed at the Russian garrison at Petro-Alexandrovsk, and they had begged him to allow the child to stay. She was, they said, Armenian and had at one time worked in the Khan's zenana. When Khiva fell to the Russians and the Khan and his household fled, she had been left behind. She had neither relatives nor means of survival nor, indeed, a name. They called her simply *Khatoon,* "the girl."

Borokov became aware that Ivana had come into the room and asked a question to which she awaited an answer. Sensing that he had not heard her, she repeated it. "Supper is served in the dining room, Colonel sir, but if you are not yet ready to eat . . ."

"I am ready."

Draining his glass, he stood up, once again impressed by the soft timbre of her voice and the flattering deference with which she always addressed him. He sat down to eat. Supervised by Ivana, his two Bokhariot houseboys served the excellently cooked meal, but he ate absently, unable to shake the woman out of his thoughts.

Uncaring one way or the other, he had allowed the child to stay on provided she remained in the kitchen out of his sight and hearing, and for the next nine years had forgotten that she existed. When he was transferred back, the Khivan couple had refused to accompany him to St. Petersburg. Too poor to feed her and reluctant to assume responsibility for a growing girl, they had begged him to take Khatoon instead. They had assured him that she was honest, hardworking, reliable and a competent cook. Concerned mainly with his own comfort, he had agreed. He had not regretted the decision.

Within a matter of months in St. Petersburg she had picked up Russian cuisine, manners, dress and language and was soon running his household. Initially he had intended to secure for her a job in the Yacht Club kitchens, but again, more by default than by design, he had let the arrangement continue and she had stayed on. To circumvent cumbersome immigration procedures, with Smirnoff's influence he had registered her as Ivana Ivanova, a Russian. She had accepted the unimaginatively devised name as she accepted everything else, without comment or complaint, and it had stuck.

By the time he was posted back to Central Asia in Tashkent, Ivana had become an indispensable component of his domestic life. Indeed, it was because he was so entirely lost without her that she even accompanied him on his occasional travels.

One of the boys presented a platter of shashlik, but with no stomach even for his favourite dish, Borokov waved it away. Ivana was, he had only recently noted with some surprise, not unpleasing to the eye. She had a tall, trim figure and a smooth-skinned, oval face with a perennially tranquil expression. He had seldom seen her smile. She spoke as she walked, quietly, without hurry. Now, as her confident fingers replenished his wine-glass, removed his bowl of borscht and rolled his napkin neatly back into its silver ring, they did so with the same economy of movement with which, he saw, she performed all her given tasks. It occurred to him suddenly that the woman must have thoughts, feelings, aspirations, needs, likes and dislikes, none of which he had ever considered, and he felt a pinprick of guilt.

"Have you been happy in my household, Ivana Ivanova?" he asked on an impulse.

"Pardon, Colonel sir?"

She could not have been more startled had he made an indecent proposal. Borokov flushed. "I merely asked if you have been happy in my employ," he said gruffly, his eyes again on the intricately fashioned silver pendant against her neck.

"Certainly, Colonel sir." The few instants were enough for her to recover her habitual equanimity. "I have everything that I need."

"There must be something else you want," he prompted, "clothes or perfumes or—whatever women normally desire."

"I have enough clothes, Colonel sir, and I do not use perfume." She coloured and he saw that she was embarrassed.

He was suddenly irritated by the exchange, irritated that overnight she should have acquired another persona. From a cipher she had metamorphosed into a flesh and blood woman—a woman someone wanted—and he resented having to waste time in thinking about her. An alien element had crept into the carefully textured fabric of his life. He was annoyed because he did not understand it.

"How would you like to go away for a month's holiday?" he asked brusquely. While he instituted inquiries to get to the bottom of this tiresome business, he decided, it would be best to remove her from Tashkent altogether.

"A holiday?" She was surprised. "We have only just returned from St. Petersburg, Colonel sir."

"That was hardly a holiday, Ivana. What I mean is, a *real* holiday away from work, a month of complete rest."

"I have nowhere to go, Colonel sir."

"Well, as it happens, there is a small family boarding house I know on the Caspian run by an old widow where you would be comfortable and well looked after. The sea air will do you good."

Reluctant and puzzled but, as always, obedient, she dropped her eyes. "Very well, Colonel sir. I will do as you order."

It was one of the longest conversations they had ever had, certainly the most personal, and he was pleased with its outcome. He rose from the table.

"I will make arrangements for you to leave as soon as General Smirnoff arrives."

Dismissing Ivana and the Dards from his thoughts, he focussed instead on other, more vital matters—matters intensely private, matters that he guarded fiercely in the secret compartments of his mind. He thought of Alexei Smirnoff and then, with a great surge of pleasure, he thought of the Yasmina.

His hand rose—as it did many times each day—and his fingers curled around the nugget he wore in a chain around his neck, the nugget Safdar Ali had placed in his palm on his last day in Hunza. He had many obstacles yet to scale, many, many daunting hazards yet to face and conquer, but if there was anything he had learned in life it was that unless one ventured, one did not gain. Having come so far, he had absolutely no intention of faltering.

In a sudden rush of energy, he marched into his study and sat down to write a terse letter.

"Dear Dr. Theodore Anderson," he wrote.

I have heard nothing from you since your response to my initial letter. I thank you for the information but it is not enough! Had I not held the binoculars in my own hands in Hunza, examined them with my own eyes, I would not have been so persistent. I must therefore repeat that unless I receive complete information from you about the matter mentioned earlier, and that too fast, I cannot see my way to providing further funds for your expeditions.

*F*irst the ghee," the cook spooned ladles of clarified butter into the pan for the dried apricot korma, "and plenty of it. Then the onions, garlic, ginger, spices, saffron, and last of all the curd . . ."

Listening with awe to the litany of culinary wisdom, Emma absorbed it as fast as it was delivered. The best way to release the colour and fragrance of saffron was to soak it in warm milk; for those who wished to avoid onions and garlic, asoefoetida was an acceptably pungent substitute;

the dried fruit must not be stoned before making apricot korma, and the chunks of mutton must be seared to retain the juices. Many a gushtav was ruined, she was warned, because the mince was insufficiently pounded. The ancillaries the cook suggested for the Kashmiri dinner were fried Bauhinia flowers, a pilaf with local black mushrooms, and *panjeeri,* a saffron-flavoured thick, sweet syrup with lotus seeds and dates, to be served hot.

It was as they arrived at the pilaf (always to be cooked last) that the lesson was rudely interrupted by the sound of a female English voice on shore inquiring if huzoor and begum sahiba were at home. Emma groaned; today, that rarest of rare days when there was harmony between Damien and her, she had no wish to entertain callers, least of all Chloe Hathaway. She was on the point of sending word that she had a headache when, floating on clouds of an unmistakable perfume, the lady herself appeared at the door of the kitchen boat.

"Ah, *there* you are, my dear!" Her smile bright and her eyes dancing, Chloe stepped into the kitchen. "I heard you were both down for the day and would have been devastated to have missed you." Without ceremony she lifted the lid of a simmering saucepan and sniffed. "*Alu bokhara* korma? Yes, Mukhtiar's speciality. I have to say, it smells ravishing." She lifted a second lid and sniffed. "Gushtav, naturally, but no aubergines, I hope? Good. Damien can't stand them, you know. Pamper his sweet tooth with plenty of pudding, won't you?"

"How kind of you to call," Emma murmured, hiding her chagrin beneath a tight smile. "Damien is not in, I'm afraid. I'm not sure when he will return."

Compared with Chloe Hathaway's faultless grooming, Emma knew she looked terrible. Her hair, lank and damp, was all over the place, her nose shiny, her crushed housegown splattered with grease and she reeked of garlic. Making the best of the situation, she politely answered questions about the menu, washed and wiped her hands and then firmly escorted Chloe off the boat vowing that no matter what, she would not be inveigled into offering an invitation for dinner.

"Would you allow me a moment or two to freshen up?" she asked easily. "I daresay I look a mess."

When she returned to the deck after a swift toilette and change into a fresh linen dress, Chloe Hathaway had made herself comfortable on the chaise-longue. Surveying the scene across the lake, she reclined gracefully, fanning herself with a tiny mauve and cream Japanese fan that matched perfectly the colours of her splendid summer dress. As Emma resumed her seat, Chloe closed her eyes, raised her perfect little Roman nose to the sun and inhaled deeply.

"Divine," she breathed, "simply divine. There is a wonderful freshness in the air here that does miracles for jaded nerves." Not deeming a response necessary, Emma merely nodded. "And, of course, for insomnia."

The offensive insinuation could hardly be missed—nor was it meant to be. "Have you ever tried a saffron-stuffed pillow?" Emma asked sweetly holding on to her smile.

"Saffron-stuffed pillow?"

"Yes, a well-known remedy for insomnia, I am assured, that Roman emperors used after a heavy meal. Try it next time you can't sleep, Mrs. Hathaway."

"Really? How very odd!"

Not knowing whether or not she was being mocked, Chloe looked put out. Turning away, she leaned her head back, again shut her eyes and continued to inhale and exhale in rhythm. Without enthusiasm Emma took note of the serene expression, the lustrous lashes against china-fine skin, the beguiling body, the facile grace of the hand holding the fan and, above all, the air of unruffled, unrufflable, confidence. Despite her annoyance, Emma felt a rush of envy; with what pains, what devotion to magical recipes the loveliness must be preserved—and how removed from her own desultory endeavours!

"Would you care for some tea?" she asked glumly.

Much to her relief, Chloe shook her head. "No, thank you. Adela Stewart expects me at the Residency in an hour. She's having the dreary Bicknell couple over and wants moral support to fend off another thrust of the begging bowl. Considering the two new commodes they've just had for the hospital from the Residency, she's perfectly justified, wouldn't you say?" She paused for breath. "*You* haven't been asked by any chance, have you, Emma—I may call you Emma, may I not?"

"Yes, of course. No, I haven't been asked."

"Well, I didn't think so. Damien and Walter don't get on at all, as I said the other day. As a matter of fact, they can't stand each other. Unfortunately, I can only stay a few more minutes or I will be late and Adela will never forgive me, especially if she's already been stung. How long is Damien likely to be?"

"I'm sorry but I have no idea," Emma said, hoping fervently that he would be as long as possible. She added unthinkingly, "He warned me that he might not be back in time for dinner."

"Oh dear—and lay to waste all your commendable efforts in the kitchen? Tut, tut." She laughed.

"He said he *might* not be," Emma amended, feeling foolish, sorry not to have devised a more credible excuse. "I know he has several business appointments to keep."

"Ah." The single syllable quivered with meaning. "I wonder what dear Damien would do without his business appointments?"

The timely arrival of a gaily festooned boat and a raucous marriage party not far from the *Nishat* drowned the comment enough for Emma to pretend not to have heard it. As the bedecked passengers spilled out onto the bank, she remarked on their festive costumes and the conversation was successfully diverted. Her prayers that Chloe might leave before Damien returned, however, went unanswered; half an hour later his unmistakable voice boomed out from the shore and he came vaulting up the landing steps onto the deck. Seeing Chloe Hathaway, he came to a halt, visibly nonplussed.

Not so his visitor. "Ah, the elusive man himself!" All charm and effusiveness, Chloe smiled an unmistakably warm welcome. "Just as well— or your bride would never have forgiven you considering how hard she laboured over the welcoming feast." She rose, walked up to him and presented him with an upraised cheek. Damien flushed, so utterly embarrassed that despite her own imperfect composure Emma felt a surge of malicious enjoyment. How would he, she wondered, respond to the intimacy from a former mistress in the presence of his bride?

He responded by ignoring it. "Well, well," he muttered, turning away to hand his coat and a package to Hakumat, "what a surprise."

"Pleasant, I hope?" Unfazed by the snub, Chloe laughed as she tapped him playfully on a cheek with her fan, transforming even the snub into a coquettish triumph.

"We will have to wait and see."

"You broke your promise to come and see me, you naughty boy!" If it were possible to pout without losing poise, Chloe managed it admirably. "I shall exact severe recompense, I warn you."

He walked over to where Emma stood and leaned casually on the railings beside her. "I've hardly been in Srinagar over these past weeks, as I'm sure you know already."

Chloe spread her fan across her face and above it arched artistically drawn eyebrows. "More than two months, isn't it, Emma, dear?" Not knowing what else to do, Emma nodded. "Well, we think it unpardonable for a newly married man to be away from home for so long, don't we, Emma dear?"

Still deriving sadistic pleasure from the embarrassment he tried so hard to hide, Emma agreed tacitly. At the same time she felt a flutter of unease: what was all this banter leading up to, anyway?

She found out soon enough.

"Why, your deserted wife was reduced to making her first journey to Srinagar yesterday all by herself! Had she not arranged to meet ever gallant, ever willing Geoffrey," Chloe continued, in her element and quite unstoppable, "the poor neglected soul would have had to explore the romantic Shalimar on her own. You ought to be *ashamed* of yourself, Damien dear!"

Emma tried to say something but could not dislodge her voice and simply stared straight ahead. Dear God, she thought wildly, was her visit to Nazneen also about to be exposed? Damien, surprisingly enough, displayed no reaction. Seemingly engrossed in a hearty dispute between two boatmen who had narrowly missed a collision, he kept his eyes on the lake. The silence could not have lasted more than a few seconds, but to Emma it was an eternity.

Chloe's eyes widened as she alternated her stares between Emma's pale face and Damien's impassive back. "Oh dear, have I said something I ought not to have?" she wailed, flicking her fan back and forth and looking stricken. "I always seem to put my foot in it, don't I, Damien dear? I had no *idea* you didn't know about their meeting in Srinagar yesterday."

"Oh but I did." Turning around lazily, Damien looked Chloe square in the eye. "Emma told me about it. In fact, I was relieved Charlton could spare the time to show her around the gardens."

Emma gulped and Chloe fumbled—but only for an instant. "In that case I am pleased not to have said anything I should not have. I certainly would not have wanted to cause any trouble." The smiling eyes were fetchingly guileless; only a glint in the depths beneath the smile gave indication of anger.

"Of course not," Damien said. "That would be so unlike you. Now, how about a drink for our visitor, Emma? Considering the energy she has expended to enlighten me on a matter of such vital importance, the least we can do is to replenish it with a glass of sherry."

Throwing him a look of pure venom, Chloe rose to her feet. "I'd *love* to stay, Damien dear," she said tightly, her smile minimally frayed, "but I really mustn't, or Adela will be very cross. Perhaps another time? How long do you intend to remain here?"

Damien glanced at Emma to provide the response.

"A . . . a day or two . . . ?"

"Good. In that case you must both come and dine with me tomorrow night. I'll invite Geoffrey too so that you can thank him personally for his kindness to your wife."

Damien raised a questioning eyebrow and again looked at Emma.

"Well, I . . . I had thought that we might . . ." Emma broke off, confused and almost in tears.

"Explore the Takht-e-Suleiman?" Cutting in smoothly, Damien scanned the splendid view of the hill across the lake. "Isn't that what you had in mind?"

"Yes," Emma said gratefully. "I've . . . I've read so much about it and now that Damien *is* here . . ."

"An excellent idea," Chloe interrupted crisply, whisking her frilly parasol off the chair. "You might as well make the most of your will-o'-the-wisp husband while he's still within sight."

As she flounced down the steps followed by Damien, Emma folded into the chair, trembling with mortification. Damien's impromptu rescue had astonished her, of course, but it was too much to hope that the matter would end there.

As it happened, Damien expressed no further interest in her clandestine visit to Srinagar, either over the elaborate dinner or after. Throughout the meal—winning high praises and eaten with great enjoyment—he remained in fine spirits and the conversation ran smoothly, at least as far as he was concerned. Horribly tense, trying hard to fathom his intentions, Emma merely picked at the food with minimal conversational contributions.

As for the sleeping arrangements, she need not have worried about those either. Soon after the coffee tray was removed from the terrace where they sat after dinner, Damien wished her a cordial goodnight, vanished down the stairs clutching a book and left her to her solitary meditations. Later, much later, as the winking lights on the lake went out one by one, the moon rode the crests of the mountains and Srinagar slept, fearfully Emma crept down the stairs and into the master bedroom.

A night lamp burned low on a side table; the quilt and sheets had been turned down, the curtains drawn and her nightgown and slippers neatly laid out. The fourposter, however, was unoccupied. Damien had elected to sleep in the adjoining bedroom and the communicating door was pointedly shut.

I shall not come to you again until you ask me to.

No, Damien would not go back on his word; but then neither would she!

Chloe Hathaway's recommendation notwithstanding, Emma slept badly. Leaden-lidded, she rose the next morning to the cheerful cooing of doves and warbling of thrushes, but they did little to resuscitate her. Unnerved by Damien's resolute silence about her escapade, she nevertheless marched bravely onto the front deck. He stood at the rails reading a letter and frowning. A cup rested at his elbow.

"Not bad news, I hope?" she asked, trying hard to sound normal.

"No." He handed the letter to her. "The maharaja writes that he returned from his winter palace in Jammu with a cold but is now much better. We are invited to tea next Sunday afternoon. His Highness appears keen to meet you."

She skimmed her eyes over the paper and returned it to him.

"Did you sleep well last night?" he inquired politely.

"Extremely well, thank you."

"I had asked Jabbar Ali to make a new mattress for the fourposter. I trust you found it comfortable?"

"Perfectly comfortable. I slept like a log."

"Good."

Hakumat arrived with a fresh pot of tea. Watching the boats on the Dal, Emma sipped in silence. The morning air was heavy with the moist scents of the lake. Pale sunshine made the waters seem translucent and the beaches were alive with willows and lemon yellow catkins. Out of the corner of her eye Emma studied Damien's expression; it gave no indication of either anger or sulk. On the contrary, his lips were parted in a faint smile. He seemed remarkably relaxed. She made another valiant attempt at conversation with a question.

"Waterways?" he echoed. "Yes, they're the lifeline of the cargo trade and there are hundreds in Kashmir. They provide a living for almost forty thousand boatmen."

Remarking on the variety of craft, she pointed to a large one that went lumbering past and asked about its function.

"That is meant to carry bulk. Grain and wood mostly."

"Won't it sink with all that weight? It looks as if it will."

"It won't. Most Kashmiri boats are flat-bottomed, with high prows and sterns, and can carry up to a thousand maunds. Those smaller ones there have a lower prow, see? The heavier, open-roofed boats carry stones and that odd-looking contraption near the . . ."

Her apprehensions growing in direct proportion to his offhandedness, Emma listened with half an ear. Finally she could bear it no longer. "About the day before yesterday, Damien . . ." she burst out.

He drained his cup and held it out to Hakumat to be refreshed. "What about it?"

"It's true what Chloe said. I did make a visit to Srinagar."

"I know. The coachman told me."

Of course—how silly of her not to have guessed that. "Well, I was bored on my own," she said, on the defensive and rushing into explanations for which he had not asked. "You had been gone weeks and I had no idea when you would return. I was longing to explore Srinagar and the Shalimar and also wanted to persuade Rehmat's father to allow her to study. I met Geoffrey Charlton quite by accident. He just *happened* to be there at the same time and, well, that is all there is to it."

"Why did you not mention it to me?"

"I wanted to please you by pretending that this was my first visit to

Srinagar, with *you*. . . ." Her voice trailed off; reading something in his face she interpreted as scepticism, her temper flared. "Oh, *don't* believe me if you don't want to! It doesn't shame you that your mistresses—past or present—have the infernal nerve to flirt with you in my presence, but I happen to meet a man you do not like quite by chance in a public place, and you are ready to believe the worst of me? Well, believe what you damn well wish! I simply don't care one way or the other." She was about to brush past him when he caught her arm and held it.

"As it happens, I do believe you." He did not release her. "I accept that the encounter with Charlton in the Shalimar was accidental; but when you invited him here for tea, it was *not*. I don't want the man in my house again, Emma. It . . ."

"My house? Oh dear me, not *ours* any more?"

He flushed and the scar on his chin shone livid against the rush of blood. "I know that you do not like me, Emma," he said quietly, "and I am forced to tolerate that. What I will not tolerate is to be made a fool of. Please keep that in mind the next time you meet Charlton. Chloe Hathaway may be a mischief-maker, but . . ."

"Oh she may be, may she?" Emma wrenched her arm free. "I thought you said she was harmless."

"What I said was . . ."

"Don't bother to repeat it, Damien." Tears of frustration threatened but she contained them. "If anyone has made a fool of you, the credit, alas, goes not to me but to a higher authority."

Running past him into the room, she slammed the door behind her. When she emerged several hours later, Damien had gone out leaving word that he would not be back for dinner. When he did return well after midnight, Emma pretended to be asleep. The next morning they returned to Shalimar, he in mocking, offensively high spirits and she in desolate silence. The trip for which she had had such high hopes had been an unmitigated disaster.

I know that you do not like me . . .

She could have wept.

*T*rout? In India? Don't be daft, Hartley—you're pulling my leg."

"Twenty-pounders, no less, 'pon my word."

"Twenty-pounders? Good heavens! At home I've never seen one larger than two pounds."

"I kid thee not—ask Wilfred Hethrington if you don't believe me. Wilfred, I say, Wilfred?" Hethrington turned to see two colonels on the

C-in-C's staff striding after him. "You've been up to the Lidder for a spot of fishing, haven't you?"

"Often."

"Eastbridge here refuses to believe that Lidder trout can grow up to twenty pounds."

"Well, my own catches have been somewhat more modest," Hethrington confessed, "but yes, you can get some that size—if you're lucky."

"There, you see, old chap? If you want further proof there's a photograph up in the clubhouse just behind the bar which . . ."

Wilfred Hethrington moved away.

It was the afternoon of the year's second gymkhana. Annandale, the largest stretch of level ground available to Simla residents and a popular venue of open-air festivities, was crowded. Organized by the Gymkhana Club, the occasion was a jolly one. There was a merry-go-round, swings, shops and game-stalls, all doing roaring trade. In the first steeplechase of the afternoon some of the horses had insisted on running round the fences instead of over them, but the tent-pegging led by the Viceroy had been a grand success. Everyone looked happy and carefree—everyone, that is, except Wilfred Hethrington.

Weaving in and out of the throng, he dutifully exchanged smiles, bows, nods and words, noting with no sense of joy whatsoever the swelling multitudes in station. Under one arm he clutched a large woolly duck with a floppy neck which he had won in the egg-and-spoon race, much to the delight of his wife who was supervising the white elephant stall. Even when not gravely disturbed, Hethrington hated the Annandale romps to which Simla was addicted in the Season. This afternoon he longed even more for the advent of November when one out of twenty houses would be vacant, all civilians gone, the temperature down to minus one and the snow-covered streets pleasantly deserted—a return, in fact, to civilised living.

Avoiding his wife's sharp eye from across the fairground, he collared a girl of about six, daughter of one of the sergeants on duty at the Viceregal Lodge, and thrust the duck into her surprised hands.

"Want a soft toy, my dear?"

The child considered the duck with disdain and thrust it right back. "Naw. It's only got one eye and the neck's *bwoken*."

Once again at a loss, Hethrington stared at a clump of snake-plants. Believed to be indicators of rain, the cobs grew straight up when the monsoons were due and turned red when they were about to end. Shielding himself behind them, he tossed the duck into a ditch on the other side and turned round—to find himself staring into the puzzled face of the Quarter Master General.

He gave an abashed smile and a stammering explanation, but Sir John had other matters on his mind. His eyes were fixed on someone near the coconut shies in conversation with Belle Jethroe. Hethrington followed his gaze to the urbane, dandyish figure of the Russian consul-general.

"Our man posted at the consulate reports plenty of activity by way of messages," Hethrington remarked. "He says he appears quite worried, the consul-general, I mean."

"Well, so would I be if I had Alexei Smirnoff posted just around the corner! When is he due to arrive in Tashkent, do we know yet?"

"Smirnoff? Any day now, I believe."

Sir John raised a hand and then dropped it in an eloquent gesture. "He's coming too close for comfort, Wilfred. In fact . . ." He stopped. "You're not, by any chance, down for the potato-in-the-bucket, are you?"

"Good God, no."

Hethrington noted with alarm the advance towards them of a pesky little French jeweller, an annual visitor who specialised in enamel boxes. Having made the mistake of considering and then rejecting one of his infernal boxes as a birthday present for his wife, he now found it impossible to shake the fellow off.

"Let's go in here, sir," he said hurriedly, "where we can talk."

They took a sharp turn past the spun-sugar stall into the trees and picking a path walked through a pleasantly dense grove strewn with pine nuts.

"Our Uzbek reports that something else appears to be happening in Tashkent," Hethrington said. "Something rather odd."

"Odd?"

"Very."

A football came flying out of nowhere, followed by a tousled young man dripping perspiration and apologies. With a curt nod Sir John kicked the ball back. "Let's try and find a spot with a little more damned privacy, shall we?"

They again changed direction to burrow deeper into the thicket of plane trees beyond the grove.

"Well?" Sir John asked, when they were reasonably secluded.

"From a conversation he overheard among the Cossacks, he reports that two men, infiltrators apparently, came to see the Baron with a request." Hethrington bent down and removed a branch obstructing the path. "It appears they wished to locate an Armenian female."

Sir John halted. "Oh?"

"They claimed to be Dards."

"Dards? What would the Dards want with her, eh?"

"They were probably lying, sir. In this game, truth is more the exception than the rule."

"Then who the blazes were they?"

Hethrington looked away. "They could have come from anywhere."

"Anywhere? *Where?* Don't tell me the entire world is suddenly mounting a hunt for one blasted female Armenian slave in Turkestan!"

Through the lattice of branches Hethrington stared at the veined rock-faces and textured scrubland glinting in the afternoon sun. Something rustled in the bushes, a large brown hare. Nostrils twitching in fury, it scuttled away into its burrow beneath the roots of a banyan.

"Far more worrying, sir," he said unhappily, "is what they offered in return for the woman."

"Don't tell me, let me guess." Sir John pressed a hand to his forehead. "Maps of the Yasmina?"

Hethrington nodded. "One of the men claimed to have been a camel groom with the caravan. He said he stole the papers from Butterfield's bag during the raid."

"Good grief!" The QMG stopped dead in his tracks.

"Quite, sir."

"Well, what the devil do you make of *that*?"

"Nothing, sir. As I said, they were probably lying."

Sir John searched Hethrington's troubled face and enlightenment dawned. His canny eyes narrowed. "Ah, so it *has* sprung a leak after all, has it?" he said softly. "This ship you had such fond hopes of steering into port with all hands safe on board?"

"We can't be sure of that yet, sir."

"Can't we?"

A further question hovered on Sir John's pursed lips, but before he could voice it a group of giggling girls came crashing through the undergrowth in search of hiding places. By the time the stampede had melted into various bushes, a junior clerk from the Department had battled his way through with an urgent message from the Club secretary. The three o'clock race was about to be flagged off and final bets were being called for in the clubhouse.

Sir John gave a quick look at his watch, a "Tch!" of irritation and prepared to run. "We'll take it up first thing on Monday morning," he said hastily. "Nine *sharp* in my office. Don't be late."

All else forgotten for the nonce, with a wave and a mumbled apology he hurried away in pursuit of the dead cert he had been promised.

Saved by the bell!

Hethrington stared at the departing back in undisguised relief. Sir John was absolutely right. Their ship had sprung a leak and was beginning to list—and there was not a single damned thing he could do about it.

CHAPTER

14

*N*ever before having been presented to royalty, Emma had no idea what to expect. When asked to provide guidance Damien was of little help with vague advice to "behave as you normally would." His airy "anything" when questioned about appropriate clothing, Emma translated into a sedate pale blue organdie with full skirt and gophered sleeves that was neither too elaborate nor too subdued.

Since their return from Srinagar, Damien's mood had remained buoyant and Emma was grateful for it. The silly argument on the houseboat seemed mercifully forgotten; neither Charlton nor Chloe Hathaway had been mentioned since. Engrossed in matters of the estate, Damien spent long hours in the office clearing accumulated paperwork or in the fields supervising the harvest and fruit picking, and Emma had taken to accompanying him. The principle on which he ran the estate impressed her: *Yus karih gonglu sui karih krao*—He who ploughs shall reap. It was not a principle that many endorsed in this country beset by despotic zamindars. More often than not, peasants earned barely enough to keep body and soul together; trapped in the nefarious conspiracy between middlemen and corrupt government officials, most remained serfs for life.

In the evenings when they were on their own, Damien's manner continued to be surprisingly affable, their conversations pleasantly civilized and the air between them distinctly less chilly.

Neither touched upon the matter of the separate bedrooms.

Since the palace was in Srinagar, it had been decided to spend the night before and after the visit on the *Nishat*. As Emma prepared for the evening in the master dressing-room on the boat, she considered the question of her wedding jewellery, wondering if it had originally belonged to Natasha Granville and been kept in that dressing-table drawer. She had vowed never to wear it again, but now, with Delhi a lifetime away, the resolution seemed to her childish. After much introspection—and knowing that it would please Damien—she eventually slipped on a sapphire and pearl necklet and matching ear drops that she had packed with her clothes. In an added gesture of appeasement she draped the *shatoosh* shawl over her shoulders. As she stepped back for a last look in the full-length mirror, a knock sounded on the connecting door and Damien walked in.

In his dark blue suit, matching cravat and shining formal shoes, he himself appeared the epitome of elegance, conservative enough to pass muster even with the Bankshalls.

"How . . . how do I look?" she asked diffidently.

He examined her from coiffure to gold sandals and nodded. "You'll do. His Highness will approve."

Do you? She bit back the question. As she climbed off the wooden stairway onto the lake bank, Damien gave her his hand and she shivered.

"Cold?"

She shook her head, drew the shawl closer about her shoulders and quickly settled back into the cushions of the palanquin, accepting once again that the traditional conveyance befitted the formality of the occasion.

Officials of the royal durbar who received them in the main hall of the palace appeared to know Damien well. He presented each in turn to her with a few words of introduction: an eminent Muslim poet, a refugee from Afghanistan related to the exiled king, a Dogra chief of protocol from Jammu, and a uniformed officer from Hyderabad on loan from the Nizam, who was now military secretary to His Highness. Escorted swiftly through corridors and antechambers and up staircases, they proceeded towards the distant destination where the maharaja's principal private secretary waited. A Kashmiri pundit dressed in white trousers and high-necked coat, he ushered them into the inner sanctum: and the royal presence.

"Ah, Damien, it is good of you to come." Dismissing the hovering courtiers with a wave, Maharaja Pratap Singh clasped Damien's hands in both of his. "I have been looking forward to seeing you again and, of course, to making the acquaintance of your bride."

Damien bowed. "I am happy that Your Highness is once more in good health after the recent indisposition."

He presented her and as Emma curtsied and then folded her hands in greeting, the maharaja appraised her with dark, dreamy eyes that seemed immensely weary.

"I am delighted to meet the esteemed lady who finally managed to pin

Damien down to a settled life," he said. "I was becoming concerned about his addiction to bachelorhood." He smiled as Emma blushed, resumed his place on the divan and crossed his legs beneath him in a gesture of informality. "Please be seated and let us talk."

Whatever her preconceived notions, Emma was struck by the simplicity of the man and his apartment, both giving little evidence of the luxury one might expect of one who ruled over a territory larger than England. He had spoken in Dogri. Not yet fluent in the language, Emma made a stumbling response and he immediately switched to Urdu.

"Since the Viceroy has decreed that more Urdu should be spoken in the state, I might as well take advantage of your wife's fluency in the language, Damien, and gain some practice."

Emma was surprised that he should have known that and said so.

"Well, I may be a spent force as far as the British are concerned, but I assure you, there is life in the old dog yet." His tired eyes shone briefly. "I might tell you, Mrs. Granville, that news of your marriage broke many hearts in Kashmir. Why, in my own palace a visit from Damien was enough to send the zenana hurrying to the windows in the hope of a glimpse."

Damien went faintly pink and made an embarrassed protest, but Emma enjoyed his discomfiture and laughed.

The maharaja complimented her on her very authentic accent and added, "But then you are the daughter of Graham Wyncliffe, I know. Someone reminded me this morning that I had the privilege of meeting him in Jammu some years ago. Regrettably my memory isn't as good as it used to be in happier days. I was sorry to read that he had passed away and in such sad circumstances."

Emma acknowledged the sympathy with a nod.

"He was last here in 'eighty-seven, the year the British set aside pretences and imposed a Resident on my state while I was still in mourning for my father. It is not a year to be forgotten." There was more than a trace of bitterness in his tone. "In fact, it was the first Resident, Sir Olivier St. John, who brought Dr. Wyncliffe to meet me."

Since the subject of British domination over his state was a sensitive one and her own political information woefully inadequate, Emma remained silent. The room, she noticed, was littered with newspapers, the *Times of India* from Bombay, the *Civil & Military Gazette* from Lahore, the *Statesman* from Calcutta, and many from England, including the *Sentinel*. It was the maharaja himself who filled the awkward gap.

"And you, Mrs. Granville, do you also take an active interest in archaeology and Buddhist history?"

Emma affirmed that she did.

"In that case, we have plenty to interest you in Kashmir, which at one time was a stronghold of Buddhism, as no doubt you already know. I hope your husband has been showing you some of our more famous sites?"

"Well . . ."

"Not yet, Your Highness." Damien chose to present his own defence. "Having been away, I have to confess that I have neglected Emma shamefully."

"Well, now that you are back, you must make immediate restitution!" He laughed and turned to Emma. "Apart from historical sites, we have many places of worship held in reverence by both Hindus and Muslims that will certainly intrigue you."

They talked of those for a while and of antiquity and its relics in general, until the doors of the chamber opened and a succession of uniformed attendants appeared bearing trays of refreshments. One of the attendants passed round glasses of khus-khus sherbet, others served the delicacies; then, leaving the silver trays ranged on a table near the window, they withdrew.

"I regret that the maharani is away on a pilgrimage to Amarnath," the maharaja said. "She would have been pleased to meet you and be able to communicate without an interpreter."

Emma politely seconded the regrets. Privately, however, she was relieved to be able to stay and listen to the men.

Taking note of the *shatoosh* she wore, the maharaja praised it lavishly. "I am told that this year's gifts for the Queen Empress are again up to your usual excellent standard, Damien. Her Majesty will approve." A wispy smile touched the thin mouth. "A true example of the great regard in which you and I hold Britain, eh, Damien?" It was difficult to miss the sarcasm.

Damien smiled. "Indeed."

"The weaving goes well?"

"As well as can be expected considering the whims of European fashion. Ironically enough, even though demand in Europe has declined, the census next year promises to show an increase in the population of weavers in the valley."

"And what do the Ali brothers have to say about the demand in Central Asia? They go there often enough to be able to assess the potential."

"Well, the potential would certainly be healthier if Russian levies did not make it difficult for outsiders to compete."

"All the same, Damien, it was a fortunate day for our weavers when your father decided to settle in Kashmir." He heaved a soft sigh and in the sag of facial muscles the grooves at the corners of his mouth deepened. "Your father did a great deal to enhance the prestige of our state in Europe, as you continue to do. The fact that you still provide gainful employment for so many craftsmen remains a boost for our famous but flagging industry."

"Kashmir gave my father sanctuary when he needed it," Damien replied. "Indeed, Kashmir has given us far more than we can ever hope to return."

Pratap Singh picked up a silver-coated almond, placed it between his teeth and nibbled. "In those days our Kashmir was a very different place, Damien, as you must have heard often enough from your father. Then, a ruler *ruled*; today, he merely dances to foreign tunes played by a Council and a Resident. He has little say in the administration of his own state."

The bitterness was now very much on the surface. Despite her ignorance of state matters, Emma was aware that intrigue was the scourge of all royal courts. Even so, there was something pathetic about Pratap Singh's helplessness. It appeared to her that he had already conceded defeat to the circumstances that had carried his life way beyond his control.

"They give Kashmir a new constitution," he continued despondently. "They make mischief within my family. I fear that what stands between me and deposition is one wrong step, that is all. I am gravely disturbed about the future of Kashmir, Damien." He glanced at the newspaper lying half open by his side. "As I am about all this disquiet in the mountain kingdoms."

Damien frowned. "It is difficult to separate truth from fiction in English newspapers, Your Highness, and there has always been disquiet in the mountain kingdoms."

"True, but when he called on me yesterday, Walter Stewart was most perturbed about this Russian's visit to Hunza. Stewart is of the opinion that they deliberately increase tension along the borders. I hope he is wrong, Damien. I would hate the British to find an excuse to pour more troops into Kashmir."

"If they can't find an excuse Durand will manufacture one," Damien replied. "Kashmir and its border kingdoms are crucial to Britain, and if"— he shook his head—"no, not if, *when* Durand has his way, one by one they will vanish."

Pratap Singh heaved another plaintive sigh. "I fear terribly that you may be right. Considering how vociferous the firanghi is about his own territorial rights—illicitly acquired as they are!—he is remarkably insensitive to the legitimate claims of others. Chitral, I know, heads for a succession war when the present ruler dies, and Safdar Ali is most unreliable. Despite his smooth manners and flowery speeches, the Viceroy evaded direct answers during his visit last year and the Resident continues to be fortified with alarming powers." He jabbed a finger at a headline in a newspaper. "Do you think the Russians seriously intend a confrontation over this Hunza business?"

"No."

"Even so, Damien, our Kashmir becomes increasingly vulnerable with all these new passes they find. One day, I fear, there will be no secrets left, not even the Yasmina. Everything in our God-given battlements will be exposed and exploited." He leaned forward and put a hand on Damien's arm. "It is not our business what they do to each other in their own countries, but I do not wish to be involved in someone else's war on Kashmiri soil."

"Knowing that if a rifle fires in St. Petersburg the British hear an explosion in the Himalayas," Damien said contemptuously, "Russia uses verbal cut and thrust only to provoke, Your Highness. There will be no war."

"What about this new railway? Has that not wrought significant change in the balance of power in Central Asia? They say the Russians extend the line to Tashkent, that a new Governor-General arrives, that they bring in even more troops for a confrontation. You travelled on the railway when you returned from St. Petersburg, Damien. What was your impression of it as a machine of war?"

So, Damien *had* been in St. Petersburg. Charlton had not lied. Emma continued to listen with steady interest.

"As a machine of commerce it is formidable, true, but as a machine of war?" Damien shrugged. "The Transcaspian runs on a single-line track. It is sparingly equipped and there are frequent breakdowns. With only six thousand trucks available, the transport of vast numbers of troops or ammunition is not possible."

"Walter Stewart seems convinced to the contrary."

"And naturally works hard also to convince Your Highness! How else can he strengthen the British foothold in Kashmir?" There was a gleam of anger in Damien's eyes. "Russia has neither the capability nor the route nor the inclination for war, no matter what Britain chooses to believe!"

Easing himself back against a bolster, Pratap Singh studied Damien's face. "I can understand your own personal dilemma," he said gently. "It is uncomfortable to be caught between two loyalties."

"There is no personal dilemma, Your Highness," Damien was quick with his clarification. "My loyalty is only to Kashmir."

"Nevertheless, I am nervous, Damien. I do not want our state to become a trampling ground for foreign armies."

It was the first time Emma had heard Damien express his political views with such openness. The conversation she had unwittingly overheard in Delhi at the Prices' burra khana during dinner had been brief, but even then his sympathy for Russia was all too evident. Lost in her own thoughts, she realised belatedly that the maharaja had asked her a question that had gone unheard.

"I beg your p-pardon?" she stammered, reddening. "I'm sorry, but for a moment I had allowed my mind to wander to something else."

The maharaja laughed. "Well, I don't blame you, my dear. Politics are a sordid, heartless business. I am not surprised that someone academically inclined should have little interest in it."

"It is not the interest that is lacking," Emma protested, "it is the knowledge. I'm afraid I am not well informed enough about current events to venture a worthwhile opinion."

Pratap Singh made some other good-humoured observation, then, still worried, returned his attention to Damien. "There is something I feel I ought to mention, Damien—it is not only for Kashmir that I fear, it is also for you. Stewart does not like you."

Damien shrugged. "He is entitled to his opinion."

"You and I have many enemies, Damien," Pratap Singh said. "They wait for an opportunity to strike. I do not wish either of us to give them one. They forge letters to try to prove my secret pacts with Russia. Having been accused of treachery once, I would not take care to be humiliated again." He paused. "Nor would I you."

Suddenly it seemed to Emma that the timbre of the conversation had changed. From generalities, it had moved to the particular. Damien got up and went to stand by the window. He did not reply.

"Be careful, my friend," the maharaja warned, "you have much to lose. There are wolves out there in the jungle determined not to spare us."

"Wolves?" Damien turned around and laughed. "They are not wolves, Your Highness, merely *hawabeen*."

"But it is the *hawabeen* who are the predators, Damien, who dictate policy and make mischief with impunity. They will not leave us in peace until what is rightfully ours belongs to them."

"Tongues cannot be stilled, Your Highness, nor claws blunted."

"Defeatism, Damien? You astonish me."

"Pragmatism, Your Highness." He returned and sat down. "I merely try to come to terms with the inevitable in an unjust world."

"Do you? I wonder."

Their eyes, frankly troubled, met and held for a moment. Then with no further comment the maharaja clapped his hands and the doors opened. Two attendants entered bearing between them a heavy walnut chest, intricately and exquisitely carved.

"A small token for you and Damien," he smiled at Emma, "with my sincere felicitations on the auspicious occasion of your marriage. May you be blessed with many sons." The weary, clouded eyes lightened. "Daughters too, of course, in the image of their mother."

Emma murmured her thanks, admired the beautiful gift, and then it was time to leave. As the maharaja walked with them to the door of the apartment, he paused. Laying a hand on Damien's arm, he fixed him with a deep look. "Should you need my assistance, you know that I will help in any way that I can."

"Thank you. I have never doubted it."

It had been a puzzling encounter. Reflecting on the visit later, Emma realised that she had not understood fully the text concealed beneath the surface of the conversation and many of the nuances had gone right over her head. The truth was, she conceded readily enough, there were yawning gaps in her political education. She had not read a newspaper in weeks, knew precious little about border tensions and frontier intrigues, and was indifferent to radical changes in the political climate. In a mountain state as volatile as Kashmir, such ignorance was unforgivable, and all at once she was ashamed. It was time, she decided, to broaden her horizons, educate herself and refashion her attitudes.

"I have an appointment tomorrow morning with the Italian manager of the winery at Gupkar," Damien said after dinner as they sat on the terrace nursing glasses of port. "I will be out more or less the whole day and am not certain when I will be back. You could return to Shalimar earlier on your own or do some sightseeing here, whichever suits you better."

She opted immediately for the latter, declaring her intention to visit the Takht-e-Suleiman while she had the opportunity. Damien nodded absently. He was, she saw, preoccupied, disinclined to make conversation. Even so, she took her courage in her hands and risked a question.

"Who or what are these . . . *hawabeen* you mentioned at the palace?"

"The *hawabeen*? Those who live by rumour."

"Oh I see, literally, 'watchers of the wind.' And the predators?"

"Those who hunt on turf where they have no right."

"The British?"

"Yes."

"Why should they be your enemies?"

He shrugged. "When one is an outsider with an estate such as Shalimar, one always has enemies."

"Who in particular?" she persisted.

"Well—Stewart for one, the Resident."

"Is it not possible," she asked warily, "that your often tactless defence of the Russians might be a reason for that?"

"How Stewart might or might not react to my opinions is of no great consequence to me."

She searched his face for signs of irritation; there were none. Emboldened, she stirred another topic. "You travelled to St. Petersburg last year?"

"Yes."

"You have been there before?" He nodded. "On business?"

On the verge of saying something, he hesitated, then changed his mind. "Yes, on business."

"These sympathies you have for Russia," she pressed on in a rush of further courage, "do they stem from genuine political beliefs—or from emotional considerations?"

"You mean because my mother was Russian and worked for her country?" His shoulders lifted slightly. "Some of both, perhaps."

The ease with which he made the admission fairly took Emma's breath away. Taking advantage of his openness, she asked quickly, "You were aware of the life she had led earlier?"

"Not until after my father died. He left me a letter explaining whatever he could." Much to her relief he questioned neither her knowledge nor the source from which it had come.

"Why did she go away?"

"Why?" He gave a sardonic half laugh. "For the oldest reason in the world! She considered another man had more to offer than her husband."

"Another man she had met here, in the valley?"

"No. A cellist she had known in Peshawar, a Romanian, who suddenly arrived one day to see her. She left with him."

Surprised that they were being answered at all, more questions came tumbling out. "How did she die, *where*?"

Cradling his glass in his hands, he focussed his eyes on her face even though he stared not at her but beyond, as if at images from the past on some distant shore. "The journey across high mountains was too much for her, it sapped her strength. She was always very fragile—a tinsel fairy on a Christmas tree." He made a face. "At least, that was how my father thought of her."

"And you?" The anguished scribbles and a dozen more questions came crowding into Emma's mind. Had absolution, she wondered, ever been granted to an absconding mother? "Is that how you think of her too, a tinsel fairy on a Christmas tree?"

"No." The vision of the past vanished; his mouth tightened. "I do not think of her at all."

So, she had not been forgiven! Aware now of the anvil on which his extreme attitudes had been fashioned, Emma felt a rush of sympathy. Before she could ask another question, however, he brushed the topic aside.

"It doesn't matter any more, Emma. Childhood memories are patterns in the water, easily made, easily destroyed."

"Childhood memories are part of us, Damien." Desperate for his confidence, desperate to know him better, she refused to let it go. "They make us what we are, shape our thoughts and quirks of personality, give directions for the future."

"Hers is a long, complicated story, Emma," he said tiredly. "She was a complex woman, complex and ill-starred. What happened will take time to tell."

"We have the time, Damien!"

She held her breath as, uncertain, he debated within himself. Just as he seemed on the verge of capitulation, a cough sounded on the stairway. The baburchi stepped onto the terrace to ask for the next day's orders and the moment was lost.

Damien rose. "One of these days we will talk of it again. Now I need to prepare for this appointment tomorrow. I will have to leave early. I may not see you in the morning."

She felt overwhelmed with disappointment.

For a long while that night Emma lay in bed staring at the closed door between them. Wide awake and restless, she finally abandoned the effort to sleep and got out of bed. Sitting down at the table, she frowned in momentary thought, then picked up a pencil and scribbled a short note to Geoffrey Charlton.

*M*aracanda to the Macedonians, Samokien to the Buddhists, final resting place of Tamerlane and splendid capital of the first Moghul emperor Babar—Samarkand was once the pride of the Asian continent. Discovered by the Chinese in 138 B.C. as a thriving kingdom, it was Samarkand that primed curiosity about the Western world and gave rise to the trade route known as the Silk Road.

With its well-ordered streets, white-fronted bungalows, wide boulevards and streams, this much favoured retreat of the Tartars even now had more trees, gardens and vineyards than any other town in Central Asia. Each of Samarkand's exquisite ancient monuments related a separate chapter of history down its many centuries of conquest and counter conquest. Focal point of the town was the Righastan, one of the most gracious city squares in the world, said to be grander than the Piazza di San Marco of Venice. At an elevation of two thousand feet, Samarkand enjoyed a perfect climate. The mercury never went above thirty degrees Fahrenheit in summer, nor below zero in the depths of winter.

Recently, as the terminus of the Transcaspian Railway, Samarkand had acquired celebrity of a more modern nature. As he paced the platform impatiently awaiting the arrival of the train, it was on this proud new achievement that Mikhail Borokov's concentration was focussed.

The station house and adjacent offices had still not been completed. The battalions of local labourers were slow, their work slipshod and the piles of leftover masonry a disgusting eyesore. With work stopped for a day and the place swept and washed for the reception of the new Governor-General, however, Borokov considered he had done as much as he could under the circumstances. The Cossack regiment and the battery of artillery ranged on the tracks was smart enough, the guard of honour ready for inspection and the band well tuned to strike up as soon as the engine sounded its whistle. He hoped there would be no unforeseen hitches.

In full-dress regalia and medals, the Baron looked hot and bothered as he stood on the platform beside the local governor and other dignitaries. Every few minutes he consulted his watch, clucked and glanced longingly at the shed where his menagerie was housed. The Baroness had already left for St. Petersburg. As soon as he had handed over charge to his successor, he himself with his remaining personal staff and his precious zoological entourage would follow on the return journey of the train—and, his expression indicated, not a damned day too soon! He thought yearningly of the golden eagle fledgling that would now never be his. Borokov had been right, he conceded sadly; the younger fellow had not returned, not even to collect the woman, and they had not been able to find any trace in Tashkent of the older rascal. Aware that he had not handled the situation as he should have, the Baron had requested Borokov not to mention the matter to his successor.

A piercing whistle announced the arrival of the train and the station sprang to life. With a final glance at their weapons the soldiers stiffened their postures, the Baron shoved his watch back into its pocket and corrected the angle of his hat, and the station staff came running to take up allotted positions along the edge of the platform. The engine chugged into view. At a signal from Borokov, the band launched into the national anthem and the artillery thundered into a deafening salute to the new Governor-General.

Despite the incomplete state of the station and the onerous preparations involved, the ceremonial reception went remarkably well. All smiles and waves at the curious crowds outside the station, Alexei Smirnoff complimented the Baron on his arrangements. The Baron, nobly, passed the credit on to Colonel Borokov.

"Keeping well, I see, Colonel," Smirnoff remarked affably. "Obviously the food and climate of Asia do your health good."

It was a remark directed at Borokov's broadening waistline; sensitive about it, Borokov did not return the smile. He was grateful at least that Alexei spoke in Russian and not in French, a language in which he himself was not comfortable. French manners, styles and language were affectations assumed by the Russian elite in blind admiration of everything Gallic. Indeed, it was in deference to prevailing French fashion that Alexei called himself Smirnoff, rather than the traditional Smirnov. It was a pretension Borokov viewed with disdain.

During the ride along the metalled road to Government House, where General Smirnoff was to host a ball for leading citizens and spend the night before proceeding to Tashkent, Smirnoff expressed admiration for the road on which they proceeded.

"Matters were very different when I was last in Asia," he said. "Certainly there were no metalled roads to be seen then."

"This one from the terminus is the only one east of the Caspian," the Baron announced proudly.

"Well, I am delighted that our railway has initiated such a significant change in communications. When I was here, a telegram from Samarkand to Bokhara had to be routed through Tashkent, Orenburg, Samara, Moscow and Baku, with no guarantee of ever reaching its destination. As for the postal service, well, the less said about that the better."

Several duties remained for Borokov to attend to with regard to the evening's banquet and arrangements for the overnight stay of General Smirnoff and his staff. Finally, as he prepared to leave for the military club where he himself was billeted in order to change for dinner, Smirnoff stopped him with a raised finger.

"I would be obliged, Colonel, if you would be so kind as to take charge of my personal baggage as your special responsibility. My wife has sent some extremely valuable Chinese furniture and porcelain for my use in Tashkent. She would never forgive me if even a single piece were to arrive damaged."

Borokov's heart somersaulted straight into his mouth. Smirnoff had brought the weapons as part of his personal baggage!

"Certainly, Excellency." Somehow he smiled. "I will transport and unpack the crates personally."

"Now if you would be so kind as to wait a few moments, I will explain to you my wife's rather complicated inventory."

It was a sign of dismissal for the rest.

"I take it you understand what those crates contain, Mikhail?" Smirnoff asked crisply as soon as they were on their own.

"Yes."

"The relevant boxes are all marked 'Fragile.' "

"The obsolete weaponry we selected?"

"Some."

"And the rest?"

"Small-calibre magazine rifles." His eyes gleamed as he awaited Borokov's reaction. He was not disappointed; Borokov was astounded.

"You had no problem securing those?"

"Of course I had problems! It was only because I finally persuaded them that the rifles and powder needed to be tested in Central Asia— where they would eventually be used—that they consented to release a limited number."

"And the cannon? Safdar Ali was most insistent about those."

"Oh, rubbish! Once he sees the new riffles, he'll forget about the cannon. I know the likes of Safdar Ali, Mikhail—savages, uncouth and coarse. I'll manage him without any trouble."

I'll manage him. The use of the singular pronoun was not lost on Borokov.

"When do we plan to make the delivery?" he asked, making his own point subtly.

"Soon, soon."

Walking up to the mirror Smirnoff removed his belt, pulled in his stomach and patted its flatness with complacency. Borokov's mouth tensed at the tacit gibe, but he withheld comment. A striking figure of a man, Smirnoff was tall, hard-muscled and in excellent fitness. With his dense crop of hair, neatly trimmed beard and full-lipped mouth crowned by a linear moustache, he was said to be irresistible to the opposite sex. Certainly there were enough women in Moscow and St. Petersburg to testify to that. Two years older than Borokov, he looked at least five younger.

"I need to know how much time I have to disassemble the weapons," Borokov said, peeved by the vagueness.

"We'll talk about that later, in Tashkent. Where do you intend to store the crates?"

"I have an outhouse in Tashkent that is perfectly secure."

"And your housekeeper, what is her name?"

"Ivana Ivanova."

"She is to be trusted?"

"Completely."

"The crates will be transported to Tashkent safely, I hope?"

"Of course. You can leave the arrangements to me."

"When do you go back?"

"At dawn. I will start to load immediately after dinner."

"Good. You will be careful, won't you, Mikhail? We don't want any mishaps now considering how many palms had to be greased and how many favours granted to get these damned rifles out here."

"No, there will be no mishaps." Borokov was irritated by the patronisation. "For God's sake, Alexei, I'm not a bloody idiot, you know!"

"I hope not, Mikhail, I sincerely hope not. By the way"—Smirnoff's expression cooled—"regardless of our relationship at home, I suggest that in Central Asia you address me formally. Familiarity is likely to be misconstrued."

Borokov was deeply offended by the snub but his expression did not show it. "Of course, Excellency. The error will not be repeated."

"Good. You may go."

Borokov returned to the military club, riding hard and seething. So, Alexei planned to pull rank on him, did he! Flying past the blue-domed Russian church, past the public gardens and the artificial lake, he reined his horse at the Bibi Khanum mosque and dismounted. He needed time to ponder, to set his thoughts in order. Barely noticing his surroundings Borokov strode through the mosque into the fifteenth-century mausoleum, tomb of Tamerlane and his descendants.

It was not yet evening. The tomb's lone attendant sat outside on a stone awaiting visitors. Inside, much to Borokov's relief, the place was deserted. Tamerlane's body in the vault below was said to have been embalmed with musk and rosewater, wrapped in linen and encased in an ebony coffin. In the upper chamber, cenotaphs had been fashioned to correspond with the underground sepulchres. Tamerlane's cenotaph, the largest, was of moss green stone believed to be jade. Still simmering, Borokov seated himself on it in brooding silence.

Now that they were once again face to face, he remembered just how much he disliked Alexei Smirnoff. Unlike his kind, generous parents, to whom he himself owed so much, Alexei was selfish, conceited, a bully and sick with ambition. Even when they had been younger he had hated Alexei's smooth, supercilious manner, his flamboyance, his gross sense of self-importance and his obsessive need of acclaim. As Military Controller of the Imperial household Alexei was a big enough fish, but the pond was also big and there were bigger fish about. The prime reason he had fought so long and so hard to return to Tashkent was that here he would be a king, a law unto himself.

Borokov knew that Alexei considered him *nekulturny,* uncultured, and that stung because he knew it was true. Secretly, he envied Alexei for being everything that he was not—influential, sophisticated, socially confident. Wealthy! Secure in his privileged world, Alexei conversed easily, conducted himself with élan, matched glasses with the hard-drinking Kiev Dragoons and Red Hussars. It was Alexei who had sponsored him for membership of the exclusive Yacht Club, Alexei who had arranged for him to dine at the Winter Palace, a rare privilege. Borokov could still remember the quivering excitement of being within touching distance of a monarch who controlled the destiny of millions, including his own.

It was his misfortune, Borokov considered, that nothing in St. Petersburg was cheap. A decent meal with wine in the best restaurants cost almost as much per head with tips as the shuba he wore, and frequent invitations from Smirnoff's wealthy friends eased the burden on his meagre pocket. Borokov was ashamed to admit, even to himself, just how taken he was with the grand estates of Smirnoff's social circle. Once, in Moscow, he was invited by a Grand Duke and his family to skate on the Neva. The ice was too hard for the cutting edge of the skates, but he was enthralled to be accepted, even for a day, as part of Muscovite society. It galled Borokov that he should be so beholden to Smirnoff. The more largesse he received, the more he resented the man.

Unfortunately, his need of Alexei in the matter of the Yasmina was inescapable, and this Borokov hated most. The clandestine dialogue with Hunza had been *his* idea, but without Alexei's influence at the palace and clout with the military, the scheme could not have got off the ground. Certainly, the new rifles would not have been secured. Therefore, much as it offended his sense of self-worth to have to grovel, under present circumstances Smirnoff's patronage was as vital as was his own need for humility.

He had been poor once. He would never be poor again.

Borokov was roused from his reverie by the arrival of the attendant. It was time for namaz, the attendant said. He had to lock up the tomb and go to the mosque. Would the Colonel be long?

No, Borokov said, he was done. Slipping a coin into the man's hand, he rose and went out to where his horse was tethered.

Only those unfortunate enough to have negotiated the road between Samarkand and Tashkent aboard the most sadistic vehicle ever designed by man, the tarantass, knew the torture it inflicted. Pulled by a troika of horses, it had not a single spring with which to cushion the rump against the severely rutted road. To transport the all-important crates, therefore, later that night Borokov lined his selection of vehicles lavishly with mattresses. Since the boxes were labelled the personal property of the Governor-General and marked "Fragile," the excessive precautions raised no questions.

For civilians, who needed permits for a change of horses at the posts, the journey to Tashkent, including the halts, took thirty to thirty-six hours. Since officers of the Russian Army were exempted from permissions and their horses changed without delay at the horse-stations, they could cover the one hundred and ninety miles in twenty-four hours. Starting early the following morning with a posse of Cossacks as escort, Borokov arrived home in Tashkent in less than twenty-two.

A fresh dawn barely trembled on the rim of the horizon as he rode into his compound, and he was exhausted. Leaving the precious crates in the locked outhouse under the watchful eye of the Cossacks, he bathed and changed into fresh clothes. He did not think that his excitement would allow him to sleep even a wink, but when he dropped his head on the pillow for a catnap, he went out like a light and did not awaken until several hours later.

Refreshed by the rest, his mind sprang into instant alertness. Summoning his Bokhariot houseboy, he asked for Ivana. Arrangements for her holiday on the Caspian were now complete; she could leave the following morning.

"Ivana Ivanova, sir?" The houseboy looked surprised. "Since Colonel sir sent for her yesterday, she is naturally not here."

"Sent for her?" Borokov stared. "Yesterday I was in Samarkand, you fool—how the devil could I have sent for her?"

Confused, the boy merely repeated the earlier explanation. The man had said that she was to pack a bag and go with him immediately. Those, the man had said, were the Colonel's orders.

"Man?" The hairs on the back of Borokov's neck tingled. "*Which* man?"

"His Excellency's gardener, Colonel, sir, the Kazakh who brought us the rose bushes last week." Borokov leapt to his feet, pushed the boy aside and ran across the compound into the servants' quarters. The bedding on the iron cot in Ivana's room was neatly rolled. Some clothes hung in the cupboard and a few toilet articles were ranged in orderly fashion on the dressing-table, but of Ivana Ivanova herself there was no sign.

Borokov's hands went cold and he broke into a sweat. Weakly, cursing under his breath, he leaned against a wall. He should have known better, been more careful. He should not have dismissed the matter of those damned Dards quite so lightly!

J was intrigued by the wording of your note, Mrs. Granville," Geoffrey Charlton said as they walked up the hill. "What, may I ask, brings on this curious urge to be educated?"

Emma laughed and removed her burqua. "Well, we were invited to the palace yesterday. So much of the conversation went over my head that I felt positively embarrassed, hence the plea for help."

He threw an oblique glance at the burqua. No doubt he saw through her ploy to avoid unwarranted identification, but he did not remark on it. "Well, shall we find some place to sit?"

Gratified that her appeal for a loan of some recent English newspapers had elicited such a prompt reaction from him, she was pleased with the thick bundle he had sent in response to her note. *I plan to spend an hour or so at the Takht-e-Suleiman this morning,* he had written. *If you are free and would care to join me, I would be delighted.*

Initially she had hesitated to risk accepting the invitation. What if the ubiquitous Chloe Hathaway came to know of it, and through her kind offices, Damien?

On the other hand, she reasoned, she had intended to spend time here this morning anyway and Damien had not voiced any objections. The Takht-e-Suleiman was, after all, a public place and her intentions were perfectly innocent. Eventually, she had given in to the temptation and dismissed the minor subterfuge involved as justifiable. In Hakumat's absence she had enlisted one of the other servants to perform escort duty.

"I wasn't sure that my chitty would ever reach you," she said as they strolled over a carpet of wild flowers among the dense acacia, almond and chestnut trees that surrounded the complex. "I gave it to a cheeky little urchin who sells vegetables from a shikara on the lake and brings me the most exquisite lotus flowers. He is an engaging scamp with quite the most soulful eyes one can imagine."

"Oh, he delivered it all right. In fact, he stung me for an anna before he would hand it to me."

They shared a small laugh. "Thank you for the newspapers," Emma said. "I hope you are not in a hurry to have them back?"

He assured her that he was not.

The hill of the Takht-e-Suleiman was crowned by the ruins of an ancient temple said at one time to have contained more than three hundred gold and silver images. The original temple was built in the third century B.C. by Jaluka, son of the Buddhist emperor Ashoka, the founder of Srinagar, but all that remained now of the original structure was the plinth and a low enclosing wall. Visited a thousand years ago by the Hindu sage Adi Shankaracharaya, the hill was now also known by his name. Groups of sightseers strolled about the grounds and there was the usual complement of guides, hawkers and mendicants. They found comfortable perches on the low wall concealed by rhododendron bushes, the escort having been despatched to the bazaar for a cup of tea with instructions to return after an hour.

Charlton asked, "What is it in particular that you wish to be educated about, Mrs. Granville?"

"Well, current political events, I suppose."

"Really? I thought politics bored you."

"Oh, they do," she gave him a wavering look, "but they certainly don't seem to bore anyone else. I am embarrassed to sound an ignoramus, always the odd one out."

He withdrew a folded newspaper from his pocket. "The most recent issue of the *Sentinel*. It arrived after your messenger had left. Some of the reports might prove of interest to you."

"Your reports?"

He gave a modest nod. As Emma took the paper from him and scanned the headlines, he asked suddenly, "Tell me, Mrs. Granville, does the name Butterfield mean anything to you?"

"Butterfield?" She started to shake her head, then stopped. "Well, I do seem to have heard the name somewhere but I can't remember in what connection. Why?"

"No special reason. Jeremy Butterfield was a British intelligence agent who operated under the code name of Hyperion. He has been much in the news lately."

"Was?"

"Yes, the poor devil was murdered in the Karakorams by Hunza raiders."

"Dear me, how dreadful! When?"

"Last autumn. For various reasons the government has made efforts to bury many of the facts. The issues I have selected for you cover some of Butterfield's story."

"Which you managed to exhume?"

"Only partially. Much still remains to be told."

"Why was he murdered?"

"For the papers he carried."

"Secret papers?"

"Very! It is believed that in his final message to Simla he claimed to have discovered and charted the Yasmina."

"The secret Hunza pass?"

"Yes. Anyone with time for the romp and money to pay for it has been trying to find it, especially the Russians."

"Really? Well, ancient Buddhist monks knew about the Yasmina. There's a third-century reference to it in one of my father's texts. Surely, there must be a hundred other unknown passes in the Himalayas?"

"Possibly, but none quite as elusive and hence militarily strategic as the Yasmina. The superstitions that surround it frighten most people off—ogres, fairies, demons, witches weaving spells and spewing curses, abductions. Nonsense, of course, but Hunza encourages the legends to fend trespassers off and so far they seem to have worked. Even so, I'm astonished that Younghusband, Elias or our pundits never quite managed to sniff it out."

She shaded her eyes with a hand against the sun. "Pundits? Not *priests,* surely?"

"No, not priests—Indian agents trained by the Survey in Dehra Doon. They are known as pundits because many are teachers by profession. Able to mix freely with local communities, pundits are a formidable source of intelligence. Nain Singh, for example, one of the first to penetrate Tibet. He won an RGS gold medal for his work as a cartographer."

"Ah yes, I remember reading about him in one of the old RGS journals. He explored the gold fields from which Tibetans mine dust to gild their idols and tankhas, if I recall correctly."

"Yes, at Thok Jalang. Disguised as a merchant, he travelled with his instruments concealed in the false bottom of a wooden chest. The distances measured he recorded on his string of prayer-beads."

"On his prayer-beads?" Emma laughed. "You take advantage of my ignorance, Mr. Charlton! How does one record anything on a string of prayer-beads?"

Not far from them, a blind beggar sat playing a haunting melody on his santoor. Charlton rose, tossed a couple of coins in his lap, then resumed his place on the wall.

"Agents use special strings of a hundred beads instead of the traditional one hundred and eight of the Hindu *rudraksha.* The round number makes calculations easier and no one notices the difference. To measure accurately they are trained to take even paces. Nain Singh's pace, for instance, measured exactly thirty-three inches so that two thousand paces added up to about a mile. After each pace, one bead is slipped forward; after a hundred, a smaller bead threaded on an attached string is advanced; and then the cycle is repeated. All tools of espionage, fabricated in Dehra Doon in the Survey's workshop, bear special markings not discernible by a layman."

He went on to describe to her some of the other extraordinary baggage agents carried. Even though not terribly interested, Emma listened politely. As he spoke, slowly and with deliberation, he watched her with curious intentness, his eyes never leaving her face. Emma had the odd impression that he was appraising her, attempting some private assessment of his own, and it made her uncomfortable. Averting her eyes, she kept them fixed upon the lake and the town of Srinagar stretched out below. Something he said tugged at her memory but she could not quite place it.

"My goodness, such melodrama outside the realms of fiction," she exclaimed lightly when he had finished. "Who would believe it?"

"Not many, Mrs. Granville, not many"—he smiled—"but it does exist, believe me, it does."

The hour she had allocated to the rendezvous, Emma noted with regret, was drawing to a close and whatever remained of it before the servant returned she decided to spend in summary exploration. At the back of the old temple site was a small tank, the roof of which was supported by four limestone pillars. It was as they were examining the partially obscured Persian inscription on one of the pillars that Geoffrey Charlton suddenly said, "About the other day, Mrs. Granville . . ."

It was their first encounter since they had met in Shalimar Baug. Although the previous occasion was still very much in Emma's mind, she had deliberately refrained from mentioning it.

"Yes, Mr. Charlton?"

"If I overstepped my bounds to cause offence in any way, I do most sincerely apologise. On reflection I cannot help feeling that I should have kept better counsel, exercised greater discretion."

"You did not overstep your bounds, Mr. Charlton," Emma assured him. "I would have heard about Natasha Granville sooner or later from my husband. Besides, since it was I who forced you into making the revelations, I deem you entirely free of blame." She added half jestingly, "Indeed, if there are any more dark secrets to which you are privy, perhaps I can persuade you to reveal those, too?"

He considered the question with the same solemnity with which he had her others. "Whatever remains is not for me to say, Mrs. Granville, it is for your husband."

"Oh, then something *does* remain, does it? Well, let me guess—these subversives who live in India and foment disaffection about England, could it be that among them you include my husband?"

He gave not even a hint of amusement. "Why do you ask?"

"Well, since my husband's mother was Russian and a spy," she said teasing a little, "and Damien himself does have strong sympathies with his Russian cousins, I should imagine he is a prime suspect where subversives are concerned."

He still did not smile. "Tell me, Mrs. Granville," he asked, abruptly evading the question, "when you married your husband, did you know that he was half Russian?"

"Naturally!"

"And that he had strong anti-British views?"

"Good heavens, everyone who knows him knew that! Damien has never made a secret of his distaste for the Empire." There was something in his expression that Emma could not quite fathom and her smile faltered. "There are many Britons whose mothers are not Russian, Mr. Charlton, who also do not consider Russians to be mortal enemies. After all, we are not at war."

"Oh but we are," he said softly, "we certainly are. There are many kinds of war, Mrs. Granville. What Russia wages is the most pernicious type because it is covert. She has no need to send agents to India, she is free to solicit them *in situ,* from within."

Was that in answer to her question? The inference, nonetheless, was unmistakable, and she looked at him in astonishment. "Dear me, you are serious! You suggest that one of those solicited is my husband?"

He did not reply immediately but stood gazing into space. Then all of a sudden his expression lifted. He smiled. "No, of course not," he said easily. "I was speaking in general terms."

"Well, I am relieved to hear it! I was beginning to think that what Mrs. Hathaway accuses you of is true—you do see Russian agents behind every chinar."

He joined in the laugh and surrendered with a bow.

"In the interests of gallantry I will let you have the last word for the time being, Mrs. Granville. Once you have been through the newspapers, perhaps we can revive this most stimulating debate."

It was on the way back to the lake a while later that the forgotten snippets returned to Emma's mind. Butterfield, for one. She remembered where she had first heard the name: at the Prices' burra khana in Delhi as she unwittingly eavesdropped. She also remembered what Suraj Singh had said, that he had measured the corridors at Shalimar with his *paces.* How very curious!

Charlton's insinuation about Damien, on the other hand, was too preposterous for words. She dismissed it immediately. Even so, a shadow of it lingered stubbornly enough to leave her marginally disturbed.

*H*olbrook Conolly was at his wits' end.

More than half his time in Kashgar was up and he was none the wiser about the Armenian woman. Overt inquiries were, naturally, out of the question and covert investigations in the bazaars had produced nothing significant. The only firm conclusion he had reached was that the woman was not in Kashgar, at least not yet. It was possible, of course, that she was being kept somewhere else, away from the capital, but being a perennial optimist he chose not to consider that yet.

Nevertheless, he had been far from idle. He had been to Shahidullah and despatched a message to Leh about the Taotai's fanciful conditions. Assuming that the Taotai would bring the woman to Kashgar sooner or later, he had devised detailed plans for eventual flight. Everything now was in readiness except the core: that mysterious nameless, faceless female on whom it all hinged.

It was ironical, therefore, that the person who should prove to be the catalyst for his coup de grâce—quite unknowingly, of course—should be the Russian consul, Pyotr Shishkin.

Even though Shishkin always referred to him as "Dr. Conolly" and his manner was unfailingly courteous, Conolly was not fool enough to believe that the suave Russian accepted him at face value. Devious and immensely crafty, Shishkin worked hard to keep a permanent British representive out of Kashgar and had so far been admirably successful. He must have heard by now about the advent of the Dards in Tashkent; had he also learned, Conolly wondered, that the Taotai was after the same woman?

Whatever his private suspicions about Conolly, socially the Russian consul was a generous and good-humoured host. Since Conolly's Russian was more than passable, Shishkin delighted in political banter over their monthly games of chess. However, while playing along with the banter like a good sport, Conolly never made the mistake of letting his guard slip. On the evening in question as soon as the splendid meal at the Russian consulate was over, Shishkin called for the chessboard to be set in place.

"Well, Dr. Conolly," he said as he poured out the snifters of brandy, "when should we expect British troops to pour into Tashkent through the Yasmina?"

"Any day now, sir," Conolly replied in the same vein. "I hope your Cossacks are in good trim for the coming war—which we will win, of course."

"Ah, but first you will have to find those maps your people have so carelessly misplaced, no?" The Russian roared with laughter and Conolly offered a manful grin.

The battle commenced. Chuffed at having won the first game, as Conolly rose to stretch his legs a petulant Shishkin voiced a request. One of his cook's many parasitical relatives living on the premises and sponging freely on him had been injured in a drunken brawl at the chai khana and he suspected that the wound had been inflicted by a knife.

"I would have thrown the rascal out on his ear had the cut not been deep and already festering. I certainly don't want him to die on the street and create a diplomatic incident with the Taotai, who, as you may know, smells sinister plots where none exist. I wonder therefore if you would be good enough to have a look at the man before you leave, Dr. Conolly?"

It was indeed a knife wound and unprepossessingly ugly, as Conolly discovered later in the man's quarter. Still stinking of mulberry wine, the injured man, a Kazakh, lay groaning in considerable pain. Fights were by no means uncommon in the taverns, but these were hardy men and Conolly was not unduly worried. As he cleaned and medicated the cut, he reprimanded the man mildly.

"It was not my fault," the Kazakh whined. "Padshah forced me to drink more than I should and provoked me into the fight."

"Who is Padshah?"

"A cousin on my father's side and a good friend, except when he drinks. Then he goes wild and starts to throw his money about."

"A man of means, eh?" Conolly made conversation merely to diffuse the sting of the iodine.

"Means? Hah!" The man snorted. "As poor as a beggar's mongrel before he went to Tash—" He broke off and bit his underlip.

"He was in Tashkent, was he?"

The man shifted uncomfortably, then gave a reluctant nod.

Discarding one blood-stained swab with his tweezers, Conolly picked up another. "What was he doing in Tashkent?"

The man threw a nervous glance at the door. It was shut. "Working for the fat man. In the palace gardens."

"Well, no wonder he was well paid. The gardens are quite extensive, I hear."

"It wasn't only that, but I cannot say more." The man's jaw firmed. "It's . . . it's a secret, you see."

"Uh-huh?" Conolly's heart beat marginally faster. Unrolling a clean bandage, he bound the wound and immobilised the arm as best he could. Then he sat back and regarded the man thoughtfully. "You are *sure* it was this Padshah who knifed you?"

"As sure as the hair on my chest!"

"And it was he who started the fight?"

"Of course! Everyone can vouch for that."

"He attacked you without reason?"

"On my mother's grave! He *leapt* at me like a tiger . . ."

"Since you can prove that he was the aggressor," Conolly interrupted, "and since he does have plenty of money, Padshah will have to compensate you for the injury."

"Oh?" This entirely novel aspect of the matter had not struck the Kazakh before. His eyes first widened, then gleamed and finally turned sly. "I am entitled to compensation, am I?"

"Certainly," Conolly affirmed solemnly. "It is the law. If you like I will personally ensure that he makes reparation, as is your legal due. Where is he to be found?"

"Chini Baug." The reply could not have come more promptly or with greater eagerness. "His Excellency has made him head gardener as a reward for his services in Tashkent."

A lucrative post at the state guest house? Conolly's breath quickened. The stench of something fishy had never smelled sweeter in his nostrils, but his face showed not a trace of expression. Knowing that nothing impressed the illiterate more than to be commemorated in black and white, he took out his pad and pencil.

"I cannot promise anything, but if I am to do my best for you I need to know everything that happened in Tashkent."

The Kazakh again looked worried. "Padshah said *no* one must know about that. . . ."

"No one will know except me," Conolly assured him, "and I promise not to tell a soul."

Used to prizing intimate information out of shy patients, five minutes later Conolly had the entire story.

He returned to the chess game bland-faced but walking on air. The woman had been abducted from Tashkent and as of yesterday was in Kashgar. What bloody luck! Before he could exult much longer, however, he came in for a shock.

As they sat down for a final game at Shishkin's insistence, over refilled glasses of French brandy and a plate of delectable savouries, the consul asked, "Incidentally, Dr. Conolly, have you heard the latest?"

"About what, Mr. Shishkin?"

"The Taotai has got himself a new concubine."

Conolly stilled. "Really?"

"A round-eye, no less! To keep her hidden from his wives the old lecher has her secreted in Chini Baug." He chuckled, gave a salacious wink and neatly whisked Conolly's king's pawn off the board. "Some highly entertaining political capital to be made out of *that* little bijou, would you not say?"

Conolly's stomach gave an almighty heave. The unexpected entry into the picture of Pyotr Shishkin was sudden and unnerving. Obviously not yet aware of all the ramifications, the Russian made light of the matter—but not for long.

Damn!

The crux had arrived sooner than Conolly expected. He saw with sinking heart that now he had no option but to abandon caution, take appalling risks and plunge in blindfolded. In his mounting perturbation he marched his queen straight into an ambush, found himself checkmated and the score levelled.

He hoped fervently that the defeat was not a metaphor for the trial that loomed immediately ahead.

$\mathcal{D}$usk was falling when Emma returned to Shalimar. Suraj Singh was still away and Damien, delayed in Gupkar, would return goodness knew when. Just as well; she had unfinished business to attend to. Back in Edward Granville's apartment later that night, she made straight for the desk.

Fragmented glimpses through an unexpected peephole into the childhood of an enigmatic husband she could not understand had been poignant but still too few to satisfy. Damien might have denied his mother forgiveness, eradicated her image from the house, left her rooms and possessions to decay, but—as Emma had sensed last night—the grief was not forgotten, only locked up and hidden away out of sight. In this too, she saw, Nazneen had been right. No matter how hardened the front Damien chose to display for his own reasons and for her benefit, his core was honey-soft and not too difficult to detect.

The dusty pile of folders in the top drawer of the desk, old estate records, Emma set aside after a cursory inspection. The middle drawer revealed no discarded photographs, no consolidated family albums; but she was lucky with the last drawer, the bottom one. Stuffed carelessly at the back were several packets of yellowing envelopes with English stamps, all addressed to Edward Granville in a hand not yet fully mature.

Damien's letters home from boarding school!

As her interest flared, so did her conscience. The letters were private, was it right for her to pry into their contents? On the other hand, the correspondence *was* more than two decades old, Edward Granville long dead and her motive by no means idle curiosity. In trying to learn more about her husband as a boy, she merely sought to understand him better as a man, to improve prospects for a more congenial marriage. Setting aside her qualms, Emma extracted a first letter. It was dated 7 October 1871, and ran to over two pages.

Composed with respectful formality as part of a weekly duty enforced by the school, the letter trembled with unexpressed emotion. It was clear that Damien hated school. Founder's Day, he wrote, was boring, the interminably lengthy lecture by the chief guest on How to Set an Example even more so. He had developed a cold, consequence of a damp boating picnic on a lake under a chilly drizzle, and the weather was depressingly dull. There followed a series of glum complaints. The housemaster's right arm had been exercised rather too strongly, too frequently and (in his opinion) quite unjustly; he had trouble sitting down. He had not done well in a chemistry test because he could not understand the subject; a wounded baby hedgehog found in the garden and since delivered of further torment by death had left him bereft. If he hated anything more than school it was a sixth former named Ruggles who tweaked his ears, stole his pencils and made him shine his boots. Could he please not do chemistry and take up painting instead?

He had made friends with another new boy in his dorm. Nicknamed Hammie—short for Hamlet, no less!—his new chum was an enthusiastic member of the school dramatic society whose parents were in Rangoon, where his father, a doctor, ran the military hospital. The boys called Hammie a sissy and him a nig-nog. Please, could he have a *real* map to prove that Kashmir was bigger than Scotland? Thrown together in common misery, Hammie and he had become blood brothers and shared each other's tuck. There were heartfelt pleas for news of home, copious instructions about various pets left behind—specially his mongrel, Sasha—and what to do in case of sickness. Please, could he come home at least for a holiday next year?

The early letters were all in the same vein, filled with homesickness, but later the tone started to change. The underlying heartache and pleas for more news were still there but the refrains were less desperate. Kew Gardens, which they had visited on an outing, were captivating, although he thought the orchids at Shalimar were bigger and better. He had won first prize in drawing and Hammie had excelled in *The Way of the World*. They had each fought Ruggles and between them given him a bloody nose, a well-bruised shin and a chipped molar. The caning that followed was considered well worth it because Ruggles no longer called him a nig-nog or tweaked his ears and had finally conceded that Kashmir was bigger than Scotland. Someone called Percy whose family lived in Redcar had *six* (heavily underlined) brothers and *two* (also underlined) sisters, all of whom he had met. They were a merry lot and he envied Percy his large, jolly family.

Somewhere along the way there was also an unenthusiastic mention of relatives in Somerset, a spinster aunt and an uncle who were his English guardians. Stern, joyless and forever disapproving, they never smiled and whispered behind closed doors. It was not difficult to guess that Damien was referring to the paternal side of Edward Granville's family, obviously unforgiving of the scandal in Peshawar and Edward's choice of a Russian wife.

What wrought a sea-change in the tone of subsequent letters, Emma saw, was a visit to France (with Hammie, of course) to Edward Granville's maternal relations. One of the French cousins owned an estate at Saint-Ouen near Paris and was a successful manufacturer of embroidered black shawls for which he imported fleece from Tibet. It was while describing the long hours spent observing the weaving process that Damien came most alive. It was his favourite pastime, he wrote wistfully, because it reminded him of home.

In none of the letters was there mention of his mother.

It was now quite late. Tired out by the bumpy journey from Srinagar, Emma could barely keep her eyes open. Two unread packets remained. They would have to wait, she decided, until a subsequent opportunity occurred. Well pleased with her night's efforts, she stretched and yawned and smiled, more at peace with herself than she had been since she had arrived at Shalimar.

CHAPTER

1 5

British Agent Brutally Slain in the Karakorams!

*I*t was the first *Sentinal* headline to catch Emma's eye as she settled down to read the newspapers Geoffrey Charlton had supplied, and to whom the front-page story was ascribed. Reports in subsequent issues claimed that confidential documents in Butterfield's possession had not been destroyed but stolen, that there was much more to the affair than had been revealed and that the government was involved in a sordid conspiracy of silence. Following a flood of outraged protest and wild rumour, Charlton wrote, the India Office had been forced to make a few more details public, but many questions remained unanswered.

Her curiosity well stirred, Emma read on.

Elsewhere in the papers were mentioned names she half recognised, events she had not heard of and political references she could barely identify. Much space was devoted to the Yasmina and its arcane legendry, the caravan raiders of Hunza, and Mikhail Borokov's dalliance with the whimsical Mir. The barbaric execution was described with gory explicitness from second-, third- and fourth-hand accounts. Colonel Algernon Durand and the Gilgit Agency figured prominently in the reports, as did Kashmir, pivotal to the border problem. The maharaja's loyalty to the Crown was questioned and his alleged correspondence with the Tsar condemned.

There were complex political analyses, fiesty editorials, a spate of indignant letters and cautious, incomprehensibly verbose statements from Whitehall. "Certain circles" hinted that Butterfield's loyalty was suspect and that the lost papers were already in St. Petersburg. Others lauded him as a patriot and a martyr. Some reports rang with authority, others leaned heavily on opinion, conjecture and, indeed, guesswork. There were a great many quotations from "reliable sources," "informed officials who wish to remain anonymous" and "someone close to the Intelligence Department." Pride of place was enjoyed by that loyal friend of every journalist, the ubiquitous "A. Spokesman."

Brickbats were hurled in equal measure at both sides. The Russians were flagellated for double-dealing and skulduggery, Westminster and the Indian government for everything from "masterly inactivity" and conceal- ment to deception and incompetence. A tabulated history of Russia's in- vasion plans for India ennumerated plots devised and discarded over the past century. Prophets of doom and latter-day Cassandras predicted that the appointment of an ambitious, ruthless Governor-General in Tashkent would precipitate fresh plans for an invasion. A pre-emptive counter of- fensive was advised before the Russians grabbed the Yasmina and swarmed down the Himalayas. The Opposition thumped tables and demanded res- ignations. There were calls for a general election.

Overwhelmed by sheer weight of wordage, Emma's head whirled. All this was happening on her own doorstep and she, snug in her ivory tower, knew nothing about it!

She had read Charlton's earlier series of articles on Central Asia with im- mense enjoyment, of course, but had skipped the political commentaries. Now as she read every word, she was struck by his fiery prose, his cuttingly sar- castic wit, the vehement passion with which he pursued his bête-noir, Russia, and the doggedness with which he followed and ferreted out information. A report in a rival paper commented sneeringly on Charlton's prodigious mem- ory and the fact that he could retain and reproduce something after having read it only once. It was mentioned gleefully that he had even been arrested once for having taken gross liberties with a secret document.

Emma was as fascinated by the deluge of information as by the rapid broadening of her political horizon. At the same time, she was confused. Among Charlton's exposures there were references and innuendoes that she still could not comprehend entirely. She had learned a great deal—and yet not enough. To fill in the gaps that remained, she needed to see Charl- ton again one final time; the question was, how without inviting Damien's wrath?

As it happened, the solution appeared unexpectedly and from a most unlikely source.

The following morning a visitor arrived from Srinagar, Mrs. Mary

Bicknell, who, together with her physician husband Malcolm, had founded and ran the Mission School and Hospital. Despite Chloe Hathaway's derogatory remarks, they were both respected figures in Kashmir, for the little hospital had done yeoman service during the frequent floods, fires and cholera outbreaks in town. Emma had intended to visit the institutions to help in the Bicknells' good work but had simply not got around to it yet.

A small, sparrowlike woman with untidy grey hair held together with an arsenal of pins, Mary Bicknell was certainly an unusual sight. She arrived wearing gum boots, wide-brimmed straw hat and a crushed muslin dress that had obviously never known starch. On her forearm swung a gunny sack and a basket filled with gardening implements. Disdaining ceremony, she introduced herself in a rush.

"You will have to forgive me, my dear Mrs. Granville, for descending on you out of the blue, but you see, I've come for my Perganum—with your permission, of course. Mr. Lincoln, your manager, told me in church last Sunday that there is a fresh batch in the south by the stream, so I hurried here, chop, chop, before it lost its potency as Perganum is wont to do in the summer. I know exactly where it is because I've been there before."

"Perganum?" Emma looked blank.

"Oh dear, how foolish of me—of course you have no idea, have you? *Perganum harmala*, what the Kashmiris call *Isband*. You see, my dear, I make herbal medicines for our hospital. Mr. Granville has been *very* kind in letting me run loose on his estate from time to time because what you have here is a virtual pharmacy—certainly your *Aconitum heterophyllum* is quite the best I've seen anywhere in the valley."

Enlightenment dawned and Emma smiled. "I see. You are a botanist, are you, Mrs. Bicknell?"

"Oh yes, although many of my recipes are what some call," she winked, "old wives' tales. Anyway, I find traditional remedies very effective and the proof of the pudding is in the eating, isn't it? Well, my dear, do I have your permission to proceed?"

"Of course. In fact, if you would be kind enough to give me a few moments to change my shoes, I'd be happy to come with you. I know very little about medicinal plants and would love to learn more."

They set off enthusiastically to spend a pleasantly informative morning trampling through birch thickets, juniper shrub and tall grasses, poking behind rocks, peering in crevices, happily cutting and snipping and pulling out roots along the stream banks.

Despite her haphazard appearance, Emma soon realised, Mary Bicknell was a well-qualified woman with a wealth of knowledge about plants. The old wives' tales, in fact, had all been tried and tested and had yielded inexpensive cures for many common ailments. *Cuscuta,* the local *kakilipol,* worked as an effective laxative; *Viola serpens*—salt flowers, since they used to be exchanged for their weight in salt—was an expectorant to decongest the lungs; *Salvia*—*janiadam* to the Kashmiris—was an excellent diuretic.

"And see this?" Parting the bushes, Mrs. Bicknell dived in gleefully. "*Berberis lycium,* an astringent. Invaluable in cases of cholera which festers, positively festers, in the bazaars."

By noon, Mrs. Bicknell's sack was full and she declared herself as pleased as punch with her little haul.

"Would you care to join me at luncheon?" Emma asked as they returned to the house.

Happily shedding clods of earth all over the hallway carpet, Mary Bicknell agreed at once.

An entertaining guest—quite unlike the grim picture Chloe Hathaway had painted—Mrs. Bicknell kept Emma well amused with her lively chatter. Her husband, Emma learned, was not only a skilled physician but also an erstwhile champion pugilist. It was he who had introduced the bicycle into the valley and encouraged its use as a safe and inexpensive mode of transport.

"The hospital is really quite small with only twelve beds, but we feel it does fulfill a very desperate need in the town. As a matter of fact," Mary Bicknell blushed and turned charmingly coy, "Mr. Charlton has been kind enough to write an article for his newspaper about our humble efforts in the Vale. We are, of course, greatly honoured. He has accepted to come to tea next Tuesday to take photographs. Perhaps you would care to join us?"

Emma was delighted to accept.

Three weeks had passed since Ivana's disappearance.

The missing gardener, discreet enquiries by Captain Vassily had revealed, was a Kazakh, one Padshah Khan, who had resigned from his job three weeks ago and left for his village to be with a dying mother. Where this village might be, no one could say; guarded questions about a possible female companion (without Ivana being mentioned by name, of course) brought forth guffaws and lewd remarks but nothing more.

Fortunately, Ivana's absence was easy enough to explain: she had merely left for a holiday on the Caspian.

There was now absolutely no doubt in Borokov's mind that the reason for the visit of the Dards was to conspire with the Kazakh in Ivana's abduction, but the *motive* behind the elaborate exercise he could not even begin to guess. If the abduction made little enough sense to him, a connection between Ivana and the Yasmina made even less. Was there a connection at all—or was it hogwash? The trouble was that he simply did not know, and it was this not knowing that troubled him the most. If by some freak of circumstance the Dards had managed to secure Butterfield's "lost" papers, had he been in station at the time it was *he* who would have benefitted from the exchange! Once again he cursed both his luck and the Baron in equal measure.

All in all, Borokov felt angry and frustrated as he made his way to the palace in response to a first summons from Smirnoff. It was a dreary night, grey, damp and depressing. He pulled his coarse shuba closer over his ears, peeved that Smirnoff should be able to afford sables while he himself made do with racoon bought after hard bargaining for a miserable two hundred roubles. Aside from anything else, without Ivana his household was falling to pieces. The rooms had not been dusted properly in days, the food brought to the table was inedible, and thieving fingers lifted everything within sight the minute his back was turned.

Nothing seemed to be going right for him, nothing.

"Have you opened the crates?"

It was Smirnoff's first question after they had settled down in the study until recently occupied by the Baron. The room now displayed many photographic comemmorations of Smirnoff's moments of personal glory, showing him in full military regalia in the company of the Grand Dukes and Romonovs and other scions of old families who dominated the St. Petersburg court. There was a signed photograph of the emperor and empress. Violently envious, Borokov tried not to look at it.

"Yes, Excellency."

"Examined and listed the weapons?"

"Yes, Excellency."

Smirnoff lifted an eyebrow. "Well?"

"I am pleased, of course," he said, adding out of pure pique, "although I cannot imagine how brand-new rifles can possibly be delivered with the British watching our every move."

"Can't you?" Smirnoff smiled. "No, perhaps not, but then imagination was never your strong point, was it, Mikhail?"

"One hardly needs imagination to foretell Angliski reaction," Borokov retorted, seething and determined to pick holes. "They will consider it an act of war."

"As faint-hearted as ever, eh? Don't you think that depends on the strategy used for the delivery?"

"What miraculous strategy will permit the crates entry into Hunza without anyone noticing?"

"I do not plan an entry into Hunza."

"Then what? We make the delivery at Shimsul?"

Smirnoff sighed. "Oh, Mikhail, Mikhail . . . is that as far as your ingenuity will stretch? Think, man, think!"

Borokov regarded him coldly. "The lists are still incomplete, Excellency," he said. "I have no time to waste in guessing games."

Smirnoff selected one of his specially ordered cheroots from a silver box, struck a match off the top of his boot and lit it. He did not offer one to Borokov. Looking amused and in no hurry to explain, he sat down and swung his legs on to the table.

"When Mikhail Skobelev was military governor of Ferghana, he devised a plan for an invasion and sent it to Kaufmann, governor-general at the time. Did you know that?"

"Of course. It was common knowledge."

"The plan was to mount a three-column attack with twenty thousand men who would march to the Pamirs from three bases, PetroAlexandrovsk, Samarkand and Margilan. The third column would then ascend the Alai from Ferghana and proceed through Pamir passes into Chitral and the Kashmir valley."

"Skobelev's plan did not work," Borokov reminded him shortly. "The attempt was aborted."

"Ah, but he did manage to prove one very salient point: high altitude in the Pamirs does not necessarily impede the progress of heavy artillery."

"And is that how you intend to transport this consignment to Hunza, across the Pamirs?"

"The weapons will not go to Hunza," Smirnoff said, still playing cat and mouse. "It is Hunza that will come to the weapons."

"To Tashkent?"

"Don't be a fool, Mikhail," Smirnoff snapped, suddenly irritated. "Of course not to Tashkent! Now think, what is Hunza known for?"

Feeling like a child at nursery school, Borokov controlled his temper with an effort. "Slaughter, slavery and loot, what else?"

"*Exactly!* Therefore, we will assist them in their noble endeavours. We will organise a caravan and Safdar Ali will arrange to pillage it. As simple as that."

Borokov's breath caught. He was startled, indeed, shocked by the sheer impudence of the plan. "By what route?"

Smirnoff swung his legs off the desk, flung open a voluminous map and laid it across the desk. "This." He stubbed a series of red dots one after the other. "Khojend, Margilan, Osh and then Gulcha, on the new road. From here it is three marches to the Taldik Pass, which at a little over eleven thousand feet is easily negotiable. Beyond is the Kizil Su river, where the route forks east to Irkishtam and Kashgar and south to the Murghab and Pamirski Post."

"The final stretch will involve climbing glaciers?"

"Frightened already?" Smirnoff regarded him with ill-concealed scorn. "Perhaps. We will leave Safdar Ali to decide that."

Borokov fell silent, his mouth dry. The plan was as rash and flamboyant as the man. The question was, would it work?

"Why not?" Smirnoff countered when he voiced scepticism. "Similar subterfuge worked for Alikhanov, why not for me?"

Eight years earlier, Alikhanov, an impulsive Muslim Caucasian, had taken to the oasis of Merv a caravan consisting of his men disguised as traders. After detailed reconnaissance and some clever manipulations, he had annexed the oasis for Russia without a single drop of blood being spilt.

"You plan to recruit genuine merchants for the caravan?"

"A few. The rest will be Cossacks disguised as European traders. It will be publicised widely that the caravan carries expensive cargo from Bokhara to Leh—silver pommels, embroidered *shabrakhs,* leather belts, dagger sheaths, green snuff and copper and brass vessels and, of course, bullion—enough to tempt any raider."

"Where will the raid take place?"

"That too is for Safdar Ali to decide. His men will make off with the crates; they will be pursued by our Cossacks, who will then meet them at a pre-designated rendezvous."

"You will trust Safdar Ali with the crates?"

Smirnoff's steely eyes bored into Borokov. "Is there anything unusual you noticed while unpacking the rifles?"

"Yes. The crates contain no ammunition."

"Precisely. The cases with the cartridges and the smokeless powder will remain with the Cossacks. They will be delivered only after we have occupied the Yasmina."

"And you are confident to be able to do so?" Even though impressed by Smirnoff's eye for detail, Borokov was determined not to show it. "Occupy the Yasmina despite the glaciers, I mean?"

Smirnoff's mouth curved in a smile. "There are two ways into every pass, Mikhail," he said softly, "and two ways out. If the southern entry is along the glacier area, then the other must be to the north, equally well concealed."

"The Chinese border runs through the Kun Lun. . . ."

"We will use the fifty-mile gap between Afghanistan and Sinkiang. Until the boundaries are decided, it remains no-man's-land."

"You consider that the operation can be kept secret from the British and the Chinese?"

"Why would we want it to be secret? Caravans are a daily occurrence along the Silk routes; why should not this one be?"

"What will happen to the merchants, the *genuine* merchants?"

Smirnoff shrugged. "One or two will be allowed to survive to give testimony at the inevitable investigation that will follow. The rest will be dispensed with."

Borokov's pulses raced as he fell silent. Alexei had thought of every-thing—it was a brilliant scheme! He wished he could have thought of it instead.

"Safdar Ali will want trials," he said.

"There will be no trials."

"He will not accept the rifles without first testing them."

Smirnoff drew deeply on his cigar. "You know little of mountains, Mikhail. Every mountaineer is aware that at high altitudes a gun shot is enough to start an avalanche and sound travels far and fast. Safdar Ali will have to trust me, that is all."

Borokov scowled. Smirnoff knew of his dislike of mountains, his fear of heights and how difficult his lungs found it to breathe rarefied air. Had not everything, everything in his life, depended on it, he would not have driven himself to make that diabolical journey to Hunza.

"How can we be sure that the pass we are taken to *is* the Yasmina?" he asked, trying not to show his anxiety.

"My dear Mikhail, Russian maps of the Pamirs are revised every year and each new pass discovered is included. So long as it is an undiscovered pass unknown to the British, what does it matter?"

"No, any unknown pass will not do, it has to be the Yasmina!"

Smirnoff raised an eyebrow. "Has to be? Why?"

Borokov controlled himself. "The Yasmina is part of Himalayan folk-lore," he said, forcing a smile. "The British have sought it for years. Its discovery will bring more glory to the discoverer, more fame, more acco-lades. Perhaps a medal from the Royal Geographic Society. A place in history."

It was an argument, he knew, that would appeal to Alexei. And it did. "Well, perhaps you are right, Mikhail. Anyway, we will see when the time comes."

"When will that be?"

"In September. To be precise, the twenty-sixth." Borokov looked at him questioningly and Smirnoff offered a self-conscious smile. "Don't you remember? September the twenty-sixth is my birthday. It has always proved auspicious for the start of a new venture."

Yes, he remembered now. The superstitions to which Russian aristo-crats, including Smirnoff, subscribed never ceased to astonish Borokov.

During his social interludes in St. Petersburg and Moscow he had been appalled at the mumbo-jumbo believed and practised in Smirnoff's inner circle.

"What happens *after* the occupation—the British will sit and watch in silence?"

"Oh dear me, no, by no means in silence!" Smirnoff gave a contemptuous laugh. "Their pin-striped overlords in Whitehall will wave furled umbrellas and howl like jackals. Their editors will write editorials, their parliamentarians will shout themselves hoarse in Westminster and there will be deafening diplomatic roars, but nothing more. Once we have a foothold in the Yasmina, they will not be able to dislodge us from the Himalayas."

"Safdar Ali approves of your plan?"

"He will. His emissary arrives here within the week."

"And does His Imperial Majesty approve?" Borokov asked slyly.

Smirnoff's jawline tautened. "The Russian Empire was not won by composing memoranda in triplicate for the palace, Mikhail," he said coldly. "It was won by the initiative of individuals who grasped their chance when and where they saw it. They *spat* on red tape, so do I. The unwritten law is to succeed, that is all. His Imperial Majesty's approval will come in good time. You have been in Central Asia long enough to know that."

Indeed, Borokov did.

Riled by the overbearing conceit, he still kept himself in check. "You truly consider that we will be able to retain the Yasmina without retaliation?"

Smirnoff strolled to the fireplace and stood warming his hands with his back to Borokov. "Have you read MacGregor's book?"

"Of course."

"What do you think of it?"

"What every patriotic Russian thinks, that it is highly offensive, an insult to our nation."

"So offensive, in fact," Smirnoff said, "that it deserves a fitting response. Having swallowed much of India, Burma and the rest of the subcontinent, Britain has the gall to preach moral propriety to us, to *us*! MacGregor actually accused us of acquisitiveness. Well, perhaps it is time to prove that he was right."

In the silence that followed, Borokov waited. Smirnoff made no mention of his own role in the scheme. Not willing to compromise his pride with a blunt question, he turned to something else.

"The road from Osh is far from complete. It has not yet reached Gulcha."

"I am aware of that, and that is where you come in, Mikhail. You will leave tomorrow for Osh. A message has already been sent to the Commandant to expect you. You will hire more men, make them work longer hours and ensure that the road is complete when we need it. Naturally the Commandant must know nothing of what is planned. I will think of a way to pack him off somewhere when the time comes." He looked at the clock and dismissed him. "That is all for the moment, Mikhail."

As he walked back home slowly, almost in a trance, with each step he took Borokov became increasingly aware of a chilling probability; by the time he reached his house the probability had turned into a certainty.

Smirnoff had no intention of including him in the campaign.

The conviction came suddenly, in a flash, and with immense force. He had seen it in Alexei's eyes, those evil, feral eyes he had known so well for most of his life. The responsibility of the road was being offered to him as a sop, a humiliating crumb from the great hero's table. Well, he was damned if he was going to accept it! The original plan had been *his*; how dare Alexei try to exclude him from it altogether? Rage welled within Mikhail Borokov, a terrible, tearing rage at a betrayal that filled his mouth with bile and seared his gut with a great ball of fire.

The Yasmina was his! Before he let Alexei snatch it away from him, he would see him hung, quartered and consigned to perdition.

Privately he cared not a broken rouble for Russia's empire; it could rot and go to hell. The only thing he cared about was *this*—his fingers curled around the gold nugget safe and snug against his heart. Safdar Ali might be an uncouth savage not to be trusted out of sight, but with the nugget he had sent him a clear message, a message Smirnoff knew nothing of, nor ever would.

He had been poor once. So help him God, he would not be poor again!

Borokov arrived home to find that a messenger awaited him with a letter, Ismail Khan, Theodore Anderson's courier. It was too early for the letter to have come in response to his own recently sent message and Borokov received it without enthusiasm. Expecting it to contain the usual bleatings for funds for interminable expeditions, he read it at a glance. To his astonishment, the letter contained no request for funds. Indeed, the news it conveyed was so unexpected that his knees trembled and he had to sit down to retrieve his balance.

If Theodore Anderson was to be believed (and why should he not be?), Borokov no longer needed Alexei Smirnoff or the Dards or Ivana Ivanova. He no longer needed anyone. All he needed now was faith in himself, the courage to take his destiny into his own hands and do what his will dictated.

Features twisted with malevolence, eyes glowing with triumph, Borokov raised his face to the sky and thrust his fists upwards. One of Alexei's many superstitions was that it was inauspicious to be wished good luck at the start of a new venture.

"Good luck, Alexei, good luck," he hissed into the wind. "Again and again good luck, you double-crossing *bastard*!"

He laughed and laughed.

Had Mikhail Borokov known that his own run of good luck had only just begun, he would have laughed even louder.

*W*alter Stewart's response to his telegram was so full of reassurances that Hethrington was positively alarmed. Since his arrival in Srinagar, the Resident reported, Geoffrey Charlton had remained very quiet, indeed, almost reclusive. He was writing another book which was to be published in the spring. Most of his time, therefore, was spent reading, thinking, writing, exploring the valley and minding his own business.

"Like hell!" Hethrington glared angrily at the rain outside pelting the slopes and puckering the surface of the lily pond in a heavy monsoon shower. "He's up to something, I feel it in my bones. Why else should he lie low after Yarkand and Leh?"

"And Cawnpore," Nigel Worth added.

"Oh yes, we mustn't forget Cawnpore!"

"I meant to tell you, sir, that while I was in Jacob's shop yesterday," Worth said, "I accidentally overheard Mrs. Price mention to Colonel Hartley that Charlton had tiffin with the Stibberts in Cawnpore. The Prices are here from Delhi for the Season, as is Mrs. Stibbert, who is Mrs. Price's sister and the wife of Major Stibbert posted at the Ordnance factory in Cawnpore. If you like, sir, I could do some discreet probing for more information. Mrs. Stibbert and Mrs. Price are at Peletti's every afternoon for tea."

"Oh, probe away by all means," Hethrington said nastily. "Sometimes I wonder why we bother with a telegraph at all when the human tongue works faster without costing a damned penny."

It was precisely at that moment that Burra Babu walked in with a duly decoded message delivered an hour earlier by a dak runner, which put paid to all further talk about Charlton. Conolly's message despatched from Shahidullah some weeks ago was lengthy, explicit and—with a full report of his second meeting with the Taotai—also alarming.

"That's all we need," Hethrington groaned, "for the Chinese to get into the bloody act! Well, the QMG will certainly have something to say about *that,* I promise." He shot out of his seat and made for the door.

Five minutes later, Sir John did indeed have a great deal to say as he colourfully expended his awesome wrath. Eventually he calmed down enough to ask, "Capricorn believes the woman might already be in Kashgar?"

"Or soon will be."

"How the devil did the Chinese find her in such short order?"

"Presumably because Central Asian walls are even better endowed than ours, sir," Hethrington offered drily. "Since the Russians only have to sneeze for the Taotai to catch cold, the man obviously has an army of informers working overtime."

"Who the devil gave him the extraordinary idea that we are about to occupy the gap through the Yasmina—Shishkin?"

"Very likely, sir. Since Shishkin reads English newspapers, as Capricorn has observed, all he needed was to plant a seed and let normal Chinese nervousness fertilise it into a forest."

"Is he aware of the Chinese interest in the woman?"

"Capricorn thinks not, sir, at least not at the time the letter was despatched."

The QMG was not at all pleased. "If Capricorn has fond hopes of abstracting the woman from under Chinese noses, I can only conclude he has lost his bloody marbles. Considering the bargaining power they expect from the maps, they're hardly likely to put her on display like a plum ripe for the plucking." He grabbed a pencil and tapped it hard on the table top. "With Younghusband and MacCartney poised for a fresh thrust at Kashgar, the last thing we want is a diplomatic incident."

Nigel Worth ventured a cough.

"Yes, Captain?"

"If Capricorn *does* manage to get the woman, sir—and he is, as we know, very resourceful—the Chinese may not be inclined to make a song and dance about it considering the fact that she is a Russian subject. Pyotr Shishkin, for one, will certainly demand to know how she happened to be in their custody in the first place. I doubt if the Taotai would encourage such a confrontation."

The QMG grunted and rose to stretch his legs. "Well, then, presuming that Capricorn does by some miracle get his lunatic plan off the ground— what route is he most likely to take on his way back to Leh?"

"Either across the Taklamakan to Yarkand and then through the Karakorams, sir," Hethrington said, "or the dak runners' route across the Pamirs. In both cases he will latch onto a caravan for part of the way rather than risk the journey on his own. If he can evade Chinese Army patrols until a Khirgiz village, the Khirgiz will help. They loathe the Chinese and Capricorn has good friends among them."

"If he can survive that far." Sir John sat down heavily and closed his eyes. "We can't afford to lose another political agent, Wilfred. We'll be bloody crucified!"

"I know, sir," Hethrington agreed unhappily. "Capricorn will need help."

"Most definitely. Army patrols will have to be positioned at strategic points near the passes—and you know what *that* means, don't you?" Sir John voiced the unspoken thought that hung above them like the sword of Damocles. "The C-in-C will have to be informed about the Janus project."

There was a moment of thick silence. Then Hethrington shook his head hard. "No, no army patrols! A Geological Survey team is at present in the Kun Lun. We could recruit their assistance. Being ignorant of the background, they pose no danger to our security."

"We can't keep your project under wraps forever, Wilfred," the QMG warned. "As it is there will be hell to pay. If we are pipped at the post and the maps do end up with the Russians . . ." He thinned his lips and left the rest unsaid.

"It's a matter of another month, sir," Hethrington said in a tone of urgent entreaty. "Capricorn is not irresponsible. What he plans is risky, but if anyone can pull it off, he can. We must allow him that chance. If worse comes to the worst, he'll simply . . ." He faltered.

"Simply what?"

"Well, simply leave the woman behind."

"And force us back to the starting gate?" Sir John gave him a piercing look. "If that is to be the case, Wilfred, you do realise what it would mean for the Department, don't you?"

It was a rhetorical question. Without the woman the Department was doomed, their reputation mud and Whitehall would have a perfect excuse to pare their budget down to its bare bones—if there remained a Department at all.

Hethrington sighed and murmured something.

"Canteen?" Sir John picked up a word. "What canteen?"

"Just a thought, sir." Hethrington sighed. "It wasn't important."

Sir John drummed his fingers on the table for a moment, then suddenly came to a decision. "All right, Wilfred, I'll let you have your month—but not one single, solitary day more. If we don't have those papers in our hands by the end of thirty days, it's all over. The project will have to be laid before the C-in-C, the Foreign Secretary and the Viceroy, and we will have to face the consequences." He got up. "Now, get the fastest runner you have and send a message to the Geological Survey chaps. Let Crankshaw have a copy as an added precaution."

Back in his own office, somewhat revived by the reprieve, the Colonel got down to immediate business.

"We have to put on our skates, Captain, and get our behinds off to Ladakh, chop, chop. We leave first thing in the morning."

"Yes sir! I'll get the arrangements started right away."

"Oh, and Captain?"

Nigel Worth halted. "Sir?"

"The next time you dream up a fancy project, do me a favour and keep it to yourself, will you?"

After the Captain had left, Hethrington peered into the lowering sky still busy wreaking vengeance on the Simla hills. Outside the window there was not a single monkey in sight. He wondered vaguely where they went when it rained.

A month: thirty days. That was all he had left to conjure up what was beginning to look more and more like a miracle. Calculating the odds against success, it occurred to him that a transfer to the Meerut mess might not be such a bad idea after all.

T here is something I want to show you on the estate," Damien said over breakfast. "A surprise."

He had returned from Gupkar the previous night and in his return Emma had felt an undeniable rush of pleasure. Over a cordial dinner they had exchanged news; the Italian manager of the winery had been forth-coming, Damien said. They made an excellent Barsac and Médoc from vines imported from Turfan, in China. Because of their shape Turfan's grapes were known as "mare's nipples," and had supplied China's Tang dynasty with its earliest wines.

Emma reciprocated with an account of Mary Bicknell's visit and how much she had learned from her about indigenous medicinal plants. Then, not because he asked but to expunge her own conscience, she added an abridged account of her visit to the Takht-e-Suleiman.

The far south-eastern corner of the estate towards which they set out after breakfast contained a small plot that was barricaded behind a high wall. Suraj Singh had given Emma to understand that it was one of the store houses meant for housing the more expensive variety of rice, and she had taken him at his word. Now, as Damien unlocked the gate that led into the enclosure, she saw that what stood revealed was anything but a storehouse for grain: the ruins of an old monument half concealed by the undergrowth.

With a cry of surprise she started towards it, but Damien cautioned her with a gesture.

"Those bushes are infested with snakes and scorpions. I doubt if they would take kindly to being disturbed."

Stepping back quickly, she peered through the tangled branches. "What was it, a temple?"

"Yes. I instructed Suraj Singh not to let you see it until I could introduce you to it formally."

"Do you know how old it is?"

"Eleven hundred years or so. In all probability it dates back to the eighth century, to the reign of Lalitaditya."

She picked up a piece of broken masonry. "Limestone?" He nodded. "My father used to call this style of architecture Arian, from 'Aryan' and what the Greeks call 'Araiostyle.' There seems to be more beneath the ground than above." Vastly excited, she scraped away a layer of soil with the tip of a branch. "Have you never considered having these ruins excavated?"

"Frequently. In fact, I was wondering if you might be interested to take charge of the excavations."

"I?" She was thrilled. "Oh, Damien!"

"Well, would you?"

"You *know* I would! When?"

"Whenever you wish."

"Next summer? Just as soon as I can get the book completed. First of all, we will have to take advice from the experts at the Archaeological Survey. Then we will need to assemble a team, but before that I think we should . . ."

As she planned enthusiastically, Damien listened with flattering attention.

It was a glorious day, perhaps in more ways than one. The grass on which they sat was warm and smelled fresh from last week's rain. On a shady slope beneath spreading walnut trees they ate a picnic luncheon of lamb chops, thick chappatis roasted on hot, oiled stones and fruit. Replete and wonderfully content, Emma sat on a boulder enjoying the uninterrupted vision of green slopes. Damien reclined on the grass leaning on one elbow. Around them the air hummed with muted sound, the buzz of honey bees, whisperings of the wind and the crisp responses of overhead leaves. Languid with drowse, Emma closed her eyes.

Damien laid his head back on the grass, stretched out and stared up at the sky. "Why did you go to see Nazneen?"

Emma jerked awake. "You heard that from her?" she asked, instantly jealous.

"No. Nazneen is no longer in Srinagar." Without opening his eyes, he shifted positions. "Little happens in the valley that I do not hear of one way or another. Well, why?"

"Does it matter?"

"To me, yes. I am curious."

"Well, since you said I had a great deal to learn from Nazneen," she said drily, "you could say my reasons were educational."

"And did you learn anything?"

"As a matter of fact, yes."

"What?"

She shook her head. "I think even Chloe Hathaway would agree that secrets between a wife and mistress should remain secret."

He coloured, then rose and brushed off both the grass on his britches and the subject. "Ever done any trout fishing?"

She smiled, pleased to have scored a point. "Now and again, but I was not aware that trout were native to Kashmir."

"They are not. The fingerlings came from England, from the Queen, in fact, and were introduced in the Lidder as an experiment. Now there is talk of importing rainbow trout from Canada for the Telbal valley waterworks and pike for the Dal and Manasbal lakes. I had a few trout from the Lidder released in this stream some years ago and they seem to be thriving."

As they made their way down the heavily wooded path that led to the water, Hakumat returned from the house with the fishing gear. It was cool in the shade, alive with birdsong and sudden flashes of colour. On the bank of the stream, Damien went down on one knee to inspect the waters.

"I see one or two big fellows. Come on, you may be lucky."

"Me?" Emma shook her head. "I'm hardly dressed to splash around fishing for trout."

"Why not? All you need is a pair of waders."

"I'm not going midstream in this dress," Emma said firmly. "If it shrinks and rides up to my knees, I'll look a sight."

The problem was finally settled with a compromise. She agreed to cast a line perched on a flat boulder that jutted into the stream. As she did so, she narrowly missed the bushes.

He laughed but conceded that for a first throw it would pass.

"If I get a bite I won't know what to do," Emma said. "Don't wander away too far."

He stretched out again, crossed his arms beneath his head and closed his eyes. As luck would have it, five minutes later she had a bite. Trying clumsily to rewind the line, Emma let out a yell. Damien jumped up, slipped into his waders and strode out into the stream. Digging both hands into the thrashing waters, he scooped out the fish struggling frantically to get off the hook. "It's a trout all right, a handsome fellow at that." He bore it to the bank, gaffed it neatly and removed the hook from its mouth.

Emma shuddered. "Is it dead?"

"Very." He held it up for her inspection. "I'd say about two pounds. Not a world record but certainly good enough for tea."

They explored the ruins again, poking and prying in the shrubbery with long sticks. Much of the temple was indeed underground and Emma was enchanted by the prospect of her own dig. On a high slope behind the ruin a herd of diminutive deer grazed. *Rous*—Kashmiri musk deer, Damien told her. Hunted ruthlessly for their musk, they had become scarce, which was why he was trying to breed them on the estate even though their natural habitat was much higher.

"A creature weighing twenty or thirty pounds is slaughtered to get at the musk pod, *nafa,* which weighs no more than two tolas but fetches astronomical prices from attar makers."

"Has the experiment proved successful?"

"Fairly. If spared by the gun, musk deer breed early and can multiply rapidly. Those three or four there with the spotted backs and sides are kids; they were born here."

She was again surprised at the extent of his knowledge of his environment and greatly moved by the quiet passion with which he loved and preserved it.

Later, again incomprehensibly hungry, they speared the gutted trout and mounted it on a stake near a fresh fire. When its skin was crackling crisp and its flesh done to a turn, they ate it with their hands. Emma licked the last succulent flake off her fingers declaring that even the charred bits were delicious.

"You like fish?" Damien asked.

"I love it!"

"Good. Fish are an important part of diet in the valley. In fact, many believe that it is fish that makes Kashmiri women so fertile."

Was the remark pointed at her as a reminder? Emma was not sure but it brought a touch of colour to her cheeks. She got up, walked to the stream and washed her hands in the ice-cold water. Dusk was falling and cold night winds were starting to stir; there was a sense of peace about the evening. Emma shivered and hugged herself, wishing she had thought to bring her shawl. Standing by the noisy little waterfall, she did not hear Damien's footfall behind her and started as something warm was draped about her shoulders—his jacket. Looking up at him, she smiled. As they strolled up to the top of the hillock towards their horses, in the not so far distance a jackal howled and others took up the call.

"Are there many large animals about?" she asked.

"No more than elsewhere. Animals are more frightened of us than we are of them."

"Army officers from Delhi used to come to the valley to hunt on their way up to Gulmarg. Is the shooting here good?"

"One has to go higher for the really big cats, even higher for ibex and markhor. Around Gulmarg, which is desolate, one does come across leopards and the occasional tiger, but only in the summer. When it turns cold they move down into the valleys."

They were interrupted by Hakumat, who materialised with an envelope and handed it to Damien. As he read the letter contained within, Damien's loose, easy mood underwent a startling change. Standing rock-still, he stared blindly into the darkening mountain masses, his face a mass of colliding emotions. Beneath his shirt, his shoulder muscles were perceptibly tight.

"What is it, Damien?" she asked, alarmed. "Is it bad news?"

He looked at her vacantly. "What?"

She repeated the question. He shook his head, but she knew that he had not heard what she had asked. A frown creased his forehead, a trace of impatience, as if he were unwilling to have his thread of thought disturbed. In silence Emma surveyed the aquiline profile, the unruly sweeps of hair ruffled by the wind, the ramrod-stiff back, the hand balled into a fist curled around the letter. Suddenly she ached to touch him, to reach out and smooth away the lines on his brow, to take the clenched fist between her palms and press comfort into it. The urge was so strong that for an instant she almost did so, but then, fearing rejection, she restrained herself. Lost in a private world that did not include her, he seemed unaware of her presence. Unhappily she made to turn away.

"Where are you going?" Before she could move he had circled her wrist with his hand.

She halted. It was a triviality, this tenuous physical contact, but it again made her throat dry. She did not pull her hand away. "It seemed to me that you would prefer to be alone. . . ."

"No, I would not prefer to be alone."

For a trembling instant their gazes levelled and held. On the point of saying something, something significant, something that *would* permit her entry into his world, he again faltered. Letting fall her hand, he walked away down the hill. Confounded by his unreadable mood, she ran after him and blurted out something, anything, to keep the channel of communication open.

"Mrs. Bicknell has invited me to tea next Tuesday."

"Uh-huh."

Touched with guilt at her true motive in accepting the invitation, she asked, "Would you . . . care to join us?"

"No. I have to go away tomorrow."

"*Again?*" She was dismayed. "Where?"

"Gupkar. I'm sorry but they simply are not able to produce all the figures I need before I invest in the project."

"Then let me come with you up to Srinagar," she begged, shaken by the intensity of her disappointment. "I can do some more sightseeing and wait on the boat until you return."

He shook his head. "Not this time, Emma. Perhaps the next."

She knew that he was concealing the truth and once again the familiar pain rose in her heart. She fell silent.

hini Baug, the Chinese state guest house, was a large, castellated double-storyed building situated away from the heart of the town. It was surrounded by well-trimmed hedges, cultivated lawns and flower gardens, now the domain of the convivial Padshah Khan. Having thoroughly cased both the Taotai's palace and the guest house under cover of darkness, with time running out fast Conolly leapt into action.

He knew from experience that Chin Wang, the Taotai's head cook and a frequent source of information, would be the last to leave the palace kitchens at night. Crouching beneath a high wall well concealed by bushes, Conolly waited for him to emerge from the rear gate closest to the kitchen houses. He did so well past midnight—carrying his lantern in one hand and his daily bag of illicit booty from his employer's larders in the other. Conolly clamped a hard palm down over his mouth and dragged him into the bushes.

"Wh . . . !"

"Not a sound, my friend," Conolly warned as he slowly eased off his hand. "I need help."

"No!" The man shook his head. "I cannot risk getting into trouble any more and losing my job."

Conolly remained unperturbed; this was how all their business transactions started. Wordlessly he produced a cloth pouch and tinkled it against the cook's ear.

Chin Wang gulped and looked around. "Not here, not *here*." He hastily pulled Conolly down a rough-hewn path and into a deserted coal-house. "Well, what is it this time?"

"I hear a new guest has arrived at Chini Baug."

"I know nothing about Chini Baug," Chin Wang muttered, his eyes glued to the pouch. "Guests come and go all the time."

"They also eat," Conolly said. "Since Chini Baug has no cooking facilities, food is sent twice daily from your palace kitchens."

The man shrugged. "So?"

Conolly jingled the coins louder. "There is enough in here to get you anywhere you like, even back to your home in Canton."

"No, not this time!" Looking longingly at the pouch, Chin Wang headed for the coal-house door. "This time it is truly dangerous. I refuse to get involved."

"Very well then," Conolly heaved a sigh, "you leave me no option but to speak to your wife."

"My wife?" The man laughed. "What does *that* old bag know about what happens in Chini Baug, eh?"

"Nothing. Even less, in fact, than she knows about your cosy little arrangement with the frisky filly with the big bosom who works in the Taotai's laundry."

The cook paled. If he was frightened of the Taotai, he was frankly terrified of his wife, an overblown, ferociously jealous woman who had once chased him down the bazaar with a pitchfork threatening assault on a most vital part of his anatomy.

"I mean it," Conolly said. "If you do not answer my questions, I will not only inform your wife of your liaison but grant her my sharpest surgical knife with which to do the needful."

Chin Wang's knowledge of Chini Baug improved miraculously. Yes, he confirmed sullenly, there was a new guest at Chini Baug and yes, food was being despatched for her twice every day.

Her! Conolly held his breath. "Who is she?"

That he did not know, Chin Wang said, because it was not his responsibility to take the food, just to cook and pack it. He only knew it was a woman because the maid of one of the mandarin's wives—aunt of the girl with whom he had the, um, "arrangement"—had been recently sent to Chini Baug for special duties.

Conolly's spirits soared; his optimism had not been misplaced. If the woman in Chini Baug was indeed this Armenian—and who else could she be?—then at least half his problems were over. He marvelled that Padshah had been able to smuggle her out of Tashkent despite its rigid security, but then the Taotai's agents were as devious as any Russian border guard and thirty pieces of silver were universal currency.

"The man who takes the food to Chini Baug, what is his name?"

"Genghis. He's the Taotai's personal servant."

"You've never delivered it yourself?"

"Only once."

"I know how many guards are posted outside Chini Baug—how many inside?"

"Four or five."

"Where?"

"All over the place." The cook's eyes stole towards the cloth pouch and he licked his lips. "Inside the rooms she is guarded by that dragoness of a maidservant."

"Has the Taotai been to see the lady?"

"Yes. The first day."

"Did you hear about what was discussed?"

"Nothing. The woman had been drugged, they say. They also say she is his new mistress, a white-skinned round-eye at that." He spat disgustedly on the ground. "I presume she is to be removed next Monday since the order for food thereafter stands cancelled."

Next Monday, only four days away!

"Removed where?"

The cook shrugged. "Who knows?"

Conolly dug inside a pocket and pulled out a rough plan he had made of the guest house. "To which room are the meals delivered?"

The cook sighed, raised his lantern and indicated a spot.

"Good. Now next Sunday night *you* will deliver the food. . . ."

"No!" Chin Wang was horrified. "Genghis will not permit it."

"If Genghis is ill, he will have to permit it."

"But he is not ill!"

"He will be." Conolly placed a packet in the man's hand. "Slip this into his midday meal on Sunday. Don't worry, he won't die, only wish he had by the time his bowels stop running. Once he's off to the fields, he won't return in a hurry."

"I won't do it!" the cook wailed. "Genghis is a Mongol, a brute of a man, that's why he's called Genghis. He's got hands like bear paws and a temper that . . ."

Conolly cut him off with a tantalising swing of the pouch. "Sunday is the day of the ram-fighting contest and the black sheep is to be presented to the winner by the Taotai, which means everyone will be at the contest. With Genghis ill, no one will question or even notice your evening errand."

"And what about the banquet that follows for which I have to prepare . . . ?"

"You have seven assistants. Let them do the preparations."

"No. I absolutely refuse to be implicated!"

"You won't be. When questioned later, you will simply tell them the truth, that on the way to Chini Baug you were accosted from behind by two men who made off with the food. You did not actually see your assassins but they sounded like Russians."

"Assassins!" The cook went quite pale. "I will be hurt?"

"No, no, of course not. You will only *pretend* to be." He swung the bag to and fro so that the coins jangled.

"Quiet, for God's sake, *quiet!*" The man made a grab for the pouch, partly to still the sound and partly because he could resist it no longer.

"Not yet." Conolly moved the pouch out of his reach. "About the rest I will instruct you later."

"My God, there is more?"

"A few last-minute details. Bring the food to the apricot orchard behind Chini Baug on Sunday night at seven. I will meet you there." As the man opened his mouth to protest, Conolly shoved the pouch into his hand and the protest died. "This is just a deposit, more when the job is done."

Hugging the pouch to his chest, the cook started to moan. "If the Taotai ever finds out . . ."

"He won't, not if you do exactly as I say."

". . . he will kill me!"

"So will I—if there is anything left of you after your wife has had her way with the knife."

It was by no means a perfect plan but it was the only one Conolly could think of. The risks were insane, the weak links many—not the least being this snivelling rascal on whom, unfortunately, so much depended. Chin Wang could, of course, be lying; the woman could have already been moved. Worst of all, he could get cold feet at the eleventh hour and not show up at all. However, with time short and the complexities many, Conolly had no choice but to take his chances where he found them. And pray that with God's grace he would beat Pyotr Shishkin to the draw.

In a region starved of medical facilities, even an unqualified doctor invokes gratitude in patients he has treated and cured. As such, Conolly was constantly being given modest gifts and heartfelt offers of free services in lieu of payment. That evening when he visited the young Baluchi couple whose daughter he had managed to save from pneumonia, they received him with genuine warmth. Too poor to make payment and greatly beholden to him, the young father, a dak runner, had tearfully offered any future service that might be in his power to perform.

"Khapalung near the Suget Pass?" he asked, when Conolly made his request. "Yes, of course I know it."

Conolly placed a sealed envelope in his hand. "Seek out a Khirgiz called Mirza Beg and give him this letter. It must be delivered at the earliest."

The young man accepted the assignment willingly.

With the time to leave Kashgar now close at hand, Conolly could not deny a sense of sorrow. He had received much affection from these simple people who had placed their trust in him and accepted him at face value. What would they have to say when they heard about his act of desertion? Sadly, there was no time for regrets and he could not provide explanations.

*O*nce again on her own, Emma turned her attention to her father's papers. In spite of all her efforts, however, her mind wandered and she found it difficult to concentrate.

She could think of nothing but Damien.

Gradually a framework was beginning to evolve within which to understand him better. The skeletal bones were acquiring flesh, the dark crevices starting to lighten and the ghostly substance to assume a three-dimensional human form. Despite the lack of physical intimacy and felicity in their marriage, there was a growing closeness between them. She could not put a name to her own feelings yet, but they produced in her a sense of such well-being, such contentment, that she was afraid to scrutinise them in case they vanished. Suddenly she wanted to purr like a cat!

Abandoning the effort to concentrate, she decided instead on a final visit to Edward Granville's apartment. Two packets of Damien's letters remained, and if this visit too failed to produce the elusive photographs she sought, she would assume that they were either stored elsewhere or destroyed, and abandon the mission. With the air between them clearer and Damien so much less guarded, she could even consider asking him about them outright when he returned.

The letters sent home by Damien in his final two years at school were varied in content and articulate in style. School events and outings were glossed over impatiently and replaced by enthusiastic reports about holidays in France with Hammie. Much time was being spent now in the weaving factory on his father's cousin's estate and the letters spilled over with newly acquired terminology, "twill-tapestry technique," "espoline weave" and "Ternaux shawls." France had once imported special goats from Khirgiz tribesmen, he had discovered, but only 500 out of a thousand had survived the journey, and this had distressed him greatly. At one grand exhibition in Paris, shawls from Kashmir were being much admired and he declared himself frightfully proud, as if reporting a personal achievement.

At other times there were boisterous romps in the vineyards and forests and on the lake, and it was in the company of his young cousins that Damien seemed happiest. There were horses on the estate; he and Hammie spent all day in the saddle. His French, he declared, was almost perfect; he had swotted hard and scored well in the final examinations. Next year, when he and Hammie finally returned home—he to Kashmir and Hammie to Rangoon—Hammie would stay with them for a month at Shalimar. He could hardly wait. The news about his dear Zaiboon's illness was heartbreaking. He pleaded with his father to take good care of her and make her eat lots of fruit, cream and walnuts.

Obviously, the scarred, embittered child had matured; the sharp corners and cutting edges of loss had rounded. Strangely enough, it seemed to Emma that in sharing Damien's childhood, even vicariously, she too had somehow mellowed. Deep within herself she sensed a new softness, a pleasing tranquillity, an entire range of emotions and instincts she had not experienced before.

Love . . . ?

Never having been in love or known an intimate relationship with a man, she had no means of identifying what she felt. Amorphous and tender, like a seed taking root, the feelings still struggled to take shape. Perhaps Damien was right after all. Perhaps what grew with time in a marriage was love (not gout!), like a pinhead bud coaxed into blossom by a slow, steady sun. However one might choose to label them, the gently sweet aches were warm and uplifting, and they brought in their wake an odd sort of happiness unlike any she had ever known.

And what about Damien's feelings for her? These too she was too untutored to decipher. Nevertheless, desperate for reassurances, she sought comfort in surmises; he had known about her before he went to Delhi, had spoken of her kindly to Nazneen, had pursued her single-mindedly into marriage. Indeed, looking back from a distance, she was amused at the absurd lengths to which he had gone to secure her agreement. Here too, she was forced to admit, his judgement was right; had he proposed outright, would she have accepted him at all? Thinking about her own intransigence during those forgettable days, she could now afford to laugh at herself—how childish her behavior seemed, how unnecessary!

She wished with all her heart that he were home.

Replacing the packets carefully in their original place in the drawer, she made to leave. Thought of those undiscovered photographs, however, still nagged. In two minds, she considered the prospect of the second column of drawers. She was tired, but having come so far would it not be a pity to give up now that there were only these left to search?

She sighed and reached for her screwdriver.

The seed catalogues, old invoices and brochures of various exhibitions stored in the top and middle drawers were of little interest. The final drawer, the bottom one, was filled to the brim with thick folders which also she viewed without enthusiasm. Nevertheless, she put both hands beneath the pile so as not to disturb the sequence and tugged gently. As she did so, she noticed something white and soft wedged at the far end of the drawer, a rolled-up piece of mull. Carefully she worked the cloth free and within it something rustled. Shredded paper?

Curiously, she unravelled the cloth and removed its contents: a sheet of blank paper wrapped around an extraordinary confusion of curly paper strips entangled with each other like confetti. The plain white sheet in which the strips were held had some writing on it, just a name. It was a name she recognised.

Jeremy Butterfield.

Quickly smoothing out one of the strips, she examined it in the spill of the lamp. The paper was packed tight with scribbles. For an instant, just an instant, she stared blankly at the odd configurations. Then she froze.

The writing that stared back at her was her father's!

Her instinctive reaction was that she had made a mistake. Pulling the lamp closer, she peered harder at the cramped characters. No, she was not mistaken; the hand she knew as well as her own was, indeed, that of her father.

But that was impossible!

Emma sank back into the chair, her bewildered eyes riveted to the untidy nest of paper strips on the desk. She made no effort to read what was written on them. In any case, she could not; her vision was unfocussed and the characters blurred.

Although she had no recollection later of having done so, she must have replaced the hasp, locked the desk and then the door to the apartment. She was surprised suddenly to find herself upstairs and back in her study, the knot of papers tightly clutched in a damp palm. For a while she stood by the open window staring out into the misty night, absorbing the dark, feeling its cool texture against her cheek. Silently the night stared back, offering no answers, no explanations to help fit her mind around a dawning reality still too gross to comprehend.

She hugged herself tight to stop the trembles. Willing herself into an unfeeling calm, she lit a lamp, placed the papers on the her desk and extricated a few strips. She ironed them into flatness and examined them closely. One word leapt into clear focus.

Yasmina.

Something cold and sinister stole over her like a shroud. What had begun as a small spear of bewilderment had assumed frightening proportions. She was overcome by a wave of sickness, a terrible sense of impending disaster. What connection had her father had with the Yasmina? She had never seen these papers before, had not even known of their existence. How then had Damien? And how had they come to be in his desk at all?

Why?

CHAPTER

16

*R*estricting himself to essentials, Conolly started to pack: gun, money-belt, writing materials, field glasses, kukri, compass, water flasks, some food and minimal clothing. His declared intention to visit patients in the northern villages, as he regularly did, was received without surprise by the young lad who served as his assistant. The bulging medical portmanteau, saddlebag and attaché case passed unnoticed.

"I will be away for three days," Conolly said, as he concluded his usual long list of instructions. "If I am needed by patients beyond the lake, I might be further delayed."

The following daybreak he set out northwards, taking care to attract maximum attention en route. At the border post, where he was known, he halted for chai and a chat. Had they heard, he asked casually, that Russian hooligans had been seen sneaking across the border near Irkishtam? The alarmed border post guards confessed that they had not and hastily set about instituting inquiries.

Having spent the day attending to a long line of patients in the first village, Conolly made known his intention to proceed to the other side of the lake where more patients awaited. Halfway to the lake, soon after dark, he doubled back to Kashgar by a longer and less frequented route. He arrived at the city's northern gate close to the dawn and made straight for the public cemetery. Gingerly picking his way to a previously selected place of concealment, he remained in the cemetery until the following evening.

The first phase of the plan successfully completed, Conolly now prepared for the second.

Considering his misgivings about Chin Wang's intentions, he was overwhelmed with relief the following evening, Sunday, to see that greed had triumphed after all; soon after the appointed hour of seven the cook arrived in the apricot orchard behind Chini Baug. The festivities at the palace were in full swing, Chin Wang reported. No one had questioned his errand. As predicted, Genghis had disappeared soon after midday and had not been seen since.

"The rest of the money?" The cook held out his hand.

"Not yet, there is more to be done. Take off your clothes."

"What?!"

A fresh bargain had to be hastily struck before the outraged cook agreed to part with his clothing.

"Now wait for me here till I return," Conolly said, tossing the shivering man his own overcoat.

"The money?"

"When I return."

Dressed in Chinese clothes and cap, his face heavily muffled, Conolly took charge of the shoulder balance on the two scales of which rested the food containers. Sending up a silent prayer, he marched boldly up to the main gate of the guest house.

"Open up, open up," he demanded. "I've brought the lady's dinner."

One of the guards gave him a suspicious look. "Who are you?"

"Li, Chin's new assistant."

"Where is old Genghis then?"

"Sick—or pretending to be. As if I haven't enough on my hands already with fifty for dinner and seventy chickens . . ."

"All right, all right, get on with it!"

The gates opened, and still grumbling, Conolly entered.

The suite of rooms Chin Wang had indicated was enclosed by neatly trimmed hedges containing a pretty rose garden. Obviously, Padshah Khan—away for his nightly tipple at the chai khana—worked well at earning his rewards. Conolly passed two more guards; both waved him on without a glance. On the verandah outside the rooms, a middle-aged Chinese woman with hostile eyes and an air of authority sat with her elbows on the balustrade. She glared at him and Conolly burrowed his face further into his muffler.

"Who are you?" she snapped.

"Li, the new helper."

"Where is Genghis?"

Repeating his complaints, he grumpily unloaded the containers, making it clear that he had no time to stand and gossip. She took charge of the food, remarked tartly on his foul temper and ordered him to wait for the containers. With his heart beating like a kettle-drum, Conolly squatted in a corner of the verandah and used the forty-minute interval to prepare for his next move, the most crucial so far. By the time the woman returned with the containers, he was ready. In haughty silence she dumped them on the floor before him and turned to go back to the room.

"Er, wait a minute," Conolly said.

"What is it now?" She stopped halfway to the door.

"Is this your napkin or did it come from the palace?"

He held up a piece of cloth. As she lowered her face for a better look, he put one hand behind her head, pushed forward hard, and with the other clamped the cloth tight against her face. She struggled like a tigress, but only for an instant or two. As the chloroform started to take effect, her eyes rolled up, her knees buckled and she became limp. Tossing the napkin aside, Conolly dragged her into a corner of the verandah behind the balustrade, tied up her hands and feet and placed a secure gag about her mouth. Then he picked up the napkin and ran into the room.

So far so good. Now came the difficult part.

The next few moments, Conolly knew, were the weakest part of his plan. He had no idea how the woman in custody would react to his sudden arrival. She might demand explanations, waste precious time. She might even scream and resist physically, in which case he would again have to make use of the chloroform. If she was already drugged with opium, he still faced the unenviable prospect of lugging her dead weight across the back garden, over the wall and into the orchard, all without being seen by a roving guard.

At first glance, the room he entered appeared to be empty. Then, in the light of a solitary lamp, he saw a figure standing by the barred window opposite the door. On a table lay the unwashed plates and remains of the meal. More than that he had no time to note, for the woman turned.

"There is no time now for explanations," he said urgently in Russian in what he hoped was a reassuring tone, "but if you want to escape from here, you must come with me quickly."

Staring at him with wide, frightened eyes, she remained rooted.

"Listen," he said, forcing himself to sound calm, "these men who brought you here are *bad* men who mean to harm you. I have come to take you to safety."

She still made no response, but her wide, stricken eyes wandered over him as she surveyed his unprepossessing appearance.

Conolly hastily uncovered his face. "Don't worry, I am not Chinese. I am a . . . a friend of the Colonel. He has sent me to fetch you back to Tashkent, but we must hurry!"

Finally she spoke, also in Russian. "Where is this place?"

"Kashgar. The Chinese brought you here from Tashkent."

"The gardener said the Colonel had sent for me."

"He lied. These men are enemies of the Colonel, of Russia, of the Armenian people. . . ." He felt like an ass but he also felt his panic mount. "You . . . you *must* come with me!"

"Where is Colonel Borokov?"

So that was his name! Padshah Khan had, apparently, known him only as the Colonel. "In Tashkent."

"He knows that I have been brought here?"

"Yes. It is he who arranged everything for your journey back."

"To Tashkent?"

"Yes, yes, to Tashkent. But there is no time to lose, we must go immediately or the guards will come and then the Colonel will be very angry. Trust me, please!"

That seemed to strike a chord, for without another word she went into the inner room and returned a moment later with a small case.

Conolly almost fainted with relief. "We must be very quiet. You must do as I say. . . ."

"The Chinese maid . . ."

"Taken care of."

In the verandah he grabbed the unconscious woman's legs and started to drag the formidably bulky form back into the room. Without waiting to be told, his newly acquired protégée took hold of the arms to help in the heaving. She now appeared relatively calm, only her eyes shone bright and her breath erupted in rapid little gasps. They laid the maid's body on the bed, tied it to the frame and snuffed out the lamp. Hurrying onto the verandah again, Conolly bolted the door behind them. With the door closed and the light extinguished, wandering guards would simply presume that, dinner over, both women had retired for the night.

As Conolly reloaded the containers on the shoulder balance and prepared for flight, one of the guards suddenly sauntered round the corner. Just in time, Conolly pushed the erstwhile prisoner down behind the balustrade and readjusted his muffler.

"They've eaten, have they?" The guard stood poised on the bottom step, ready to ascend.

"Yes and, as you can see, gone to bed." Before the man could negotiate another step up, Conolly had run down with his sling. "I was just about to take the containers back."

The guard's eyes gleamed. "Genghis always lets us have the leftovers," he said pointedly.

Conolly hesitated and glanced nervously over his shoulder. "All right— so long as the old harridan doesn't see you. Go and eat in the guardroom, all of you."

Greedily, the guard grabbed the sling. "Wait for the containers."

"The containers?" For a split second Conolly went blank; this was a problem he had not foreseen. Thinking quickly, he said, "Er, don't worry about the containers, I'll collect them in the morning. They have plenty more at the palace."

It took Conolly another five minutes to leave through the front gate and run around to the orchard at the rear of the house where Chin Wang waited shivering in his underwear beneath the great coat. They retired behind the bushes to conduct the exchange of clothing.

"Well, is that all?" Chin Wang asked.

"Yes."

"The rest of the money?"

Conolly handed over a second, heavier pouch.

The cook grinned. "Can I go now?"

"Yes."

"Have you told the two men not to hit me too hard?"

"Yes."

"Where are the empty containers? If they are not returned, they'll think I've stolen them."

"Don't worry, they're with the guards. I've told them they'll be collected in the morning."

The cook eyed him anxiously. "You *swear* I will not be implicated?"

"Not as long as you stick to your story. You were attacked by two men on your way to Chini Baug. You have no idea who this Li might be but he was obviously in league with the criminals. When you regained consciousness, you were lying in a ditch half naked with your clothes scattered about you, and the food containers were gone. Beyond the fact that they spoke Russian, you know nothing about your assassins. Remember—don't be in a hurry to get back to the palace. Take your time."

Gleefully the cook turned to hurry away with his hard-earned dues. As he did so Conolly picked up a dead branch and hit him hard on the back of the head. With a loud groan he crumpled into the bushes. Conolly waited a few moments and listened, but nobody came to investigate. Once again he was galvanised into action.

From inside a cluster of bushes he pulled out a wooden handcart fitted with a platform and retrieved two bundles from the undergrowth. He had purchased the cart for a hefty price two days ago from a washerman whom he had successfully treated for a painful crop of carbuncles, his alleged purpose being to indulge a sudden passion for gardening. The bundles of old clothes he had bought in the flea market for a non-existent family of poor patients. Unrecognisably garbed, under cover of rain last night he had concealed the cart—its wheels well oiled—in the orchard, praying that no one would find it. No one had.

He changed into a long belted coat, baggy trousers and a turban, and added his own clothes to the pile. Running across the orchard he climbed over the back gate and returned to the guest suite, assured that the guards were all in the guardhouse busy stuffing themselves. The woman sat waiting patiently in the verandah exactly where he had left her.

"Good girl," he murmured, pleased.

With the guards still quaffing, the return to the orchard presented no problems. Five minutes later they had both vaulted over the gate into the safety of the orchard at the spot where the cook lay. The girl recoiled, staring at the unconscious figure in horror.

"He's not dead, only temporarily out of action," Conolly said comfortingly. "It's too complicated to explain now but he has been well paid for his trouble."

Ten minutes later Chin Wang had been artistically laid out in a ditch dividing the orchard from the rutted road together with—for good measure—a somewhat moth-eaten Russian racoon fur hat also purchased from the flea market.

That done, Conolly paused to scan their surroundings. To the north, across a stream, lay a line of buff-coloured loess cliffs crowned by a huddle of mud houses. Beyond were fields and more orchards and the Taklamakan desert. To the south-west, in the far distance, glistened the snowcaps of the Pamirs and in the west, on a clear day, one could see the ranges of the Tian Shan. Camel bells tinkled restlessly somewhere in the night, probably in the caravanserai in the bazaar, but otherwise all was quiet.

He turned to the woman. "Are you warm enough?"

"Yes."

"There is plenty more woollen clothing here if you are not. Now get onto the cart."

She offered no argument. Pulling her knees up under her chin to adjust to the length of the platform, she lay still as Conolly covered her with piles of clothes. The hour was late; a fine grey drizzle had started and the night was foggy. There was no one about. It seemed to Conolly that it must be at least midnight, but when he consulted his watch he was astonished and relieved to see that it was not yet nine.

With luck, by the time dawn broke they would be crossing the fringe of the Taklamakan on the way to Yarkand.

Forcing himself not to hurry, Conolly wheeled the cart down the road away from Chini Baug in the direction of the Yarwakh Durwaza, the north gate of the town. There were a few stragglers about and someone waved at the familiar sight of the washerman trundling his laundry-cart late at night on his way back from the river.

The cemetery where Conolly had concealed himself during the day stretched on both sides of the road for at least a mile and a half beyond the north gate. He picked his way carefully in the uncertain starlight between the thousands of tombstones, past the mosque with its dome of green tiles, until he eventually arrived at his previous place of concealment, a mausoleum.

One of hundreds belonging to the more affluent, it had a wide, arched entrance and free space between the cenotaphs. He pushed the cart in, held his breath and listened: he was greeted by a low, slightly aggrieved neigh from deep within the shadows, and he exhaled with a whoosh. Local superstition ensured that no one would venture into this vast city of the dead after dark unless they had to; obviously those who had died that day had done so with a thoughtful sense of timing. His horse, tethered where he had left it earlier in the evening, had not been discovered. He brushed the clothes off the cart.

"Are you all right?" he asked, concerned.

The woman raised her head and nodded.

"Do you have a pair of strong boots?"

"In my box."

"Good, put them on. And these." He handed her a thick woollen jersey and a pair of stout trousers. "You will need them in the desert." Opening his portmanteau, he extracted a pair of surgical scissors and looked at her uncertainly. "It will not be safe for you to travel as a woman. . . ."

She took the scissors, undid the thick plait wound about her head and with minimal hesitation sheared it off at the base. Watching in silence Conolly marvelled at her pragmatism, her tacit understanding of their plight and lack of feminine vanity. So far there had been no time to examine her closely, although from the quality of her voice he could tell that she was young. Now as he studied her face in the light of the lantern, her extreme youth surprised him. She was a mere slip of a girl, perhaps not even twenty.

Having cropped her hair into acceptable shortness, she wrapped the scattered tresses in a scarf and handed them to him. "We had better bury these. It would not do for them to be found here."

He nodded approvingly, stuffed the bundle into the bulging saddlebag and led his horse out of the tomb. When he returned a few minutes later, she had changed into the trousers and coat, wrapped a scarf around her head like a turban and transformed herself into a surprisingly credible young lad.

Conolly laughed. "Oh yes, you'll certainly do."

He wedged the handcart tightly behind the cenotaphs in a dark corner. It would be days, perhaps weeks, before it was discovered.

"Incidentally, what is your name?"

"Ivana Ivanova."

He frowned. "A Russian name?"

"It is the name the Colonel gave me."

A host of other questions hovered on Conolly's lips but there was no time for more.

The shortest distance between Kashgar and Yarkand, two hundred miles, was across the western fringe of the Taklamakan desert. To venture into the old town where the caravanserai was located was out of the question. Conolly had therefore made arrangements with the caravan leader—a Yarkandi and an occasional informant bringing news from Tashkent—for him and a companion to join the caravan a few miles into the desert.

Conolly was aware that the woman's disappearance—and, in due course, his own—would be investigated thoroughly. The Taotai was not a fool; but considering his nervousness about Russian infiltrators, Chin Wang's sorry tale would make him first mount inquiries at the border. Later inquiries would lead them to the northern villages to confirm his own visit and several days would pass before the deceit was discovered. By that time, he and the woman would be well beyond Yarkand and the Chinese border. Or so Conolly fervently hoped.

In Turki, *Taklamakan* meant "he who goes in does not come out," and with good reason. The desert was notorious as a graveyard, a communal coffin for thousands of bodies preserved in the sands. Those with fertile imaginations swore that at night the spirits revived and through the winds whispered spine-chilling tales of how long-forgotten men and monarchs had met their gruesome ends. Conolly was not a superstitious man, but it was not until they were within sight of the mound of ancient bricks that was their rendezvous point with the caravan that his breathing eased.

As they sat down to a sparse meal and drank thirstily of their water, Ivana suddenly made a remark. "You have taken a great deal of trouble over me."

Not knowing how to respond, Conolly merely smiled.

"Why?"

"Because your, ah, Colonel, has commanded me to."

She considered that in silence. "Who are you?"

"Let us just say that I am a friend."

She nodded and asked no more questions, not even his name.

Her unquestioning acceptance was somehow touching, like a child slipping her hand into that of a trusted parent, and all at once Conolly felt uncomfortable. What would she have to say when she found out the truth: that he had lied to her, that he was taking her not to Tashkent but to Leh?

Once again he wondered who she was, this mysterious woman—girl!— who did not even know her true name. Why was she so important to everyone? And how the devil could anyone as innocent and untouched be involved in as brutal a business as international intrigue? There was no time to probe for answers.

*T*o sleep was unthinkable.

Emma waited for the numbness to recede, then rose from her desk, splashed iced water on her face, washed her blank sleepwalker eyes and re-seated herself. Somehow she had to survive the shock and rediscover her mind. It was all she had left, her ability to think; she could not compromise that now. Forcing herself into logical thought, she started to disentangle the assortment of strips that lay scattered on her desk.

The paper, she recognised, came from the type of lined foolscap notepads her father had used. The sheets had been cut along the lines and the strips were of more or less equal size. In all there were thirty-five strips, both sides of which were covered with tightly cramped writing. Laying them side by side, she set about fitting them together much in the manner of a jigsaw puzzle.

Used as she was to her father's impossible scrawls, these were especially difficult to decipher. The characters were small, the handwriting inconsistent and sentences ran haphazardly into each other as if written with unsteady fingers. There were continuations all over the place and the fact that the strips had been cut after the writing made the task even more laborious. Nevertheless she persevered, and gradually, a coherent pattern began to emerge out of the confusion. The patchwork document was not extensive, a mere seven full sheets in all. Placing the strips in sequential order, she numbered them in red for future reference.

The detachment she tried to invoke was not easy. Every once in a while she paused and laid her head back against the chair. Sooner or later, she knew, her heart would revolt, but she could not risk rebellion yet, not yet! When the task was finally completed, she got up, drank thirstily from a carafe and again washed her face to shock her mind into dispassionate thought.

Then she sat down to read what her father had written.

17 June, 1889: *The north flank of the Biafo after two days slow march. A hideous, bone-chilling climb. Here the glacier is about two miles wide, a frightening crossing. Desolation unimaginable. A savage, primaeval place, a* dead *place, yet filled with sound and move-ment. Crashing boulders, thundering avalanches, primordial upheav-als within the mountains, frightening earth shifts that seal old crevasses and cut open new. Glacial surface heavily ridged, waves in a frozen sea. Deep, sub-surface ice pools of pale green. Staring cre-vasses plunge into darkness, their walls spiked with long, green icicles as sharp as rapiers. The region is alive, a world coming apart. Behind lifting mists the cliffs and rockfaces block out the day. Bitter, bitter cold.*

The blizzard again brews. Visibility low. Bingham and the rest must follow! The cold hollows me out, freezes blood and breath and every cell in my body. I am lucky. A hole in the rock, a cave above a ledge, offers shelter. This is where I sit crouching now as I write. Light is filtered and fades fast. The blizzard rages. It will last all night. Food enough for four days. No fire.

18 June: *Blizzard dying. No sign of the others. Visibility still poor. Oh for some chai! Must not complain.*

19 June: *No hint of Bingham! Are they lost or am I? Arctic weather but a pale, milky sun. I have a visitor, a boy. He is from Hunza, speaks Burishaski and is greedy for my binoculars. I must be careful. I do not wish to lose them. He says this is* bad place, *repeats many times but cannot explain. He is Mohammedan; does he refer to some infidel Buddhist monastery? I grill him but he knows nothing of a monastery. What is this "bad place"? I finally have it out of him. Yasmina, he says. Of course I do not believe him!*

There is no pass that I can see, but he is insistent. He says he will show me in exchange for my binoculars. I refuse. I know he is trying to trick me. All the same, I look through my binoculars to where he points. There is a break in the rockface, a crack barely visible to the naked eye. What is it? I cannot tell, but it looks very strange.

20 June: *Sunshine, not warm but bright, blue sky. The weather has cleared. The snows are blinding, less desolate, less sinister. I am dazzled by the grandeur of this awesome realm. The boy has gone. So also my binoculars! I am desolate but can do nothing. Today, I know, Bingham will find me. I must not wander. I wait and think of what the boy said. I cannot restrain my curiosity. I have clambered up a slippery slope to the north, a thousand feet, I calculate. Narrow, zigzag path. Stony. Large boulders. A precarious shelf. I am now more*

than fifteen thousand feet above sea level. Temperature, my instru-
ment says, is forty-five below.

Ahead is that slim crack, the rockface sliced as if by a giant bread
knife. Opening narrow, no more than ten feet. Perpendicular rock
walls turn inwards at the top, almost meeting. Uneven, slippery
ground, sharp rock edges, deep pits, heavy encrustation of ice. I step
carefully, slowly. Gully curves to the west. Echoes. Little light. Thin
line of blue overhead. Eerie feeling, malevolent, brooding. I am not
comfortable. The weather closes again, it is dark. I cannot go on, I
retrace my steps. Almost noon.

The gully fills with light, sudden and unearthly. I am fearful, but
it is the sun at its zenith directly overhead. Veils of sunlight drape
the walls and they glisten. Wetness? The light passes and the gloam
returns. It is twelve minutes past noon. Must eat sparingly. Dried
meat. Last of the chappatis. God's mercy!

I return to the shelf. Must climb the outside wall but not today.
No strength left. Gradient tricky. I am exhausted. Tomorrow, if I am
alive. Does the gully lead to the Yasmina? Don't know. Alas, no
instruments, only an altimeter. My life ebbs with my strength. I
wonder if it is not ordained. There is devilish intent in this inhuman
world and I am trapped with no intelligence higher than mine to
guide me. I fear it will not. I have trespassed where I should not
have. The gods will not forgive.

22 June: Frozen. Head reels. No more food. I lose my legs. Must
reach snout of glacier. Can I? Heaven have mercy on my soul. God
bless my family. Tell them I cannot . . .

The handwriting dissolved into squiggles of illegibility and then petered
out. It was the end of the diary, the end of her father's final testament.

The end of his life.

Alive with grief and a larger, more devastating sense of loss, Emma
once more strangled her emotions. The luxury of tears was still not to be
had; there were questions to be asked, answers to be found, knots to be
untangled. Searching for solutions, she unlocked her repository of sorrows
and allowed her mind to regress.

The return to Delhi of her father's team had ended weeks of agonising
uncertainty. Two months later, the Lieutenant-Governor called with the
cruel news that extinguished the last of their hopes: Graham Wyncliffe's
body had been found by tribesmen in a crevasse on the Biafo. After having
buried it, the kind men had carried the information to the Commissioner
in Leh, from where it was telegraphed to Delhi. Too stricken at the time
to ask questions, she had digested nothing beyond the fact that her father

was dead. There were glowing tributes in the newspapers; the Lieutenant-Governor read the eulogy at a moving memorial service under the aegis of the Archaeological Survey. Streams of sympathetic visitors descended upon Khyber Kothi and their own dazed grief obliterated all else.

Then, many weeks later, came the mysterious delivery.

A large, roughly trussed bundle addressed to Graham Wyncliffe was left by two Buddhist monks with the watchman at the gate of Khyber Kothi. Before they could either be questioned or thanked, they hurried away, and subsequent efforts to trace them proved futile. When Emma examined the contents of the carpet bag—for that was what was in the bundle—she did not recognise any of them. Certainly neither the bag nor its contents belonged to her father. With no further interest in it, she stored the bag in a tin trunk in the annexe to her study and forgot about it.

Until now.

Abstracting the bag from the trunk in which it had lain forgotten for so long, Emma once again emptied its contents on the table and examined them. Her second, more careful inspection only confirmed her earlier conclusion: none of the clothes, shoes, toilet articles or solitary prayer-wheel in the bag had belonged to her father. Stuffed into a cloth pouch were some papers—bills, inventories, orders for an assortment of goods and a list of names and addresses in Aksu, Bokhara and Samarkand. At the back of an invoice her father's name and address were scribbled, although not in his hand, and this she had overlooked earlier. She studied carefully other names mentioned, but they still meant nothing to her—with a single exception. A bill for Khotan carpets was made out to one Rasool Ahmed.

She knew now from Charlton's reports that "Rasool Ahmed" was the pseudonym used by the dead British agent Jeremy Butterfield. If the carpet bag had belonged to Butterfield, why then had it been sent to her father? By whom? Even more confounding—the Yasmina *had* been located, the diary proved that. Why then did the government continue to deny it? And why was the discovery being debated as that of Butterfield with no mention of her father?

Emma's head whirled. None of it made any sense to her, least of all the possibility that her father could have had any connection with Butterfield and his intelligence activities, which she dismissed as palpably absurd.

Daybreak touched the leaden, lowering skies. A cold rain fell and the dawn chorus struck its first plaintive chords. Throwing open the doors of her balcony, Emma stepped out into the frigid dampness to gaze aimlessly into the nothingness of the mists.

All night long she had forbidden her thoughts to dwell on Damien, forced herself to think only of the papers. Still unable—unwilling—to accept the implied reality, even now she forced her thoughts into trivia: a loose tassel on a curtain needed stitching; she was to look at sales figures for the paddy crop today; a character reference was to be written for Qadir Mian's son to train as a medical orderly at the Mission Hospital.

Eventually she could sustain the delusion no longer. The burden was too heavy and her resistance snapped.

Damien had lied to her!

Surging questions held behind barricades on her little mental island of safety burst forth in a flood. Yes, Damien had lied, had been lying to her all along. She had not had an inkling about her father's discovery; how then had he? And when had the papers come into his possession? How and where and why?

All at once the problem assumed frightening dimensions of quite another magnitude. Behind her tightly shuttered eyes, dark, awesome suspicions swirled in circles like eddies going nowhere. Fighting despair and filled with liquid pain, Emma searched blindly for answers. She cared nothing about the Yasmina, nothing about its strategic worth or its politics. All she cared about was Damien, and he had deceived her, manipulated her, used her.

She started to die.

Laying her head down on the desk, she finally wept.

What Gilgit was to Britain, Osh was to Russia. Gulcha, the final Russian post before the Trans-Alai mountains, lay twenty-seven miles beyond Osh and was soon to be connected with it by road. From there, it was three marches to the Kizil Su river for an army, but less, Mikhail Borokov assessed, for a man riding out alone. Declaring that he wished to spend the day by himself to explore the terrain and assess the quantity of explosives required for the road, he had politely declined the Commandant's offer of an escort.

He arrived at the highest point of the Taldik Pass from where the distant view of Mount Kaufmann was quite magnificent. Marginally less than twelve thousand feet, the pass overlooked the plains of the Kizil Su river to the south, where the path forked between the Russian fort at Irkishtam and Kashgar, and on the right to the Murghab and Pamirski Post.

And ahead, somewhere in the bosom of the terrifying infinity of the Himalayas, lay his ultimate destination: Srinagar.

Borokov turned one final time to look behind him. Hidden under the far, far blanket of cloud lay Tashkent and the green valley of the Ferghana where he had spent many happy holidays roaming the cotton fields. His eyes filled with tears; he would never again see St. Petersburg, never again set foot on Russian soil. But then, angrily, he brushed away the tears and the memories. Having come thus far he could not, would not retract. He had to press on. The Yasmina was *his*; Smirnoff had no right to it.

He started the descent to the river.

On the far bank of the Kizil Su ponies grazed in green pastures and lazy Khirgiz herdsmen dozed with no more than half an eye on their sheep. Knowing that the cold, pure air of the mountains sharpened appetites, Borokov bought a sheep for twenty roubles, waited while it was skinned and gutted, and set off again with the carcass slung across his saddle. The sheep would last until he could purchase more provisions and a horse at the Khirgiz village he had marked on his map on his reconnaissance trip earlier. In any case the plains were thick with wild duck, partridge and hare; he would not starve.

He proceeded to the isolated spot on the river, well concealed by out-crops of rock, that he had previously selected. Removing his uniform, he hung it on a skeletal branch, slung a well-filled nose-bag round his stallion's neck, a warm blanket across the saddle and tethered the animal to a bush. He would be sorry to see the last of his horse, a trusted friend and companion, but to retain him would arouse suspicions and he did not dare take the risk.

He took a deep breath and set about completing what he had started. Changing into a thick, warm shirt, voluminous trousers and quilted jacket, he wound a scarf about his head. Borokov was not a vain man; he rarely thought about himself in personal terms. If there was one thing he regretted, however, it was his face. Unmistakably Slav, it was flat, with high cheekbones and a splayed nose that were difficult to disguise. He admired agents who could assume second identities, speak native lingos and pass themselves off as local merchants. Men like Jeremy Butterfield. His own communicative prowess was limited to a smattering of local dialects and he could disguise his thick accent as little as he could his face.

Once dressed, he surveyed without enthusiasm the endless wastes of snow, rock, and hideous glaciers around him. He was submerged in mountains, high and hostile, mountains that he hated and feared. Would he ever escape from their clutches alive? Slinging his heavy pack on his back, he threw a final moist look at his horse and set off on foot as fast as the stony, zigzagging, desolate paths would allow.

The alert for him, Borokov calculated, would be sounded in the morning. In a day or two they would find his horse, his clothes and some possessions scattered on the river bank. The hunt for his body in the fierce torrents of the Kizil Su would soon be abandoned as hopeless. A frantic message would be despatched to Tashkent. Smirnoff would pretend shock, grief, but privately he would be relieved not to have to share his glory with a lesser mortal. A touching memorial service would be held in his honour. Smirnoff would mouth a few platitudes, perhaps even shed a tear or two for public consumption. His belongings would then be packed and sent to Kharkov to his old biddy of an aunt, his sole living relative, who would sell them off to earn a few roubles, and that would be the end of that.

Basking in his private vision, Borokov felt his spirits rise. He began to feel an odd sort of weightlessness, a measure of release. He owed nothing, owned nothing. Forever free, he had ceased to exist. His life had come full circle.

He did not know exactly when he started to sense that he was not alone. He could see no one but his sharp ears caught subtle indications of another presence—a rattle of stones, the croak of a startled raven taking wing, a sudden inexplicable hush. He plodded on without stopping, but by the time night fell he was convinced that he was being followed, or at least that someone was walking behind him. Petty thieves and brigands abounded in the mountains. With no intention of being robbed of all his savings scraped together rouble by rouble over the years, he patted his money-belt and reassured himself that it was still securely tied.

Arriving at the cave he had located on an earlier trip, he lit a lantern and ensured that no beasts of prey lurked in its cavernous bowels. It was a deep cave, comparatively warm and with a second opening at the rear that led upwards and out. Whistling unconcernedly, he gathered brush-wood, started a fire and set the sheep to roast on an impromptu spit. His altimeter showed a height of little more than seventeen thousand feet and his temples had started to throb. Nevertheless, he forced himself to remain alert with his revolver within reach and his eyes never far from the mouth of the cave. When the mutton was part roasted, he cut off a hunk and masticated, more out of duty than pleasure.

Dinner done, he arranged his sleeping bag, partially doused the fire, extinguished his lantern and as quietly as he could clambered up the opening at the back of the cave. As he already knew, it led to a sort of ledge that overlooked the entrance directly underneath. Choosing a secure vantage point, he waited.

An hour passed before he heard the muted sound of a dislodged stone rolling downhill. Someone was coming up the path! An animal? His grip on the revolver tightened. Then in the eerie silence, finally, came the whisper of a first cautious footfall. The moon, not yet full, threw down enough light to see by. Over the lip of the cave roof, on the ground below, he saw a shadow detach itself from the dark with a flash of steel. The dagger of a tribesman? He could not tell yet if the man was alone.

The shadow moved again and Borokov heard the soft swish of clothing. He peered deep into the gloom and waited. The intruder, now clearly visible and seemingly alone, crept towards the entrance. When he was directly below, Borokov jumped to land unerringly on the crouching back. Under his weight the stalker collapsed soundlessly and lay still. Making sure that he was not feigning unconsciousness, Borokov relieved him of his dagger, dragged the limp body into the cave, and tied the hands and legs securely with rope. He then revived his fire, set a can of water to boil and once more sat down to wait. By the time the man started to stir, Borokov was sipping a tepid mug of brick tea. He rose and tossed a handful of icy water across the stranger's face. Spluttering, the fellow jerked awake and returned to full consciousness.

"Who are you and why were you following me?" Borokov asked sternly in Turki. The youth—for that was all he was—moaned but gave no answer and Borokov repeated his question.

"I was not following you," the intruder replied sullenly in the same language. "I live near here. I was going home to my village."

"Liar!" Borokov grabbed his revolver. "Why then did you come up to the cave?"

"I was curious. I meant no harm."

"You are Khirgiz?"

"Yes. We graze our sheep near the river."

Having incapacitated the fellow, Borokov wasn't sure what to do with him next. Unarmed and well trussed, he seemed harmless enough. With luck perhaps he could even turn the intrusion to his advantage.

"I am going to untie your hands," he said, speaking in the same hard voice in order to sustain his authority, "but one false move and you're a dead man. Understand?"

The herdsman nodded.

"You know these mountains well?"

"As well as the nose on my face."

"Good."

Borokov rose to his feet and in so doing staggered a little. The rarefied air had again made him dizzy and the physical exertion had shortened his breath. He leaned against the cave wall, closed his eyes and gulped in lungfuls of air to restore his breathing. Then, annoyed to have a witness to his discomfort, he straightened sharply. He removed the ropes that bound the Khirgiz, watching out for unexpected moves, but the man made none. Once free he shambled off into a corner, wiped his face with a none too clean cloth and sat down to rub the circulation back into his limbs.

Filling two tin mugs with the pale yellow liquid, Borokov offered him one and took one himself. Even lukewarm and salty, the chai was invigorating. Still having difficulty in breathing fully, Borokov felt his eyes droop.

He was determined not to close them, but deprived of oxygen his head reeled and his lungs panted. He must have dropped off for a while for when he opened his eyes again his breathing was normal and he felt noticeably better.

There was no sign of the Khirgiz.

With a muted curse Borokov sprang to his feet, picked up his lantern and ran silently to the mouth of the cave. Outside, squatting on his haunches behind a rock, the infernal fellow was in the process of investigating the contents of his leather sack.

Enraged, Borokov leapt at him and hit him hard with his fist.

"Oh, *Christ*!"

The oath exploded in English. Reeling back, Borokov picked up his lantern and thrust it close to the befuddled face. "Good God!" he breathed. "You are Angliski?"

Dazed by the blow, the injured man offered no answer.

Borokov grabbed hold of his collar, dragged him back into the cave and slung him roughly against a wall. What rotten bloody luck! "Now, tell me the truth," he hissed. "Just who the hell *are* you?"

He still spoke in Turki. To his further surprise, however, the man replied in diffident Russian.

"A soldier."

That much Borokov had already deduced; few civilians ventured into the mountains without permission, certainly none on their own.

"Why were you following me?"

"I was obeying orders."

"Whose?"

"Those of my commanding officer."

"For what purpose?"

"You were involved in the construction of the new road from Osh to Gulcha. I was told to keep an eye on it."

Well, that made sense enough. Always fearful of a Russian invasion, the British interpreted any road building in the mountains as a preparation for war. In this case, of course, they were right! The soldier answered questions so readily that a chilling thought occurred to Borokov.

"You are not afraid to reveal your clandestine activities to me, a Russian officer?" he asked, assuming an expression of severity.

The Englishman grinned. "No. I saw what you did at the river. You don't want your own people to know that you are not dead, do you?"

His worst fears realised, Borokov's hand curled around his revolver. "I have a good mind to kill you just for that, you prying son of an Angliski whore!"

"That would not be a good idea," the soldier retorted. "You are outside Russian territory. Here *our* influence prevails. To have an English escort could be a safeguard for you."

"So that you could hand me over to the nearest English post?"

The Englishman laughed. "Have you any idea how far the nearest English post is from here?"

Weighing that silently, Borokov saw that what the man suggested sounded not unreasonable. To travel through these murderous mountains without being detected would not be easy, especially for an indifferent climber. One way and another, he would certainly be better off with an English guide. An idea occurred to him.

"Listen," he said, his heart thumping, "as long as you behave you have nothing to fear from me. I do not wish to harm you, why should I? After all, we are only rivals, not enemies. Men who push pens in London and St. Petersburg and dictate policy are not the poor soldiers who have to fight in these murderous mountains. Why should we behave like two dogs after the same bone?"

The Englishman frowned, unsure of what was coming. "Well?"

"Do you know how to get to Srinagar?"

"Srinagar?" He looked surprised. "Why would a Russian soldier want to get to Srinagar?"

"For three reasons—I, me and myself! I have nothing more to do with the Russian Army. As far as they are concerned, I am dead."

The soldier speculated, his expression wary. High altitudes addled the brains of those unused to mountains and the Rusky looked extremely unwell; could it be that he was losing his mind?

"You have business in Srinagar?"

"Yes. Personal business. I go purely as a civilian."

Never before having met a Russian soldier, the Englishman was uncertain how to tackle the situation. He had been trained in solid blacks and whites; he had no idea how to deal with in-between grey. It could be a trick, of course; he had been warned never to trust a Russian, *any* Russian. On the other hand, if rebuffed, the man could turn violent. Having already witnessed the theatrically staged suicide—proof of the man's tottering mental balance—he decided to humour him.

"Very well," he said, "but if this is merely a ploy to reach Kashmir and make trouble . . ."

"It is not a ploy, I promise." Borokov smiled his most winning smile and extended his hand. "Mikhail Borokov, erstwhile Colonel in the Russian Imperial Guards—or do you know that already?"

The soldier started. No, he had not known the name of the officer he had been watching for days. He had heard of Mikhail Borokov, naturally— General Smirnoff's stooge who had made mischief in Hunza. Dismayed by the man's identity, he was even more at a loss. After brief hesitation, however, he reluctantly extended his own hand. "Lieutenant David Wyncliffe. Queens Dragoon Guards."

Wyncliffe!

Borokov was stunned. "Wyncliffe? *Graham* Wyncliffe's son?"

David nodded.

Borokov was beside himself with excitement. Oh sweet Lord—was there no end to his good fortune today? "It was your father who discovered the Yasmina!"

"My father?" It was David's turn to look stunned. "How in heaven's name do you deduce that?"

Possessed by the sheer joy of the moment, Borokov laughed. "Happenstance, my friend, sheer *happenstance.* I had thought that my stars had deserted me, but they have not. Those binoculars . . . I saw them in Hunza with my own eyes after the execution!"

"What binoculars?" Sure now that the altitude was playing tricks with the Russian's brain, David was again nervous.

Borokov contained his elation. "Your father's. His initials were on the pair the boy stole from him near the Yasmina, the boy who was executed. Safdar Ali showed them to me. It was not Jeremy Butterfield who discovered the pass, it was your father."

David sat down heavily. He was dumbfounded by what the man said, not sure that he believed any of it. "You knew of my father?"

"No."

"Then how did you manage to guess that the initials were his?"

"I didn't. I have a contact in India who did."

"Who?"

Borokov shook his head. "Even in this insane game we play, there are some rules that must be honoured. I cannot reveal my source."

He now regretted having cursed Anderson and withheld funds for his expedition. Had it not been for Anderson he would never have heard of Graham Wyncliffe nor, indeed, of his daughter. He had written to Anderson about the binoculars on his way back from Hunza. Having known the dead archaeologist and his itinerary, Anderson had identified the initials easily. The poor old sod had done his best to get those papers from the Wyncliffe girl; it was not his fault that she had cunningly kept them from him, then married and moved to Srinagar.

Another idea suddenly flashed through Borokov's mind. No, not an idea—an inspiration! It made this blessed Angliski seem like manna cast down from heaven, an angel descended. It was no longer of any relevance to him who had discovered the Yasmina, or even where the papers might be. The sudden flash had come so unexpectedly, with such little warning, that it produced a wrench in his guts and he clutched at his stomach.

"Colonel Borokov?" Alarmed, David snapped out of his daze. "Are you ill?"

Eyes shut tight, Borokov sat himself down carefully, lowered his head between his knees and inhaled deeply. Presently the spasm passed and he breathed normally. "No, I am not ill." He straightened with slow care. "On the contrary, I have never felt better in my life. On reflection I find that there is no need for you to take me to Srinagar after all."

"Oh?"

"You will take me instead to the Yasmina."

David gasped, now totally convinced of the man's insanity. "How on earth can I?" he cried. "I haven't the faintest clue where the damn pass is! Besides, why should I?"

Borokov appeared not to hear him. Glacially composed, he walked up to where David sat and stood facing him. "According to the obituary in your London *Times,* your father's body was discovered on the Biafo. The geologist, Bingham, testified that they were two marches out of Ashkole when Graham Wyncliffe separated from the rest of the team. Given half a march more considering the difficulties of the glacier, we could pinpoint the Yasmina within a manageable radius."

"Difficulties? Manageable radius?" David started to laugh. "Colonel Borokov, I see that you are not a mountaineer and have not the faintest notion of the region. If you had, you would tremble at the mere mention of it. No one who has not been there can even begin to conceive of the size of the glaciers or the frequency and depth of their crevasses. Good God, Colonel, these glaciers are at the core of the greatest, most pitiless, most malignant mountain system on our planet! Even if I knew how to get there, which I do not, to attempt it would be certain suicide!"

"Nevertheless, that is where we will go," Borokov said calmly. "If you are half as adept as your father, as a guide you will serve my needs perfectly, especially since I can never hope to find another. Tomorrow morning we will proceed to the nearest Khirgiz encampment to assemble porters, pack beasts, food and equipment. The Yasmina, naturally, will not be mentioned." He smiled faintly. "Considering that it was your father who found the pass, does not the irony of our adventure strike you as truly poetic?"

It did not! If anything, it struck David as truly terrifying, for he saw that the Russian was in deadly earnest. In his madness he had lost all touch with reality. He spoke calmly enough but his eyes shone with a fervour that was almost maniacal.

"I may be Graham Wyncliffe's son and a good mountaineer," David said, in a frantic bid to make the lunatic see reason, "but I am also a soldier in Her Britannic Majesty's armed forces. To conspire with a Russian officer and trespass across restricted territory would be an act of treason."

"On the contrary, it would be an act of patriotism that could win you a medal." At his bewilderment Borokov's smile broadened. "We will avoid the towns and restrict ourselves to unbeaten paths. We will both travel as we are, dressed as Khirgiz nomads. Naturally, you will do the talking when we make our purchases."

"No!" Horribly alarmed, David stood up and his quivering jaw clamped down in a stubborn line. "I'm sorry but I simply *cannot* afford to risk my life, your life and my career by participating in this . . . this preposterous escapade."

"You cannot afford not to, Lieutenant Wyncliffe," Borokov said gently. "As I said, my motives are personal, not political. I should also point out that your participation is asked for not as a favour but as a soldier's duty and part of a fair exchange."

"Fair exchange for what?"

"For Alexei Smirnoff's plans to capture the Yasmina."

*I*t was the time known in Kashmir as *ador,* when the valley had thirteen days of rain. The pervasive scents of wet earth and sweet musk melons enriched the air. The ruby red flowers of the pomegranate, the last of the summer fruit to ripen, had blossomed and dropped; soon the trees would be ready for the plucking.

In the long, punitive days since Emma had found her father's papers, much had fallen into place; what remained mattered little. Something had been terribly wrong from the beginning; it was just that she had not seen it. Blinded by vanity, stupidly and to her own satisfaction she had explained the inexplicable. Damien had once accused her of valuing herself too little. In ascribing to him motives that flattered her own worth she now saw that she had valued herself too much.

She could never show her face again to Geoffrey Charlton, but yes, he had been right; she did desperately need a friend!

Damien had been aware of her father's discovery before he had married her, before he had even come to Delhi. The careful baiting of the trap and its inexorable closure—all were according to plan, an overture to a predetermined composition orchestrated to perfection. And in executing his plan he had taken away everything from her, her confidence, her self-respect, the very foundation on which she had so diffidently and precariously balanced her future.

Damien had used her. He had been using her all along.

Crushed by the very callousness of the conspiracy, Emma simply could not absorb it. Thoughts trapped inside a careening brain fluttered like moths against a mesh. With each passing day the flux of emotions thickened and deepened and the pain was intolerable, as if from a physical assault. Now, finally, came the last act of self-destruction, the quickening of memories she dreaded.

She started to re-live everything that reason told her to forget, each remembrance a pitiless incision into the centre of her being. Fragmented images crowded her mind like reflections in shards of a broken mirror. She remembered the interludes they had shared, such as they were, the promise of closeness, the nascent understanding of eloquent silences and exchanged glances, the trembling hopes she had encouraged herself to build secretly. The night of the wedding.

Her life dissolved further.

Forcing the fulcrum of her natural sense of balance back into place, she fought hard to regain her equilibrium. Each day she detached herself further, sieving rampant feelings, watching her own disintegration from an ever-increasing distance. By the time Damien returned, she had rectified the tilt of her world. The insulation was again in place, a sheet of hard winter ice across a heaving, restless pond.

He returned late one night. From behind locked doors, Emma heard him move about in the adjoining apartment. An hour later came the sound she awaited—the creak of a floorboard on the landing. He was going down to his father's apartment! Giving him a start of half an hour, she followed.

It was time for a confrontation.

She entered boldly through the unlocked corridor. The door to Edward Granville's apartment was open. Strengthened by a nerveless inner calm, she walked in. Damien stood by the desk; both its flaps were unlocked and some of the drawers had been extracted from their slots. A lamp, its flame high, was positioned on the table. There were piles of folders scattered on the floor.

Bathed in shadow, she leant against a wall to watch. He bent down over the bottom drawer and groped within with quick, anxious movements. She heard him mutter something, an oath, then watched him yank the drawer out and turn it upside down on the desk. It was as he finished scrambling within the contents and stood staring at them in angry incomprehension that she finally spoke.

"Is this what you are looking for?"

He spun around and in the ghostly silence she heard the release of held breath. Strolling up to the desk, she placed something on it: a Buddhist prayer-wheel. It was of brass and beautifully engraved. Removing the lid, she spilled the contents onto the desk, surprised that her legs should be so steady, her voice so level and her cold fingers without even a tremble.

He stared at the tangled web of paper strips on the desk but did not reach for them.

"I found the papers, Damien, the Yasmina papers."

He remained stock still and silent, momentarily nonplussed.

"The papers belonged to my father. I have a right to them." She pulled out the chair and sat down. "Initially the ball of tightly curled strips meant nothing to me, but then I recognised the container whose shape they had assumed."

His eyes were watchful but he still made no comment.

"You are a very determined man, Damien. You came to Delhi for the sole purpose of securing my father's papers. Your efforts are to be commended." She leaned back, her gaze not leaving his face. "The papers were concealed in this prayer-wheel, Jeremy Butterfield's prayer-wheel. It was in his carpet bag delivered to us by . . ." She paused and smiled a little. "But then you already know about that, don't you?"

She waited for him to speak, but he merely continued to watch with steady interest. If his persisting silence was meant to unnerve her she refused to let it.

"You found the papers easily enough in my study because you knew exactly where they were hidden. You had plenty of time to look for the carpet bag in the trunk. Having found it, you removed the papers and left the wheel where it was. Is that not what happened?"

"You tell me." He spoke for the first time. "After all, you seem to be the one with all the answers."

It was neither a denial nor an admission. Observing her from afar, he leaned back against the desk, crossed his arms and waited.

"Not all, Damien, not yet, but most of them. To return to your devices in Delhi—you arranged the little charade at the gaming-house because blackmail was your only option, the only way you could get to me and through me to these papers. You were right, Damien." She laughed, but the humour tasted sour on her tongue.

He seemed about to speak again. She cut him off with a gesture.

"No trite excuses, Damien, please no more lies. Don't insult my intelligence more than you already have." She interlaced her fingers to keep them from shaking. "You knew about our straitened circumstances, everybody did. You also knew that I would not accept your proposal unless forced to. Nevertheless, you were supremely confident of eventually getting what you wanted—and why not? The trap, after all, was irresistibly baited.

"You paid Highsmith to fix the game, to befuddle my brother with drugged drinks so that he would lose Khyber Kothi. Indeed, you were so certain of success that you even arranged for Sharifa and Rehmat to come to Delhi before you left Shalimar, which is how they arrived with such despatch. The study too was planned in advance to ensure that all my papers were in one room and easy to locate. You even spoke to Nazneen about me before you left."

"So?" A muscle twitched in his cheek. "Like everyone else, I too had heard of the waspish Emma Wyncliffe. *Unlike* everyone else, however, I rather looked forward to being stung."

She ignored the ill-timed flippancy. "I also know now precisely when you abstracted the papers from the wheel."

"Oh?" He lifted a quizzical eyebrow.

"The first time we were in Srinagar." She relieved her throat with a hard swallow. "Instead of going to the emporium to meet Jabbar Ali, you raced back to Shalimar to search my study in my absence—your first opportunity to do so. Lincoln confirms that you *did* return that morning, supposedly for a forgotten file. That is why you needed to take Toofan with you, the fastest horse in your stables." Her smile was as steely as her unrelenting eyes. "No wonder you were in such high spirits all the while—you had good cause to be!"

He reached for his pipe tucked into his belt, struck a match and lit it. "Neatly worked out and very plausible, I have to admit. Of course there is more, isn't there?"

"Yes, there is more." Claps of thunder bounced across the hills. She waited until the echoes subsided. "How or why my father's diary found its way into Jeremy Butterfield's prayer-wheel I have no idea, but it did. Prayer-wheels are what intelligence agents use to hide their secret papers."

"Are they now? Another of Charlton's tutorials?"

"No one else knew where the papers were concealed," she said, disdaining the diversion, "how did you?"

"You mean, with all your exceptional powers of deduction you haven't worked that one out yet?"

"Perhaps because the powers are not exceptional enough!" She rubbed her eyes with the back of a trembling hand. Destabilised by his unshaken composure, her own threatened to slip. "Who *did* you steal these papers for, Damien—the Russians?"

"If that is what you choose to believe." He turned away and started to rearrange the disarrayed folders.

"What would *you* choose me to believe?" she cried. "That everything that I have said is untrue?"

"Why the devil should I choose what you should believe? That privilege is yours entirely."

She sparked with quick anger. "Just answer one question honestly—can you look me straight in the eye and swear that *none* of what I have said is true?"

He paused in what he was doing, turned and did exactly as she suggested, looked directly into her eyes without a blink.

"No."

One syllable, the coup d'état! She felt a sudden tearing grief, a pervasive sense of helplessness, but then with effort she steadied herself and the weakness passed.

"To get those papers you sold your soul, Damien," she said quietly, "and into the bargain, mine. If they were important enough for you to destroy my life, at least I have the right to know *why*."

She waited with agonising hope for some word of denial, some sign of outrage, hurt even, but there was none, only indifference.

"You have already worked out the reason. Frankly, I couldn't better that even if I wanted to." Turning his back on her again, he began to replace the drawers in their respective slots.

She stared at the arrogant back with flaring hate. "What you stole and kept from me was my father's dying testament," she said fiercely, "the record of the last week of his life. Had I not found it by accident I might never have seen it, might never have even *known* of it!"

"Yes." He swung around and for the first time his face showed expression. "You will have to believe me when I say that *that* I do most profoundly regret. The papers were to be returned to you."

"Once copies had been delivered to the Russians?"

"Since you were not even aware of their existence," he said, not answering her question, "I had blithely assumed that you would not miss them."

"You tried to ensure that I never did become aware of their existence—why else would Suraj Singh lie about these floors?"

"Yes, he lied on my instructions, but I see now that I underestimated both your quest for knowledge and, indeed, your proficiency with a screwdriver."

"What I was looking for . . ." she began and then stopped. How cleverly he tried to divert the guilt and the thrust of the argument! What she had looked for was immaterial, what she had found was not! Her fury blazed higher. "I had a right to the last words my father left—how *dare* you steal away my inheritance!"

"I dared because I had to." His tone was flat. "I can say nothing more in my defence, Emma, take it or leave it. Nevertheless, I do owe you an apology, a monumental apology. I was . . ."

"An apology? Is that *all* you owe me?" She was outraged. "After driving heartless bargains with helpless debtors, you have the gall to settle your own debts so cheaply?"

"There is a great deal at stake. . . ."

"For you but not for my father? Why should it be concealed that the Yasmina was *his* discovery? Why should Geoffrey Charlton not publish that it was Graham Wyncliffe who . . ."

She did not see him move but suddenly he had her arm in a vice and the words died in her throat. "Is that your intention," he asked softly, "to give the papers to Charlton?"

"That alarms you, doesn't it!" Her skin erupted with fear but she hid it behind a taunt. "You know that once he exposes you, you will be arrested, tried as a traitor and sent to jail—and Shalimar will no longer be yours."

He released her arm with a jerk and walked to the window. A cold, steady rain still fell outside leaving wet, glistening snakes on the glass. He stared at them for a moment. "I leave for Gulmarg tomorrow," he announced abruptly. "When I return, you will have your explanations."

Explanations, apologies—was that all it took to repair a broken marriage, a broken life? Sick with disillusion, she gave him a last look of despair. How could she ever have thought that she loved him, that she would want to make him love her? He had cheated her of everything she cherished, left her pitifully diminished in her own eyes. Unable to grapple with the agonising imponderables that had taken over her life, all at once she was defeated.

"When you return," she said, "I will not be here."

Sweeping the paper strips back into the prayer-wheel, she appropriated it, turned and walked out of the room. He did not try to stop her.

CHAPTER

17

Crouched under the inadequate shelter of a rocky ledge below the snout of a glacier, David sat skinning a pair of rabbits. He scanned the bleak, icy landscape around him with little enthusiasm. At more than fifteen thousand feet the cold was awesome.

In this apology of an encampment their inadequate tents were buried deep in soft, fresh snow. With forty-five degrees of frost under canvas, lashing blizzards and vicious winds, it was impossible to be warm. They slept in layers of woollen underwear, sheepskin coats, fur boots, fur cap and muffs purchased by Borokov at exhorbitant prices from a Khirgiz encampment. To assemble men, mules and provisions they had bargained furiously, bribed outrageously and told lies. The name of the Yasmina was not even whispered by mistake.

Once in Sinkiang in the jurisdiction of the Amban of Yarkand, they had headed for the peaceful valley of the Sariqol through which flowed the Yarkand river. Snuggled serenely in the green glens, yellow meadows and shady leas were tidy mud houses with neat wooden fences. The cattle were healthy, the orchards rich and the hills redolent of the sweet scent of lavender. Wide fields heavy with barley, wheat, corn and lazily grazing sheep under a golden haze of sun completed the picture of pastoral perfection. David had spent time here earlier building bridges with the local people and the welcome they received was warm, the hospitality generous. Chinese military patrols were frequent, but since the Sariqolis hated the Chinese there was no danger of betrayal.

That, sadly, had been days ago. Now with the pastoral idyll over, they were again in the real world trudging precariously and wearily across grim, gruesome terrain in pitilessly variable weather. The region they negotiated was uncharted. There were no maps, the tracks were haphazard and hazardous and they could still be surprised by a patrol. The lesser known trails and unbeaten paths that Borokov insisted they follow were positive death traps.

Moreover, on the ascents and descents the sudden changes of temperature were physically devastating. If at two in the afternoon up on a summit they stood shivering in sub-arctic weather, three hours later they sweltered at ninety-six degrees Fahrenheit and through the rarefied air the fierce sun caused fearful burns on the skin. It was impossible to regulate clothing. One either boiled and suffocated or froze and went blue.

Borokov had been the first to succumb to the wild fluctuations of temperature. Stricken with fever, vomiting and blinding headaches, he lay in his tent only half conscious and several of the porters had followed suit. With their stocks of fuel desperately low, they were reduced to eating foul-tasting, half-cooked meat while the numbing cold bit deep into the spirit.

A hoarse shout sounded from Borokov's tent. David scrambled to his feet and hurried to answer the summons. He crawled in through deep snow, brushing crusted flakes off his face. Curled in a corner and burning with fever, the Russian lay huddled beneath a mountain of clothing shivering convulsively. His breathing was worse than before. His crippled lungs rasped with the effort of inhalation and his lips were blue. Weakly, he asked for water. As David held the glacial cup to his lips, he saw that the man's forehead was speckled with frozen globules of sweat and his eyes, red and fiery, were unable to focus.

"How many more miles?" It was a question Borokov asked a hundred times a day and David's glum response was always the same.

"Many."

"We will get there. We *must*. I need to sleep well tonight, then we can press on in the morning."

"I know these mountains, Colonel Borokov, you don't." David made yet another attempt at persuasion. "Many of our porters have abandoned us. We have only three mules left and we are almost out of fuel and food. We cannot go on."

In a burst of energy Borokov jerked up, grabbed his collar and clawed at his throat. "You do not understand, Angliski," he croaked, "we *can* go on, we *must*!" He fell back panting.

The man, David could see, was desperately sick. Let alone the highest, most treacherous glaciers in the world, he would not be able to negotiate the slope up to the next pass. He could also see that Borokov was demented, past logical thought. With the taste of fear again strong in his throat, once more David fell silent.

He fed the stricken man a tablet from their medical pack and watched as he slipped into restless sleep. Every once in a while Borokov broke into incomprehensible mumblings as he thrashed about in his private nightmares. David listened carefully in case he mentioned Smirnoff, but he did not. All he deciphered was one word repeated frequently: *zolata.* It was the Russian word for "gold."

Not knowing what to do, David sat and watched Borokov in helpless silence. To abandon the Russian to his fate in this icy inferno was unthinkable. Apart from the fact that he dared not lose sight of him, it was simply not done. The information Borokov claimed to possess could be the fantasy of a lunatic—but it could also be true. Somehow he had to cajole the Russian into revealing what he knew before time ran out altogether; but for the moment he was trapped.

Crawling out of the tent, David dispiritedly joined the few remaining porters who sat trying in vain to stoke a dying fire. He desperately needed help—but from whom, where?

If it had been bad so far, David knew that ahead it was worse. There were more semi-frozen rivers to cross over glassy stones, always a step away from death. At each crossing the pack beasts would be unloaded and the baggage carried manually. On the high slopes there were few footholds. Animals would have to be held on to for dear life; it was impossible to ride. Also, they were now dangerously close to the Hunza hunting grounds. Even in these godforsaken wilds, news had a habit of travelling fast. They could be attacked and killed long before they reached the next slope, let alone their mythical destination.

Borokov's dream of the Yasmina was hopeless!

All the same, David could not help feeling a curious compassion for the haunted man within whom burned such an unquenchable fire. Despite everything, the Russian's courage and indomitable inner strength had to be admired. Whatever private demons he harboured, it was they who gave him the ferocious will to carry on, to make a mockery of the limitations of his suffering body.

Borokov called out again and this time he was awake. Incredibly enough, he seemed better. His eyes were clear and well focussed and his voice sounded strong. Struggling up into a sitting position, he asked for something to eat and David poured out a tin mug of half-frozen brick tea. Borokov grimaced but drank thirstily and ate a few mouthfuls of the nourishing mulch before pushing the mug away. He lay back, closed his eyes and breathed in even cadences.

"You are right," he said without opening his eyes. "I am too sick to continue. We cannot go on."

Too surprised to speak, David gasped out a cloud of frozen air.

"We will turn back tomorrow," Borokov added. "Tonight I would like to sleep long and well to build up strength for the return."

Weak with relief at the eleventh-hour deliverance, David mopped the sick man's brow. "You have made the right decision, Colonel. I will make sure that your sleep tonight remains undisturbed."

Borokov opened his eyes. They were distant and dreamy. "The gods have spoken," he said sadly. "The gold is not for me after all."

"Gold? Where?"

"In the Yasmina."

David almost laughed, wondering if the man was raving once again. But the Russian's eyes were filled with tears.

"There is no gold in the Yasmina," David said kindly.

Borokov seemed not to hear. Putting his hand under his layers of clothing, he pulled out his nugget and held it up in silent triumph.

"This came from the Yasmina?" David asked.

"Yes." In the deepening dark, the whites of his eyes glistened. "Now it will belong to Smirnoff."

David was instantly alert. "Smirnoff is after this . . . this alleged gold?"

Borokov did not reply. He lay back again and closed his eyes. Outside, a mule hee-hawed and the men fought loudly over their frugal pickings, but he did not hear them. His lips were curved in a thin smile and his thoughts were a lifetime away.

He had heard of Nain Singh and Tibetan gold years ago from Theo Anderson when they had first met in Baku. It had been a convivial evening and Anderson had been very drunk. Centuries ago, Anderson said, Herodotus had written about veins of Himalayan gold and the enormous rodents that dug it out of the mountains. Nain Singh, a Survey of India agent, had confirmed the existence of huge ingots in the Tibetan gold fields, some weighing as much as two pounds. The field was so productive, he had reported, that even in winter they employed six thousand miners and paid them thirty rupees for each ounce of gold dust mined. The ingots, however, were returned to the soil in the belief that they contained life.

According to the miners, Anderson had said, there was only one other gold vein of comparable richness in the Himalayas, and that was in the Yasmina Pass.

Borokov had been fascinated but also sceptical. Whatever doubts he might have had, however, were eliminated the day Safdar Ali had pressed the shapeless lump of yellow metal into his palm. The Hunzakut, he knew, panned gold dust from the river in the Hunza gorge; why then should there also not be gold in the Yasmina? On his next visit to St. Petersburg he had gone to the library and read a Russian translation of Nain Singh's report as published in the Royal Geographical Society journal in London. Even now, every detail of the report remained etched in his memory. Indeed, it was his dream of the Yasmina gold that had driven him on, given his life substance, purpose, direction.

Each time his resolve slipped, he remembered his early destitution in Kharkov, his demeaning childhood in foster homes cleaning pigsties and chicken runs, feeding off cheese rind and half-cooked offal. The memory of those days still haunted him, filled him with revulsion. It had forced him to grovel before Alexei because without Alexei's help his dream was dust and Yasmina's gold could just as well be on the moon.

"Listen!" Borokov sat up struggling, his lips blue with the cold. He pulled David closer and put his mouth against his ear. With their film of ice, his cheeks had gone rigid. "About Alexei Smirnoff . . ."

"Yes?"

"You must stop him!"

"I?" David's heart hammered in his ears. "H-how?"

"Write it down," Borokov hissed, "write it all down, every word." As David continued to gape, he flailed his arms angrily. "Hurry, hurry . . . write, damn you, *write*!"

Mutton-fingered with the cold, David fumbled frantically inside his voluminous coat to grab his notebook and pencil. Forcing himself into calmness to conserve his limited strength, Borokov started to talk. He spoke quickly and softly and without emotion. Several times the pencil fell from David's frozen fingers, but clenching his teeth he carried on. When the Russian was done, he fell back, all his strength gone.

"We will make an early start tomorrow," David said, alive with new energy. "The sooner we reach Simla the better."

Borokov made no response. He was already asleep.

Outside, the temperature had dropped further and the cold was breathtaking; in his euphoric daze, David hardly noticed. Burying his face deep into his sheepskin, he squatted by the exhausted embers around which men and beasts huddled, and to the men's amazement, recklessly piled an armful of mule-dung cakes onto the dying licks of flame. He put on a pot of snow and when it had melted tossed in the rabbit meat. It would take hours for the water to boil and the meat would remain inedible, but no matter; by the infinite grace of the Lord their nightmare was almost over.

As he sat staring into the flames, he thought again of what Borokov had told him about his father. In the beginning he had been uncertain, but eventually, for a very good reason, he had dismissed Borokov's information as false. If it were true that his father had discovered the Yasmina, despite the tension between them, Emma would have told him. It was as simple as that.

After he had eaten, he crawled into his own miserable little ice-bound tent. The vile taste of half-raw rabbit flesh fouled his mouth and made his stomach heave. He felt stiff, cold and uncomfortable, but his spirits were high. Once they were back in Simla, he would turn Borokov over to the Department and wash his hands of the ghastly affair. His relief after weeks of corroding tension was so intense that he fell asleep almost instantly. He did not open his eyes again until bright light filtered through the canvas and forced him awake. Shocking the drowse out of his eyes with a handful of snow and rinsing out his rancid mouth with another fistful, he hurried out to tend to his companion.

The tent was gone; so also was the Russian.

He had left, the porters informed him, before dawn with one mule, a small pack, a walking stick, his box of instruments and the remains of the half-cooked rabbit. He had paid them their dues, thanked them for their efforts and told them he would not be returning.

The mad Russian had set off alone in search of his gold!

*G*oing through the motions of packing, Emma sat in her bedroom swamped by boxes and cabin trunks. Her hands moved mechanically, her mind unaware of what they did. Surveying the unintelligible mess, not knowing what to do next, she banged the lid of a trunk, sat down on it, and crippled with heartache hugged her knees.

Why had Damien done this to her? It was an inane question; she knew why.

A moment later Sharifa came in with a calling card and Emma congealed; Geoffrey Charlton at this hour of the morning? Despite her show of bravado to Damien, she dreaded the prospect of facing Geoffrey Charlton. She had already written to Mrs. Bicknell regretting her inability to join them for tea. Her panicked reaction now was to return the card, make some excuse and turn him away. But then on the reverse of the card she noticed his scribbled message: "I need to see you *urgently* and in private."

What urgent tidings did he bring that demanded privacy? What else had he unearthed about Damien's shamefully shady life?

With valiant effort, she pulled herself together, reminding herself that Damien's sins coming home to roost were no longer her concern. Indeed, if they did, it would be no more than he deserved. She washed her face, brushed her hair and changed into a fresh muslin frock. Touching her waxen cheeks with rouge, she dabbed perfume behind her ears, shut the door on the litter of boxes and ordered the parlour fire to be revived. When he walked in a few moments later, she faced him with perfect equanimity.

"Why, Mr. Charlton, how nice of you to call," she said pleasantly. "Please do be seated. Tell me, what brings you here so early in the day and requires the privacy of my sitting room?"

"To intrude on you seems to have become a habit with me," Charlton replied, containing his apology in a rueful smile. "Were not the matter sufficiently urgent to warrant the intrusion, I would not have disturbed you." He took a seat, smoothed his hair and coughed behind a hand. "Urgent and, of course, confidential."

"Oh?" Emma clung to her own smile. "In that case perhaps we should have some refreshments while we discuss it." Summoning Sharifa, she ordered a tray. Dispensing coffee and cakes would help to keep her hands conveniently active.

Charlton wasted no time in small talk.

"As I mentioned to you once before, Mrs. Granville, last autumn I was in St. Petersburg at the same time as your husband."

"So you did, Mr. Charlton."

"We happened to meet at the Yacht Club where I was a guest of our military attaché. Your husband was dining with some high-ranking Russian Army officers. They were deep in conversation. In Russian, of course. This was, I learned, not his first trip to Russia. Having been in Kashmir I knew Damien Granville by reputation, of course, but now I was genuinely intrigued. How was this Englishman, I asked myself, so much at home in Russian company? More to the point, for what purpose?"

"My husband does belong to both countries," Emma forced herself to intone dutifully, wondering why she should still consider it necessary to devise alibis, "and he does have business connections in Russia."

"Perhaps not only business connections, Mrs. Granville." His tone was casual, even lazy, but his eyes were not. "I learned subsequently from an obliging waiter that much of the conversation at their table that night was to do with one Colonel Mikhail Borokov. Your husband, it appeared, was most keen to make his acquaintance. Perhaps you remember the Colonel's name from some of my reports in the *Sentinel*?"

Emma widened her smile. "Oh dear, are you about to tell me again that my husband is a Russian spy?"

He rose, stood with an elbow balanced on the mantelpiece and sidestepped the question.

"In Delhi earlier this year," he continued, "when I discovered that your husband was also in station, I set about learning more about him. It was then that through my sources in the army I heard about Edward Granville, his extraordinary wife and how he came to acquire this"—he waved his arms at the window—"splendid estate in Kashmir. As for your husband's reasons for being in Delhi . . ."

He paused and, briefly, so did Emma's breath.

". . . but I fear that I put the cart before the horse. I beg of you to bear with me a moment. Now that you are, presumably, familiar with the background as reported in the press, I need to regress somewhat. To Jeremy Butterfield, in fact, the dead agent I mentioned to you the other day."

The coffee arrived and Emma was grateful that she had ordered it. As she poured, her hand shook. Charlton appeared not to notice.

"You see, Mrs. Granville," Charlton resumed when the cups and petit-fours had been dispensed, "I was never entirely satisfied with the lame explanations offered by the Intelligence Department for the loss of Butterfield's papers—as you must have gathered from my dispatches."

"Sugar?" Emma asked. "Two lumps if I recall."

"Yes, thank you. Even though the air was thick with rumour when I was in Simla, I found that there prevailed a curious conspiracy of silence in the Department. Lips were buttoned, hatches firmly battened down, and I was fobbed off with evasions. Since the papers had been destroyed in the raid, the Department maintained, Butterfield's claim about the Yasmina was dubious. Nor was there an iota of truth, they insisted, in the rumour that any maps he might have had were in Russian hands, or likely to be, et cetera, et cetera."

He laughed and resumed his seat. "Have you ever been to Simla in the Season, Mrs. Granville?"

"No."

"Well, it's an unreal *Alice Through the Looking-Glass* kind of Wonderland populated by Cheshire Cats and Mad Hatters. The universal goal—fortunately for me, as it happens—is to acquire secrets, anyone's, and then share them with the true zeal of a socialist." He gave her a deep look. "Tell me, Mrs. Granville, does the name Lal Bahadur mean anything to you?"

It did not. She shook her head.

"Lal Bahadur was the Gurkha who accompanied Jeremy Butterfield on that last mission, the man who carried his final message back to the Department. Curiously enough, I found that Bahadur, like the Cheshire Cat, had since vanished. Why? Nobody could say. Where? Nobody would say. Through friends I eventually tracked him down to Cawnpore, to the Ordnance factory, where he had been quietly transferred. Bahadur was cautious but being a simple, honest man, not a very good liar. What I eventually managed to extract from him was, to put it mildly, staggering." He drained his cup and replaced it on the table. "The subject to which I must now refer will undoubtedly refresh your grief, but since it cannot be avoided I hope you will forgive me once again."

Emma sat still, her face carefully blank.

"You see, Mrs. Granville, it was not some anonymous tribesmen who found and buried your father's body on the Biafo glacier, it was Jeremy Butterfield."

Emma paled, but with remarkable self-control showed no other reaction. Now that she saw the connection, a hundred anguished questions came to mind, but some canny instinct told her that she must not ask them, not until she had heard everything.

"Your father's name was suppressed for the same reason that Butterfield's findings were denied: those elusive papers. To admit that the Yasmina had been located meant to admit also that the papers were missing. That was unthinkable. There would be a national outcry and the government would be crucified. So in their usual clod-hopping fashion, Simla chose instead to stonewall."

The nightmare, Emma saw, was about to intensify. Refusing to let the prospect cloud her perceptions, she forcibly restrained her personal anguish and, like a good hostess, refreshed Charlton's cup. He stirred the coffee and sipped appreciatively.

"Lal Bahadur confirms that with your father's body Butterfield also found his notebook. The Gurkha is unaware of its contents but says that when Butterfield read it, he was hugely excited and disappeared with his instruments. On his return he immediately despatched Bahadur back to Simla with his wooden chest and an urgent message. Bahadur has no idea of the rest." He leaned forward. "It was your father who discovered the Yasmina Pass, Mrs. Granville, and Butterfield confirmed his findings. Unfortunately for Butterfield, he was seen near the Yasmina by Safdar Ali's assassins, stalked and finally killed." His eyes bored deep into hers. "His papers, however, survived that raid."

In the silence that followed, Emma rose and unhurriedly picked up from the table the crochet tablemats she was in the process of making. The coffeepot was empty and she badly needed something to hide the tremble of her hands. The gaps in the mosaic of her information were being filled in too swiftly to be assimilated.

"Simla maintains that Butterfield had his papers in the carpet bag and that the raiders destroyed them." Tucking his thumbs in the armholes of his waistcoat, Charlton eased back. "Well aware of how agents operate, I knew that this was poppycock. What I unearthed later in Yarkand and Leh confirmed it."

He again stood up, walked to the hearth and reached for the poker to stoke the fire even though it blazed perfectly.

"Still nervous of involvement, the merchants who had travelled with Butterfield refused to talk to me. However, I had better luck with a garrulous muleteer who, when offered the lubricant that oils the human tongue best,"—he rubbed a forefinger and thumb together—"talked most willingly. The Muslim merchants, he said, had refused to touch 'Rasool Ahmed's' two infidel possessions, a Hindu rosary and a prayer-wheel. Being a Hindu himself, he had had no such qualms when asked to pack them in the carpet bag. The rosary, he confessed cheerfully, he kept to give to his mother. What subsequently happened to the prayer-wheel he did not know." Laying his head back, Charlton stared up at the ceiling. "I daresay you know a great deal about prayer-wheels, Mrs. Granville?"

Emma carefully dropped a stitch off her crochet-hook and took her time to retrieve it. "Yes, Mr. Charlton. My father specialised in their study."

"Ah, then you will recall what I told you the other day at the Takht-e-Suleiman, that like rosaries, prayer-wheels too have special significance in intelligence work."

"Really? I'm sorry, I don't remember."

"Don't you, Mrs. Granville? No matter. We will come to that later. As I also mentioned that day, all tools of espionage manufactured in Dehra Doon bear special markings. Since the muleteer's mother had indignantly refused to accept a rosary with only a hundred beads, he was happy to make a few extra pice by selling it off to me." He dug a hand in his pocket, pulled out the rosary and offered it to her. "As you can see, the distinctive marks are here, near the tassel."

"I have no reason to doubt you, Mr. Charlton," Emma said, declining the offer. "I know how thorough your research always is. Anyway, what does all this have to do with me?"

"A great deal, I'm afraid—but first things first." He replaced the rosary and steepled his fingers under his chin. "In Leh, despite his recent purification in Mecca, when given the right lubricant the mullah's tongue wagged equally promptly. Yes, a prayer-wheel *had* been part of Rasool Ahmed's belongings, he admitted. Wanting only to be rid of it before he went on to Haj, he had consigned it and Butterfield's carpet bag—not to charity, as the Department maintains but to Buddhist monks on their way to Gaya via Delhi. Having some knowledge of English he had deciphered a Delhi address among Rasool Ahmed's papers attached to a name, probably scribbled by Butterfield himself." He unsteepled his fingers to brush a crumb off his lap. "The name and address, Mrs. Granville, were those of Graham Wyncliffe." He stopped. "Need I go on?"

"Why ever not, Mr. Charlton?" she asked, surprised at her sudden surge of confidence. "I am most anxious to hear the rest."

"You already know the rest, Mrs. Granville."

"Oh? And how do you calculate that, Mr. Charlton?"

"Despite your consistent and very credible air of innocence, none of what I have said is unknown to you. As a journalist, I have learned that far more eloquent than what people say is what they do *not* say—and you, Mrs. Granville, have been noticeably silent. And, I might add, surprisingly unsurprised."

Laying down her crochet-hook, Emma took a moment to study Geoffrey Charlton with dispassion. The smile was still silken, even winning, but the charm was tarnished. Beneath the skilfully cultivated veneer of modesty, she saw, burned the consuming, ruthless fires of ambition. She wondered now why she had not noticed them before.

"And now, Mrs. Granville, we return to Damien Granville's reasons for being in Delhi." The deep blue eyes were as cold as marbles. "Amazingly, my investigations exposed a most incredible string of coincidences. Individually, they meant little. Together, they opened an entirely new avenue of exploration that had not even occurred to me. Piecing together the information I now have, let us consider these coincidences in chronological order."

Splaying the fingers of a hand, he started to pick them off. "One, the prayer-wheel in which Butterfield hides the papers is delivered to Wyncliffe's daughter in Delhi. Two, Damien Granville, self-confessed Russophile and son of a notorious Russian spy, also takes up residence in Delhi. Three, Granville takes to frequenting a gaming-house where he plays cards with one David Wyncliffe who just happens to be the son of Graham Wyncliffe, secret discoverer of a pass badly wanted by Russia. Four, David Wyncliffe loses heavily, his house in fact, plunging the family into a desperate situation. However, all is not lost because, four, lo and behold the gambling debt is generously cancelled and, five, Damien Granville marries Graham Wyncliffe's daughter."

He lowered his hand and again flashed even, white teeth. Emma was astonished that she could have ever thought that sly, feral smile boyish!

"*Quod erat demonstrandum,* would you not agree, Mrs. Granville?"

With resuscitated courage, she not only grasped the offensive but actually managed to evince amusement. "Are you asking me to believe, Mr. Charlton, that whereas you claim to know all these alleged facts and coincidences, the Intelligence Department does not?"

"The Department!" He dismissed them with a grimace of contempt. "A bunch of myopic bureaucrats governed by incomprehensible sub-clauses. They are behemoths, Mrs. Granville. They move in tandem, slowly, lugubriously, with lunatic caution, particularly when trapped in a mesh of lies and facing nasty publicity. I, on the other hand, travel light, alone, quietly and swiftly."

"Well, perhaps *too* swiftly, Mr. Charlton," Emma retorted, angered by his arrogance. "Even assuming that your fairy tale has the slightest connection with reality, how did my husband discover that the alleged papers were in this mythical prayer-wheel, pray?" It was a question she had asked Damien, a question to which she still had no answer.

"Probably the same way that I did," he said, his gaze steady on her face.

"Probably?" Emma laughed. "You mean there is actually something about which you are still unsure?"

"I mention that as one probability."

"And the other?"

"That he learned about the papers from you."

She was startled into speechlessness.

He sprang up to walk up and down the parlour. "Forgive me, Mrs. Granville, but I can think of no tactful way to say this. It was well known in Delhi that you were articulate and intelligent but with few prospects of marriage. With little money, a sick mother and a wayward brother on your hands, you jumped at what Granville offered—an end to spinsterhood, financial security, and, into the bargain, cancellation of your brother's debt." He coughed delicately. "In exchange for the papers, of course."

"I see." She was too shocked even for anger. "So, it was *after* you had given your own imaginative interpretation to these alleged coincidences that you decided to seek me out through the kind offices of Mrs. Hathaway and beg me to accept you as a friend?"

He flushed. "Your husband is a traitor who intends to sell the papers to a potential enemy," he snapped. "To expose treachery one uses whatever means happen to be at one's disposal."

"And your own motives, Mr. Charlton, are they purely patriotic?"

"As I once told you, I am a journalist and a realist. I neither profess nor pretend patriotism. Your father was British, with loyalty to Britain. His papers . . ."

"My father was a scholar, an international citizen, with no time for narrow parochialism."

"Nevertheless, what he discovered belongs to Britain, Mrs. Granville, and the British public deserves to know about it."

"Ah, so you wish to acquire and publish the papers merely as a service to the nation, is that it?"

"No. I am not an altruist either. To be the first to publish the Yasmina papers would be a scoop any journalist would kill for."

"Since you appear convinced that what you have discovered is the truth, why then have you not published it yet?"

"For two very good reasons. First, without documentary proof of the

Yasmina, I would be laughed out of court. And second," his face shone with triumph, a triumph he now saw no reason to hide, "it was only last night that I finally confirmed, beyond any reasonable doubt, that your husband is already involved in negotiations with the Russians for the Yasmina papers."

There was a terrible ring of truth in his tone. He was, Emma knew, too shrewd a journalist to make so confident an assertion without proof. If she remained expressionless it was only because sheer pride gave her the strength not to expose her sense of shock to this hateful man.

"May I ask how and from whom you have managed to procure this alleged confirmation?"

"By means too arduous and too complex to bear enumeration, Mrs. Granville, and naturally I cannot reveal my source. Suffice it to say that if one knows how to provide the right triggers and suffers endless patient hearings, sooner or later most people can be induced to make unintended revelations." He added softly in a purr that was almost catlike, "I want those papers, Mrs. Granville."

She gave an involuntary laugh at the impudence. "Just like that, Mr. Charlton?"

"Oh no, not just like that. For a consideration, naturally."

"More lubrication?"

"If you like. The lubricant in this case would be that your husband's role in the affair and, indeed, your own will not be revealed, nor how I came to acquire the papers and from whom."

"And if I refuse?"

"Then you will both be exposed. Having brought disrepute to Kashmir, your husband will lose Shalimar and be expelled from the state. Stewart has enough powers to ensure that."

She chilled further but did not respond.

"Possesion of these papers is an act of theft, Mrs. Granville. To sell them to a hostile power is an act of high treason. Your husband will be arrested and undoubtedly convicted, as will his co-conspirators—Suraj Singh and the Ali brothers, Hyder and Jabbar, who have been his willing middlemen in Central Asia over many months. And, of course, yourself."

Emma stared at him in disbelief. Geoffrey Charlton had been stripping their lives bare with the help of Chloe Hathaway and her gossip-mongering friends in Delhi while enjoying her hospitality, soliciting her confidence and beguiling her with offers of friendship! She was outraged.

Rising to her feet, she pulled herself up and regarded him with open contempt. "I might once have considered you a friend, Mr. Charlton—and I am truly sorry to find that you are not—but I do not have those papers. Even if I did, you would be the last person to whom I would give them.

Now please leave my house and do not take the trouble to return. If you do, I will have you thrown out."

He breathed hard, eyes narrowed in anger. "Very well, Mrs. Granville. Walter Stewart signs the search warrant in the morning. The house you so proudly claim will be torn apart, room by room, and the papers found and confiscated. Until then, you yourself will remain confined to your apartment. Two guards from the Residency will be posted outside your door to ensure that you remain where you are. Others have instructions to search anyone trying to leave the premises." The bitter resentment he had been at such pains to suppress now exploded. "Why do you go to such self-destructive lengths to protect a man with whom you share no love? A man who bartered your life for political gain and won you at a gaming table?"

Her hand lashed out and the back of it struck him across the face with all the force she could muster. Taken by surprise, he clamped a palm to his mouth and cursed. Quick as lightning, she ran to the table and retrieved her Colt from a drawer.

"Get out, Mr. Charlton," she said quietly, "or I promise I will put a bullet through your right kneecap. I am a good shot, I am not likely to miss."

He started to back away. "This is not the end, Mrs. Granville, just the beginning," he spat out venomously. "Tomorrow I return with the warrant. The papers *will* be found—and Shalimar will no longer be yours."

The handkerchief he held to his mouth, she noted with considerable satisfaction, was stained red. With a purposeful *click* she removed the safety catch of her Colt.

Charlton hesitated an instant more, then shrugged, swaggered out and slammed the door behind him.

So as not to risk running into Chinese patrols alerted by the Amban of Yarkand, except for a brief halt to purchase necessary supplies, Conolly decided to by-pass the oasis.

In the Yarkand bazaar outside the caravanserai, they stopped just long enough to buy provisions and other essentials for the journey ahead. He and Ivana both ate hungrily at a Chinese roadside stall where everything, even the noodles, was freshly made to order, and rested for an hour or two. Then, without wasting any more time, they pressed on along the southern Silk Road, a pleasantly shady avenue that ran for miles south of Yarkand.

Because they travelled light, they also travelled fast. Riding hard over as many as thirty three miles a day, they replenished their meagre provisions from passing caravans. Due to their head start, they had so far remained undetected; but certain that they would be pursued, Conolly remained cautious. Therefore, it was not until they had negotiated the Sanju Pass, the first of the five high passes to Leh, that he finally halted to consider the safest route to follow.

The newly discovered route to Leh through the Karakash valley, across the Aksai Chin plains and along the Changchenmo river, was less known and hence less frequented. On the other hand, the dead, desolate Aksai Chin would force them to remain for hundreds of miles at altitudes of fifteen thousand feet and above in a flat, barren wilderness. It would add days to their journey, sap away their strength and their energies, and he was not sure that he, let alone Ivana, could survive it. Reluctantly, therefore, he opted for the traditional route through the Karakorams.

Their most serious obstacle, however, was yet to come: the Suget, second of the passes which marked the end of Chinese territory and was guarded by an extremely well-manned fort. Once past the Chinese border, they could afford to slow down and join another caravan, but not until then. Perched on a plateau high above Karakash plain, the fort was enclosed on three sides by sharply rising mountains and impossible to approach without being seen. Wedged between two large stones on the approach, Conolly knew from previous visits, was an ominous warning: *Anyone crossing the Chinese frontier without reporting himself at this fort will be imprisoned.* Even if news of the abduction and their flight had not yet reached Suget, it would be foolish to take chances. To avoid the fort they needed to make a long, arduous and dangerously wet detour; but he could see no other solution.

"Are you frightened of water?" he asked Ivana.

"No."

"Can you swim?"

"Yes."

"Good."

He waited until dark, then giving Shahidullah a wide berth they headed west to the Yarkand river. Here on the deserted banks he unwrapped the essential equipment he had purchased and set to work. He pumped air into the large buffalo skins with a pair of bellows and tied their mouths tightly with rope. He then secured Ivana to one, himself to another, their belongings to a third, and knotted them all together.

He took a deep breath. "Say a prayer, Ivana. We need divine intervention to survive."

"I know you try your best. I am not afraid." She looked at him squarely. "Thank you once more for all that you do for me."

He winced but saw that this was neither the time nor the place for explanations. He lifted a hand and at the signal they plunged together into the icy waters. At the end of a long rope tied round his neck, the horse, strangely fearless, slipped in behind them. Picked up by the currents, they were whirled away swiftly and smoothly. Knowing that there were rapids ahead, Conolly breathed a silent prayer of his own. If they did not die of the cold by then, they had a pretty good chance of being battered to death against the rocks around which the rapids raged.

It was a harrowing journey. Entirely at the mercy of the rampaging currents, they were buffetted mercilessly, missing death several times by a hairsbreadth. As they raced onwards through the dreadful timelessness of the dark, their lives passed out of their control, every ounce of energy directed towards simply keeping their heads above water. Somewhere along the way the rope holding the horse broke and they lost sight of him, but there was no time to mourn as they continued to bob and whirl and swirl along for a terrifying eternity.

Finally the rapids ended; the waters subsided and settled into a stream. Clinging onto their impromptu rafts, they paddled with their hands as frantically as their depleted strength would allow. Hours later—or perhaps minutes, there was no way of telling—they collided with something hard and soft at the same time: the opposite bank!

With creaking muscles and almost the last breath left in his lungs, Conolly clutched the serpentine roots of a tree with one hand. With the other he plucked away at the knots in the ropes until they loosened and then hauled himself up onto the bank. By the time he had done the same with Ivana and their baggage, his nails were torn and bleeding and every part of his body screamed in protest. Gasping for oxygen as he coughed and spluttered and expelled water from his lungs, Conolly collapsed on the bank. Drenched to the skin and shivering, he gave a final gasp and lost consciousness. His last waking thought was of Ivana, but he had the strength neither to turn his head nor to call out. The life-saving buffalo skins sped away into the invisible dark to continue their onward journey into the unknown.

His first sight on recovering consciousness was of a lightening eastern horizon. Painfully, he struggled up and looked around. Close to the edge of the water, he saw, Ivana lay in a heap with her eyes closed. He could not tell if she was breathing. Oh God, was she dead? He stumbled to his feet, ran to her and touched her face with frantic fingers.

"Ivana?"

Her eyelids fluttered minimally, but she did not raise them. He picked her up and, almost collapsing again with the effort, carried her further up the bank under a tree. He looked around for signs of human habitation but in the cold, lifeless desolation there were none. He had no idea where they were but he did not care.

They were alive and no longer on Chinese soil!

Above them the sky turned a pale, hesitant blue. Soon the sun would rise, bringing with it life-giving warmth. It promised to be a day of revival. Conolly wanted to jump up and throw his arms about and dance in exhilaration, but his eyelids were weighted down with stones. He let them drop. Like Ivana, he slipped into the sleep of the dead.

Hours later, when the day was half done and filled with sunshine, he roused himself with difficulty and propped himself up on aching elbow joints. Some distance away, Ivana sat in the sun drying herself. Her eyes were closed and her head rested on one arm balanced on a rock. He called and she looked back.

"Are you all right?"

She smiled weakly and nodded.

When their belongings were dry, they changed into fresh clothes and hungrily devoured strips of soggy but very welcome sun-dried yak meat. All through their flight Conolly had guarded four precious articles almost as jealously as he had Ivana: his field glasses, a map, his revolver and his compass, all rolled tight in rubber sheeting. Miraculously, all had survived their long immersion in the river with only minor damage. The loss of his horse was a severe blow, but there was nothing he could do about that.

He now surveyed the surrounding terrain through the field glasses. According to the position of the sun and his compass, he calculated roughly where they were and the direction of their next destination, hoping that the message he had sent earlier from Kashgar had arrived safely. Then, with their few belongings slung across their backs, they started their weary trudge in a south-easterly direction.

A day and a half later, to his overwhelming relief, Conolly discovered that his Baluchi friend from Kashgar had not let him down after all and the message had indeed been delivered. At the Khirgiz encampment a few miles west of the town of Khapalung, his friend Mirza Beg waited with his customary welcome.

*T*he fact that two large, bewhiskered Dogras in uniform were positioned outside the door of Emma's private apartment caused a furore among the staff.

"What is happening, begum sahiba?" Sharifa whispered, darting nervous glances through the open door where other staff, with pale, anxious faces, hovered uncertainly. "They say that more soldiers are on the way to surround the house. Who are these men, begum sahiba?"

Smiling as reassuringly as she could, Emma firmly closed the door. "The guards are from the Residency and are here at huzoor's request. There has been some talk of bandits in the region and huzoor wishes to secure us and the estate in his absence. Please tell everyone there is nothing to be concerned about."

She hoped fervently that they would believe her. The last thing she wanted at the moment was a panic; there would be enough of that tomorrow when the search of the house began.

"How many guards are there?" she asked Sharifa.

"Two in the corridor. The others are not visible from the house."

"Well, I suppose they are concealing themselves in the grounds so as not to alert would-be intruders."

Behind her forced calmness, Emma's thoughts raced. What was she to do? What *could* she do? Suraj Singh was in Gulmarg, and Lincoln, the estate manager, had taken a large consignment of canned fruit to Srinagar for despatch to Amritsar. There was no one else she could take into her confidence. Once Charlton had secured the search warrant, it would be a matter of time before he found the papers, regardless of where she concealed them. In the desperate circumstances of the moment, even the packing was forgotten.

Somehow a message had to be reached to Damien!

Whatever the differences between them, however determined she was to abandon this fraudulent marriage conceived in greed and formalised in deceit, Emma knew she could not leave without at least warning him. So far, her conscience was clear; she was not prepared to stain it by letting Damien lose his damned Shalimar by default. To maintain a semblance of normalcy, she ordered her usual luncheon and forced herself to eat it. Later, through the afternoon, a hazy plan started to form in her mind and gestated slowly. By evening she knew exactly what she had to do.

The guards, still positioned in the corridor, showed no sign of deserting their posts and would, no doubt, remain until Charlton returned with reinforcements in the morning. Ordering Sharifa to arrange food for the two men, for herself she ordered an early—and somewhat unusual—supper of parathas, buttered bread rolls, fresh and dried fruit and cheese. Once the meal arrived, she dismissed Sharifa and Rehmat.

"I did not sleep too well last night," she said, "and I do not wish to be disturbed. I will ring in the morning when I need you."

She locked her doors securely and set to work.

Her first-floor parlour overlooked a side garden. To ensure privacy to the apartment, part of the garden was screened by a line of trees away from the path to the kitchen houses. Removing the sheets from her bed and adding several more from the linen cupboard, she knotted them together in a fairly satisfactory chain. At one end of the impromptu ropeway, she tied a heavy book. The other end she secured around the wrought-iron balustrades of her balcony, praying that the masonry would hold.

She then packed her uneaten supper in thick paper and oilcoth, poured the paraffin from one of the lamps into a silver hip flask—the only un-breakable container she could find—and wrapped it in a pillow-case. She tied the various items together with lengths of braid edging cut off the canopy of her fourposter. Changing into thick riding britches, warm wool-len vest, long johns and a quilted jacket with a hood, she slipped two pairs of fur-lined gloves into the pockets of the jacket. Her feet she protected with a pair of heavy, fleece-lined boots. Finally, she removed the papers from the prayer-wheel and returned the wheel to the cupboard. By eight o'clock, she had completed all her preparations.

Following their own evening meal, Emma knew, the servants usually gathered in their courtyard to take their ease and gossip around a bonfire. When she felt the time was right, she extinguished her lamps and cautiously lowered the line of braid and its attachments from the balcony. The heaviest item, the silver flask, hit the ground first with a soft thud. She waited a moment; apart from the rustles and squeaks of bandicoots scurrying for safety, there were no other sounds, and she repeated the process with the other items. Then, thrusting her hands into a pair of gloves, she confirmed the strength of the impromptu ropeway, climbed onto the balustrade rail, closed her eyes in a prayer and started to slide down.

The descent was alarmingly swift. Even before she had a chance to be frightened, she had landed in the shrubbery with a hard *thump*. Taking a few moments to regularise her breath and hammering heartbeat, Emma looked around. The half moon rising above the trees was at the moment a disadvantage, but she saw that later on it would be a help. She could see no one, nor could she hear the crunch of patrolling feet. All the same, eyes seemed to watch from everywhere, and she shivered.

Crawling out of the shrubbery and keeping to the shadowed verges, she inched towards the large barn on the far side of the orchard. No longer in use, it was now a storehouse for broken machinery and discarded odd-ments. She reached it without incident. Crouching against one of its timber walls, she sprinkled the base with paraffin from her flask and set a match to it. As the bone-dry planks flared, she ran to the safety of a thicket and waited for the fire to attract attention.

By the time the shouting began, the blaze had turned into an inferno and the roar of crashing timber filled the night. People came running from all directions and there was chaos everywhere. Silhouetted figures scurried back and forth with splashing buckets and pails and water cans. Someone shouted to Sharifa to inform begum sahiba and earned a quick reproof. Begum sahiba, the maid declared firmly, was not to be disturbed, no matter what.

Emma smiled and hurried on.

Keeping to the peripheral belt of trees, she crept towards the stables in the opposite direction to the barn. With the grooms busy with the fire the stable house was deserted and she soon had Zooni saddled. During one of their many tours of the estate, Suraj Singh had pointed out a bridle-path that threaded through the saffron fields, circumvented the main gates and joined the wider track outside. In the confusion and dark no one noticed the lone rider wading through a sea of saffron towards the main road. Half an hour later, she was safely on her way to Gulmarg.

All around liquid night stretched black and silent over the valley. The half moon in which she had reposed such faith had let her down and gone into hiding behind a cloud. It was piercingly cold. Sharp wind blades cut through her quilted jacket into her flesh and icy air drove needlepoints into her eyes. Later, it would rain. The tracks were rough, even rougher after the turning at Narabal, and a pack of jackals, sounding dangerously close, howled behind her. Remembering that according to Damien big cats roamed the slopes around Gulmarg after dark, in her mouth Emma tasted corroding and all pervasive fear.

Why am I doing this? she asked herself bitterly. *Why am I suffering this torment for the benefit of a man who has done nothing to earn it?*

She could offer no answer reason would accept.

*T*he Khirgiz encampment was situated on the banks of an eggshell blue lake alive with wild duck, water-fowl and long-legged cranes. Standing beside the entrance of his splendid *akoi,* the round tent of the Khirgiz, Mirza Beg greeted Conolly with a welcoming smile.

They embraced.

"Us-salaam-alaikum," Mirza said. "My home is yours. Use it as you will."

"Walaikum salaam." Conolly grinned, tight-throated with relief. "I am forever in your debt."

No, no Mirza Beg protested, it is quite the reverse.

During Conolly's last visit here, Mirza's third wife had gone into a long and difficult labour and he had helped as best he could with medicine and practical advice through the midwife. Finally, a healthy son had been de-livered—Mirza's first after three daughters—and since then Mirza had attributed the twin blessings of his wife's survival and the birth of an heir to Conolly.

"I have collected everything you asked for in your letter for your on-ward journey, including horses," Mirza said. "But you must stay a while. I insist."

"Well, perhaps a day or two," Conolly agreed, more than willingly. "After that we must press on, for we are awaited in Leh."

They stayed for four days, succumbing to their host's persuasions with scant pretence of reluctance. The luxury of warm beds, spacious tents, generous hospitality and freedom from fear of pursuit was not easy to resist, and Conolly did not even try. Two passes still remained to be crossed, including the Karakoram. But once they were revived and well rested, he hoped that under the protection of another caravan, they would survive those too. After the long, harrowing haul from Kashgar the encampment was akin to Omar Khayyám's paradise, the wilderness indeed made heavenly beneath the boughs with freshly baked bread, succulent game meats and endless glasses of *khumis,* the traditional Khirgiz liquor made from mares' milk.

One of Mirza Beg's many brothers, a musician, provided nightly entertainment on the *ngara,* the ancient drums once used for royal proclamations, to which they sang and danced. All around were serene, green pastures, for the Khirgiz loved their horses and claimed that it was here that the saddle and stirrup were first devised centuries ago.

The Khirgiz earned their livelihood by catching and training eagles and by making hats of fox and badger pelts. Up on the hill slopes, where the hunting was particularly good, herds of kayang grazed among flocks of chakor and rock pigeon. In between the ice and gravel of the higher reaches, amazingly, there were bright-hued flowers; purple foxgloves, blue daisies, a possible yellow cowslip and one that Ivana swore was a violet.

Having finally abandoned her boy's disguise, Ivana was lodged in the tents of the zenana. There was much silent curiosity about her, but, perhaps on instructions from their considerate host, no one asked uncomfortable questions. Never having been in an environment such as this, Ivana herself was initially dazed but later quite frankly enthralled.

It was their last evening at the encampment. They lounged by the lake, savouring for a final time the glory of a fiery sunset and the clear, luminous pink waters that reflected it. On a nearby pasture a herd of *yaboo* horses nibbled young grass; floating on the wind were the dusk calls of homing birds and the tinkle of camel bells. On the surface of the lake slim, long-legged cranes, storks and ducks stretched lazy wings and prepared to retire for the night, untroubled by human presence.

A family of ducks sailed past close to the shore, casting coy looks in their direction. Curious to test their tameness, Conolly waded into the shallow waters and tried to catch one, but the entire family vanished beneath the water in a trice. Plunging in after them he managed to grab hold of one, and much to her delight, offered it to Ivana.

As she sat stroking the duck sitting nervously in her lap, she asked suddenly, "How near are we now to Osh?"

It was a question Conolly knew would come one day and he had been dreading it. "Osh?" He looked away, unable to meet her innocent, unsuspecting eyes. "Quite near."

"We arrive soon?"

He nodded.

"The Commandant is a friend of *my* Colonel. When he learns that you too are a friend, he will convey us safely to Tashkent."

Sick with guilt, Conolly murmured an excuse and walked away along the lake's edge.

One way or another, during the past weeks he had learned a great deal about Ivana. The precarious, tension-filled journey had made them live in strange intimacy and without formality. Together they had huddled in caves around inadequate fires, shared sparse meals and slept almost side by side because in the wilderness privacy was a luxury. Through it all Ivana had remained remarkably self-possessed, compliant and uncomplaining. As was her habit, she spoke little and listened carefully. She never questioned his decisions, content to go where taken and do as she was told. All her life, Conolly realised, she had served others, obeyed orders and thought little about herself. For some reason, this pained him.

He had questioned her closely about her life and she had replied willingly and freely. Borokov had obviously treated her well, for she spoke kindly of him. Unexposed to the complexities of the world, however, she had little knowledge of how people lived and thought outside the narrow confines of her own experience. He had never met a woman as guileless and as unaware of herself. Sometimes at night when she thought he was asleep, he knew that she cried softly to herself, but he never saw evidence of her tears and whatever her fears she never voiced them to him. She called him "Mr. Conolly."

Here in the encampment where their daily lives were comparatively regular, he discovered she had habits that were touching. Despite his embarrassed protests, for instance, she insisted on folding his clothes, smoothing out his camp bed, cleaning his washbowl and, much to his horror, shining his heavy, bedraggled boots each night. When they ate, she insisted on serving him.

She had been in St. Petersburg with the Colonel, she told him, and quite awed by its glitter and glamour, its beautifully gowned and coiffured ladies and handsome, uniformed gentlemen. She had cooked for them, served them, observed and admired them from afar, but she had never spoken to them. It was not her place, she said, to converse with such fine people as an equal.

Sometimes, not often, her artlessness exasperated him, but he had lost his temper with her just once. "Don't you know *anything* about the world?" he had demanded irritably when she confessed ignorance about some trifling, commonplace matter. "Haven't you read any books at all?"

"No." She had lowered her eyes and stared at her hands. "I do not know how to read."

He had been shocked into silence and his heart had filled with pity. He had never shouted at her again. She was like a child, untouched and vulnerable, and like a child she reposed total faith in him.

How was he to tell her that he had lied, that he had never laid eyes on her Colonel, that they were headed not for Tashkent but in quite the opposite direction, for Leh?

"Who the devil *are* you, Ivana?" he burst out, angry not with her but with himself.

The question startled her, and as always when unsure, her hand rose to her neck and curled about her silver pendant. "You know who I am," she whispered, wide-eyed and fearful. "I am Ivana Ivanova."

It was hopeless. She simply did not understand.

He suddenly decided that he could not suffer the deception any longer. That she was a pawn in some larger game, he knew, but he had no idea of the players any more than she had. Considering her singular lack of self-importance, had she known of the extraordinary stakes being offered for her by the British, the Chinese and in all probability the Russians, she would have been terrified.

"There is something that I think you should know," he said now, deciding that it had to be said quickly, firmly and bluntly. There was no other way. "We are not going to Tashkent."

She stared at him in incomprehension.

"Have you heard of the Yasmina Pass?"

"No."

Speaking slowly and quietly, he related to her everything that he knew. It was not much but it was certainly more than she did. She listened, as she always did, with full concentration and without interruption. She made no immediate comment when he had finished. Then she asked, "Where will you take me if not to Tashkent?"

"First to Leh and then to Simla."

She had not heard of either. "Why?"

He smiled sadly. "You will have to believe me when I say that I have not the remotest idea."

She excused herself, rose, deposited the duck gently back into the water and walked away from him. She strolled by herself on the lake bank for a long while, throwing crumbs to a flock of chirruping birds that followed close on her heels. When she returned, he saw that she had been crying.

He was deeply distressed and made an effort at reassurance. "Don't worry, once we are in Leh we will get to the bottom of the mystery. Please, please trust me, Ivana."

"I do trust you," she said tearfully, and apologised for her unhappiness, begging him not to think of her as ungrateful. "You are a friend, I know, and if I behave badly it is because I have not had a friend before."

He felt the size of a worm.

Just at that moment Mirza Beg came hurrying to where they sat. "Quick," he said, greatly agitated, "you must hide. Horsemen approach. It could be a Chinese patrol."

Conolly's blood went cold. "Here? But we are well outside Chinese territory!"

"Do you think that matters to them?"

"How many are there?"

"I cannot see clearly, but by the dust being kicked up I would say at least ten horses. Hurry, hurry, my friend. I will show you a place where you will be safe."

He pointed to the lake and Conolly nodded. Being familiar with Chinese incursions, it was obviously a contingency for which Mirza Beg was already prepared.

Even so, Conolly hesitated. "If they suspect your complicity in having harboured fugitives, your lives will be endangered!"

"Do not concern yourself about us, my friend. Everything has been taken care of. No sign remains of your presence. Even if it does," he gave a knowing wink, "the Chinese enjoy *khumis* as much as we do and there is plenty to be had. Now, hurry!"

Conolly did not share in his optimism but there was no time to argue.

At the edge of the water Mirza handed him a sheaf of long, hard, hollowed-out reeds and took charge of the shoes and sheepskin coats they removed; also Conolly's revolver. Tying their voluminous garments around them to stop them from floating up, they waded in and made for a bank of tall water-plants. The water was shallow but ice-cold. For a moment Conolly could hardly breathe. As they submerged themselves up to their necks, he passed a handful of reeds to Ivana. She put one in her mouth and looked at him and he nodded. The thundering of hooves was now dangerously close. Without another word they submerged their heads and crouched low among the tangled grasses, their feet just touching the lake bottom.

The Taotai was obviously more persistent than expected!

The submarine world was eerie in the half-light. Through the dense foliage, patches of a pale, wavy sky showed overhead, but save for the thunderous beats of Conolly's own heart and his rasping breath as it passed through the reed, all was silent. An eternity passed. Entombed in a pale green universe of wriggling, darting shapes and flitting shadows, Conolly felt sick with despair. Had it all been for nothing, doomed to end like this?

Without any warning at all, he suddenly felt pressure on his head, the fumbling pressure of moving fingers. A human hand, fingers spread, groped beneath the water, found the reed and pulled it roughly from his mouth. Caught without breath and expecting to die momentarily, Conolly shot out of the water, arms outstretched and thrashing wildly. Sweeping aside the grasses, he lunged upward and outward, his fingers flying through space in blind search of a fleshy target. If he had to die, was his immediate thought, he might as well make a fight of it and take a couple with him.

Before Conolly could contact anything remotely like flesh, however, he found both his own wrists manacled in a grip that rendered him immobile.

"Whoa, whoa—steady *on,* matey! What the bloody 'ell do you think you're doing?"

An English voice!

Choking and spluttering, jerking his head to get the water out of his eyes, Conolly stared blearily into a thicket of ginger hair sprouting out of a ruddy face and a pair of indignant blue eyes. The thicket moved, an orifice opened and his wrists were released. A fat, beefy hand shot out to grasp his.

"Dr. Conolly, I presume?"

CHAPTER

18

Sir John Covendale sat in his study sipping a Cognac. It was past midnight and Lady Covendale had long retired. The room was in darkness; he made no move to light a lamp. Lounging on his favourite couch with his feet outstretched, he warmed the snifter between his palms, sipping with appreciation but absently. Presently he got up, ambled to the window and stood listening to the rhythms of the rain. The drizzle that had started earlier as he walked home had settled into a steady downpour. He was glad to have missed it.

He had spent the evening at Snowdon with the C-in-C. They had shared a working supper of cold meat sandwiches and iced beer over a stack of pending files and again discussed the Royal Commission report. The Commission had recommended the abolition of the post of Commander-in-Chief and its replacement by a Chief of Staff responsible directly to London. Not yet certain of their own reactions, they debated the matter endlessly.

Deeply pensive, Sir John returned to the comfortable sag of the couch, lowered himself into it, loosened his collar and tossed off his shoes. The infernally hard regulation chairs they made do with in the Department produced creaking aches and the warmth of the plump cushion behind his back was soothing. As always on a Saturday night, revellers returning home from sundry jollifications on the Mall were proving boisterous. Vaguely irritated, he laid his head back, subjected the ceiling to a hard stare and again thought about the evening.

"Where did you say Hethrington had gone, John?" Sir Marmaduke had asked as he was about to leave.

He had not said, but a direct answer to the direct question could hardly be avoided. "Leh, sir."

"I see." Evidently not yet satisfied, the C-in-C started to stroll alongside him down the winding path that led to the Mall. "I know that your Department moves in mysterious ways, John, much in the manner of the Lord, but what transpires behind my back and is being kept from me with excessive secrecy worries me. I would like to be assured that the secrecy is for a good reason, a *damned* good reason."

Even through the swirls of mist, the limpet gaze felt sharp on Sir John's face. Taken by surprise and glad of the dark, the QMG coughed. "Well, sir, we . . ."

"I have no intention of forcing you into a corner, John," the C-in-C interrupted impatiently. "Just tell me off the record—does all this have anything to do with the Butterfield business?"

Sir John's hesitation was remarkably brief. All in all, it was a relief to clear at least part of his conscience. "Yes, sir."

"And do we risk getting more egg on our faces?"

"Only if we fail, sir."

"Are we likely to?"

"No, sir. At least"—Sir John took a deep breath and stopped.

Sir Marmaduke gave a bark of a laugh. "The obstacle course between the cup and the old lip, eh?"

"Well, yes, sir. As in all operations there is an element of risk, but an acceptable risk."

"Can you give me your word on that?"

"No, sir. All I can give my word on is that everything possible is being done to recover the papers."

"Ah, so they are *not* lost to the four winds in the Karakoram gorges after all!"

"No, sir."

"I didn't think they were," Sir Marmaduke grunted smugly, "notwithstanding intrepid efforts to convince me otherwise. Well, then, when *am* I likely to have the pleasure of your confidence?"

Sir John flushed at the sarcasm. "At the end of the week, sir."

Recapitulating the conversation, the QMG shifted uneasily on the couch. *At the end of the week!* That was all Hethrington had left to get his hands on those blasted papers. Well, he bloody hoped it would be enough. If not . . .

He nipped the thought in the bud. It had been a long day; he was tired, the cognac was smooth and it went down easily. He yawned, again laid his head back and allowed his eyelids to droop. Almost immediately— or so it seemed to him—he was rudely jolted out of his drowse by a commotion that sounded alarmingly close, right outside his front door, in fact. Annoyed, he leapt up and regardless of stockinged feet marched out into the hallway. Street drunkenness got worse with each successive Season. It was disgraceful; he would have to speak to the Commissioner about it.

"*Koi hai?*"

Bellowing for the servants, he unlatched the front door and flung it open. However, before he could do the same with his mouth and read the drunken sots their fortune, a noisy tangle of arms and legs came hurtling out of the darkness to crash through the doorway and land a few inches from his feet.

He leapt back with an oath. "What the *blazes!*"

"Who is it, John?" Lady Covendale called down anxiously over the bannisters. "Are the chowkidars not there?"

Just as several servants came running, the heaving knot resolved itself into two belligerent and highly vocal chowkidars, clutching between them what at first glance appeared to be an animated dirty laundry-bag.

"*Yeh sab kya tamasha hai?*" Sir John roared. "*Kon hai yeh?*"

"We don't know who he is, sahib," one of the watchmen gasped holding his quarry in a viselike grip. "We caught him trying to climb over the gate. When asked, he refused . . ."

"C-Columbine, sir." He was cut off by a hoarse croak from the laundry-bag as it wrenched itself free and resolved itself into human form. "Columbine r-reporting back from d-duty, sir . . ."

"Columbine?" Sir John peered suspiciously. "Good God, Wyncliffe!" Momentarily speechless, he stared at the mud-encrusted clothes, thickly matted hair and beard, bloodshot eyes and roughly bound hands and feet. "What are you doing here? I thought you were somewhere on the Murghab?"

Wyncliffe took a faltering step into the hallway and stood swaying on his feet. "S-Smirnoff, sir," he whispered. "September twen . . ." It was as far as he could get. The eyes rolled, the knees buckled and he collapsed in a heap on the doormat.

Recovering fast, Sir John waved aside the watchmen and went down on his knees beside the unconscious man. "*Pani lao, juldi,* juldi, *aur lady sahib ko bulao!*"

"Coming, dear, coming!" Lady Covendale hurried down the stairs. "Goodness me, who on earth is it? Anyone we know?"

"Wyncliffe. David Wyncliffe." Having felt a weak pulse in the limp wrist, Sir John lifted each eyelid in turn and ran his fingertips up and down the limbs. "Nothing appears to be broken but he's badly frost-bitten. The hands and feet are absolutely raw. We'd better get him to bed and send for the Major."

Half a glass of water was forced into the slack mouth, the unconscious man carried into the downstairs guest room, hot-water bottles slipped under the quilt and a highly confused chowkidar despatched to the army hospital.

"Where in heaven's name did you send him, John, for the poor man to be in this most dreadful state!"

Even if Sir John had considered it professionally ethical to offer a response to his wife's reproof, which he did not, he would not have been able to. Shaken as he was by the sight of the injured man, mention of Smirnoff had left him quite unnerved. Wyncliffe was a recent recruit, still fairly wet around the gills. His initial assignment had come from Crankshaw, a relatively simple job of surveillance of the new Russian road. Why then had he reported to Simla instead of to Leh and risked putting Crankshaw's nose out of joint? That at the moment, however, was the least of the QMG's concerns. Wyncliffe had obviously stumbled upon something he considered of crucial military importance, something to do with Alexei Smirnoff.

Bloody hell!

It was, of course, impossible to question Wyncliffe in his present sorry state. The interrogation would have to wait; but intuition honed over many years in the service told Sir John that whatever news Wyncliffe brought spelt trouble for the Department—and the last thing the QMG wanted at the moment was more indigestible fare on his plate.

As it happened, answers to the unasked questions arrived sooner than expected.

"You're right, sir, no bones broken," the Indian Medical Service Major confirmed after the patient had been examined, given medicines, sponged and bandaged, "but the frostbite is wicked and he's severely malnourished, starved, in fact. I'd say he's damned lucky to be alive. He'll be hors de combat for a few weeks, naturally, but on the whole there's nothing wrong that solid food, a good long rest and careful nursing won't be able to set right. I'll arrange for him to be removed to hospital in the morning."

Sir John frowned. "Is that absolutely necessary, Major? As long as it is not medically inadvisable, I would much rather keep him where he is."

The doctor scratched his chin, then nodded. "I understand, sir. No, it would not be medically inadvisable. I'll leave my medical orderly behind to take care of the nursing." He extended a hand in which was held something wrapped in thick layers of rotting cloth smelling not unlike an advanced case of athlete's foot. "We found this strapped to the Lieutenant's chest, sir. We had to remove it in order to sponge him. Goodnight, sir. I'll look in again first thing in the morning."

Ordering the lamps to be lit, Sir John hurried into his study with the packet. Carefully he unwound the rotting cloth, sent it off to be incinerated and inspected what emerged from within, a sodden notebook. Disregarding the high smell, his wife's irritated summons to bed and his own fatigue, he again made himself comfortable in the sag of the couch and started to read. Through the night—or whatever remained of it—he perused Wyncliffe's jottings slowly, with unwavering concentration. By the time he had ingested Mikhail Borokov's astonishing revelations, dawn light had started to creep across the hills and a new day had begun.

Even though his eyelids were weighted with lead, his back as stiff as a pikestaff and every joint in his body sore, Sir John's mind had never been more fully awake. He was too appalled even to contemplate the prospect of sleep.

*T*he clustered stars in the night sky were reassuring but the darkness on earth was uncompromising and frighteningly silent. An army of black clouds growled menacingly in the north and a chill wind whistled around Emma's ears, scything easily through her muffs and jacket. The smell of rain in the air was overpowering. It was difficult to believe that a vale so warm and vibrant in sunlight could turn so sinister at night. She had not been on this road before. The track bordered with poplars and rice and maize fields was straight and flat and the gradient mild, but in the filtered starlight the ruts and potholes were difficult to see, and in spite of Zooni's surefootedness, the going was slow. In the murky distance, far ahead, glinted the snowy caps among which nestled the Gulmarg valley.

At an elevation of more than eight thousand feet, Gulmarg was three and a half thousand feet higher than Srinagar. After Tanmarg, Emma knew, the ascent over the final few miles would be steep and treacherous, especially if it rained. The tortuous zigzag of footpaths was threaded through thick forests of blue pine and in the dark the precipices would be doubly menacing. About the predators Damien had mentioned Emma tried not to think at all.

The rumbling from the cloud bank came closer and a moving veil obscured the stars. Her single lantern was vastly inadequate; she could barely see her hand before her face. Even though the rhythm of Zooni's clip-clopping hooves did not falter, she had no idea how long it would take to reach Tanmarg. Crouching low in the saddle, she consigned her fate to the mare's capable care, closed her eyes against the gusting winds and plodded on.

She did not notice the cluster of huts that was Tanmarg until she was upon it.

It was almost dawn and the village was beginning to stir. Behind it, outlined against the brightening sky, towered the mountains, their decapitated peaks like icebergs floating on an ocean of mist. A light flickered in an open doorway; above it stretched a crude gunny sack awning. A chai khana! Even though to stop was to lose precious time, she simply could not go on without a rest, a welcome cup of hot tea and some food. She banged on the door and it opened almost immediately.

"I would like refreshments for myself, and a nose-bag, water and a rub-down for my horse."

The sleepy-eyed, tousle-haired woman stared a moment, then nodded and opened the door wide.

The room was small and still cosy from the residual warmth of last night's fire from the open stove. As the woman set about reviving it, a yawning, equally dishevelled youngster, probably her son, went to lead Zooni away to the back. Emma sank onto a wooden bench and closed her eyes. Her body was numb with cold, her mind a blank. By the time the tea arrived, so did the rest of the family. Intrigued by her presence, they stood around staring with unabashed curiosity.

Unpacking the food she had brought in her saddlebag, Emma ate hungrily. Gradually the warmth from the stove resuscitated her frozen limbs and breathed life into her taut body. The tea, fresh and scalding hot, tasted wonderful; as it revived her stomach, it also dulled her senses. Unable to keep her eyes open, she laid her head down on the table and closed them.

She did not know how long she dozed but it could not have been for more than a few minutes, for the empty tin mug clutched in her palm still felt tepid. Refreshed by the catnap she slowly returned to full wakefulness, noticing in the process that someone had walked out of the shadows to stand opposite her at the table.

Geoffrey Charlton?

Certain that she was dreaming she peered blearily at the apparition as she whispered the name, but then he gave a courtly bow and spoke.

"At your service, Mrs. Granville. We do seem to meet in the most unlikely places, don't we?"

Emma's eyes jerked wide open as she stared at him in horror. *Oh dear God!* "Wh-what are *you* doing here?" she gasped, trying to leash her panic.

"The same as you, Mrs. Granville. Enjoying an early morning cuppa after a hard night's ride."

"How did you . . . ?"

"Know that I would find you here?" He smiled, pulled out a chair and sat down. "Well, where else would a dutiful wife in your circumstances be, if not on her way to warn an unaware husband?"

"You followed me!"

"On the contrary, it was you who followed *me*." He was amused by her bewilderment. "I had calculated that it would only be a matter of hours before you devised a way out and headed for Gulmarg. What better place to await you than this warm little oasis?" He raised his mug in a mock toast. "You are a brave, extraordinarily resourceful lady, Mrs. Granville. I salute you."

"You lied about the search warrant!"

"A small ruse, I admit, but it achieved its purpose."

Sickened that he should have been able to read her with such ease and accuracy, she sat before him silent and defenceless.

It had all been for nothing!

Charlton's triumphant eyes swivelled unerringly towards the saddlebag that lay exposed between them on the table. "I have waited long and very patiently for what is in here, Mrs. Granville," he said softly. "I would like to relieve you of its contents now, if you please."

He reached for the bag. She would not have been able to stop him even if she had tried. Her fingers, still clasped about the mug, were numb and useless.

Charlton emptied the contents of the bag onto the table, impatiently brushed aside the food, and pounced on the envelope she had secreted at the bottom. Hiding her despair, Emma watched in helpless silence as he placed the strips of paper—in sequence and so thoughtfully numbered—side by side, smoothed them out with his palms and started to read. As his gleaming eyes darted greedily from side to side, she could almost taste his excitement, feel the tremble in his body and hear the wild rhythm of his heart as if it were her own. As the finger following the haphazard lines of characters moved uncertainly, she noted with minimal satisfaction the gap in his teeth where a canine should have been.

"You have no right to these papers," she said dully.

"Neither has your husband."

"But *I* do—and the RGS does!"

He laughed. "Let us not delude ourselves, Mrs. Granville. The bald truth is that no one has a right to reports of Himalayan explorations except the government, no matter who funds them."

He resumed his reading. Emma could see that he made little progress and was becoming increasingly irritated by the illegibility of the scrawls. The brief rest, the food and tea had revived her strength and beneath her apparent composure her mind again raced.

"Considering that you are unfamiliar with my father's handwriting," she said, "how do you know that these papers are genuine?"

"Don't take me for a fool, Mrs. Granville—had they not been, neither you nor the papers would be here." He fumbled again inside the saddlebag, then re-examined the strips. His eyes slitted. "Genuine but incomplete. Where are the rest of the papers?"

"The rest?"

"Sketch maps, location, elevation, measurements. Details of the Yasmina, Mrs. Granville, *details!*"

"My father carried no instruments."

"But *Butterfield* did! Butterfield was a trained cartographer and surveyor. It is inconceivable that after having confirmed your father's findings, he should not have recorded his own!" In his agitation he had raised his voice and the woman's husband looked up from behind the stove with a questioning frown. Charlton controlled himself with an effort, but his face was taut with rage.

"Where are Butterfield's papers, Mrs. Granville?"

Emma could think of no response to give him. She had never seen Butterfield's papers, indeed, had not even thought to look for them. The shock of suddenly coming across her father's handwriting had driven all other thoughts from her mind. She saw, however, that what Charlton said was valid; of *course* Jeremy Butterfield must also have left notes—but where were they? Still lying overlooked in the desk? With Damien in Gulmarg?

"These are all the papers I have," she said quite truthfully. "I know nothing of any others."

He breathed hard as he battled his fury, then grabbed the papers in a fist and leapt up.

"Don't underestimate my resources, Mrs. Granville," he grated. "And don't ever forget that I can still deprive you of your precious Shalimar if Butterfield's papers are found on your premises." He shoved the papers back into the saddlebag and tucked it under his arm. "Or," he added, "in your husband's possession."

"Where are you going?" she asked in alarm.

He gave her a look of such contempt that she recoiled. "Where do *you* think, Mrs. Granville?"

Before she could even take another breath, he had vanished.

he notebook, sir, you have it?"

Sir John nodded at the anxious face on the bed. "Yes, I have the notebook, Columbine. The doctor found it when you were about to be sponged. Being an honourable man, he did not read it."

David Wyncliffe groaned and fell back on the pillows. "Thank God for that! I was afraid it might have disintegrated by now. I must apologise, sir, for giving you and Lady Covendale such an unholy fright the other night, but I heard that both Colonel Hethrington and Captain Worth were out of station and I didn't know where else to turn."

"You did absolutely the right thing, Columbine."

"The notes, sir—have you had a chance to go through them yet?"

"Yes." The QMG stood up. "We will talk about that later when you are sufficiently recovered."

"I am sufficiently recovered now, sir," David said eagerly. "If you don't mind, sir, I would rather get it all off my chest while it is still fresh in my mind."

"Well, we already *have* it off your chest," Sir John smiled. "The notebook could not have been better secured."

"About Colonel Borokov, sir, there is more, much more to tell. I couldn't put it all down because my fingers were frozen."

Sir John scanned the earnest, open face for a moment. Washed, wearing fresh clothes and well rested, he certainly looked alert enough, even though his hands and feet were still tightly bandaged. Not having considered that Wyncliffe would be up to facing questions for at least another week, he was delighted by the offer after only two days. A précis of Borokov's revelations had, of course, been rushed to the Viceroy, the Foreign Secretary and the Commander-in-Chief and their reactions were as expected: the Viceroy was circumspect, the Foreign Secretary noncommittal until he had heard everything, and the Commander-in-Chief as enraged as a wounded bull in a ring. Just as well Hethrington was away!

What Wyncliffe had stumbled across through sheer chance was dynamite, pure dynamite, and the sooner a preliminary informal interrogation was held the better.

"Very well, then, since time *is* of the essence, we may as well get down to it." Sir John briskly resumed his seat by the bed. "Your notes were remarkably explicit considering the conditions prevailing but, naturally, I want to hear everything, every little detail that you can remember."

He called for writing materials, ordered a pitcher of fresh lime juice and asked the medical orderly to wait outside. Decreeing that they were to be disturbed only if the house caught fire, he then locked the door, settled down at the bedside table with a wad of paper and several sharpened pencils, and pronounced himself ready.

"Don't rush, young man. Take as much time as you want and start at the beginning, from the day you saw Borokov at the river."

With so much having happened unexpectedly and in a relatively short period, David Wyncliffe did indeed take his time over the telling. It was a comprehensive account, cogent and well remembered, and he needed little prompting. Each time Sir John fell behind with the writing, he lubricated his throat with sips of sweet lime juice and waited. Very painstakingly, Sir John recorded the blow-by-blow narrative, interrupting only to ask the occasional question. When they had finished, it was almost lunchtime.

Sir John laid down his pencil, flexed his aching fingers, cracked his knuckles and walked around the room to return the circulation to his legs.

"You are convinced Borokov spoke the truth?"

"Yes, sir. He had no reason to lie."

"Why does he want Smirnoff to believe that he is dead?"

"I gathered there was some sort of falling-out, sir. Borokov did not elaborate but I got the impression that he had cause to feel betrayed."

"September the twenty-sixth, eh?"

"Yes, sir. Smirnoff's birthday, a day he considers auspicious."

Sir John turned to glance at the calendar positioned on the desk behind him; 26 September—thirty-three days away!

"Where do you think Borokov went after he left you?"

"Almost certainly to the glaciers, sir."

"Without guides or maps or, indeed, equipment?"

"Yes, sir. Borokov was possessed by that pass, sir. He thought and spoke of little else. He was terrified that Smirnoff would get there first and rob him of his gold. We hunted for him over several days as much as we could but it was hopeless. The weather was vile and he was in pretty bad shape already." He heaved a deeply felt sigh. "He's probably dead by now."

"His interest in the Yasmina, *was* it just the gold?"

"Oh yes, sir. The poor sod was past pretending."

"He will be disappointed, of course—not that he will get there at all. There is no gold in the Himalayas. A small amount of dust is panned here and there, in the Hunza gorge, for instance, but certainly not enough to make a man wealthy. Tibetan gold, of course, is another matter."

"He knew all about that too, sir, but nothing could change his conviction that there *was* gold in the Yasmina. He wore the nugget all the time, almost worshipping it like some sort of magic talisman that would transform his life. He was determined to strike it rich, sir. Once, he said, he had even mounted a team of Russian officers to dig for ancient Chinese gold believed to be buried in the Taklamakan. They found nothing and one of the officers perished in the effort."

"You say he initially asked to be taken to Srinagar?"

"Yes, sir."

"Why?"

"He did not explain, sir. He said it was personal business."

Sir John frowned, not liking the sound of that. "Well, let us assume that you had managed to guide him to the pass and that there was gold in it—what then?"

"Then he wanted to be escorted here, sir, to Simla. He intended to deliver the information about Smirnoff in person."

"Not gratis, surely!"

"No, sir—against safe-conduct to Bombay, a passport in a new name, a passage to Argentina and a promise of secrecy from his own people."

"I see."

"He had always dreamed of owning a mansion and hundreds of acres of land, sir, of raising sheep and horses and hosting lavish parties. More than anything else he said he wanted to be his own master, dependent on no one for favours. That is what he hoped the gold would bring him, sir, self-sufficiency, dignity." Strangely moved, David felt his lip quiver. "I have to say, sir, that there was something pathetic about the man. It wasn't crass greed that drove him on, it was exhaustion. He was just tired of being poor."

Giving him an absent nod, Sir John gathered up his papers and prepared to leave. "The hierarchy already has the broad facts, of course. Tomorrow we will finalise your comprehensive report and table it for thorough discussion." He gave the tightly bandaged feet an uncertain look. "Keeping in mind the time factor, when do you consider you will be up to a formal interrogation?"

"As soon as the doctor allows me out of bed, sir."

"You will, of course, be on crutches for a while."

"Yes, sir. The doctor mentioned it." He gulped. "If I made mistakes, sir, it was because I lacked the experience to deal with a situation that was beyond my training and capacity to handle."

"A man can do no better than his best, son," Sir John said gently. "Considering the diabolical circumstances, you reacted with pragmatism and extreme courage. With or without experience, in the wilderness a man has nothing to fall back upon but his common sense. You used yours well. I have no doubt His Excellency will endorse my opinion. Certainly, we can all be proud of you."

David's underlip again quivered. He tried to say, "Thank you, sir," but could not.

"Well, once the interrogation is over, a month's leave will not be difficult to arrange. Perhaps you would enjoy a holiday and some good hunting up in Kashmir?" Recollecting himself, the QMG broke off in some confusion. Good God, considering to whom his sister was married, that would certainly not do!

"If it is all the same to you, sir," David said, bridging the awkward gap as he dropped his eyes, "I would rather take the furlough in Delhi with my mother."

Sir John was relieved. "As you wish."

David hesitated. "Sir, do I have permission to ask a somewhat . . . forward question?"

"Well?"

"Is it true that it was my *father* who found the Yasmina?"

Whatever it was the QMG had expected, it was not that. "Who told you that?" he asked sharply.

"Colonel Borokov, sir."

"How in hell did *he* know?"

David told him about the binoculars and Borokov's anonymous contact in India. "Is it true, sir? Was it my father?"

Sir John considered a moment, then nodded. "Yes. It was—but for reasons that need not concern you, the matter is not to be discussed with anyone yet."

"I understand, sir." David fidgeted with a corner of his bed sheet. "Does my . . . my sister know?"

Another tricky question. Not having known himself, he was obviously perturbed by the thought. Well, whatever the truth between brother and sister, in view of his splendid performance the boy did deserve to be put out of his misery.

"No, son. Your sister does not know."

David's brow cleared. "Thank you, sir. I was sure that if she did, she would have told me."

"Your father's connection with the Yasmina is still classified information, Columbine," Sir John again warned crisply. "I trust you will remember that."

"Oh yes, sir, absolutely, sir."

Something was still troubling him, Sir John saw. "When the government is ready, your father will be given due credit, I assure you."

"It's not that, sir." David looked away. "For personal reasons I would rather not reveal, sir, I just want to say I am . . . glad that my sister does not know."

Comprehension dawned and Sir John's eyes narrowed; so *that's* what the lad was worried about, his brother-in-law's less than salubrious reputation. Well, he certainly had cause to be!

Back in his study in a grim mood, Sir John called for iced beer, some lunch on a tray and again ordered that he was not to be disturbed. That a *Russian* should have known about what they had gone to such lengths to keep from their own people had come as a nasty jolt. However, the fact that the information had obviously not been passed on to Smirnoff (or they would have heard about it, by gad!) was a compensation. Perhaps Wyncliffe's instincts were right; perhaps Mikhail Borokov *did* play a lone hand after all.

With Worth and Hethrington both away, Wyncliffe's extraordinary testimony could not be entrusted to anyone from the Department. Despatching a note to his office to say that he would be working at home, Sir John heaved a sigh and resigned himself to the task. However, by the time he had completed several copies of the transcription many hours later, his mood was quite different—surprisingly cheerful, in fact.

He had been struck by an aspect of the matter that he had not considered earlier. It not only relieved the ache in his knuckles but also lightened the weight on his mind. Whatever explosions might detonate in Whitehall following Wyncliffe's report, the consequences for the Intelligence Department could only be salutary. Many sceptics still openly questioned its usefulness and dismissed it as a fanciful luxury. What Wyncliffe had unearthed would change all that; not only would the Department gain stature and respectability but, much more to the point, a decent budget.

The bothersome fly in the ointment remained Hethrington's precarious project, the outcome of which still hung in the balance. Not for a moment could it be forgotten that "the obstacle course between the cup and the old lip" was still to be run.

As a good racing man himself, Sir John never underestimated the importance of the home stretch.

Under the pewter sky the morning was grey. The Gulmarg valley was shrouded in mist, the air cold, dank and insidious. There were few people about. In the thick fog Emma could discern little except disembodied trees and ghostly outlines of scattered wooden roofs clinging to the hillsides. Which one was Damien's? She had no means of knowing.

On the final stretch of the journey there had been no time for thought other than that of survival. The climb was terrifyingly steep and the unmarked paths slippery. It was only because of Zooni's miraculous confidence and the grace of an unseen hand that she had managed to remain in the saddle. Charlton had inferred that he too was headed for Gulmarg for a confrontation with Damien. Had he followed her? Preceded her? In her renewed sense of disorientation she was too worn out even to think.

She became vaguely aware that Zooni had stopped. With a tremendous effort Emma tried to focus her senses. They had halted, she saw, before a large iron gate. In a flash of insight she recalled that the mare had been born and reared in Gulmarg—obviously, memories of her first home had not been forgotten! Sliding down from the saddle, she pushed open the gate and stumbled through. Behind her the mare neighed gently, then broke into a trot and veered to the right. Following blindly, Emma presently found herself in a stable house where several horses were tethered in the stalls. One, a shiny black hulk with fiery eyes and flaring nostrils, she recognised instantly: Toofan!

Not waiting for the startled grooms as they hurried towards her, she turned and with a spurt of energy ran through the slush towards the hazy outlines of a house barely visible through the mists. There were lights in the windows but the curtains were drawn. Walking to the front door, she balled her fists and banged against it with all the strength she could muster. The door opened and in her furry vision a figure appeared, Suraj Singh. Ignoring his astonished exclamation, she ran past him and through the very first doorway that loomed ahead. It led into a parlour. A log fire crackled in the hearth; it was wonderfully warm. Seated in a wing chair, reading, Damien looked up as she flew into the room.

"Emma!" Dumbfounded, he half rose. "What on earth are you doing here?"

"Geoffrey Charlton, he . . . he . . ." She staggered forward, managed to reach a table and leaned on it with palms flat down and head lowered. "Charlton," she whispered, her spasmodic breath barely enough for the words to be heard, "coming here . . . rest of papers. Search warrant . . . confiscate Shalimar. No time for . . ."

She lost her breath and her voice died. Just as Damien reached her side, her legs gave way. Blackness descended, and as limply as a rag doll, she folded into his arms.

*M*aurice Crankshaw was not in a good mood.

Columbine, he had just learned, had reported back to the QMG rather than to Leh, and he was most displeased. Seconded to and paid for by his office, the fellow had no damned business traipsing off to Simla without express instructions. The flimsy that had arrived from Sir John was cryptic, uninformative and, indeed, offensive. The affront deserved to be returned in kind and, by Jove, it *would*. So as not to waste a pleasant sense of grievance and let his anger dissipate, he grabbed a pen and sat down to compose a fitting riposte. If the errant agent did not return to base ASAP, he wrote angrily, he would have him marked AWOL.

It was as he sat weighing the relative merits of "over my head" and "behind my back" for verbal potency that the door opened and Holbrook Conolly walked in.

Irritated by an interruption he had expressly forbidden, Maurice Crankshaw looked up, opened his mouth to issue an eloquent rebuke, then clamped it shut again. He scanned Conolly slowly from head to toe with no change of expression. For all the reaction he showed, the agent could have stepped in from the next room for a routine consultation. Returning his attention to his draft, Crankshaw selected "behind my back" as the more incisive and laid down his pen.

"So those geologists finally found you, did they?"

Used to the Commissioner's habitual crustiness and not to be outdone in nonchalance, Conolly was unfazed. "Yes, sir—not to say that we were by any means lost."

"Where?"

"In Mirza Beg's encampment."

The Commissioner nodded complacently. "I told Hethrington that was where you were most likely to hole up. Well, about time, too. Considering the general lunacy of your antics, I was beginning to think you had bought it. Since we've just paid for one, the last thing we can afford at the moment is another memorial service. Well?" He peered behind Conolly from above the rim of his glasses. "Not come without the *baggage,* I hope?"

Conolly's expression cooled. "Miss Ivanova awaits in the antechamber, sir," he said distantly. "Not having the faintest idea why she has been brought here—any more than I have—she is understandably nervous."

"Well, had you spent less time quaffing *khumis* and more on the road, you might not have missed Hethrington. He left for Srinagar last week. She would have certainly been a sight for his sore eyes, I can tell you."

He waved Conolly into a chair. Conolly opened his mouth to speak, but it was too late; Crankshaw had picked up his pen to change "AWOL" to simply "absent" and was again lost in feisty composition. Conolly had no choice but to wait.

They had arrived at the Leh caravanserai early that morning and had immediately headed for the office of the Joint Commissioner. The closer they came to Leh, the more disturbed Ivana had become. Confused and insecure after learning the truth—whatever there was of it—she asked questions that Conolly still could not answer, falling just short of tearfully begging to be taken back. Not having any means with which to comfort her, he was totally at a loss as to how to deal with the situation.

"How will they receive me?" she asked unhappily as they rode the final few miles into the heart of the town. "In Tashkent they say the English are snobbish and do not like us."

"Do you find me snobbish?"

"No, of course not, but you are different. You are a friend."

Conolly sighed. "So is old Cranks, or at least he will be once he gets to know you. He does bark a lot, I admit, but he's never bitten anyone yet. At least not that I know of."

She touched her head with its scraggly hair growing unevenly like an unmown lawn. "What will Mr. Oldcranks think of me? And what will his lady wife when she sees me in these dirty clothes?"

"Lady wife?" Conolly guffawed. "You think any lady would consider marrying the old hedgehog? Besides, the man is a dyed-in-the-wool bachelor. The very sight of a female gives him the shingles—and, I daresay, vice versa. He's looked after by a Tibetan housekeeper who won't give a damn what you look like. Er, his name, incidentally, is Mr. Crankshaw."

None of which, of course, was especially reassuring. By the time they arrived at the office, Ivana was too petrified even to enter.

Crankshaw completed his telegraph, blotted the paper and snapped shut the folder.

"The young lady—she is in good fettle, is she?"

"As good as can be expected, sir."

"She behaved well?"

"She behaved impeccably, sir."

"No fainting fits, tantrums, hysterics and whatever else females have outside the confines of their boudoirs?"

"None, sir." Conolly's manner assumed a touch of frost. "Miss Ivanova conducted herself throughout in a most exemplary manner. Her strength of character was admirable and her composure never less than perfect. No other young lady that I know would have endured what she did with such lack of complaint. She is apprehensive, naturally, as is only to be expected under the circumstances, but by no means distraught."

"I see." Crankshaw's thicket of brows shot up and bristled with eloquence. "In that case may I also have the pleasure of making the acquaintance of this worthy paragon who seems to have made such a profound impression on you?"

Pinking a little, Conolly hastened out to fetch her. He returned a moment later and Ivana crept in fearfully behind him. "Presenting one Armenian lady, sir, as ordered by the management," he announced with a flourish. "Miss Ivana Ivanova."

"Hmph." Crankshaw polished his glasses, replaced them on the bridge of his nose and subjected Ivana to a prolonged visual inspection. "You've led us quite a merry dance, young lady," he said severely. "I hope you realise the trouble the British government has gone to in order to rescue you from the Russians?"

Not understanding a word but alarmed by the tone as much as the look, Ivana moved closer to Conolly.

"I don't think 'rescue' is quite the right word, sir," Conolly pointed out drily. "Perhaps 'kidnap' might be more appropriate."

Crankshaw dismissed the technicality with a *tch!* "Sit down, sit down," he said testily. Understanding the gesture, Ivana hastily dropped into a chair. He addressed her again. "No worse for wear then, are we?"

"She doesn't speak any English, sir," Conolly said, resuming his own seat across the desk and crossing his arms firmly. "Since she has no idea why she has been put through all this torment, perhaps some explanations might . . ."

"Later, Capricorn, later. First things first. Having got used to cushy living, I suppose you're starving as usual?"

His stomach gave an ominous rumble and Conolly conceded the good sense of the suggestion with alacrity. "Now that you mention it, sir, I wouldn't say no to some breakfast. Neither, I'm sure, would Miss Ivanova."

"Tea, ham, eggs, toast, marmalade and leftover quail pie do you?"

Conolly gulped. "I would certainly say so, sir, thank you. A good, sound kip on a bed without resident population would also be greatly appreciated."

Crankshaw's mouth creaked with the effort of a smile. "Well, consider all that done—except for the order of priority." He crinkled his nose and brushed it with a finger. "First, get my housekeeper to find you both some fresh clothing, you pong all the way to bloody Simla. Second, ask the bearer to put a light to these infernal rags *outside* the house, then both into a hot bath for a good hard scrub." He glared at each in turn. "Separately, of course."

Conolly heaved a sigh of pure bliss.

When he was again on his own, Crankshaw settled back to re-read the draft he had composed. As he read, his huge hands absently caressed the barren expanse of his scalp as if in propitiation of the deity of hairlessness. Although the crest showed no sign of growth, there were bushy grey tufts above each ear and his lovingly groomed whiskers were abundant enough. His skin, thick and corrugated, looked not unlike one of his housekeeper's well-browned shortcrust pastry pies.

A thought occurred; Crankshaw scratched a crusty cheek and smiled slyly. The Janus project was the brainchild of the Intelligence Department. He had been roped in (much against his will) only because without him Simla didn't have a hope in hell. Well, if Columbine had chosen to report to Simla, then Capricorn had opted for Leh, which made it a *quid pro quo*. Handled judiciously, the situation could even turn out to be lucrative—a prospect not to be scorned considering the pittance on which he was expected to run the bloody place.

Honour restored, he scrunched the draft in a fist, tossed it into the waste-paper basket and set about formulating a second message in a mood rather more conciliatory.

Bathed, fed and rested, over dinner that night Conolly was relieved to find Ivana in a less dejected frame of mind, due perhaps to the maternal ministrations of the housekeeper. Her face looked less pinched, the wide eyes a little less frightened and a smile or two had appeared. The housekeeper had produced a brightly coloured traditional Tibetan dress for Ivana and some old shirts and trousers for him. It was arranged that Ivana would stay with the housekeeper's predominantly female Tibetan family, which satisfied the demands of both propriety and convenience.

Visibly uncomfortable in the presence of a young woman on his undefiled premises, at dinner Maurice Crankshaw gave Ivana the benefit of a few barks and yelps, then—much to her relief—ignored her for the rest of the evening.

"Flatulence, eh?" Listening to Conolly's account of his adventures in Kashgar, Crankshaw chuckled. "I wonder what the windy old coot will do now without his magic potions?"

"Whatever he does, I wouldn't like to be standing behind him when he does it," Conolly replied, and they roared with laughter.

"When can I have your written report?" Crankshaw asked.

"Er, day after tomorrow, sir?"

"What's wrong with tomorrow?"

Conolly bit his lip. "Tomorrow, sir, I thought I might escort Miss Ivanova up the hill. She has never been to a Buddhist monastery before."

Crankshaw waggled a finger in his face. "Corrupted by easy living, eh?" he growled. "Oh, all right, all right. But if it's not on my desk first thing the day after, Capricorn, you can be sure I'll have your guts for garters."

"Yes, sir, thank you, sir."

"Miss Ivanova recovers well? Comfortable where she is?"

"Sir. Of course, it will take her time to adjust." He added before he lost the advantage, "About the explanations, sir . . ."

"*After* the report, Capricorn," Crankshaw said firmly. "Now, what about the expenses?"

"I have a list of them here, sir."

"Yes, I'm sure you have. Well, I've been thinking, Capricorn. Since your escapade was engineered by the Intelligence Department, it is only fair that Hethrington should make the reimbursements. How much did you spend, anyway?" Conolly mentioned a figure and Crankshaw launched into a tirade. When he had finished, he heaved a long-suffering sigh and shrugged. "Well, all said and done, I suppose it was worth it."

"Being in the dark about the facts," Conolly pointed out coldly, "I wouldn't know, sir."

Ignoring the bait, Crankshaw got up, yawned and bade them good-night. "Oh, by the way, Capricorn," he added casually, as they were about to disperse, "I told Hethrington right at the beginning that if anyone could get the job done without making a bloody mess of it, it was you. I thought you might like to know that."

Coming from Maurice Crankshaw, it was exceptional praise indeed. Holbrook Conolly was quite overwhelmed.

A brash, alien sky stretched across Emma's inner horizons. Awake and yet not awake, she hovered on the rim of consciousness, slipping in and out of fevered dreamscapes. Slowly, one by one, the nebulous neth-erworlds drifted away and with an effort she prised her eyes open. Dazzled by a shaft of sunshine, she shut them again quickly and winced. She strug-gled to sit up.

"Lie still."

Damien stood watching her from the shadows. She lay back, spent, and forced her eyes open again. He walked to the windows and adjusted the curtains. The morning glare transmuted into a restful dark, touched with soothing orange from the low fire in the grate.

"Feeling better?"

Murmuring something, she ran her tongue over arid lips and took note of her surroundings. She was on a fourposter under a plump eiderdown in a room that was warm and wood-panelled. Overhead, thick oak beams supported a slanting roof. There were patterned wool rugs on the floor and flowered chintz curtains at the windows. She lifted the quilt and peered at her oversized nightshirt in puzzlement.

"You were drenched, your clothes needed changing. I'm sorry, but a nightshirt was the best I could do." He came to stand by the bed. "You rode up all the way from Shalimar?"

Memory came sweeping back like a winter wind.

Charlton!

She raised herself on her elbows. "Geoffrey Charlton was waiting for me in Tanmarg," she whispered, wide-eyed and frantic. "He took away my father's papers."

"Alone?"

"He had the house surrounded, Damien. He said Walter Stew . . ."

"You should not have come alone." Agitated, he barely listened. "You could have been attacked, killed. It was not safe."

She clenched her fists and stared up at the beams. "I had to warn you. Charlton said he . . ."

"First some broth. It will do you good." He picked up a cup from the table and offered it to her.

"Don't you understand?" she cried, pushing away the cup. "Charlton *knew* I would be carrying my father's papers, he *took* them from me. There was nothing I could do to stop him."

He replaced the cup, sat down at the foot of the bed and regarded her solemnly. "Did you really want to?"

For an instant she could not understand what he meant, then she remembered their terrible confrontation and with a shudder squeezed her eyes shut.

"Never mind," he said. "Tell me what happened. Charlton came to Shalimar?"

"Yes." Taking hold of herself, without looking at him, she related everything that had transpired. "He was angry because I did not have the rest of the papers. He assumed that *you* had. He was coming here to get them—did he?"

"Yes. You were asleep. I saw no reason to wake you."

"You have the papers?"

"Had. I gave them to him."

For an instant, just an instant, she was stunned. But then remembering the brutal reality between them, she wiped the astonishment off her face. She had not been able to fathom this man through all these many months; it was unlikely that she should do so now at the end of their, what?, association, acquaintanceship? She could not think of the appropriate word. Suddenly, her insane dash through the wilds alone, in the middle of the night, seemed laughable. She had achieved nothing, merely made a fool of herself. The barrier between them was too high, too far above her head. She should not have tried to scale it. She should have not allowed herself to forget that Shalimar was no longer her concern—any more than was Damien.

He was staring at her, puzzled. "You took all these frightening risks just to warn me?"

"Yes, but I see now that I need not have."

"No, no, I didn't mean that," he corrected himself. "I am overwhelmed that you should have made so valiant an attempt to . . ." He broke off, confused. "I hardly know what to say."

"There is no need to say anything," Emma assured him stiffly. "Since I did not want to leave with the loss of your property on my conscience, my motives were entirely selfish."

"Nevertheless, I am beholden to you."

She turned her back on him. "I wish I had never laid eyes on those papers," she said with sudden bitterness. "It would have been better to remain ignorant and blissful rather than . . ." She buried her face in the comfort of the pillow without completing the thought.

He did not remark on her observation. He asked instead, "Do you feel sufficiently recovered to come downstairs for a while?"

"No."

"There are some people I would like you to meet."

"I have no wish to meet anyone."

"You have made so singular an effort on my behalf, I would be grateful if you would consider extending it to this one final favour."

She turned. "Who are these people you want me to meet?"

"You will see."

"I have no clothes to wear. I can hardly appear in company dressed in your nightshirt!"

"I think we could extend ourselves to a dressing-gown, a woollen vest and a shawl or two."

He spoke lightly, almost offhandedly, but beneath the casualness she could detect urgency. Not really concerned any more and too tired to argue, she made a gesture that he accepted as affirmative.

"Thank you. Now drink this."

She took the cup from his hand and sipped. The broth was thick, hot and in all probability delicious, but she could taste nothing.

CHAPTER

19

Swathed in a quilted dressing-gown, oversized woollen stockings, and shawl, Emma awaited Damien's guests without enthusiasm. She felt like an Egyptian mummy—and no doubt, looked like one—but Damien had insisted and she was too ill to protest. A revived log fire sent licks of flame leaping up the chimney and Hakumat bustled around fussing with this and that. Suraj Singh, as always, stood by like a watchful centurion.

"Comfortable?" Damien draped a blanket across her knees.

"Yes, thank you."

"Good." His smile fell just short of his eyes. "One final request—listen first, then ask questions."

"If that is what you wish."

At a sign from him, Suraj Singh went out and returned a moment later to usher in two men, both dressed in Indian Army uniform. Brusque and formal, the officers shook hands with Damien. No words of greeting were exchanged, only their cold, guarded eyes indicated their tensions.

"Colonel Wilfred Hethrington and Captain Nigel Worth from the Military Intelligence Department," Damien said, presenting them to her. "My wife."

If she was at all surprised, Emma did not show it. They bowed in turn over her hand, both clearly embarrassed. In the light of what Charlton had told her, their embarrassment was, of course, understandable. She did not remind Captain Worth that they had met in Delhi at the Prices', neither did he mention it.

"My wife decided to join me for a few days," Damien said. "Unfortunately, she was caught in a downpour and runs a fever."

They murmured polite platitudes, then seated themselves at the table set in a corner. Hakumat materialised with a samovar and cups of *qahwa* were passed around amidst stilted exchanges and cemented expressions. As the door closed behind the bearer Damien walked to the desk, opened a drawer and withdrew from it a thin, narrow brown envelope. He placed it on the table before the Colonel. There was no preamble, no small talk, no social nicety. The hostility between them was evident.

Cheeks pallid, hands clasped tightly in front of them, the two officers stared unblinkingly at the envelope. Neither made a move to pick it up.

The Colonel cleared his throat. "I take it this is everything, Granville?"

"No. Only Dr. Wyncliffe's diary." Colonel Hethrington glanced in Emma's direction, then quickly looked away.

"The rest?"

"When your side of the bargain is complete."

"It is complete. Proof arrives shortly."

Damien stilled and his expression changed. For an instant he looked stupefied, as if in a trance. Then, excusing himself, he went out of the room, leaving behind an awkward silence. Quietly, Suraj Singh slipped out after him.

Your side of the bargain.

Emma stared into the fire. He had dared to enter into a bargain using *her* father's papers? Fleetingly she was incensed, but only fleetingly. With so much lost, did it matter? She decided that it did not.

The Colonel sucked in his breath and reached for the envelope. He slit it open, pulled out the papers and laid them flat on the table. He took the first page, his acutely alert eyes darting from side to side as he read, then passed the sheet to his aide and went on to the next. There was no sound in the room save for the rustle of paper, the steady *tick-tock* of the wall clock and the soughing of logs in the grate. One slipped onto the hearth with a hiss and a shower of sparks. Emma rose and replaced it in its former position with a pair of tongs. Neither man looked up.

The joint persual over, Captain Worth re-folded the papers and returned them to the envelope. He gave her a sidelong glance but she had already averted her face.

Damien returned once more composed, his features reconstituted in their earlier phlegmatic mould. Only his cheeks showed a rush of colour and his eyes shone startlingly bright.

"This is a transcript, Granville," Colonel Hethrington said. "Where are the original strips?"

Positioned by the window with an elbow resting on the sill, Damien appeared entirely engrossed in a pair of foals being exercised in the paddock by a stable boy. For a moment he seemed not even to have heard the question, but then he answered it.

"I think you should know, Colonel, that Geoffrey Charlton was here."

The Colonel inhaled sharply. "May I ask why?"

"For the same reason that you are."

"And?"

"I gave him the original strips."

There was an incredulous silence. Eyes glazed, both officers froze in a tableau. Vaguely surprised that he had not revealed her own unthinking part in Charlton's sordid game, Emma remained silent. With unsteady fingers, Colonel Hethrington groped in his pocket for a kerchief and dabbed his forehead. He did not speak, perhaps because he could not.

It was Nigel Worth who first found his tongue. "Are you quite *mad,* Damien?" he asked, his voice hushed with horror.

"Not mad, Nigel. Expedient."

"But why in God's name, *why?*"

"For an excellent reason. Charlton had a gun and I had no burning desire either to kill or be killed for the greater glory of your damned Empire."

The Colonel recovered his speech but his hands still shook. He thrust them under the table. "Whatever your opinion of the Empire, Granville," he said, cold with fury, "those papers happen to be the classified property of the government. Even to be in possession of them is a criminal offence."

"What I am in possession of, Colonel, is unauthenticated copies. The property of the government is with Charlton."

"Which you bloody well gave him!"

"Considering the departmental Pandora's Box you would have to open to prove that, Colonel, I don't think you can afford the luxury of indignation. A Pandora's Box, by the way," he added pleasantly, "about which, in all probability, your Commander-in-Chief knows nothing."

Colonel Hethrington gave him a baleful look, then his shoulders fell. Within the space of an instant he seemed older, more defeated, his jowls hanging loose and heavy with strain. "My initial instincts about your chum were right, Captain," he said tiredly. "I knew he was not to be trusted."

Stung by the insinuation, Nigel Worth leapt out of his chair, his expression equal parts of outrage and anguish. "You gave me your word, Damien! You promised, dammit, you *promised*..."

"There is another reason," Damien said.

"Sit down, Captain!" Hethrington commanded as he again mopped his brow. "Now that your Janus has revealed his darker face, I suppose we might as well hear what he has to say. As much for his sake as ours he had better make it good, *damn* good. The other reason, Granville?"

Nigel Worth sank back into the chair with a groan.

"You might recall," Damien said, "that after the Russo-Turkish War and during the Congress of Berlin, Charlton held a part-time job at the Foreign Office in London while continuing to write for the *Sentinel*."

"So?"

"Overhearing that details of an Anglo-Russian treaty were to be leaked to *The Times* by the F.O., and having access to the document, Charlton published its contents the following day in the *Sentinel*. He was arrested for theft of confidential government documents but subsequently released because no papers were found either on his person or at his premises. With his remarkable memory, he had reproduced the salient points of the treaty almost verbatim after having read them only once."

Catching the drift, Colonel Hethrington's frown deepened. He leaned forward. "Are Butterfield's notes in code?"

"No. He probably didn't have time to encode them."

"And the writing on both sets of strips, is it legible?"

"Only just. Before he can commit them to memory, Charlton will need time to decipher the notes."

Nigel Worth brightened perceptibly and the Colonel straightened his back. "What time did Charlton leave?" Hethrington asked, getting down to business at once.

"About three hours ago. He should be in Srinagar by nightfall. Considering the strain of the journey here and back, I should imagine his first priority will be sleep. With no idea that anyone apart from Suraj Singh, my wife and myself is aware of his visit, he certainly will not expect to be searched."

Colonel Hethrington reached for his notebook. "Send both our sepoys off to Srinagar with this chitty for Stewart," he instructed Worth. "Once the search warrants are issued . . ."

"*Not* Walter Stewart!" Damien sliced him off. "His Highness will arrange for the warrants."

"His Highness? Good God, man, I am not authorised to go above the Resident's head to the maharaja!"

"No, but I am."

"Departmental procedure does not . . ."

"Confound your departmental procedure, Colonel!" Damien snapped. "You know damn well Stewart and Charlton work together with their big guns trained on me. I'm simply *not* having Stewart involved in any of this, no matter how rigid your blasted protocol!"

Hethrington compressed his lips in annoyance. "I gave you my *word,* Granville, that your Shalimar would not be at risk!"

"I don't trust the word of the Intelligence Department any more than it does mine," Damien retorted with ill-concealed contempt. "For your information, Colonel, Suraj Singh is already on his way with my letter requesting His Highness to do the necessary. He will be delighted, I have no doubt, to put Stewart in his place and settle Charlton's hash. You will have your original papers by tomorrow."

Colonel Hethrington bristled. "You had no damn business to approach His Highness without our authority, Granville!"

"On the contrary, Colonel, I had *every* damn business! As it happens, the Yasmina is located within Kashmir, still an independent state not entirely down the British gullet. You do it my way—or Charlton publishes the papers with my blessings. It's no skin off my nose, believe me."

"By *Christ*!" Hethrington exploded. "How dare you try to dictate terms to the government! Considering you worked for me, Granville, your temerity can hardly be . . ."

"I did not work *for* you, Colonel," Damien amended icily, "nor ever will. We made a single arrangement for mutually selfish reasons. That arrangement is now at an end. We owe each other nothing."

Arrangement.

Yes, that was the word that had been eluding her, Emma saw. It summed up their marriage precisely; an *arrangement* (also now at an end) for mutually selfish reasons.

"And what about our friendship?" Nigel Worth demanded heatedly. "That counts for nothing? We had unwritten rules, Damien, and you broke them. You and Hyder Ali hare off to Tashkent illegally . . ."

"Because you refused me permission to go legally!"

". . . spin a cock-and-bull yarn to that ass of a Baron and actually offer him the maps. Then you leave Hyder behind in hiding and now you take it upon yourself to . . . to . . ." He spluttered to an angry halt. "You betrayed us, Damien. I . . . I *trusted* you, dammit!"

"Don't be an idiot, Nigel, it is because I have *not* betrayed you that you stand to get your papers tomorrow." Dismissing the accusation with an impatient wave, Damien walked over to the desk and from it abstracted a second envelope. This he did not lay on the table but merely held up for inspection.

"A transcript of Butterfield's notes. Everything he could possibly squeeze into his prayer-wheel: descriptions, elevations, latitude, longitude, sketch map and measurements—in other words, cartographical information about the Yasmina Pass." He opened the envelope and withdrew its contents with a flourish. "May I?"

No response came from either of the officers. In the quivering silence only a horse dared to neigh outside in the paddock, that too briefly. Despite her scant interest in the strategic value of the pass, Emma found herself gripped by the sheer scope of the moment.

"To satisfy himself," Damien began, referring to the paper but not reading from it, "Butterfield walked to the end of the gully Dr. Wyncliffe had explored and did what Dr. Wyncliffe was too weak to do: climb its exterior face and look down into it. Butterfield confirms its height as two thousand, three hundred and seventy-six feet, slightly above Dr. Wyncliffe's estimate. He then walked along the top of the crack to the gully's northern end, a distance of one and a quarter miles." He lifted his eyes briefly. "It is what he found at the end of the gully that constitutes the crux of the discovery. Butterfield's own words describe it best."

He flipped over the page and started to read:

The topography here is volatile, a magnificent-ugly primaeval world trapped in an eternally continuing cycle of creation and destruction. Overnight gigantic avalanches divert and re-divert massive rivers of ice, form underground lakes, split open crevasses into the entrails of the earth, dam valleys and send torrents thundering down gorges. There is constant upheaval. The clamour is deafening and terrifying, and the earth moves without warning.

The gully itself, the Yasmina Pass, is a sinister place, freezingly cold, dark, hostile and bestrewn with ice and boulders. The Hunzakut are right, it is the epitome of evil. One senses it in one's bones. It is touched by the sun only at noon, that too for a few minutes. The surprising reality is that the Yasmina is not difficult to find, only difficult—nay, impossible!—to discern unless one looks for it, so well does the crack of its opening merge with the rock.

Early explorers believed that there were tunnels under the Himalayas half a mile deep. Perhaps at one time, before glacial changes transformed the region, this was one of them. When I arrived at the far end of the alley—for it is hardly more—I was faced with a prospect I had not considered, no one had: rockfall. I found myself confronting a wall of frozen boulders compacted with the ice of ages— a formidable barrier impossible to penetrate, dislodge or circumvent. On the other side—as I had already seen—sheer ice slopes plunged down hundreds of feet.

Damien stopped. "The sketch map, statistics and geological information you can see for yourselves." Replacing the papers in the envelope, he tossed it onto the table before them.

"This, then, gentlemen," he concluded softly, "is the secret of the Yasmina—the secret the beleaguered Hunzakut fought so long, so savagely and so hopelessly to protect—the fact that there *is* no Yasmina. If the pass existed once, glacier changes and topographical volatility have ensured that it no longer does. In her great wisdom, Nature has blocked it and placed it beyond the reach of any human agency. It could have happened last year, or a century or a millennium ago. No one knows and no one ever will."

It was a devastating revelation, a reality so unexpected, so immense, that for a while its significance could not be fully ingested. Plunged into private confusion, both officers remained motionless as they tried to come to grips with it. Unaware that the future course of Central Asian history was about to be re-fashioned, only the wall clock ticked on in blithe rhythm.

Colonel Hethrington was the first to shake off his paralysis. Easing himself back in his chair, he started to laugh.

"Well, I'll be damned!"

Damien returned to the window. "Hunza had no resources with which to fight either of its neighboring bullies," he said. "All it had were two assets, the Yasmina—and insatiable imperial greed. It exploited both for as long as it could, and—you must admit—did a damned fine job of it too!"

Colonel Hethrington swung forward, made a cat's-cradle of his fingers and propped his chin on his knuckles. "Much as it pains me to say this, Granville, I cannot disagree with you entirely. If anyone is inclined to shed tears over the passing of that pernicious pass, I can assure you, it isn't me. And now that the bubble has finally been pricked, perhaps we can forget about it and get on with our blasted jobs." He disentangled his fingers, pushed back his chair and stood up. Captain Worth did likewise.

"Good." Damien stopped them with a gesture. "Now that we have at least minimal agreement on that, Colonel, there is something else I think you ought to know."

Ever alert to nuances, the Colonel frowned. "Why do I have the feeling that I am about to hear something I would rather not?"

"Because," Damien replied equably, "you are."

They sat down again and Nigel Worth cursed under his breath. Strolling across to the table, Damien leaned on it with his palms.

"Even though they both behave as if they do, neither Britain nor Russia owns the Himalayas. The truth about the Yasmina is the monopoly of no one, therefore details of the find are now on their way to St. Petersburg. They will be delivered anonymously to the *Novoe Vremya* and the *Morning Post*. Having nothing to fear from *their* laws, I should imagine the Russians would be delighted to publish the scoop of the century."

Had the clock not chimed the half hour a moment later and restored life to the inanimate, the disbelieving hush might have continued indefinitely. Emerging out of her stupour, Emma stirred, worked herself into a sitting position and through a feverish haze stared unblinkingly at Nigel Worth.

"I know who you are," she said, finally breaking her silence. "You are *Hammie,* Damien's school friend from Burma, aren't you?"

*M*aurice Crankshaw had very definite rules about how reports should be written—or rather, how they should not be written. There was to be no hyperbole, no adverbial and adjectival clutter and no vulgar colloquialisms. Facts were to be stated clearly and succinctly. The text, in no-nonsense Queen's English with due deference to the tenets of grammar, was to be restricted to essentials. Flights of fancy were expressly forbidden.

Therefore, for all the excitement his account generated, Conolly considered he might just as well have conjugated Latin verbs. The mild protest he ventured left Crankshaw unimpressed.

"Well, how do you expect a government report to read, Capricorn, like Shakespearean sonnets to the Dark Lady?"

"No, sir, but the way it sounds nobody will read it without falling asleep after the first paragraph."

"Nobody will read it anyway," Crankshaw assured him, "except you, me and a handful in Simla in what is known—laughably, I might add—as the Intelligence Department. Reports are not adventure yarns for schoolboys, Capricorn. They are archival records compiled to convey a sense of history to future generations, to commemorate inspiring examples of imperial initiative and enterprise for the benefit of those who come after us. We don't want posterity to remember us as mindless moon-calves, do we?"

Conolly couldn't speak for Crankshaw, of course, but for himself he could not have cared less how posterity remembered him, if at all. To add to his growing irritation, the matter of Ivana still remained unexplained. Each time he tried to pin Crankshaw down, he was met with the same testy prevarications.

"All in good time, Capricorn, all in good time. She's not running away any more than you are. The report first, then the ancillaries."

Apart from the fact that it riled him to have Ivana dismissed as an "ancillary," he had completed the report yesterday morning as ordered and a summons from the Commissioner was still awaited. Vetted and approved with only two adjectives, one arguably overheated phrase and a split infinitive excised, it had finally been encoded and telegraphed to Simla, and that was that.

What now? Conolly wished he knew.

In the absence of David Wyncliffe on medical furlough in Delhi, Conolly was billetted in his rooms in the bungalow. After existing on the edge for weeks, the sudden cessation of activity produced in him an ennui, a sense of anticlimax. As he sat brooding on the verandah in the early after-noon contemplating his—and Ivana's—uncertain future, he felt restless and unusually dispirited.

During their five days in Leh he had met Ivana only thrice, each time under the disapproving eye of Crankshaw's ogress of a housekeeper, who had chaperoned her also to the monastery. Although comfortably housed and well cared for, to him Ivana seemed forlorn and his heart went out to her. He longed to talk to her, reassure her about the days ahead—wherever they might be—but the opportunity had simply not arisen.

Fed up with the uncertainty of the situation, he decided that one way or another the truth had to be forced out of the Commissioner, and soon. He made up his mind to demand, yes, demand, explanations that very evening.

As he sat quietly seething and watching a procession of well-oiled saffron-clad Buddhist schoolchildren pass along the road, Conolly suddenly sensed a presence behind him. He turned to see Ivana standing by the rails. With a sudden rush of pleasure, he stumbled to his feet.

"Ah, I was just th-thinking about you," he stammered, tongue-tied in his surprise. "Er, are you well?"

They had shared so much over the past weeks, survived so traumatic a common experience, yet now that they were by themselves and face to face he could think of not a thing to say.

She answered seriously enough, "Yes. Very well. And you?"

"As well as can be expected, I suppose."

"You do not like it here?"

"No. I am not used to doing nothing. I don't even know what my next assignment is to be."

"You will be leaving Leh?"

"Well, yes, I suppose so."

"Where will you go?"

He shrugged. "Persia, Afghanistan, Turkey—who knows? Anywhere except Kashgar. The Celestial People can be most un-Celestial when it comes to absconding agents who also happen to be kidnappers."

She did not smile. "You do not care where you are sent?"

He considered the question. He had not cared earlier, no, but now the thought of routine preparations for a new journey, a new identity, a new game with new rules, depressed him.

"No," he sighed. "One assignment is very much like another."

"Like the assignment to bring me here from Kashgar," she said mis-erably.

"Well, yes. I mean, *no,* of course not!" He forced a smile. "What I meant was that agents like me are rolling stones. Once we start to gather moss, we might as well pack it in."

She lowered her head and two tears trickled down her cheeks. "I will not see you again."

He was incredibly touched, once again charmed by her honesty and lack of artifice. Moving close to her, he impulsively put a hand on hers, longing to take her in his arms and kiss her to death, but not daring to with the office next door and Crankshaw's peon looking on.

"There is no need to be frightened, Ivana," he said earnestly, deliberately misunderstanding her. "I won't leave until I am assured that you are in, well, good hands."

Even to him it sounded lame and horribly trite. In whose good hands? Where? He turned away unhappily. Over the past weeks he had held her life in his own hands many times, but now, all at once, she was no longer his concern. The prospect of such total amputation was intolerable; when he turned to tell her so, however, he found Ivana gone. He had never felt so low in all his life.

Despite his abrasiveness and the awesome acidity of his tongue, Maurice Crankshaw was a popular man in Leh with a vigorously active social life. Hardly a week went by without an invitation either to attend some private ceremony or other or to preside over a public function. Conolly was therefore greatly chagrined to find that evening as he prepared to collar the Commissioner that he was not only off to a wedding feast but expected Conolly to accompany him. It was only because Ivana was also included in the invitation that his temper eased somewhat.

Well, so be it, Conolly decided grimly. Whether old Cranks liked it or not, he would broach the subject at the feast—and damn the consequences!

The occasion was a Tibetan betrothal. The groom, an orphan boy of ten, was to wed an older woman from within his family in traditional fashion. The bride would first perform the duties of a nursemaid and then, when the groom was older, of a wife. Later, if he so wished, he could acquire a younger consort. The complicated rituals were presided over by the head Lama. In keeping with tradition, Crankshaw had made a joint offering on all their behalves of gram flour, ghee, dried fruit, a length of saffron cloth and a silver rupee. It was a colourful, boisterous occasion and festivities were likely to continue through the night.

Never having seen anything like it before, Ivana was fascinated by the rituals and Crankshaw's explanations as translated by Conolly. The religious ceremonies over, the guests got down to the real business of the day. The *korey*, or loving-cup, filled with the local tipple called *chhang*, started to be passed around. Etiquette decreed that the goblet be drained each time and consequently much hilarity prevailed. Very soon Crankshaw started to turn noticeably merry.

Every time Conolly opened his mouth to stir the subject of Ivana, the goblet reappeared. By the end of the third round, he himself was beginning to feel distinctly lightheaded and after the fourth he had trouble focussing his eyes. Then Crankshaw started to sing a Tibetan love song and Conolly saw that it had to be now or never.

Before his Dutch courage—and his senses—evaporated altogether, he began firmly, "About the Armenian lady, sir."

As guests of honour they sat some distance away from the rest, but even so the noise was cacophanous. Crankshaw stopped singing and cupped his ear with a hand. "Eh?"

Conolly repeated his question and Crankshaw nodded. "Well, as a matter of fact, Capricorn, I did want to tell you about your next assignment."

"Oh." His heart sank. "Afghanistan, sir?"

"No, Capricorn, not Afghanistan. The Pamirs. You are to assist Francis Younghusband in negotiations for the demarcation of the fifty-mile gap. Since you know the region and are proficient in both Chinese and Russian, you could provide invaluable help. Now, about Kashgar . . ."

"I cannot go back to Kashgar, sir!"

"I am not suggesting that you do, Capricorn—if you would kindly let me finish. I was about to say that since you have studied the commercial potential of Sinkiang, a word with Younghusband and MacCartney might also be useful before *they* go to Kashgar—that is, if they are let in at all after your little caper about which, I can tell you, neither is particularly amused."

It was, of course, a grossly unfair observation, but bent on more vital issues, Conolly let it pass.

A thunderous roll of drums announced the start of an extempore verse contest. The women of the family, in the meantime, had cajoled the coy bride into coming forth to sit beside her youthful husband, who, bored with the proceedings, had fallen asleep. The bride, a mature lady thrice the age of the somnolent groom, took her appointed place with much oohing and aahing, and the groom was hastily nudged awake. Immediately, two of the men burst into song amidst hoots of laughter and excited prompting, rendering conversation even more of a penance.

"Now, before you go to the Pamirs, Capricorn," Crankshaw said, raising his voice above the din as he downed a fifth cup of *chhang,* "I have another assignment for you, a short one. You are to go to Srinagar."

"Srinagar?" Conolly focussed on his superior's face with an effort. "To what purpose, sir?"

"To what purpose does anyone go to Srinagar?" Crankshaw asked irritably. "To inhale salubrious air, to trek, to commune with nature, to drink *qahwa* (try it this time with a tot of gin), to nibble lotus seeds and walnuts, and when one is bored to tears with a life of hedonism, to meditate on a houseboat fanned by nubile maidens. Frankly, Capricorn, my heart bleeds for you, but I don't want to see you back here for another month. Talking about Srinagar, I remember when I was on the Dal in 'seventy nine, the . . ."

"What about *Ivana*, sir?" Conolly cut in with a measure of desperation. "What is to happen to *her*, sir? Where is she to go from here?"

"I've just told you, Capricorn—it is *because* of the lady that you have been ordered to Srinagar. Don't you ever listen?"

The bridal couple approached to pay their respects. Crankshaw rose to his feet somewhat unsteadily to compliment the matronly bride on her beauty, the yawning groom on his miraculous good fortune and the host on the excellent quality of the *chhang* (which immediately fetched another round), and sank down again.

"I have now been authorised by Simla," he said after due justice had been done to the goblet, "to put you fully in the picture with regard to Miss Ivanova. You are to escort her to Srinagar and deliver her safely into the hands of one Mr. Damien Granville—her brother."

*E*mma's fever persisted through the week. An army doctor up from Srinagar prescribed tonics to revive her body, but there was little he could do to repair her spirit. Despite Damien's attentiveness—or perhaps because of it?—she remained despondent. Summoned from Srinagar, Sharifa and Rehmat arrived with clothes and other requirements and a highly solicitous Suraj Singh was never far.

In spite of the detachment she had tried so hard to cultivate, the extent of her exclusion from Damien's parallel life had left Emma shaken and unbearably wounded. She wished that it were not so, that she could distance herself from him as successfully as he had from her, but she seemed unable to do so. That she had been wrong in branding him a Russian agent was to her of little consequence. It made no difference for which side he had spun his callous web of entrapment. What had already been explained was secondary; for what was primary, no explanations were acceptable. Stubbornly she asked no questions, and equally obdurate, Damien volunteered no answers.

Secretly, however, in the deep, aching silences of her mind, Emma still hunted for excuses and alibis and inadvertently overlooked interpretations. She could find none.

How could she ever forgive him?

As soon as she was sufficiently recovered, she requested Damien to make arrangements for her return to Delhi. He accepted that as he did all her requests, without question. When he went out of the room, she wept.

It was on the second day of her convalescence, as she sat in the garden flicking listlessly through a periodical, that Captain Worth came to see her. The spell of bad weather had passed. The morning was warm and sunny. In the terraced garden sloping down the hillside the combined scents of freshly mown grass, of pure mountain breezes and the sheer abundance of nature were sweet.

"I return to Simla tomorrow," Captain Worth said as he seated himself in a cane chair facing her. This morning he was not in uniform but in flannels and blazer. "I could not leave without saying good-bye."

Despite the assumed informality, Emma was not deceived. Knowing that Damien was away for the day in Khillanmarg, Nigel Worth had deliberately called in his absence.

"I see that Damien has told you about our schooldays in England."

"Yes." Emma let the presumption pass.

"He must have also mentioned that we are still close friends."

"I recognised you from a school photograph in Damien's study." She made an effort to smile. "I notice that he doesn't call you Hammie any more."

The Captain grinned. "For good reason. He knows I'd shove his teeth down his throat if he did."

She shared in his laugh and offered refreshments, a glass of fruit juice, perhaps? He accepted, inquired after her health and wished her a speedy recovery. She thanked him and asked politely if Colonel Hethrington had left for Simla. He confirmed that he had. She questioned him about his interest in dramatics, did it still persist? He confessed that it did, and at her prompting waxed eloquent about the latest production at the Gaiety.

The small talk exhausted, there was an awkward lull. Then Nigel Worth cleared his throat and got down to the purpose of his visit.

"I stayed back because I wanted to talk to you, Mrs. Granville."

She had guessed that, of course. "Oh?"

"Colonel Hethrington has ordered me to apologise most sincerely for the anguish caused to you and your family by everything that has happened. Had he not been in a tearing hurry to return to Simla with the papers, he would have apologised in person. He will be writing to you shortly."

He waited for her response but she made none.

Anxious to make amends, he pressed on. "You see, Mrs. Granville, we could not possibly acknowledge your father's extraordinary discovery until we had recovered . . ."

"Yes, I know," she interrupted. "Mr. Charlton was kind enough to explain all that to me."

Noting the cutting edge he winced, and Emma felt a stab of perverse satisfaction. After all, Captain Worth and his Department did have a great deal to answer for.

He said quickly, "Colonel Hethrington has authorised me to make whatever clarifications you wish, Mrs. Granville. Please feel free to ask questions."

Hakumat arrived with a jug of fresh orange juice. She waited until he had poured out two glasses and left, then asked the question that had been exercising her the most.

"Will my father now be given official credit for the discovery that cost him his life?"

"Yes, but only after a suitably worded statement has been approved by the Council of Ministers."

She picked up the magazine and stared hard at a page. "The threat to Shalimar that Mr. Charlton made—was that genuine?"

"Very much so. The sheer weight of circumstantial evidence Charlton had collected against Damien was incredibly damning. Had Charlton published it and accused him of treason, regardless of Simla, Stewart would have overridden the maharaja and requisitioned the estate in a jiffy. He's had an eye on it for months for his own personal use."

"And now?"

"The Resident has been ordered to leave well alone."

"Will he go to prison?"

"Charlton? Regrettably not. To make a cast-iron case we would have to expose . . ."

"The Pandora's Box?"

"Well, yes." He smiled faintly. "The QMG will not allow that. Charlton will be given a stern warning, asked to leave Kashmir and not permitted to return. The Department needs to keep its secrets, Mrs. Granville"—he took a sip of the juice—"and Damien must be protected."

"In spite of everything?"

Nigel Worth sighed. "Damien is his own person, Mrs. Granville—as perhaps you realise better than anyone. I knew at the outset that we would not be able to leash him. I just hoped he wouldn't run totally out of control."

"You consider that he did not?"

"Well," he shrugged philosophically, "it could have been worse."

"With the maps on their way to Russia? I doubt if Colonel Hethrington would agree!"

"Perhaps not. Even though the maps are of no use to anyone, Damien did behave outrageously. On the other hand," he spread his hands, "the Russians would have discovered the truth sooner or later. As Abraham Lincoln said, you can't fool all of the people all of the time."

Her thoughts already elsewhere, Emma looked back through a fog of distant, opaque memories. It all seemed so long ago. "Tell me, Captain Worth . . ."

"Nigel, please."

". . . Nigel, why did you not approach me directly for the papers?"

"We did." He gave her a deep look. "We authorised Damien to make you an offer through the Nawab—without revealing the true reason to the Nawab, of course. You refused it."

"Oh." Emma shifted uneasily. "Why then did you not take me into your confidence? Had I known of their strategic value, I would have surrendered them willingly."

He stared into his glass. "The papers were highly prized, Mrs. Granville. We feared that if . . ." He faltered.

"That if I realised their value, the price would go up?"

His colour heightened. "Frankly, yes. Your family was—forgive me for saying this—not in a happy financial situation, and the resources of our Department were sorely limited."

"I would not have *sold* my father's papers for all the tea in China," she informed him warmly.

"We were not to know that then, Mrs. Granville."

He spoke matter-of-factly enough, but Emma could see that he was profoundly embarrassed. Well, so he deserved to be. All the same, she could not help feeling sorry that it had fallen on him to discharge such a thankless duty. In spite of everything there was something disarming and likeable about Nigel Worth.

"If you had only trusted me," she sighed, "it would have saved so much"—she almost said "heartache"—"trouble."

"We were debating just that when I learned in Delhi that you were about to turn the papers over to Dr. Theodore Anderson. We could not risk that. You see," he inched his chair closer, "Dr. Anderson is suspected of receiving Russian funds for his expeditions in return for information."

"Good heavens, you mean Dr. Anderson is a *spy*—?"

"Oh dear me, no! In essence he is just a harmless old boy. The information he supplies, as far as we know, is trivial. On the other hand, he has been acquainted with Borokov for years. In the light of Russia's dalliance with Hunza and Anderson's own financial constraints, a sale of the papers might have proved tempting."

"How did he find out about my father's discovery anyway?"

"That, I'm afraid, we don't know yet. Perhaps through Borokov, who might have stumbled across something in Hunza."

So that was why Dr. Anderson had initially turned down her request for help and then suddenly changed his mind.

"Well, I could hardly have given Dr. Anderson papers of which I myself was unaware."

"We couldn't be sure that you were, Mrs. Granville," he reminded her gently.

"Why then did you not arrest me?" Emma asked, partly in exasperation and partly in jest. "After all, you did Geoffrey Charlton!"

"We considered that, too," he replied in all seriousness, "but the resulting publicity would have been self-defeating."

She fell silent.

"When Damien approached me for help, Mrs. Granville," he went on earnestly, "he was desperate. So, as it happened, were we. It was imperative that the papers be recovered *quietly,* without fuss."

Ah yes, hence the inspirationally named *Janus* project—obviously Nigel Worth had known his friend better than she herself had done.

"Anyway," he continued hurriedly, "I introduced Damien to Colonel Hethrington. The meeting was not a success. The Colonel was dead against the project."

"Also dead against Damien, it would seem."

"Well, the dislike was mutual. Damien loathes imperial officialdom in any form, and knowing about Natasha Granville and Damien's dubious reputation, the Colonel refused to trust him. But by then we were all grasping at straws. Ivana's trail, which Hyder Ali followed, had muddied even further. It appeared that . . ."

"Ivana?"

"Yes, Damien's sister."

Emma sat up slowly. Damien had a *sister*—?

Seeing the pallor of her face as the colour fled, Nigel went very still. "You didn't know about Ivana?"

Emma tried hard to conceal her enormous sense of shock, but could not. She shook her head. Caught unaware by the admission, he did not know how to respond to it. The bitterness must have shown in her eyes, for alongside the confusion in his there was compassion.

"Well, until five years ago, neither did Damien." Making a valiant bid to repair the damage on behalf of his friend, he asked hesitantly, "Would you . . . would you like me to tell you about Damien's sister?"

Emma's throat was thick with tears. What was the point now? Sensing the unhappiness she tried so desperately to hide, he asked no more questions but started to tell her anyway. Still stunned, she was too demoralised to resist.

"Before she died, Natasha Granville's old maid, Zaiboon, revealed to Damien that his mother had been . . . well, *enceinte,* when the Romanian cellist suddenly arrived and tempted her away. Edward Granville never knew that he was to be a father again; his wife had not told him. The caravan in which Natasha and her companion travelled was attacked by bandits in the Darkot Pass. He was killed and she was abducted and sold into slavery. When the man who bought her learned of her condition, he sold her off to someone else. Eventually, perhaps because she was very beautiful, she ended up in the zenana of the Khan of Khiva. It was here that she produced her child, a girl, and died a day later."

It was a terrible story, far worse than any Emma had expected, and she was horrified. "How on earth was all this discovered?"

"Piecemeal and over the years, put together with great perseverence by Damien and the Ali brothers, Hyder and Jabbar. Their mother was a Bokhariot with extensive family in Central Asia, all of whom helped. Initially, not knowing quite where to start, Damien began his search St. Petersburg."

"Is that why he went to Russia?"

"Yes, twice. The authorities were courteous but also highly suspicious of the half-English son of Natasha Vanonkova, a woman they considered had deserted her post and betrayed her country by marrying an Englishman. They had, they claimed, no record of her having returned to Russia. His subsequent inquiries in Central Asia yielded even less. Since the Russian annexation of Khiva, all those held in bondage had been freed. There was little interest in a female slave dead twenty years and Damien's own information was, to say the least, tenuous. His mother could have died before giving birth; the child might never have been born or been born dead."

Resentments forgotten for the moment, Emma was profoundly moved. "But she was born alive, did survive and has finally been found?"

"Miraculously, yes. It was one of Hyder Ali's uncles who unearthed an old midwife in Samarkand known to have been in Khiva at one time. The woman remembered that an Armenian slave in the zenana had indeed died after delivering a girl child about two decades earlier, although she could not say what had happened to the child."

"Armenian? Surely, Natasha Granville was Russian, was she not?"

"Oh she was, but fearing arrest by her own people she had passed herself off as Armenian. Of course, Damien only found that out later. The child survived, it was subsequently learned through a man employed at the time in the Petro-Armendarisk barracks as a cook, because of the kindness of a Khivan couple who had worked there for a Russian officer. He did not know the name of the officer, long since transferred out anyway, but his wife remembered something curious." He leaned forward. "I know Damien has removed it, but have you ever seen his mother's portrait? The one that used to hang in the formal drawing-room?"

"Yes."

"Did you happen to notice the pendant she wore?"

"A silver filigreed swan?"

"That's the one. The man's wife said that this Armenian child in the officer's house had worn some sort of ornament round her neck, a silver pendant of a bird. It stuck in her memory only because it was unusual, looked incongruous on her and she was surprised that it had not been stolen. She also remembered that the child was called, simply, *Khatoon*, 'the girl.'

"Well, on the offchance that his mother might have been wearing it when she left, Damien made a drawing of the pendant for Hyder to circulate in the region, but with no luck. No one knew anything about the child or what had happened to her since. It was only when Damien returned to St. Petersburg last autumn that the trail once more revived."

"When Geoffrey Charlton first met him . . ."

"Ah yes, that too." Nigel gave a wry laugh. "Well, in spite of that rather unfortunate circumstance, Damien did have an amazing stroke of luck. One of the Russian officers he met mentioned that a certain Colonel in the Imperial Guards had in his employ a young housekeeper when he was posted in St. Petersburg. He remembered that because someone had remarked on her culinary skills over the baccarat table. As far as the officer could recall, however, the woman was Russian, not Armenian, and he had no idea of her name. The Colonel was now posted in Tashkent, he said, and suggested that Damien contact him there."

"The Russian Colonel being Mikhail Borokov?"

Nigel was quite surprised. "As a matter of fact, yes. How on earth did you know that?"

"Through something Mr. Charlton said."

"Ah! Well, what Charlton picked up that night at the Yacht Club was the second most vital component in his dossier of circumstantial evidence. The most vital he finally managed to extract from one of the errand lads at the Ali brothers' emporium. It was about Damien's reckless trip to Tashkent."

"Was that where Ivana was found, in Tashkent?"

"Well, no, not exactly." Nigel Worth stroked his chin and frowned. "You see, in the meantime—just to complicate matters even further—Jabbar Ali had unearthed a *second* possible trail that led to Sinkiang, where a wealthy Chinese silk exporter was reported to have secretly acquired an Armenian concubine. As it happened, the second trail was a dead end, but since that was not known at the time, it also had to be pursued.

"And this," he pulled a long breath, "is where the Department came in. Through our agent in Kashgar we undertook to investigate the Sinkiang business."

"In return for the surreptitious abstraction of the papers!"

He coloured. "Er, yes. Unfortunately, we had no one reliable in Tashkent," he carried on hastily, "which is why when Damien received that message in Delhi from Hyder Ali the day after your wedding, he . . ." Nigel broke off and peered into her face. "But you don't know about that either, do you, Mrs. Granville?"

"No."

The day after your wedding. Yes, she remembered that day—how could she not?

"One of Hyder's cousins in Tashkent," Nigel explained, again trying hard to conceal his discomfiture, "had reported that Borokov did have a young Russian housekeeper, but he baulked at further inquiries. Borokov was a high-ranking officer on the Baron's staff. If caught asking questions, he could be arrested. Well, this being undoubtedly the most hopeful lead yet, in a wild impulse Damien decided to follow it himself. To be fair, he *did* ask permission to approach Borokov officially, but Colonel Hethrington threw a fit and put his foot down." He shrugged. "Well, Damien went anyway. Illegally and in disguise."

"You knew what he planned to do?"

Nigel smiled tightly. "No, but I knew Damien and what he was *likely* to do if the need arose. I was furious and, I might tell you, scared out of my wits."

"He would have exchanged the papers for his sister?"

"Oh, absolutely! It was sheer luck that both Borokov and his housekeeper were away in St. Petersburg and he was stuck with having to improvise with that imbecile of a Baron. Fortunately, the Kashmiri markhor buck he had taken with him—purchased at exhorbitant cost and with great foresight—got him off what could have been an extremely painful hook. Colonel Hethrington was, of course, livid. He had never trusted Damien's motives anyway."

"And you still did?"

"Yes, I did." Nigel's chin firmed. "Damien despises politics, always has done. He doesn't give a tinker's damn about the tug-of-war in Central Asia. All he wanted was his sister who, Hyder Ali finally confirmed, was indeed Borokov's housekeeper. Being there illegally, Hyder had to proceed cautiously, in secret and very, very slowly. By the time he had the confirmation, it was too late. Both Borokov and Ivana had vanished, she for an alleged holiday on the Caspian and he on a posting to Osh. Shortly thereafter it was learned that Borokov was dead."

"But obviously not the trail!"

"No, not the trail." Nigel shook his head, smiled and sat back. "However, the rest of the story is not mine to tell, Mrs. Granville, it belongs to

Holbrook Conolly, our erstwhile agent in Kashgar. It is he who must receive the credit for bringing Ivana back and restoring her to her family. Given his inimitable style and personal involvement, I have no doubt he will make a much better job of the remaining narration than I possibly can."

Emma lay back on the chaise-longue. Staring up at the benign blue sky and its brushwork of frothy cloud, her eyes were moist. She was deeply affected by the tragic saga; whatever her own tribulations, it was impossible not to feel compassion for the blameless young girl so brutally buffeted by fate merely through an accident of birth. At the same time, Ivana's story intensified her own tearing sense of isolation and she was filled with loneliness. With what unswerving determination Damien had excluded her from every aspect of his life that held meaning!

It was unlikely that Nigel Worth would not sense her inner pain or, indeed, its immediate cause. "Damien grew up believing that he was an only child, Mrs. Granville," he said, in stout defence of his friend. "It was the profoundest regret of his life. His quest to find his sister was a desperate need—an obsession, if you like—in an extremely solitary life."

Evidently not solitary enough to be shared with his wife!

Torn between loyalty to a friend and the need to make further clarifications, Nigel struggled inwardly but could not bring himself to trespass on territory so intensely private. Recognising his dilemma, Emma bit back her own sense of betrayal and reassured him with a smile.

"Where is Ivana now?" she asked.

"On her way to Gulmarg from Leh with Conolly. It will give her tremendous courage to see you here when she arrives, Mrs. Granville. Who better than a warm, understanding sister-in-law to welcome her into a home and family she has never known?"

Emma was filled with a terrible sadness. *When she arrives, I will no longer be here.*

With a mind icily calm in the acceptance of her imminent departure, Emma resumed her packing. Closeting herself in the fierce privacy of a sorrow pride would not allow her to share with anyone, least of all Damien, she avoided him whenever she could. He on his part made no effort to seek her out. Between them lay an impassable gulf, a wasteland of accidentally colliding glances and stilted communication. With an entire blighted lifetime to bury and mourn, when they did converse it was in banalities.

"Suraj Singh will escort you back to your mother," Damien said as she prepared for the return journey.

"Yes."

"It will be cold on the way. Keep plenty of warm clothing handy."

"I will."

"Do you have enough boxes for your books?"

"Yes, thank you. The same that you arranged earlier."

"Good. If you need any more . . ."

"I will let you know."

"Do."

It was impossible!

The evening before her departure Emma went for a last stroll through the pine forests of the circular walk that surrounded Gulmarg. The slopes were covered with bluebells, moon daisies, forget-me-nots and buttercups. The village was once known as Gaurimarg after the deity of the meadows, but in the sixteenth century a king had changed its name to Gulmarg, "meadow of flowers." Two Englishwomen dressed in riding britches walked by holding the reins of their mounts. They smiled and nodded and Emma smiled back. Gulmarg was fast becoming a favourite watering hole of Europeans, especially of those inclined to sport.

When she returned from the walk, it was to find Damien sitting at the desk in the parlour, writing. He had had an appointment, he had told her, at the Gulmarg Golf Club with an army officer who planned the laying of two golf courses. Obviously, the meeting had concluded early. Not having expected to find him home yet, she halted uncertainly in the doorway.

He did not look up. "The club secretary sends his salaams and asks if you would kindly agree to judge the dressage at the Horse Show on Saturday."

She took her time to slip off her cloak, remove her gloves and reconstitute herself. "That is very kind of him, but by Saturday I will be gone."

"You could delay your departure by a week."

"No. I don't think that would be possible."

He fidgeted for a moment with his papers, then, finally, turned to face her. "Is this what you really want, Emma, to return to Delhi?" It was the first time he had asked the direct question.

"Yes."

"I see. Well, in that case I suppose I had better give you the explanations I promised."

More explanations! She shook her head. "Enough has been explained already. I have no need to hear more."

"Not even about my sister?"

"Since Nigel Worth was kind enough to relate to me the entire story, I can save you that trouble too."

As soon as she had said it, she was sorry; it sounded hard and unfeeling and childishly sullen. She removed her overshoes, sat down on the couch and stretched her palms over the fire.

"Why did you not tell me about her earlier?" she asked wearily.

"Would you have been interested if I had?"

"Of course I would have been interested!"

"Really? There seemed to be so little about me and my affairs that did interest you."

It made her angry that even at this late hour he devised alibis to salve his conscience.

"That you should have kept from me such an . . . an *integral* part of your life is unforgivable!" she burst out, unable to hold the outrage so carefully leashed for days. "You deliberately cloaked everything in secrecy—even something as trivial and stupid as repairs to this house!"

"Until her *mulki* status could be formalised, I intended to keep my sister in Gulmarg." If he was perturbed by her outburst he gave no hint of it. "The concealment was necessary."

"Concealment from me, your wife?"

"No." He picked up his pen. "Concealment from Geoffrey Charlton."

She stared at the stretch of his back, startled. "You believe I would have betrayed your confidence to Geoffrey Charlton?" That hurt more than she would have thought possible. "How could you even *consider* that?"

"How? Having thrown his name at me often enough, I think you can answer that better than I!" He folded a sheet of paper, slipped it into an envelope and set about addressing it.

She averted her face. "I was angry, Damien. I felt cheated and abandoned. Had I been told the truth earlier . . ."

"I had intended to tell you everything the day I returned from Tashkent," he said, not letting her finish. "However, when you flaunted Charlton in my face and locked your door on me, I realised I would be a damn fool to risk it."

"My interest in Geoffrey Charlton was purely academic!"

"*His* interest in you was not! Charlton is a highly skilled professional busybody. He knows how to excavate secrets—especially from adoring females who imagine themselves cheated and abandoned. He also excels at insinuating ideas and planting insidious little seeds. He could see perfectly well how enamoured you were of his charm, how impressed with that shy, smarmy, little-boy smile he cultivates to such advantage." He gave an angry snort of a laugh. "A little less smarmy since you deprived him of a canine, but smarmy nonetheless."

Listening to the tirade, Emma suddenly realised something she would have earlier considered impossible. "You were *jealous* of Geoffrey Charlton?" She was too amazed even to laugh.

"Not in the *least!*" He leapt out of his chair to lope across the floor with leonine strides. "I was simply surprised that a woman of your allegedly intelligent perceptions could not see the man for what he was—an ambitious, unscrupulous, scheming opportunist who made use of you for his own selfish ends."

"And *you* were not?" It was out before she knew it.

He stopped in mid-stride. "You really believe that, do you?"

She was dismayed that without any desire to do so, she should have revived the stale debate. Not knowing how to retrieve what had slipped out, she assumed the offensive. "Well, you *did* blackmail me into marrying you!"

"Yes."

"And you *did* bribe that foul man Highsmith to drug my brother so that he would lose that hand."

"Yes."

"You pumped Chloe Hathaway for gossip about me from Delhi . . ."

"Yes."

". . . only as groundwork for stealing those papers."

"No."

He *still* lied to her! Picking up her cloak and gloves, she made to go upstairs to her room.

"Wait. There is something I would like to show you."

Without meaning to, her footsteps faltered.

Unlocking the lower portion of his desk, he abstracted from it a large box wrapped in brown paper and set it on the table.

"Open it."

"What is it?"

"A gift."

"A *parting* gift?" she asked scathingly.

"If you like."

"You don't have to . . ."

"*Open* it!"

If only to avoid another blistering argument she walked to the table, examined the package without interest and stripped the wrapping off it. As she opened the cardboard box that emerged, her heart stopped. In it reposed an object with which she was extremely familiar: a silver clock, on the back of which was engraved a tribute to her father from his colleagues at the Archaeological Survey of India.

She sat down, suddenly unsteady on her feet. "Wh-where did you get this?" she asked faintly.

"From the mantelpiece in your drawing room at Khyber Kothi."

"Oh." Not knowing where else to look, she continued to stare stupidly at the clock.

"Suraj Singh needed to deprive you of something reasonably valuable to make the burglary credible. The typewriting machine was too bulky and got stuck in the window, so he settled for the clock."

"It was *Suraj Singh* who broke into our house?"

"Twice. The first attempt was unsuccessful, the second was not. Until the mountaineering accident in which he broke his leg, Suraj Singh was a pundit employed by the Survey of India in Dehra Doon. A pundit . . ." He stopped and stretched his eyebrows to their limit. "Do I need to explain that, or has Charlton done so already?"

A painful blush crept over her cheeks.

"Ah, I see he has. Well, having worked as a pundit, Suraj Singh can recognise the Survey's tools of espionage with his eyes shut. Butterfield's prayer-wheel, stuffed in the carpet bag stored in a trunk in the annexe to your study, he identified immediately from its markings. He removed the papers from it—your father's as well as Butterfield's—and left the wheel where it was." Walking to the hearth, he lowered himself into the rocking chair. "So you see, Emma, when we married I already had the Yasmina papers."

Even if she could have thought of something to say she would not have been able to. She closed her eyes to shut out Damien's bland face and another loomed large in her inner vision, her brother's.

Oh merciful heavens!

Watching her silently as he rocked in the chair, Damien had the grace to allow her her moment of shame.

She felt sick, humiliatingly close to tears. "If you were so . . . so desperate to marry me, why did you not propose like a *gentleman* instead of mounting that ludicrous charade?"

"How—since you refused even to let me call on you?"

"You could have persisted!"

"And if I had, would you have accepted me?"

"I . . . I might have. Stranger things have been known to happen."

"Not *so* strange! You despised me, found my attitudes repellant, remember? Or, at least, professed to." There was a sharp, metallic glitter to his eyes. "The truth of the matter, I soon saw, was that the arrogant Emma Wyncliffe, icon of intellectual superiority, spirited spinster celebrated for her disdain of society and her whiplash tongue, was too big for her britches by half. She begged to be taught a good, hard lesson. I decided that it would be my pleasure to provide it."

"Well then, why bother to marry me at all?" she cried, stung. "After all, you already had the papers!"

He squinted at her across the tips of steepled fingers. "You believe that a man would want to marry you only for an ulterior motive? You still value yourself so little?"

"No, I didn't mean that, I meant . . ." She shook off the thought. "It doesn't matter what I meant."

Clasping his hands behind his head, Damien gazed up at the ceiling. On the wooden beams a play of light and shadow from the dancing flames choreographed an impromptu ballet. For a while he sat watching it in pensive silence. Then his face softened. He sighed.

"My mother was a very beautiful woman, Emma—beautiful enough to be displayed on a mantelpiece like an ornament, like your silver clock. I grew up surrounded by beauty, *her* beauty. There were pictures of her everywhere." His eyes bored into her. "Is that what you were hoping to find in the desk, photographs? To see what she was like?"

She replied with a minimal nod.

He returned his stare to the ceiling. "She was like a drug, addictive and cumulatively fatal. My father was besotted with her. He gave her whatever he could, whatever she wanted. She reciprocated by deserting him. When she went, she took away everything that was important to him—his self-respect, his reputation, his stature as a man." He smiled tightly. "Also what was important to *her,* most of the jewellery he had given her. Damaged irredeemably in his own eyes and with no will to live, he simply withered and died."

Lost in a bygone era, Damien sat re-living the few cold wisps of memory that still haunted, no longer bitter but deeply sad.

"Not all beautiful women are faithless," Emma said carefully, "any more than all . . . plain women are the epitome of wifely virtue."

"Perhaps not." Shrugging off the melancholy, he raked his hair. "When I returned from England I was swamped by images of her perfection, submerged by them, so much so that I could hardly breathe. Finally, I removed them all and burned them, every last one of them—except for the portrait. That, somehow, I could not bring myself to destroy." His eyes still bored into hers, strangely anxious. "Do you understand what I am trying to say?"

Did she? Trembling on the brink of comprehension she could not absorb his meaning fully, not yet. She maintained a wary silence.

"When my father died, I swore that I would never marry either for beauty or for love," he said flatly. "Unfortunately, the vow did not prove quite as easy to keep as I had imagined."

Inside the pit of Emma's stomach a butterfly fluttered, a whisper of something warm. She did not let it surface.

"If you truly wish to return to Delhi," he said, curtly abandoning the thread, "I cannot stop you. Nor would I want to."

"Is that not what you also truly wish?"

He walked to the window and peered out. "Since you ask"—struggling hard, he managed to extract a syllable from somewhere as if with a pair of forceps—"no."

The whisper of warmth uncoiled, expanded and radiated. "You would like me to stay?"

Through a pane of glass he glared fiercely at a hapless groom. "*Yes, damn you!*"

Within her something else stirred, like a summer sea breeze, leaving ripples of contentment. But she was not done yet.

"Why?"

"Why? I would have thought that was self-evident—Ivana will need you."

"That I am aware of. Is that your only reason?"

"You *know* my other reasons. You had them all in Delhi."

"Because I am the most courageous woman you have ever met, the salvation of the memsahib in India? Because I am the only woman who doesn't bore you entirely to tears? And—let me not forget the *pièce de résistance*—the only woman qualified to bear your genetically perfect children?" She laughed. "Come, come, Damien, there have to be better reasons even for a marriage of inconvenience!"

"You are still convinced that there are not?"

"I am not entirely convinced that there are!" Tired of saying what she did not mean and not saying what she did, she asked boldly, "What about you, Damien, will *you* also need me?"

He did not look completely away but shifted his focus slightly to something behind her. "Naturally. That can be taken as said."

"Not until it is said."

"Even though in your monumental perversity you will not believe a single word I utter?"

"If I consider that what you say is true, of course I will."

"Well, would you believe me if I said that even before we met, I had made up my mind to marry you?"

"Without ever having seen me? No, I would *not!*"

"What if I said I *had* seen you—several times, in fact?"

She frowned. "Where?"

"At the Nawab's house. Coaching his daughter with enormous patience, enormous care. I found that most . . . inspiring."

"I see." Her heart gave another little bounce; she steadied it. "You were frantic to marry me because you were inspired by the way I taught?"

"Among other things."

"What other things?"

He flung up his hands. "Must you have every damn reason spoken out loud?"

"Yes, *every* damn reason!"

Whatever her mistakes and misjudgements—and there were many!—she saw no reason to forgive his excesses quite so easily. The words she had been denied for so long—words to which she had a right—had to be said. He had to be made to pay for all her heartache, for all the lies told, for all the subversions and evasions sustained over those despairing months of deceit.

"Well, would you believe me," he asked between clenched teeth, "if I told you that by the time we actually met—*collided,* rather—in that miserable village on the Jamuna, in spite of your atrocious beige dress and frightful topknot, I knew that no other woman would ever satisfy me again? That I absolutely *had* to have you?"

Emma blinked. Was he drunk?

He strode back to the table to tower above her, eyes ablaze and nostrils flaring. "And would you believe me if I said that by the time you had read me my fortune, those devilish blue-green eyes, that vitriol-tipped tongue and the crusading fervour with which you marched your cannon into battle had ruined for me every other wretched female on earth? By *heavens,* you infamous creature," he roared, thumping the table so hard that both Emma and the cardboard box jumped, "you owe me compensation for that!"

He stormed away to resume his pacing.

Emma eased herself back in her chair, dazed, starting quietly to enjoy the explosion of temper, the savage pride that induced it and the fact that it was she who compelled him to confess. Ignited by inner smiles, her eyes threatened to sparkle and she lowered them.

"Would you also like me to specify," he raged, "the recompense I might consider adequate for having been reduced to monogamy?"

"No," she assured him quickly, "I don't think there is any . . ."

"Oh, but I think there is!" With long, swift strides he returned to the table and sat down opposite her. "On our wedding night in Delhi I found myself quite surprised—trapped somewhere within Emma Wyncliffe's impregnable edifice of priggishness and propriety, I saw to my astonishment, was a wanton begging to be released!"

She was horribly shocked. "You found me *wanton?*"

"As one of your more redeeming virtues, yes. Ice mixed with fire—a miracle of physics but, alas, in imbalanced proportions. The ice, God knew, needed no help from me. The fire, on the other hand, could do with a little coaxing which, as compensation, I would be pleased to supply. Provided, as made clear earlier, I am *asked.* He whisked his pipe off the desk, lit it and puffed furiously. "You wanted damned reasons—will these do for the moment?"

Oh Lord above—*would* they do!

"Perhaps," she said. "For the moment."

She got up and returned to the couch by the fire. With a mind clogged with words, she could think of not one more to say. Plunged in frowning thought, for a while Damien remained where he was. Then he laid down his pipe and came to position himself beside her on the couch. His rage had evaporated; his mood was subdued, sombre.

Unsmiling, he touched her cheek lightly. "I realise there is much for which I need to be forgiven, Emma," he said, his voice low. "In a way I suppose you were right. It has been a travesty of a marriage for which I am more to blame than you, but at least I have never made the mistake of deluding myself that you loved me."

Emma stared at him in disbelief—was it possible that so clever a man could be so blind? "No," she said crossly. "Of course not."

"I may not have the patience to wait until the onset of gout," he continued with an uncertain half-smile, "but do you think that, given enough time, some day you *could* learn to love me?"

The diffidence, the humility, the underlying anxiety—all were so unfamiliar that Emma's eyes welled. Suddenly she ached to be done with words, ached to touch him and be touched by him—but one more loose end still remained.

"Only enough to engage the senses?"

"Enough to *devastate* the senses!"

"And the heart?"

He sighed. "You strike a hard bargain, Emma Granville. Well, I daresay some similar disturbance in the region of the heart wouldn't do it any great harm either." At last, at *last,* he took her hand, enclosed it in his and searched deep within her eyes. "*Could* you, Emma?"

The moments went by in pulse beats; the thousands of words trapped in her throat remained unreleased. Her vision filled with his face, leaving no space for anything else. There was a taste of wine in the air, a scent of summer roses, and in her ears the music of a hundred unashamed celestial choirs.

A smile surfaced and touched her mouth. It illuminated her face from within, like a Chinese lantern, and made it glow. Raising the hand wrapped around hers, she laid it against an incandescent cheek.

"Perhaps," she said. "Some day. Given enough time."

EPILOGUE

*F*ollowing clearance from a baffled Russian Foreign Office, on 20 September 1890 the *Novoe Vremya* and the *Morning Post* published on their front pages detailed maps and information about the Yasmina Pass.

Neither newspaper revealed the circumstances in which the information was received. Both credited it to "confidential sources in India." In a bid to avoid possible egg on their faces, both challenged Whitehall to dismiss the claim as a hoax. The discovery was attributed jointly to Dr. Graham Wyncliffe and Jeremy Butterfield.

No response appeared to be forthcoming from Whitehall.

Official reaction in various capitals was as expected. Privately as confused as everybody else, publicly St. Petersburg scorned the claim as another example of British chicanery. In Kashgar, the Taotai disdained interest in the Mandarin translations Pyotr Shishkin presented but read them avidly after the Russian left and was livid. More as a slap in Shishkin's face than because of newfound love for Britain, he forthwith granted George MacCartney and Francis Younghusband permission to visit Kashgar. The matter of the absconding British agent did not come up for discussion.

MacCartney and Younghusband arrived in Kashgar in November 1890 and spent the winter months at Chini Baug. Despite violent opposition from the Russian consul, in due course MacCartney was accepted as Britain's official representative to the Celestial Empire and Chini Baug as the British consulate. He was to remain in the post for the next twenty-six years.

Enflamed by the cipher from his Foreign Office, Alexei Smirnoff flew into an almighty rage in Tashkent. He stormed and thundered for three days, much of his wrath directed at Mikhail Borokov for dying before he could be blamed for the disaster. Spewing awesome venom on Safdar Ali's quaking emissaries he disbanded the caravan, aborted his campaign, then had the Hunza delegation dragged to the border and physically ejected off Russian soil.

Patiently awaiting the arrival of the caravan at his fort in Shimsul, Safdar Ali remained unaware of events as he plotted where, how and when best to slaughter the Russians once the rifles were seized. It was only after he returned to Hunza many weeks later empty-handed and in murderous mood, and his envoys crept fearfully back from Tashkent, that he learned of the abysmal truth. The envoys were immediately executed.

At the government secretariat in Simla, an atmosphere of hushed horror prevailed. White-faced civil servants scurried up and down corridors and peons flew back and forth between ministerial rooms bearing bulging despatch boxes. In the Intelligence Department offices further down the Mall, however—regardless of volleys of incensed ciphers arriving thick and fast from London—the mood was markedly tranquil. Apart from a quiet sense of deliverance and a certain modest satisfaction, on the whole it was business as usual.

And in London, Whitehall went quietly mad.

When the dust finally settled and a semblance of sanity returned to allow for dispassion, it was realised that the situation was perhaps not quite as dismal as initially envisaged. The publication of the Yasmina papers was embarrassing, certainly, but in view of the reality the "scoop" was of little consequence and the "challenge" deserved to be ignored. The true mine-field was the testimony of Mikhail Borokov. How precisely, it was debated endlessly at No. 10, should (or should not) Her Majesty's government react to the exposures (if at all)?

Finally, after many miles of ciphers drafted, discarded, despatched and received and much midnight gas expended, the Cabinet arrived at a consensus. The exposure were made by a Russian Army deserter of dubious repute in a state of dementia in extremely bizarre circumstances, who was, in all probability, genuinely dead by now. Since the Yasmina was no longer strategic and no *actual* damage had come of Alexei Smirnoff's endeavours, it was agreed that Mikhail Borokov had lied. The headache of another tedious protest to St. Petersburg was thus averted, the prospect of more frightful publicity diverted and Borokov's testimony accorded a hasty (and permanent) burial in the India Office archives.

At the same time Lord Castlewood, the British ambassador in St. Petersburg, was directed to bring the matter informally (and tactfully) to the attention of Tsar Alexander the Third. Given no evidence to substantiate either the plot or Smirnoff's involvement, His Imperial Majesty dismissed it as a figment of Simla's over-active imagination. He suggested politely that it would serve the cause of Asian peace better if in future Britain abandoned her favoured sport of shadow-boxing and stuck to cricket.

A month later Alexei Smirnoff was quietly recalled from Tashkent. An announcement in the Russian Court Circular made it known that in recognition of his noble services to the Central Asian empire, the Ministry of the Interior was pleased to post General Smirnoff to Irkutsk as Governor-General of Siberia. A subsequent announcement regretted greatly General Smirnoff's inability to accept his new position for reasons of ill health. On medical grounds therefore he had been relieved of all official duties and advised a long convalescence. Retiring to his affluent estate outside Moscow, Alexei Smirnoff spent his remaining years writing his memoirs, devising clandestine strategies for future invasions of India and breeding prize pigs.

The following year, 1891, the Russian heir-apparent, Crown Prince Nicholas, paid a state visit to India. Apart from a near-collision in the Himalayas where six hot-headed Russian officers made an abortive bid to annex the Pamirs, relations between the two empires showed steady improvement. Reluctantly, Russia wrenched her sights away from India and trained them instead on Afghanistan.

In its exploration of the glacial region and the Yasmina Pass, the Survey of India mountaineering team confirmed the findings of Wyncliffe and Butterfield. Both men were jointly awarded posthumous gold medals by the Royal Geographic Society. On closer examination, the "glistening walls" of the Yasmina reported by Wyncliffe were found to contain traces of gold, although the extent of the vein could not be established.

Exposed and on public display, the Yasmina remained a subject of debate in the British, Russian and Indian press for months. Gradually public interest in the pass waned, mention of it became sporadic and then ceased altogether. Eventually, save in the mournful songs and legends of Dardistan, the Yasmina was forgotten.

The Janus affair was never made public, nor revealed in its entirety to the Commander-in-Chief of the Indian Army.

Nothing more was heard of Colonel Mikhail Borokov—at least not until another two years had elapsed.

At the last ball of the 1890 Season at Viceregal Lodge, seeking relief from the crush inside, Sir John Covendale found himself sharing a patch of garden with Sir Marmaduke. Still highly disgruntled, after some desultory social exchanges the C-in-C reopened a subject that had continued to nag.

"That anonymous letter, John—damned rum show, what?"

"Indeed, sir."

"Left on the F.O.'s doorstep with the milk bottles, eh?"

"So the rumour went according to our ambassador."

"I'm surprised it was published at all!"

"Well, as we know, it was touch and go at the Russian Foreign Office. All said and done, sir, we were bloody lucky they published it when they did. Had they not, and had Columbine perished with Borokov's testament, we would have found ourselves plunged into very nasty hostilities indeed."

"Nasty, eh?" The adjective was not received kindly. "I hope you realise, John, that whichever treacherous bastard leaked those papers to the Ruskies did me out of a damn fine war. I would have enjoyed thrashing the blasted Beluga out of Smirnoff!"

"My apologies, sir," the QMG murmured. "We'll try to do better next time."

"I suppose it's all water under the bridge now, but between you and me, John—how many beside the Granville woman *did* have access to those papers?"

"No one, sir. Being unaware of their existence, she herself had no cause to open the wheel."

"So your report claimed. And the Rusky husband?"

"Half-Rusky, sir. Well, since she knew nothing, neither did he."

"You still maintain your help to locate the Granville girl had no connection with any of this?"

"Yes sir. We already had an agent in Kashgar; the offer was made purely on humanitarian grounds."

An imperially garbed bearer arrived with a selection of Havanas on a silver salver. The C-in-C nodded; the bearer circumcised two with a silver cutter and presented a light.

"One way or another, sir," the QMG commented as they lit up, "it goes to show one can never put too high a price on happenstance in this odd game."

"Happenstance? Good God, John, is that how your Intelligence Department does business, through *happenstance*?"

"Intelligence *is* happenstance, sir: something overheard, stumbled across, glimpsed round a corner by someone passing by. In this instance, Columbine just happened to be in the right place at the right time."

"Hmph." Sir Marmaduke stared at him hard and long. "Tell me truthfully, John, now that it is all water under the bridge—you *honestly* have no idea who sent the letter to the Rusky rags?"

Sir John met the stare head-on. His own did not waver, neither did his conscience.

With or without official knowledge, the Intelligence Department would continue to move in the manner of the Lord—and honesty would have very little to do with it. Mysterious ways were the essence of their game, a game in which risks were lethal, stakes high and the end the only justification of the means. They had broken rules, taken insane chances, lied and prevaricated; but at the end of the day they had prevailed. A major military conflagration had been averted, Charlton's tricky little bomb de-fused and the Yasmina papers—whatever their worth—retrieved without a whiff of publicity. Commanders-in-Chief came and went with the political tides; the Intelligence Department would remain as long as the Empire did.

"Haven't the foggiest, sir," he said firmly. "As our report concluded, the leak must have occurred in Leh before the wheel was delivered to Mrs. Granville."

Colonel Hethrington too had cause for complacency.

Thanks to the support of the QMG there were promotions in the offing, whispers of a mention in the New Year's Honours List and for the Department a sizeable increase in subsidies. The C-in-C's trenchant rebuke following publication of the papers had left him simmering, certainly, but it had been a small price to pay for everything that was achieved.

Most reviving of all, the Indian government was packing up for a return to Calcutta; soon Simla would be deserted.

Joy of joys, the Season was over!

If there was a single cloud in the cerulean expanse of Colonel Hethrington's skies, it was Captain Worth's sudden madness. On the threshold of a hard-earned, well-deserved crown on his epaulette, the bloody fool had opted to resign his commission and dedicate himself to the stage.

"You would rather be an actor than a major in the Indian Army?" Hethrington was appalled.

"I already am an actor, sir," Worth reminded him sedately. "I merely seek to formalise my profession."

"You'll starve," Hethrington promised with vindictive pleasure. "You'll live in rat-ridden garrets on beans, cheese-parings and dry bread, not knowing where the next stale loaf is coming from."

"I don't think so, sir. Belle—ah, Mrs. Jethroe—has generously consented to become my wife. Having been a successful textile manufacturer in Manchester her husband, the late Mr. Jacob Jethroe, left her a legacy of half a million pounds."

"Half a mill . . . !" Hethrington was all but speechless. "You will not be ashamed to live off money left by your wife's previous husband?"

"No, sir. For one's art one must consider no sacrifice too great, no compulsion too demeaning."

Hethrington mouthed a colourful curse and resigned himself to the inevitable. "Well, I suppose I'll have to do the decent thing and wish you the best of luck," he said ungraciously.

"Oh no, sir! In the theatre when we want to wish someone luck, we say, 'Break a leg.' "

"Is that so! And what do you say when you want someone to break a leg, eh? Oh, never mind, never mind. When do you want to leave?"

"The last week of November, sir, if that is convenient."

"Well, it *isn't* convenient, but never mind that, either. Where do you go from here?"

"Belle and I are expected at Shalimar for the Christmas season, sir. We hope to sail for England in the spring."

"I see. Well, try not to make a complete ass of yourself if you can help it," Hethrington growled. It was a lame parting shot, but it was all he could think of at the moment.

Left on his own, he morosely contemplated the future. He would miss Nigel Worth; they had made a damned fine team. Facing him now was the dreary prospect of scrounging for a new aide, endless interviews with gormless youths who couldn't tell a fly-paper from a flimsy, and the insufferable penance of licking the best of the bunch into decent shape.

Since there was no justice left in the world, he decided glumly, he might as well take the day off and go fishing.

*A*t Shalimar, there was much to celebrate that Christmas.

Gone were the mood of decay, the hollow echoes of sadness, the poignancy of waiting rooms where no one waited. Fresh winds gusted through airless corridors. Locked suites abandoned the debris of the past and new life flowed into dead spaces. In the coming festivities there was promise of abundant fulfilment, of laughter and music and dancing feet, of a house alive with human presence.

Ivana and Holbrook were the first to arrive. Before the passes closed for the winter, Margaret Wyncliffe came with the Purcells, followed by Nigel Worth and Belle Jethroe. John and Jenny were expected shortly from Calcutta and David, now off crutches and a Captain, was to join them later.

It was said that a medal was in the offing for valiant service rendered over and above the call of duty. It was a time to rejoice, to mend fences, to make peace and count blessings. Above all, it was a time for thanksgiving for the merciful return of the daughter of the house after so long and arduous an odyssey.

Settling down nervously in her mother's refurbished apartment, Ivana Granville took time to come to terms with the bewildering acquisition of an alien family, a new home, language and country. Due to the infinite patience, understanding and attentions of a loving brother and sister-in-law, however, by the time Christmas came, her diffidence had begun to erode as steadily as the severed threads of their destinies re-joined. With her air of serenity, her charming innocence and her lack of self-awareness, she brought to Shalimar an added dimension, an enrichment as vibrant and pervasive as the paisleys on Qadir Mian's beautiful shawls.

The announcement of Ivana's engagement to Holbrook Conolly was made by Damien on Boxing Day. The wedding, at his request, was deferred for a year to allow Ivana's tender roots to take hold and family bonds to strengthen. Much to everyone's relief, Conolly decided to resign from his hazardous job in favour of a position with the Revenue Commission in Srinagar.

With new relationships on the anvil and so many fresh chapters opened in so many lives, the time for grudges was over. Graham Wyncliffe's silver clock was proudly displayed on the drawing-room mantelpiece with explanations to David given and accepted easily. At Emma's insistence Natasha Granville's portrait was returned to its rightful position alongside that of her husband, and restless ghosts of a bygone age were finally laid to rest.

*T*he Commander-in-Chief of India might have been done out of a damn fine war, but Colonel Algernon Durand of the Gilgit Agency was not. As relentless a medal hunter as Alexei Smirnoff, when the military road was ready, so also was Durand.

The subsidy promised to Safdar Ali was never intended to be paid, nor was it. "All my savages are going wrong," Colonel Durand had written to his brother, Sir Mortimer Durand, after his return from Hunza in 1889. Two years later, by the end of 1891, the time had come to whip the erring "savages" into rectitude.

It was decided to extend the military road through Hunza and Nagar, allegedly to counter the threat of a Russian invasion following their incursion into the Pamirs. When the Mirs protested, they provided Durand with a perfect excuse to attack.

On 1 December 1891, under Durand's command, Gurkha and Imperial Service troops equipped with a battery of seven-pounder mountain artillery and a Gatling gun marched into Nagar. There was fierce resistance at the Nagar fort of Nilt and later from Safdar Ali's troops entrenched in the Hunza fort with jezails, breechloaders and home-made ammunition, but by 22 December it was all over.

Safdar Ali and his family fled to Chinese Turkestan. His fort was ransacked, its contents auctioned at Gilgit and one of his half brothers more amenable to Britain installed in his place. Furious at the loss of Hunza, which they considered theirs, the Chinese tossed Safdar Ali into prison. Eventually he was released and given permission to settle in the Yarkand valley, where he lived in comfortable exile with twenty-two of his wives and all his children. He was never to return to Hunza.

With the veil finally whisked off the face of the Yasmina, the ancient prophecy of the Sufi mystic had come to pass: Hunza had ceased to exist as a nation.

In Srinagar, Pratap Singh was finally deposed and his brother, Amar Singh, enthroned as Maharaja of Kashmir.

It was the beginning of the end for Dardistan. One by one, under one excuse or the other, the Dard chiefs of the five mountain kingdoms were tamed or replaced by pliable puppets. Dardistan and Kafiristan were carved up and divided between Britain and Afghanistan. Both gained vast tracts of additional territory and tighter control over the Himalayas and its passes. By 1896, British domination of the north-western regions of India was complete.

It primed British hubris to believe that they had brought Pax Britannica to the Himalayas. Durand's campaigns were celebrated for their many acts of bravery resulting in three Victoria Crosses to British officers; but even by Britain's standards of colonial duplicity, they were inglorious wars and recorded as such by many. Commendable acts of courage were performed also by Indian sepoys who had to be satisfied with the Indian Order of Merit, the highest award for gallantry for which native soldiers were eligible.

Approximately a year after Durand's campaign, a minor news item appeared on the back page of the Lahore newspaper, the *Civil & Military Gazette*.

Under the ice of the Biro glacier, not far from the Biafo, it reported, an Austrian mountaineering team had discovered the frozen, well-preserved body of a white male aged about fifty. The corpse was dressed in Khirgiz clothing and about its neck was a gold nugget threaded through a chain. Since no mountaineer had been reported missing and the dead man carried no papers, his identity could not be established. The body was found two marches away from the Yasmina Pass.

Except for those in the Intelligence Department, the item meant little to the few who noticed it.

In a final irony, a subsequent official survey of all passes leading into Hunza concluded that a Russian military advance through any of them was a practical impossibility. Two years later, that view was confirmed by the Pamir Boundary Commission, but too late to bring consolation to the dispossessed rulers of the north-western states.

In the autumn of 1891, a month after Ivana became Mrs. Holbrook Conolly and left for Srinagar to set up house, Emma sat in the orchard at Shalimar reading a London newspaper.

The season of mellow fruitfulness softened the valley with pastels and washed the skies with sunshine. There was richness in the drifting sounds and colours, in the murmurings of autumn light, in the drowsy air weighted with fragrance. A fine mist of rain had come and gone, leaving behind a luminescent moistness. As she read, Emma smiled. Her compilation of her father's papers published by the RGS, including the Yasmina diary, had attracted another encouraging review and she was gratified.

Striding across from the estate office, Damien came to lay a kiss on her forehead, drop two letters in her lap and fling himself down on the lawn.

"Don't lie on the grass," she said as she laid down the newspaper and poured him a cup of *qahwa* from the samovar. "It's still damp."

He rose obediently, transferred himself to a chair and retrieved the newspaper. "Another favourable notice?"

She nodded, handed him the cup and started to read her letters. "Ivana has begun to write exceedingly well," she said. "The war with English phonetics continues but a major battle with syntax seems to have been won." She read through her second letter and looked quite delighted. "David got the job, Mama writes. Brigadier Hethrington has been pleased to accept him as a replacement for Nigel. I should imagine the decoration helped." She paused, toying once again with a recurring thought.

"No." Pre-empting the thought he knew so well, he lowered the paper. "No more excavations until my son arrives."

"Your son will not grace us with his presence for at least two months yet," Emma protested. "Besides, your son may well turn out to be your daughter."

"Not if he knows what's good for him, he won't!"

Emma laughed, picked up her embroidery frame and shifted her bulk into a more comfortable position. Lost in private thought, she sat for a while with the frame forgotten and her eyes riveted to Damien's face.

He again lowered his newspaper. "Why are you staring at me?" he asked. "Is my nose shiny?"

She smiled. "I've just thought of a question I've always wanted to ask but could never remember to—how *did* you get that scar on your chin?"

"Why? Is it important to know how?"

"Well, I was told so many theories about it in Delhi that I'm curious, that's all."

"You might not like the answer when you hear it."

Recalling the options Jenny had enumerated, Emma hesitated. A duel for a lady-love's honour? A brawl with a cuckolded husband? A somewhat more respectable skirmish with Afghan tribesmen?

"We agreed not to have any more secrets between us, Damien," she said bravely. "Whatever happened, I think I can bear it."

"Oh?" His eyes twinkled. "Well, then, since you insist—I slipped on a cake of soap in the bathroom."